A PLAGUE OF GIANTS

There were . . . I don't know how many. More than I could count. All tall, pale, and dressed in clacking bones. Some with swords, some with spears—the tools they had used to slay the people of Möllerud and Hillegöm . . .

I had a glass knife. They had swords and spears and arms that were half again as long as mine, plus bodies that weren't slowing and breaking down. Combat wasn't an option, even at one-to-one odds, much less one-to-hundreds or thousands. But the Lord of the Deep had given me a kenning and now an opportunity not only to avenge my people but perhaps learn something that would help rid us of this scourge . . .

A PLAGUE OF GIANTS

Book One of the Seven Kennings

KEVIN HEARNE

www.orbitbooks.net

ORBIT

First published in Great Britain in 2017 by Orbit

1 3 5 7 9 10 8 6 4 2

A CIP catalogue record for this book
is available from the British Library.

ISBN 978-0-356-50959-4

Printed and bound by CPI Group (UK) Ltd, Croydon CR0 4YY

Papers used by Orbit are from well-managed forests
and other responsible sources.

MIX

For Kimberly,

who was first to tell me that the Raelech bard had

some good stories in him.

Thank you always for your love & support.

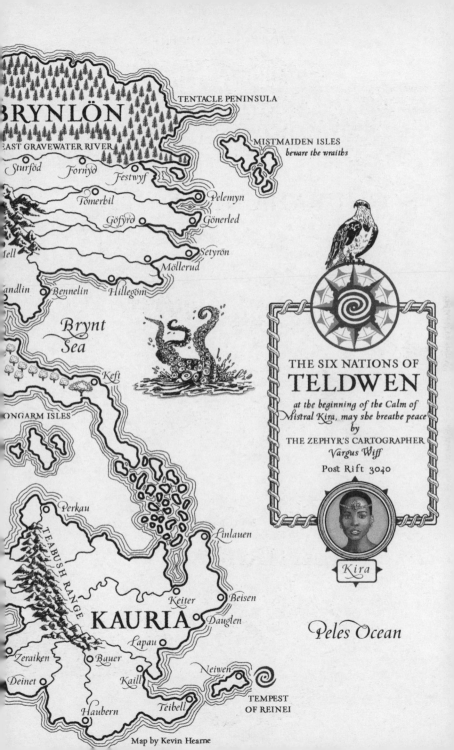

Dramatis Personae

FINTAN, BARD OF THE POET GODDESS KAELIN: Raelech bard assigned to perform daily for the people of Pelemyn, telling the story of the Giants' War.

DERVAN DU ALÖBAR: Brynt historian tasked to write down the Raelech bard's tale. Widowed, providing shelter now to a family of refugees.

GORIN MOGEN: Hearthfire of Harthrad, determined to secure safe haven for his people.

NEL KIT BEN SAH: Fornish greensleeve of the White Gossamer Clan, opposed to Gorin Mogen's scheme.

KALLINDRA DU PASKRE: Daughter of a Brynt merchant. Fond of honey-apple bacon.

ABHINAVA KHOSE: Son of a hunting family in Ghurana Nent, struggling with how to tell them that he doesn't want to hunt anymore.

MELISHEV LOHMET: Viceroy of Hashan Khek, the southernmost Nentian city. To him falls the task of repelling Gorin Mogen. Plagued by a persistent health issue.

TALLYND DU BÖLL: Tidal mariner of Pelemyn, widowed mother of two boys.

GONDEL VEDD: Kaurian scholar of linguistics. Married, fond of mustard.

MEARA, STONECUTTER OF THE EARTH GODDESS DINAE: Young stonecutter engaged to a soldier in the garrison in Baseld. Likes to play in the mud.

CULLAND DU RAFFERT: Brynt spice importer in Fornyd, compelled to seek an abrupt career change.

Day 1

THE BARD BEGINS

When we encounter a voice that moves us on an emotional level, by turns wringing tears from our eyes and plucking laughs from our bellies, there is an ineffable quality to its power: all we know is that we like listening to it and want to hear more. But when we encounter voices we find loathsome, we usually can pinpoint why without difficulty: too nasal, too whiny, too steeped in anger or sodden with melancholy.

The bard's voice was the ineffable sort.

He planted himself behind the battlement facing the peninsula, where the vast sea of refugees swirled around their tents, and raised his hands from his sides as if to embrace all the people who had washed up there because of the war. Then he turned slowly as he spoke, including the city in his address as well: "Good people of Pelemyn, I am Fintan, Bard of the Poet Goddess Kaelin." At once, eyes swiveled to lock upon his form or heads tilted in the far corners of the city to hear his disembodied voice better; conversations subsided, and other magics seemed to begin their work. His beaming face elicited a kindred response and lifted moods; the cup of watery beer from a nameless keg that I had in my hand suddenly tasted like the crisp, legendary brews of Forn; pleasant aromas of fresh food were accentuated and wafted about on the wind, and the less pleasant whiffs of unwashed bodies and rotting garbage faded away.

"It is my life's work to tell stories," the bard continued, his smile gone now and replaced with an earnest tone. "And no one else can tell you what I have seen. This great war of our time has indeed been terrible, and I am still struck with its horrors, waking up in the night sweating and—well, I am sure I don't have to tell you."

No, he didn't. Most of the people on Survivor Field were still wearing the same clothes they'd been wearing when they'd had to flee their homes. They were all dirty and ragged now, and purple hollows lay under their eyes, testament to lost sleep, lost loved ones, just . . . loss.

"But I am also struck by the sudden heroism of people all across the continent. For I have come from the other side of it, the western front, where I participated in the great battle below the Godsteeth." A tide of exclamation greeted that announcement, and I marveled that it came from far out on the peninsula and from the streets of the city as well. He was not shouting—his volume was what one might use for a toast at a fair-sized dinner party—yet no one had difficulty hearing him.

"Yes, I witnessed that and much more. I can tell you exactly what happened in the Granite Tunnel—" Here the people sent up another cheer. "—and I can reveal that a peace-loving citizen of Kauria, acting at the behest of Mistral Kira, long may she reign, has had a secret role to play in this war and indeed may have finally found a way to bring it to an end. It is why I am here now." That earned him the loudest roar yet, and he nodded at Survivor Field, assuring them that what he said was true. "Friends, I have permission from the pelenaut to tell you that there is a fleet on its way here from Kauria this instant. And it is coming to pick up the two allied armies that are marching this way across the mountains—one from Rael and one from Forn—and together they will sail across the ocean with your own forces to answer the enemy in kind for what they have done to us!"

The emotion that news tore from the throats of the assembled would have drowned out even the power of his kenning. It was angry at first, not directed at him but at distant shores, a tide of people who had lost almost everything and hungered for a balancing of the scales, and then it lightened, morphing into jubilation as people felt hope for the first time in months. They hugged one another, danced in the mud, tears streaming down their faces as they punched the air with their fists, for it was good news at last instead of another dose of despair, and I was not immune to those feelings. I lost track of the bard for a few minutes as I surveyed Survivor Field and then crossed to the other side of the wall and saw the same celebration happening in the streets of the city.

People skipped out of the buildings to embrace and smile and savor the sight of teeth that weren't bared in a snarl or a cry. I could not see my own house from the wall, but I imagined that even Elynea might be grinning right then, and I was sorry to miss it; she had never looked anything but haunted since she and her children had come to live with me. And when the bard spoke again, his voice cutting through the noise as people were trying to find their second wind, he was no longer standing on the wall, half hidden by the crenellations, but was up on an improvised stage a few mariners had cobbled together out of crates. "But our relief and the enemy's defeat will not arrive tomorrow or even the next day. It will take time for it to get here and even more time to prepare the voyage. I am told it could be up to sixty days. In the meantime, the pelenaut thinks it wise that you all hear what has happened elsewhere, for it is doubtful you have heard more than rumors. He has asked me to share what I know with you all, and he is listening as well. I am therefore engaged in your service, and I will tell you the tale in the old way, performing each afternoon until the sun sets. I hope you will take heart, as I have, from the small victories against overwhelming odds, all of which allow us to be here today, to be here tomorrow, and, gods willing, generations hence, to tell these stories again."

The bard had to pause here for another swell of applause, and while he did, a young woman stepped onto the stage of crates with a giant flagon and presented it to him, speaking a few words in his ear that did not carry like the bard's voice. Fintan dipped his head in thanks to her, and then his voice floated again on the wind.

"It seems that Brynlön's reputation for generosity is well deserved! Master Yöndyr, owner and brewmaster of the the Siren's Call in the city, gives me a flagon of Mistmaiden Ale—purely medicinal, I'm sure—and lodging at his inn for the length of my engagement! Thank you, sir!" Appreciative noises were directed at Yöndyr for having such excellent sense, and I imagined that other inn owners were cussing themselves for not thinking of it first; the Siren's Call had just received the best advertising possible. Smiling as he did so, Fintan took the opportunity to tip the flagon and then wipe the foam from his upper lip. He then returned the flagon to the woman and wrapped himself in an air of dramatic doom, saying, "Listen." Everyone I could see on either side of the wall stood rapt, many of us grinning at him in anticipation despite the fact that he had advertised details of a war we already knew too well. It didn't matter because we were all children again, waiting to be told a story, and we had hope now that it would end well.

"Like all tales worth the telling, I shall begin at the beginning—but your beginning, not Kauria's or Forn's or anyone else's. We'll get to them later. We're going to start with the reason this city still stands—your own tidal mariner! So take some time, friends, wherever you are. Fill your cups, visit the privy, do what you must so that you can be free in a few minutes to bend an ear for my tale—come closer to the wall so you can see me if you are out of my sight! If you're thirsty, I can confirm that Yöndyr's Mistmaiden Ale can slake a thirst like nothing else! I'll begin soon!"

An afternoon of entertainment with one of our own featured as the heroine? Maybe with snacks and beer? We couldn't wait! Everyone began to move and talk at once, and there was a general rush for food and drink on either side of the wall, all other occupations forgotten. Master Yöndyr, no doubt, was delighted.

"Let us begin," Fintan said, his voice spreading effortlessly across the city and the peninsula a few minutes later. "I'd like to invite someone very special up here: Pelemyn's tidal mariner, Tallynd du Böll. Tallynd, please join me."

A woman in a military uniform stepped onto the makeshift stage with Fintan to thunderous applause, favoring her left leg as she did so. She had insignia that I had never seen before, which I at first assumed was due to her blessing but which I learned later meant a new military rank. She had kind eyes, a weary smile, and close cropped hair going gray at the temples. She waved to the refugees on Survivor Field, and Fintan indicated that she should speak.

"Say something. I'll make sure they hear you."

"Oh. Well, hello?" Her voice carried for a league thanks to Fintan's kenning, and she received cheers in response. "Wow. Okay. I want everyone to know that I have shared both my duty log and my personal thoughts with Fintan prior to this. Except I'm sure he will organize it all much better than I ever could or did. Anyway: it's the truth of things, and I'm glad that he will tell it all. It's not the sort of tale you may be thinking it is right now. And you should know it."

Fintan pulled out what looked like a small black egg from a pouch tied to his belt and held it up between his thumb and forefinger. He cast the egg at his feet, and black smoke billowed up in a column, shrouding his body completely until his form resolved into an exact copy of Tallynd du Böll, uniform and all, growing a couple of inches in the process. Fintan was a fairly short, dark man—his skin not quite as dark as that of we Brynts—distinguished by an overlarge nose perched above a generous mouth in a narrow face. It was therefore quite a shock to everyone to see him transform into the distinguished savior of our city, stand right next to her, and say with her voice, "Thank you, Tidal Mariner."

She gasped—everyone did, honestly—and she said, "Oh, drown me, do I really look and sound like that?" Laughter from the crowd. "Never mind. Thank you, Fintan." She waved again and stepped off the stage,

and the bard told us, as Tallynd, what really happened the night the
giants came.

*T*allynd

Before my husband died five years ago, in a moment mellowed by
drink and the puff of a Fornish gourd bowl, he asked me what price I
thought we would all pay for the peace we'd enjoyed for so many
years.

"What are you talking about?" I asked him. We were sitting in our
small fountain court behind our house, and I was idly using my kenning to curl the water in twirling spirals before they dropped into the
reservoir below. He hunched forward, leaning elbows on knees, and
withdrew the pipe from his mouth, squinting through the smoke and
waggling the stem at me.

"You have been in the military for what, four years now? And you
have yet to fight a single battle. There's always a price to be paid for
that."

"Why must *we* pay it?" I countered. "Perhaps the price was already
paid by those who came before us."

He bobbed his head to either side, admitting the possibility. "Perhaps you're right," he said. "We read all those stale histories in school,
you know, and I don't doubt that they scrubbed away a whole lot of
blood and pain. Countless tragedies happening to families like ours, all
reduced to a sentence or three, while pages were devoted to what this
ruler ate or what that rich person wore." He snorted smoke through
his nostrils. "But I still think we have it coming to us, love. And I worry
about it. Because when it comes, you'll be the first to greet it."

I laughed at him then. I did! I remember it so clearly now, though it didn't seem important then. Because in that time, in that place, when he was so handsome and I wanted to have another child with him, when the sun was setting and bronzed his beautiful dark face, I could not conceive of war. I could not conceive of it, in fact, right up until it came to me first, just as he said it would. But by the time it came, he was long returned to the ocean, and our two boys were eight and nine and barely remembered him. I thought that was the worst tragedy in the world until the Bone Giants sailed over my head.

Normally I'm on duty during daylight hours, but by request of the fisher clave I was mapping the crab beds and taking note of the feeding habits of other nocturnal species in the waters north of the peninsula, keeping an eye out as always for any ship-sinking predators. I was in deep water far offshore when I heard, or rather felt, the slicing of keels through water on the surface at moonrise. It was an anomaly since no boats should have been in the area during the course of my mapping. Even allowing for fishermen who ignored the boundary buoys, it was far too much turbulence for one or two rogue net trawlers. I rose to investigate.

During the ascent, I realized the number of keels was not merely an unusual grouping of boats but a massive fleet of transport ships of strange origin. Upon breaking the surface, I saw that they definitely were not a Brynt fleet. Nor were they of Raelech or Kaurian construction or any recognizable profile. They were broad-bottomed sailing ships outfitted with oars, though at the moment they were under full wind from the east. The decks mounted no harpoons or other visible weapons. They were, however, packed with people. Tall, thin people with bone armor on their torsos and arms. They looked like ribs. I also saw handheld weapons, swords of some kind. They all had them, and they were all looking ahead at the firebowls atop the walls of Pelemyn and the smaller lamps along the docks. Unless I was mistaken in the moonlight, their skin was pale and they had painted their faces to look like skulls.

Turning my head to the right, I saw that several ships had already passed by my position and were entering the harbor. All I could see in the moonlight at that distance was the sails, not the people, so I could not tell for certain that this was an invasion in progress. But the stark evidence before me shouted that this was no friendly trade embassy. Cargo ships aren't packed bow to stern with armed and painted men.

Swimming closer to the nearest ship on a tightly channeled current, I called out to them: "Who are you? I am the tidal mariner of Pelemyn and require an answer."

Someone replied in a strange language, and that was when I found out they had a few spears, too: three of them plunked into the water around my head, and I do not think I could have been more shocked if they had actually hit me. They were most definitely hostiles, and they had just triggered the war protocols. I was authorized—required, in fact—to use the powers of my kenning to apply coercive and lethal force against an invading fleet.

And I admit that it took me a few moments to process that. I had to look toward the docks again, take in the enormity of the dark shapes in the moonlight, realize what they intended, and say the words out loud to make myself believe it was happening: "This is an invading fleet. Invading us. Right now."

Up to that point, I had never used my kenning for anything but peaceful purposes. Scout the spawning grounds up and down the coasts, map the crab beds for the fisher clave, make sure the currents kept the coral reefs well fed—that had been my duty. But right then I needed to kill as many strangers as possible to protect my city. It is a disorienting transition to make—I mean from peace to all-out war in the space of a minute—but somehow classifying it as my "duty" every bit as much as my peaceful occupations helped. It didn't make it easy: it just made it possible. If you drape the word *duty* over *murder*, well— you can hardly tell it's murder anymore. Add the words *in wartime*, and the word *murder* simply disappears.

How, then, should I do my duty? Summoning large waves to wash men overboard would be inefficient and tax my system so much that I would age quickly and become useless. Better to use funneled, targeted currents similar to what I used to propel myself quickly through the water.

My first effort to capsize the nearest boat gave the occupants a scare but didn't succeed. A bit stronger, then: triple the force I would use for myself, applied to the right side of the keel, amidships. Over it went, bodies thrashing in the cold water, and I felt a small ache bloom between my eyes. It was not entirely without cost, then, to focus that kind of pressure, but it was a small cost. Propelling myself to the site, I drew out a black volcanic knife chipped from the flows of the Glass Desert, ideal for water work, and opened some long gashes along the limbs of these unnaturally tall invaders, passing through them to get to the other side, where another boat awaited my attention. Blood in the water would bring the bladefins along to finish the job I had started. Probability of a feeding frenzy was high.

As I repeated the process on the next boat, tumbling tall bodies into the deep, the true size of the force seeped into my consciousness, chilling me far more than the water did. It was no mere raiding party but an army of many thousands, capable of sacking the city. Had I been sleeping at home rather than on duty in the water, most if not all of them would have already landed before I could do anything. I could only hope that the mariners on night patrol would be able to handle those who slipped past me while I did everything I could to prevent any more from landing.

After the second boat, I zipped through the waves back to Pelemyn's docks to take out the leading ships—the fewer that landed, the better. From there I worked my way back out, always taking out the nearest boat first. Even if some of the invaders managed to swim for shore, they would be cold and weary and demoralized when they tried to attack the walls and would be attacking singly or in very small groups rather than large waves.

Once near the docks, I saw that three ships had landed and a small horde of skeletal giants were disembarking, swords held high, removing all doubt about the nature of this fleet. I wanted to go ashore and help or raise the alarm but knew that my priority had to be preventing the rest from landing.

The ache between my eyes grew incrementally with every ship I scuttled, and I was breathing heavily after three. After the fifth the bladefins and other predators had homed in on the blood and were finishing what I had started. More blood meant more predators on the way; they could chew through the army for me if I could just get them into the water.

I had to dodge several bladefins myself, but they never came back for a second pass when there were so many other easy targets thrashing about, practically begging to be eaten.

And they *were* eaten. The invaders screamed underwater, but still I heard them, garbled bubbles of terror popping in my ears as jaws sank into them, their severed limbs and intestines floating past me in clouds of blood, each drop a siren call to frenzy for everything in the ocean possessed of more teeth than brains. Seeing and hearing that hurt me, for even then I doubted I was doing the right thing. Had we spoken the same language, I wondered, could we have avoided it all?

They did not look as if they had come to talk, and that was what my duty told me. But even if my duty stood tall and proud like the cliffs of Setyrön, waves of guilt kept crashing against them, determined to wear them down as I dumped ship after ship into the ocean and men flailed and gasped and died. And every effort I made to force water to do my will drew days of my life away, unseen like the undertow of tides yet felt and feared as all forces of nature should be. Aging quickly was the price I had to pay for my blessing, and I swore to myself when I first swam out of Bryn's Lung that I would never regret using it in my country's defense—still: ninety-seven ships and pain like a nail in my head. There had probably been a hundred men or more on each boat. Whoever these tall foreigners were, they had sent ten thousand men against us without warning or, so far as I knew, any provocation from us. They would have completely overwhelmed us had I not been on duty.

When the last ship capsized and the pale figures cried out, knowing what awaited them in the deep since they saw what had happened to all the others, I took a moment to simply tread water with my own muscles, bereft of my kenning, weary beyond anything I had ever known. The firebowls of Pelemyn were not even visible where I was, which told me I was far out to sea. Returning to the docks meant I would have to weave through the feeding frenzy, but it was necessary: better to dodge bladefins than krakens. I was in deep enough waters that I would have to worry about true monsters, and a disturbance in the currents beneath me hinted that one was approaching, attracted by all the blood.

That prompted me to wonder: How did such a fleet cross the ocean without falling prey to krakens? If I had felt the fleet's passage on the surface, then surely the krakens would have.

I skimmed the floor of the ocean on the way back, opting to swim underneath the ongoing frenzy but unable to avoid seeing some of the aftermath. I saw a crab scuttling across the ocean floor with a pale chewed hand clutched in its claws. That was a hand that had belonged to a man who had used it to greet his friends once, or hug his mother, or offer a gift of love or perhaps an apology. Now it was food for a crawling thing in the ocean, and I had made that happen.

Ninety-seven hundred deaths on my head if my estimates were correct. And it was all duty. Not murder.

Per protocol, I had to report directly to the pelenaut after using lethal force, so I would use the Lung's underwater locks to get to the city Wellspring from the harbor. I did surface briefly to see what was happening at the docks and immediately saw the bodies of a few mariners and citizens lying sprawled on the boards. The firebowls illuminated a battle for the walls in progress—the invaders had actually reached the top without benefit of towers or ladders. The ghoulish giants swarmed on top of one another, making ladders out of their own bodies, quick and lithe and horrifying like snow spiders—if spiders could wield swords! Once I saw them confronting our mariners at the top, I worried that we might lose the city to these mere three hundred, because one of them, dressed in no more than bones and rags, hacked down a mariner by first splitting his shield and then carrying the blow through to cave in his skull through the helmet.

I had never seen the like; that took incredible force. Their weapons were swords in the sense that they were blades attached to a hilt but were nothing like any sword I had seen before. Only one side had been sharpened, and the blade angled up to a ridge, then back down again. Viewed from the side, the sword looked like a child's drawing of a mountain, albeit a gently sloped one. Their long reach and that design, coupled with good steel, clearly gave them a deadly advantage. There were only a few of them up top as yet, though more were ascending, and they were mowing through mariners like cutting summer wheat. I almost decided to climb out of the water to give what help I could, but someone had raised the alarm with the garrison, and a squadron of archers arrived on the south side as I watched. They let loose a flight, and the giants went down, their scant armor doing little to stop the arrows. Another flight aimed at the base of the human ladder buckled it, and the pile of them collapsed to the ground. They wouldn't make it back up the wall again. Confident that the garrison now had matters in hand, I ducked down beneath the waves and cycled through the Lung's locks.

I emerged in the Wellspring behind the coral throne, in the pelenaut's pool but around a little-used corner. None but one of Bryn's blessed could navigate the locks without drowning, but the egress was guarded by a mariner anyway—one who had a spear pointed at me until she recognized my face. She raised it and apologized once I gave her a tired grin in greeting. "We're feeling some pressure here, Gerstad," she said, addressing me by my military rank rather than my kenning.

"As you should be," I said, dripping on the floor a moment before wicking away the moisture with a thought, dropping it back into the pool. "I have a report for either the pelenaut or the Lung. May I see one or both?"

"Certainly. I can't leave my post now but please proceed."

"Thank you. Before I go—how old am I?"

"Your pardon?"

"How old do I look?"

The mariner shrugged, uncertain. "Midthirties?"

That was a relief because I'd appeared to be in my midthirties before the watch began. Well, maybe my younger thirties, but midthirties wasn't bad. I felt older and slower and wanted nothing so much as a cup of tea and a day or three of sleep, but that would have to wait. I trod down the short hall with the pool's feeder channel on my right and rounded the corner to find the pelenaut pacing in front of his throne and his wall of water. The Lung was there, too, along with several military personages of higher rank than mine—even the Könstad was there—and some others I did not recognize. Before I could say anything or salute, the pelenaut spied me and interrupted the Lung. "Ah! Gerstad Tallynd du Böll! So glad you're here! Please come, report."

I recounted what I had done and the reasoning behind it and watched for signs of disapproval. I couldn't tell if I had done the right thing: they all wore masks of grim stone, and I was giving my report without knowing the full situation outside. Had any of the invaders made it into the city? When I finished, Pelenaut Röllend said, "Thank you, Gerstad. Könstad du Lallend."

"Yes?"

"Please fetch me an update on our casualties and dispatch the rapids while I talk to the Gerstad for a moment."

He motioned me to follow him and led me around the corner to his pool behind the throne, the same way I had entered. He dismissed the mariner on guard there and waited until we were alone, and then, much to my surprise, he hugged me.

"There is no doubt you have saved Pelemyn tonight," he said. "Thank you. I was asleep until moments ago and would not have been able to stop them as you did."

"Normally I would have been asleep, too."

"We were fortunate for sure. I know you must be tired, but I can't spare you now. There's more to do."

My headache flared at the mere thought of more water work, but I tried to smooth away the wince on my face and keep the pain out of my voice. "Of course, Pelenaut Röllend. What can I do?"

"I'm worried that we weren't the only target. I need to know as soon as possible if other cities were attacked. If they haven't been, then we need to warn them that an attack may be coming."

"Down to Gönerled, then?"

"No, I'm sending a couple of rapids there. I need you to go up to Festwyf with all possible speed." I had to swallow my fear at those words, and he saw it. "I know that's asking a lot." He was asking me to move so quickly through the water that I essentially became it and in the process stripped away years of my life. I had told my boys often that this day might come, but now that it was here, I doubted that they truly understood; already I had lost some time, and who knew how much older I would be when I came home?

"It's your prerogative to ask," I said, and once I got past my visceral reaction, I agreed it was necessary. Advance warning might be the difference between saving the city and losing it. "May I beg a small favor in return?"

"Of course."

"Look after my boys while I'm gone. I was supposed to be home in time to take them to school, and if I'm not there—" They had already gone to sleep one night and woken up without a father the next morning; I didn't want them to lose another parent the same way. They would be worried regardless, but maybe someone could reassure them.

"Done," he said.

"Thank you. And . . ." My question died in my throat. "Never mind. Time's wasting."

"No, go ahead and ask. You've certainly earned an extra question. A promotion, too, once we have the luxury of ceremony again."

"Do you know who these people are? Or why they attacked us?"

The pelenaut shook his head. "I've never heard of them. Haven't managed to even see them yet, but I'm told they're definitely not Hathrim."

"No. These are not like any giants we've seen before."

A helpless shrug from the pelenaut. "I had no idea they existed. Which makes me wonder where they came from and how they knew we existed."

"I'll seal my questions in a jar, then, and open it later. Currents keep you safe, Pelenaut Röllend."

"And you, Gerstad du Böll."

I was back in the ocean minutes later, headed north, pushing water in front and pulling it down the length of my body, sleeving myself through the deep, but this time I pushed and pushed until the resistance faded and the water welcomed me as part of it, my uniform slipped away and foundered in my wake, and I became the tide rolling in to Festwyf, where the fresh sluice of the Gravewater River fed the Peles Ocean. I lost time traveling that way—so much time—and more prosaic things, like my glass knife. I didn't pull out of the tide trance until I hit the freshwater. There I slowed down, felt the sharp ache of a year's strain on my organs and bones—quite possibly more—and surfaced.

Festwyf was quiet, and for a moment I harbored a hope that all was well. The firebowls still burned on the walls and the docks as they should. But upon closer inspection, there were bodies slumped over the walls near those fires. There was blood in the river and corpses bobbed near the docks. And at those docks, stretching back into the ocean, was an anchored fleet of the giants' ships.

But there were no screams or sounds of fighting, nor were there sounds of a victory celebration. In fact, there were no sounds of a city at all, even those which a city at night might be expected to make. There was only the sound of water, and this was the first time in my life when I did not find it comforting.

I swam closer to the docks and pulled myself out of the ocean, concluding that there was no reason to be worried about my modesty when everyone was dead. I saw that there were both Brynt and giant bodies littering the area, but far more Brynts. The giants had surprised Festwyf as they had surprised Pelemyn, except that Festwyf had had no tidal mariner here to keep them from landing. The other two tidal mariners, aside from Pelenaut Röllend himself, were to the south in Setyrön and Hillegöm; one could only hope they were in a position to do as I had done.

When I came to the first dead invader, who had three arrows through his chest, I crouched down to examine him a bit closer, since I'd had no chance previously. They were pasty men, seven to nine feet each, possessed of stringy muscles and little else. They had no armor whatsoever on their legs—no pants either, which I thought vaguely obscene—and only rudimentary fibrous material strapped to the soles of their feet. They wore bands of cloth wrapped around their loins and then a basic undershirt belted to it. On top of this they had tied a sheet of flat rib bones to the front and back of their torsos. Said bones were too large and wide to be human as I originally feared. They had also tied smaller sets of these to rest on top of their shoulders and to protect their upper arms. No helmets, but not for lack of steel. Their swords were well made. Except for the handles; those were wrapped in poor cloth rather than leather. With a start, I realized they had no leather at all. Even their belts were made of woven fibers.

I mentally added to the giants' list of contradictions: Though their boats were crude, they had enough sophistication at sea to coordinate an attack at multiple sites on the same evening. But none of them remained on their ships—they were all silent, anchored hulks. So where were the invaders now?

I took the giant's sword—a bit heavy for me, but it might prove useful later—and padded barefoot across the planks of the docks to the city walls. No one challenged me. The gates were open, and piles of the dead stared up at the sky or lay sprawled in positions they would never adopt in life, and each one of them said to me that I would find nothing different beyond. They were right.

Inside the city there was no sign of survivors apart from lit buildings. I investigated a few of them to see if anyone remained inside, but in each case they turned out to be untended candles or fires burning low, illuminating a massacre of the inhabitants. The Wellspring was littered with the bodies of the city's leaders. And I discovered that many people had been slain in their beds, efficiently murdered in their sleep.

Bryn preserve us, they had killed the children, too.

So these giants were not fond of war cries and waking up the populace. In fact, much of Pelemyn might still be unaware the city had been attacked if they were living far from the ocean walls. I thought about what I'd seen so far at both Pelemyn and Festwyf: Any person the giants saw was a target. Beyond that they had no clear military goals. They weren't loading their ships with material goods, so it wasn't our wealth they wanted, nor did they want to conquer and rule. They certainly gave us no diplomatic warning. They simply came to wipe us out. No threats or bluster or even an overture of diplomacy. Just blades parting skin and sawing flesh.

"What did we do to deserve this?" I wondered aloud, stunned. "Why slaughter us all?" The dead gave me no answers.

There might have been some survivors hidden away—I dearly hoped there were—but it wasn't my mission to conduct a search and rescue. I had to find the giants, and they had already moved on. I had to move also, even though all I wanted to do was weep for the dead.

Back to the Gravewater River. I dived in with the giant's sword and sleeved myself upstream, keeping my head above the surface and my eyes turned to the southern shore. The Merchant Trail there was wide and would allow an army to move quickly. I found them only two leagues away, setting up a camp under moonlight and torchlight. They had raided for food at least and had a significant train behind them—everything pillaged from Festwyf, right down to the carts. I could make no accurate count but was sure there were many thousands, and they sprawled for a good distance along the riverbank. They obviously planned to move at speed down the Merchant Trail and attack the river cities in turn. They had no siege weapons and needed none, counting on surprise and their overwhelming numbers to win.

My orders were to report on Festwyf and the army's whereabouts; technically, I had all I needed and should return now. But the pelenaut had also mentioned warning Festwyf if possible. I couldn't do that now, but I was the only person who could warn Fornyd that there was an army bearing down on them in time to make a difference.

I didn't know who was running Fornyd in the pelenaut's name, but he or she would probably want some evidence of my report despite my kenning and in whose name I worked. I hoped the sword I carried would suffice.

Moving away from the riverbank toward the center where I'd be able to go a bit faster, I was just beginning to sleeve myself upriver when a giant shouted in surprise. My eyes tracked the sound to the shore, where I spied a slack-jawed brute relieving himself, adding his own stream to the river's. His painted skull face gaped at me in disbelief. I could have simply moved on and probably should have, but instead he became a target for all my frustration and rage over what I'd seen in Festwyf. I wanted someone to pay for it, and he had been there. He had taken part in it. And he was in front of me now.

"So much blood you've spilled," I growled at him through clenched teeth, though I'm sure he didn't understand a word. "Drown in it!"

His body was largely made of water, as all creatures were, and I called to small pockets of it on either side of his chest, just a short pull, about the length of a finger joint. The blood burst from the vessels in his lungs and began filling them up with every beat of his heart. He tried to shout again but coughed wetly instead, and then he gurgled, collapsed, and died. I waited to feel better, for some sweet rush of justice or vindication, but it never came. That life, taken in anger, had not been my duty. I still regret it even though he quite probably deserved it.

I didn't resume my full-speed pace upriver because I wanted to scout as I moved. Three times on the way to Fornyd I stopped, woke up camps of merchants sleeping in tents by the bank by shouting at them, and told them to head to Fornyd immediately or they would meet an army that would slaughter them. They didn't question my authority; I floated in the river without being moved by its current or visibly swimming against it, and they knew that tidal mariners would not appear out of the river if it wasn't an emergency.

At the gray croak of dawn I arrived at the riverside docks of Fornyd, looking at it the way the invaders would: a fat fish that practically jumps into your stew pot. The walls were not especially high or thick compared to those of the coastal cities. It would fall quickly if taken by surprise. Even with warning it might fall quickly. The giants would be atop those walls in no time, and there were more of them in that army than there were perhaps in the entire city; Fornyd was more of an ambitious town than a city, a trading hub for the farmers who sprawled out to the south and east and west.

The Lung's Locks had not been used in years, perhaps not since my last visit when I was doing my river tour as a new tidal mariner. They had crusted over with sediment, and it took some work to open the outer hatch. Inside, however, the locks were unusually clean. Cleaner than Pelemyn's, and Pelemyn's enjoyed frequent use. The sleepy mariner stationed at the other end was mightily surprised to see me emerge, however. He jumped and made an undignified noise and only then remembered that he was supposed to be professional should a tidal mariner ever show up.

"I—uh. Sorry, mariner. *Tidal* Mariner. Sorry. How can I help?"

"I came at speed with urgent news. If you could provide me a robe?"

"Oh! Yes! Of course! Sorry again!" He turned to the wall behind him, where a robe waited precisely for occasions such as this. He plucked it off the hook and held it out, politely keeping his head turned toward the wall. When I had pulled myself out of the pool and wrapped the robe around me, he escorted me to the Wellspring and begged me to wait while he summoned the city's quartermaster. It was still quite early, and she wouldn't have risen yet.

She appeared less than a minute later, a woman in her forties with hair cropped short like mine, a blue robe hastily thrown on and still knuckling away sleep from her eyes but anxious to hear what I had to say. I liked her immediately—I had been kept waiting in the past by others.

"Yes? What's the matter?"

"Gerstad Tallynd du Böll, sent by the pelenaut," I said by way of introduction.

"Quartermaster Farlen du Cannym. What news?"

I held up the giant's sword and said, "About ten thousand giants carrying these are headed this way. Festwyf is already lost, and you're next."

Her nostrils flared briefly and her eyes widened, and then she visibly controlled herself and clasped her hands together. "Hathrim are coming here?"

"No, these aren't Hathrim. They top out at nine feet, I'd say, rather than twelve. They crossed the ocean. We've never seen them before."

I explained the night's events and respectfully suggested that her duty must be to warn not only the people of Fornyd but the other river cities and perhaps even Rael. Pelemyn was a safe place for people to run if they wished; I could speak for no other cities yet since the situation was still developing, but Pelenaut Röllend would keep it safe in my absence.

"Use archers, or pikemen if you must," I offered. "Keep them at a distance because at close range they will win with their reach and these weapons every time. I'll leave this with you so that your mariners can test it."

"Leave? You're leaving?" A note of panic might have crept into her voice and expression. She didn't seem the type to boil over quickly, however. Perhaps it was only stress, which would be understandable.

"I must report back to the pelenaut and tell him about Festwyf. I'll also tell him that I warned you and that you will hopefully warn the other river cities."

"Of course; you can be sure of that. But . . . I have so few mariners here. Hardly any of the blessed, just a few rapids. We cannot possibly hope to stand against ten thousand."

"I know, Quartermaster. But this isn't a war you have to win by yourself. Pelenaut Röllend would never expect that. This is developing too quickly for anyone to help you—and I'm sure that's by design. They are trying to move so quickly that each city is taken by surprise.

But now you have the opportunity to save many people. Reduce the enemy's numbers if you can. And seriously consider evacuating. If the invaders follow the pattern of Festwyf, they will leave the city intact, taking only food. They have no cavalry, and they don't know the surrounding area like you do. They're simply coming up the road and killing whatever's in the way. So my advice is to get out of the way."

She took a deep breath and nodded once on her exhalation. "I understand, Gerstad. Head for high ground when the floodwaters come."

I knew Fornyd was in good hands then. "Exactly. What are floods but Bryn's admonishment that we should build better? Let the flood pass over and rebuild in its wake." I bowed. "And if I may make a suggestion, hide all the wells you can. Make them drink from the Gravewater. Since they're not from around here, they probably don't know how it got its name, if they know it at all."

Her head jerked in surprise. "Oh! Yes, we'll do that."

"May the currents keep you safe."

"And you as well."

She was calling for her mariners and longshoremen before I left the room. I returned the robe to its hook and cycled through the locks to the Gravewater. Once there, I pushed myself past the flesh, becoming one with the tide again and flowing back to Pelemyn. I was using the Lung's Locks for the second time by midmorning. The same mariner who'd been on duty during the night was still there. She looked worried this time as she helped me out of the pool.

"What?" I said. My voice was dry and scratchy to my own ears. "How bad is it?" Once I had wicked away the water and the mariner had settled a robe about my shoulders, a coughing fit racked me and everything hurt. Stabbing pains in my abdomen like a harpoon in my guts. Needles in my fingertips and toes. A vise squeezed my spine and all the muscles in my back, and my legs didn't want to support me. I knelt at first, and when that was too much, I slumped sideways, curled up into a ball.

"I . . . it's nothing, Gerstad. Forgive me," she said. "Welcome home. Just catch your breath." She patted my shoulder a couple of times as if

I were a child. We both felt awkward about that, but she clearly didn't know what else to do.

"Tell me," I gasped, lying in a fetal position on the deck. We were still behind the coral throne, and no one else yet knew I had arrived unless my coughing fit had alerted them. "I need to know before I see myself in a glass. Before the others see me, too, so I can deal with their faces. Yours is a kind one." She pressed her lips together and shook her head. "Please. You'll be doing me a favor."

Grimacing, the mariner told me, "You look to be in your midforties now, Gerstad. Well, maybe the downstream half of it. I'm sorry."

Almost fifty, then. I had looked to be in my midthirties when I woke up. But in truth I am twenty-nine.

I wondered if my boys would even recognize me when I got home. But before I could think too much along those lines, I nodded, said thank you, and extended my arm. The mariner grasped it and hauled me to my feet. I leaned on her for a moment, and she was patient while I collected myself.

"All right," I finally said, standing straight and clutching my fists at my sides. "To the Wellspring to report. Currents keep you."

"And you."

I don't even remember giving that report. I remember the shock and pity that flowed across the faces of the pelenaut and the Lung when they saw me. I remember them saying that Gönerled had been lost as well and remembered that my sister lived there. I know there was more, but nothing stuck in my memory.

"I need you to go home and rest now," Pelenaut Röllend said. "You're dismissed until the morning."

The walk home across cobblestone streets was slow and painful to my knees, and though the sun was shining, I pulled up the hood of my robe and kept my head down to avoid encounters with people I knew. The last thing I wanted was to talk about what happened and why I looked so old.

People were still going about their business like it was any other midweek morning. Buying apples in the market and haggling over the price of cooking herbs. Apprentices running errands for their masters and laughing at ribald jokes. It was still too early: they had no idea that entire cities had been wiped out last night and might not even know that Pelemyn had escaped the same fate by lucky chance. They'd all know by the end of the day. But right then the blissful normality was a living memory of what Brynlön had lost. They wouldn't be like this tomorrow or the day after that or for many days to come. For me it was like experiencing the past: these people were already ghosts from a better time.

And seeing them so happy, knowing it was to be that way for only a little while longer, and knowing that so many more were simply gone, like my sister, I wept.

There had been no time to weep before, to feel the enormity of it, because duty had given me no choice. And there had been the anger, of course. But on that lonely walk home, the only one aware that these were the final hours of what we once were, I could feel it. The sorrow bubbled within me until I could hardly breathe. I tried not to sob aloud and draw stares. I wouldn't want to ruin anyone's last few minutes of happiness.

But when I got home and closed the door behind me, I held nothing back. I simply dropped to the floor and cried for Festwyf and Gönerled and the others. For my sister and the mariners who'd died on Pelemyn's walls and the people down by the docks. For my shortened life and knowing that I'd have to shorten it further before this was done. For the years I wouldn't be with my boys. I knew I would never live to see my grandchildren, and I cried for that. And I knew that if I didn't do my duty, then I wouldn't have grandchildren at all, nor would anyone else.

And the worst part was not knowing the answers. Who were these giants, and why had they attacked us? How was it possible to cross the ocean in such huge fleets?

Picking myself off the floor, I shuffled wearily to the kitchen and found a note from the next-door neighbor: "Boys are happy and off to school. Sleep well! —Perla"

And underneath that was written:

"Checked on them personally. They are safe. —Föstyr"

Thank the currents for that. I wondered if school would even continue for much longer. This might be their last day of bliss as well. I hoped it would be a good one and worth remembering. And I hoped that when they got home, my boys would love their older mother as much as they loved their younger mother from yesterday.

I wiped away tears from my cheeks, hoping nobody had seen me lose control, but then realized I was not the only person weeping. Seemed like everyone was because we *did* remember those last few hours of happiness before the news of the invasion, how sweet and peaceful life had been. And when the bard dispelled his seeming, the roar from Survivor Field grew and grew, not so much for him but for Tallynd, for she came back to the stage to wave and blow kisses at us. She was crying, too, and I understood why the bard had had to tell that story for her. How could anyone expect her to relive that as a performance? That gray at the temples I'd seen before—I thought stupidly that it reflected her true age. Like most people I'd heard that our tidal mariner had saved us the night of the invasion, but I had no idea what that involved or that she was a twenty-nine-year-old widow with two young boys.

All blessings have their particular curses, I'm told. Hygienists never age the way tidal mariners do, for example, but they become absolutely paranoid about contaminants and infections and scrub themselves constantly since they perceive impurities in almost everything.

But sacrifices like Tallynd's should be recognized and rewarded. And just as I was thinking I should create the most glorious gift basket of all time for her, Pelenaut Röllend appeared and joined Tallynd and Fintan on the precarious stack of crates. He *had* the most glorious gift basket for her in his hands, which satisfied every Brynt's dire need to give her one right then. Fintan projected both of their voices, and that was when I learned what that insignia on her uniform meant—it was indeed a new rank, and she wasn't a Gerstad anymore.

"Second Könstad Tallynd du Böll, almost everyone within hearing right now owes their life to you, and they know it. If I don't give you this gift basket *right now*, your house will be buried with them tomorrow." Cathartic laughter and cheering. "Please accept this from a grateful pelenaut and a grateful people."

She sort of laugh-cried, a chuckle followed by a sniff, and took it from him. "Thank you. Thank you all. This is the best gift basket I've ever received, and I will cherish it. It will have a place of honor in my home."

There was more applause for her because she deserved all we could give, but eventually she and the pelenaut waved and departed, leaving Fintan alone on the stage.

"There will be more tomorrow," he assured us as the sun was setting. "But these will be stories from the far west! Until then, may the gods of all the kennings keep your loves!"

Cheers followed the bard as he stepped down off the crates and took a long draught from the flagon of Mistmaiden Ale; the woman from the Siren's Call had never left. He thanked her and asked her to lead the way to Master Yöndyr's establishment, then he turned to me.

"Coming, Master Dervan?"

"Absolutely."

Day 2

ERUPTION

Before we go forward, we should probably go back. My association with Fintan had begun the previous day, when he arrived at Pelemyn in the company of a Raelech courier and ruined what was shaping up to be a pleasant day of boring logistic details. Couriers didn't normally cause a stir, but this one had become annoyed when she wasn't ushered immediately into the pelenaut's presence.

That was the explanation of the breathless mariner who burst into the Wellspring, helmet askew, to seek guidance on how to proceed. The pelenaut flicked a finger at his Lung, Föstyr, and the old man stepped forward, arched an eyebrow, and pointed out to the mariner that he had left out why the courier had been detained. Normally couriers *were* brought immediately to the throne.

"She's with a bard, sir, and insists that he be allowed to accompany her."

Silence for a few seconds, and then the pelenaut asked Föstyr, "Presumably there is some problem with the bard?"

The Lung nodded once, the wattles under his chin rippling at the sudden movement. "An old law, sir. Raelech bards aren't to be trusted."

The pelenaut frowned. "How old is this law? Rael is our ally, and this bard is escorted by a courier of the Triune Council, is he not?"

"It's a very old law, sir."

"Then let's move on and flush it down the shit sluice. Bring in some extra mariners if you think it prudent but allow the courier and bard to approach."

Föstyr rattled off some orders and there was a general scramble to obey, and the pelenaut looked back at me and smirked briefly, sharing a moment of amusement that the same muscle-bound bullies who used to slap him around as a child now thought of nothing but his safety.

Pelenaut Röllend and I had been childhood friends and used to get beat up by the same bands of fish heads in our youth, before he got his kenning and became politically powerful. After he closed the university out of necessity—my office and classroom were lodging for refugees now—he brought me to court to be a historian of sorts during a historically significant time, since his usual court scribe had been drafted to help administer the families staying in Survivor Field and record the many deaths they reported. My fingers were ink-stained and cramped from sitting at a desk behind and to the right of the coral throne and scribbling down everything I could, but I was grateful for the work and the cot to crash on when I couldn't bear to face Elynea and proud of the leader my old friend Rölly had become.

He didn't sit on his throne very much; he tended to pace in front of it, fully engaged in the governing of the country, especially now that we were fighting for our very survival as a people. "Water which does not move stagnates," he explained. And when he wasn't forced to govern from (or in front of) his seat of power, he toured the city in disguise, taking only a discreet bodyguard along to "solve problems upstream" before they could flow down to him in the Wellspring.

Once she was admitted, the courier proved to be an unusually tall and striking woman, her hair pulled tightly from her face and gathered in the back with a golden torc and a pair of goggles dangling around her neck. Her rust-red leather armor—and the bard's as well—was spattered with the guts of insects, the visible drawback to a courier's kenning. The ability to run so fast that insects became a hazard simultaneously thrilled and disgusted me.

The bard stood a step behind the courier when she halted in front of the throne. She nodded to the pelenaut and said, "Pelenaut Röllend, I am Numa, Courier of the Huntress Raena," in that strange formal protocol the Raelechs used: always their given name, profession, and patron goddess. She told him about the approaching armies that were supposed to join with us and mount a counterattack against the Bone Giants, which would have been very interesting to me if the bard hadn't been there with her. I confess I missed some of the details because I was far too curious about her companion—which probably proves that I am not the best court recorder.

Bards and couriers were elite castes in the Raelech system, which allowed only seven and twenty of each to exist at any time. Couriers we saw often, but I doubted anyone in the Wellspring had ever seen a Raelech bard before. He had a pack on his back with a couple of stringed instruments sticking up out of the top, a rather full pouch of something at his belt that was far too big to be a purse, and a pleasant, confident expression that I envied. I would not be so comfortable meeting the ruler of another country.

"Very well," Rölly said when the courier's official message ended. "What other news do you have for me?"

"Only an introduction, sir, and a request for lodging this evening. I will return in the morning to take any reply you wish back to the Triune Council." Numa took two steps back so that the bard was closest to the throne, and she gestured to him. "My colleague in service to the Triune and my lifebond, Fintan." Her smile as she introduced him was proud.

The pelenaut was not the only one who had to squelch a look of surprise at that personal addition. Fintan was not conventionally handsome, and the top of his head reached only to Numa's chin. They did not appear to be well matched, but that only increased my curiosity.

Rölly stopped pacing, netted his fingers together, and nodded once at the bard. "Tell me why you are here, Fintan."

"I . . ." He flicked his eyes back at his wife, who nodded in encouragement. "I am a gift of sorts from the Triune Council."

"A gift?"

"It would be more accurate to say I am on loan. I am to go with the Raelech army once it arrives, but in the meantime, I am to provide my services to the people of Pelemyn free of charge."

"Your services?"

"Entertainment, sir."

"What? Singing and dancing?"

The bard shuddered at the thought of dancing and said, "The occasional song, perhaps. But mostly it will be the tale of how we got here so that we will know where we are going."

Pelenaut Röllend's eyes widened. "You presume to know where this is all headed?"

"No, sir. The future always waits until the present to reveal its plans. But the past can clarify our goals for us sometimes, help us say goodbye to those we haven't let go, even realize that we need to change. That is the magic of stories. And my kenning allows me to tell stories better than anyone else, if you'll allow me a moment of immodesty."

"I don't understand. The Third Kenning is of the earth, but the Raelech blessed are known for erecting stone walls and destroying them more than anything else. How does that allow you to tell stories well?"

"Bards do have an unusual adaptation to the kenning, sir," Fintan replied, and flicked his eyes to his wife. "We share one with couriers, in fact: a perfect memory, the memory of earth. Crucial to storytelling and to relaying messages alike. But where couriers are gifted with extraordinary speed, bards are gifted with extraordinary voices. Our voices can be heard for a league if we wish it, and we can also take on the voices and likenesses of those we have met. It allows us to tell the story of the earth and the people on it."

"You can change your appearance? I have heard rumors of this tal-

ent but have never seen it. My Lung informs me that we have a law
against it."

"I'm well aware, sir. Most of the nations do out of an excess of caution. It's why we bards are rarely seen outside the borders of Rael. May
I have your permission to demonstrate this aspect of my kenning?"

The pelenaut nodded, and Fintan fished in a pouch to produce one
of his black spheres, about the size of a small egg—at that time we
didn't know what it was. When he pulled it out, Föstyr barked and four
mariners sprang forward, spears pointed at the bard's throat. Fintan
froze and Numa protested as more mariners surrounded the pelenaut
and moved him back from the perceived threat, but Röllend demanded
that they leave the bard untouched and then, somewhat exasperated
behind a wall of flesh and armor, asked Fintan what he might have
there.

"My deepest apologies for not explaining first. It is a natural rock we
extract from the Poet's Range, easily broken and hollow inside, that
will release a gas that allows me to cast a seeming."

"How does a gas allow you to cast a seeming?"

"I am imprinting it now, as I hold it, with the form and voice I wish
to take."

"Whose?"

"Yours, Pelenaut Röllend. I thought it might be amusing."

"You thought it would be amusing to impersonate the pelenaut?"
Föstyr roared. His anger caused some of the mariners' spear points to
twitch, and Fintan's eyes shot back and forth between them.

"I am reevaluating the humor now, and I admit it does not hold up
well to inspection. My comedic instincts are below average at best."

Rölly shot me a glance that indicated that he thought the bard's
humor was perfectly serviceable. "Remain still," he said, "and explain
precisely what you were about to do with that rock."

"I was going to throw it onto the toe of my boot, where it would
break, and once the gas rose and adhered to my form, I would seem to
be you. If I may be allowed to continue under the close supervision of
your mariners, you will see how easily the illusion is pierced—ah, no.

Not pierced. Poor choice of words." The bard tried to make eye contact with the mariners without moving. "Please do not pierce anything, gentlemen."

"Very well. Mariners, please take a step back and let the bard enact exactly what he spoke." As they did so, Pelenaut Röllend added, "Make sure that rock goes to your feet and nowhere else, sir, or my mariners may misinterpret your intentions."

"Understood."

Once given room, Fintan tossed the pellet down, the gas rose up around him, and he copied Pelenaut Röllend's form perfectly, growing a foot in stature and changing his clothes from the Raelech rust and brown leathers to the Brynt blue and white tailoring. He smiled broadly and spoke in the pelenaut's own voice, "You are looking very fine today, sir, if I may say so."

After the gasps of awe at this demonstration I followed the gaze of Föstyr, who was turning his head back and forth to judge the accuracy of the copy. If he found a flaw, he didn't say so.

"Well done," the Lung said. "And how do we banish this seeming?"

"Any physical contact or a strong wind can blow it away. Or rain, for that matter. It is easily dispersed. Please ask one of your mariners to clap me on the shoulder or shake my hand or any other nonlethal contact and watch what happens."

Föstyr chucked his chin at one of the mariners, and the man reached out with his left hand and laid it on the bard's shoulder. The fabric of the tunic parted like vapor, his hand sank out of sight as if into a cloud, and when he removed his hand, there was a hole in the pelenaut's seeming through which we could see Fintan's leathers somewhat below. The seeming of the pelenaut said, "Thank you, that will do admirably," and his voice changed from Röllend's baritone to Fintan's tenor by the end of the sentence. "You see, I never physically change my shape—it is all an optical illusion—and the seeming cannot survive physical contact." The seeming began to warp and slide in disturbing fashion as the gas lost the surface tension keeping it together. Fintan slowly raised his own left hand and wiped at his face so that we could see him again, and after that larger breach was made, the seeming came apart much more quickly over the rest of his body. "When I perform, I have a different gas that disperses this more quickly. These gifts of the poet goddess are intended to help me tell stories, not practice espionage, and it is easily countered."

"But you understand why it leads to mistrust," the pelenaut said.

"I do, sir. That's why we wished to be forthright with you," the bard said, and the pelenaut asked the mariners to back off.

"This story you wish to tell," Föstyr said. "Can you give us the short version?"

"Certainly." Once Fintan outlined the broad swaths of his tale, it was quickly decided to accept the bard's services and allow him to meet Tallynd du Böll. The pelenaut grew enthusiastic about what it would do for the city's morale—the prospect had already visibly improved his own—and then he startled me by whipping his head around in my direction.

"Master Dervan. Come forward, please." I laid down my pen and rose, clasping my hands behind my back to hide my stained fingers, then limped as quickly as my old knee injury would allow. The pelenaut signaled with an arm that I should stand beside him, and once I did, he presented me to the bard. "Numa and Fintan, this is Master Dervan du Alöbar, lately of the university but currently my court historian. I would consider it a personal favor, Fintan, if you would allow him to record your tale for posterity."

If the bard was as surprised as I was by the request, he hid it well. He was so smooth that I wondered what it would take to rattle him; even the spear points had only made him careful. "A pleasure to meet you, Master Dervan," he said. Numa said nothing but nodded at me when our eyes met. "And of course you are welcome to write it down. Should I be worried about the speed of your handwriting?"

The pelenaut smiled and answered for me. "He will do his best, and of course you shall approve the manuscript."

That elicited an answering grin from the bard. "An opportunity to

improve on my performance! A dangerous incentive to offer a poet."
His eyes slid over to me, amused and clearly teasing me. "We could be
editing for years, Master Dervan."

"So be it," I said, infected by the bard's good nature.

"Excellent," Pelenaut Röllend said, and then he deftly handed the
Raelechs off to Föstyr to see to the details of their lodging for the evening while he recessed the court for a few minutes and drew me with
him behind the throne to the Wellspring's water wall. Normally this
fell in an unbroken curtain of water that made only a pleasant background noise, but there were rocks set in the wall and Rölly used his
kenning to split the stream again and again around those rocks to
make the water drop as noisily as possible into the drainage basin and
thus obscure our conversation from any nearby ears.

Rölly threw an arm around my shoulders and said in a low voice,
"Welcome to the world of intrigue, Master Dervan. That man is a spy
for the Triune Council. A very politely introduced spy but a spy nonetheless. And you get to watch him."

"What?"

"You're perfectly suited for the job."

"How can you say that, Rölly? I'm an historian. I study things in the
past so I don't have to deal with people in the present."

"Remember to keep your voice down," he cautioned. A recessed
court did not equal an empty one. "And you weren't always an historian. You were an excellent mariner before your injury forced a career
change. And Sarena must have taught you a thing or two."

My jaw dropped. Sarena had been a spy for Rölly and for his prede-
cessor as well. Publicly I had presented her death as the result of a
tragic fatal disease, but the two of us and the hygienist knew that she
actually had been poisoned at some point with a slow-acting agent.
Her liver failed over a period of weeks, and we had no idea who had
done it or when precisely she had been poisoned. A representative
from almost any country could have been responsible; someone had
wanted her removed permanently from the diplomatic corps and had

been exceedingly clever about it. She had shared some of her professional life with me as she weakened, knowing the end was near, but it was nothing like training.

Turning down my volume but turning up the desperation in my expression, I said, "A thing or two doesn't make me perfectly suited. I don't know what to do. I can't fight well or keep secrets or anything." I could hold a spear or sword but could not be expected to hold my ground. I could still walk without a cane most days, but my right knee would buckle at any pressure more strenuous than moving slowly forward.

"You don't know any secrets, so it's not a problem," he said, and that was true. Sarena had never shared anything sensitive with me. "And you don't need to fight."

"What am I supposed to do?"

"Have lunch with the guy every day and write down his story. Add in what you want about what's happening here. Ask him questions about Rael or whatever you like. He'll ask you about yourself and the city."

"And I'm supposed to answer?"

"Of course. Tell him the truth. Even about Sarena if he asks. I'm sure he already knows, and there's no way we can hide our situation here when he can see it for himself."

"What's the catch?"

"You can't sleep in the palace anymore. You have to go home, Dervan."

My stomach churned at the thought of it. "Why? I prefer it here, and I don't mind the cot."

"I understand your home is fraught with memories of your wife. But you have dammed up your emotions long enough, and you need to let them flow again. You can heal from this, and you will. That is what I say to every Brynt alive right now." He squeezed my shoulder and found my eyes. "Look, my friend, this is history happening right now. It needs to be written down, and I trust you to do it. You told me once about the people who always write the histories. Who are they again?"

"The victors," I said, and he smiled at me.

It was a bit dizzying to have another sudden change in my career—from mariner to scholar to court scribe to pseudo-spy with the country's fate possibly stranded in a tidal pool. But I remembered to count my many blessings: the majority of Brynts had lost far more in the invasion than their comfortable careers.

Elynea had lost practically everyone she knew except for her children. Her husband and her neighbors had all been hacked to component parts by the Bone Giants just outside the walls of Festwyf. Her husband had gone outside that night to investigate alarming noises and shouted at her to pick up the kids and run, don't look back. Spurred by the fear in his voice and the cries of others, she had done just that, barefoot and carrying nothing but her children.

They woke up screaming for their father most nights.

The kids seemed happy, though, when I arrived at my wee cottage with some fresh fish and a bag of rice practically plucked off a Fornish grain barge that had just docked. Through the window I saw (and heard) that Tamöd was pretending to be a tidal mariner diving for pearls and Pyrella was impersonating an unusually argumentative oyster. Elynea watched them from a chair at the kitchen table, eyes puffy and red but not actively weeping or even frowning. She wasn't smiling either, but perhaps the antics of her children would make that happen soon. I paused, feeling somewhat guilty at interrupting their peaceful moment by walking into my own house. But the fish wouldn't be getting any fresher that way.

I knocked on my door as a warning and called out a friendly hello. They startled and then relaxed, the kids shouting *"Dervaaaan!"* by way of welcome. Elynea rose, self-conscious, and looked about the kitchen and living area, perhaps to make sure nothing had been damaged by her inattention.

"Oh," she said, "we didn't expect you."

"I didn't expect to be here either. Things have changed a bit at the palace."

"They have? Not for the worse, I hope."

"Too early to tell. Hopefully it's for the better. But I won't need to work quite as much. Occasional morning meetings, but mostly I'll start at noon from now on and be finished by the early evening."

"That actually sounds like a better job. Is it?"

"We'll see. I start tomorrow."

Tamöd and Pyrella regaled me with tales of the tidal mariner and the oyster while Elynea and I tiptoed around each other, anxious not to invade the other's privacy. She pretended she hadn't been crying, and I pretended I didn't notice.

"Perhaps, if you will be here in the morning, I could look for a job," she ventured over dinner.

"While I look after the kids? Sure, I can do that."

"Thank you," she said, and then said practically nothing else the entire evening as if she felt she had trespassed enough.

Elynea made an effort to look confident and capable in the morning, and I think she pulled it off. Her curled cloud of hair was pulled back from her forehead with a white headband, and she wore a deep orange tunic with a white belt and brown pants tucked into boots.

"That's new," I noticed.

"Donated to me by the kind woman across the street."

I wished her luck and assured her that the kids would be fine, and she left in what I supposed passed for good spirits.

She returned at noon, defeated, her voice grating like a millstone. "There's no work to be had. At least no work for me. So many desperate people looking. Some of them can still smile, though." She shook her head. "I don't know how they do it."

I was silent for a few moments, thinking about how I managed it. When I thought of Sarena, watching her die slowly and helpless to prevent it, I found it impossible to smile, too.

"I think . . . maybe . . . ?" Elynea turned to me, waiting for me to finish. "They have figured out a way to forget temporarily." Her eyebrows climbed, and she shook her head at the impossibility of this. "No, I know you can't ever forget such a huge part of yourself," I assured her. "It's always there, an enormous thing—like the palace. But sometimes, you can go into a tiny room, lock the door behind you, and that vast, overwhelming sadness is on the other side. It'll always be there, and you can't stay in that locked room forever. But maybe, while you can't see it, you can forget about it a tiny while and discover something to smile about before you have to emerge and face the enormity again. And then, who knows? Maybe you'll find more and more rooms to smile in, and over time the character of the palace changes until it's the sadness that's locked in those tiny rooms and not the happiness. Maybe that's what healing is like."

Elynea stared at me, a plateau of sorts that I hoped might end well, but she dissolved into a loud sob and ran into my bedroom, slamming the door.

"Or maybe my skill with extended metaphors leaves much to be desired," I said.

"Why did you make my mom cry?" Tamöd shouted.

"You're so mean! I hate you!" Pyrella added, and the two of them ran to the other bedroom and followed the example of their mother by slamming the door as forcefully as they could. Sadness and anger behind the doors.

"Shit," I said. This was why I preferred history. All the shouting was in the past, and none of them had been shouting at me.

This is not to say that Elynea and her children were not welcome to my home; with my wife lost the winter before the invasion, I had more space than I needed, and sharing it was the least I could do in a time of crisis. Sharing any more than that, though, was impossible. Perhaps she saw the yawning empty place in my chest that Sarena used to fill and speculated about moving in there, and maybe she wondered if I could occupy the space in her heart where her husband used to live. It was a terrible idea: neither one of us would be anything more than a squatter. I counted on my new work to distract me from such matters and give me an excuse to stay out of her way. We would all be better off if we respected one another's emptiness.

But as I began to make myself a solitary lunch before heading to the wall for the bard's first performance, I resolved to write this story as you see it set down now. The bard would have his story, and we would have ours. There is heroism to be found in great battles, it is true: warriors with stable knees who fight and know that they will die for an idea or for the safety of loved ones back home. But there are also people who spend their entire adulthood at a soulless job they despise to make sure their children have something to eat that night so that one day those kids may lead better, more fulfilling lives than their parents. The warrior and the worker both make sacrifices. Who, then, is more heroic? Can any of us judge? I don't think I'm qualified. I'll let history decide. But I do not think we should leave it all up to warriors and rulers to speak to the future. We all have our stories to tell, and since I've been granted permission by Pelenaut Röllend himself, I will add a few of my own to the bard's.

The space on either side of Pelemyn's western wall looked quite different when we returned for the bard's second performance. By midafternoon, the closest lots on the exterior of the wall had been cleared—the pelenaut sent longshoremen to help the dislocated families move—and wood benches had been hammered together and arranged in rows to provide dense seating. The longshoremen also helped food and drink vendors set up an alley of stalls behind the benches, including one from the Siren's Call, while hygienists worked with a visiting Raelech stonecutter to construct a row of public privies and tie them into the sewers.

It wasn't the plodding drudgery of day-to-day living; people worked with a purpose, with small tight grins on their faces, anticipating the fruit of their labors. I knew because after I met Fintan for our first lunch and faithfully wrote down everything he had said the day before, there was an hour or so to spend before he spoke again, and I decided to help however I could. I wound up helping a family from Göfyrd relocate to another plot so that the privies could be built underneath their original campsite. It was something of a chore for the family and me, but they felt, as I did, that the bard's story would turn out to be worth it.

The structures inside the city were not so easily moved, but building owners with a view of the wall put out chairs on roofs or rigged scaffolds in some cases so that they could see, and even though their view would consist primarily of the bard's backside, there were people willing to pay for such seats.

Once I returned to the wall, I saw that someone had constructed a sturdier stage for the bard as well. Instead of a hastily assembled stack of crates, he had several square layered platforms, like a cake, that allowed him to be seen above the battlements. He climbed atop it, threw his arms wide, and let his voice ring out through the city and beyond it. "Hello, friends! Are we ready for day two?"

An answering roar assured him that the city was. Or almost. It was already clear from my vantage point on the wall that the benches would not come close to providing enough seating for everyone in Survivor Field who wished to see the bard. Many more clogged the area in front of the stalls, and a seething mass of heads could be seen beyond that point, people streaming in to get closer once the bard spoke. They didn't absolutely need to—his voice clearly carried to wherever they were—but they wanted to lay eyes on the people he seemed to be, however distantly. It would be a challenge for the pelenaut's men and women to solve.

"Before I continue the tale I began last night, I wish to give you time to settle in, as it were, for a fine afternoon's entertainment. I see people streaming in from far off in Survivor Field, and I am sure some of you are currently occupied in some kind of work or another and cannot simply drop it. And so I will sing you one of the old Drowning Songs that my master taught me when I was an apprentice." An appreciative noise swelled from the crowd.

"I do not know if you knew this," Fintan continued, "but the Brynt Drowning Songs are popular in Rael. They speak of dangers and poor decisions and teach your children well how to survive the sea. They also have the benefit of being short, which makes them easy to remember." He had brought a small handheld harp with him, and he plucked a major chord, its notes singing across the city.

"I was reminded of this one by Master Yöndyr's Mistmaiden Ale. Haven't sung it in many years, but perhaps you will recognize it. This is 'Mistmaiden's Kiss,' though of course the Mistmen are equally dangerous and you can switch the gender to suit you." He struck a different chord, a haunting minor one, letting the notes fade in the air before he launched into the lyrics:

> In the chill gray of a Barebranch morn
> She came to me like curving coils of vapor;
> Out of the air's moisture was she born
> With skin like onion paper.
>
> Pale, hungry, lithe, and beckoning,
> With a breathy sigh she begged a kiss,
> But on her lips lay a reckoning
> And a trip to the abyss.
>
> I fought my lust and tried to run,
> But it was all for naught in the end;
> I kissed her and it's done,
> So into darkness I descend.

His rendition gave me chills, and I shuddered, thinking of the wraiths that haunted the Mistmaiden Isles and how terrible it would be to join them. Fintan caught my expression and grinned. "Good that we heard that one on a bright sunny day, yes?" Laughter from the city as he carefully put his harp aside.

"Right! I have three tales for you today. Just as we bards rarely leave the borders of Rael, Fornish greensleeves are rarely seen by anyone outside their country. They don't like to leave their forest as it gives them that fish-out-of-water feeling, and even when they do, they avoid outsiders. I imagine it's because people stare at them. And if you aren't sure why that would be the case, well, I'll show you. Meet Nel Kit ben Sah," he said, producing a black sphere from his pouch and tossing it at his feet.

A ripple of awe spread through the crowd when they saw the pale figure revealed on the stage, diminutive and blond, sheltered from the sun all her life from living under the vast canopy of Forn. Her clothing was brown yet mottled in a pattern that would allow it to blend into the bark of most trees. Over her shirt she wore a hunter green waistcoat, also broken up into a pattern that would deflect eyes and keep her camouflaged in the canopy. She carried a bow and had a quiver of arrows strapped to her back—none of which was the awe-inspiring part. We had a few Fornish immigrants living in Pelemyn and their traders often visited our port, so it wasn't her size or pale skin that amazed everyone. It was the living bark on her arms and legs that drew gasps from the crowd. No other kenning wrought such a transformation on the blessed. The moss growing on the bark of her arms gave her the green sleeves of her kenning's namesake, and mushrooms like miniature white shelves grew on her shins. (I wondered if she ever ate them, and as soon as I thought of it, I knew it was the sort of question you would never, ever ask her if you wanted to live.)

Nel

My cousin Pen Yas Min has abruptly been granted permission to seek her kenning! I am filled with the excitement of planting season tripled, when you have a handful of seeds and can envision the bounty that will spring forth months later, but there's also the worries about weather or blights that could ruin the harvest. It is a period pregnant with potential, and I love such moments for their mystery.

Her parents were originally against it, but someone must have changed their minds—perhaps my great-uncle, Mat Som ben Sah, our clan's only other greensleeve. He may have reminded them of the prestige that comes with having a blessing, and with that prestige came economic opportunity. And Pen did not fail to remind her parents that seeking a kenning was not only her dearest wish but that younger Seekers typically enjoyed more success than older ones.

So they held the farewell ceremony, bidding goodbye to their child and she to them in case she was taken by the roots, and I think by that time her mother was genuinely excited for her and at peace with the decision. Her father had more difficulty performing his part of the leave-taking with open petals. He doubtless hoped Pen would grow closer to the family trunk, and I think he would have trimmed her ambitions if he could, kept her like treasured topiary, beautiful and safe but ultimately the reflection of the gardener's will rather than the will of the Canopy. Should Pen be taken by the roots, I feared he would blame his wife for it; so many people thought it appropriate to prune the branching of others and could not bear to watch others grow as their natures suggested.

Pen and I traveled together on the Leaf Road to the First Tree in Selt, and I was pleased with her sure-footed progress and unaided stamina. Should she be blessed, both her agility and her stamina would improve.

The road widened the closer we got to our capital, and we saw the increased traffic that justified it. Merchants and craftsmen and harvesters and herbalists, scions with their students following branches of thought to their ends, and the occasional benman like myself who nodded to me as I passed.

Pen tapped my shoulder after one such encounter, her eyes large with wonder, and asked me, "Was that a thornhand?" I was surprised at first that she had never seen one before and then realized she would have had no occasion to before now. They were almost all stationed on the southwestern coast closest to Hathrir, defending against timber pirates, whereas our clan was in the northwest foothills of the Godsteeth. "Yes, it was."

"How do they sleep?" she asked, worried about the thorns growing at the base of their skulls and spreading out down the spine and over the shoulder blades.

"On their stomachs, usually. Some of them manage to sleep on their sides. Depends on how they arrange their arms," I explained, for the tops of their forearms were thorny as well from near the elbow all the way to the backs of the hand.

"Have you ever seen a thornhand fight?"

"No. We've been blessed with peace, so there's been no call for them to transform. I might see it someday, but that's no cause for joy."

She was silent for a while, considering. It was possible that she might become a thornhand herself and have that difficulty sleeping. Possible that she might be called upon to fight the Hathrim and leave the Canopy to do it. And also possible that she might spend her life prepared for a fight that never came. When people sought the Fifth Kenning, they often hoped to be a grassglider or a greensleeve or even one of the specialized culturists while willfully ignoring the chances of becoming a thornhand. That was why she would see more of them when we arrived at the First Tree: every Seeker should know the fullness of her odds before being presented.

The Leaf Road turned from a mixture of hardwoods to exclusively silverbark branches, and I knew we were close. Our progress slowed because we had so many more people to weave through, but I don't think Pen minded at all. She was enjoying the strangeness and wonder of Selt, seeing the vines and ladders trailing or dangling all around the Leaf Road that led to merchant and craft huts, clan halls, or private homes. Such things existed in the White Gossamer Grove in the north, but not on this scale.

We reached the ring of sentinel trees that guarded the First Tree, and two members of the Gray Squirrel Clan stood there, blocking the Leaf Road that led to the trunk. Only greensleeves could go any far-

ther, and only those who had business to conduct in the sway and
spoke for their clans. We halted in front of them and bowed.

"Bright sun to you both. I come with a Seeker. Where shall I take
her?"

The one on our left nodded, an older woman. "Northeast side today,
shortly after noon. You should have time to make it."

That was a good piece of luck. Had we missed it, we might have had
to wait up to a week before the First Tree was ready to accept Seekers
again. We thanked them and circled around to the north, pausing at
the Silver Leaf Public House to take in some greens and juices. There
was a gathering of Black Jaguars in one corner whom I recognized
because Pak Sey ben Kor was with them, along with one other I'd seen
before at the Second Tree in Pont. I wondered what brought them to
the First Tree. But then I saw that all their attention was pointed at a
young man about Pen's age. A clan send-off for their own Seeker, then.
One with some fairly close ties to Pak or else he would not have made
the trip. Well, good for the young man: I hoped he would serve the
Canopy well.

I was fortunate not to be spotted by the Black Jaguars during our
repast, but once Pen and I departed and made our way to the Seeking
ground, we could not avoid Pak Sey ben Kor's notice. Especially since
he was the personal escort for his clan's Seeker and joined us underneath the First Tree's canopy. There were sixteen Seekers all told, each
from a different clan and escorted by a greensleeve. To the Gray Squirrel record keeper I introduced Pen as my cousin and offered her as a
Seeker to the First Tree on behalf of the White Gossamers, and it was
thanks to a similar introduction that I learned that the Black Jaguar
Seeker was Pak Sey ben Kor's nephew. He looked confident about his
Seeking, though whether he truly was or was merely pretending to be
I could not tell. Most of the others, including Pen, had a very sensible
sequence of expressions cycling on their faces, from excitement to uncertainty to dread and back again.

Rich and loamy soil squished pleasantly between our toes. The
Seekers all disrobed and stood waiting in a cluster an arm's length

away from one another on all sides. When the Gray Squirrel attendant nodded to us, we greensleeves each extended our shoots into the earth and spoke to the roots of the First Tree, introducing our Seekers again and sharing our love and pride and hope.

The earth rumbled and croaked beneath us as the roots of the First Tree stirred. Pen looked down at her feet, where the soil churned, and then up at me, tears shining in her eyes and a curious half smile on her face. I remembered that feeling. Being taken by the tree is a wondrous admixture of the sun and all the horrors of night, for you are struck by the immense power it represents and how very small you are in comparison, feeling all the hope for a blessed life along with the terror of dying in darkness.

Brown roots spiraled out of the soil and twined around the Seekers as they stood still. And then, when they were all wrapped up and began to descend into the earth, drawn down to be blessed or devoured, there were some last looks at their clansmen and then up at the Canopy and what little sunlight filtered through the leaves. For approximately half of them, it would be their final chance to see the sun.

By long-standing tradition we greensleeves withdrew our shoots as soon as the Seekers disappeared beneath the surface and ascended to the lowest branch above, there to wait out the time until we reunited with our clansmen or carried sorrowful news back home.

It was a tense and fearful time made longer by uncertainty. They were all down there long enough to suffocate. Except that the blessed would be brought into symbiosis with the Canopy and sustained during the process. So our clansmen might already be dead after a few spare minutes or else going through the racking pain of mutation. We would not know until they rose from the earth or did not. It was the lot of birds to chirp and chase one another, the lot of others to smile and eat and sleep and fight and lie with one another, but it was ours to worry and hope.

An hour passed, and the Red Horses were blessed with a new grass-glider, a grinning young woman who waved at us as soon as she emerged. The Yellow Bats got a new culturist blessed with the ability to husband teas, an economic boon for sure. The Blue Moths sprouted a new thornhand. And the blessed were slowly returned, one by one, until seven greensleeves had departed with their newly blessed and nine of us remained on the branch. It would not be unheard of for nine of sixteen to be taken by the roots. It would be almost common. But there might yet be a new greensleeve to arise from the earth, or a thornhand. We had not passed the time of no return: the Gray Squirrel record keeper would tell us when we could extinguish our hope. So I continued to wait . . . and hope. And so did Pak Sey ben Kor.

We nine stared at the earth, willing it to bubble and shoot forth hands and then the heads and bodies of our clansmen, returned to the air to serve the Canopy for the span of a lifetime. But nothing happened. The soil remained still, and the sun continued to sink toward the horizon. My throat began to close, and I fought back tears that wanted to spill for Pen.

Not yet. She could still emerge.

My eyes began to dart back and forth between the ground and the Gray Squirrel recorder who kept the time. She was looking at a sunstone to determine when the longest recorded time of blessing had passed, and I wondered how accurate it could possibly be, denials already building in my mind. The First Tree couldn't have taken Pen. If the Gray Squirrel had one of those new clockworks from Rael that ticked away the moments as its gears turned, that might be more accurate than squinting at a half-seen shadow underneath a silverbark's canopy. She raised a finger and took breath to speak, and I thought, *No, not Pen. Not Pen.*

"The time has passed, greensleeves," she said, looking up at us. "Your clans have honored the First Tree."

Not Pen.

"Wait! Look!" Pak Sey ben Kor shouted, pointing at the earth.

It was moving. And I was in time to see pale fingers erupt from the soil and clutch at the air. Then a second hand, both arms—and they were arms covered in silverbark. "It's a new greensleeve!"

I gasped and stared, unblinking. The Gray Squirrel had spoken too soon. Or else this was the new record for longest blessing. Who did those arms belong to?

Blond hair like mine and a face racked by pain emerged—it was Pen in all the first agonies of the blessing! I cried out in relief, and my fists shot up to the sky. I nearly fell off the branch in my excitement. "Pen! You're blessed!"

I dropped down from the branch and ran to her, steadying her before she could fall. Most new greensleeves couldn't walk for the pain in their legs—I certainly couldn't. The Gray Squirrel came over with a modesty blanket that wouldn't cover up her bark, and together we helped her to a recovery lift. She wept and asked me why it hurt so much.

"The symbiosis isn't complete yet. You'll be in pain for another couple of weeks while your body adapts to the silverbark. But getting you to full sun is important now. We have just a couple of hours before nightfall."

"Why didn't you tell me it hurt so much?"

"Would it have stopped you from wanting to be a greensleeve?"

"No."

"Then there was no point. I know it might not feel like it right now, but you have been truly blessed, Pen. When the symbiosis is complete, you'll feel that blessing every day. I know I do."

The Gray Squirrel whistled and shook a rope vine to signal to the attendants up top that it was time to do their jobs. The lift began to rise, and the Gray Squirrel stepped off, leaving me alone on the lift with Pen. I spared a quick glance back at the branch where we had waited; it was empty now. Pak Sey ben Kor and the rest of them had departed, disappointed, no doubt, with hearts crushed by grief. I was sorry for them and their Seekers but also wondered if this might not be the first hint of the Black Jaguar Clan's autumn. Their summer of rule had been long and prosperous, but perhaps they had become complacent and the First Tree wished to make a point. Or perhaps there was no significance to it at all. They were a large clan and no doubt had many Seekers throughout the year. One or two or three taken by the roots would be expected. But if they lost Seekers consistently, then—well, I suppose it didn't matter that much. The White Gossamers had no consistent presence at the First Tree and none at all on the east coast at Keft. I didn't want to be that presence, and I doubted Pen did either. I wanted to serve the Canopy in the field more than the sway, and I thought my cousin was of like mind. Or would be once the pain subsided.

"Will you . . . stay with me?" she managed to say through clenched teeth.

"Just tonight, then I must get back to my duties. You are supposed to make your own way home anyway, trusting root and stem to guide you. But we have much to talk about in the meantime, and that will be a pleasant distraction from the pain. You're going to love how the sun feels, trust me. Ah, here we are." We arrived at the high-branched station of the Gray Squirrels operating the lift, and they nodded at us as they continued to operate the pulleys and lift us higher, above the First Tree's topmost leaves. The full afternoon sun hit Pen's silverbark on her arms and legs, and she gasped.

"Oh! Oh, that's better. I mean it still hurts, but not as much. I can at least think now."

"Then think about this: you're one of the White Gossamer Clan's three greensleeves now, Pen Yas *ben* Min."

Her wince of pain wilted, and a smile blossomed in its place. She even managed a chuckle. "Thank you, cousin."

"Thought you might enjoy that account of a Seeking," Fintan said, dispelling the seeming with a shattered green stone that sent up a corresponding plume of green smoke. "We will hear more of Nel and Pen in days to come. But now I will take you back to the night of Thaw 17, 3041. Some of what I will say comes directly from the journal of Hearthfire Gorin Mogen, some of it from eyewitnesses, and some of it, I admit, is the privilege of a poet." A few titters greeted this last. Dipping his hand into his belt pouch, he withdrew a seeming stone and imprinted it. "Though kennings are not hereditary and the giants insist you do not need to be blessed to become a Hearthfire, some blessed member of the Mogen family has ruled Harthrad for the last hundred and thirty years, and it is from that island that the finest smiths in the world can be found. Say hello to a leader of the Hathrim."

Despite his warning, no one was prepared for Fintan's transformation into a pale-skinned, broad-boned giant. He disappeared in black gases, and his new bulk rose out of it, a colossus twelve feet tall with a square, black-bearded face punctuated by ice-blue eyes and a snarl. He was wrapped in the fur of some massive white-pelted animal, and when he roared, people screamed. I might have been one of them. He laughed at us, enjoying the fear and no doubt relishing the power of his kenning. When next he spoke, it was in a gravelly rumble entirely unlike his normal pleasant tones.

Gorin Mogen

The only reason I didn't kill the lad who woke me was that he did it from the door and closed it on the dagger I whipped from under my pillow and threw at his face. I am prone to violence beyond reason when I am woken from a sound sleep. The rest of the time I like to think I have a reason for my violence.

"Hearthfire, you have urgent matters of state to attend to," he shouted through the door. My dagger still quivered in the wood. Real Fornish wood, not glass or steel. The damn door to my bedchamber was worth more than much of my Hearthroom.

"The matters of state can urgently hump a sand badger until the morning," I growled, and my hearth stirred beside me, sensuously stretching and curving in ways that soothed my sharp edges. I did not want to leave her.

"We would not wake you if it were not dire."

Since Sefir hadn't yet been fully roused, there was no reason to continue the argument and risk waking her, too. I slid out of the sheets, cursed silently, and allowed the moonglow streaming through the skylight to guide me to a chest on which was folded my favorite ice howler fur. Draping it about me, I opened the door and glowered at the lad who'd been sent to fetch me. I didn't know his name, but he knew enough about the expression on my face to skitter out of throttling distance.

"Your advisers wait in the Crucible, Hearthfire."

"Understood. Begone."

He scampered away, and I stalked down the halls to the Crucible. Rumblings from Mount Thayil vibrated through the walls of glass and rock.

My advisers were there as the boy had promised, but none would meet my eyes. My feet must have been in a sorry state, judging by the mournful gazes directed there. These men would plunge their hands into lava for me, charge a wall bristling with archers at my command, but they would not look me in the eye. I sighed and wondered if I would ever meet another again—apart from my hearth—who could match my stare for more than a heartbeat.

"Well? What is it? Report." They shuffled their feet and made throat-clearing noises, and one or two ventured a mumble but spectacularly failed to say anything intelligible. The news must be dire indeed for them to remain so taciturn—especially when they were in full armor and I was wearing nothing but a fur.

"I have never punished anyone for speaking truth," I said quietly. "Nor will I now." I paused, and after none of them took the cue to speak, I continued in the same low tone. "I have never punished anyone for remaining silent, either. But if you don't tell me why I'm not in bed with my hearth, I'll let you all take a swim on the Rift side of the island; is that clear?"

Their very beards trembled. It was Halsten who managed to speak first, an orange-haired, overmuscled houndmaster who braided his mustaches with silver thread. He was openly mocked for his vanity but secretly envied if I guessed correctly.

"Hearthfire, it's the volcano . . ."

"Has it blown?" I snapped, my eyes narrowing.

"No, no, not yet," Roffe assured me. No one would ever confuse him with Halsten. Roffe's beard was brown and curly and spread like a fan to cover his chest. "But the firelords assure us of an eruption today."

"A huge one," Volund added, somehow managing to convey that this tiny fact was the most important ever uttered.

"I see." If I had leisure, I would make sure to ask the firelords monitoring Thayil why I got less than a day's notice of the end of my realm. "Our crops?" We had planted only a week ago, but already some seedlings were sprouting.

"Total loss," Halsten said. And with less than a day to work at it, there would not be time to transplant anything.

"The city?"

"The same. We must abandon it if we wish to survive."

"Teldwen's tits!" I cursed, and as if in reply, the ground quaked beneath us and the sky boomed with a thunderous explosion, shattering the skylights in the Crucible. The stone pedestals set throughout the Crucible shook, toppling the priceless glass sculptures to the floor and exploding the heirlooms of my line. My sire's works, his sire's, my own, and my son's recent master work exploded into slivers and shards across the polished marble. "Apparently I am not to be given enough time to get dressed."

They didn't hear me over the cacophony rolling through the sky. My father had warned me this day might come, and his father before him. And the firelords had warned my sires just as they had warned me: Mount Thayil would erupt again, violently, and when it did, there would be little hope of saving the city. So my grandsire had been the first Hearthfire to commission the building of transport ships, a fleet to be used for nothing except evacuating the entire population of Harthrad on short notice. The project had consumed plenty of treasure, and there were those who showered the family name of Mogen with ridicule because of it. Why do we have a functional port and a fleet of glass boats that generates no revenue whatsoever? Why are we paying men to build and maintain empty ships that are in some cases older than anyone alive? Why are we storing perfectly good food and water when we could sell it or consume it? I expected that the owners of those sneering voices would be eager to board the ships now, and a small part of me wanted to make them grovel first. But that was truly the small part of me; I knew that some of those giants would be my staunchest defenders once I saved their lives.

"Give the evacuation order," I shouted in an attempt to be heard. "Bring only tools, weapons, armor, coin, and family members. Leave everything else behind. People who refuse to leave everything else behind will be left behind."

"Yes, Hearthfire!" my men chorused, and then Roffe followed up. "Where are we going? Tharsif or Narvik?"

For the first time I had cause to smile. "We're not staying in Hathrir, brothers. You know very well none of the other Hearthfires will welcome us—especially Winthir Kanek. My very presence in Tharsif would be a challenge to him. And the other islands in this blasted archipelago cannot sustain us. So we're going to Ghurana Nent, north of the Godsteeth, bordering Forn but south of Hashan Khek."

"We're invading?" Volund's voice was strangled with surprise and a note of hope.

"No, Volund; armies invade, and they attack the native populace. We're refugees, you see, so we're settling. Settling in a land with bountiful natural resources we won't have to import anymore. Close to a mountain that won't explode on us and full of metals and close to our Fornish trading partners in Pont. Closer still to forests we can harvest ourselves. We will all build new hearths and prosper. And our excuse for all is the eruption of Mount Thayil. Thus we turn a disaster for our generation into a boon for our heirs. We plead innocence and beg for charity, and all the while we build defenses, and by the time the Nentians realize we don't plan to ever leave, they'll discover that they have a hare's chance in a falcon heath of making us. This was my grandsire's plan, passed on to my sire and passed on to me. Think on it," I admonished, waggling a finger, "but say nothing. Have everyone get safely in the sea and then follow my ship, telling them only that I'm leading them to safe harbor. Is that clear?"

"As glass, Hearthfire," Volund said. He was smiling now, and so were Roffe and Halsten. They finally saw what my grandsire had seen—that this eruption, long expected, wasn't the end for us but the beginning. Indeed, it was a much-needed spur to our withers, urging our people off this blasted rock to a land large and rich enough for the Hathrim.

The air boomed again, and I had to shout to be heard. "We will speak more in private once we arrive. I must retrieve my armor and tell Sefir we're leaving. Halsten, don't forget the damn hounds and some livestock. We will need them eventually. See you at the docks." My advisers turned to relay my orders to the city, moving in a strange sort of pantomime. Normally I would hear the creak and clank of their armor as they moved, but all was lost to the bone-shaking roar of Mount Thayil.

Roffe never made it out. A black boulder of volcanic basalt plowed through the ceiling and obliterated him, and the impact vaulted Halsten and Volund a good distance away. Had my grandsire not built so well, the entire structure might have collapsed on us. As it was, we had no time to bid Roffe a proper farewell, not if we wished to survive ourselves. We needed to get out fast and hope that everyone with some kind of kenning made it to the boats.

Harthrad has a goodly measure of firelords like myself and a number of lesser lavaborn but no furies like some of the southern cities. In Ghurana Nent there will be few opportunities for our young giants to visit the fires of Olenik, to burn away the child and be reborn immune to flame and heat. I have not spoken of it yet to anyone, but I think it is vital for our long-term survival that we find the Sixth Kenning, which some believe is a fable but which logic insists must be there. For without it—or at least reliable access to the First Kenning in Olenik—we will flicker and wane as a people until we are snuffed. Better that we find the Sixth Kenning and gain dominion over animals. Think what we could do then with our hounds! Discovering it would be a great gift to my people and a fine legacy.

I gave the Crucible one last look as Halsten and Volund got to their feet. All the beautiful glass blown by the Mogen line was destroyed, and the stained windows cracked and slid out of their iron frames, shards tinkling in silence compared with the thunder in the sky above. The gold and glass throne would melt in a lava flow, the stone of my hearth would crack from the quaking earth, and all my material wealth would burn except for the large sack of gems I would take to finance the building of a new city. Raelech stonecutters weren't cheap, but they worked fast and loved nothing so well as riches from the earth. Even with their help, my people faced a trial of flame ahead.

As my world fell about me and I ran to my bedchamber, I laughed as I realized that I was looking forward to it.

The giant's fingers reached into a different pouch and pulled out a green pellet, and Gorin Mogen in his ice howler fur shrank and disappeared, replaced by Fintan the Raelech bard, looking very pleased with himself and enjoying the reaction of the crowd. He threw up his hands.

"That was the origin of the western front of the war: an eruption and the execution of a plan crafted long ago. South of here, on the Brynt coast, one possible origin of the eastern front and all our woes occurred on the very next day—Thaw 18, 3041! My discovery of it was quite accidental, and had a certain seventeen-year-old merchant's daughter not kept a diary, it would have been lost forever. Let us see what happened, shall we?" He plucked out another black sphere and held it high. "Ladies and gentlemen, I give you the delightful Kallindra du Paskre."

This time a slim Brynt girl with large sleepy eyes, cool dark brown skin like mine, and tight curly hair allowed to grow into a cloud around her head emerged from the black smoke. She wore a light yellow tunic belted over blue pants and the slip-on sandals that we Brynts tend to favor over all other footwear. Her sardonic tone and faint grin suggested that she was perpetually amused by the world—but only because she was laughing at us, not with us.

Kallindra

We've just had the strangest encounter.

A sunburned woman crouched over a campfire as we came around the bend in the road leading to Setyrön, and she became defensive when we approached. She backed away from the light, drew a knife from a sheath, and eyed us warily like we were bandits.

Perhaps she was only embarrassed. She had almost nothing on.

Perhaps she'd been sunbathing. It was a beach, after all, and a rather nice one. It was the last gasp of twilight now, but she might have fallen asleep in the sun. I couldn't believe it, though, because this trade route was fairly well traveled, and I saw an odd watercraft of some kind pulled up onto the sand; she might well have been burned in the boat.

Checking on the reaction of my parents, I saw Father's jaw drop, and Mother closed his mouth with an audible chop as his teeth clicked together. Jorry, seeing this, clicked his own jaws shut, and I found that part amusing, but the rest of the scene was uniformly odd.

The woman was more than seven feet tall and moved with the sort of grace one sees in professional dancers. She was lean and looked hungry; slim muscles stood out on her arms and legs, and she didn't have a trace of belly like normal women do. It was like she was saying she'd never make room for a child in there. She looked half starved. Well, more like seven-eighths. Around her bony hips she had tied a piece of coarse cloth, but that was all. I think it was Jorry's first look at bare breasts, and he must have been so disappointed. He'd doubtless dreamt that his first pair of breasts to ogle would belong to someone shorter and rather more friendly and perhaps not so dreadfully pale. The woman didn't have the milk-white skin of the Fornish, but there wasn't anything like a respectable color to it either. It was difficult to assign a shade to it with the deepening darkness on one hand and the firelight on the other, but we could tell she wasn't from Brynlön or Kauria. She couldn't even be a Raelech or a Nentian. It was like all the richness of her life had been drained away.

Father slowly got down from the wagon and held up his hands to show he meant no harm. He asked the woman if she was all right in the trader's tongue and got no reply. Without advancing, he repeated the question in Brynt, Kaurian, and even Fornish, all to no avail.

I thought he should have tried the Hathrim tongue, for she was almost tall enough to be one of the giants and everyone knows they're pretty pasty bastards, but I don't think Father knows their tongue well, if at all. I know only a few words myself, but I will hopefully learn more soon at the trader clave in Setyrön.

The woman kind of spat something out—I thought it might have been a sneeze at first—but then we realized she'd tried to say something to us and it made no sense in any language we knew.

"I beg your pardon?" Father asked.

The woman made the spitting noises again, and her tone made it clear that she was annoyed. Father gave up.

"I don't think she wants to buy anything," he said drily, climbing up to the driver's seat. "I'm not going to waste my time with someone who looks ready to fillet me."

"Shouldn't we at least show her a tunic?" Mother asked. "We have the supply, and she's got the demand if anyone does."

"Do you see a purse on her, my love?" Father asked. "I honestly think she could use a few pies more than clothes. Looks like she hasn't eaten in a year. Jorry, load the crossbow in case she gets any ideas."

Jorry and I were inside the wagon as usual, watching all this from some very purposefully constructed gaps between the planks.

"The crossbow? You want me to shoot her?"

Father turned in the driver's seat and frowned at Jorry's tone. His eyes tried to find us even though it was as near dark as made no never mind and all we could see was the reflected firelight on half his face. He knew we could see him well enough, though. "A pair of tits can rob you just as easily as a pair of balls, boy. It doesn't matter that one is prettier and less hairy than the other; you hear me? You're still broke at the end of the day and on your way to starving."

Mother scowled at the phrasing but couldn't argue with the lesson. My brother said, "Yes, sir."

My father will never be welcome at any Wellspring for saying such things and neither will I, but I love him for always speaking truth to us, harsh or embarrassing or sorrowful as it may be. But I think his forthright manner makes him a trusted trader; the du Paskre name will always be honored at the clave if not at the watered courts of the quartermasters. Jorry scrambled to get the crossbow ready.

Father took the reins from Mother but didn't snap them until he heard the crossbow cocked. The strange woman watched him warily, not moving, still in a defensive stance. When father snapped the reins and clucked his tongue at the horses and the wagon began to move, the woman cried out and took a few steps toward us. She dropped the knife and spread her long arms away from her sides, empty-handed, and her tone was pleading instead of angry.

Calling a halt and reining in the horses, Father eyed the woman and then searched the darkness for possible confederates. We carried valuable goods but weren't prosperous enough to go around hiring Raelech mercenaries to guard the wagon, so plenty of footpads thought we were ripe for the picking. Sighing as he handed the reins to Mother, he got back down.

"Keep the bow trained on her, Jorry, but don't fire unless I say so or unless someone attacks me. Kallindra, load another bow just in case."

I didn't answer but moved quickly to obey. We had a tiny lantern to see by, nothing else. I did my best to keep an eye on what was happening while I did this. The woman had frozen with her arms outstretched. Father duplicated that posture, keeping out of Jorry's line of fire. When she saw him spread his arms, she exhaled in relief and smiled as she dropped her arms. Father didn't smile back, but he nodded at her and slowly returned his arms to his sides.

Under his loose brown trader's robes, he wore a mail shirt and a lamellar tunic of the sort Nentians favor. He had small daggers strapped to either forearm, hidden by his sleeves. He wouldn't be able to stand up to a soldier, but neither was he as harmless as he looked.

The woman tried to appear friendly now, but she was clearly nervous. She waved an arm at the sky and said something that sounded like a question. Father shrugged and gave a tiny shake of his head. She could have been asking if he was enjoying the fine weather or asking about constellations for all we knew.

She looked crestfallen for a moment, then tried something different. She pointed to herself and spoke about six syllables very slowly. Father repeated them, but she shook her head and repeated only the last two, again pointing to herself.

"Motah," she said. Or something like it.

"Motah," Father repeated, and she smiled. The first few syllables must have been the equivalent of saying "My name is" in her language. But now that I think of it, maybe *Motah* was the name of her people or the word for "tall daft naked woman." Mother keeps saying I shouldn't assume, and she's right; it's bad for business.

"My name is Lönsyr," Father said. "Lönsyr."

"Lonzeer," the woman said, by and large bungling the vowels and swapping a *z* for the *s*.

"Close enough, sure," Father replied.

The woman began pointing at the beach and asking questions, her eyes hopeful. Father told her she was concerned with sand, and then a beach, and then a coast when she seemed unsatisfied. The woman danced around in a circle and shrugged. Remembering the strange boat that I could no longer see in the darkness, I spoke up for the first time through the side of the wagon.

"She wants to know where she is, Father."

"What? Hmm. I think you may be right, Kallindra." He spoke to the woman again. "You're in Brynlön. This is Brynlön."

The giant woman cocked her head at him. "Lonzeer Breenlawn?"

"Oh, fire and mud," Father groused. "This will take all night!" He held up his hands to the woman in what he hoped was a universal signal to wait. "Excuse me for a moment." He stalked back to the rear of the wagon.

"Kallindra, fetch me a map of the continent. Jorry, keep her in your sights."

"Yes, sir," we chorused. I rummaged through a trunk for a recent map of Teldwen drawn by some Kaurian to celebrate the crowning of their new mistral, and once I found it, I slipped it through a gap in the planks for Father to take. There was no need to open the back door; security always. The woman hadn't moved during this time. She waited patiently.

When Father returned to her, he squatted down and unfolded the map on the sand near her campfire. The woman's face lit with a large smile and showed off a few crooked teeth. Father started by pointing at the cities nearby—Möllerud and Setyrön—and then jabbed repeatedly between them and said, "We are here."

Motah, if that was her name, grinned and made affirming noises and then suddenly clocked Father upside the head with her elbow. He fell over, stunned, and she ran out of the firelight toward her boat, taking the map with her.

"Hey!" Jorry shouted, and he fired the crossbow into the dark in her general direction but must have missed. We heard no grunt or scream, only the sound of a boat hull scraping across the sand. There was no use wasting another bolt. We couldn't see anything past the fire.

Father sat up and cursed loudly to let us know he was all right, and Mother laughed at him. She even slapped her thigh.

"You see there, Jorry?" he roared. "I just got robbed by a pair of tits." Mother nearly fell off the wagon from laughing so hard.

I wonder sometimes what kind of parent I will be with the examples I have to follow.

I also wonder where that woman was from. She was so very strange. We will have much to talk about at the clave when we get there.

When it was clear that Fintan had finished speaking in Kallindra's personage, the crowd murmured among themselves instead of applauding, but he seemed to expect this. He nodded at Survivor Field as he took shape in the green smoke and said, "Fascinating, isn't it? One invasion caused by an eruption and another that may have been facilitated by a chance meeting. Of course we don't know that Motah—or whoever she was—ever made it back to her home successfully. But I happen to know that there were other scouts like her, perhaps a large number of them, and we don't know how many of them managed to secure a map. As I said, a recording of this encounter only came to me by accident. What else the Bone Giants learned of us and how they learned it is a mystery to be solved later." Fintan held up a finger and waggled it back and forth as he spoke.

"I am fascinated by Kallindra's record not because it is the history of the blessed or of the military or of some political leader but because it is the record of an ordinary person who had no idea what was coming. And ordinary people have their stories, too, don't they? You all have your stories, I'm sure!"

A roar from Survivor Field answered him.

"I thought so. That is all for today, so let the story tonight be of fine drink and finer company! Tomorrow we will hear more from Nel Kit ben Sah and find out what was happening in Kauria and Ghurana Nent!"

Day 3

THE CREATURE IN THE DUNGEON

I didn't sleep well and woke before dawn. I made a cup of tea and sat at the kitchen table with my hands folded around the Raelech porcelain, part of a set my wife had been gifted long ago, feeling the heat seep into my fingers and watching the steam rise from the surface in a sort of nonthinking haze. I didn't notice Elynea emerge from my bedroom until she pulled out a chair and sat across from me, murmuring a soft good morning.

"Good morning," I replied. I hadn't seen her or the children since they had all slammed doors yesterday to demonstrate their displeasure with me. When I had come home after the bard's performance, the doors were still closed and the house was quiet, and I didn't want to disturb them. I stretched out on the couch after a cold meal of bread and smoked moonscale and began a string of short uncomfortable naps that passed for slumber. The cot in the palace had been easier on my back. "Can I make you a cup?"

"I want to apologize," Elynea said, her eyes downcast but her voice firm. Tea apparently would be a distraction when she had apologies to make.

"There's no need," I said, and she looked up. "Truly. I'm sorry I upset you and the kids."

Her eyes dropped back to the tabletop, and she traced a slow pattern on it with her finger. "I know you didn't intend to. You were right that healing will be slow. Here we are nearly a year past the invasion, and I'm only now beginning to think of rebuilding my life. I think perhaps the well of my patience had run dry after my job search yesterday morning and I needed time for it to refill."

"I understand," I said. "You're welcome to search again this morning if you and the kids can stand it. I'm free until a half hour before noon."

"Thank you," Elynea said, her voice fervent. "I'll change and go right away. I don't wish to be a bother to you any longer than necessary."

"We're all bothered these days," I said. "But you're far less of one than you think. Your welcome is still fresh and clean here."

Elynea made a grimace that might have been an attempt to smile in gratitude and disappeared into the bedroom to change into the same orange ensemble she had worn yesterday while I set about making breakfast. She woke the kids and told them all was well and she would be back before noon, adding to Pyrella that she should try to teach her younger brother something today. They were sad to see her go but distracted themselves soon enough after they had eaten.

If Tamöd's play was any indication of his future, he would seek a kenning as early as he could. He wanted to be a tidal mariner with all his being.

Pyrella, I noticed, never pretended to have a kenning. Perhaps she was simply playing foil to Tamöd, but I noticed that she chose to oppose him with defensive creatures or those which renewed themselves easily. She was the oyster in a shell, or a sea turtle, or even everblooming algae but never an aggressive predator like a bladefin or a longarm. Tamöd even asked her to switch. "Come on, be a kraken," he said, and she refused. "But it's no fun beating up algae," he complained, and as soon as he did, Pyrella changed the game on him as if she'd been waiting for him to say that. I suspect that she had.

"Maybe you don't have to always beat things up," she said.

Tamöd looked lost. "What else is there?"

"There's growing."

The seven-year-old scoffed. "Tidal mariners don't grow things, stupid!"

"Of course they do. Nothing grows without water."

"I know plants grow with water, but that's not something a tidal mariner does!"

"They do, but they're sneaky about it. Tidal mariners influence the currents, right?" Pyrella prodded him.

"Yeah, so?"

"All the food that ocean plants and animals need is carried on the currents, and tidal mariners use those currents to help everything grow faster, which helps feed us, too. There's even a song about it! The Current Chorus. Do you know it already?"

"No."

"I can teach it to you. Or everything I know anyway. All the tidal mariners know the whole thing."

That hooked him. If the tidal mariners knew it, he wanted to know it, too. "Okay!"

My house was an endless repetition of the Current Chorus after that, but I didn't mind. I knew firsthand that the education system had been dissolved in the flood of refugees and if children weren't taught by clever older siblings or their parents, they wouldn't be taught at all. I and a few of my erstwhile colleagues had thought of trying to establish an open-air school somewhere on Survivor Field, as all the city's school buildings were currently occupied by families, but none of us could figure out how to get paid and eat at the end of the day. Education had become a luxury item no one could afford.

I taught them both the last few verses, which Pyrella hadn't learned yet, and they proudly sang the whole thing to their mother when she returned. Halfway through it, she finally smiled for the first time since I had met her, and when I left the house to meet Fintan for lunch, they were all laughing together, and that might have been a first, too, since the invasion.

I was smiling to myself as I walked, shaking my head a bit in wonder. No well-meaning words or kindness of mine had pierced Elynea's
depression in months, but an old children's rhyming song had. I think
it must have been the chorus:

> Currents bring us food today,
> And to creatures in the bay,
> While we sing and dance and play,
> Currents wash our poop away.

Yes, indeed. Indeed they do.

At my first session with Fintan he was very reserved and had little to
say to me besides reciting his tale more slowly for my dictation. I had
thought that perhaps his earlier easygoing manner had been an act for
Rölly and that like many performers he was dour and reserved while
not on stage. But during my second lunch with him he proved quite
eager to talk over our food, and I had to reevaluate the first day: he had
merely been watching and absorbing his new surroundings, and now
that he had become somewhat oriented, he was ready to probe.

"Forgive me, Master Dervan, but is it true what I've been told? You
are married to Sarena du Söneld?"

"Who told you that?"

"I dined with the Raelech ambassador to Brynlön last night, and he
mentioned it."

"Did he also mention that my wife has passed?"

Fintan blanched. "No. No, he didn't, and I'm so sorry to hear it. I
would not have brought it up if I had known."

"Why *did* you bring it up?"

"I remember my master speaking of her once. He met her in Killae
and praised her wit."

"Really? When was this?"

"Three years ago."

Well before her death, then. She made at least two trips that year, I think. I remember she complained that one of the members of the Triune Council at that time had been more than unusually stupid."

"Huh. And you merely wished to pass on your master's compliment?"

"Well, I had intended to notice out loud that you seemed to be a couple wedded to diplomacy as well as each other, not unlike my own wife and myself, but now it already seems like one of the most inept pratfalls in the history of conversational gambits."

"I'm not a diplomat of any sort."

"Oh? Your position in the Wellspring, then—?"

"Is both recent and temporary," I finished. "I used to teach at the university," I added, anticipating his next question.

"Ah, but the university is closed. I understand now. Well, I'm not much of a diplomat either. I nearly got myself skewered when I first arrived, and now I've quite likely offended you and who knows who else since I've been here."

I assured him that I was not offended. "Though I can't speak for others," I said.

He grinned at me and gave a soft chuckle. "I will take what relief I can, then."

Sarena's few lessons to me on her deathbed came back to me as Fintan spoke. "The Raelechs are so very affable," she had told me. "They want every conversation to be as pleasant as milk and cake. Too much of that sugar will make you sick, though. A little milk and cake can make you happy, but it's easy to go too far with them. You have to remember they're our allies, not our friends, and even friends don't always watch out for one another like they should."

Bryn of the Deep, I miss her. And I was already seeing what she meant. Fintan was quite likable but clearly calculating behind all that good nature; though he made light of planning what to say to me, the fact was he *had* planned it in a way that ensured we would be speaking of politics sooner rather than later.

I could not fault him, though; I was calculating, too. Perhaps I could dive deeper under the surface than he could. The challenge of outwitting him excited me, as I imagined Rölly thought it would. Hopefully my enthusiasm wouldn't lead me to drown.

The wooden benches had been expanded and were already filled to capacity when we arrived for the afternoon performance. A cheer greeted the bard when he stepped up onto his stage with his harp.

"Friends! Fifteen minutes until we begin! One of our tales will be set in Kauria. Their love of peace permeates everything they do—even tending their gardens. So today I will sing you a brief hymn sung by gardeners and farmers alike before they tend their crops or their flowers and herbs, and then we will get to the stories. This is 'A Gardener's Ward Against Discord.'

> *Bees will sting,*
> *Ants will bite,*
> *Birds shall dive*
> *And nothing shall thrive*
> *When Anger, Spite,*
> *And Impatience arrive.*
>
> *Still your wrath,*
> *Calm your mind,*
> *You should know*
> *Your garden will grow*
> *When you are kind,*
> *Reinei's wind will make it so.*

"Let me introduce you now to a young Nentian man," the Raelech bard said after the fifteen-minute waiting period. "I had occasion to speak with him earlier, and his story will be free-form as it progresses, but for this first appearance I will share with you one of his journal entries, verbatim, dated Thaw 21, 3041. His name is Abhinava Khose."

The copper-skinned Nentian lad who took shape in the bard's smoke was tall and lean yet muscular; he would bulk up soon as he matured into an imposing man, the sort that does not stand so much as loom in your presence. He had a broad nose and the long, straight black hair of his people falling to his chest. His leathers, flared at the shoulders, were dyed in tans to blend in with the grasses of the Nentian plains. He wore khernhide boots that indicated privileged status, and his voice was a smooth baritone.

Abbi

This is my last day pretending to be a proud Khose hunter.

I don't think what I feel matters to anyone but me, but I must tell it to someone. Since I have no one to tell—or no one who will care—I will tell it to this small journal. I think my aunt gave it to me years ago when I was a child, thinking I would draw something cute in it and make memories for my later years. It has collected dust until now, but I am glad to have found it again. I will fill it with memories that fall short of adorable but will perhaps prove invaluable to me later on. Though I am still quite young, already I can see how I change as I age, looking back at my old self at fourteen and fifteen and wondering what that kid was thinking. So perhaps what I write today will help me some years hence. More likely it will make me laugh at my own foolishness.

I have walked seventeen years under Kalaad's blue sky, and my father says I should choose a bride soon. He says it like I should choose a melon in the marketplace for breakfast, which I doubt the girls would appreciate. When we are in the city, he keeps pointing at girls and say-ing, "How about her?" and I shrug my indifference, never saying what I really think.

That one's eyes are flat dead things.

That one has a voice like claws on stone.

That one smells like borchatta soup.

And none of them are the boy I love. He is the son of a chaktu butcher with whom my father frequently does business because they were schooled together. He is so strong and beautiful but has never shown any interest in me, so I imagine that someday soon his father will talk to him like mine does and have him choose a bride like she was some kind of breakfast fruit. A bridefruit.

That day is coming for me also. And then I will have to tell Father—and Mother, too—that I have no interest in women except as friends. I am *sakhret,* and so their dreams for me are not going to work out the way they hoped.

Father will be angry at first, but I hope not frightfully so. He will be more upset that I didn't tell him sooner than upset by the thing itself. What will anger him far more is telling him that I don't wish to be a hunter like the rest of the Khose men since before the First Kenning. The whole family is to go out tomorrow on the annual khern hunt, and I would rather do almost anything else. Clean the stables. Walk alone in the Gravewood. Choose a bridefruit. Ugh.

I cannot pinpoint the moment when I stopped wishing to hunt ani-mals or even eat them. Maybe it was the scream of a khek hare or the terrified bleating of a gut goat. Some creature's peaceful grazing inter-rupted by violent death so that we could graze later on its flesh mari-nated in a slow-cooked sauce and turn its hide into boot leather. I simply do not want to make my life's work ending the lives of other creatures. He will say it is the way of animals to hunt and eat other animals, and that is true. But I have no taste for hunting anymore.

That is not to say I have no skill at it. Or that I have skill at anything else. I do not know what else I want to do, and if I tell my family I don't want to be a hunter, I know that's one of the first questions they will ask me: *What else will you do, Abhi? How will you put food on the table if you do not put a spear through its neck first?*

And I don't know for sure. Go to Rael, perhaps, where they have the Third Kenning and their Triple Goddess to match and know who they are as a people. There is no national identity crisis there. The Earth Shapers are so very grounded, ha ha. I have no interest in pursuing their kenning, but perhaps I could apprentice myself to a bee-keeper . . . ?

Kalaad in the sky, I need to think of something better than that! Father will stomp me into the grass if I tell him I want to keep bees.

Maybe a farmer. Something he doesn't fully understand but he respects. I need to be ready with an answer when he hands me a spear tomorrow and I refuse to take it.

Whatever happens, I know my life will be much different when the sun rises than it is today, and I thought I should record a small part of it before it's gone forever.

"That was short, I know," the bard said, "but diary entries are rarely much longer. Soon enough Abhi will long for the days when all he had to worry about was the annual khern hunt. We will come back to him tomorrow but return now to our greensleeve, Nel Kit ben Sah, who has left her cousin to recuperate and returned to her duty on the western coast."

Nel

Coastal patrol is a mixed blessing. On the one hand, we are always looking out into the sun and never drinking the twilight peace of the canopy, but on the other, there's a decent chance we'll see something strange at least once a week.

Yesterday in the night, for example, one of the Hathrim mountains bloomed into the sky. The ash blossom could be seen in the dawn, spreading and flattening in the blue and promising gray rain on our green forest. We think it is Mount Thayil above Harthrad, though we cannot be sure. But I have never seen anything so strange as what I saw early this morning. I don't think I've even heard of such a thing.

In the black hour before sunrise, flickering lights danced on distant waves. Many tens of tiny fires moving north on the surface of the ocean.

I knew it could only be one thing: Who else builds ships that can stand the scorch of fire? Only the giants do this. Lacking trees, they build glass boats and burn putrid blocks of compressed vegetables and dung in large steel bowls and keep the blaze going forever with the talents of their firelords.

Seeing their trade barges pass in the night is common. But those ships keep fairly close to the shore and move in ones and twos, and we can hear the beat of the drum and the grunt of the oarsmen as they pull their way through the water. These were far out—so far that I would not have seen them without the fires—and making no noise that I could hear over the susurrus of the tide. And there were far too many of them to represent a trade convoy. In all my years of patrol I have seen no more than six rowing together. These were many tens.

What could it mean? Follow the branches until you get to the trunk: the ash blossom was indeed Mount Thayil, and it represented the death of Harthrad. The Hathrim had to evacuate their land. But instead of going south to other Hathrim cities, Hearthfire Gorin Mogen was moving his people north. *All* of his people. To where?

I doubted that he would be so foolish as to make landfall on Forn, though we should be wary of it regardless. Desperation can drive anyone to madness. Or maybe it wasn't mad; if he planned to cut down our trees and return south, the potential income from such a timber raid might be significant enough to finance the building of a new city.

Panic seized me at the thought. We didn't have any thornhands up here in the north since the Hathrim timber pirates typically attacked our southern shores, so who could stop him? I couldn't do it all by myself.

That branch, I decided—I hoped!—was unlikely. He wouldn't conscript his entire population into piracy and risk them against our defenses. I mentally leapt elsewhere: the vast stands of pine on the north slopes of the Godsteeth were unguarded by the Nentians and represented unthinkable riches. What if he landed there, clear-cut as much as he could ship, and then sailed south to start anew? The death cries of the trees would be horrible, but I don't think the Canopy would move to prevent it, and that might be the same calculation Mogen already made. I could hear the arguments of the cautious now: We should not risk our roots for trees outside our borders. If the Nentians cannot be bothered to worry about their resources, why should we? It is Forn we are pledged to protect, a fact no one can dispute, and so the Canopy will allow an unspeakable desecration and I will have nightmares and feel the bite of axes in my limbs for weeks after it happens. My eyes fill up just thinking about it.

The trees from our side of the Godsteeth would be even more profitable, of course, and we would need to patrol the passes in great numbers to make sure the Hathrim never harvested so much as deadwood without permission.

When morning came, they extinguished their fires and I could see nothing, sunlight glinting off water and distance disguising details. But there was no question that this had to be reported to the Canopy. Greensleeves up and down the coast needed to know about this, and if the Hathrim were heading for Ghurana Nent, the Nentians needed to be warned, too. They might not care as we did about the clear-cutting, but they would care about their borders being breached.

The details and the thinking cannot be communicated well by root and stem, so I am on my way to report to Pont in service to the Canopy, breaking my journey to record this and spade a small meal down my throat, dangling my feet over the edge of the Leaf Road. No doubt

some other greensleeves will be there, adding their branches of understanding to the problem. With any luck, Pen might be well enough to
travel now and meet me at the Second Tree. I would be proud to introduce her to everyone. And if I can convince the Canopy to defend the
northern slopes of the Godsteeth from wholesale slaughter, I will.

A flash, a cloud of green smoke, and Nel Kit ben Sah dissolved all too
soon. The bard bowed to Survivor Field, saying, "More from Nel tomorrow. But now I must introduce you to Gondel Vedd, a linguist at
the Senn College of Languages at the University of Linlauen in Kauria.
Please excuse his initial appearance—he will clean up nicely later, I assure you."

Once Fintan cast down his next black sphere, a Kaurian man, mildly
stooped and on the edge of elderly or, to be charitable, in very late
middle age, looked around in wonder. He was bald on top, his remaining hair was white and unkempt, and he had a mustard stain on his
tunic. He didn't look particularly brilliant or heroic but did have a
quick intelligence in his eyes. His voice surprised me; it was a high
tenor but strong and confident.

Gondel

A hammering fist on the door woke me after a fitful two hours' sleep,
and it was still black as tar in my rooms. I'd stayed up until my last
candle guttered out, reviewing ancient texts on the origins of the
Rift—again—and my eyelids felt weighted and sticky as if someone
had poured honey on them as a practical joke. "Gondel Vedd! The
mistral requires your counsel!" a voice boomed, followed shortly

thereafter by more pounding. Apparently Her Grace wanted answers on the Rift, too. Or else I was in serious trouble. My husband grumbled, and I felt him burrow underneath the covers next to me.

I stumbled blindly out of bed, kicked over the chamber pot, and groped my way toward the front door. An impatient cyclone frowned at me when I opened it. He held a lantern up to my eyes, and I squinted at the sudden glare.

"You're Gondel Vedd?" He sounded disappointed, as though he'd expected someone much more impressive. My parents would have sympathized. They'd always expected me to be much more impressive as well.

"Yes, I am he. How may I help you?"

"The mistral requires your presence at the palace. I'm to bring you to her immediately." He said this quickly, as if the speed of his tongue could lend greater urgency to his mission.

"Is my head to be struck off?"

The cyclone blanched, the question taking him by surprise. He considered it seriously, though, unable to appreciate the absurdity—for why would the mistral need to decapitate men when she could simply feed them to the ocean?—and then said in reassuring tones, "I doubt it, Scholar. That form of execution is only practiced by the Nentians."

"Ah. You relieve me excessively. Let me get dressed. What time is it, Cyclone?" I called.

"Two hours before dawn, I think."

"Too blasted early," my love mumbled.

"You could show some concern here," I whispered to him.

"Mmf. Can't be mad at me. I'm unconscious."

"You can be sure we'll talk when you're conscious, then."

What had happened that the mistral needed to see me at this time of night? Perhaps she needed my aid translating something in the old language. I hoped it was something simple like that. I could see no other positive reason for sending a cyclone for me at this hour. Mistrals do not bestow medals and titles on scholars before breakfast. Or after it, if we are to speak honestly.

"Has the mistral not slept?" I asked.

"I'd be surprised if she had, what with this—well. You'll see."

Interesting. Whatever had happened today had little to do with me, then. Until now. "I'm sorry to hear of her unrest. But the wind will bring us peace," I said, taking comfort in the ritual phrase.

"We breathe it as we speak," the cyclone answered automatically.

I shoved my ancient shanks into some breeches and hastily pulled a tunic over my head. Finding my belt proved problematic, and I could almost feel the cyclone's impatience boiling over as I scrambled to find it.

"What are you doing, Scholar?" he called from the doorway. "We must be on our way."

Finding my boots was no problem at all. I nearly tripped over them, and I yelped in fear. That was a broken hip narrowly escaped. And Maron slept through it, ripping out a tremendous snore.

"Are you all right, Scholar?"

"Yes, a moment. Almost ready." I was probably a mismatched horror, and the fops at court—if any were awake—would mock me mercilessly, but on the whole I counted it better than appearing nude. Careful searching allowed me to find the pitcher of water on my bureau. I poured some into the washbasin next to it and splashed my face, then tried to tame my hair by drowning it so that it hung from my scalp like sodden clumps of wool.

"All right, we can go now," I said, returning to the front door. The cyclone's face suggested that his second impression of me was worse than the first.

A chariot awaited in the street, and we managed to travel three whole blocks before the cyclone brought up my family.

"Forgive me for asking," he said, "but—"

"Yes, Tammel Vedd is my brother," I interrupted, "and no, we are not very much alike."

"Oh. Well. Um. Great man, your brother," and then he added, "Sorry," perhaps realizing he'd implied I wasn't a great man or as if he thought I might not agree.

"No need to apologize. It's true that my brother is a great man. But for all that, we do not speak very much."

It was a bald statement of fact that didn't assign any fault, but I knew the cyclone would assign the blame for our chilly relationship to me. The wind of conversations about my brother always blew in the same direction, but I was always grateful when they got to this point, because the awkward silence that followed for whoever was with me was a blessed silence in my mind. I am as proud of him as I should be, but I do not enjoy constant reminders that I am the lesser son.

There were only occasional Hathrim firelamps in the streets, and so we traveled in near darkness, much of Linlauen's beauty shrouded in black, thin clouds obscuring the stars. But the gentle and omnipresent wind from the ocean kissed our faces, freshness with an aftertaste of salt, and the distant crash of waves on the base of the cliffs was a soothing counterpoint to the clack and rattle of the chariot on the cobbled street.

Descending from the summit of the university grounds, we followed the winding trail of the coastal road through an expensive merchants' district and then past the soaring spires of noble houses before ascending again to Windsong, Kauria's seat of power and monument to the glory of Reinei.

Once we arrived and the cyclone transferred care of the chariot to the palace hostler, I thanked him for his escort. The young man examined my face for signs of sarcasm but found none. "It's only my duty," he mumbled. Then, remembering his mission, he spoke briskly. "Come. The mistral bade me hurry." He led me through a labyrinth of passages and narrow guarded doors until we entered the Calm from a small niche to the west of the mistral's dais, which stood in the center of the circular room. The legendary tones and chimes of the wind hummed and tinkled as currents of air were circulated through the traps and tunnels of Windsong, but at present the Calm did not live up to its name. There were at least a score of people in the room, all bunched to the north of the dais, most of them talking over one another, but all conversation ceased when the mistral's attention slid to our entrance. And with her attention came everyone else's.

I recognized the mistral's chamberlain, Teela Parr, and a Priest of the Gale named Borden Clagg, but the others were strangers. Nobles and merchants speak the languages of money, fashion, and power, and those are the only three languages with which I have little acquaintance.

The cyclone bowed before her, and I looked down until she deigned to recognize me.

"Mistral Kira," the cyclone said in a rich, full tone he'd never used with me, "Scholar Gondel Vedd, as you requested."

"Thank you, Carlen," she said as I was wishing I'd taken more care in dressing. Unlike my poor cell at the university, the Calm was very brightly lit, and it cast into sharp relief the many wrinkles in my tunic and highlighted the spectacular mustard stain on my right breast. "It seems we caught you at a bad time, Scholar. We would not have disturbed your rest had there not been great need."

"Please excuse my disheveled clothes. I was given to understand that haste was at a premium. How may I serve the mistral?"

I'd only ever seen portraits of her before, hanging in the university library; in person she was stunning. Tall and slim, Mistral Kira wore the traditional sky blue color of Kaurian leaders, a length of light cotton fabric wrapped cleverly about her body and chased about the edges with strips of soft yellow and sharp orange. It was fastened with silver brooches at her right shoulder and left hip. The silver sapphire crown shone at the top of her forehead; from this towered a magnificent headdress in blue, yellow, and orange, adding another half meter to her height. Eight thin silver torcs circled her neck, but she wore no other jewelry, not even rings. Her skin was as dark as mine but unblemished as yet by time.

"Begin by speaking plainly," she said. "I need not be reminded constantly of my title. I am told you are a linguist."

"Yes, Mis—ahem. I am. Fluent in all six modern languages."

"That is all? I was told you know the ancient tongue as well."

"I do, yes. Uzstašanas is a mother tongue to the modern languages spoken today."

"Excellent. I'm glad to be so well informed. Nobody told me of your fondness for mustard, though." She arched an eyebrow at my tunic, and the assembled courtiers laughed on cue. That was okay, I thought. I still had no idea what I was doing there, but I was willing to suffer some official ridicule and the laughter of fools if it meant I could avoid the dungeons.

"Scholar, I'm afraid I must send you to the dungeons," the mistral said.

My face fell, and I think I aged past my life expectancy in the second before she continued.

"But not as a prisoner, you'll be glad to hear." Yes, if she could have mentioned that part *before* my bowels liquefied, I would have been glad indeed.

"Oh," I managed to reply.

"An interesting situation has arisen, and we require your skills. My chamberlain will fill you in on the details, but I wished to meet you and make clear that I am very interested in what you may discover down there. I am sure you will do your best work, and I thank you in advance for enduring the coming hardship."

"Hardship?" I repeated.

"Farewell, Scholar. I look forward to your report. Do be quick, for there may be something we need to act on immediately, but do not be so quick that you ignore details. Teela? If you please."

The chamberlain stepped forward and took my arm, guiding me to another door behind the throne. There were a bewildering number of them back there, each with its own guard. It occurred to me as we were about to walk through it that I hadn't said farewell to the mistral. I swiveled my head around in an attempt to give my audience a sense of closure, but I saw that the mistral was talking already to someone who was dressed in an absurdly aggressive shade of purple.

"Don't bother," Teela Parr said, recognizing the thought behind my glance. "And don't worry; you did well. Most people babble or weep or even swoon the first time they meet her. She has that effect on people."

We entered the famous Silverbark Room, named for the four pieces of furniture made from the prized Fornish silverbark tree. Tales of its splendor do not do it justice. On a Nentian rug that rested on a floor of Raelech marble, two chairs faced a small sofa with an exquisite tea table between them. The legs of the chairs, sofa, and table were carved with the leaf silhouettes of different rare plant specimens never seen alive by anyone who wasn't Fornish. The pieces represented a nearly priceless gift from the Black Jaguar Clan, the current rulers of Forn. These rested in the center of the room, which had vaulted ceilings and a series of stained glass windows high up opposite the door. Two windows were left clear and open to allow for a pleasant draught of ocean air through the room.

There was a silver tea service set upon the table with sachets of loose-leaf black tea from Perkau, and the chamberlain asked me how I took mine.

"Milk and honey," I said.

"Please, sit," she said, gesturing to one of the silverbark chairs. I felt it would almost be criminal to sit on such a work of art, but apparently I was headed to the dungeons whether I sat or not. I sank into it, and the upholstered cushions cradled my bones with almost sinful luxury. A soft sigh of pleasure escaped my lips, and the chamberlain looked up from pouring tea and smiled.

"Nice, isn't it?" She looked to be slightly older than the mistral, perhaps in her early thirties, but she was not quite as tall. She had large eyes and a narrow nose, and her hair was curled tightly in rows and gathered in one long braid held by three silver rings, which fell all the way to her waist. If I remembered correctly, she was from one of the Finch houses, but she wore the mistral's osprey on the left shoulder of her tunic.

"Very nice," I agreed, and thanked her for the tea.

"I'm afraid the mistral might have scared you a little bit back there," she said, leaning back into her seat with her lips curving in faint amusement over the rim of her teacup. "The hardship will be the time you must spend in the dungeon itself, with no breath of Reinei's peace to sustain you. We will do what we can for your comfort, but there is only so much one can do with a dungeon."

I nodded sagely as if I knew all about the challenges of creating comfortable dungeons.

"We have a special project for you, Scholar. A very odd person washed up on one of the islands in the archipelago on the ocean side."

That last part hardly needed to be said. People never washed up on the Rift side. The longarms or the bladefins always got them.

"Washed up as in dead?"

"Nearly so. More like a shipwreck. Except it's better described as a glorified rowboat. And the strange man we found in it doesn't speak a word of Kaurian."

"I begin to see why you might need me, then. But surely you have translators available, diplomats who usually handle this sort of thing."

"Usually we do. But he isn't speaking any language they know. One of them theorized he might be speaking the ancient tongue, so we had to go digging for civilian linguists, and you were at the top of the list."

A knock sounded at the door, and a young page came in with folded garments across his arms. "The mistral sent me with a change of clothes for the scholar. She thought you might wish to change before you go downstairs." The clothes were neatly pressed and of much finer quality fabric than I was used to. The tunic was a copy of the chamberlain's—a sort of palace livery, really, for the page was wearing the same thing—a light desert tan with a sky blue sash running diagonally across the chest and an osprey clutching a fish embroidered at the top of the left breast. Resting on the tunic was a small unopened jar of imported Fornish mustard.

I smiled. "Please tell the mistral I appreciate both her courtesy and her wit."

My parents used to tell me, in concert, that I was far too smart for my own good. They tried to discourage my love for language early on, and

I was forced to sneak away to the university library at night to explore nautical records in the language of the Brynts, learn the few plant songs available in the percussive syllables of Fornish, and exult in the musical, rolling rhythms of the Nentian plains on the rare occasions when they put into port. At the time, in my youth, I naturally thought my parents' brains were contaminated with dung. How could intelligence, a natural advantage, ever prove to be a disadvantage?

Only as we descended into the dungeons did I concede that they might have had a valid point. It was dank, the air mildewed and moist, heavy with the reek of chamber pots.

Had I listened to my parents, I would not be here. I would have traveled down to the Tempest of Reinei in my sixteenth summer, said the words to the Priests of the Gale and had the words said to me in kind, and then I would have walked to the edge of the cliff and thrown myself into the howling swirl, a literal leap of faith that Reinei would bless me with the kenning of the wind. A short while later, I would have emerged under my own power and joined a profession commensurate with my Windclass, or I never would have emerged at all, dashed against the rocks or dumped into the sea like so many others. Either way, I wouldn't be in a still dungeon, charged with speaking to a foreign stranger.

But I consciously chose this Windless life. It was the only way to guarantee I'd have a life, after all, since the Tempest takes as many as it blesses. It blessed my younger brother and took the older one. But neither of them ever visited a dungeon out of the comfort of the wind. And Teela Parr clearly did not want to add a visit to her duties. "I have to get back to court," she said, stopping outside the door, "but let me give you a conversation piece to get you started."

The chamberlain produced a book bound in matted reeds, the paper inside of a strange texture to my fingers. The cover had a circle of leather glued in the center, hand-tooled to read ZANATA SEDAM in embossed letters. I read them aloud, and Teela asked me if I knew what it meant.

Frowning, I said, "The second word looks like it's close to two different numbers in the ancient language, but I don't know what the first word is at all." I flipped open the book and found a tight, flowing script using the ancient alphabet; a few words looked familiar, but none of them were immediately recognizable except— "Fire!" I said.

"What? Where?"

"This word here. *Vatra*. That's 'fire' in the ancient tongue."

"So you can read it?"

"I can read that word. Let's see if there are any others . . . yes. Here is *voda*. That's 'water.' "

"Very good, Scholar. But what about the rest of it?"

I tore my eyes away. "You gave it to me less than a minute ago."

"What I mean is, do you recognize the language?"

"It's drifted away from the ancient tongue like all the languages have over the centuries, but perhaps not as far as ours has. Certain words resist change because of their frequency of use, like numbers and everyday nouns. If they shift at all, they shift in pronunciation or at least share the same roots as older versions of a language, but it's rare to develop completely different morphology—"

Teela held up a hand to stop me. I guess I had been babbling a bit. "Just tell me if you can read it now or later," she said.

"Later. Once I talk with him, I will have a better idea of how long it will take."

"Thank you. I will let you begin. But be careful. Do not let him get his hands on that book."

"Why not?"

"Because the cyclones were at great pains to take it from him. He wants it very badly. So we want to know why. Is it a diary or what?"

"There's no way it's a diary."

"How do you know?"

"It's a completed work. Same script throughout. The handwriting is consistent with someone copying a text. Which means this probably has religious significance to him."

"Holy writ? Like *Reinei's Wind*?"

"Kaurian sailors never leave port without it, right? It's not so difficult to imagine that this sailor would also bring with him a volume of comforting thoughts."

Teela Parr nodded. "All right. I'll come back to check on you soon. Good luck."

I tucked the book underneath my new mustard-free tunic and followed the guards down into the damp and dark. The stranger waited in a single large cell. It was one of the nicer ones, with decent lighting and fresh matting for his sleeping tick. He had eaten his fill three times, I was told, so much that his stomach visibly bulged. A table and a chair already waited in front of the cell with a stack of paper on it, along with a fresh quill and ink pot.

Seeing the foreigner reminded me of my childhood, when I laid eyes on a teabush serpent for the first time: a sense of childish wonder coupled with a twinge of fear that this new thing in the world might be dangerous. He was too tall to be Fornish but a bit short to be one of the Hathrim. His skin looked pale and sickly to me, but I suppose sickly always goes together with pale in my mind anyway, and I am certainly no healer to judge these things properly. Apart from the slight bulge to his abdomen, he had a skeletal appearance, sharp-bladed cheekbones scraped clean and hollows under his dark brows, ribs starkly outlined on his torso. He definitely couldn't be a stunted Hathrim; they had stocky builds and were fond of their beards and leather. His only clothing was a broad strip of cloth like a bandage wrapped around his hips, fastened with a length of coarse rope. And it was his choice to remain immodest, for I saw a folded set of fresh clothes resting in his cell.

Extraordinary. A new race of people from somewhere across the ocean. How had he ever managed to cross it?

He eyed me with suspicion at first, leaning against the wall to my left with his arms crossed in front of his chest and his right leg crossed in front of his left.

"Hello," I said. "My name is Gondel." I tapped my chest. "Gondel."

I got a glare for my trouble at first, but my expectant expression must have persuaded him to respond in kind. He tapped his chest once and said, "Saviič." The *ch* sound at the end of his name told me that they were hewing to the old alphabet.

"Hello, Saviič." I held up my right index finger. *"Jedan,"* I said. Then I lifted fingers in succession and continued to count to ten in Uzstašanas. *"Dva, trik, četiri, pet, šest, sedim, osim, devet, deset."*

Saviič uncrossed his arms and took a couple of steps forward as I spoke, then shook his head when I finished. He began counting as well, correcting my poor pronunciation, or rather correcting the ancient words into his modern equivalent. The first four numbers had changed to *jed, duv, tri,* and *čet,* and *sedim* had changed to *sedam.* Interesting and encouraging. But what he said next was unintelligible babble to me. I think my lack of comprehension showed on my face, because he sighed in frustration. Remembering that the title of his book contained the word *sedam,* or seven, I withdrew it to begin discussing it with him.

Upon seeing it, he cried out and rushed the bars, startling me and causing me to stagger backward until I ran into the table and toppled onto it, beyond the reach of his long arms. I made an undignified noise and eventually landed on the floor, where additional noises and my continued flirtation with a broken hip brought the guards to the cell with spears pointed toward the prisoner. "It's all right, I'm fine, just help me up," I said. "The chamberlain wasn't kidding. He really wants that book back."

One of the guards hooked a hand under my arm and hoisted me to my feet. I thanked him and seated myself at the table a safe distance from the bars. I straightened the paper and righted the ink pot that had tumbled on its side during my fall—luckily the cork had been in place. Placing the book in plain view on the table but well out of his reach, I smiled at Saviič to reassure him that I was not annoyed and pointed at the title. *"Zanata Sedam.* What is *zanata?"* I circled the word with my finger and then pointed at it, repeating my question so that Saviič would know I wanted to know that word. I saw that he was paying more attention to the guards than to me, so I asked them to retreat while I spoke with him.

"I won't be falling down again," I told them. "Thank you."

With the menace of the spears removed, Saviič focused his gaze on the book and on my question. He sniffed and rubbed at his bare chin, refolding his arms and thinking about the problem for a few seconds before answering. Then a half smile formed on his face as he met my eyes. He held up a finger. *"Zanata jed: Vatra."* Fire.

A second finger appeared. *"Zanata duv: Vjetar."* Wind.

The third finger went up, and he said, *"Zanata tri: Tilo."* That was the earth. He was naming the elements, so *zanata* must mean "elements." As expected, for the fourth finger he said, *"Zanata čet: Water,"* that was water. But if the title was *Zanata Sedam* and he had named the four elements we all knew, what were the other three?

With all five fingers extended he continued: *"Zanata pet: Bilje."*

"Bilje?" I repeated, frowning.

He nodded. *"Deh. Bilje."* That couldn't be right. *Bilje* was a catchall term for plants, and they weren't an element. Unless he wasn't referring to elements after all. Still with a half grin on his face, he raised a finger on his other hand and said, *"Zanata šest: Zivotinje."* Animals.

"Reinei give me breath," I said. "Are you talking about kennings?" Of course he didn't understand my Kaurian. He shook his head and continued, holding up seven fingers.

"Zanata sedam: Vječnast."

I didn't recognize that word. But I couldn't give up now.

Uncorking the ink pot and snatching up the quill, I quickly scribbled out childish illustrations of fire, water, earth, and wind and then wrote the old words next to them and showed them to Saviič, confirming what each one was supposed to be. *"Deh, deh,"* he said, nodding each time. I drew a flower for a plant and then pointed at the osprey for the animal, and he confirmed those as well. I then wrote the word *vječnos* and rose from the table, coming around to hand him paper, quill, and ink pot, asking him to draw what that word meant. With all the examples he already had and a large blank space to fill in, he knew precisely what I wanted. But he waved me off and spewed a river of words at me, only a few of which I might have recognized but couldn't place into any meaningful context. His body language proved to be much better. He tapped his skull and shrugged, communicating that he knew of no way to draw the meaning of the word. It must be an abstract concept rather than a common noun.

That was all right. I knew the title of the book and already suspected that it would give the fops in the Calm plenty to talk about. Reinei blow me down, it would give the whole world plenty to talk about! Returning to the chair side of the table, I sat and penned a quick message to the mistral's chamberlain: "Reinei's wind has brought us something remarkable indeed. I know not yet whether it is for good or ill, but the title of the book is *Seven Kennings*. Not six—seven! Same order as we count them. Sixth is for animals. Seventh is unknown as yet."

I didn't quite know what to add after that. Several profanities and exclamations came to mind, and I almost wrote one of them down when I realized that this piece of paper might become part of history. I would not want to be remembered as the man who wrote "great lakes of longarm shit!" to the mistral's chamberlain, so I confined myself to adding a few surplus exclamation points—and ended with "Learning more."

Folding it and handing it to one of the guards to deliver immediately into the hands of Teela Parr, I then began to write down my recollection of these events while they were still fresh in my mind, for I sensed that a full accounting of my labors would be demanded sooner rather than later, and being thorough might allow other eyes to notice something of significance that I, in my haste, might have missed.

I sent the other guard to fetch a set of children's primary language cards, the kind with pictures and words underneath them in large letters, and another ink pot and quill for the prisoner to use when he had need. I will learn the language of this strange, bony giant from across the sea, and maybe Kauria will be the first nation to secure access to the Seventh Kenning, whatever and wherever it was.

I looked up to check on Saviič and found him staring at me with curiosity. I smiled back at him. "This is good," I said. "How do you say *good*, Saviič? *Dobar*?"

He wasn't sure what I meant, so he tilted his head and ventured a guess. *"Dobro?"*

I grinned and nodded. *"Dobro. Deh.* This is *dobro."* Maybe we could let him out of there once we could speak well enough to let him know we just wanted to talk and read his fascinating book.

He smiled back, and I almost wished he hadn't. His teeth were rotten, and he laughed unpleasantly as he said, *"To če biti dobro kad smo osvojiti svih sedam zanata."* I think I have that right; I asked him to repeat it so I could translate it later. Anything said with that much menace deserved a closer look.

When the bard dismissed the seeming of Gondel Vedd, there was quite a bit of noise but only distracted applause; everyone was eager to discuss, or rather shout about, the revelations of the tale—that the Bone Giants were not illiterate savages but religious zealots, and they knew of a Seventh Kenning. *A Seventh Kenning.* I think many people might have missed the last few paragraphs of that particular story because they couldn't contain their surprise once they heard about it. Unlike Gondel Vedd, I will write down a couple of exclamations I heard on the wall because that's history, too:

"Fuck me with a kraken cock! A Seventh Kenning!"

"I couldn't shit harder if you fed me week-old shellfish!"

It's hard to imagine what that kenning might be, however, since the Bone Giants displayed no magical talents in their invasion. Foremost in my mind was the question why we hadn't learned of this captive earlier: the Kaurians had done us a disservice by keeping it to themselves. Fintan picked up on such sentiments, especially the angry epithets spewed by one reactionary mariner nearby who thought that the Kaurians had allowed us to be attacked and hadn't behaved like allies at all, and addressed it.

"Some of you may be thinking right now, with the benefit of hindsight, that the Kaurians should have told us immediately of their discovery. But remember that they had no idea of what was to come.

They had a single strange man in captivity and the same language barrier that we faced. Except that they had a way to solve it. We will check back with Gondel Vedd later to see what he learns, but you already know the most important bit: not only is there a Sixth Kenning, there's a Seventh! Or at least the Bone Giants think there is. They didn't use one when they attacked—they just had surprise and overwhelming numbers—but maybe they're looking for it. Maybe the source of the Seventh Kenning is hidden somewhere on this continent, along with the Sixth, and that's why they have come: they want it for themselves. It is food for thought, yes? We'll continue tomorrow!"

Fintan and I parted for the evening, and I smiled on the way home, savoring the idea of a Kaurian fleet transporting our armies across the ocean to strike back. And since the bard had mentioned that Gondel would at some point join us—he'd no doubt go with us if he could speak the Bone Giants' language—I'd have to put together a suitable gift basket for our meeting. Perhaps themed around some fine mustards.

Elynea and her children surprised me when I came home by not being there. And neither were most of my belongings.

Day 4

KINDLING

The first thought I had upon seeing my looted house was that Elynea and the children would have no place to sleep except the floor because the couch and the beds were all gone. Then I worried that I would have to sleep on the floor, too, and Bryn of the Deep, it looked pretty rough. Only after that did the thought enter my head that maybe Elynea had something to do with the robbery.

Unworthy of me, perhaps. Unjustified by any facts other than the single one that she was not in my house at a time when she usually was. But I supposed there would be no reason to stay in my house in such a state if she had gone out and come back to discover it this way.

Not everything was gone. My writing desk still squatted in my bedroom, together with my materials and papers; that was a mercy. Such things were worthless to desperate people right now, but beds and couches were in short supply out on Survivor Field.

So, apparently, were bathtubs. Mine was gone, the drainpipe to underground sanitation sluices sticking up out of the tile like a lightning-struck stump. I cursed, and it echoed off the walls. I still had a commode, at least. And although they had carried off my wardrobe, they had tossed my clothes out of it first, leaving them scattered about on the floor.

My pantry was bare, every scrap and crumb of food pillaged. I supposed there must be far hungrier people than I who needed it. My dishes and silverware were missing, too. Recognizing a pattern, I saw that most of my personal items remained but all the housewares and basic needs had been stripped. If it was indeed Elynea who was responsible for this, I didn't begrudge her a bit of it, though I would have liked to hear how she explained such behavior to her kids.

There was nothing to do but inform the constabulary and make inquiries with my neighbors, not in any hope of recovering my possessions but merely to let them all know it had occurred, and perhaps my neighbors would beware and take steps to make sure it didn't happen to them.

Dame du Marröd, the nice widow across the street who'd given the orange tunic to Elynea, had seen nothing.

"You didn't notice some dodgy types removing my bathtub and furniture?"

"I was knitting a pair of socks for my grandson and listening to that bard fellow tell his story," she said. "And the young men I have staying with me were all out working or looking for work today. I'm sorry, Master Dervan." She sniffed a couple of times, uncertain and a touch worried. "Do you need a bath now?"

"No, thank you, I have much else to do. I might take you up on it later, though."

"Of course, dear."

When the constable arrived, one Master du Bartylyn, he let me know that I should not hold out any hope of swift justice. A slightly pudgy and avuncular gentleman with a beard going gray and a nose that looked like it had been broken more than once, he had a voice that was both tired and sympathetic. "There's been a rash of these types of robberies recently. This is the fifth one this week. We haven't recovered anyone's belongings yet, and I'm doubtful we will. Everyone's moving in and out all the time with this refugee situation, and nobody looks twice at furniture moving now. It's so commonplace that you'd have a difficult time distinguishing between lawful and criminal furniture moving, you know?"

"Right. How does one move furniture suspiciously these days?"

The constable chuckled. "Well, you're being quite sensible about it. The last family screamed at me for not instantly returning their grand-mother's candelabra to them."

Shrugging, I replied, "I suppose it's nothing to scream about com-pared to what most people have lost. I can't summon too much out-rage when they left me my work and my clothing."

"A man with perspective! That's rare. Well, if we do find anything, we'll be in touch. Thanks for reporting it in any case. Helps us estab-lish a pattern."

"And if you see Elynea or her children?"

"Same thing: we'll let you know."

I returned to the palace to sleep on my old cot for the evening and let a mariner know why I'd returned and ask him to please inform Rölly. My friend the pelenaut had me join him for breakfast in the morning, sending a longshoreman to take me to a small private dining room. He had decided that morning that everything was orange, or at least he would be, dressed head to toe in varying shades of it. It wasn't a traditional palette for Brynlön, and I wondered if Rölly had lost a wager.

We bade each other good morning and sat at the table, and a long-shoreman promptly set glasses of orange juice in front of us. I wasn't going to comment aloud on the overload of orange, but after that I couldn't resist.

"Are we celebrating citrus today?"

Rölly looked down at his outfit and smirked. "A Kaurian ambassa-dor arrived last night with a shipment and I'm meeting with him later today, so I suppose we are." He plucked at his tunic and snorted. "Ev-erything you see on me was a gift from him in the past few years."

"No. He's been giving you orange clothing every time he visits?"

"Yes, he has. I'm trying to visually communicate to him that perhaps it's time to be a bit more thoughtful. You think it's too subtle?"

Shaking my head and chuckling, I said, "I'm so glad I don't have your problems."

"Yes, you should be. But I understand you have your own. Your home was robbed?"

I let him know what happened and asked to resume my residence in the palace, but he surprised me by stating that he'd have some longshoremen bring me a cot and a chair for my writing desk instead. "I'd really rather you weren't in the palace, Dervan. Föstyr tells me that—well, never mind. I am purposely sheltering you from what's happening here."

"I don't understand why."

"This bard is going to be trained in reading facial expressions. He'll be able to tell when you're hiding something. I need your reactions to be genuine and open."

"Reactions to what?"

"Whatever he says. He will say some things just to see how you react."

"Huh. That might explain yesterday. He brought up my marriage to Sarena as if she were still here."

The same longshoreman as before arrived with plates for us, and after the pelenaut thanked him and he left, he ignored the food and leaned forward, eyes boring into mine. "Tell me exactly what he said as best as you can remember." I told him, and he leaned back when I finished, wagging a finger at me. "You see? He has already begun."

"Begun what?"

"He's assuming you're a trained spy because of your close ties to both Sarena and myself. He will be looking for tells that you are trained, and he mentioned Sarena entirely to gauge your reaction."

"You mean he already knew about Sarena's passing?"

"Of course he did, Dervan! The Raelech ambassador he mentioned visiting was *at her funeral.*"

I felt an ache bloom between my eyes. I'd been so foolish to think I could match wits with a trained bard. "I'm really not suited for this, Rölly."

"You're fine. Ask him something for me next time, will you? Pretend you know nothing about the Triune Council members—"

"I won't have to pretend."

"That's good. Ask him who they are and what they are like. Listen but also watch his face as he describes them. Does he make small expressions of disgust when he thinks of any of them? Does he blink his eyes a lot or look elsewhere when talking of one of them? Notice everything."

"Why? Is there something going on with one of the council members?"

"Maybe and maybe not. I don't want to say anything because you can't give away what you don't know. Just be openly curious and clueless. And watchful."

We didn't say much after that, just fell to feeding our faces, but my mind whirled with so many questions that I didn't even notice what we ate. Something fishy.

I spent the remaining hours of the morning back at my house, picking my clothes up off the floor and folding them into neat piles. I stacked them on top of my writing desk, having no other place to put them. Then I sorted through the papers that had been casually perused and tossed aside with little interest. I had to reorder my manuscript, but nothing was missing; in fact, I found something extra. It was a note from Elynea that she evidently had left on my writing desk, thinking I would have seen it there immediately.

> *Master Dervan:*
>
> *I didn't get a chance to tell you before you left, but during my job search this morning I ran into an old friend from Festwyf. I thought he had perished with most everyone else, but he is in a stable situation here and has room for us to visit. We'll spend*

the night there and try to return tomorrow before you leave for
the afternoon.

—E.

So perhaps that was what had put her in the mood to smile yesterday. And perhaps she hadn't been involved with the robbery after all but merely made it possible by leaving the house unoccupied—and unlocked—in the afternoon.

I heard the creak of my front door, followed by a gasp and Pyrella's voice: "What happened?"

Tamöd, with a note of outrage, cried out, "Where's all his stuff?"

"Lord of the Deep," Elynea said, and I entered the living area to find them frozen in the doorway with wide eyes.

"Welcome back. I'm glad you're well. I was worried," I said, waving her words that were still clutched in my hand, "and I just found your note."

"Are you moving?"

"No, quite the opposite. I'm staying no matter what, it seems. But I've been robbed. Everything's gone except my desk and clothes."

"Oh, that's terrible."

"You mean there aren't any beds?" Pyrella asked. "Where will we sleep?"

"The longshoremen walking up behind you have the answer to that, I believe."

Four longshoremen, obviously sent from Rölly as they were wearing palace corals, arrived with a total of four cots, four chairs, and a basic square wooden table. One of them remained behind to install a new lock on my door, one of the expensive ones forged from Hathrim steel. Elynea and her children stood mute the entire time, trying to stay out of their way.

"I'd understand if you wished to find lodging elsewhere," I said after the longshoremen had all departed.

"No, no. The kids have been happy here."

I noticed that she didn't include herself in that happiness.

"But you had good news? You found a friend?"

A smile. "Yes, a neighbor of sorts who lived three farms away from ours, Garst du Wöllyr. He lost his farm and land, of course, but he was always good with tools and has started over here as a carpenter. Making furniture, actually. He might be able to help you get some bed frames if you would like."

"That would be lovely. I'm sure the comfort of these cots will leave much to be desired. Perhaps you could inquire what that might cost when you see him next." I did not have inexhaustible funds and could not count on my friend to refurnish my home for me beyond what he already had provided. What he had delivered had no doubt been intended for someone on Survivor Field, and I would have felt guilty accepting it save for the fact that Elynea was one of those survivors.

"I will. Actually . . ." She stopped and looked down.

"What?"

"He might have a job for me. Mostly painting or staining assembled pieces. Some sanding, perhaps some other finishing work."

"I didn't know you were a woodworker."

"I'm not. But I might as well learn a new skill since I cannot tend goats I do not own or land I do not possess."

"And he'll pay you for this? It's not an unpaid apprenticeship?" I would have an objection to make if this Garst was looking to take advantage of Elynea's desperation.

"No, it's paid. I can't formally apprentice with him since he's not a master anyway. But there's so much demand for pieces right now and people are so strapped for cash that they can't afford master-made items anyway, so Garst has all the work he can handle. Most people are willing to take them raw, but if I finish them, we can charge a bit more, and with increased production he can take on more work."

"I see. Well, that certainly sounds good if you've planned what to do with Tamöd and Pyrella."

"I was hoping we might continue our arrangement where you looked after them in the mornings. I would go to his shop before dawn and return before noon when you have to leave."

I nodded. "That would be fine most days except for the few I have to have breakfast meetings. Perhaps we could ask Dame du Marröd to help on those occasions or someone else you might know."

"Dame du Marröd would be perfect if we can convince her." She looked down at her kids, stroking Pyrella's hair. "You two liked her, didn't you? You wouldn't mind spending just a few hours with her once in a while?"

"That would be okay, Mommy," Pyrella said. Tamöd was somewhat doubtful.

"Does she know any tidal mariners?" he asked.

I felt a small upwelling of hope on behalf of Elynea; a job would help her move on more than anything else. But since I had been so abysmally wrong about everything I thought yesterday, I wondered what I was missing now. Where was Garst du Wöllyr getting his lumber, for instance? And if he needed help finishing pieces so badly, why had he not already hired someone else from the vast pool of labor clamoring for work right now? It bore investigation, but I didn't want to pry or sour what could potentially be a great blessing. Rather than swim against the currents, I would swim with them and wait.

I met Fintan at the Siren's Call and purposely took him to eat at a Kaurian café, guessing that they'd have fresh ingredients from their homeland since a boat had come in the previous night loaded down with citrus and who knew what else.

On the walk over there through Pelemyn's streets, I neglected to tell him that my house had been robbed; he'd ask what happened to the pages I'd written thus far, and I'd be forced to explain that they'd been tossed around but not destroyed or taken. A fortunate thing, that, considering what I had been writing, and perhaps doubly fortunate that I had a better lock on my home now. Taking even further measures to hide the manuscript as it was completed might be wise. Perhaps an enchanted Hathrim lockbox, one of the fireproof ones, hidden away somewhere beneath the floorboards. Rölly might have one I could use.

"How has the Siren's Call been treating you?" I asked him as we squeezed past a crowd of people shouting at a fishmonger for his freshest catch. "You said the ale was good, but what about the rest?"

"It's been delightful. I sing one song when I walk in after the performance on the wall, and then I eat and drink for free the rest of the night. People want to tell me their stories, and I want to listen. It's a perfect arrangement, really."

"What have you learned from these stories?"

"Lots of different accounts from the northern cities along the Gravewater River. The Bone Giants seemed intent on raiding the outlying farms as much as the cities."

"Makes sense. The way I hear it, they were pretty hungry."

"But they were also degrading your ability to withstand a siege of any kind," Fintan pointed out.

"It never came to that."

"True enough. Have you ever seen one of them in the flesh?"

"No. They never got over Pelemyn's seawalls. I've only heard tales. Have you seen them?"

"Aye. But that story is weeks away. I began in the west and didn't come this way until somewhat recently."

As I suspected, the Kaurian café had some fresh limited-time specials: spicy grilled shrimp and baby longarms over cilantro lime rice pilaf and even garnished with lime wedges. Citrus like that was hard to come by in our part of the world. Fintan was impressed, and I thought it was a boon to know what had just arrived at the docks.

Though I supposed I shouldn't have been surprised, Fintan was recognized by the server, a dour gentleman with a short beard and an expansive forehead. His face lit up in a brilliant smile as his eyes took in Fintan's Jereh band.

"Reinei give me breath, you're him, aren't you? The Raelech bard?" Fintan beamed at him. "I am, sir."

The Kaurian gushed for a minute and welcomed us both and rushed away to tell the owner of the establishment that we were there. She emerged from the kitchen, smiling widely, and insisted that our lunch was on the house and it would be her privilege to serve whatever we liked from the menu. We ordered the lime-squeezed special.

Once they left our table, my expression of wonder caused Fintan to flick a finger at my face. "Close your jaw, Master Dervan. You could hurt yourself."

"Does this happen to you all the time?"

He shrugged, a tight smug grin on his face. "Let us say *most* of the time. It will be like this from now on, I expect. If they somehow miss that my skin is lighter than a Brynt's and my hair is straighter, then the Jereh band is a giveaway that I'm Raelech, and if they know their colors, then they can easily put together the rest even if they've only heard me, never seen me."

My eyes flicked down to his Jereh band, which all Raelechs wore to signal their status through the polished stones set in a bronze or gold torc wrapped around their biceps. They forced all foreign visitors to wear one while within their borders, too. There were always three main stones that echoed the ritual of their formal introductions— patron goddess on the left, rank in the middle, and profession on the right. Fintan's Jereh was citrine for the poet goddess Kaelin, amethyst for the master rank, and then another citrine stone representing the bards. His wife, Numa, wore a ruby for the huntress Raena, a master's amethyst, and mother-of-pearl for her profession, linking it visually with the Triune Council, whose members also wore mother-of-pearl on the right side. If you knew the Jereh table—as all Raelechs did— you'd be able to tell at a glance who you were dealing with, and I saw the practicality of that.

"How many people know the colors, would you say? I mean, how familiar are Brynts in general with the Jereh table?"

He winced and sucked at his teeth. "I can point to any fish in the sea and a Brynt can name it for me, but most of you can't tell a Raelech miner from a beekeeper without a guide. And that's not a knock against you; it's the same wherever you go. Most people who aren't Raelechs don't know more than the few colors they might see in their daily lives, you know? They know the colors for merchants, certainly, and the blessed craftsmen who are typically employed abroad, like stonecutters and masons, and people in government know about couriers and diplomats, but otherwise we usually have to say out loud who and what we are. Most people miss the relationship status, too."

"What? I didn't even know—where's that?"

Fintan reached across with his left hand and tapped the metal with his finger. "Gold means I'm married, bronze means single."

"Ah. I have a feeling you brought that up because someone missed that signal."

He nodded. "I have been the subject of spirited flirting at the Siren's Call. When I tell them that I'm married, they are utterly surprised even though I advertise it clearly. It's simply ignorance."

"Sure, I understand. Maybe I can help a bit with that. Would you mind helping me write down a current Jereh table? For an appendix, perhaps. I don't know it all myself."

"Certainly. It's changed in the last five years anyway." There was a small bowl of fruit on the table—citrus, of course—and as I got out my writing materials, Fintan casually removed an orange and held it in his palm, considering it. "Do you know what this color signifies in Rael?"

"No."

"We use the same stone—a special orange garnet—for millers, merchants, coiners, and thieves."

His eyes fixed on mine as he said "thieves," and I almost laughed. Rölly had been right; he would say things merely to gauge my reaction. I'm sure he knew that Pelenaut Röllend was dressed entirely in orange that day and furthermore knew that I'd had breakfast with him in the palace.

"Fascinating," I said. "A reminder to merchants, millers, and coiners that they're being watched at all times?"

"Yes." He dropped the orange and sighed. "I know how they must feel now."

That did elicit a chuckle. "I am not watching you so much as enjoying your company," I said, acknowledging that I knew he was being watched but carefully making no comment about it.

"True. Aside from performing, it's my favorite part of the day. Thank you for that. Shall we fill out the Jereh table now and see if we can work faster than the kitchen?"

"By all means."

That kept us busy until the food came out; it was utterly delicious, and Fintan promised to mention it on the wall, which pleased the owner no end. I waited for him to pull my chain again to see what flushed, but he had no further prodding scheduled, and I didn't feel like asking him about the Triune Council just yet. That could wait. We worked over drinks, chatted with the Kaurian staff and some other customers who wanted to talk to Fintan, and then it was time to return to the wall. Inspired perhaps by our earlier conversation and a desire to forestall further flirting, he shared a Raelech children's song about growing up couched in the colored stone markers of their social hierarchy.

> Jade and marble till we're twelve,
> Into studies we will delve
> And earn our brown apprentice stone,
> Keep it till our craft is known
> Then step into our journey blue,
> Grow until we're ready to
> Go test for master amethyst,
> If we're lucky we'll be kissed
> And marry someone wise and bold,
> Turn our bands from bronze to gold.

"Today we begin by checking up on Kallindra du Paskre, the trader's daughter who chronicled her family's encounter with one of the Bone Giants. I mentioned at that time that the du Paskres weren't the only ones to see them in advance of the invasion. Kallindra's family had been on their way to a trader clave in Setyrön, where she learned more."

He cast down his seeming stone and took the form of the sleepy-eyed teenage girl. Whereas before she had worn a wry smirk, she now appeared almost jubilant about something.

Kallindra

I cannot tell you who was most excited in my family to finally reach the trader clave in Setyrön, nor can I tell you who hid their excitement best. I would like to think I won in both categories, but Jorry caught me smiling once too often for no apparent reason.

"You can stop pretending you don't care about the clave," he said. "I see you there smiling like a kid at a tide festival."

"I wasn't smiling about that," I said, scowling at him.

"Then what?"

"Dad getting robbed the other night."

Jorry frowned. "That's hardly anything to smile about."

"Mother sure smiled about it. She nearly died laughing."

"But we were robbed."

"And we'll remember it well, won't we? It was an excellent lesson for us all. I can't remember half the things our parents have tried to teach us, but I'll never forget that."

Jorry snorted and allowed himself a half smile. "No, I guess not."

In truth I was smiling because the clave was one of the few times and places where we could relax. It was safe and everything smelled good and tasted delicious, and those things are the fundamental building blocks of a great day. And we had many such days to look forward to.

Father, however, stopped thinking claves were safe a couple of years ago. Ever since I came of marriageable age, in fact. Nope, not a coincidence! He seems to think I would abandon the family at the first proposal, and so he tries to forestall any attempted courtship with his looming presence, following me around most of the time. That was all right with me. I'm not chafing to be free just yet; I have yet to find someone who suits me. The handsome boys my age tend to be more than a little doltish, and older unattached men tend to be unattached for good reasons. I'm not sure marriage would suit me, anyway. Men so far appear to be more trouble than they're worth.

The clave was being hosted by a farmer outside Setyrön who had yet to plant his crop for a fall harvest and wasn't using his field for anything else. He'd pocket a healthy sum for letting us trample all over it and enjoy clave prices in the bargain.

When we pulled up to the posted, gated entrance to the farm, there was a friendly greeter there to take our entrance fee and register us.

"Ask him, Father. Ask him."

"All right! Patience!" he said, then turned to the greeter. "Could you tell me if the du Lörryls are here yet, sir?"

The young man smiled. "You're not the first to ask. They are indeed. I think you'll find them already busy."

Jorry and I clapped and made high-pitched noises of excitement. We passed on to find a spot to park our wagon, necessarily taking a spot on the periphery. It wouldn't be the periphery much longer; more wagons would arrive and form rings around us.

"Go on, kids," Father said. "See where everything is and find our friends. I'll expect you back in an hour, and then I'll want you to take me to the du Hallards, Kallindra."

Jorry and I shot out of the wagon like bolts, clutching our purses with the few coins in them that Mother had given us when Father wasn't looking. I think Father knew, though; he was too shrewd with his money not to know where it all went, which made me wonder why he pretended not to know.

We called out greetings to families we knew who worked the inland routes, and they called back. We depended on them to supply us with wool and honey and wax, and they depended on coastal traders like us for fish oils, inks, imported goods, and so on. I asked the du Nedals where we could find the du Lörryls. Dame du Nedal smiled at us and said, "You want that honey-apple bacon, don't you?"

"My mouth is already watering," I said.

"Yours and everyone else's. You can almost smell it from here. They're frying it up two rows over and north. Hurry before it's gone, now."

We thanked her and dashed between wagons, turned to our right, and spotted the line. We joined it gladly and knew it would keep growing. The du Lörryls had found a farmer somewhere upstream from Göfyrd who made the world's best bacon and furthermore dealt exclusively with them. They got premium prices for it, and deservedly so. We always bought some at every clave and never held on to enough of it to resell, though Father claimed every year he was going to buy five stone of it and make a fortune marking it up.

"You smell that, Jorry?" I said. We both took obnoxiously loud, deep whiffs of the air, making little wafting gestures with our hands around our noses. "Smells like bacon." And money. And earth ready for replanting. And perfect contentment, that sublime moment when you're at peak anticipation for something and you know you'll get it soon. I often think that moment is better in some ways than getting the thing itself: it's the awareness of your own joy at being alive and that the gods of all the kennings have blessed us, even those of us who never seek a kenning.

The couple in front of us were strangers and we gave them tight smiles of greeting, but Mella du Bandre came along a few seconds later and joined the line behind us. Her family was coastal like ours, working between Setyrön and Gönerled, and we competed in a friendly manner with them for customers in Setyrön. She had a hug for me and a shy smile for Jorry. His smile in return was a bit goofy as he stammered out a hello, and I could see already that this present awkwardness would be fertile ground for future teasing. I take my sisterly teasing duties very seriously because it's so much fun.

Mella had grown up and filled out a bit since last I saw her, so it's no wonder that Jorry noticed. She had pretty eyes and a quick wit that I'd always appreciated. If Jorry managed to win her consent, I'm sure both of our families would be delighted to see them matched.

"How have the tides treated you?" Mella asked. "Wash up anything interesting?"

"Yes, but why do you ask?" I said, because I sensed it wasn't a casual query. "Have you seen anything strange?"

Mella nodded, "Yes, but you go first."

Jorry caught my eye and gave a tiny shake of his head. Perhaps he didn't think I should share the fact that we had been robbed. But it was only a map, not our entire inventory. And if there had been more people like that strange woman—Motah or whatever her name was—I wanted to know about it.

"The tides brought us a very tall woman who looked like she was starving."

Mella gasped. "A woman! We saw two different men, also very tall, and we could see their ribs. And strange skin."

"Strange how?"

"We couldn't tell if they were pale with sunburned skin or just naturally kind of reddish."

"It was the same with the woman we saw!"

"Did she have a little boat?"

"Yes, though we didn't get a good look at it."

"Did you understand anything she said?"

"No. What about the men?"

Mella shrugged. "We had no idea what they were talking about."

"Did they buy anything?"

"No, but I don't think they had any money. They were almost naked." Her eyes flicked to Jorry. "Was she naked?"

Jorry's face was priceless. Panic and indecision and then a silent plea to me to save him from speaking.

"Mostly," I answered. "She seemed to be lost."

"Same with the men. Makes me wonder if there was a shipwreck out there somewhere and they were the only survivors."

"Did you show them a map?"

"We didn't have one."

Jorry found his voice. "Any idea where they might have been from?"

"No; that was the weird thing. If you assume they were sunburned pale people, that means they had to be Hathrim or Fornish. But they didn't look or speak like either one."

"You're sure they weren't Hathrim?"

"Quite sure. My brother speaks their language fluently, and he didn't recognize a word they said."

My initial excitement and wonder at finding someone else who'd run into the strange people turned into uncertainty and a touch of worry. "Do you think we should be telling someone about this?"

"Like who?"

"Well, I don't know. Our parents for starters. You tell yours we saw one, too, and we'll tell ours what you saw. I have to think someone would want to know that we're seeing people no one has ever heard of before."

"Well, yeah," Mella said, "but—"

"What can I get you?" a voice broke in. We had inched our way to the front of the line as we talked, and now it was our turn to order bacon from Master du Lörryl. Jorry insisted on buying a few slices for Mella, and the strange people were forgotten between their flirtation and the delightful baskets of greasy meat.

I remembered them later, of course, and even mentioned to Father that the du Bandres had run into two lost giant men on their route. But he was too preoccupied by the absence of our best friends among the merchant families to pay any real attention.

"They're not the only ones lost," he grumbled. "Are you sure you looked everywhere for the du Hallards, Kallindra?"

"I am, Father, but I will gladly search the clave again if it would ease your mind."

"I think it would—but take Jorry with you. And don't just look; ask about. Maybe they're running late, but maybe they're nearby and need help, too. Thieves like to take advantage of traders going to claves when they can, you know."

"Yes, I know very well." Anticipating his next words, I said, "I'll be careful, and I'll return soon."

We didn't find the du Hallards that night but discovered why they were late the next day. Just after midmorning, Jorry and Mella were smiling and practically drooling on each other near the Glorious Bacon Wagon, as they had taken to calling it, and I was utterly fascinated by how they seemed to grow more stupid with each passing moment. But then news rolled through the clave like high tide: Tarrön du Hallard had stumbled into the clave on his own, half dead. No word on why or where the rest of the family was.

"Father will know," I said, and the three of us hurried back to our wagon, thinking he'd be able to give us the truth. He gave us more than that: he put us to work immediately, because Tarrön du Hallard was there, cradled in Mother's arms, and there was a crowd of people around the wagon, trying to get a look at him, and all of them were asking questions.

"Get rid of these people!" Father hollered at us once we pushed through. "Tell them you'll give them the facts when we have them but right now we need to get him well. He can hardly tell us what happened when he's unconscious."

"Shall I fetch a hygienist?" Mella asked, and Father said several people already had gone to do just that.

We spent a good while just trying to disperse people with promises to report as soon as we knew anything and then fending off new arrivals as they came. Though the du Hallards were closest friends with us—Father had known Umön and Lyra since they were kids together—the whole family was well loved in the clave. Tarrön was a couple of years younger than me, and I think that Father and Umön had been hoping we'd take a liking to each other. He was nice enough and told a good joke, but I'd never felt attracted to him, nor, so far as I could tell, was he attracted to me.

He looked to be in pretty dire condition, though I'd only caught a short glimpse of him in the back of the wagon before Father stepped in front to block the view and discourage precisely that sort of gawking. But poor Tarrön! His lips were swollen and bloody, his clothing was shredded and his skin bruised and lacerated, and there was a nasty gash across his scalp that probably would leave a scar through that pretty, poufy hair of his—okay, so maybe I felt a *tiny* attraction to him. But he's still a kid. And so am I, technically. Let's simply observe that we both have potential.

The summoned hygienist finally appeared to assess the damage. Mother had given Tarrön water, of course—first thing you do—and attempted to clean him up a bit with boiled rags, which the hygienist approved. But he'd lost a lot of blood and used up all his strength just trying to get to the clave, and there was definitely contagion in the blood he had left.

"I know you want to speak to him," he said, "but he is in poor shape. He needs time to rest, and I'll need time to cleanse his blood."

That didn't really satisfy anyone, but we couldn't argue the facts. Obviously something horrible had happened, and Father requested that we get both the constabulary and the mariners at Setyrön involved. Normally we took care of our own business at the clave and didn't want outside authorities involved, but everyone wanted to find the rest of the du Hallards.

Tarrön woke on his own from a bad dream in midafternoon. Mother and I were with him in the back of the wagon along with the hygienist. His head began to turn back and forth in troubled sleep at first, a prelude to his horror, then he sat up, fully awake, and screamed, "No!" And then when he realized where he was and with whom and that he was safe, he just wept, and it pulled tears out of my eyes to see him so upset.

"You'll be fine, Tarrön," Mother said, pulling him to her, and Father, who'd been outside, appeared at the back and peered in.

"Can you tell us what happened?" Father asked. "Where's your family?" Tarrön simply shook his head and took great shuddering breaths, holding on to Mother. "Were you attacked by bandits?" Another shake of his head.

"Really, we should let him rest," the hygienist said. "Perhaps a tea with a soporific would do."

Unsure why I spoke, I blurted out, "Did you see a pale giant, Tarrön?" and he startled, eyes turning to me, and caught his breath. The barest nod. "We saw one, too. Halfway to Möllerud. Where did you see one?"

"Nuh, not far," he managed. "Road to Göfyrd. Top of the peninsula. Due north of here."

"Sunburned? Starved?"

"Uh huh."

"What's he talking about?" the hygienist asked. "He saw a Hathrim?"

We all ignored his question, and Father said, "Did the giant do this to you, Tarrön?"

His eyes shifted to Father and welled with fresh tears. He pressed his lips together, and they trembled, trying to hold back another sob. He nodded once.

"Bryn drown me . . . and your family? Umön and Lyra and your sisters?"

Tarrön couldn't keep it in after that. He gave one disconsolate moan and dissolved into sobs.

The hygienist's mouth dropped open, and he turned to Father for confirmation. "He's saying a Hathrim murdered his family?"

"Not a Hathrim. Something else."

"That's three encounters we know of if you count Mella's," I said. She had left by that point, and I hadn't thought to ask her precisely where they had seen their giant or what had happened afterward; we'd been distracted by bacon.

"What did he want, Tarrön?" Mother asked.

He gulped and sniffed. "I don't know. We couldn't understand him. He talked for a while and then just—started killing us. I fought back, tried to choke him, but he got loose, took off in his stupid boat."

The story came out in little spoonfuls after that. Tarrön had come to the clave for protection instead of going to the city, since he realized that no one might believe his story and then he'd be blamed for his family's deaths. But we knew he was speaking truth; he would have our backing, plus the du Bandres, if the constabulary wished to make anything of it. Once word spread around the clave, another family confessed to seeing one of the strange giants.

When the Setyrön constable showed up, she was willing to believe that Tarrön was innocent and had fought off *somebody* . . . but she seemed oddly unmoved that four coastal traders had encountered what sounded like a new race of people from across the ocean.

"You can't get across the Peles Ocean," she said in a flat tone that communicated her disbelief. "What you saw was probably a tall Fornish pirate. I hear they have little colonies scattered around the archipelago, maybe even on the Longarm Isles. Been there ever since the Rift, you know, isolated, maybe a bit . . . uncivilized."

Father scowled. "You think they're Fornish pirates? If that were the case, why would they be landing all the way up here? By themselves, in four different places, speaking a language that sounds nothing like Fornish, and somehow growing two or three feet taller than normal while looking like they haven't eaten in months?"

The constable shrugged. "I don't know. I admit I'm speculating. I'll ask around and see if the mariners have seen anything strange. We'll make sure your family is given proper rites, Tarrön. And if we run into these giants who aren't Hathrim, we'll contact you."

Her attitude didn't fill me with confidence that anything would be done, but there was nothing to be gained by pushing her further. We assured her that Tarrön could stay with us until he recuperated and we could get him to family in town.

The episode cast a pall over the rest of the clave. Even the honey-apple bacon didn't taste so good anymore. Jorry remarked in a rare effort at thought that tragedy sort of has its own aftertaste.

"I know what you mean," I said, "but it feels more like a sponge that soaks up your happiness and squeezes it out somewhere else. It makes everything that's good just a little bit . . . less."

There were few in the audience who couldn't relate to that sentiment, but Fintan didn't allow us much time to dwell on it. "Let's jump back to the west now and see what Nel Kit ben Sah did next," he said.

My report at the Second Tree did not go as well as I had hoped, but neither did it go as badly as I had feared. It is an enduring truth of life that we must all struggle for our place in the sun, and I am content to stretch out my arms until my leaves collect that which I require.

For most of my life the Black Jaguar and the Blue Moth Clans have been able to go to the Second Tree and have their words accepted without question. I want that to be a reality for the White Gossamer Clan before it is my turn to die and become one with the roots of Forn, and perhaps this is an opportunity to take a step along that branch.

While I ran along the Leaf Road to Pont, word came through root and stem from greensleeves to the south that Mount Thayil had indeed erupted and Harthrad was a total loss. The ash cloud would trail south to fall on most of Hathrir, though some would inevitably coat the southern coast of Forn. It's as if Mount Thayil coughed and soon it will make all of Hathrir sick.

If the Hathrim are smart, they will hire Kaurian blowbags to funnel the ash into the Rift. Cyclones, I mean: that's the proper term, and I should use it.

When I arrived at Pont, the merchant clans were already discussing the probable boon to Fornish farmers this eruption would bring; dead Hathrim crops meant a lot of hungry giants, and they would need our produce. But no one was talking about what happened to all the giants in Harthrad, or if they were, it was with pity, because they assumed that they all died in the eruption.

I swung up higher into the canopy once I reached the Second Tree, struggling to find a space where I could send out my shoots and join the sway. There were far more Black Jaguars than there needed to be. They couldn't all have something important to contribute; they just wanted to drink up all the news and choke out the roots of other clans. Pak Sey ben Kor, that sour cabbage, actually questioned my presence as though I had no right to join the sway like any other greensleeve.

"Why aren't you on the coast?" he said, making it sound like an accusation.

"Because I have new mulch for the garden to help us all grow."

He snorted in disbelief. "Doubtful. You're a dormant seed."

I'd been prepared to allow him a thorny word or two because he lost his nephew at the Seeking, but my sympathy evaporated at such a stark insult. I told him he had no nuts in his shell and swung up beyond his voice. He would fight me in the sway on general principle, so there was no use fighting before.

I found an unoccupied branch that was high enough that it protested under my weight. I guessed I would be part of the sway in both the figurative and the literal sense.

Caressing the bark of the Second Tree with my fingers and humming in pleasure, I took a moment to appreciate the blessing of being a greensleeve. Odious clan politics aside, I always know my place in the Canopy, and it's a good one, an important one to the ecology of the forest even if I am not so important in the hierarchy of humans. The First Tree gave me an equal voice, and the Black Jaguars and Blue Moths could not shut me out, much as they would like to.

Pressing my palm flat against the living bark of the Second Tree, which was carved with ridges and festooned with mosses and mushrooms, I closed my eyes and felt the solid patience of the silverbark, the determination to grow and remain, to be nurtured and nurture in return, to give shelter to the small and be sheltered itself by the surrounding canopy and the forest of Forn, to share in the strength of intertwined roots and interests. My bark sprouted, shoots slithered into the bark of the Second Tree, and I joined the sway.

The minds of the Black Jaguars and Blue Moths were there, of course, and I felt them also at the First Tree and on the far coast in Keft as well. But luckily they were not all. I also felt the presence of greensleeves from friendly clans: the Red Horses, the Yellow Bats, the Gray Squirrels, the Invisible Owls.

Sending quick love and acceptance of all in the Canopy and my pledge to defend it with my life, I announced that I brought news from the coastal watch north of Pont. *I believe I have seen the giants moving toward Ghurana Nent,* I said. *Many tens of boats passing in the night. It was no trade fleet. I think it was the entire population of Harthrad. They had fires on the water, and only the giants do this. I think they are going to land on the north side of the Godsteeth and cut down the unprotected trees there to finance the building of a new city.*

Much discussion ensued and requests for further details. I had little else to offer, and there was never any question of deception on my part—just questions about my judgment and how I interpreted what I saw. Condescending doubts and suggestions that I might have imagined it all.

See and judge for yourself, I replied. *A fleet that size deserves watching even if it is not the people of Gorin Mogen.* Pak Sey ben Kor suggested I might not have seen a fleet of ships but rather a migration of sea creatures that emitted their own light from within as some creatures were known to do.

Should we not confirm? I asked the Canopy. *If it is the Hathrim, then surely Forn has an interest in their destination. Our northwestern region has no thornhands garrisoned at all, only greensleeves and a few grassgliders.*

Pak Sey ben Kor could hardly argue that we should ignore potential threats to the Canopy or our allies in Ghurana Nent, and so it was quickly decided: the sway ordered him and Tip Fet ben Lot of the Blue

Moths to accompany me north in search of this fleet to confirm its existence and final destination if possible. They are not ideal companions and will try their best not to see anything at all, so I must show them something undeniable or my whole clan will suffer for it. Pak Sey ben Kor was quick to let me know that as soon as I withdrew my shoots and descended to the Leaf Road.

"You may have won a small victory in the sway," he said, sneering at me, "but when we find nothing, your clan will not be able to dodge the shame of your foolishness any more than the earth can dodge the rain."

Tip Fet ben Lot was only marginally less threatening. "I hope for your clan's sake you are right, Nel," he said. He might have added my name to seem friendly, but somehow it conveyed the opposite of friendliness. "The White Gossamers have some good people, and I would hate to see their honor stained in service of a delusion." I bit back an angry retort. I had made a report according to my duty, not as a political maneuver, yet they had cast it as such.

Pen Yas ben Min arrived with a triumphant smile before we set out, and her appearance curdled Pak Sey ben Kor's already sour expression. She'd been blessed by the First Tree, and his nephew had fed the roots. Rather than accept his nephew's faults—or his own, since he'd been the one to present him—he'd resent Pen's excellence.

She shone with health and new growth, her symbiosis complete. Moss hadn't begun to grow on her silverbark yet—that would take a season or two, and its lack would mark her as newly blessed for a while— but she had budding mushrooms on her shins. "How was your journey?"

"Full of wonders," she replied, beaming at me.

"I'm so glad you made it here in time. We were just about to leave on a scouting mission."

"Yes, if we could get on with it," Pak Sey ben Kor said. Pen's face fell at his rudeness, but I caught her eye, kept a polite grin on my face, and gave her a tiny shake of the head to tell her not to respond.

"Certainly, benmen. Let's be on our way."

I set a brutal pace and told them to keep up, a command with which they had considerable difficulty. They were not used to exerting them-selves, having spent so much time dangling on branches and talking rather than doing. It was probably petty of me to enjoy their panting and especially Pak's eventual entreaty that I slow down, but if so, I think I can live with that particular guilt. Pen, as I suspected she would, kept up just fine.

"Why are we moving so fast?" she asked me after the first hour.

"It's more peaceful," I explained. "They can't sow their poison if they haven't breath to speak."

We camped for the night and filled our bellies with fruits and seeds. When we reach the sentinel trees on the border with Ghurana Nent, we will borrow horses and any other weapons we may need for our scouting. Some of my clansmen will be there and will join us, no doubt. Cousins I have not seen for seasons but close to my roots, and in their eyes I will see if I have grown straight and true on my own— I am only five years senior to Pen, after all. Perhaps the Black Jaguars and the Blue Moths will not be so eager to disparage the White Gos-samers when they are outnumbered. Perhaps, if the Canopy is well served by my watch, the White Gossamers will climb again. I would dearly love to be the sprout of that new growth.

Even in the company of wilted men like Pak Sey ben Kor and Tip Fet ben Lot I exult in running the Leaf Road, where every step brings new smells and sounds and I can feel the filtered sun dapple my skin through tiny gaps in the leaves. The blessing of the First Tree flows through me, energy singing ballads in my blood and urging me onward in ser-vice to the Canopy. My two companions gave up on asking me to slow down, realizing it didn't reflect well on them, and instead I waited for them to catch up periodically, wordlessly pointing out that they were not so superior after all and it was fortunate for everyone that the White Gossamer Clan protected this stretch of the western coast in-stead of the Black Jaguars or Blue Moths.

My clan members waited for us at a sentinel station at the base of the Godsteeth. They had not seen the Hathrim fleet pass by, nor had they received any word of timber piracy north of Pont, and my political rivals seized on this news as proof that I had misinterpreted the evidence of my eyes.

"The lights must have been sea creatures, as I said," Pak intoned as if he were quoting wisdom straight from the roots of Forn.

"Or the ships passed by too far from this shore to be visible," I replied. "We will ride north of the Godsteeth to be sure." The terrain would not allow us to follow along the coast—the rocks of the Godsteeth broke up the canopy and produced large gaps in the Leaf Road—so we'd travel inland a short distance to the nearest pass between the peaks. I ignored Pak's grumbling and insistence that this was a waste of his time and greeted my clansmen, two of whom—Yar Tup Min and Kam Set Sah—were close cousins. They weren't benmen, but they were expert horsemen who patrolled and harvested the area's fat spider silks and reported any trouble to the greensleeve on station.

Kam and I had grown up together but hadn't seen each other since I set out for the First Tree and became a greensleeve. He was taller than me now, though just barely so, his hair bleached white by the sun and his skin tanned by regular exposure out of the shade. He threw his arms around me and kissed my cheek, his whiskers tickling, then he stepped back and admired the silverbark on my forearms and shins.

"You wear the forest so beautifully," Kam said. "We are all very proud of you, Nel."

"Thanks. But are you proud of your sister, Yar?"

"What of her? I was just about to ask about the Seeking." He looked worried, and I smiled at him.

"She's come back to you as Pen Yas ben Min."

Pen had taken to some higher branches above the Leaf Road to keep it a surprise, but now she swung down on a vine and landed next to us, her silverbark plain to see. "Hello, brother," she said.

"Pen! You're a greensleeve!"

She chuckled. "Yes, I'm aware."

Yar rushed forward to hug her, crying happy tears, and their reunion was one of those rare slices of perfection when you feel all your life's trials are mere shadows thrown by the brilliant light of that moment.

Once they parted, Yar said, "I don't have any expectation that you'll be able to stay, but I'm very glad you had reason to visit us." He flicked his eyes to my winded companions. Startled into remembering my manners, I introduced Pak and Tip and my clansmen welcomed them, according them honors they probably didn't deserve, but that is the White Gossamer way, and in truth their courtesy shamed me. I should be as gracious as they were—I was, once—but that simple meeting demonstrated to me that my conduct has deteriorated since I've become a greensleeve. It would be easy to blame it on the low standards set by the Black Jaguars, but I don't need a giant's glass to see my own faults and I am not one to shrink when the sun provides me light. Henceforth I shall follow my cousins' good example and recall that honor lies more in the giving of it than in the expectation of receiving it—even if Pak and Tip are perfect toads and know nothing of honor.

We descended from the Leaf Road to the forest floor and visited the stables, where Kam invited Pak and Tip to choose their horses. Pak chose Kam's favorite horse—I could tell when Kam blinked—but my cousin only smiled and said we would be ready to ride in the morning.

"Kam. A word?" I said as Yar led Pak and Tip to their nests in the canopy for the evening.

"Sure." I waited until I was sure we were alone before speaking any more.

"How many net launchers do you have here?"

"Enough for everybody."

"Okay, that's good. Offer them to Pak and Tip tomorrow but don't be surprised if they refuse them. However, I'd like to make sure all the White Gossamers carry them. Bring them all. I'll take two."

"Of course. But why, if I may ask?"

"We haven't had to fight giants up here in the north for a long time. Never in my lifetime, in fact."

Kam's eyes widened. "Are you expecting a fight?"

"No, I'm merely preparing for one. I'm thinking we might have trouble bringing them down with arrows. They are strong enough to wear very heavy armor, and even if they don't, who's to say a single arrow will bring them down? They're more than twice our size. If someone sinks a shaft into us, we'll go down, but would a giant?"

"Oh." Kam's mouth opened a little bit as he thought about it. "That's right; we tend to think of fighting in the forest borders where we can call on root and stem to join in. And usually there are thorn-hands. But we'll be on the other side of the Godsteeth."

"Open land. There are trees on the slopes, of course, but nothing like a Leaf Road."

"But you could still call on the plant life there, right?" he said, gesturing to the symbiotic evidence on my arms.

"Yes, but it wouldn't be the same. Not as quick to obey, not as strong. And if I'm right, Kam, the Hathrim are going to be out on the plains."

My cousin twitched. "The plains?"

I nodded. "Treeless plains. The giants are not used to trees, remember. They don't think of them as shelter, only as fuel. As *timber.*" I shuddered, despising that word: a Hathrim root, of course, that implied trees were good only for building or burning. "So they wouldn't think of hiding on the slopes. We'll find them wading through the grass."

"You realize that we qualify as food out there, right? And the horses, too?"

"Yes, I know. Out in the open like that we'll be at a disadvantage. That's why I think the nets might help."

"What are we trying to accomplish?"

"We're just scouting. We find the Hathrim and report on what we see. But we have to find them, Kam."

"Why?"

"The Black Jaguars and Blue Moths are out to discredit me and, by extension, the entire clan. Everything they say makes that clear. They want us brought lower than we already are. They don't want us to threaten their position again."

Kam scoffed and narrowed his eyes. "We were children when that happened."

"So were they. But they remember."

My cousin folded his arms. "You're making it sound like we have more to fear from them than we do from the giants."

"We do, Kam. The Hathrim might want to kill us, but these other clans—they want to disgrace us."

"I think your priorities could stand some examination, Nel."

"Our reputation outlasts our bodies. You know this to be true. My parents are gone, yet I am paying for their actions. We all are."

"That's not the way I see it, cuz. I mean, sure, they got treated like weeds in a vineyard, but apart from missing them every day, the arguments of the past don't affect my life in the slightest. I have a profession and may have a family soon, and there isn't anyone trying to take that away from me. Clan politics aren't my concern, nor are they the concern of most people. It's only you who have to deal with that. The curse of being blessed, I guess."

It was my turn to scoff at him, remembering how much I enjoyed running on the Leaf Road. "I don't feel cursed."

"Time to start acting blessed, then?" my cousin said, his eyebrows raised so high that they nearly melted into the hair on top of his head.

"Yeah," I admitted. He'd scolded me well, and it was what I needed. "I've missed you."

"I've missed you, too," he said, and clapped me a couple of times on the back. "We'll find the giants, and all will be well. I mean, with the other clans." He winced. "Not sure about the giants."

And that wry, halfhearted joke of Kam's almost put me on the same side as Pak Sey ben Kor and Tip Fet ben Lot: I hoped we wouldn't find the giants at all, and my reputation and the clan's could grow mold. Because if we did find them, it wouldn't just be the Nentian pines in danger. It would be Kam and Yar and Pen and whoever else would be joining us tomorrow.

I didn't like the way this tree was branching, but I had no way to prune it.

"Speaking of Hearthfire Gorin Mogen, let's catch up with him and the fate of his migration northward."

Fintan's transformation into Hearthfire Gorin Mogen evoked a much louder response than it had the first time; more people could see him now. But unlike previously, the giant wasn't cloaked in an ice howler fur but rather in his customary slate gray lava dragon leathers shot through with streaks of black and maroon, tied with a dark blue belt and a steel buckle engraved with the Mogen crest. His beard, too, was different in that it appeared to be groomed and gathered at the bottom with two heavy gold ties.

$\mathcal{G}$orin Mogen

We came to fresh shores on the first day of the new year—the first official day of spring in 3042. An auspicious beginning for the Hathrim in the Nentian plains. Or perhaps I should think of them as something else. "The Mogen plains" has a pleasant sound to it. Perhaps in a month I will wake up feeling arrogant and declare it.

The vast stands of timber on the northern slopes of the Godsteeth beckoned to us in the wind. Never have I seen such riches! They will fuel a new age of prosperity for our people, and our hearths will smell of woodsmoke again instead of stinking blocks of compressed weeds and vegetables.

Thinking of hearths, I called my son Jerin to me before we set foot on the beach and charged him with forming a crew to harvest the first wood for our new home. We would need not only fires but docks for our fleet, for we would be dependent on the sea for a while and rocky beaches are not gentle to glass-bottomed boats. He predictably recruited his betrothed, Olet Kanek, and her small train of followers who had come with her from Tharsif to await the wedding. Her relationship to the powerful Hearthfires of Tharsif and Narvik would provide us a political and economic boost: They would be our first trading partners, no doubt, and perhaps provide us with new settlers. And once Winthir Kanek decided we had the right to be here, all the other Hearthfires would hasten to agree.

Volund hauled his thick blond braids and some of my gems aboard a ship and continued north to Hashan Khek, where he would hire Raelech stonecutters to come down and throw up some walls and basic structures for us. I told him to lie and say the work was for a new settlement near Tharsif. If he sailed cleverly and timed it right, returning under cover of darkness, the Raelechs might not even realize they were building on Nentian soil.

Taking stock of our population as they filed off the boats was a sobering task. I had hoped to save more. The lack of warning doomed many.

But the culling might end up saving us in coming months, horrific as it is to say. I do not think we could support Harthrad's entire population here, having no existing infrastructure on which to build. As plentiful as the game is in Ghurana Nent, it is not sufficient to support so many giants for long. The sea will provide for a while; only when we have reliable crops coming in will we be out of danger. But what potential exists in this land!

Trees on the mountains for the taking. Metal inside the mountains to be scooped out. Fertile land for us to tame and ocean waters that have rarely been fished. We will sow and we will reap a future undreamt of in the minds of Hathrim, who have so long thought themselves confined to Hathrir—who have, for too long, shied away from taking what is here to be taken.

That is, if we do not combust out of sheer stupidity.

Once we got a communal hearth going—a row of fires, really, over which we were roasting our first meal slain by Halsten's pack of hounds—I was forced to let the new head priestess of Thurik speak to the people as soon as the sun set. Or at least there was no reason to deny her. If I'd known what she would say ahead of time, I might have simply cut out her tongue, but the old priest, lost in the explosion of Mount Thayil, had never given me cause to worry before.

She was a different creature from old Durif Donorak. Where he was staid and musty, she was a riot of color and energy. All the lavaborn draped themselves in the fireproof leathers of lava dragons out of practical necessity, but she wore a fitted corselet fashioned from their spiny tails, and at the center of it she wore a harness of blown glass chains that looped over her shoulders, under her arms, and about her waist and were clipped front and back to a brushed bronze and copper circle of Thurik's Flame, similar to what I wore on my own armor. But the chains had been heated and treated to reflect different colors—the entire spectrum if I wasn't mistaken—and she used this to dazzling effect. When she stepped near the fires, her shaved head gleamed in the light, and the glass chains shimmered over the lava dragon scales. Putting a finger between her brows, she sparked it, and the whale oil she had smeared over her shorn skull ignited, setting the glass chains to gleaming. That made for quite the visual; Durif had never indulged in such theatrics. She had a chain leading from her right nostril to her ear as well and additional chains around her neck. Only ten feet tall, but she dressed and carried herself to command attention.

"We gather around Thurik's Hearth for comfort," she said, her voice ringing like a hammer striking steel. "And a comfort it is. That's one of the many uses for fire. It can give us a sense of safety and protect us. But we know better than all Hathrim now how destructive it can be as well. And while we mourn the loss of our homes and especially the loss of our friends and family, after every fire it is our duty to consider what comes next. Do we rebuild? Do we move on? How best to proceed? For one of Thurik's most sacred commands to us is to use fire as a creative force more than a destructive one, to craft tools so fine that they are themselves works of art."

There were some nods and grunts at this, and the priestess lifted a finger. "And while we are creating, we must not forget to build for strength as well. And we do that by burning away our impurities."

The response to that was far louder than I expected. I realized I might have misjudged the mood of the people and shot a startled glance at Sefir, who stood next to me. She gave the barest shake of her head, reminding me that my every move was watched by more than one pair of eyes, and I quickly mastered my expression. It would be better for me to watch the expressions of others.

"We are allowed a short time here, a safe place to huddle around the hearth and think well. When the ash from Mount Thayil is cleared, we will return to build again—but build what? I urge you to consider the blessing hidden in the tragedy: we have an opportunity to show everyone, like no generation before us, that the people of the First Kenning are also first in civilization."

Nostrils flaring, I craned my head around, seeking out Halsten and beckoned him forward. He stepped up, the silver threads in his mustaches somehow still immaculate, and I spoke in low tones for his ears only. "I need to speak to this new priestess tonight. Do you know her name?"

"I do not. But I'll find out."

"Good. Bring her to me soon."

The priestess wrapped it up quickly after that with an exhortation to think on the path ahead more than the ruin behind, and the brevity and clarity of her message was so well received that my stomach soured. She would be a problem—and not an easily solved one. I had to eat and be merry after that, suffer through the farce of communal, convivial warmth when all I wanted to do was take an axe to something. The meat we shared of some nameless herbivore brought down by the houndsmen was tough and poorly seasoned and stuck between my teeth.

Sefir and I chose a place away from the main crush of the camp, a spot near the foothills of the Godsteeth where we could pitch a tent and hear about the aches of others. Sefir took care of most concerns regarding settlement and supplies; she had organized much of the provisioning herself, and she had a mind for details, hailing as she did from Haradok, where nothing but logistics allowed them to survive the frigid southern winters. She would make an excellent Hearthfire in my stead should it become necessary. I could not pretend that I would not be a target for much longer.

Halsten ushered petitioners to and fro, and when the fire priestess arrived, it was I who spoke, but Sefir was at my side, listening intently. Halsten introduced her as Mirana Mastik. "Honored to meet you, Mm—La Mastik," I said, remembering the church honorific for lavaborn at the last moment. "Your ascension to Keeper of the Flame came under regrettable circumstances, but I am sure you will guide our people wisely."

"I am honored to meet you, Hearthfire Mogen," she replied. She had thin, almost nonexistent lips, as if she were hiding them. "I certainly did not expect to lead Harthrad's population. I am a transplant, after all, from Tharsif."

"Indeed?"

"Yes. I came to Harthrad with Olet Kanek. I was her personal cleric."

I shot a glance at Halsten, annoyed that he hadn't told me this ahead of time, and he gave a tiny shrug. But perhaps this was fortuitous. If the new head priestess of the church was intimate with my soon-to-be daughter-in-law, that might make her more willing to work with me.

"Your delivery of Thurik's Flame is somewhat unusual," I said. "Or is it common to set your head on fire in Tharsif?"

"It is a fairly common practice there," she admitted. "But some priests are more vain about their hair than others." Her eyes flicked to Halsten's silver-threaded mustaches, and I almost smiled. "I do not expect others to follow my example, of course. I simply follow the path that Thurik has blazed for me."

The ego required to utter such statements always took my breath away. "Thurik blazes your path?" I said.

"Of course."

"You are suggesting that Thurik made Mount Thayil erupt and wipe out our city so that you could be head priestess of the survivors?"

She did not pale at the insinuation or stammer. No, she laughed at me.

"I did not say that in jest, La Mastik."

"Please forgive me, Hearthfire. We were speaking of my shaven head, not Mount Thayil. To jump from one to the other was surprising. I make no claims that Thurik arranged matters here to suit me or that he killed my elders to give me a promotion."

She handled that well, and unlike my advisers, she managed to look me in the eye as she spoke. Admirable.

"Then tell me, if you will, what path you believe Thurik is blazing for us now. I found your earlier words interesting."

"Which words, Hearthfire?"

"The ones regarding a wise use of our resources and the people of the First Kenning becoming first in civilization. You spoke aloud my wish for the Hathrim: not only to be first in our size or first in appetite but first in craft and culture. We have been wood-starved and resource-poor for so long that we could never hope—until now—to build a society equal with our stature. I have long held that the power of fire should allow us to shape and forge our own destinies as it shapes glass and metal, but fire needs fuel, and here we finally have enough of it to make a difference."

She frowned, and her head tilted slightly. "Build a society? You speak as if you intend to stay here."

"And why shouldn't we? What better place for a new Hathrim city than here?"

She spoke with a tone of patient disbelief, as if I were some child. "This place belongs to Ghurana Nent. We cannot stay."

"We most certainly can," I growled. "There is only a piece of paper signed by our ancestors that defines where we can build and thrive. And it says we can only build in treeless wastes, where we most certainly will never thrive. Time to set that nonsense aflame."

"That nonsense will have serious consequences if you flout it," La Mastik said. "I cannot condone it."

"I'm not asking for your approval. Or anyone else's."

"Clearly. But you're putting all our lives in danger acting alone like this."

"We won't be alone for long. You're from Tharsif, and so you must know that Winthir Kanek is a Hearthfire of my mind. That's why he sent his daughter to marry my son."

La Mastik's brows drew together, and a corner of her mouth turned up. "Are you sure about that, Hearthfire? It's true he may be in favor of expanding his territory, but I rather think sending his daughter to you announced his intention to expand into Harthrad next."

My hand twitched toward my axe, and Sefir grabbed it and inter-locked my fingers with hers, a seemingly loving gesture. Which it was. She saves me so often. "He's welcome to expand into Harthrad now. It's a lava flow covered with a thick frosting of ash. I think he'll prefer to profit from the trade we can offer. The first shipment of lumber should do much to convince him. And if you wish to depart with that shipment, La Mastik, you're welcome to do so."

Her eyes narrowed. "A kind invitation, Hearthfire. But I'll remain to minister to Olet Kanek and the good people of Harthrad who have no other spiritual guidance. I notice you have not tended Thurik's Flame since I came to Harthrad."

"The crush of responsibility prevents me. But never fear, I'll make sure someone attends in my stead and pays rapt attention to your every word."

"I have no doubt."

"Speak all you want about rebuilding strong and well, La Mastik. But I hope we'll hear no more from you about returning to Hathrir."

That finally fueled some anger in her, and she pointed a scolding finger at me. "Thurik's Flame is not subject to the governance of a Hearthfire. You cannot prevent me from speaking my mind."

"You are quite correct. And you cannot prevent me from splitting your unprotected head with my axe."

Her hand dropped, and she sneered at me. "Ah. So it's a naked threat, then."

"I dislike threats. They carry the implication that one might not fol-low through on them. Do spout what other fire you wish, La Mastik, but speak another word to my people about leaving here or one word

against me and I *promise* you will be dead moments later, consequences
be damned."

Her eyes shifted to Sefir, searching for assistance, perhaps, or some
sign that I was insincere. She would find no help there. When her eyes
returned to me, she said, "I appreciate your candor, Hearthfire."

"And I yours. We both want the best possible lives for these people.
Let's focus our efforts on making that happen." I pointed a finger at
the ground. "Here."

When her thin lips pressed together she almost appeared to have no
mouth at all, just an unbroken mask of skin beneath her nose. I waited
for a retort, some blast of defiance, but she only nodded once.

"I'll bid you good evening, then," she said, and Halsten escorted her
away. Sefir told him to wait a few minutes before bringing anyone else
forward. Once the priestess and the houndsman were out of earshot,
Sefir kept her voice low and spoke her concerns. "What are you hoping to kindle here, Gorin? Confronting her like that could complicate
matters."

"She would also be a complication if I did nothing. Better to control
the fire when it starts than let it burn freely. You saw her at the hearth.
She has far too much charisma. Let her continue to preach about returning to Hathrir and that's all we'll hear about."

"Fair point. But she'll go straight to Olet now and blacken your
name for this. She may try to get the marriage called off."

"Let her. I only agreed to the arrangement so as not to provoke
Winthir. Let Jerin choose his love and be chosen in turn, as we did."

Sefir hummed with pleasure. "That would be my wish for him. And
if he truly likes Olet, then . . ."

"Of course, of course. It's too soon to tell."

"You should make some art with him as soon as possible. New glass,
new steel for our new city. Inspire others with your fire and hers will
be doused."

"That's a fine idea. I'll begin building a smithy tomorrow."

"Good." My bride released my hand and turned around, surveying
the site. "Are we settling our hearth here, then?" We were slightly ele-

vated above the rest of the plain and could see the dozens of campfires spread out beyond us, stretching to the beach on our left. Behind us lay the roots of the Godsteeth, inestimable riches in fuel growing on their slopes. An excellent spot: the view was priceless, yet we were not so high that people would think we were looking down on them.

"It suits me well if it suits you. But then I am well suited wherever you are."

Sefir smiled at me and ran the tip of her finger along my jaw, through the beard. "Gorin?"

"Yes?"

"Have you been reading Raelech romances again?"

"Shh! Halsten might hear."

Sefir laughed low in her throat, and her eyes sparkled at me. "He might, but he would never dare speak of it."

"He'd better not."

"I am content, Gorin. We will build our new hearth here, and it will be the envy of the world. Give it time and fire and the hammer and you will see."

The orange glow of open hearths didn't look like much at that time, but I knew Sefir was right.

This humble refugee camp will be a great city someday. I should probably start thinking of a name for it.

Once he returned to his normal form, the bard paused for a drink and then raised both hands, a seeming stone in one of them.

"Now I need to introduce you to a new figure, Melishev Lohmet, the viceroy of Hashan Khek and closest Nentian government official to Gorin Mogen's occupation of his country. His city is many leagues away from the Godsteeth, but the responsibility to confront Mogen will still be primarily his."

The black smoke curled around the bard, and his tailored Raelech silhouette faded away to be replaced by a formal Nentian tunic, the kind with excessively flared lapels that roamed uphill to the shoulders and around them, providing a stage of sorts for the new glossy black hair that fell to the middle of his torso. Pale green with silver accents to let the hair shine, the tunic was belted at the waist with a silver sash embroidered with vertical lines of gold thread. Very fine clothing indeed, but the viceroy's expression failed to reflect similar refinement. His broad cheeks and generous nose were pinched in a scowl, and his voice dripped contempt like bitter syrup..

Melishev

I despise unctuous shits, yet I am surrounded by them.

And I am sure that there is someone in Hashan Khek who envies my position as viceroy, but if they knew what I had to deal with, they might reconsider.

I have demands from authority in Talala Fouz that have nothing to do with reality.

I have transient families that enjoy the city's services and drain its coffers yet never pay taxes.

Corrupt merchants do the same and profit immensely by it but then pull out their giant hairy balls, plop them on the dining table of my welcome hall, and complain that I'm not doing enough for them.

I have a military that can't be trusted to do anything but sleep on duty and eat everything.

I have the responsibility to defend a huge portion of the country with that same military.

And the Raelech stonecutters, whose services come at great cost, are taking far too long to expand our walls.

I also do not understand this extreme discomfort whenever I urinate.

But who am I kidding? The entire city envies my position because they are surrounded by shit of a slightly different stench from mine and think the viceroy never has to smell any of his own. They think I live a privileged life—and they are right. I certainly do. My boot closet is probably second only to the king's. But that does not mean I am free of worries.

I have material comforts and no security. People see the material comforts and believe I must have security, too, but no, that is not the case. I only have a finer bed, a chef to cook my food, a man to taste it for poison (after which it is cold), and a safe place to dump it all when my body is through with it.

These privileges, no doubt, are very fine indeed: a safe dump should never be scorned.

And yet I think the stress of my existence will end me. If the king doesn't send an assassin to kill me first. I'm on his list now, I can *feel* it, because he knows I covet that cushy chair of his. But he needs a good reason to replace me. He would find it very convenient if I died, but if I do something he can label as a failure of leadership, that will serve as well. If I don't get the city expanded on time, that might be all the excuse he needs. Even a dip in revenue could spell my doom if it's big enough, and now it might be here.

That simpering wine-soaked liaison to the merchant clave, Badavaghar, claims that we have lost our trading partner in Harthrad in a single night and this will create a costly deficit in the treasury; they imported a lot of our goods. New trading partners will have to be secured in other Hathrim cities if we want their glass and steel and terms might not be as favorable as before, and so on. I banish him to the cellar where he can marinate in his favorite cask, leaving me to think. I climb the dank stone steps of the tower, spiraling ever up and misted with sea spray under the open windows, until I can look out at the entirety of the city without obstruction or interruption. The cry of seabirds and the bustle of industry reach my ears, and underneath it the dull whoosh and hiss of the ocean, but that is all.

Strange, looking out at Hashan Khek from the Tower of Kalaad, to think that the city might be in any kind of danger, economic or otherwise. It is a vista of prosperity viewed from on high, the beasts of the plains all safely deterred by our walls, and it is easy to imagine that everyone below is happy and fulfilled. Rooftops shield the people from rain and their rulers from the reality of the streets.

I know that they suffer. I know that they need more room and that the farmers and herders outside the walls need more protection. That's why I approved the expansion of the city at great expense. And if we don't make up this sudden trade deficit, we won't be solvent and the king will shove a hot poker up my anus before he kicks me outside the walls for the animals to eat. He won't care that a volcano melted and buried our revenue stream.

Dhingra bursts into my tower study while I'm meditating on what to do next. "Viceroy, the Raelech stonecutters are gone. They've been hired away."

That means the city expansion is on hold indefinitely—another reason for the king to serve me whole to a family of harkha weasels. "Who hired them?"

"Hathrim—I mean the ones from Harthrad. The Raelechs left a note. Said they'd return in a month to finish with no further payment required."

"The ones from Harthrad? But Badavaghar just told me that Mount Thayil killed them all."

"Yes, but Badavaghar needs help to find his boots in the morning."

That was certainly true. The drunken sponge needed help to take them off at night, too. "Wait a moment, Dhingra. We may have a problem here that could solve all my other problems."

"I don't follow."

"I've been given two steaming piles of shit news mere minutes apart: Harthrad was destroyed, but the survivors just hired my Raelech stonecutters out from under me. What does that tell you about the direction the survivors sailed?"

My chamberlain's eyes widen. "They didn't stay in the south. They're in the north!"

"And they would be foolish to land in Forn, correct? That would be about as smart as sliding your penis into a monkey's cage to see if he tries to pull it off. But we have all that empty land between us and the border."

"You think they've landed in Ghurana Nent?"

"I think it's *possible*. And if our trading partners have become invaders, I'd like to know sooner rather than later. Fetch Badavaghar out of the damn cellar and bring him to me under the skylight. We'll use him to find out what's going on."

Descending from the tower, I smile to myself, hoping the Hearthfire was dumb enough to invade us. That would start a war. The king wouldn't replace me in the middle of a war. And if I wound up winning that war, well . . . I might as well be the new king. I *would* be the new king.

I beat Badavaghar to the skylight and wait for him, standing in front of my throne. He shuffles into my presence a few minutes later, asking how he can serve. His speech is slurred; he had taken my caustic suggestion to drink some more as a command.

"Outfit a fast ship with a lot of food but only ten swords. It'll be an honor guard for someone from the merchant clave. Someone who has—or had—a lot of money tied up in Harthrad. Who's into their glass and steel?"

"Chumat hash—or rather *had*—shignificant glassh holdings," Badavaghar says right away, and after a moment's thought adds, "Panesha buys finished shteel pieces but not so much raw material from them."

At least the sot knows his clave. Perhaps his only redeeming feature. "Either or both will do. Find out where the survivors of Harthrad have gone and reestablish ties. Offer our aid now in return for favorable terms in the future. They've hired our Raelech stonecutters; tell them they'd better make sure they return here to finish the job they started or I'll be lodging a formal complaint with the Triune Council. And if Chumat or Panesha wants to visit any other Hathrim ports while they're down there and spread their assets, so be it. But the survivors of Harthrad need to be found first, am I clear?"

His hands lift up to the sun shining through the glass ceiling. "As the sky when Kalaad shmiles upon us, Viceroy."

"Good. And tell the ship captain not to take the safe route down. I want them to hug our coast on the way south and watch for anomalies."

"What sort of anoma-loma-nomalies, m'lord?"

"Giant ones."

Badavaghar gapes at me, his brain trying to attach meaning to my words. His yellow teeth flash when he finally gets it. "Oh! Because the Hathrim are giants. You did a . . . you made a pun. Hee hee hic!" He belches after his hiccup and apologizes for that but not for getting smashed on my wine. Kalaad save me from unctuous shits.

Fintan offered a sardonic twist of his mouth to the spectators sitting on the wooden benches below the wall. "His leadership style is a bit different from Pelenaut Röllend's, yes?" Laughter from the crowd. "More from him later. Let us stay in Ghurana Nent, though, and see what happened next with Abhinava Khose."

Well, my life is certainly different now. I'm so glad I took time to write down something before I left the walls of Khul Bashab.

Our wagons are pulled by wart yaks, and since they are notoriously slow, we are hunters built for defense rather than speed. We never sneak up on anything and never outrun anything. We make a lot of noise, try to smell delicious, and the predators of the plains come to us, leaping onto our spears without ever thinking that perhaps they might be the prey.

But for three days we trekked south from the city with very little to show for it. My father grew more annoyed with each passing day and my mother and sisters grew more sullen, and I supposed I joined them in a sulk, Father's annoyance hanging over all of us like grim thunder-clouds exhaled from the Godsteeth.

My uncle Navir tried to cheer Father up last night by pointing out that his "shitty ass was more attractive than his face lately." His gambit failed to improve my father's mood somehow, but the rest of us found it amusing and laughed about it once we were safely out of Father's hearing.

We've seen no kherns and very little else to hunt, so I've had no op-portunity to address my desire to be anything but a hunter.

Well, that's not true; I could bring it up at any time. But my thinking is that if I bring it up as they're going to hunt, they won't be able to discuss it for long. They'll have to go after the prey before it escapes, and that will be *my* escape. Besides, I still have to think of what else I want to be. Maybe I could go to the university in Ar Balesh—or almost anywhere else—and find something worthy of study. I'm beginning to think that hunting for a livelihood will be more difficult than hunting on the plains.

What's changed for the better is that I won't have to hear about choosing a bride anymore. Over breakfast this morning Uncle Navir was talking about my cousin Favoush getting married soon, and inevi-tably his eyes slid over to me and a grin spread across his face. "What about you, Abhi?" he said. "When will you pick out a woman?"

"Never," I blurted out in front of everyone. "I'm *sakhret*."

It wasn't the way I'd planned to tell them, but their reaction wasn't what I expected either. A great cry went up from everyone around the campfire, not in outrage or shock but in appreciation and with many congratulatory slaps on the back for my uncle. Everyone was smiling but me. I didn't understand what was happening until people started handing my uncle money.

"Wait," I said. "Did he just win something?"

"We've had a standing wager for a year now," Father answered, smiling for the first time in days. "We had to get you to admit you're *sakhret* without directly asking you."

"What? You mean you knew?"

"We've known a long time, Abhi," Mother said, and she stepped around the campfire to embrace me and kiss my cheek. "We were just waiting for you to tell us." As soon as she released me, Uncle Navir crushed me in his arms to thank me for ending the suspense and filling his purse while I was at it.

I was happy for Uncle Navir and grateful beyond words that my family loved me unconditionally. It should be a gift freely given to all, a thing taken for granted, but I knew many *sakhret* never felt such acceptance. Quite the opposite. And that made it so much harder for me to tell them that I never wished to hunt again, to reject their way of life and a large part of their identity when they had already given their blessing to a large part of mine.

But the day would come, and it would come soon. We would find the kherns, and when that happened, I would wager my family had never thought to place another wager on my refusal to pick up a spear.

"What happened next to Abhi and his family will take up the majority of our time tomorrow," Fintan said. "And I assure you that none of them would have bet on it happening."

Day 5

KHERNS AND HOUNDS

A groan accompanied the creak of the door when Elynea returned from her first day of work. She had a hand on her back and a wince of pain crinkling her brow.

"That bad, eh?"

With her free hand she pulled out a small leather bag and shook it. Coins made music inside, and she managed a tiny smile. "Not that bad."

"Good. Save it all. Eventually you'll be able to get your own place somewhere."

"I think there's a mariner waiting for you outside," Elynea said.

"What?" I peeked through the window, and sure enough, there was a blue and white uniform. Maybe he wasn't there for me specifically but rather was a security detail. He was smiling and nodding at passersby on the street. "I'll go see what he wants. It's time for me to go anyway."

I gathered my paper, quill, and ink pot and left Elynea in the kitchen with her kids, making them lunch from a few staples I had ventured out to get that morning. The mariner was indeed waiting for me.

"Master Dervan, good day. I'm to escort you to the bard."

"No need. I already know my way to the Siren's Call."

"He's not there. He was moved to a safer location last night."

That stopped me. "Safer location?"

"I don't have many details, unfortunately, but I'm sure he can fill you in." He pointed in the opposite direction we would have taken to the Siren's Call. "This way if you're ready."

"Absolutely. Lead on."

The benefit of living in a city blessed by the Fourth Kenning is that the streets and buildings are usually clean, disguising some of the markers of poverty one might normally see in other cities. One has to look at the size of the homes, then, the lack of decorative touches, the hollow cheekbones, the worn hems, and the baggage hanging under the tired eyes of the citizens to spy their struggle. It was into such a neighborhood that the mariner led me; some of them were no doubt longtime residents of Pelemyn, but others were refugees like Elynea's family. Curious eyes followed our progress, and a few children asked for coins; I had nothing to give them, unfortunately.

Fintan was waiting for me, scowling, outside an inn of questionable structural integrity. Again, like all things in Pelemyn it was fairly clean, but the wood trim was rotting and in need of new paint at the least, if not replacement; I guessed that at one time it had been blue. The second floor appeared to sag somewhat in the middle to my eye, and I would not like to set foot in there without some advanced carpentry to repair it first. The shingle outside was also faded and in need of paint, perhaps fortuitously so. The chipped and weathered sign depicted a silhouette of a cloven-hoofed animal in a state of nearly supernatural arousal, which made more sense once I squinted at the faded words underneath until I could make out that we had arrived at the Randy Goat.

"Why am I at this festering sore of an inn?" Fintan demanded of me, dispensing with his usual greeting. He was accompanied by a pair of mariners, who stood at rest behind him.

"I was hoping you could tell me," I said.

Fintan cursed and rounded on the mariners. "You told me all would be made clear once Master Dervan arrived."

"Apologies, sir," one of them said, a hulking lad who spoke softly. I think his arms might have been thicker than my thighs. "I should have said all will be made clear at your luncheon. A third party will join you."

"Which third party?"

"Will you follow us, please," the mariner said, ignoring Fintan's question. Having little choice, we trailed after the mariners to one of Pelemyn's celebrated luxury establishments along the docks called the Steam Spire Loose Leaf Emporium. It was in fact a series of small tearooms clinging to a central tower with two elevators inside controlled by steam-powered hydraulics, one for diners and one for service. Bell-pulls let the workers in the elevator room know where and when to take the elevators, the steam for which was generated by thermal vents on the ocean floor. Those who preferred the stairs could take them if they wished.

Each of the tearooms held only four tables, all windowed and suspended over the bay, affording beautiful views. Much of the city's—or indeed the kingdom's—expensive business got handled there. The menu offered the finest imported Fornish and Kaurian teas and delicacies as well as the best local seafood available. Usually there was a wait of an hour or more even with reservations. We were ushered immediately to the topmost room, the Kraken Tea Suite.

The pelenaut's Lung, Föstyr du Bertrum, sat behind a round table covered with a white cloth, which appeared to have been composed for a still life painting with tea service, silver bowls of fruit, and miniature frosted tea cakes that I could not believe anyone still had the ingredients to make. Föstyr looked uncomfortable and almost afraid to touch anything. Or perhaps I was projecting my own feelings onto his face.

His bottom lip, jutting out like a pink precipice, stretched into a joyless smile at our entrance. "Masters Dervan and Fintan!" he boomed. "Come, join me. Can I pour you some tea? It's the Sif Tel variety grown by the Red Horse Clan in the southeastern lowlands."

Dazed, we both nodded to him, and he visibly brightened at the opportunity to serve us. Porcelain clinks and liquid sloshing noises filled the room as we took our seats, which were upholstered in the tanned hide of some unfortunate creature from the Nentian plains, no doubt. Three other tables occupied the room, but they were empty. The mariner escorts exited via the elevator so that it was just the three of us. The bay stretched out below, jewels of sunlight winking from the surface of a rippled ocean.

Föstyr set our tea before us, a rich golden brew, and exhorted us to enjoy it.

"You first," Fintan said. The Lung grimaced but said nothing as he sampled the tea and something from each bowl as well as a bite of each cake. That task done, he spoke.

"An unfortunate necessity, for which I apologize."

"What is going on?" Fintan asked. "Why was I whisked away to a sty like the Randy Goat with no explanation?"

Föstyr sighed and dabbed at the corners of his mouth with a napkin before answering. He deliberately placed his palms on the table and looked directly at the bard. "For your own safety. We received threats against your life and wished you to see the sunrise, so you were discreetly relocated and an impostor spent the night in your room."

"And what happened to the impostor?"

"He lives, but only because he was expecting the visitor who tried to slit his throat as he slept."

"No!" I exclaimed, but the other two men ignored me.

"Start at the beginning," Fintan said, crossing his arms and pointedly not enjoying the repast laid out in front of him.

Föstyr looked as if he'd been asked to eat something repellent, but after a short pause he began. "Very well. About an hour after your tale yesterday we received an urgent visit from the Nentian ambassador, who said that the few Nentian nationals we have living in our fine city did not take kindly to your portrayal of either Melishev Lohmet or Abhinava Khose."

"I assure you that my portrayal of Viceroy Lohmet was as kind and generous as I could make it."

"I have no doubt. But the idea that one of their leaders might be a heartless shitsnake disturbed some of them greatly, and they decided they would rather not hear you speak of it anymore."

"That comparison," Fintan pointed out, "is somewhat disrespectful to shitsnakes. But the best way these citizens thought they could ensure that I never spoke of it again was to kill me?"

"You have a quick mind. They fear you will tarnish their good name in the city. The ambassador warned us that your life might be in danger, and they were very anxious to add that the Nentian government was not to be held responsible."

"I fail to see what good name these Nentians might have if they're the sort to hire assassins. You have no other details?"

"There was the suggestion that your portrayal of the viceroy either is an outright fabrication or that you somehow gained unauthorized access to his private documents, since there is no way he would share such sentiments with you freely."

"It is true that he never asked me to read his diary, and it was in fact stolen from him, but not by me, and I only read it because I was bored. Anything else?"

"Nothing except complaints about the obvious anti-Nentian slant of your tale."

"I don't understand. How was the portrayal of Abhinava anything but positive? He's thoughtful, properly respectful of his family—"

"The ambassador claimed that some small-minded Nentian citizens were not so accepting as the young man's parents were about his sexuality."

Fintan pressed his palms into his eyes and muttered, "Goddess give me patience!"

"They don't serve patience here, but this tea really is quite lovely," Föstyr said, picking up his cup and slurping from it. "You should try some before it gets too cold."

The bard dropped his hands. "Well, if they objected to what little they've heard so far about the viceroy, they're going to soil themselves over what's to come."

"I imagine they will," Föstyr said, nodding agreeably. "So we must move you around, you see."

"I'm not changing my tale to please them. That would betray my duty to the poet goddess."

"You will note, Master Bard, that I did not even suggest it."

"I'm not here to promote the agendas of any government—even mine. I'm here to tell this story, and it's going to be uncomfortable for everyone because war is bloody uncomfortable."

"I understand."

"Do you? What happens to me when I present some of Brynlön's closer allies in a less than favorable light? You have little to do with the Nentians, but what if I offend the Black Jaguar Clan in Forn or point out some embarrassing facts about Kauria? That might threaten your little tea party here. You're already dependent on imports for food and other necessities with most of your economy wiped out. They could put pressure on you to silence me."

"My government won't hurt you."

"But it might cease to protect me from others; is that it?"

Föstyr deliberately dabbed at the corners of his mouth before replying, perhaps to give himself time to think. "We are not so unworthy as you suggest. The pelenaut is invested in your tale, and so are the people. It's all they talk about, and it's frankly a relief, because they're getting answers from you that we could never give them. They've stopped asking what we're going to do next, and that's giving us time to work instead of answer questions all day. We're very grateful to you, Fintan; you are the finest of distractions."

It occurred to me that we did not know for sure that any of this was real. We had no proof except the Lung's word that the Nentians objected to his story or that an attempt was made on Fintan's double last night—or even that they put a double in place. I was not about to bring it up, however. Instead I asked, "Am I still allowed to take him wherever I wish in the days ahead?"

"Yes," the Lung replied, and reached for a tea cake that no one else seemed intent on eating. "It's good that you visit the city and that Fintan talks about it, beneficial for everyone to hear that we still have a functioning civilization, however strained. We will, however, discreetly follow and provide some extra protection."

"I'm already being followed everywhere," Fintan said, his voice rising, "and you're not very discreet about it."

Föstyr appeared not to notice Fintan's irritation and replied affably. "It's for your own good. Can't protect you if we don't know where you are."

"You could protect me better by simply housing me in the palace."

"Please forgive us for that," the Lung said. "We would not want to accidentally leave any private or sensitive documents in your view when you were bored. Can't be too careful around someone with a perfect memory."

Fintan's face twisted in disgust as if he had smelled something foul while Föstyr favored him with a tiny smirk.

"I think I will have some of that cake," I said, desperate to break the tension.

"Excellent," Föstyr said, placing his hands flat on the table and pushing himself up. "I'll leave you two to your work. You have the room to yourselves until it's time to perform this afternoon. Farewell."

"Thank you," I said, and Fintan remained silent. He sulked for a while, and I let him. He could sit there with his arms crossed and listen to the clink of my fork on my plate if he wished. I set aside the dishes when I finished and moved myself to the next table, getting out my materials. When I had my ink pot uncorked and my quill ready, I looked up to see Fintan staring out at the ocean.

"It's strange," he said, his voice soft. "Looking out this window, you'd never think there was anything wrong with the world, that everything's a blue-green paradise watched over by clouds. You'd forget that people are absolutely miserable starting ten lengths behind us and extending far inland."

"I suspect that's one reason this establishment is so popular."

Fintan snorted. "Too true. When your only view is one of such peace and beauty, you can believe the happy lie that the rest of the world is just so. Well, my duty—our duty, I suppose—is to make sure people look through plenty of other windows. Let's be about it."

We climbed the steps up to the wall a bit earlier than usual, and the stands were not quite filled when Fintan hopped onto his makeshift stage. He employed his kenning and broadcast his voice across Survivor Field and the city. "Friends! My tale is going to be somewhat longer this afternoon, so I'll be starting directly. It will be so long, in fact, that I worry about your health, sitting down for so long. So let's get plenty of exercise now, shall we? Instead of singing today, I'll be playing a Raelech instrumental guaranteed to get you dancing and lose a stone or so of weight in the process."

He got everyone clapping—a magnificent sound to hear thousands of people clapping in unison—and then performed a scorching number on his hand harp while singing a wordless percussive beat that complemented the clapping.

At first I was too shy to dance myself because everyone could see me on top of the wall. But soon I realized no one cared and flailed about with everyone else, albeit with my upper body only; my knee wouldn't take much else in the way of dancing. When the song ended and the bard called out for fifteen minutes' rest until he began his tale, we were all sweating and out of breath and needed the break.

The bard hopped up onto the stage after taking a few long draughts of ale and said, "Let's travel back to the west, where several decisions altered the course of our history, beginning with our hunter who no longer wished to hunt, Abhinava Khose."

Abbi

We finally found the kherns, and close behind them followed the moment when I had to inform my family that I wouldn't be hunting with them. It was not merely unpleasant: it was the end of my world.

Uncle Navir spotted them coming. They were only a plume of dust above the plains at first, a small cloud on the horizon to the southeast, where the headwaters of the Khek River began their long journey to the ocean. It was the mark of their passage, earth and grass churned up by the pillars of their legs and thrown into the air by their tapered snouts. We were skirting an island of broad-trunked nughobe trees in the sea of grass because you never go into that darkness: you make the animals inside come out if they want to eat you, where you can see them before their teeth sink into your flesh. But we had circled around it from the north side and traversed its western border with not so much as a howl from a wheat dog. It was once we began to swing around to the south that my uncle shouted and pointed to the khern cloud in the distance. Father climbed up on top of our wagon and shielded his eyes from the sun, and when he was satisfied that he really was looking at a boil of kherns, he unpacked his smile and spread it out for us to see.

"Great Kalaad blesses us! It is a mighty boil at last! The Khose will get to be hunters after all!" My mother was driving the wagon, and he bent down to kiss the top of her head. "Move us away from the trees.

We don't want anything coming at us while we are busy with the kherns."

And so the wart yaks were turned due south and goaded to increase their speed by a step or two, and my aunt and my cousins did a little dance in the grass while Uncle Navir for some reason thrust his hips repeatedly in the direction of the khern cloud. He stopped when his daughter asked him what he was doing.

My sister, Inasa, laughed at him and then turned to me. "Come on, Abhi. Let's get ready." I joined her at the back of the slow-moving wagon, but not to get ready for the hunt. My preparations looked similar but were intended for something much different. We had field bags for hunts like this when we would be away from the wagon for extended periods. Usually they were filled with twine and snares and implements for simple meals. I loaded up on the simple meals.

I packed many water skins, so many that Inasa said I would spend all my time draining my bladder and miss out on the hunt. I also carried a very small cooking pot filled with a bag of dry beans, along with a separate bag of root vegetables and a few onions, a box of salt, a blanket, and a firestone enchanted by a Hathrim sparker. She picked up her bow and quiver, but I left my spear alone. I had a hunting knife on my belt for defense; the spear would be useful against larger beasts should I be attacked by one, but it had become a symbol in my head and I didn't want to touch it again.

When I left it behind, Inasa pointed it out. "You forgot your spear, Abhi!"

"No, I didn't. I won't need it."

"We're hunting kherns! Of course you'll need it."

"No. You will see. But thank you, Inasa. You are the best of all possible sisters. I love you."

She flinched as if expecting an attack, and when none came and she saw I was being serious, she cocked her head and narrowed her eyes. "What is wrong with you? What have you eaten recently?"

I grinned at her. "I love you regardless of what I eat."

"Yeah, but you don't usually say it."

I sighed and said, "It's a truth and a fault. One I'm trying to remedy. I should remind you more often."

Inasa stared at me, her mouth hanging open, so rather than shock her any more I strode to the front of the wagon to remind my mother. She trailed after me, calling my name, while I called Mother's.

But Father's voice cut through both of ours, assuming it was an unimportant sibling squabble. "Everybody gather over here for your duties!" he yelled from the other side of the wagon, so I reversed course to jog around the back—it's unwise to step in front of wart yaks. Inasa tried to grab me, but I dodged around her and continued on, joining Father and Uncle Navir and all my cousins to the right of the wagon, keeping pace with it so that Mother could hear.

"This looks good. It's a big enough boil that we might get two, maybe even three. Two would give us a handsome profit, and three would be astounding riches. As always, we need to flank to either side and pick off the ones in the back. Navir, take your family around the near side, and I'll go with Abhi and Inasa on the far side."

"No," I said.

"Shut up, Abhi," Father said.

"I'm not going."

My uncle told me to shut up next. "It's not the time for jokes."

"I'm not joking. I'm staying with the wagon."

Everyone's eyes traveled up and down my body, looking for injuries. "What's wrong with you?" Father growled. "Stub your toe?"

"No, I simply don't want to hunt anymore. I'll stay and watch the wagon and protect the yaks. But I won't seek out another creature's death."

My family physically recoiled from me as if I had announced I was diseased, and then their expressions hardened, taking their cue from Father. But he was the only one who spoke.

"Tell me you're joking, son," he said, crossing his arms in front of him.

"I'm not."

"You're a Khose. That means you're a hunter. That's it."

"I think it's time that Khose meant more than that."

"Like what, Abhi?"

It was the question I'd dreaded and still didn't have an answer for. "That's what I plan to figure out."

"There's no need. I've figured it out for you. You either come with us and help this family of hunters prosper or you leave the family."

Inasa gasped. I think my cousin Pandhi did, too. But it was no less than I expected. Father can be stark and uncompromising at times, and I assumed that this would be one of those times. And I also knew from experience that there would be no arguing with him. There was only submission or walking away.

"I want you to know that I love you all," I said, looking around at the faces of my family. "But I will not hunt. And I can do both of those things: love you and hunt no more." I returned my eyes to Father and finished, "If you will let me."

Father's lip curled in a sneer. "Contribute nothing but say you love us? Your actions don't match your words. If you want to contribute nothing, then contribute it elsewhere. We will not support you."

I nodded once, carefully keeping my emotions packed away in my field bag; I planned to open it later. "Farewell," I said. "Good hunting."

Pivoting on my heel, I faced north and began to jog toward the island of nughobe trees, the water skins heavy and sloshing around as I moved. Mother cried out in confusion, unable to believe what had just happened; Inasa called after me and took a few steps, but Father barked at her to let me go and her footsteps halted. Mother pleaded with him, Uncle Navir said something and so did my aunt, but he said they had a hunt to finish and they could worry about me later.

All of that went as expected, and painful as it was, I had prepared for it. I had prepared to walk all the way back to Khul Bashab by myself and start a new life in peace with other creatures and hope that one day, after they had some time to recover from the shock I had given them, my family would talk to me again.

But then the ground began to shake and thunder and the shouts of my family changed their tenor, and when I turned to look, the distant dust plume of the kherns was closer—too close—and the largest boil of them I have ever seen was not merely traveling but stampeding directly at our wagon. We had taken our eyes off them during my selfish drama and thus had little warning.

There could only be one reason why: something was pursuing the kherns from behind. The Khose were not the only hunters on the plains. Though in fact the hunt was off now; there is no stopping a khern stampede except the will of the kherns themselves. The only thing my family could do was run. It was the only thing I could do, too.

I turned ninety degrees and headed straight east, hoping to get out of the path of the kherns and let them pass me by. Outrunning them would be impossible.

There were dozens of the gray-skinned behemoths—perhaps more than a hundred beasts spread out and churning the earth, snorting and trumpeting and running full speed, heads lowered, their great black curved horns thrust forward and ready to ram anything, including our wagon and the wart yaks tied up to them.

Wart yaks stand six feet tall at the shoulder, and their horns are dangerous. But though they're strong and sturdy, they're not particularly fast. And they're half as tall as a khern, less than half the weight, and far less than half as fast. I didn't think they stood a chance of surviving the charge of the kherns. What chance, then, did my family have?

They ran to the sides, as I did, to try to beat the edge before it overwhelmed them. But they had been on the other side of the wagon—my uncle's family ran in the opposite direction from me. But Mother jumped down to run in my direction, perhaps to warn me, because I saw her waving her arms over my shoulder as I ran. Father came after her, climbing over the wagon and doing his best to catch up, but they were far closer to the boil than I was. I saw the wart yaks begin to panic, saw the twelve-foot-high wall of horn and meat thunder closer, saw my mother open her mouth in a scream I never heard over the rumble of the kherns, saw her see me looking back at her as I ran, and she reached out to me, mouthing my name and something more as she realized she would never make it, my father behind her, shouting as well, and then my parents disappeared under the boil of kherns, the wart yaks were plowed under, the wagon splintered into pieces and got chewed up by the stampede, and it came for me, growing larger, quaking the earth beneath my feet. I hardly had breath to make noise, but I did, limbs pumping as fast as I could make them, my field bag flapping madly in my wake and tears leaking out of my eyes as I ran for my life. And I wasn't alone: other creatures in the path of the boil were flying if they could or running to get out of the way—a stalk hawk, a covey of gharel hens, a saw-beaked owl taking wing in the daylight, plus rodents and serpents and lizards scrambling through the grass.

I cleared the edge of the boil by no more than a couple of lengths, the turbulence of the last khern's passage knocking me off my feet. For a moment I expected to be trampled anyway, but the beasts kept going, and I struggled upright on shaky legs to get my bearings.

The boil was far broader than it was deep. It had flattened out in response to the pursuit of a sedge of grass pumas, perhaps ten of them anxious to make one of the kherns go down and then prevent it from ever gaining its feet again. Most of them stopped and converged on the wart yaks; that was the way they operated sometimes, never bringing down a khern but taking advantage of whatever the kherns brought down in their stampede. But of course the wart yaks weren't the only victims. The grass was flattened where the kherns had passed, and so I could *see* them, broken and crushed and smeared on the plains *because of me,* when not five minutes ago I had told them that I loved them all—

I don't think I ever made noises like I made right then. Whimpers at first and then a long, sustained cry of denial when I could catch breath enough to voice it. That cry drew attention, however. One of the pumas was having trouble getting its fair share of yak meat with all the others crowding around, and it looked up with interest while all the others were feeding. It decided I looked delicious and easy to catch and arrowed through the grass in my direction.

There was no outrunning it. It was coming specifically for me, and for a moment I thought, why not? Why not die with the rest of my family? Since I had been the one to distract them from the danger and take their eyes off the boil, should I not pay the same price in blood?

But then I supposed I didn't want this sedge of pumas to be the end of all the Khose. They are not bright creatures, only savage and unafraid of anything. I have had more than one jump at me in the past and die on my spear. I missed my spear now.

I pulled out my hunting knife and shifted my field bag to the front, holding it up just below my chin with my left hand and gripping the knife with my right. The grass puma leapt at me, mouth open, going for my throat, and I raised the bag and fed it to him as he came, going down to the ground so that he would land on top of me. That was what he wanted and what I wanted, too. He tore into the bag instead of my throat, his teeth bursting through a water skin instead of my skin, and I stabbed him repeatedly with my knife as he got a mouthful of water and nothing else. I wasn't trying to kill him, just make him decide to eat something else. After five or six stabs I must have hit something that really hurt. It jumped up and back from me, ripping the knife out of my hand and bounding away with it still lodged between its ribs. It left me alive but deeply scratched, weaponless and with a lot less water to drink when I was days away from home.

There was no going after it because it staggered back to the other grass pumas, making a noise between a wail and a roar. I was making similar sounds, but more from grief than from physical pain. The other pumas had enough to occupy them, so they ignored both me and my attacker. Still, I needed to get out of there; more predators and scavengers would be coming this way, following the scent of blood. I didn't have a goal in mind except to live long enough to mourn them properly, to release them to the sky, and then, perhaps, Kalaad would take me or show me what to do next. The pumas wouldn't go into the island of nughobes—even the kherns wouldn't go in there. They were already swerving around to the west to avoid them.

The canopy held its own dangers for me but nothing as immediate as the pumas; soon there would be packs of scavenging wheat dogs and then a cloud of blackwings descending to pick over the bones. And once they had all gone, maybe then I could return and pay them the honor they deserved and beg their spirits for forgiveness.

I ran in an awkward crouch away from the pumas, half in staggering grief and half in hope that my back didn't crest above the grass and give me away to any other predators nearby. My breath heaved raggedly out of my lungs and my eyes streamed and my nose, too, if I am honest, and I felt trickles of blood down my arms and sides from where the puma scratched me.

Nothing chased me into the canopy, and the temperature cooled noticeably as soon as I entered the shade. The broad trunks spread out with long, heavy branches that drooped all the way to the ground, allowing almost any creature to climb up into the trees with ease. The branches of the nughobes always hid more dangers than the ground, which was carpeted with the leaves of many seasons, which smothered almost all undergrowth aside from a few low-light ferns.

I didn't stop once I made the border of the island but kept going inside; the truly dangerous creatures inhabited the periphery so that they could hunt in the plains or the interior. The fact that none of them had attacked our wagon didn't mean they weren't there; it simply meant they were more likely nocturnal.

I ran until I could run no more, when all I could hear was the rasp of my breath and the plodding of my tired feet, heavy with loss. I stopped in the middle of a triangle of trees, scanning the branches quickly to make sure I was not about to rest in the middle of a howler colony. I should have taken more care, but I was too exhausted to be careful.

Collapsing to the ground and folding my legs beneath me, I inspected the contents of my field bag, which had been ripped and chewed but not ruined by the puma. Two skins still had water in them; the rest had been punctured. That alone made my survival doubtful past a day or two. I didn't know where to find fresh water between here and Khul Bashab. Unless I returned to the wagon and found more unbroken skins, surviving until the city was as likely as a kraken grazing on dry land. The jerky and all the beans remained, but with little water to cook the beans they were almost worthless. And even if I had water, without a weapon for defense my death was almost certain. The chances of crossing the plains without running into something with sharp teeth and an appetite were extremely small.

But the journal my aunt had given me remained along with my quills, and my ink pot was still intact because it was made of thick Hathrim glass.

I began writing what had happened while I was still breathing hard, sorrow springing fresh in my eyes. I will never forgive myself should I live to return to civilization. My family had died because of my selfishness.

The sun is sinking to the horizon, shadows darkening in the forest.

A flicker of movement in the trees. Is that—?

Kalaad's judgment is upon me. I am in the middle of a nest of bloodcats, their fur camouflaged against the bark of the nughobes. They were asleep when I arrived, but now they stir and I can see them moving where I didn't before. They will smell me soon if they haven't already. They will certainly see me when I move. There is no escape; they are too fast and too many. They will hunt me down together, and I have nothing to keep them at bay.

So be it. It is only fair that I be food for them when I have made food of so many other creatures on the plains. It is natural, and it may even be justice.

Teldwen will prosper without me, I am sure. Farewell.

A cry of dismay rose on the wind when the bard returned to himself. "Don't worry," he reassured his audience. "That is not the end of Abhinava's story. It is only the end for today. Meanwhile, near the Godsteeth, Gorin Mogen's plans took shape while most of the rest of the world wondered if he was still alive." When he took the seeming of

the Hearthfire, more than doubling his size, the giant looked pleased
with himself.

orin Mogen

Shaping steel is all about the application of heat and pressure. Shaping
the hearts and minds of a population is similar, except instead of the
hammer and tongs, one uses words and gestures, and they generate
their own heat and pressure. Before Mirana Mastik could sow any
more discontent and get people thinking of sailing south, I gathered
the survivors and told them to make themselves comfortable for the
season at least.

"The ash continues to rain down from Mount Thayil and spread
south to any place we might think to land to start afresh. If you were
inclined to think of Thayil's eruption as some kind of judgment or
punishment—and I am not one of those—then the judgment will
hang over Hathrir for the entire season. So we must remain here, sow
and reap here, build here, and yes, even prosper here. We have no other
choice. Very soon, there will be no patch of sky in Hathrir where the ·
sun is not blotted out by ash. I have brought you to the best possible
place to start anew. So let us begin!"

I gestured to Jerin. "My son, Jerin Mogen, will begin building a proper
hearth for Thurik's Flame under the supervision of La Mastik herself!"

Applause broke out for this, and I grinned. Let her complain now
when the very first thing I commanded was to do honor to her god.

"And I will personally build our first smithy so that we may create
the Hathrim glass and steel the world hungers for!"

More applause.

"There is employment for everyone here. Trees to be harvested. Land to be sown. Animals to be hunted. An entire city to be built! For though this is Nentian land and we are guests here, they will no doubt approve of our industry and be grateful to us for developing land they have long thought too wild to be tamed. And honestly, when the Nentians see the benefit of having quality glass and steel on their doorstep—in effect, becoming an exporter of it instead of an importer—why not let us remain here in this land of abundance, in harmony with them? Think of the new era of prosperity we will all enjoy—and again, what other choice do we realistically have? We could not choose when Mount Thayil erupted, but we can choose how to react to it, and I, for one, choose not to cower in defeat but to rebuild and prove, as La Mastik said, that the people of the First Kenning are first in civilization!"

No one had anything but shouts of approval for that sentiment, and La Mastik's opening play was effectively neutralized for the moment. Once we had something built and the people felt they had something to fight for, it wouldn't matter that I had spouted pure dragon shit about living in harmony with the Nentians.

Sefir would see to logistics as she always had, getting people to work; it was her particular genius, and she had done far more to make Harthrad an economic powerhouse than I had. She knew what needed to be done, and I provided her with a motivated labor force since my talents tended toward politics and persuasion.

Before Jerin and I got started on our construction projects, I took hounds up into the hills with him so that we could talk away from the eyes and ears of others. We gave them rein to pick up trails, and when they caught the scent of prey and lowered their heads and ears, asking permission to hunt, we grinned at the danger, gave the hounds a chuff of approval, and held on.

There are few rushes that can match riding upon such concentrated power and ferocity. Especially through a forest where the low-hanging branches threatened to knock us off our mounts or spear us—neither of us was wearing full armor, just the customary lava dragon hide. My hound cut too close to the trunks of a few old scaly pines, brushing my legs against them, scraping off chips of bark and bruising me through the leather. It was not long, perhaps only a minute, before our bone-jarring progress revealed the prey: a squalling herd of spotted khek-alopes bolting from where they'd bedded down for the day, spraying panicked shit out of their asses as they ran before the oncoming teeth, and the hounds tore into the back of them, jaws snapping over necks, severing spines, taking out ten and letting the rest go. We called them to a halt, dismounted, and dragged the kills into three piles. Three khekalopes each for the hounds and four to take back to camp.

We unsheathed our blades and began to dress them, sawing through hides and scooping out entrails. A perfect time to talk—anything to take the mind off the squelching of intestines and the sloppy chop-licking and crunching noises the hounds made.

"So tell me how Olet is feeling," I said. "I've not seen her since she first came to Harthrad."

Jerin grunted and sniffed, which meant he was thinking about it. "Resentful, if I'm reading her right."

"Of you?"

"Not necessarily me. Maybe. More resentful of you and her own father for putting her here, for depriving her of the chance to choose her own future."

"That's created a chill between you?"

"Oh, a mere chill would be nice. I think she arrived in Harthrad upon a glacier. And I don't blame her. If she discovers that she likes me, then it will please both you and her father, and she's not in the mood to please either of you."

"I see. And how do you feel, son?" Silence. Or rather, not silence but the savage tearing of flesh and the splash of blood and no words. "You can tell me how you feel, Jerin. I must know the truth of things to make informed decisions."

"I feel resentful as well, because you feel entitled to make these 'in-formed decisions' about my life and hers."

"We've discussed this before. Your union will prevent us from going to war with Winthir Kanek. You're saving lives."

"Yes, we've discussed it before. Or at least you talked and I listened. All very noble, Father. But it doesn't stop Olet and me from feeling like your playthings. It doesn't stop me from feeling acutely embarrassed to be in her presence, knowing that she wouldn't care to be breathing the same air as me if it weren't for you."

"All right, back up. How do you feel about her? Separate from me and her father?"

"How can they be separate? She is Olet Kanek, daughter of Winthir—"

"Forget who her father is and who your father is and just think about her for a moment. What do you think of *her*?"

Jerin sighed. "Her eyes possess a keen wit, and she carries herself like a well-trained fighter. That's about all I know. She has not spoken to me beyond the most formal, distant responses. And I will not force my attentions on her when they're not wanted—even if that's conversation."

"I think perhaps I see." Sefir and I watched five of our children jump into the lava boil at Olenik, and only our youngest, our last hope to continue the Mogen line, climbed back out lavaborn. And we raised Jerin to believe that by forging his future as a Hearthfire he would forge a better future for many people. Winthir no doubt did the same with Olet. Little wonder that they chafed at these circumstances, in which they were unable to shape matters as they wished. "Your best hope is a slow kindling based on respect, which may, in time, flare into something more. Perhaps if you speak to her frankly, as you are doing now, you can acknowledge the awkwardness and control it because you name it. She may yet prove to be a blessing. But if it doesn't work out and she is of the same mind, you may have *my* permission, at least, to be free of the commitment. Winthir Kanek may take insult from it, and we may fall to fighting, and should that happen I honestly do not know which of us will emerge the victor, but we can let that hammer fall when and where it will. You have jumped into fire for your mother and me. We would not condemn you to a life of unhappiness."

The sounds of sawing flesh stopped, and I turned to look at Jerin, who had cocked his head, unsure if he'd heard correctly. Black-bearded and blue-eyed like me, he was already strong and still packing on muscle. Shorter than me by the width of a finger. Kinder than me by the width of an ocean yet still able to fight and sail well. His crew regularly stole from Winthir Kanek's timber pirates based in Tharsif—or at least they used to. They'd have to stop that now, but at least there was no need for it anymore.

"That's . . . unexpected. And appreciated."

"It's also deserved, son. I couldn't ask for a finer boy."

We bent to our work in silence for a while, savoring a moment of accord.

"The hammer's going to fall here soon enough, Father. The Nentians, and I imagine even the Fornish, will object to us being here. Do you know if we can win that fight?"

"I have no doubt of it. It's a fight the Mogens have been planning for a long time."

"But you made it sound earlier like the Nentians will welcome us."

"Yes. They will prove me wrong, and we'll go to war. But the rest of what I said was absolutely true. There is not a place in Hathrir so fine as this. Should we try to start a new city in Hathrir, it would be under the cloud of Thayil's ash, and should I decide to challenge another Hearthfire, I would win nothing better than what we have here. This will be a splendid city because we'll make it so."

Satisfied and packing the dressed kills on the hounds, we took our time returning, and I admired all the timber as we descended. My timber. It was a day of hope and fine promises, one of the best in memory.

Volund somehow snatched three Raelech stonecutters away from Hashan Khek and played it perfectly. They arrived at dawn the next day, we told them they were in Hathrir, and they were gullible enough to believe us. Landlocked as they were and wedded to the earth, they had no knowledge of the sea and took our word for it. They probably could not conceive that we would have stones big enough to lie about something like that. Or else they were blinded by the stones we offered in payment.

Sefir got two of them started right away on the outer walls she'd laid out with a wood frame for the foundation, the earth underneath it already salted. Volund had brought a shipment of quicklime with him, and a couple of men mixed and poured it ahead of the stonecutters, who lifted massive hunks of rock out of the earth with their kenning and shaped it into a solid wall. Once the living stone was set upon the lime, it was cut off from the earth and the stonecutters could no longer manipulate it except via direct touch, and they also could not undermine the salted earth below the wall. We'd never let them touch it after it was built; they'd have to walk through fire first. Judging by the rate they worked, we'd have our city walled up in ten days, possibly less.

Jerin directed the remaining stonecutter to fashion irrigation canals for the crops and sewers underground. We were also going to make sure we had a deep and protected well within the walls. While the Raelechs worked, I summoned Halsten and Volund to my hearth to discuss our next moves.

"What else did you bring from Hashan Khek besides the quicklime?" I asked Volund.

"Brewing supplies and smithing tools—the basis of all civilization." He produced a bottle of grain alcohol and waggled it for us. "And I brought something to tide us over until we make our own."

"What can you tell me about the city?" Volund's mouth twitched in a sneer of disgust. He looked tired, or perhaps it was only his beard. Normally it was the most energetic part of him, brushed and shining with oil, but now it was dry and scraggly like summer wheat. He spat into my hearth, a summary judgment.

"Miserable from top to bottom. They live like shitsnakes."

"Who's the viceroy there now? Still Melishev Lohmet?"

"Yeah. Worst of the lot."

"Well, he's going to be curious about us now that you've stolen his stonecutters and put a halt to whatever he had them working on. How long do we have them?"

"As long as needed, Hearthfire. They were impressed with your gems."

"Good. We need to restrict their access to others and warn everyone who does come in contact with them not to speak of this place as Ghurana Nent. Though I doubt it, they might quit as soon as they found out, and I don't want to risk it. And we need to let fishermen and houndsmen and anyone else who might make contact on our borders know that they should call this a refugee camp instead of a city, at least in front of any outsiders. And you left a couple of men behind to plead our case to the viceroy?"

"Yes. They will have done so by now."

"Excellent." I turned to my master of hounds. "Halsten, have you got the patrols straightened out yet?"

"The plains patrols are settled and simple, Hearthfire. Still working on the wooded foothills. It's difficult going in there for us since the trees grow too close together in some places. It will take time to weave in and out and scout a path."

"Yes, I'm aware of the difficulty. Mark trees to be cleared and we'll make that path a bit wider."

"Of course."

"Good. Volund, I'm putting you back on the boat—but don't worry, I'll let you sleep and oil your beard first."

He gave me a weary grin. "My thanks, Hearthfire. Where am I going?"

"Down to Tharsif. Hearthfire Kanek needs to know his daughter survived the eruption and the wedding to my son will happen as scheduled, but it will be here. Issue him an invitation to our new city."

"We're going to tell him it's a city and not a refugee camp?"

"Yes. It needs to sound like a destination and a trading center, not a collection of campfires. So you will tell Winthir Kanek I have a new city up here, a city with plenty of fuel, and he is welcome to send emigrants and traders if he wishes."

"He'll send you his dregs and criminals and a spy or two," Halsten warned.

"I know. But they'll be model citizens or we'll give them a fresh grave." I turned back to Volund. "You're going down with a load of timber, and that should buy some things we need. I will give you a list before you go. Nothing like timber to establish that this is for real."

Volund nodded. "And what name shall I give him for this city, Hearthfire?"

"I've been thinking about that. If we give it a Hathrim name, that will only make the Nentians bristle. Give it a Nentian name and that gives us some leverage with everybody, the veneer of legitimacy. You're better with the Nentian tongue, Halsten. How would you say 'Giant Plains' in their language?"

"Uh." He scrunched up his face. "I think you'd say 'Baghra Khek.'"

"That is fantastically ugly. I love it. Volund, tell Winthir Kanek that the Hearthfire of Harthrad is now the Hearthfire of Baghra Khek and would like to resume trade as before, except now with timber."

"It's a fine, hideous name," Halsten said, rising to his feet and extending his right fist. He poured the remainder of his drink over it and then sparked it up. "Shall we light a tower and write it in fire?"

"Aye!" Volund said, springing up and setting his clenched fist on top of Halsten's. I added mine on top of theirs, and on the count of three, we opened our fists just enough to create a sort of chimney out of our stacked hands, allowing air and a gout of fire out of the top. As it spiraled orange over our heads, fanned and shaped by our combined powers, the city of campfires saw its name spelled out in the flames.

Presumptuous of us, perhaps, but ideas and names are at times far more important than substance. A collection of buildings cannot inspire people to action, but the ideas behind them, the associations with their names—those can be so powerful that people will fight to the death for them. That was exactly the power I needed.

"Meanwhile," Fintan said, briefly returning to himself before taking on another seeming, "Nel Kit ben Sah was crossing the Godsteeth to deprive the Hearthfire of that power."

el

During our journey to Ghurana Nent, Tip and Pak predictably trailed complaints behind them like thorny vines:

"Why don't we use the Leaf Road as long as we can?"

"Why do these horses smell so bad?"

"Why are you looking at me like that?"

Because you need to get used to riding a horse before we find the Hathrim. Because horses don't bathe in perfumed oils like you. And because you are rotten fruit.

I didn't say any of that aloud, of course, but I certainly thought it, and I know I wasn't the only one thinking along those branches. I traded a look with Kam, and we rolled our eyes at their ridiculous whining. We ignored them most of the time, but when Pak Sey ben Kor directly addressed me, demanding to know why we must operate in such foul conditions, I carefully composed my features and answered him in bright tones: "I see no foul conditions, good benman," I said, using the formal term for the blessed. "Why, I see only sun and a chance to serve the Canopy. You and I and benman Tip have been blessed by the First Tree, and I'm delighted to suffer any hardship in return, especially one so small as riding a horse up a steep mountain. Do you not feel the same?"

Yar and Pen chortled, and Kam smiled broadly. "I'm equally delighted," he said, "and I'm not even blessed. It's a beautiful day in Forn."

Pak scowled and was about to reply when his horse sneezed for perhaps the tenth time since he had climbed on her back.

"I worry about the good benman's horse, Kam," I said. "Does she normally sneeze so often?"

"No, but she seems fine otherwise."

Yar saw where we were heading and chimed in. "I do not think she is used to smelling such concentrated florals. What's that delightful perfume you're wearing, ben Kor?"

"It's . . . never mind."

The complaints from Pak and Tip stopped after that, and I felt good about handling it without descending to their level of nastiness. The White Gossamers believed that one could be both strong and gentle, and I had forgotten the latter in my time away from home. It was good to be with my clansmen again.

We had a party of eight all told and ten net launchers. Pak and Tip refused to carry them as I assumed they would, but Kam and I carried two each.

Two members of the party were new acquaintances. Both were clansmen, but I had never met them before. They were younger, and their eyes shone as they took in my sleeves and Pen's upon our meeting that morning.

"We have two greensleeves again!" one said.

"What do you mean, 'again'? We have three now."

Kam cleared his throat. "Mat Som ben Sah returned to the roots last week, Nel."

"Oh!" My hand flew to my mouth. "I had not heard. I'm sorry, Kam." Mat had been his grandfather. I hadn't known my great-uncle all that well, but he had been kind to me on the few occasions we'd met—especially once I was blessed with my sleeves—and I'd been looking forward to seeing him again. I supposed he must have been much older than I realized. Everything does indeed have its own season.

"No, I'm sorry. I thought you already knew," he said.

"We can remember him later," I assured him, since there were introductions to be made.

The two clansmen were young men who had no plans to seek a kenning. One was fascinated by the sea and wished to be a trader, forsaking the Canopy for extended periods. The other wished to be a mushroom farmer and couldn't tear his eyes away from the specimens growing on my legs.

So we were an odd bouquet of people leaving the Canopy and crossing over the westernmost pass of the Godsteeth in search of giants. The air became stark and cold, and I felt as if I were walking through emptiness even though there were still plants and peaks around me. I saw that Pak and Tip felt uncomfortable, too—they felt the change as I did, felt vulnerable outside the Canopy—while the others smiled in the abundance of sunshine.

There was a stretch of barren ground in the saddle of the mountains where our horses' hooves clattered over dark shale and the sound echoed back to us, hollow and haunting. Only in a few crevices where some soil had accumulated did we see thin tongues of grasses; lichens on the rocks were the only other greenery. When we began to descend on the other side, we saw trees again, but they were softwoods like pine and juniper with evergreen needles rather than leaves. The horses trod on a carpet of needles as we picked our way down, and the smell was invigorating if lacking in complexity.

Sparse at first, the trees grew denser as we descended, and I felt less exposed. In some places our horses barely fit between the trunks, for this forest had never been touched so far as I could tell. Birds and squirrels cried out their alarms at our trespass. Some hours later, as afternoon crept by and shadows lengthened, the trees thinned out and the land flattened until we suddenly emerged from the forest and there was nothing ahead but grass to the horizon, not a single tree to be seen.

"Horrifying," Pak Sey ben Kor declared. I don't know if I would have gone quite so far, but it wasn't pleasant.

"Ugh," was all Tip Fet ben Lot had to say. It was fortunate that they were not our ambassadors to Ghurana Nent.

"Well, I see no Hathrim," Pak said. "Or anything else. We've wasted enough time on this foolishness. Let's return."

"We haven't searched the coast yet, benman," I said. "We need to head west and perhaps travel some distance up the shore before I'll be satisfied that the Hathrim do not threaten our borders. Like you, I don't want to find them. But if Gorin Mogen does threaten the Canopy, it's our duty as greensleeves to discover that threat before the first axe swings in our direction."

The Black Jaguar's eyes seethed with hatred, and his mouth twisted in a snarl. He didn't like to be publicly schooled on his duty as a greensleeve, but I had said it more for young Pen's benefit than to shame him. I turned my horse west and urged it to pick up the pace somewhat. We rode two abreast so that we wouldn't be vulnerable to isolated attacks from plains creatures, and we skirted the tree line so that our left sides were less vulnerable; we'd be able to see anything approaching on that side before it leapt on us because the needles choked out most of the undergrowth. The grasses on our right could hide any number of dangers.

We managed an easy trot into the sun, a pace that ate up the unfamiliar ground but didn't strain the horses. It jarred our bones, but I had no problem enduring that if it would get us our answer more quickly. Pak Sey ben Kor pointedly brought up the rear, refusing to ride anywhere near me. That was fine; he could mutter curses to himself if he wished.

Tip Fet ben Lot rode next to me, a smirk on his face about which I carefully did not ask him. Eventually he could not keep his amusement to himself. "You haven't made a friend with Pak Sey ben Kor," he said.

"He was never going to be my friend. The Black Jaguars hate the White Gossamers, and that is all he cares about."

"Is not the reverse also true?"

"We are aware of the Black Jaguars' feelings, but we have the Canopy to serve, and *that* is what the White Gossamers care about. I for one would welcome reconciliation with the Black Jaguars, but that appears beyond my powers."

"Perhaps my clan could help." The plain disbelief on my face caused him to add, "I'm being serious."

"If the Blue Moths wish to broker a peace between our clans so that the Canopy may thrive, that would be fine. But if you have in mind some scheme where the White Gossamers would be indebted to the Blue Moths for services rendered, then I will respectfully pass."

Tip snorted. "Don't be so naïve. Favors are currency in politics."

"No, I'm not naïve. I understand the game you're playing, ben Lot. I just refuse to play it."

"You'd rather let your clan languish in obscurity, then, when you were once so bold?"

"That wasn't me. My elders strayed out too far on the wrong branch; it broke, and they fell. I'm a bit more cautious. Canopy first, clan second, and myself third." I didn't mean to chide him with the oldest moral maxim of our people—I'd recited it as *my* guiding principle, not as an indictment of his behavior—but I supposed he took it as a personal insult. Perhaps he had been putting the Canopy third and that was why he huffed and reined in his horse, dropping back a rank or two and urging Yar Tup Min to join me at the front.

My cousin grinned knowingly and couldn't pass up the opportunity to tease me. "It's a good thing you don't have political ambitions, Nel," he said, "because you're making friends about as fast as furry swamp fungus."

I was about to retort when movement ahead caught my eye. Far ahead—straight ahead—a grand moss pine that was only a splinter in the distance toppled over into the plains, silhouetted against the sun, a silent death drowned out by the sound of our horses. I couldn't see what caused it, but I could guess. I signaled to everyone behind that we needed to halt, and once we did, the other greensleeves asked why. I turned my ride around, as did Yar, to face the others.

"I saw a tree fall ahead. Maybe it was natural. But it's more likely the Hathrim cut it down."

Pak Sey ben Kor sneered and said, "A fallen tree that no one else saw is not proof the Hathrim are here."

"I know that. We're going to take a closer look. But we're going slower, and I recommend getting weapons ready." I pulled out one of my two net launchers and hefted it in my right hand before guiding my horse west once more, forestalling any more debate. I let the horse walk at its own pace instead of trot and heard the others follow. The land ahead was not entirely flat; it had waves to it, the trailing roots of the Godsteeth causing gentle rolls of land and hiding the ocean from our view.

We couldn't see anything for a while as we negotiated a small valley in the foothills, but when we crested the next hill, we had a beautiful view of the ocean and all the Hathrim glass boats flashing in the sun. We lined up, taking it in, and saw what could only be called a settlement. Walls were rising out of the grass, visibly growing as we watched, which indicated that they must have Raelech stonecutters working for them. A large swath of ground appeared to have been plowed and planted, soon to be irrigated with water diverted from a stream into a canal that another stonecutter was shaping as we watched. I saw him, a tiny ant of a man at this distance, with the equivalent of a swollen grub beetle looming over him. Seeing a Hathrim next to someone of normal stature is always sobering.

"Are you all seeing this?" I said. "That's an entire population of Hathrim on our border building walls in front of us. Cutting down these beautiful old moss pines and occupying land that belongs to the people of Ghurana Nent."

"I sure see it," Yar growled.

"I do, too," Pen said, and then Kam echoed her.

"I see it," Tip Fet ben Lot said, "but I can scarcely believe it. This is illegal. I mean it goes far beyond a timber raid. It could be called an invasion."

"Invasion?" Pak Sey ben Kor sounded incredulous. "I hardly see an army there. I agree the Hathrim shouldn't be cutting down trees or occupying the land without permission, but it looks like a peaceful settlement. It's not a martial force, and the Raelechs are there helping them."

"I think you've delved to the roots, ben Kor," I said, privately noting that since the Hathrim existence was now indisputable, he had immediately thought of how to cast them as harmless. Later he would insinuate that I was worrying about nothing. I needed to get at least Tip Fet ben Lot to agree that such a group on our border was dangerous. "How will we report this to the Canopy? An invasion or an illegal occupation?"

"I think those are both inflammatory characterizations, ben Sah," he said.

"What would you say, then? Surely this is more than a family camping trip."

"Don't be ridiculous."

"Can you think of any legal reason for a force this size to be here?"

He didn't answer the legal question but focused instead on my word choice. "I think calling it a force is stretching the meaning of the word."

"Pick your own noun for that very large number of Hathrim, then, and tell me if you think they have legal standing to be building walls and canals and what looks like docks in Ghurana Nent. Have you or ben Lot perhaps heard through diplomatic channels that the Nentian king has authorized the Hathrim to build a new city here?"

"No, I haven't," Pak said. Tip shook his head to indicate he had heard nothing either, and Pak continued. "If they *are* here illegally, the Black Jaguars shall certainly support action against them."

"So you believe there might be legal justification for their presence?"

"I'm not saying either way, ben Sah. I'm saying we have no grounds for pursuing punitive action until we know more."

"Let's review what we do know," I said, "just to make sure we're all agreed on the facts. I saw fires on the ocean pass by my post the night after Mount Thayil erupted. They were headed north. Here, to the north of my post, we find a very large group of Hathrim and a fleet of glass boats docked on the coast of Ghurana Nent. We know that Harthrad had a fleet of glass boats for many years. We are therefore most likely looking at the survivors of Mount Thayil's eruption. Yes?"

"Most likely," Tip Fet ben Lot said.

My clansmen agreed, and ben Kor grudgingly said, "Agreed that it is most likely, but by no means certain."

"I would agree that confirmation is necessary, ben Kor. But should this prove to be the citizens of Harthrad, there can be no justification for them landing here. They should have sailed to one of the other Hathrim isles or else to the main continent of Hathrir. Unless they negotiated a secret treaty with Ghurana Nent that we don't know about that gave them permission to land here, this is a breach of Nentian borders. An invasion, in other words. Wouldn't you agree?"

"Burrs and weeds!" he exploded. "You can't throw around words like *invasion* so casually! It's that kind of talk that starts wars!"

"It should start vigorous diplomacy first," I said. "And I think this situation requires plenty of vigor. We don't want a population of lavaborn with this much fuel for fire so close to the Canopy."

"No. No, we don't," Tip Fet ben Lot said, and I was glad that he at least appeared to be thinking of the Canopy first now. He'd support my view of things in the sway should it come to that.

"Let's just confirm who these Hathrim are and what they want before we start assigning them motives from a distance," ben Kor said. "That's all I ask."

"Uh, I think we've been spotted," Pen said, her finger pointing ahead of us and to the left. We'd all been looking down to the right, where the settlement was, and therefore hadn't seen the movement.

Three houndsmen emerged from the trees perhaps a hundred lengths away, fully armored and wielding the long-handled axes that they liked to swing down at the tiny heads of people like us.

For a few seconds, all was still. The houndsmen halted when they spied our party, and the horses froze as if they hoped the hounds wouldn't see them. It was the first time I had seen the Hathrim hounds in person, and they were nothing short of terrifying. A cold shudder shook my limbs, and my jaw dropped. Such monsters should not walk in the world. I had seen kherns once, great horned beasts twelve feet tall at the shoulder and deadly on the run but ultimately herbivores and not interested in attacking other creatures. These hounds were nearly as large—and they would have to be to support the giants on their backs. They were saddled and harnessed like our horses but also armored in the front to deflect arrows in a head-on charge. Their coats were largely gray and short, dotted with patches of white and black, and their mad eyes were yellow. When their lips drew back and they snarled, their teeth appeared to be larger than my head. The horses shied, Kam's reared and whinnied in fear, and the hounds each barked once in concert. That was my first clue that it was not to be a diplomatic meeting.

"Straight up the hill, into the trees!" I shouted. "Go!" The party turned their horses and goaded them, a hardly necessary encouragement, but I held on to mine for another couple of seconds, waiting to see what the houndsmen would do—they had reins as well. Seeing that we were only eight Fornish people on horses and no threat to their encampment, they could hold back if they wished. They could raise an empty hand and talk. Or, if they saw that we were only eight small people and would rather we disappeared, they could order an attack.

I don't speak the Hathrim tongue, but when they shouted, kicked the sides of their hounds, and raised their axes high, it wasn't for parley. They sprang forward, and I turned my horse uphill and told her to go, wondering if I would ever see another sunrise.

Kam's horse was the farthest uphill, he being the one who had spooked first, and close behind him were Pen, the boy who wanted to be a mushroom farmer, and Pak Sey ben Kor. The hounds would have to go through us first to get to them—more specifically, me. But Tip Fet ben Lot and Yar Tup Min were only slightly ahead, and in front of them ran the would-be sea trader.

Within seconds it became clear that the hounds were faster than our horses. There would be no outrunning them, and Tip Fet ben Lot saw this as soon as I did. Awkward as it was, he had just enough of an angle to twist around and fire off a shot with his bow. And he actually hit the lead hound on the run, one that was bearing down on me, which I found a remarkable feat of marksmanship. But the shaft glanced off the armor between the eyes, causing the hound to flinch and then focus on Tip instead, shifting its angle of pursuit slightly to close on his horse.

I heard their snarling between the hoofbeats of the horses, felt their hunger and my fear, and knew that if we simply ran, they would take us down one by one. And being rearmost though only slightly behind ben Lot, I would be first to fall.

When the lead hound was almost within lunging distance of ben Lot, I twisted in my saddle and shot the net launcher at it. The gossamer net, crafted of spider silk harvested and spun by my clan, was nearly unbreakable by blunt force. It was made to ensnare smaller animals, but it spread out and the hound ran directly into it, tangling his legs and falling face forward to the ground. That launched the giant on its back through the air directly at ben Lot's back, and he sheared the Blue Moth in half with his huge axe before crashing to the ground himself in an awkward clatter of armor. The horse sprinted onward, uncaring that its rider was now only legs and intestines and listing in the saddle to the left. I shucked my second net launcher out of its sling, turned in the saddle, and fired it at the next closest hound coming after me. Its front legs tangled and froze as if rooted, and its momentum, suddenly halted, was such that its rear end flipped over, tossing its rider to the earth before landing on him, audibly snapping bones, though I could not tell if it was the hound's bones or the giant's or both.

While I was focused on him, the third hound passed me by, and I faced forward just in time to witness Yar Tup Min and his horse snatched up into the jaws of the hound and tossed into the air, blood spraying from their bodies and already dead before they crunched to the ground. The houndsman swept his axe at the would-be sea trader and took off his head, then the hound snapped at his horse and killed it, too.

"Use your nets!" I shouted. Pak Sey ben Kor didn't have one, but Pen and the mushroom enthusiast did. They pulled out their launchers, turned, and fired at the final houndsman as their horses struggled uphill. The young clansman's shot sailed high, but Pen's net settled around the hound's head, and it tossed about, trying to shake it off. Its legs remained unbound, and if given enough time it would win free, especially with its rider's help, and resume the chase.

"Kam! Your nets!"

My cousin wrestled his horse from a full panicked gallop to a canter, then turned it around and whipped a launcher from its sling. The houndsman was trying to free his hound from the net, but the creature thrashed around so much that he couldn't get a grip on it. I slowed my horse, coming up behind him, and brought up my own bow to bear, pulling an arrow out of my quiver. My shot, though carefully aimed, missed the houndsman because of a last-second lunge by his hound. I'd do better to aim for the beast.

Kam had two launchers, like me. He shot his first net at the hounds-man, which prevented him from swinging his axe, and then he drew closer, pulled out his second launcher, and aimed for the hound's front legs. Once it was tangled up and it went down, both it and its rider howling in frustration, ben Kor and I poured arrows into its vulnerable side and into the houndsman until their struggles ended. The other two houndsmen had died along with their mounts, the force of their collisions with the earth snapping their necks or something else vital. Large beasts moving that fast weren't meant to stop that suddenly.

Tip and Yar and the trader boy whose name I am ashamed to admit I could not recall were all dead. I wanted to sing the songs and give them back to the roots but knew we wouldn't have time to do it properly. Our clash surely had been heard by others, and they would be coming soon, or else they would when the patrol did not report in. Pen's chest was heaving and tears streamed down her face as she saw Yar and his horse lying downhill. I felt the pricking of tears in the corners of my eyes, too, but they would have to wait.

"We have to keep going," I said. "The Canopy must know as soon as possible that the Hathrim have a military presence here."

"What?" ben Kor said. "What about our people?"

"We have to leave them. We still have a mountain to climb and can't be sure we'll make it without a significant lead—you saw how fast they moved. If we don't make it back, then that gives the Hathrim more time to dig in, more time to plot an invasion of our shores."

"We can't simply leave!" Pak protested. "Tip was my friend!"

"And Yar was *my clansman!*" I yelled at him, refraining from pointing out that he had not fought at all to save the friend he cared so much about now. "And Pen's brother! But it's Canopy first, benman; you know that! We have to get back to Forn and let them all know through root and stem that we have been attacked by houndsmen, and what's more, there's a whole host of Hathrim just a few hours away from our border. Imagine the damage a few firelords could do to the northern hardwoods before we'd have time to muster a response."

He spluttered, "They would never attack us."

"I'm sure you thought they would never settle north of the Godsteeth either. And now they have this incident that they can use as an excuse to retaliate. Because of course they won't say that they attacked us; they're going to say we attacked them! What if this isn't just Gorin Mogen, ben Kor? What if this is a plot among all the Hearthfires to wrest the Fifth Kenning from us to fuel the First?" Both Pen and Kam gasped at the thought. It was an ancient fear among us all. The Black Jaguar squinted at me. "You're saying this was planned?"

"Yes." It galled me to have to fertilize his ego, but prudence dictated that it was the only way to get the harvest I wanted. "You're good at this kind of thinking. What would the plan be?"

His eyes fell to the back of his horse's neck as he thought about it. "Wait for Thayil to erupt and move to Ghurana Nent as refugees, harass our northern border and draw our forces there, and then the rest of the Hearthfires strike massively in the south."

"Or some variation on that theme, yes! Our strategists can run scenarios and plan countermeasures. But only if they know about it, right? So we have to go."

"All right," he said, all his anger gone as he nodded. "We will go and report together. But if we can risk the time and bring the fallen back to their roots," he said, jerking his chin downhill, "it would not only be proper but galvanizing for the Canopy. You see that, yes?"

Fine. A compromise. He would argue away any time I thought we'd save—he already had. It was a terrible risk, but he was right about the effect it would have: Tip's death would motivate the Blue Moths for sure. Since we were outside Forn and leadership consisted of we two, no silverbark except that which grew on our limbs, I extended my left arm, moss up, simulating the sway. "I see and agree. Accord?"

He paused, looking down with surprise at the offer to proceed as suggested. He was used to arguing for days before achieving anything in the sway. But perhaps, like me, he was realizing that we would no longer have the luxury of days to argue. He touched his right arm to mine. "Accord."

"You get ben Lot, I'll get my cousin, and Kam, will you get our clansman? Quickly."

"I should help," Pen said, her voice rough and filtered through a sob as she took in the body of her brother.

"No, we need your eyes and ears for approaching Hathrim," I said. I dreaded every second of returning downhill, knowing that if any other houndsmen appeared, we'd be every bit as dead as Yar Tup Min and the others. Net launchers only had the single shot, and I had no arrows left.

I had plenty of tears for Yar, though, like Pen, and a forest of regrets that I hadn't saved him. If I had said something to the Hathrim, would that have stopped them? Not sure what good it would have done unless they spoke Fornish. I didn't speak their language.

Getting him on the horse was not all that difficult, but lashing him so that he wouldn't fall off took more time than I thought we could afford. My horse snorted in outrage at the extra burden, but she wanted to leave the scene as much as I did, and soon enough we were clambering uphill again with no signs of obvious pursuit. Pak was able to recover only the top half of Tip because the dead man's horse was still running uphill with his lower half bouncing in the saddle.

We spoke little on the trek back to Forn, our voices failing along with the light. The horses picked their way through the needles and rocks with little guidance from us, and it wasn't until we were nearly at the pass again that we heard them coming.

It was a single bark in the darkness, followed by another, that alerted us that we were followed.

"Go!" I shouted. "Quickly as you can!" We spurred our horses onward, but they were already tired; their breath sprayed wetly out of their nostrils, and they managed only a labored trot, whereas Pen's horse, not burdened down, leapt into a full gallop. Good. Perhaps she would make it if we did not. At first I felt like I might be able to run faster than the horses, but they soon realized what those barks behind us meant and sped up. After a few minutes of panicked flight, we crested onto the bare shale of the pass, and had we sufficient light to see it, the Canopy would have been there, welcoming us. Pen and the surviving clansman were far ahead, perhaps already safe; it was only Kam, ben Kor, and myself who lagged behind.

The barks were closer now, though; the houndsmen were gaining much too fast, and I doubted we would make it. But perhaps this close to the Canopy I could do something about slowing them down. Except I would have to dismount to do anything; the vegetation could hardly help me if I was floating above the earth on a horse's back. The others didn't even see me rein in and hop off my horse since I was the rear guard. Time to make that duty mean something.

Slapping the horse on the flank to send it and Yar's body after the others, I ran alongside it for a short distance until it outpaced me. I kept churning after it, starlight and sound guiding me, hoping that soon I would find a patch of ground that wasn't solid stone, a layer of topsoil through which I could call on the powers of my kenning.

The clatter of the horses' hooves on the shale kept me from hearing anything of the hounds beyond their barking; I couldn't tell how close behind us they actually were. But then the sound of the hooves changed as they hit the high mountain turf, and I knew that the soil I needed wasn't far ahead. The collected thumping of their gait matched the hammering of my heart, and I took big heaving gulps of air to give myself as much energy as possible, straining against muscles that had tightened up after hours on horseback.

Reaching into my vest for a sealed inner pocket, I remember thinking years ago that I'd never have occasion to use the dormant seed waiting there inside a slim wooden box. It was given to me by Mat Som ben Sah once I'd adapted to my silverbark; every greensleeve got them from an elder of his or her clan. I remember feeling awed at its appearance as he placed it in my palm; even as a seed, the carnivorous bantil plant looks hungry and vicious, having a scalloped red hook and thorn to it. Animals that were too strong for the vines to take down took seeds with them, snared into their fur or flesh, and soon the seeds burrowed in and bloomed, consuming the animal from within and taking root in the soil where it died and then consuming any scavengers that came to feast on the corpse. It grew very quickly that way, converting blood and tissue into its own and growing more thorny vines tipped with toothy blooms that were really mouths.

"Plant it shallow, Nel," Mat told me, words issuing from behind the impenetrable thicket of his gray beard. "Cut a finger and give it a single drop to get it started. More if you need it to grow big quickly."

I would definitely need it to grow big quickly, and I would have to channel a huge amount of energy from the Canopy to do it. It would cost me a year or so of my life to accelerate the bantil's growth to the extent that it would even stand a chance of stopping the houndsmen. But if it would save Pen and the others and guarantee alerting the Canopy before Gorin Mogen's plan could take root? That would be worth it.

The jarring shock of stone ended, and spongy loam cushioned my feet. It was an island of soil in the rock, or more like a pool, blown into a water-carved depression and then rooted there by lichens and eventually grasses, and I could feel that it connected to the soil of the Canopy. I remembered seeing these areas trace up the hillside from Forn, hollows of vegetation streaming between ridges of shale.

The horses' hooves faded in and out like the staccato barks of treetop apes, sometimes falling on stone and sometimes on turf. They were getting close to the Canopy. But the houndsmen were gaining. The barks were louder, and I heard massive claws scrabbling on the rock and the clanking of armor. Was I already too late?

Whipping the box out of my vest, I spun in the turf and knelt, poked a small depression with my finger, and upended the box over it, careful lest the hook of the seed get caught on my own flesh. I tossed the box away and pulled out my knife, slicing the tip of my left middle finger and holding it over the seed. Six drops and I pulled away, getting to my feet and stepping backward as the seed exploded into ravenous life, a small feral red mouth springing up a couple of fingerlengths even as roots shot into the earth. Hungry, the bloom of teeth searched for more blood, more meat, but that was not how the bantil plant would grow now. It would be fed from the Canopy itself at my direction.

Silverbark shoots dipped down from my legs and sank into the earth as I walked, picking up again before they tore as my movement demanded, pale tendrils that moved like the spokes of a wheel, communicated to the Canopy, requested energy, received it, and delivered it again to the roots of the bantil plant.

Mat Som ben Sah had told me what it was supposed to feel like, and he had been told by his elders, and they by theirs, because no greensleeve of the White Gossamer Clan had done this for generations. But the lore was clear: "If you're directing the energy properly, you will feel as if you're burning from the inside," he told me.

He was right, but it wasn't burning like the Hathrim burn or like any fire I have known. It was the day's sunlight channeled through my core, and although I did heat up and break into a sweat, it was not painful but enervating, as if I had not eaten for days—a strange sensation to feel such exhaustion when I was funneling weeks of growth through my cells.

Yes, it was weeks, for the bantil plant grew eight, perhaps nine feet high, a seething mass of thick, murderous vines, and its mouths faced north naturally, for it could sense the oncoming meat of the houndsmen, a far greater meal than I could ever provide; it would never eat me anyway since I enjoyed the protection of the Fifth Kenning. Seed hooks flashed in the starlight as vines snaked along the ground, hoping to snare a passing animal. They would have their greatest hopes realized soon enough.

Hounds do not track plants. They track animals like me, focus on their prey, and never think about vegetation as being dangerous or edible. So even if they smelled the bantil plant growing in front of them, they had no reason to be wary. And at the speed they were climbing over that saddle in the mountains, the houndsmen wouldn't see it in time. But maybe they would hear ben Kor shouting from behind me, no doubt already safe under the leaves of the Canopy: "Ben *Sah*! What are you *doing?*"

Four mounted houndsmen bounded over the pass into Forn, and unable to see well, one of them ran directly into the bantil and went down howling in a tangle of snapping vines, its rider soon enough adding his screams to the hound's as the blooms fed on them both. The other three passed by but brushed against the trailing seed vines.

I broke my connection with the Canopy, withdrew the silverbark roots into my legs, and staggered as the energy left my body. One of the hounds either saw or smelled me and pivoted to charge, allowed to seek a target by his rider. I knew I wouldn't be able to dodge, much less fight such a beast on foot with only my hunting knife. I was too tired even to try. All I could do was collapse, and I did, the hot breath of the hound blowing my hair and its stench filling my lungs as it snapped its jaws above me, missing by inches as its trunklike legs passed me on either side.

The houndsman yanked his ride around to try again, and I thought perhaps I could manage a feeble roll, but I doubted it. The two other houndsmen were circling about, taking in their dying counterpart and realizing that I probably had something to do with the bantil plant.

A couple of steps more from each, and then their hounds yelped in unison. One sat to chew on one of its feet, and the other two spun in a circle at some irritation, bewildering their riders. I knew precisely what the irritation was: bantil seeds burrowing into their flesh and eating them. Only one of the giants had the sense to dismount and get clear. The others tried to hang on and get control of their hounds, but that didn't work out well for them. The hounds flopped onto their sides, desperate to get at their feet, and that trapped their riders underneath them. The bantil seeds were young plants now, growing and eating fast, and soon enough they'd send roots into the ground, lash their prey to the earth, and feed until they could feed no more. I was not quite trapped in a circle of four bantil plants, but very nearly so. They might not burrow in and finish me, but those toothy blossoms might take a bite of me before they realized I was off limits.

The single giant that had avoided the bantils retreated and watched his feet as he ran. When he got close to the first monstrous bantil I had planted and its trailing vines blocked his path, he shouted a curse and pointed his axe, and flame traveled up the handle to the head and sent a gout from the blade, lighting the vines on fire. He was lavaborn—and he alone, since none of the others had set anything alight. And it was precisely that ability that was so dangerous to the Canopy. The bantil vines blackened and shriveled, and he stepped across them into safety before stoking the flames higher and making sure the entire bantil plant would be consumed—along with his erstwhile companion, who had stopped screaming but was still being eaten. I lost sight of the giant after that; he was hidden behind a wall of flame and writhing vines. He left the others to die, I noted, but perhaps he realized there was nothing he could do to save them now. A strategic retreat was his only option, and it was mine as well.

My muscles wouldn't obey me, though. I couldn't get up; channeling all that energy had wiped me out, and the fire most likely would move faster than I could. No matter; the others had escaped and would warn the Canopy of the danger, and I had served the Canopy above myself as a greensleeve should.

I lost some time in the darkness, a blissful time when the screams and the flames all faded, and woke up as someone grunted and tried—unsuccessfully—to lift me onto a horse. It wasn't Kam Set Sah or Pak Sey ben Kor. It was my cousin Pen Yas ben Min.

"What're you doing?" I mumbled.

"What needs doing," she replied. "Pak was saying you shouldn't have sprouted the bantil plants and Kam was telling him he has the brains of a puffweed, and neither of them was saving you. Can you just help a little bit? Get yourself draped across the horse and I'll walk you down."

She gave me an undignified push on the rear, and I scrabbled weakly across the saddle, draping across it much like a sack of barleycorn. There were no sounds of dying now from the hounds or their houndsmen, only the sound of the fire behind me and the three other young bantil plants feeding on their kills and growing at their natural rate.

"Have you seen the last Hathrim?"

"The lavaborn? You mean he got away?" Pen asked.

"Unless one of you killed him, yes."

"We didn't see him come our way. We just saw him briefly as a silhouette and assumed you must have gotten him after that since he didn't start any more fires."

"No, he didn't need to," I said. "I think he just wanted to get away, like us."

"I'm glad he did." She took the horse's lead to guide us downhill, watching out carefully for any scattered bantil seeds or vines that might have slithered across her path since she had passed. She had a bright yellow glow bulb in one hand to help her see, brighter than the ones I was used to.

"Where'd you get that glow bulb?"

"Jak had it with him."

"Who?"

"Jak Bur Vel. The boy who wants to be a mushroom farmer?"

"Oh. Sorry, I think it's me who has the brains of a puffweed."

"He's really into fungus like this. Told me all about the Silver Carp Clan that harvests these in the caves near the Raelech border."

She was talking fast, obviously nervous, and I listened to her talk about Jak and his strange fungus collection so that I wouldn't have to listen to the bantil plants eating. Pen might have been talking for the same reason. I grunted in appropriate places as we picked our way downhill to the Canopy, where the others waited. Jak and Kam were relieved to see me and heaped praise on Pen for rescuing me. Pak Sey ben Kor, I noticed, said nothing as they helped me off the horse and braced me between them. I met his eyes and asked him a question.

"Did you report what happened already through root and stem?"

"Not yet."

"Then let's do so now, together, as agreed."

"Let's talk first about what you just did," the Black Jaguar said, pointing at the fire. "You used your bantil seed, and now there are hundreds more of them up there. You've effectively turned the pass into a major hazard."

"The lavaborn are a major hazard to the Canopy," I replied. "And thanks to the bantil plant, the one they brought with them never got this far."

"He's going to get reinforcements."

"And so will we. I think we should request them now and not wait for the sway to suggest it."

"You don't seem to realize that you've quite possibly provoked a war."

"They were hunting *us*, ben Kor, trying to prevent *us* from reporting their presence. The provocation was all theirs—we acted in self-defense only. And now it's up to us to inform the Canopy and let our diplomats try to find a solution before anything else burns."

He seethed, knowing I was right and hating me for it. And now that we were out of immediate danger, he was ready to twist events to spite me. I don't think he honestly disagreed with anything I said; he simply couldn't stand the fact that I was correct and he was wrong; it was a poisonous mindset. And that is what happens to people who do not put the Canopy first.

"Come. Let's report as agreed." The roots of my silverbark lengthened and dipped into the soil of the forest, and seeing this, Pak Sey ben Kor had no choice but to join me. He dismounted and his own roots snaked into the ground, and we spoke through root and stem to all of Forn. By dawn, even the greensleeves in Keft would know what happened here, and they would spread the news to the Raelechs and Brynts and Kaurians. Gorin Mogen's sneaky invasion would soon be simply an invasion, and the world would not let him get away with it.

Fintan waved to the crowd. "Tomorrow we will find out what happened to Abhinava and the bloodcats!"

Day 6

THE BLOODCAT

When I returned home after the tale, Elynea was sitting up straight in a chair and obviously waiting for me.

"Good, you're here," she said. "Kids, go outside and wait for me. I'll be out directly."

As they filed past me to the door, Tamöd waved and said, "Bye, Dervan." Pyrella said nothing but gave me a brief hug. And after the door closed behind them, I turned to Elynea with a question on my face, but she wouldn't meet my eyes.

"Dervan, you've been so kind to let us live here, and we're so grateful," she said. "And I know it's not your fault, but this isn't the best place for my children anymore. We're going to move in with my friend Garst du Wöllyr."

"You mean your new employer?"

"Also my employer, yes. He has room for us, and since he's in the furniture business, he has, well . . . furniture. Real beds for the kids instead of cots."

I forced a smile onto my face. "Of course. I completely understand."

She stood and clasped her hands together before her, finally looking up at me. "I wanted to tell you in person and not leave a note."

"That was nice of you," I said. "I might have worried. I wish you all good fortune and happiness, and of course please let me know if there's anything else I can do for you."

"You've been a blessing to us as it is. Thank you." She stepped forward until she was directly in front of me, her eyes downcast again. Then she placed her hands on top of my shoulders, stretched up on tiptoe, and quickly kissed my cheek. "Goodbye."

I stood there dumb as she exited and the door clacked shut behind her. The house seemed especially empty now even with me inside of it. I was alone again, a prospect I had in the past weeks looked forward to with relish, but now that it had happened, I recalled the stark fact that it is truly horrifying to be so alone. I still missed Sarena, and now that Elynea and her kids were gone, now that I couldn't lounge in the palace and chat away the time with mariners and longshoremen, now that I had nothing but bare walls to look at and four cots and four chairs for my use only, my home felt like the Mistmaiden Isles, a place no one ever visited, populated entirely by ghosts.

Shuffling to the kitchen, thinking that food might distract me, I opened the pantry without enthusiasm and saw no comfort there. There was none to be had. I closed it again and announced to the walls, "I'm going out."

Locking the door, I strode briskly to the Randy Goat, the sagging and practically derelict inn where Fintan had spent the previous night. It was dark inside, the weak light shining in the oil lamps dirty somehow, and it smelled of urine and grease and bad decisions, but it was full of loud unwashed people ready to talk and share a joke, their tongues loosened by drink and their senses of humor in keeping with the inn's name. I paid for a room and a round for everyone and thereby ensured that for one night at least I would not feel like the old man in the stories about Blasted Rock who grew so lonesome in his lighthouse that he went mad and became four different people in his head.

Fintan was in a much better mood than I when we met the next day at a bacon bar, the invention of a Brynt businessman that was becoming popular in both Rael and Kauria. The idea was simple: You could order tea, bacon, eggs, cheese, and bread, all of the highest quality, or nothing. You could order a plate of shark shit before you could order fruit, and they were always out of shark shit.

The bard owed his fine spirits to his stay at the Coral Reef, an establishment that bordered on the luxurious, and unlike me, he had enjoyed a restful night's sleep.

"Apart from the usual nightmares," he said, though I didn't inquire further. He was solicitous about my obvious hangover and turned out to be a patient companion, not feeling it necessary to fill up silence with talk while I recovered. We slurped tea and inhaled bacon and egg sandwiches until I felt closer to human, though I'm sure I didn't look it. Perhaps I could use that to my advantage, catch Fintan off guard. Might as well get around to asking what Rölly wished me to.

"Who's on the Triune Council these days?" I asked him, breaking the silence. "I don't even know."

A single eyebrow hiked up his forehead for a better view, then slid down as he leaned back in his chair. "Well, the senior member is Dechtira, who will be missed when her three-year term ends this year. In the middle is Clodagh, and—" He halted, blinking his eyes a couple of times and then deliberately clearing his expression. "Well, I suppose I don't have much to say about her. The newest member is Carrig, and he seems a decent sort. Tough to predict where he'll throw his vote, though. Sometimes he's with Dechtira, sometimes with Clodagh, which I suppose is a good thing. Provides some balance."

"So that means Dechtira and Clodagh are often on opposite sides of any given issue?"

A furrow appeared between Fintan's eyes. "You wake up with a hangover and the wrangling of the Triune Council is what you want to talk about?"

"No." I shook my head and chuckled somewhat sheepishly. "Desperate for conversation, I suppose. Though I am genuinely curious about something else." I took a sip from my tea, which had begun to grow cold, and set it down with some disappointment. "Do you ever miss Numa?" I asked him.

"Every day."

I nodded. "I understand that completely. Your heart is a harp string, and every day the memory of your love plucks at it. So here's what I want to know: How do you bear it, being alone?"

He thought in silence before answering. "I don't think loneliness is a thing that can be borne: it's so heavy and crushing for something that is essentially emptiness. It's like being trapped beneath a boulder, this immovable weight that presses your ribs and slowly steals your breath. And so it must simply be endured, and you do that by looking away. I hope you will not be offended if I admit that I am looking away right now. Every minute she's out of my sight, I am looking away. But never fear—that boulder of crushing emptiness will still be there when you look back."

I snorted. "That's the least of my fears." But his advice was well taken. I pulled out my paper and ink. "Think I'll look at my work for a while. We have a lot to write down from yesterday. Ready?"

"Absolutely. Let us look elsewhere together."

My fingers had begun to ache by the time we finished, and I was grateful when Fintan assured me that the day's tales would not be quite so long this time. The bleacher seats below the wall were packed an hour before he arrived, and I doubted many of them moved when he gave them the quarter-hour warning.

"This song is a rather grisly one that Nentian parents sing to their children. When I've heard it done, they try to make it cute—the tone is delightful, it's a catchy melody, and there's usually some tickling at the end to make the child laugh. But the lesson sticks with the children as they get older. Or if it doesn't, they most likely won't get older."

Sleep on the ground and die
On the plains of Ghurana Nent!
Your body is a meat pie
To the eels of Ghurana Nent!

Chew and chew, chew and spit,
Flesh eels can't get enough of it!
Tasty meat, tasty meat,
Just lie down and they will eat . . .

You up!

The grin on the bard's face was wicked as he retook the stage. "We'll begin today with the scheming of Viceroy Melishev Lohmet."

Melishev

Chumat set sail with a troop of lackeys to discover where Gorin Mogen's people had gone, but he's not far over the horizon when I receive two different people telling me precisely where the Hearthfire is: squatting on my land in territory I'm supposed to defend, just as I both feared and hoped.

The pale, whimpering Fornish ambassador tells me first, shrouded in green robes and moving in an almost visible cloud of florals. Her name is Mai Bet Ken, and she might have been pretty if she weren't so deathly white. Her voice might have been pleasing were it not so soft that it could almost be bruised if I coughed. She projects weakness, and it annoys me that she represents my strongest ally at the moment. No one else is close enough to render any assistance. The capital would move slowly if it got around to moving at all; I'll have to do what I can with the resources I have for now.

"Viceroy Lohmet," she says in a breathy whisper, "the Canopy wishes to inform you, should you not already be aware, that a sizable force of Hathrim have landed on your southernmost shores, almost on our border."

"A military force?"

"Partially. We know that they have lavaborn and houndsmen since our scouts were attacked by them. We think—"

"Wait a moment. What were your scouts doing in my territory?"

"Forn has a vested interest in keeping the lavaborn away from the Canopy, and it also has an interest in enforcing treaties. We sent a small scouting party—a mere eight people—to find what happened to a fleet sailing north after the eruption of Mount Thayil, and they found the survivors of Harthrad camping on your land. They were discovered by a patrol of houndsmen and immediately attacked."

She provides precious few details on the settlement: her people ran at the sight of houndsmen as any sane person would. But they had accounted for themselves quite well; they lost three against a total of six monsters and their riders. Put my army in the field and I'd probably lose twenty men or more for each houndsman and count it a bargain.

We could use more intelligence for sure. And if a Fornish party of eight could take out six houndsmen, then I wouldn't mind them sending in a few more scouting parties like that. Let them get chewed up and turned into epic piles of dog shit and do our work for us. That would give us a fighting chance, perhaps. I paste an expression of sincere gratitude on my face and clear my throat to make it sound warm.

"Ambassador Ken, Ghurana Nent appreciates your information and would welcome more. You have my permission—now and retroactively—to cross our borders for purposes of scouting the Hathrim invaders. It is in both of our interests to purge them from the plains. I must communicate with the king, of course, before agreeing to anything else, but you can be sure my attention is fixed on solving this problem."

She bends at the waist and whispers that she's glad to be of service to Ghurana Nent. She assures me that she will relay my desires back to the Canopy and will no doubt have much to discuss with me again soon. Then she floats out of the room—or seems to, since her long robes conceal her feet and drag on the floor—but leaves the stink of her perfume behind her. I order the room aired out while I climb the tower to think again, but as before, I'm interrupted. It's clear I'll never have another moment's peace until we kick Gorin Mogen back into the sea.

Dhingra answers my scowl at his entrance first with a smirk and then with a wide grin; he is often amused whenever I am not, and he looks highly amused.

"Back under the skylight with you, Viceroy," he said. "We have two Hathrim who urgently wish to speak to you."

"Hathrim? Are they Mogen's people?"

"I think they might be."

"How delightful. Make them wait a moment, and when you show them in, offer them tiny little chairs to sit in."

Dhingra snorted. "It shall be as you say."

"And make sure there's a couple of squads of men in there with crossbows."

"Oh, yes, they're already waiting for you."

And so they are: twelve leather-faced and ornery men on either side of the throne, a dozen for each giant. Dhingra knows how I like things done. Incredibly, even with the stink of soldiers lining the walls, the floral scent of the Fornish ambassador still lurks in the reception hall. And when the Hathrim duck through the double doors at the other end, their heads scraping against the ceiling and then the skylight, I can see their massive nostrils twitch at the smell. Their eyes dart uncertainly among the crossbowmen, wondering which one of them might be responsible for the perfume.

The planks of the floor groan under their heavy booted feet, and

Dhingra, true to his word, comically offers them simple wooden chairs that would instantly splinter to kindling if they sat on them. They look down at him in disbelief, wondering if he's joking, but he keeps a magnificent straight face and so do I when they turn to me.

"Thank you, no," one says, and the floorboards squeak in protest when they take one knee in front of me and still remain taller than anyone in the room. They both have large, bushy beards, one blond and one red, and eyes as blue as the famous waters of Crystal Pond upriver. They look half wild and disheveled, though I discern after speaking with them that this is probably intentional. They are doing their best to look desperate and in need.

The blond one's cheeks are flushed and fat, and he might have eaten four whole hogs for breakfast. He introduces himself as Korda Belik and does all the talking; the red beard just nods and tries to look somber while his companion spins a story.

"Thank you, Viceroy, for seeing us," Korda says. His Nentian is accented but perfectly understandable. "I won't waste your time. You may have heard already about the eruption of Mount Thayil. Most of Harthrad died within the first hour, and hot molten rain and ash fell out of the sky to the south, forcing the few of us who could make it to boats to head north and land in the safest place we could think of: Ghurana Nent. We now throw ourselves upon your mercy and your famous generosity, hoping you will allow us time to regroup and perhaps aid us with a shipment of grains so that we may not starve."

I stare at him, astounded at his gall. I let the silence lengthen until he clears his throat, uncomfortable.

"I have questions, Korda," I said. "And I want you to answer as quickly as possible. Just facts. No embellishing."

"Understood."

"I am saddened to hear about the loss of so many Hathrim, but I know not how to gauge the depth of this tragedy. You said your numbers are few. How many of you, precisely, are now occupying my land?"

"I cannot give you a precise number—"

"Then give me your best estimate. Give or take a hundred, I won't mind."

"Viceroy, I was sent here instantly by Hearthfire Gorin Mogen upon our nighttime landing, and we had no time to count heads before I left."

What a pile of yak shit. "I will need a number if I am to estimate how much grain to ship you, Korda."

That traps him. "Say a thousand, then, Viceroy, though that is most certainly high." The red beard nods vigorously.

That means that number is most certainly very low. Hundreds of starving giants sounds manageable. Thousands of giants sounds like a recipe for panic, and they do not want me to panic yet.

"Very well. And where am I sending this grain?"

"The southern edge of your coast, just north of the Fornish border. We were too exhausted to travel any farther, and we also had no wish to alarm your citizens with our sudden appearance."

I give him a cheerless smile. "My thanks. And how long does Gorin Mogen plan to stay in my country with his thousand giants, Korda?"

"Just until the ash clears away and we can safely return to Hathrir. I believe all the cities are suffering now."

"Again, help me with a number. How long?"

He shrugs massive shoulders. "Two months, perhaps three."

"Two months should suffice for the dust to settle. So two months' grain for a thousand giants, is that correct?"

"Yes, Viceroy."

"Dhingra, I will want to discuss the specifics of that with you after this."

He dips his chin. "As you say, Viceroy."

"Korda, you will remain here as my guest. Your friend there will go back with the shipment of grain and some of my men to deliver my personal condolences and promises of continued friendship to Hearth-fire Gorin Mogen."

I pause to let Korda respond to my bald statement that I'm effectively taking him as a hostage. He's a smooth one: he only blinks once.

"Of course, Viceroy."

I turn to the red beard. "You will inform Gorin Mogen in the very plain terms that I am using now that he and all other Hathrim must be out of Ghurana Nent in two months' time regardless of how much ash and molten rain may be ravaging Hathrir. After two months you are no longer welcome guests and the sad victims of fate we are happy to succor in your most dire hour. At that point you are trespassing and will be treated as trespassers. Is that clear?"

The shoals of Red Beard's facial hair mash together in the space where his mouth is supposed to be. He's biting back an angry retort. But Mogen has them trained well. After a moment, he gives a curt nod and says, "It is."

"Do you have a ship?"

Korda answers. "No; our ship returned ahead of us with some emergency supplies. We were going to beg passage south on a merchant vessel in exchange for work."

"Good. You'll go on my ship, then," I say to Red Beard. "I'll have a room for you at the Pelican by the docks. They have Hathrim-size ceilings. These lovely gentlemen," I say as I gesture to the crossbowmen on the right, "will escort you there." Pointing to the crossbowmen on the left, I continue, "And these fine worthies will escort you, Korda, to our largest room here, and should you need anything in particular, please ask one of them and it will be brought to you."

They make noises of gratitude and depart with their heavily armed escorts. Dhingra sidles up to me once the doors close.

"Load only ten bags of grain into the hold and call it a clerical error, assuring them that we'll give them more."

"Will we?"

"Of course not. But make sure Red Beard delivers that two-month deadline to Gorin Mogen. Take the best head count you can, especially of their military forces, and get back up here as soon as possible. Set sail tomorrow."

"As you say, Viceroy."

"And make sure Korda and Red Beard don't leave their accommodations. They are still guests but guests with restricted access. Bring them whatever they need to be comfortable."

"Aye," he says, and then sneezes. "Sorry. Perfume."

"Yes, I need some air."

We part: he to work, I to the blessedly scentless Tower of Kalaad to compose a missive for the king. Something along the lines of "We've been invaded, send help."

I'll have to summon the tactician and tell him to get his boys ready to fight lavaborn giants wearing the world's strongest armor. And I'll have to resume my own military exercises. There will be a necessary diplomatic dance before we trade blows, and if Kalaad smiles on us, maybe it will work. But it is more likely to end in death and wailing families of the fallen. Giants aren't known for backing down until you drop them on their backs by force; sooner rather than later I'll have to ride out and trip them up myself. Can't stay here in my tower if I want to rule the country from a more pleasant spot than this backwater town that smells of borchatta guts and cabbage ass. No, when I ride out to deprive Gorin Mogen of his throne, it will assure me of mine . . . so long as we win.

I chuckled softly as Fintan dismissed the seeming of Melishev Lohmet. That little vignette would annoy both the Nentians and the Fornish. He certainly wasn't holding back for fear of criticism. Looking down at the bleacher crowd, I saw many of them shaking their heads and discussing the viceroy with their companions. His opinions were odious, but many had laughed at the image of offering small chairs to the giants.

"Elsewhere in Ghurana Nent," the bard said, "Abhinava Khose was making a new friend." When he took on the young hunter's seeming, he was bloody and bruised and his field bag hung in tatters from his shoulder.

Abbi

I cannot explain why I still live. It makes no sense. I should be making my way through the digestive systems of about thirty bloodcats now, but instead I'm cursed to live a while longer.

The bloodcat that moved first stretched and stood on the branch, looked directly at me, then gave a short cry that was almost a bark, waking up the others. The branches of the nughobe trees around me writhed, the rest of the bloodcats revealing themselves once they moved. Their ears, pointed triangles with tufts at the tips, rose above their heads as they saw me. Without moving anything but my head, I noted that they were on all sides and must be behind me as well.

They were beautiful creatures. I had only seen dead ones before, their reddish-brown furs brought in by other hunting families that specialized in the dangers of nughobe groves. Bloodcats rarely strayed into the plains. But they possessed a more pleasing shape than grass pumas, more attractive pelts, faces that could be called cute until they revealed their teeth, and pointed, tufted ears that were almost adorable. The bloodred eyes that gave them their name were difficult to classify as kind, however.

One by one they descended from the branches, almost noiseless save for the noises they chose to make. They began to circle me clockwise, waiting for me to move or show fear, but I had none because I already counted myself dead. What I felt instead was grief for my family, sorrow that I would never see my sister smile again or my uncle tease my father or my aunt spontaneously decide that the best possible thing she could do was dance in the middle of the plains to music only she could hear. I wept and wished the bloodcats would hurry up and end it, but they kept circling and growling at me. I had never heard of such a thing.

"Come on!" I finally shouted at them, and that did it. Their muscles bunched and their ears flattened against their skulls, they hissed and charged. Sitting passively on a carpet of leaves, I should have been dead seconds afterward. The first one bowled me over flat onto my back, claws raking my chest, and then the rest of them descended to feed. But their teeth bit into my shoulders, arms, legs, and ribs, a single bite from each of them. None ever attempted to tear my flesh away, and none of them bit into my throat as they would have done instinctively if they wished to kill me. They bit and scratched and made me hurt everywhere, and then they all gathered together in front of me in a mess of fur, laid down in the leaves, and licked themselves as if they had no other pressing business. As if they had not just attacked and left me there to bleed.

I thought at first that perhaps I was delirious from blood loss and was hallucinating all this as I was being eaten and soon my vision would wink out and the nonsense would end. But no, the licking continued, and I would like to observe here that there is nothing quite so maddening as the loud lapping of genitals.

"What's the matter?" I said to them. "Don't I taste good?"

I received no answer, of course. And then I understood: I wasn't giving them a chase. They wanted to hunt me. They were playing with their food as cats are fond of doing. That meant if I wanted to die, I'd have to get up and run for it. So I did: I staggered to my feet, lurched a few steps, and discovered that lurching was the best I could do with my injuries. I lurched straight away from them. Looking over my shoulder, I saw that a couple of the bloodcats had turned to watch me run, but most hadn't even interrupted their ritualistic laving. Bewildered and feeling quite weak in any case, I stopped running. Perhaps they were simply not hungry and wanted me out of their nest, nothing more. Possible, I supposed, but unlikely; I had heard that bloodcats were extremely territorial. Their behavior was utterly baffling.

Still, having been given a reprieve, I resolved to behave as if I had a chance of surviving after all and putting my family to rest. My field bag was largely shredded, my water skins destroyed and my food eaten or lost, but it still held my journal and ink, the firestone, and the remnants of a blanket. It might allow me to return to the plains, make camp, and have nothing to worry about except scaring off a few blackwings in the morning. My spear could have easily survived the khern stampede, and maybe a few water skins remained as well, or at least a knife. I should be able to find someone's knife near the wagon.

It was a very long series of lurches, during which I imagined that the bloodcats would simply track me down and finish me off when they were hungry again. Or something else, drawn by the scent of my blood, would put me out of my misery. I heard the yips and howls of a pack of wheat dogs approaching at one point, but after I hoped aloud that they wouldn't find me, their cries veered off and faded in pursuit of something else. Kalaad must want me to live long enough to do right by my family.

I kept going in darkness, navigating a slow path by the stars peeking through the leaves. Once I reached the plains, I stopped, gathered some dead wood, and built a fire under the branches of the last (or the first) nughobe tree. I had nothing to eat or drink, a body covered in scabbed wounds that might fester sooner rather than later, and only prayers to defend myself should anything wish to eat me.

The plains were silent, though, and having little else to do, I took out my journal and wrote by firelight, hoping that seeing these events put down in words would allow me to understand it all.

I can tell you now: writing didn't help. I still don't know why I'm alive.

There is a bloodcat curled up next to the fire directly across from me. A few minutes ago it approached from behind, purring deep in its throat, and when I turned and saw its red eyes glowing, I scrambled around the fire, putting the flames between myself and those teeth.

It was a laughable move. The bloodcat was much faster than me and could easily chase me down from one direction or another. But like the entire nest of them earlier—perhaps it was from the same nest—it had no interest in killing me. It sat down and regarded me with its head canted to one side as I stood on the balls of my feet, knees bent, ready to dodge one way or the other. Not that my injured leg would let me do much but shift a few inches in any direction.

"Don't eat me," I said, but the bloodcat only purred louder, then toppled over sideways and writhed in the tamped-down grass where I had been sitting, pawing the air as it scratched its back.

I looked around to see if anyone else was seeing what I was seeing, but of course I was alone. Alone with one of the most feared predators of the plains. Behaving adorably.

Perhaps it was a trick. A distraction. I stared into the darkness of the nughobe forest, but it was impenetrable, especially to my fire-blinded eyes. "Where are your friends?" I asked it. "The rest of your nest?"

The bloodcat stopped wiggling and came to rest right side up, its ears at attention as it looked at me. It swung its head back to the nughobes for a few seconds, returned its eyes to me, then looked away and sneezed.

"You're here alone? You came to see me all by yourself?" I asked, then wondered why I was bothering to speak. But the cat rolled over, presenting its belly again, and made that low rolling noise of contentment in its throat.

"You are very strange," I said, and the cat kicked out with its back legs as it stretched, pushing my journal and ink bottle a few inches away. Once I saw that, I wanted the journal in my hands to write this down so that proof would exist somewhere that such an encounter as this was possible. (And if I wake up later and check the journal and see these words in black and cream, I will know it really happened. And if they are not there at all, I will know it was a dream.)

"Hey. Mind if I come over there to pick that up?" I asked, pointing to the journal. The bloodcat righted itself, looked to where I was pointing, then got to its feet and moved a short distance away. Extraordinary. "Thanks," I said, and cautiously moved around to pick up my journal, ink, and quills. Once they were in hand, I returned to where I'd been standing and sat down, flattening the grass beneath me, sitting with my back to the plains. The bloodcat watched all this, and when I was settled, it moved back to where it had been stretching, curled up, and placed its head on its paws, red eyes watching me. I began to write all this down, and at some point the bloodcat closed its eyes. I am not sure if it sleeps, but I have no desire to rouse it.

I wish that I could sleep so fearlessly out here. I don't think I will sleep until my body gives me no other choice. We will see at dawn if the bloodcat is hungry.

The fire had burned down to a few red coals, and at some point I must have nodded off for a few minutes or hours. The bloodcat remained. I was still in one piece, felt somewhat better, and miraculously had not woken up covered in insect bites. The sun was not up, but the sky was gray and I could see well enough to move.

"Hey, friend," I said, and the bloodcat's eyes opened like two more coals and blinked. "I would like to visit my family now. Would that be all right with you?"

If it wanted to have me for breakfast, it could. But it stuck its rear in the air and stretched. I rose and did the same in a more human fashion. I hoped that if it let me live, I'd find some water; I was parched. That didn't mean I had nothing in my bladder. I stepped away, turned my back, and took care of it, looking over my shoulder at the bloodcat. It was still occupied with loosening its muscles.

Finding the wreckage of the Khose train wouldn't be difficult. The path of the kherns was clearly visible as a swath of flattened grasses not far from the nughobes. All I had to do was follow it back to where they'd smashed into the wagon.

When I finished, the bloodcat completed its morning stretch, yawned, and then looked at me almost expectantly, its tail swishing idly in the air. "Well? Shall we go together?" I said, pointing in the general direction of the wagon. "Or is this where we part company?" The bloodcat simply returned my stare, tail moving of its own volition. "All right, I'm going. Come along if you want," I said.

I turned to the plains and began to walk, muscles tight but not as painful as the night before. I had improved from a lurch to a slight limp, and my arms had their full range of motion with only a few minor stinging complaints. I thought it remarkable to be feeling so well.

After twelve steps or so I heard the bloodcat move, only a whisper but still audible in the silence of the early dawn. An unmistakable hiss of liquid told me the animal had its own bodily functions to complete. What would it do next? Disappear back into the nughobes and rejoin its nest? Sprint at my back and bring me down?

It did neither of those things. Before I had taken another twenty steps I heard a soft whisper of grass grow louder, and then out of the corner of my right eye I spied movement. It was the bloodcat, keeping pace next to me a short distance away, tail held high and head up, sampling the air.

"You are the strangest creature I've ever met," I said, "but I'm glad you're here. I'd be all alone otherwise."

It purred, though I don't know at what. Surely not at my words.

A mess of boards and planks marked the site of my family's end. The carcasses of the wart yaks lay prone, ribs already exposed to the air after a single afternoon and evening's rest on the plains. The scavengers had been efficient and thorough. A couple of lingering blackwings crowed a lazy challenge at us, but they were full and had nothing to fight about. They flew away as the bloodcat and I approached.

The wagon had been splintered apart and its contents tumbled across the grass, but the contents hadn't been completely annihilated. There were colorful pieces of cloth strewn about, wraps that belonged to my mother or aunt or sister. Cooking utensils such as spoons and pots. I found a small knife suitable for peeling roots and palmed it in case I couldn't find anything better. A minute later I found a spear—my spear, in fact, recognizable by the dyed red leather strips wrapped around the base of the head. When I bent to pick it up, the bloodcat growled. I dropped it immediately, and the bloodcat fell silent. It stared at me, not exactly aggressive but not as relaxed as it had been earlier. *Vigilant* might be the word.

"Yeah, you're right," I said. "I left it behind for a reason. But I need a better knife than this puny thing if I'm going to survive." Odd, I thought, to be thinking about survival past the next hour or so.

I searched for the box that held our water skins and eventually found it, ruined and splintered but still vaguely boxlike. It must have been tossed in the air when the wagon came apart and never directly trampled, so it had provided just enough protection to the skins inside that they still held water. There were three of them. Not enough to cook or wash with but enough to drink if I did nothing but walk straight back to Khul Bashab. I drank half of one before I felt sated.

Continuing to salvage what I could, I found a field bag in better shape than mine and transferred my few possessions to it, adding in the water skins and a few other items, mostly dry food. The bloodcat sat down and watched me pick through the wreckage.

"You are very patient," I told it, but it behaved as if I hadn't spoken at all. The sun had fully risen and warmed the air perceptibly by the time I could no longer delay the ushering of my family to the sky.

Since I had seen the path my parents had taken, I walked in that direction first, locating my father after less than ten lengths. He was nothing but bones and rags and a stain in the grass now, his flesh all pecked and torn away. He'd banished me from the family but hadn't deserved this in return. Tears in my eyes and then trailing down my face, I tipped my head back until I nearly fell backward, staring straight up at the cloudless blue.

"Kalaad in the sky, I give you my father, who thought his son must hunt if he was to be a good son but who did love me and my family and made sure we prospered for all our days together. He is dead because I distracted him from hunting. Maybe he was right and I am not a good son. But that does not matter so much as that he is blameless and deserves to be at peace."

I hoped I was doing it right; I'd never been old enough to give anyone to the sky before. I'd seen my parents do it for their parents and my uncle do it for his father, but that was years ago and I could barely remember.

My mother's tunic had been a bright pink and was easy to find in the grass along with her remains. I cried over her, and when I thought I could keep my voice steady, I looked up to address Kalaad. "I give you my mother, who bore me and fed me and kept me in her heart for all her days. Now I will keep her in my heart for the rest of mine. May you keep her safe and free from pain for all time."

It was not a day for me to be free from pain. Walking in the other direction and sniffling, I found the rest of my family, cried for them all, gave them all to Kalaad in the sky. My aunt and uncle, my cousins, my sister. None of them survived. I took all their hunting knives and left their spears in the grass. I needed only one knife, but they were made of fine Hathrim steel and I could probably sell the extra ones for necessities if I made it back. The bloodcat accompanied me as I visited each corpse and said the words, and it remained silent when I took the knives and placed them in my field bag.

There was nothing for me to do but return to Khul Bashab and, should I make it there, figure out some way to survive without a family.

I squinted at the bloodcat, which sat on its haunches and waited.

"What do you want?" I asked it. "Don't you want to be with your nest?"

Standing on all fours, the bloodcat snorted and began to pace back and forth in front of me. Its red-brown fur, perfect for keeping it concealed among the nughobes, stood out against the pale grasses of the plains. It didn't belong out here. Neither did I.

"I'm going to walk north," I said, pointing. "Follow in the path of the kherns so long as they go in that direction. I have to make it back to Khul Bashab. It's probably four days from here depending on how fast I go. You can come if you like, but I have nothing for you to eat and only enough water for me."

"Murr," the bloodcat said in his throaty rumble, and began to walk north. I followed after, and I supposed that was my answer, though I still didn't understand how such behavior was possible. Soon we were walking side by side again, this time with the bloodcat on my left, but thinking of my family and my responsibility for their deaths prevented me from dwelling on the strangeness of it. By the time the sky had arced above us into afternoon, it no longer seemed strange. I had grown used to the creature and began to think perhaps it deserved a more dignified name than "creature."

Perhaps it already had one.

Feeling absurd, I introduced myself. "I'm Abhinava. What's your name?"

"Murr," the bloodcat replied.

"I'm glad to meet you, Murr. Thank you for your company today. Should you become hungry or thirsty, please do whatever you need to do. I'll just keep walking north and you can catch up easily."

The bloodcat angled its head to look at me for a few steps, then it uttered a short acknowledging grunt and faced forward again. We walked in silence another quarter hour before Murr's ears perked up and he darted off to the west after something. I didn't see him again until evening when I had made my camp for the night in a small thicket of woody shrubs. I had to dismantle one of the shrubs to make a serviceable fire. There were small rodents in the thicket and at least one poisonous viper preying on them, along with a portly tusked boar that seemed content to coexist with me in his neighborhood. He watched me build the fire and didn't move until Murr showed up, and then he took off with a squeal.

"Welcome back," I said to the bloodcat. "Did you find something to eat?"

"Murr." He lay down across from me and began to clean his paws with his tongue.

"Good."

I didn't know what else to say. Once he had left that afternoon, I never thought Murr would seek me out to lie by the fire again. It was definitely not natural behavior, and as I munched on a few raw root vegetables, I wondered if he would follow me all the way back to

Khul Bashab, and if so, what would happen when we approached the gates.

Murr fell asleep almost immediately, his belly full of something. I frowned and got out my journal again.

Here is a crazy idea: What if I have found the Sixth Kenning? Ha ha! No.

But consider: the first and most basic gift of any kenning is that the blessed person becomes invulnerable to that kenning's nature. The lavaborn cannot burn. I do not know what the Brynts call their blessed— the soaked? Anyway, they cannot drown. If the Sixth Kenning is related to animals in the way that the Fifth Kenning is related to plants, would that not mean that the blessed would never be eaten by an animal— the way that I have not been eaten by anything so far, starting with the bloodcats, and then moving on to the wheat dogs I heard, the complete lack of insect bites, snake bites, or any number of other hungry things, like flesh eels, that should have finished me off by now? And might not this single bloodcat's strange and somewhat friendly behavior be explained by the kenning? Murr acts at times as if he understands what I'm saying—what if he does?

Kalaad in the sky, if this is true and I am somehow the first person to discover the Sixth Kenning, what do I call myself? What are my powers? And . . . does Kalaad have anything to do with this? Why me and why now? So many questions and no one to answer them. I will have to experiment.

A strange thing happened when Fintan banished his seeming: everyone seated on the benches below the wall rose to his or her feet and applauded thunderously. The bard had received loud applause before, of course, but I had never seen Brynts behave this way. What had caused them to erupt from their seats so? The possibility that the Sixth Kenning, long rumored to exist, had finally been found? That must be it. Like them, I had to assume it was the truth—why else would Fintan include this hunter's story in his tale? Staggering, really, to hear of such a discovery happening in our time, and so recently. A new kenning with animals—that could only benefit everyone, right?

I wondered how the Nentians who disliked the bard's portrayal of their people would react. Would they finally feel pride in their countryman, or would this enrage them further?

Day 7

A STALK HAWK

Föstyr found me after the bard's tale and pressed some coins into my hand as a stipend. "Come to the palace in the morning for breakfast with your old friend," he said, and then disappeared into the crowd that was streaming off the wall into the city where all the mead and ale was.

I didn't go back to the Randy Goat or any other inn. I spent my stipend on a new bed frame, or rather a used one with a cracked beam on one side that I chose to regard as charming and well loved rather than poorly made or broken. I spent far more finding a new feather down mattress on the principle that used mattresses are an astoundingly bad idea.

I bought a bottle of spiced Kaurian rum in the marketplace two blocks from my house, a few logs for my fireplace even though it would not be so cold that night, and a small chapbook of ribald poetry by a wit from Sturföd who might or might not still be alive. It was not luxury, but it was warm and gave me a glimpse of what my home might grow to be in the future. It was enough.

Pelenaut Röllend was blessedly not dressed in orange for our meeting in the morning but in a palette of varied greens edged in black.

"Let me guess: The Fornish are coming today?"

"No, I just like green," he said. "And I've discovered that avoiding blue and white helps me stand out in the Wellspring. Lots of military in there these days, and I like to give the idea that someone is still concerned about other matters than active warfare."

We talked of trifles until breakfast was served and the longshoremen departed to let us speak privately.

"How did the orange meeting go, then?"

"I think the ambassador got the message. He came with a wrapped gift, saw me all in orange, and then said the gift was for someone else and he'd be sending some prized stock of his own tea to me later."

"Ha! Well done."

"Yes, but lying about that gift was just the beginning of a strange meeting. I asked him about that Bone Giant prisoner they have in their dungeon—Saviič, right? And he claimed to have no knowledge of it. Either Mistral Kira is keeping her own diplomatic corps in the dungeon on this after all this time or the ambassador was lying about that, too."

"Again I'm grateful to not have your job."

The pelenaut snorted. "And how does your job go? What did you learn about the Triune Council?"

"Oh. Yes, I asked Fintan about that. I'd worry about the one named Clodagh."

"Why?"

"He diplomatically chose to say nothing about her, which I think means he had nothing positive to say."

Rölly nodded. "That fits with what we've heard elsewhere."

"Do I get to hear it, too?"

The pelenaut inspected a piece of bacon, didn't appear to like the look of it, but crunched into it anyway. "She's quick to suggest military solutions to problems. She's not been able to do much in that regard because the other councillors keep her in check, but we—I mean the Fornish and the Nentians and everyone else—suspect she's been doing a lot of work in deep waters."

"Eating away at us in the darkness? Look, if you want to know what the Raelechs are up to, isn't there a better way to go about it than having me ask the bard roundabout questions?"

"There is, yes. Föstyr knows someone who specializes in that sort of thing. I needed to know where to point that particular weapon, and all the signs are pointing to Clodagh. But I asked you here for a different reason."

"Oh?"

"This threat on Fintan's life is real. The Nentians are not playing around. You need to be armed from now on."

"Armed?"

"Sword or rapier. Something. Maybe wear some chain underneath your tunic."

"I'm a target now?"

"No, he's still the target. But you're with him for much of the day, and you need to be on guard in case they try something."

"I thought that's what the mariners were for."

"They are. But it's best to be prepared."

"I'm out of practice."

"Get into practice again. Föstyr tells me they are looking for an opportunity, Dervan. You can't be complacent anymore."

Chagrin smeared my face into a wince. "I actually don't have a weapon. Haven't had one since I was discharged from the mariners."

"Easily remedied," Rölly said. "I'll requisition one for you. And *practice*, Dervan. I mean it. In fact, go see Mynstad du Möcher at the armory right after this, get your weapon, and arrange to spar with her. She's excellent with the rapier. Without equal, I suspect. She trains me. She'll do for you."

As I walked up to meet Fintan and his mariner escort outside a nonde-script chowder house, I covered up an uncomfortable burp with my fist, the ghost of breakfast haunting me with memories of thick sauces on eggs. I had spent a few hours practicing after picking up my weapon, but even that exertion had not been enough to banish the meal completely, though it was now lunchtime.

"Ah, that's the belch of a man who ate rich food at the palace this morning," Fintan said.

"You can tell?"

"No, it was just a guess. A good one, apparently. You also look worried. A transfer of the pelenaut's concerns directly to your face. And a transfer of a weapon from the armory to your hip," he said, pointedly staring at my new sword.

"Ah, yes. Being seen next to you is a dangerous thing now."

The interior of the chowder house was poorly lit except for candles in orange glass on the tables, providing pools of light that gave off an air of mystery, an air that Fintan noted with approval.

"I appreciate the atmosphere. A bit spooky, somewhat ominous, makes you wonder if any of this is legal: that's what good chowder is all about."

It made for a terrible work environment, though. We had to ask for extra candles so I could see what I was doing. Once I could see a bit better and the place filled up with locals, I relaxed. The chowder was hot and the beer was cold, and no one bothered us. Fintan determined to give them a good report from atop the wall that afternoon.

When we got there, he prefaced his starting song with a few words. "I have learned this morning that the Fornish force coming here to join our counterattack will be primarily composed of grass-gliders and thornhands." That startled everyone, including me, since I had not heard any such news. "You might not be terribly familiar with either or what they're able to do, but we'll meet some grassglid-ers today in Nel Kit ben Sah's portion of the tale and the thornhands later. In the meantime, I'll share with you a Raelech song about the First Tree."

> *Not blood but sap runs through its limbs,*
> *It has no breath to speak its mind;*
> *Yet if you threaten aught in Forn,*
> *You will very quickly find*
> *The First Tree is the Canopy.*
>
> *By root and stem it speaks to Fornish,*
> *And if they ever feel the need*
> *To Seek more power than they were born with,*
> *They can always choose to feed*
> *The First Tree of the Canopy.*
>
> *Perhaps their blood will water the roots,*
> *Perhaps it will reward their nerve*
> *And bless them with the Fifth Kenning,*
> *So that they'll be bound to serve*
> *The First Tree of the Canopy.*

The song made me shudder. The semisentience and hunger of the First Tree always left me feeling vaguely ill whenever I was reminded of its existence. Unlike the sites of the other kennings, where Seekers simply cast themselves into it, the First Tree *took* people and then *decided* whether to eat them or bless them. To my admittedly small understanding it seemed more monstrous somehow than the impersonal sites of the other kennings. I know the Fornish argument is that Bryn or Reinei or the other gods of the kennings are making decisions on who to bless every much as the First Tree, but somehow the other sites don't inspire the same horror; perhaps because it's not like the wind or water is *eating* the Seekers.

Fintan smiled after the break and held up his first seeming stone. "Let's see what Nel is up to, shall we?"

Nel

The days after making my report to the Canopy were bittersweet. I missed Yar and deeply regretted his death and the others that happened under my command.

Yet amid the pallor of death a column of sunshine speared through the shadow: the prestige of the White Gossamer Clan improved markedly as a result not only of my efforts on behalf of the Canopy but of the demonstrated success of our net launchers against Hathrim houndsmen. It's the nets more than the launchers that made the difference, but our clan now has more orders than they can fill and prosperity is blossoming for us. And my influence in the sway has increased significantly, just as Pak Sey ben Kor feared. But it was not at his expense; he and the Black Jaguars are still very much the broad leaves and drink up most of the sun.

The need for more information required a second trip, and I was tasked by the sway to lead a party of grassgliders over the Godsteeth and secure a thorough scouting report. I was to be the only greensleeve this time, which meant leaving Pak Sey ben Kor behind. That suited me perfectly.

The grassgliders entrusted to my command were a picked squad from several clans and cared nothing for politics—even better. They were professional, in fantastic shape, and a pleasure to work with. They met me at the same stand of sentinel trees our first party had left from, and we followed the same route, slowing down and picking our way very carefully through the pass with the bantil plants; they had grown naturally and spread, feasting on new creatures, and we would need to contain the growth soon but let it remain for now as a line of defense against possible Hathrim invasion. On the other side of the pass we kept high up on the mountainside, where the houndsmen were least likely to patrol among the thick stands of trees, and cut straight west on the edge of the Godsteeth until we saw the ocean.

We paused next to a grand moss pine, the sort that the Hathrim were cutting down, and the eldest of the grassgliders, Ncf Tam ben Wat, pulled pigments out of his pack and began mixing them to match the pine bark. All the other grassgliders retrieved pots of base coat pigment and stripped down to their dark undergarments. They applied the dark base that would serve as shadow and afterward would apply the lighter bark pigments on top. We had camouflage material to mimic silverbarks and all manner of trees in the Canopy but nothing for these pines, so we would have to take the time to use paint. I simply wore a custom black bodysuit and mask because I couldn't smear pigment on my silverbark, and the plan was for me to crouch down in the center of them anyway. The other grassgliders helped one another with their backs, and they were so practiced and quick that we were ready to go in an hour.

"Orient yourself on this tree," I said. "We'll leave our packs here. Hooks and spikes ready?" They nodded like animate wood, reddish brown bark scales painted on their skin and their hair dyed black like mine. I had my miniature crossbow and a few bolts treated with a paralytic developed by the Red Horse Clan. They were famous abroad for their teas and medicinal herbs, but inside Forn they were known for developing poisons.

The grassgliders formed up around me and then employed their kenning, which allowed them to make no noise when they moved on or through plant life. Since I occupied the space between them and benefited from the cone of silence they projected about themselves, I was completely silent, too. And thanks to Nef's expert mixing of pigments and the squad's practice at application, we looked from a distance like a lightning-blasted stump of a grand moss pine as long as we stayed close together.

We moved in complete silence down the mountain. We could still be smelled, still be seen, but could not be heard. Instead, we would hear any Hathrim patrols long before they were in range to see us. No one said a word until we had descended far enough to see the Hathrim encampment through the trees, and it was I who broke the silence.

"May the First Tree shield us," I whispered when I took in the breadth of the Hathrim city. For that is what it was, a city—not a camp of desperate refugees. They had paid the Raelechs to build high walls, and only our vantage point on the mountainside above allowed us to see what they had going on inside them. They might not have grand buildings erected yet, but they had the sites staked out, tiny fires that would be family hearths someday. They had the beginnings of a smithy going if I wasn't mistaken, and a long mead hall. It spoke of extensive planning; no one suffers a surprise eruption of his or her home and lays out a new city like this so quickly without thinking about it long beforehand.

The eruption of Mount Thayil might have been a catastrophe for those who couldn't escape it, but this level of organization made it clear that it was also something for which Gorin Mogen had been waiting.

"We can't have this here. They can ship all their firelords to this point, walk over the pass, and overwhelm us. Stage timber raids on our hardwoods all along the western coast from the safety of their port. No. We can't have it."

It was impossible to tell where Mogen's personal hearth was; no markers of importance or ostentation separated one fire from another. The giants all dressed alike in leathers, but I had heard that you could tell the lavaborn apart from the rest sometimes by the color of the leather; theirs had to be made out of the fireproof hide of lava dragons, which were gray creatures with black heads and a black spiny ridge all the way down to the tips of their tails, sometimes with a swirl of maroon here and there. Some of the giants had different hair colors, but I had no idea what color Mogen's was supposed to be.

They had sown crops outside the walls, so they were definitely going to be staying for months. The walls, though, were undeniable proof that they intended to claim the land as their own. One simply didn't go to the expense or trouble otherwise.

We could ruin their crops without a problem—so could the Raelechs—but they wouldn't be depending on them for sustenance. They had the sea and a glass fleet. They'd trade with other Hathrim cities for all they needed or simply cast nets off the coast, and no one could stop them. The problem of how we would ever get them to leave without a full-scale war of allied forces grew and grew in my mind until I remembered that it wasn't a problem I had to solve. I was meant to defend the Canopy, not besiege a Hathrim city on the plains. Let the strategists worry about that. All I had to do was get them the information they needed to do their jobs.

"Count everything," I said. "We need numbers above all. Look especially for hounds, realizing that some are on patrol, and also see if you can spy any Raelechs milling about; the Triune Council would like to know."

Silence stretched except for the susurrus of the ocean on our left and the sad sounds of chopping wood to our right. There were thousands of Hathrim below. Nearly ten thousand; when we consulted, the grassgliders' figures and mine varied somewhat, but we put their numbers between nine thousand two hundred and nine thousand six hundred. And with Hathrim you almost had to count every single one as a potential military threat. Any giant could kick one of us in the chest and break our rib cage.

They had sixty-five hounds, though some of them were pups as tall as me; a protected well inside the walls; and what looked like an extensive cache of grain and other foodstuffs that they had brought with them. We could see the brown bags of it piled underneath a rudimentary shelter from the rain.

I supposed the key figure beyond their raw population would be to estimate how many lavaborn they had and of what strength. Sparkers and firelords were bad enough, but if they had a fury, we might as well give up now. Mere giants could be overcome, but giants made of fire were another thing entirely.

The number of giants wearing gray or black leathers was far too high, approaching a thousand. There was no way they had that many lavaborn. But that also meant we had no way to tell what we were facing.

Nef spotted the Raelechs because of the new construction. The wall was complete—it extended all the way to the shore and enclosed a vast area, so much that I thought it would be difficult to defend, but then I thought that anything besides the Canopy would be difficult to defend. I supposed that if you had lavaborn able to set attackers on fire, that would make it easier. Or spray oil over the walls and ignite that instead; probably less effort involved.

The Raelechs were constructing siege breaks outside the walls. Deep, wide pits that would have to be spanned, and outside of those pits were shorter walls, perhaps five feet tall. A giant could step over them. And a giant could certainly fire down over them from the top of the city walls—they were building this within bowshot. But attackers would have to climb the wall and then fall into a pit that the Hathrim would no doubt fill with a trencher of flaming oil, all the while dealing with the many different ways the lavaborn could make fire rain down from the sky. The Nentians wouldn't stand a chance without our help and that of other nations. I wondered if other nations would care enough to actually send troops; it wasn't their country being invaded, after all. I knew, however, that we wouldn't hesitate. We could not abide having the lavaborn so close. Already their hearths were blazing with the wood of murdered trees.

"I want to know what those Raelechs are thinking," Nef said. "I'd like to just ask them right now, 'Do you know that you're helping the Hathrim invade Ghurana Nent?' And then, regardless of whether they say yes or no, punch them in their seed pods."

Snickers and snorts from the others: it was what we were all thinking. "Tricking them was probably the cleverest thing he did," I said. "Without those walls they wouldn't be such a threat. You guys have your counts? We should withdraw and get back to the Canopy."

Affirmatives all around, we made our slow, silent way uphill to our cache of clothes. I was mentally congratulating myself on a smooth operation when Nef heard the hounds coming a split second before the rest of us and said, "Houndsmen." Grumbly woofs off to the east, not angry or excited, just conversation. A patrol coming our way. The grassgliders looked to me for direction.

"Up the trees," I whispered. "Quick and silent."

We knew coming in we couldn't outrun the hounds, but we could outclimb them. The grassgliders had brought hooks and spikes for their wrists and ankles. My kenning would let me scale the trunks without aid, and I leapt onto the trunk of the nearest moss pine and began to climb as high as I could to get myself out of sight. I wasn't camouflaged like the grassgliders were and would stick out against the bark. Disappearing into the branches above was my best bet.

Unfortunately, outside the kenning of my companions—unavoidable in this case—I made some noise. The grassgliders rose up the trunks without a sound, visibly jamming hooks and spikes into the bark that should have sounded like chopping, but only my soft scrabbling could be heard, and it attracted the hounds. Their barks grew urgent, inquisitive, and the houndsmen riding them sounded annoyed. They probably thought their hounds had heard a squirrel or something.

I suppose I did qualify as something.

There were two houndsmen, a small patrol, and their hounds snuffled at the ground beneath my tree and the others nearby that the grassgliders had climbed. I could not see my companions at all; they had gone still and blended in perfectly with the bark of the moss pines.

I, too, had gone still, since any movement could be heard and would draw their gazes upward. I did not blend with the bark, though; I was a black blob on the tree with odd gray patches where my silverbark limbs stood out.

The Hathrim riders groused at each other as their hounds inhaled our scents. One of them kept heading uphill, following the path to our cache, and that gave me an idea—if we could get out of these trees. I was counting on the riders to eventually get impatient and pull the hounds away, but a cone fell out of the tree I was clinging to and plopped to the ground behind the closest one. He turned, located the cone, and looked up. And that was when he saw me and shouted at his companion. Within a few seconds I had both houndsmen pointing up at me and shouting. If they wanted me to climb down and be eaten, they had unrealistic expectations regarding my obedience.

It could have been worse: they had axes but no bows, and neither one appeared to be lavaborn. I guessed the latter since I had not already combusted.

But it wasn't long until one of them yanked his mount downhill toward the city, presumably to get either a bow or one of the lavaborn to smoke me out of the tree. I had a very short window in which to attempt an escape.

And this was why the grassgliders needed a greensleeve to lead them. If I could save them by sacrificing myself, I would. The houndsmen would conclude that I had drawn the hounds and eventually would move off. The grassgliders could wait in silence, camouflaged, and return to Forn without me. The Canopy would be served, and Gorin Mogen would surely be foiled. A worthy trade for my life.

This grand moss pine was not of the Canopy, but it was of Teldwen, and through my kenning I could speak to it and through it. Indeed, I could *act* through it if I was willing, and I was very willing.

Closing my eyes and sending shoots from my silverbark to merge with the soft woody flesh of the pine, I felt its strength and reach in the earth and its stolid contentment with the sun and the rain here, the birds that built nests in its branches, and the wild hogs that foraged nearby and fertilized its base every so often. I showed it the hound standing at its base, convinced it that it must be destroyed, and triggered the fusing of my impatient mind with its branching patience, catalyzing the channeling of Teldwen's energy through the earth. It moved up the tree, into me, where it was infused with purpose, and then back into the tree, directed now to spur accelerated growth and then—

—*my strong roots burst through the ground, wrapping around limbs and pulling down, down, until bones snapped and a creature cried out, but still I pulled until its limbs tore free and I took my prizes with me into the earth. Another creature landed on the ground, only two legs this time, but they must*

*be taken also. More roots erupt and seek to twine about those limbs, but they
are hacked and bitten by a blade, hateful axe hewing my flesh and spilling sap.
Bigger roots, then, and more of them, reaching higher: Wrap its limbs, trap
the axe, pull all of it down into the earth, where it will be still and silent and
feed me its nutrients for seasons to come. Yes! Yes, hush, be quiet now; it's over.*

With some effort, I opened my eyes and broke the link with the
grand moss pine, realizing that I was being kept aloft by nothing but
the shoots from my silverbark embedded in the tree. Panicking, I
lunged forward and grabbed on to the tree, then felt the ache all over
and the weakness in my muscles. Melding my consciousness with that
tree had drained me significantly. Looking down, however, I saw that it
had bought us the opportunity we needed: The hound's huge limbless
body lay still below me, and its rider was nowhere to be seen, though
the earth around the trunk was freshly turned.

"Grassgliders, move out!" I called. "We have to go before reinforcements arrive!"

My progress was slow and jerky, and I cared nothing for whatever
sound I might make climbing down. I just wanted to make it to the
ground without falling on it. I was breathing heavily by the time I got
there, and my knees were shaky. The grassgliders were all waiting for
me near the corpse of the hound.

"Ben Sah, that was incredible—hey. Are you all right?" Nef said.
"You look ill."

"I'm not ill," I said. "Just older." He was probably three or four years
my senior, but I would not have been surprised if I looked like his elder
now.

"Oh."

"Don't let the price I paid be in vain," I said. "Let's go, back to the
cache, quickly!" I pointed uphill. "Move!"

I huffed behind them, barely able to keep pace but unashamed to
strain. If we did not strain now, we might not survive.

When we arrived at our cache, I told them to just pick up their stuff
and keep running. "No time to dress! Run back along the same way
that we came in!"

I trailed behind them as we ran east along the Godsteeth, treacherous footing preventing us from moving much faster than a jog. It would be a troublesome pursuit for the Hathrim as the trees grew close together, but they would still move more quickly than we could and catch up to us long before we made it back to the pass.

But only if we remained on the same track. Keeping my eyes half on the trail and half in the branches above us, I waited until I spied a likely looking stand of pines and cedars stretching uphill.

"Stop here," I said, and they did and turned to me, wondering if I had given up. I took a few moments to catch my breath and explained. "They will track us via scent. We have established a trail already coming in from the pass. We need to let them think that we stayed on that trail so that they will keep going. But we will not stay on that trail. We are going higher into the Godsteeth, and we will lose them on the Leaf Road." I pointed up at the mixed canopy above us, which currently had nothing like a Leaf Road.

Their eyes drifted up, confirmed that it was just a random tangle of wood and needles, and then dropped back to me, no doubt wondering if I had succumbed to dementia.

"Ben Sah, your pardon, but I don't see a Leaf Road."

"Of course not. I haven't made it yet."

I had them jog a bit farther along the trail to strengthen the scent, and then they came back to the tree I had chosen and climbed first. They ascended after me with hook and spike on the side opposite the trail so that their passage might go unnoticed by houndsmen passing by. They leapt as far off the trail as possible first in an effort to leave no trace.

Once again, I sent my shoots into the bark of a grand moss pine, but this time my efforts were not quite so demanding or taxing. I was strengthening and shaping what was already there, and communicating through roots, I coordinated with neighboring trees to form a narrow wooden bridge of branches between our tree and the next.

"Stealthily we go," I whispered as the distant bark of hounds could be heard now, and the grassgliders engaged their kenning and we tiptoed across a narrow bridge, single file, from tree to tree. The grass-glider in front of me and the one behind kept my noise to a minimum, and all the while I kept speaking to the trees through my silverbark so that a walkway formed in front of us and then the branches returned to their normal state after we had passed. In this way we walked uphill, yet above the hill, until we could go no higher: the trees stopped grow-ing, and the bald, ever-snowy peaks of the Godsteeth rose above us, stark crags that might be passed but not without equipment that we didn't have. As it was, we were very cold and would have to spend a night in it.

But the stratagem had worked. The barking of hounds never grew closer than distant, and they couldn't follow our scent in the trees or even know where we had gone since we left no visible trail in the can-opy. By the time we reached the tree line, it was near dusk and we were all exhausted. I found a place where four trees grew close together and asked them to form a platform of branches for us to rest on. We were only twelve feet off the ground and a houndsman could still reach us there, but I figured it wouldn't matter—they'd never find us. The grass-gliders dressed, pulling layers over their painted bodies. Since we had only enough water to drink, we ate dry rations, and as the sunlight faded, I caught a couple of uncertain glances in my direction as the grassgliders started to think about sleeping arrangements. We were all shivering and would need to huddle together for warmth, but the sil-verbark on my legs meant I couldn't have anyone in front of me lest I damage the mushrooms on my legs. It would be best for me to settle the question before it could be asked, and there was no question in my mind who I wanted at my back: Nef.

He was efficient and skilled and possessed a calm charisma, and no, it didn't hurt at all that I'd met few men as handsome. Dark hair and deep brown eyes and a pleasant curve to his lips. Once night fell, there was little else for us to do at that elevation except survive it, so I pulled a blanket out of my pack and motioned to Nef to grab his.

As I lay on my side, knees drawn up, Nef draped an arm around my belly after asking if it was okay and I laid my arm on top of his. He smelled of cedar and sweat and fit me like the hammock at home. I was so exhausted that I fell asleep after only a few minutes, but I woke an unknown time later with a start, having dreamt I was the houndsman pulled underground by pine roots and torn apart so that my blood would feed the tree.

"What? What is it?" Nef said, keeping his voice low, half rising in the chill to match me, propped up on an elbow. My breath fogged in front of me, pale gasping clouds in the starlight.

"Nothing. Well, not nothing—a nightmare. Probably . . ." I sighed. "Probably the first of many."

I hoped I hadn't woken the others. I lay back down and snuggled up against Nef, placing his arm and mine back where they were. He was warm and safe, and a pleasant weariness returned until I drifted off, only to wake again when images of bantil blossoms eating my face made me cry out.

These were ridiculous nightmares: plant life would never behave that way toward me. But I supposed I must carry these images of death within me now that I had caused the death of others. Nef understood and did not even seem annoyed when I woke for the third time.

"I cannot sleep anymore tonight," I whispered to him. "Would it be okay if we talked? Perhaps you can project your silence around us and we won't disturb the others."

"Of course." The sound of the night muted somewhat as he employed his kenning.

"Do you ever have nightmares?" I asked him, still keeping my voice low but no longer bothering to whisper.

"Yes. Mostly about me thinking I'm being quiet but everyone can hear me. Like when—well. Promise you won't tell?"

"I promise."

"I cannot stand the thought of anyone hearing me relieve myself, so I use my kenning whenever I do. And my nightmares are about people hearing me anyway and making comments."

For some reason that started me laughing, and then, to my horror, I couldn't stop. Fortunately, Nef found it funny, too—or perhaps just the sound of me laughing was funny to him—and soon we were both carrying on until our stomachs hurt. It was far better than crying.

Feeling grateful and warm and affectionate and too late to stop myself, I realized that I had caressed the back of his hand with my fingers, an undeniable signal that he couldn't have missed. I let my fingers go slack and forced myself to relax instead of tense up and said, "Tell me about your clan. You're from the Brown Marmosets, right?"

I doubted my obvious distraction would make him forget what I had done, but I hoped he wouldn't return the gesture. Except for the part of me that did. What if he felt nothing like that for me?

He told me about his uncle Vin Tai ben Dar, the greensleeve who took him to his Seeking as a youth, who defended a stretch of the southern coast, and who never lost a single tree to timber pirates for ten years despite their many attempts. He also had a cousin who was an herb culturist, but few others were blessed. Most of his family, and indeed his clan, handled sanctioned timber exports to Hathrir. We traded stories like that until the dawn, and then, reluctantly, we disentangled and let the cold air come between us.

Despite the lack of sleep, I felt better when I rose if a little stiff in the knees. I frowned down at them, dismayed by their betrayal. I asked Nef for an honest assessment. "Tell me in the sun, leave nothing in shadow: How many seasons are written on my face?"

"It's not bad, ben Sah," he said, examining my face closely. "There are some new fine lines near the corners of your eyes. Perhaps some heaviness underneath them. But that could be exhaustion as much as anything. You are still very—"

He blinked and stopped abruptly, and I quirked an eyebrow at him. "Still very *what*?"

Nef looked away to hide a grin, failed miserably at it, then looked down. "Still very much in charge of this mission, ben Sah."

I had to laugh. "Yes. Very much. An excellent reminder. Thank you, ben Wat. To be continued, perhaps, when we return to the Canopy under less formal circumstances."

"May the sun shine on the opportunity."

He was being kind; he had that sort of face. I had to squash the impulse to kiss him, for he was right: it would be inappropriate during a mission while he was temporarily under my command.

Once everyone had risen, I thanked the trees for their comfort and shelter and allowed them to return to their accustomed form, and we descended to the ground. I allowed myself a private smile. We had scouted the Hathrim successfully and lost nothing this time except some ill-defined measure of my life span. But perhaps something new had taken root between me and Nef. Time and sun would tell if anything would grow out of it.

"To the north of the Godsteeth," Fintan said, "Abhinava Khose also had the opportunity to form a new bond."

It has been a day of incredible discoveries. First came the realization that all of my bloodcat bites were completely healed, the torn muscles repaired; even the skin was unblemished by scars or scabs. All had healed while I slept. The scratches I'd suffered from the grass puma were likewise healed. I should have had weeks of discomfort ahead of me with injuries like those, but instead it was as if they had never happened.

No: it's much better than that. I feel better than I ever have. Stronger, faster, more alert. I feel like my senses have improved. And though I cannot confirm it yet, I suspect that I have nothing to fear on the Nentian plains anymore but other humans.

My first order of business upon waking—after stretching and such—

was to ask Murr if he could understand me. He just rolled over, presenting his belly.

"Are you asking for a belly rub?" I said. He pawed at the air and said, "Murr," which was cute but inconclusive. I didn't move because if I was wrong about that, Murr might become annoyed with me. Even if I was immune to harm from animals now, I didn't want to offend him.

"If you can understand me, we need to establish a way for you to signal yes and no. That would help immensely. So let's start with that. Can you nod your head or bob it up and down to say yes?" I began nodding to demonstrate. "Like this?"

Murr righted himself, locked his red eyes on mine, and executed an awkward nod—more of a tossing of his chin than a human movement, but still, it was evidence that he understood me. Or perhaps he was just mimicking me.

"That's excellent. So let's say you wish to say no to something. Can you shake your head from side to side, like this, to say no?" I demonstrated again, and Murr watched me for a moment, then copied the movement.

I grinned at him. "Fantastic, Murr! Now, let me ask you that other question again and you answer, yes or no. Do you want a belly rub?"

The bloodcat stared at me for a few beats, then shook his head.

"No? I'm very glad I confirmed that, then. That could have been extremely awkward."

Murr performed his catlike nod.

"Do you know if I can talk to all animals, or are you special?"

He shook his head, and I realized I hadn't phrased the question very well. Did he simply not know the answer, or did he mean I couldn't talk to any other animals? I would have to be more careful with my word choice.

"Can you say anything else besides 'murr'?" At his nod, I asked him, "What else can you say?"

"Murr," he said.

"That sounded the same to me. Are you saying different things, perhaps, but my human ears can't understand the difference?"

He nodded again, and I thought that was interesting. It appeared that the kenning granted me the power to communicate clearly to animals—or at least bloodcats—but not the other way around. It required testing.

"I need to keep walking toward Khul Bashab. I'll eat something as I go. Still coming with me?" Murr got to his feet by way of answering and took a few steps north before stopping to check if I was moving yet.

"Guess you're anxious to go! Okay. Same as before: hunt when you feel like it and find me when you want. Let me make sure this fire is out and get my bag."

We covered a lot of ground that morning; I even jogged for a while since it felt so effortless. I asked Murr only one question before lunch: "Am I the first human to be able to do this—I mean talk to you and not get eaten and all that?"

He nodded, and that gave me plenty to think about. The histories that I'd heard never went into much detail on the lives of the first people to discover the other five kennings except that they had all been discovered by accident by someone ready to die—suicidal, in other words, as I had been.

Their discoveries had necessarily changed their cultures forever. And they had all lived very short lives because of a combination of circumstances. Too many people wanted them dead because of the change they represented, and they were forced to spend so much energy defending themselves that they aged a lifetime in a few months. If I was going to learn from their mistakes and avoid a similar fate, I needed to be smart about this. I stopped running for a moment when I realized that I no longer wished to die.

Looking up at the sky, I asked the silence, "What do you have planned for me, Kalaad? Is this part of a plan at all, or are you just watching an accident unfold?"

No answer, of course. I would have to continue and look back at this moment sometime in the future, assigning meaning when I had the benefit of a window to the past.

I didn't know how to use my powers yet or even what they were beyond the passive benefits that I had to admit were glorious. To walk anywhere in the plains, unafraid of predators? That's a dream practically every Nentian shared, and the wonder of it made me smile. In fact, much of the prestige of hunting families like mine came from the fact that we walked the plains and faced those predators and wore khernhide boots that only the wealthiest could afford. Any prestige I might earn because of this kenning, though, came at the cost of my family's lives. I would not have been in that nughobe grove otherwise.

That put a spear through my smile. I'd gladly give up this sense of physical well-being to have them back. I resumed my northward march, and it was some time and distance before I returned to thoughts of how to proceed.

The immediate conflict I saw was a religious one. The cultures of the other five kennings have the old gods, sons and daughters of Teldwen, to guide them in the use of their powers and order their societies. Thurik the lavaborn was first; Reinei was the wind, the peaceful counter to his brother's flame yet sometimes the goad; the triple goddesses of Rael were born of earth; and Bryn of the sea. We Nentians have Kalaad in the sky, lover of Teldwen and father of the gods, but he is not especially concerned with the Sixth Kenning or with watching over animals. What shall I do, then? Go up to the gates of Khul Bashab with Murr by my side and laugh, shouting, "Ha! That Kalaad business was a pile of yak shit all along"? That would get me feathered with arrows in no time. And it is not what I feel; I just sent my family to Kalaad in the sky, and I know they are at peace there. But there will be questions of my faith when I lay claim to the Sixth Kenning. People will question priests about what my appearance might mean, priests will question me, and I could just as easily be branded as unholy as a gift from Kalaad if I wasn't careful.

The Fornish are different; they worship no god but rather the source of the Fifth Kenning at Selt, which they call the First Tree. They do protect their Canopy with religious zeal, though. I don't think that's a path I should try to walk. I do not think I can (or should even try to) persuade people to worship a pack of bloodcats in the southern plains.

The government of Ghurana Nent will probably despise me as well. Or at least seek to control me. "Look," they will say, "we can't have you controlling animals unless it's for our benefit." I remember asking Father why the blessed simply don't run everything with all their powers.

"Because, Abhi," he said, "to seek a kenning you have to be willing to gamble with your own life. And if someone is willing to throw away their own life, then they won't hesitate to throw away others. Who would want to follow that kind of leader?"

I couldn't argue with that. But I wasn't gambling when I ran into the nughobe grove, was I? I was simply grief-stricken. That might be a meaningless distinction to most people; I don't know. But I think Father might have been generalizing there.

Outside of Ghurana Nent, the blessed *do* sometimes rule. Quite often, in fact. Never in Rael, but in Brynlön and Kauria they elect blessed rulers from time to time; I think their current leaders happen to be blessed. The Hathrim *say* that anyone can be a Hearthfire of one of their cities, but they haven't elected anyone who wasn't lavaborn for centuries.

It is a giddy, drunken thought to think of myself ruling a city or even a country. I am sure everyone would think I am too young, and they would be right. I am not wise enough to rule. I am a son who got his family killed because he never had the courage to speak up about his selfish desires until his family was in danger. But I do think life in Ghurana Nent could and should be better for its people. I don't have to be old and wise to recognize that.

That reminds me: the king has a whole wagon full of stupid policies that he says are "for our protection" since we are a country without a kenning. Will he simply abolish them once we *do* have a kenning? Or would he instead rather keep those policies and see if maybe he could make this kenning disappear by making *me* disappear? After my death he would say, "What? That Khose boy? He wasn't blessed. He was insane. There's no Sixth Kenning here."

The viceroy of Khul Bashab might think along similar lines. If I want to make sure I can't simply disappear, I need as many people as possible to know about the Sixth Kenning before the viceroy does. A very public demonstration would need to be made.

I didn't stop but did slow down to eat a lunch of vegetables at a walk. Murr slinked off through the grasses in search of his own meal, and I used his absence to experiment.

If my blessing followed the pattern of others, I would have the strongest powers possible and would take a title in keeping with it. The lavaborn have furies who can become fire and burn anything, the Kaurians have tempests who become the wind, the Raelechs have their juggernauts, the Fornish have greensleeves, and the Brynts have tidal mariners. And when they use the full power of their kenning, it ages them perceptibly. I am still as young as ever I was, I think, though I have no looking glass to see my face. My hands and skin still seem young, and my back is straight and strong. So I have yet to discover what I can do.

The Fornish are sometimes called Tree Speakers for their root and stem communication. I can sort of speak to Murr, but it's not the same thing as what the Fornish are doing at all. And calling myself a Beast Speaker sounds . . . gross.

Beast Caller, perhaps?

Wondering if I could, in fact, call a beast, I attempted to do so. I surveyed the plains around me, stretching unbroken to the horizon, and saw nothing nearby. Any animals that might be within my sight were keeping out of it under the tops of the grasses. It was universal camouflage available to all.

Picturing a bluetip prairie pheasant in my mind and feeling somewhat foolish, I said aloud, "Are there any bluetips nearby? If there are, please come to say hello. I mean you no harm. I merely wish to greet you."

Bluetips were notoriously difficult to scare up. They knew how well the grass concealed them and would fly only at the approach of four-footed predators. All swishes in the grass sounded alike, but they flushed at the sound of paws in the dirt. We'd have to practically step on them before they broke cover for us, and it was always accidental. That's why someone always had a bow ready when we hunted; you never knew when a bluetip would take to the sky.

Too late, I remembered why they didn't take to the sky if they could help it; there were also stalk hawks hiding in the grass, waiting for bluetips or other birds to reveal their whereabouts. Three bluetips erupted out of the grass to my left and banked in my direction, and before they had flown ten lengths, a stalk hawk shot out of the grass below them and took one of them down.

"Oh, no!" I gasped, recognizing that my request had exposed them to danger. I might have meant the bluetips no harm, but almost everything else in the plains did. Perhaps I could have protected it had I thought ahead. Would a shepherd with this kenning be able to protect his flock from predators, never lose a sheep, that kind of thing?

I held out my arms to either side, inviting the remaining bluetips to perch there if they wished. They did, but they looked nervous about it and minced awkwardly on my forearms, trying not to dig into my skin with their talons. They were right; it was a terrible idea.

"Go and be safe in the grass," I told them. "Thank you for saying hello."

They chirped, hopped into the grass near my feet, and waddled away. A grin spread across my face until I recalled that there should have been three of them walking around. My family should still be walking around, too. My primary talent so far was not thinking through the possible consequences of my actions. Even when I tried to think ahead, events never turned out the way I thought they would.

Perhaps calling something smaller would be better. Could I call insects? "Are there any bugs nearby?" I asked. I knew that there were, of course; I'd seen a few zipping around here and there. But after I made that general query, a dense cloud of buzzing, thrumming insects rose all around me, blocking out the sun. "Ahh! Silly question! Never mind! As you were!" The swarm of assorted flying creatures dropped back into the grasses to eat and be eaten, and I shuddered even though it wasn't cold. If the smaller creatures of the world ever organized to wipe out the larger ones, they would most definitely win.

It would be useful to know what kind of animals there were in an area—and how many—without calling them individually with a demand to show themselves. Far less annoying to the animals as well. But did I possess that ability? If so, how would I access it? The information wasn't readily available in my consciousness. I had to *do* something.

My thoughts before had focused on specific animals. What if instead I focused on an area?

I visualized myself in the middle of an area a hundred lengths square, focused my thoughts, and wondered how many creatures of any kind might exist in that space. My reward was an instant, staggering headache that made me clutch my head.

"Ahh. Okay, too much," I said aloud. The sheer number of insects in such an area would be too many to count. I tried again: a smaller area, only fifty lengths square, and a query about mammals only. The images came quickly and were blessedly pain-free: A family of prairie voles to my right. Barley shrews behind me to my left. Ahead on my left, a ratcatcher sniffing out the voles but waiting for me to pass by. Nothing else.

I tried birds in the same area next. The bluetips and the stalk hawk were there, but also a pair of gharel hens bedded down for the day off to my right and about twenty tiny fly fishers that would flock at night, skimming the grass tips for insects. I repeated the process for snakes and lizards, then spiders, and didn't ask about insects again.

There was so much hidden on the plains that I could uncover now. Of great use to me would be discovering a source of water: these animals must be drinking something.

Focusing on the stalk hawk, which was still filling its belly on the bluetip, I asked it, "Where can I find water near here?" It screeched at me, annoyed at being interrupted, but they were fast eaters and I imagined it had eaten quite enough already. "Please show me where," I said. Another screech, and the stalk hawk took wing, circled around me once, and flew to the northwest. I began to jog in that direction, and it wasn't long before the stalk hawk swooped and climbed and swooped again at a point ahead of me. I saw nothing special there until I fell into a small pond that had been completely hidden by the tops of the grasses. It was not huge—the size of my bedroom at home—but it held plenty of water that I could boil to remove any plagues that might be living in it.

I smiled and thanked the stalk hawk. My water problem was solved, and I probably had enough dry food to last to Khul Bashab. Nothing would eat me on the way there. I would live!

Until I got there, I supposed. Then what? How would I announce to the city—and thus the world—that I had discovered the Sixth Kenning? How would I do it without immediately placing myself in jeopardy? And when they asked me what underneath the sky possessed me to wander unarmed into a nughobe grove in the first place, what would I tell them about my family?

I didn't get a chance to think about it right then since the stalk hawk flew tight circles about my head and screeched.

"What? You're free to go if you wish," I said. "I'm grateful to you." I waited a few moments to see if he would react, but his behavior continued. "Would you like to stay with me?" I asked. "I am going to fill some empty water skins, and then I'll keep walking. You can wait for me there if you like," I said, pointing to the nearest lip of the pond.

The stalk hawk screeched once more and spiraled down to settle on the edge of the pond. He—she?—was a beautiful creature, tall legs for walking in the grass and her feathers all wheat colored, so that if you did not see the black eyes floating above the ground or the sharp yellow beak, you would have difficulty seeing her in the grass for most of the year. There were green-colored birds who took advantage of the spring and summer camouflage, but I had always preferred the coloration and build of stalk hawks, graceful both on land and in the air.

Drawing out an empty water skin, I continued to speak to her as I filled it. "I'll assume you're female until you tell me otherwise. What's your name?"

She didn't screech this time, merely made a short, high-pitched declaration: "Eep."

"Pleasure to meet you, Eep. I'm Abhi."

I taught her to nod and shake her head for yes and no, though she didn't have the same muscles and couldn't really shake her head. Instead she had to rotate it or twist it, which was disconcerting to watch but a clear difference from a nod.

"I'm going to a human city a couple of days' walk to the north. If you'd like to join me, you are welcome. I should warn you that there's a bloodcat who's been tagging along. He's not here right now, but he might show up later. I'll make sure he doesn't bother you, though. Want to come along for a while?"

She nodded, and I grinned. I made friends much faster out here than I did among humans.

My empty skins filled, I sloshed out of the hidden pond and took my bearings. I'd left the wake of the kherns that had killed my family since they had veered west; I was traveling across trackless grass now, but I couldn't get too lost. If I simply kept heading north, I would eventually run into the wide Banighel River, and Khul Bashab was situated on its bank.

Eep sometimes walked through the grass with me and sometimes flew. Murr rejoined me in midafternoon while she happened to be airborne, and she screeched at his appearance.

"Hello, Murr. I've made a new friend. I want you to be friends, too. Murr, meet Eep. Please don't eat her. Eep, this is Murr. He won't eat you. Right, Murr?"

The bloodcat tossed its chin upward. "Excellent. You see, Eep? We can travel together in peace."

The stalk hawk screeched once more: She was doubtful. But soon she spiraled down on my left, keeping me between her and Murr, and walked along, her head twisted to watch him. He watched her. And eventually they faced forward and ignored each other. With sunset perhaps an hour away, I mentioned to both of them that I would need to make camp soon. I had water to boil and needed a fire, and for that I needed wood.

"Eep, would you mind looking for some shrubs or trees that I might use for a campsite and then direct me there if you find some? If we're lucky we can find something to make a perch for you also. Then you can rest above the grass and see well."

She took wing, circled above us once, then flew northeast. I turned that way, and after about ten minutes she returned, calling down to me that she had found something. She banked and flew over my head in a straight line to point the way, and I picked up my pace. The sun was sinking, and our shadows stretched out for lengths on the grass.

Soon I saw what she had found: a nughobe grove, smaller than the one in which I found Murr but with plenty of dead branches for my fire and a broad, shallow stream that I thought I recognized by the color of the bed; the mud was reddish. We had forded a red muddy streambed near the end of our first day out from Khul Bashab. If this was the same one, then I was getting close. I didn't remember seeing this nughobe grove, however, so if it was in fact the same stream, I was significantly up- or downstream from where my family had crossed it; the amount of water here attested to that as well. I must have wandered significantly off true north somehow. That meant Khul Bashab was either northwest or northeast of me. When I reached the Banighel River, I would have to decide which way to turn.

But the stream water was cleaner than the pond water, and Murr sounded pleased that he would have a nughobe tree to sleep in that night. I let him pick a tree and then made my fire nearby, dumping out the pond water, boiling plenty of stream water, and refilling all my skins before getting out my journal and setting some beans and potatoes in the pot.

My basic needs are met for today. But I still don't know what I will do when I get to Khul Bashab. I worry about my ability to make plans since my last one wound up getting my family killed and I'm clearly not good at anticipating consequences. I'm afraid that Murr and Eep might suffer for accompanying me. I'm not sure that I'll ever be as safe again as I am right now.

"More Abhi tomorrow! And more of everyone's favorite Nentian viceroy as well." The bard got some wry chuckles out of that, but he was goading the Nentians. He might have a poorly developed instinct for self-preservation.

Day 8

PLAGUEBRINGER

I slept hardly at all because I was so nervous about my first lesson or sparring session or whatever my training was to be called with Mynstad du Möcher. When I had met her the previous day to acquire my requisitioned rapier and mail shirt, I was surprised by her beauty and I think my mouth might have dropped open. One does not expect, in a storehouse of tools for causing violent death, to find a face that makes one want to live.

She saw my reaction, which inspired a scowl, and then I felt like an idiot. My first thought was that she must have to fight men off, and then I realized immediately that she not only could but had. She would not be personally training Rölly in warfare otherwise.

She was taller than me. Long arms and fingers. Narrow waist, muscular thighs, a physically intimidating person even without a weapon in her hand. She had grown her hair out and gathered it in back with a tie, confident that no one would ever get close enough to grab it. Her complexion was darker than mine, dark enough to be Kaurian, but if that was her heritage, she clearly did not hold with their pacifist theology.

She barely spoke to me and avoided eye contact when I presented Pelenaut Röllend's requisition along with his request that she assess and train me to standard. She must have thought that I would try to flirt with her after my embarrassing display of surprise. She snatched the paper from my hand, read it, and then turned into the armory, expecting me to follow. She pulled out a rapier and a mail shirt from storage, thrust them at me, and then said only, "Be here at 0800 tomorrow for assessment, sir. I have much to do before then. Excuse me."

The Mynstad pivoted on her heel and left me there, clutching a mail shirt and awkwardly holding a rapier and its carriage. "Oh," I said, and then, realizing that was inadequate, added, "I'll see you then!" She made no answer but kept walking out of sight around a corner of shelved cuirasses, her boots making crisp claps on the stone floor. I sighed and shook my head; I hadn't felt so inept since my school days. I spent some time in the morning working off my embarrassment with old forms before meeting Fintan at the chowder house, and after arriving home subsequent to Fintan's evening tales, I spent more time in my bare parlor practicing. I took the forms slowly and thought I remembered the dance at least, but I felt sure my technique was rusty, not to mention my speed. My knee injury would prevent me executing the necessary footwork for some moves.

After a long time staring into darkness from my bed, I must have caught a bare hour or so of sleep before waking up to the same impenetrable gloom and mincing gingerly across the floor to light a candle by touch alone. I dropped the box of matches and gave them a good cursing. Once I finally got some light going, I practiced again until dawn. A light breakfast of fish and rice and then a limping march to the armory for me, determined to make a decent second impression since the first had been so awful.

I nodded at Mynstad du Möcher when I arrived, keeping my mouth closed. She waited for me to say something, and when I failed to say or do anything damning, she returned the nod.

"Welcome, Master du Alöbar. Please follow me to the courtyard in back."

I remembered the courtyard from my early days of service. On the other side of it was the training barracks for new recruits, which meant it was nearly always hosting exercises of one kind or another during daylight hours, and one could count on always having an audience of judging eyes.

"Did you ever serve in the military?" the Mynstad asked once we emerged into sunlight on cobbled stones.

"I did. Under Pelenaut Hönig."

"I see. Did you earn that limp in his service?"

I winced. "I was hoping you wouldn't notice that. But yes."

She faced me and for the first time looked interested in my existence. "Mind telling me how if it's not painful to recall?"

"Not at all. Time has weathered away the sharp edge of the pain. I was stationed in Grynek, manning the wall during a night watch. There was a trading wagon approaching the gate on the eastern side—carpet merchants. A pretty safe trade: nobody gets really excited about robbing them because they're bloody awkward to haul around without the wagon and bandits don't like wagons; carpets just aren't products you can turn into easy money."

She gestured with her hand to indicate that I should speed forward. I was babbling.

"Right. Well, it was a family, you see. Young children with adults. But they were happy at seeing the lights on the walls and were singing quite loudly about the good times they'd have in town. It drew the attention of a hungry gravemaw on the other side of the river."

"No," the Mynstad said, already horrified.

I nodded. "It crossed the river, mostly in a single massive leap across the deep channel, and then it walked out the rest of the way. I called for help, and everyone within hearing rushed down and out the gate to defend the family, pikes in hand. We shouted at them to run, leave the wagon behind, but the distance was too great and the gravemaw too fast. Bryn save me, the teeth—it was . . . well. It ate them. The kids first. The parents followed. And that's when we got there with our pikes—only five of us."

"It had to be hard to see."

"Yes, but it was a full moon that night and cloudless. Torches from the wagon might have helped. The gravemaw was thinking about maybe eating one of the horses and was not truly worried about us. It was attracted to their fear and their neighing while we were simply running toward it. But it was taking its time, snaking that massive tongue across them, tasting them, I suppose. The huge mouth was open, in other words. I was first, and I had a shot at a killing blow—right through the upper palate and into the brain, past all that natural armor, and it wouldn't be hunting along our riverbanks again. I was focused, I was ready, I envisioned what I wanted, and none of it mattered because one of the horses knocked me over in its fear just as I was about to strike. I tumbled, rolled with the hit, ready to regain my feet and try again, except that the gravemaw had spotted me, a nice delicious human, easier to eat in one go than a horse, and its tongue whipped out and wrapped around my right leg at the knee. It yanked me into the air that way, above its head, where I could fall into its mouth, and I felt the tissues around my knee tear right then. They never healed right, and I've limped ever since."

Mynstad du Möcher gaped. "But how are you alive?"

"Oh! My fellows saved me. The gravemaw opened wide for his dessert, and they had been right behind me. They took the opportunity to ram their pikes up into his brain through the upper palate, and I fell to the ground next to it. Broke a bone in my forearm coming down, but that healed properly."

"So it's true what they say about their natural armor? Impenetrable, so you have to kill them from the inside?"

"Absolutely true. And it's why they don't run from anything, since they're so hard to kill."

"That was good service."

I snorted. "Hardly. I couldn't save anyone, didn't kill the gravemaw, and I got injured. In fact, I got dismissed as soon as I could walk again."

"That was a poor decision by your superiors, if I may say so. You saw the danger. You called the alarm. You charged in first. That deserved commendation. Battles rarely work out the way we wish them to, so it is quick thinking and good judgment that matter outside of physical prowess. What was your rank?"

"I was a Mynstad, like you."

Mynstad du Möcher straightened and gave me the veteran's salute. "Since it seems no one has bothered to thank you for your actions, let me thank you now, years too late and far, far away."

I smiled. "That's very kind."

She flashed a grin at me, a brilliant, dazzling thing. "The only kindness you'll get from me, I'm afraid. Because now I must assess your physical prowess, Mynstad."

"I stopped using my military rank long ago. You can call me Dervan."

"Very well, Dervan. Let us review the basic forms. Side by side, we will step through them."

It was so very fine at first. My fervent practice allowed me to look respectable until it was time to lunge. I couldn't fake that or go halfway, and my knee buckled under the strain. I collapsed but didn't cry out.

"Master Dervan! Are you all right?"

"Eghh. Embarrassed but not hurt. That's a resounding *no* from my knee concerning lunges."

"Is there any pain?"

"Not much. But not much strength, either." She extended a hand, and I grabbed it, allowing her to pull me upright again.

"It's an interesting challenge," she said. "With that lack of mobility you will be hard pressed. Let us see what we can do."

We worked on upper body moves only, quick parries and thrusts or slashes to end the fight as quickly as possible. Mynstad du Möcher dismissed me after a couple of hours, enjoining me to return for additional practice for an hour whenever I had the time. I saluted her and thanked her for her time and pivoted smartly on my good leg to go meet Fintan. I was exhausted and my hand throbbed with forming blisters, but I didn't care. At least I wasn't an utter failure.

Some hours later, our work finished and energized by a mediocre lunch not worth remembering, Fintan took to the wall and greeted his audience with a strum of his harp.

"Today we'll hear all about events in the west. But first, at risk of putting you to sleep, a Hathrim lullaby—specifically one from Harthrad, as you will note from the mention of Mount Thayil. I know it's strange to think of giants cooing their children to sleep, but that's why I think such songs are fascinating."

Another strum of the harp and then:

> Hush now, heart of my hearth,
> Bank your fire for the night,
> I will keep the coals bright
> Until you wake at dawn.
>
> Hush now, heart of my hearth,
> It is time for us to rest,
> The bellows in our chests
> Are making us both yawn.
>
> Tomorrow we will be stronger
> While Thayil sleeps a bit longer,
> But now you need to close your eyes
> And dream of summer berry pies.

There were titters in the audience at the end, and Fintan chuckled with them. "I have no idea where those pies came from," he said, and the laughter grew louder in response. We'd all been thinking the same thing. "Get ready, everybody; the tales begin soon!" His first seeming transformed him into Gorin Mogen.

$\mathcal{G}$orin Mogen

Fire blast the Fornish! We lost six houndsmen and very nearly lost my son to some slithering flesh-eating plant! And because the Fornish lived to report our presence here, we are getting attention earlier than I would have wished, but the essential plan remains the same. We will lie, delay, and build our defenses until we are unshakable, and the city of Baghra Khek will stand long after I am ashes. But we must clearly devise a countermeasure to the Fornish net launchers. That tactic was both unexpected and successful. We have been conducting timber raids on their southern coast for generations now and never saw them. And maybe we should worry more about the greensleeves. A hound on patrol had its legs completely torn off, and its rider disappeared while his partner came to report one of the Fornish in the pines.

Volund has sailed to Tharsif with our first shipment of timber and should return with food and good news soon. For my ease of mind, he cannot return soon enough.

Sefir came to me with less pleasing news from the shore. A Nentian transport had arrived with one of the houndsmen whom Volund had left behind in Hashan Khek—Lanner Burgan, a stout red-bearded lad nearly my size.

"The word is that the viceroy is keeping Korda hostage," Sefir said, arriving fresh from the new docks.

"The viceroy used that word?"

"No, he's a 'guest,' but it's clear."

"How many Nentians are here?"

"Twenty or so."

"Armed?"

"Yes."

"And their ship?"

Sefir smirked in satisfaction. "Very flammable."

"Good. You know it can't ever leave."

"I do. I'll see to it on your signal. One of the Nentians wishes to talk. He has a message from the viceroy."

"Let's hear it, then, and find out what they know. But before you bring them to me, make sure the Raelechs don't get to see them or even hear about them. Find some excuse to get them on the far side of the city until it's over. Oh—and send La Mastik here right away if you can."

My hearth frowned. "The flame priestess? Why?"

"I want her head to be on fire when the Nentians get here."

"We could set our own heads on fire."

"I know, but her shaved head really makes it look more impressive than it is. Basic intimidation."

Sefir nodded, her lips curling up in a smile, and leaned forward to kiss me. "Merciless *and* a sense of theatre. I married almost as well as you did." I smiled and agreed.

A half hour later a Nentian with a dark oiled beard and long straight hair draped over a pale yellow tunic was ushered to my hearth in the company of several small men. I've been told that I could learn quite a bit about any given Nentian by examining his boots, but I've never cared enough to absorb their status markers. Lanner trailed behind and gave me a nod of respect but kept silent, taking up a position off to the side and behind the Nentians. Like the leader, they were all dressed in light-colored linens or soft cottons; I get them mixed up and cannot tell the difference. No Hathrim would ever wear such materials when there was leather to be had.

I had to suppress a smile when their eyes drifted to La Mastik, who had arrived a few minutes earlier and was standing behind me and to my right. The bearded Nentian's mouth dropped open for a moment before he remembered he was supposed to behave as if ten-foot-tall women dressed in spined lava dragon hide and with their heads on fire were commonplace.

"Welcome to my hearth," I said. "May you be warmed and nourished by it. What is your name, sir?"

"Please call me Dhingra, Hearthfire. Thank you for seeing me. I am the chamberlain of Viceroy Melishev Lohmet in Hashan Khek."

He wasted little time after that, asking questions about the walls we built with their Raelech stonecutters. "Such defenses are not usually the priority of refugees who seek temporary relief," he remarked.

"I'm merely protecting my surviving citizens from the infamous savage creatures of the Nentian plains. My understanding is that you build walls for the same reason."

There was more back-and-forth like that, his questions revealing what the viceroy most dearly wished to know: how many of us were here and how long we planned to stay. And eventually he gave us an ultimatum. We were to be guests for two months, and after that we would be trespassing.

I laughed in his face, and he scowled, taking offense.

"Two months is more than I need. Who is your god? Kalaad, is it?"

His eyes narrowed. "Yes . . . why do you ask?"

"Make your peace with him." And then with a word and a small expenditure of effort I set him and his companions on fire, head to toe. They screamed, and Dhingra at least had the sense to drop to the ground in an attempt to smother the flames. I lunged forward and stomped down hard on his head, enjoying the crunch beneath my boot. Halsten and Lanner killed the others with axe and fist except for one we let burn and scream until he dropped.

La Mastik cleared her throat as their fluids watered the earth. "Hearthfire, please help me understand why you just did that."

"Certainly. We are still not ready for an assault. Nor are we in a position to negotiate from strength. Until we are, we have to prevent the Nentians from learning our numbers and defenses."

"So it's true. You're not merely staying the season but claiming this land as your own."

"I am."

"And all your talk of living in peace with the Nentians was a slick of sand badger shit. The other nations won't allow it to stand."

"They won't be able to put together a force strong enough to defeat us now. The Kaurians and the Brynts are too far away to care, and we can handle the Fornish and Nentians and, yes, even the Raelechs."

"Perhaps. This method, though, is distasteful. It's murder."

"All great cities are born in fire and blood," I said, quoting the words of Thurik to her. "What did you think it was going to look like?"

"You are adept at quoting Thurik for someone who doesn't tend his flame."

"My father taught me that words shape people as the hammer shapes iron. Leaders bend religions to their purposes, and religions in turn bend the people who believe in them. I'm sure you already knew that last part, but if you were unaware of the former point, then you haven't examined your histories."

"Do you even believe in Thurik, Hearthfire? Tell me true."

Stepping close to her and keeping my voice low so that only she could hear, I said, "I believe in fire and in the craft of my mind and in the strength of my people. I'm told that Thurik believes the same. And in case you were unaware, I sent all six of my children to the boil at Olenik and your patroness is marrying the only one who survived. Remember that before you question my beliefs."

She pursed her thin lips, disliking my answer, but broke eye contact and passed a hand over her skull, snuffing out the flames, before excusing herself. She would move against me soon if she hadn't begun to do so already in secret. I would have to consult Sefir on the matter and prepare countermeasures.

Halsten said, "Lots of fresh meat on the ground. May I feed it to the hounds, Hearthfire?"

"Absolutely, Houndmaster. I was just going to suggest it. And Lanner, please let the Hearth know it's time to scuttle that ship. This Nentian delegation was tragically lost at sea, and we never saw them, understood?"

"Understood, Hearthfire," he said, grim satisfaction evident on his face.

"Before you go, Lanner—any chance of getting Korda out of Hashan Khek?"

He shook his head. "They have him in the viceroy's compound surrounded by a whole lot of crossbowmen."

"We'd pay a steep toll in lives, then, to save his life. We can't afford it."

"He's at peace with it, Hearthfire. He's bought us time, and he knows it. He may yet escape on his own. And if not, then we have already avenged him here tonight. My only hope is that we'll get a chance at the viceroy sometime. I'd enjoy killing him more than most."

"We will get to him eventually," I assured him. "He'll send more like this first. When they realize that pretty words on paper mean nothing, we will laugh in their faces, too. We will burn and grind them all until they agree—or the survivors agree—that Baghra Khek is our city and this is Hathrim land."

Once Fintan had dismissed the form of Gorin Mogen he chuckled as he imprinted his next stone. "The viceroy, as you may well imagine, was not ready to agree." He threw down the sphere and took on the scowling visage of Melishev Lohmet.

Melishev

Chumat and Dhingra are long overdue, and I know they're not coming back because Gorin Mogen has made them vanish. The Fornish ambassador reports that there are closer to ten thousand Hathrim by the

Godsteeth than one thousand, and that was excuse enough to float my brain in alcohol last night and enjoy the company of a professional sexitrist. After taking the most painful morning piss I can remember and staggering around my chambers with a thunderous headache, I'm ready to kill some people. Since doing so will hasten the day I can get out of Hashan Khek and see a Brynt hygienist, I take to the task with relish. Pulling on my black shitsnake boots—if ever there was a day to wear them, it's this one—I stomp over to the barracks and rouse my senior tactician, Moshenoh Ghuyedai.

He's a tough old piece of leather with salt in his queued hair and two missing teeth in the front, the result of a bar fight in which he killed three men with his bare hands. He's losing some of his muscle to fat as he ages, but there's still plenty there, and his ruthlessness is at peak.

His office is strewn with maps and empty bottles and little chapbooks of erotic poetry, half-eaten sausages, and volumes of military history written by Raelech and Nentian scholars.

"Moshenoh. That possible Hathrim invasion is confirmed. Time to round up some disposable meat."

"You mean my regulars or some fresh blood?"

"Mostly the latter. I'm going to throw open the coffers for a one-time march. Go recruit every sponging, no-good, borchatta-smelling dock rat you can. Promise them meals, prestige, and a steady income every month. Then take them down to the Godsteeth and make damn sure the giants kill them all. We'll clean up the city and trigger the Sovereignty Accords at the same time."

My killer tactician actually flinches. "That's . . ."

"An efficient use of funds, I believe, and a move that doesn't cost you any of your trained regulars. Are you the man for the job?"

His eyebrows jump briefly but settle down, and then his shoulders lift. "I guess I am."

"Good. The treasurer is expecting you. See him and follow his instructions precisely. Recruit today and tomorrow, march the day after tomorrow."

"Very well, Viceroy."

"Right now I need two dozen crossbowmen and some horses. I have to take a trip outside the walls."

I leave Ghuyedai to his work and brief the crossbowmen on what needs to happen. Twelve of the men remain at the stables to get horses ready for the rest of us, and the other twelve accompany me to the quarters of Korda, my Hathrim guest. The giant is in the middle of inhaling a box of Fornish candied figs when I enter, and I sling a winning smile at him.

"I trust everything is to your satisfaction?"

"Mmf. Yes. I cannot complain about the accommodations, Viceroy. Though I'd like to get out more."

"Perfect! That's just what I was about to suggest. I've been told that there's a rare skulk of khek foxes near our walls right now, attracted by an unusually large company of harrow moles, and thought you might enjoy seeing them. What say you to a walk on the famed Nentian plains? It's a beautiful day to be outside."

"Isn't it dangerous to walk out there? I've been told everything on the plains is meat for something bigger and hungrier."

"We'll have plenty of protection. I go out there all the time. Besides, you're lavaborn, aren't you?"

"No, I'm not."

"Ah! Well, no matter. As I said, we'll be perfectly safe."

"All right. Thank you for the invitation."

"Not at all!" I point at the half-empty box in Korda's hand. "Friendly warning: eat too many of those figs and you won't stop shitting for a week. Though maybe Hathrim can handle more of them than Nentians can. For me, it's one and I'm done."

Korda looks down at the box, counts, and realizes he's eaten ten. "I may be in trouble."

"We'll have to wait and see. In the meantime, let's go see the skulk before they're gone." We walk to the stables, chatting amiably as people like to do about other people being killed by wild animals. He tells me about a friend he lost to sand badgers back home, an uncle who lost an eye to an angry scold of knife jays, and how his sister lost her foot to the bite of a Narvikian acid roach.

At the stables, the crossbowmen all mount up and so do I, and once we get to the gates, they load up and prepare to shoot anything hungry enough to attack. They form a protective circle around the two of us, he walking and I riding. Korda has no trouble keeping pace.

We strike directly for Kalaad's Posts, eight tall lodgepoles placed in the ground with rawhide strips dangling from them. They're only four hundred lengths or so from the gates, spaced two lengths apart from one another.

Korda notices them early on, but we are so involved in trading stories about the wild beasts of Hathrir and Ghurana Nent that he says nothing until we draw close to them. "What are those, if I may ask?"

"They're boundary markers. The plains become significantly more dangerous once you pass them."

"Are we going to pass them? Is that skulk nearby?"

"I was told the skulk is visible from the boundary, so it's not far now."

"Ah! Good."

When we reach the posts, I direct my horse to the left side of the circle. Korda calls after me, bewildered: "Where are you—?" But then he cuts off as he realizes something has changed about the ambient noise. The horses behind him and to the right have stopped. As he turns to look, he sees that the crossbowmen have leveled their weapons at his torso an instant before they fire. Ten bolts hit him, mostly in the chest, though one pierces his neck and one sails wide but doesn't hit anyone else. Korda topples backward like a fallen tree and makes a couple of gurgling noises before falling silent.

"Check him," I tell the crossbowmen next to me. "Finish him if he's alive, then strap him to a post once he's dead."

If Gorin Mogen wants to make my chamberlain disappear, I can play the same game. Poor Korda must have wandered into the plains and been eaten by something. All of which will be true: scavengers will pick his bones clean in a day or two.

Once he's strapped somewhat upright, bolts removed, we hurry back to the gates. The smell of blood will be bringing teeth in our direction. Before we reach the gates, a cry comes from behind. Something's coming fast—and it turns out to be three Raelechs. One of them is a courier—an attractive one.

A brief tingle thrills up my spine, and I have to suppress a shudder. The Triune Council has dispatched a courier to *me*, not the king! She introduces herself as Numa, and she's accompanied by an absolutely useless beak-nosed bard named Fintan, who turns out, in one of life's inexplicable tragedies, to be her husband, but this disappointment is salved by her other companion, a fantastically welcome juggernaut named Tarrech, who might be able to wipe out the Hathrim by himself.

"I'm grateful to the Triune for sending you," I tell them. "My tactician will be riding south to meet this Hathrim invasion the day after tomorrow. Will you join him?"

The courier replies, "We would be pleased to do so provided that you understand that we do not guarantee our military involvement, nor do we place ourselves under your command. We will go with your forces independently as an ally to make Rael's interests plain to Hearthfire Mogen."

"What interests are those?" I ask.

"We wish to safely extricate our stonecutters who have been duped into this situation and to remind him that the Sovereignty Accords will be enforced. The first consideration may not matter to you, but we have a duty to our citizens. But we also have a duty to our friends, and the second consideration should be your wish as well."

"Indeed it is," I say, nodding, and I invite them to be my guests until Ghuyedai is ready to march.

In a couple of days they all ride out of town with a trumpet or two, families bidding them farewell and a safe return. Two thousand of the regular garrison—leaving only a soggy sponge of a force behind—and two thousand more hastily conscripted desperate people who looked upon army rations as fine cuisine. We didn't tell them they were going after ten thousand giants behind a wall. They were told they just had to kick some refugees back into the ocean.

After some wasted breath trying to get Mogen to leave peacefully, Ghuyedai would spend the conscripts freely and then withdraw. And then we could say to the world, Look, Gorin Mogen slew our people when we rightfully and lawfully tried to force him to leave our lands. He is a would-be usurper. And invader. Help us crush him now as you promised to do in that treaty you signed long ago.

I give the Hearthfire credit. He has maneuvered well to this point, but soon he will have nowhere else to move. He will either leave—highly unlikely—or defend himself and bring the world down upon his back, because we have always feared the unchecked fire of the Hathrim. Either way, Ghurana Nent wins.

When Fintan took on the seeming of Abhinava Khose next, he had a fresh set of clothes on, the tatters all gone.

Abbi

I thought the walls of Khul Bashab would be a welcome sight—or at least welcoming. But after my initial joy at spying them from a distance, they took on a different character as I drew closer until I felt something like dread.

They weren't what kept me safe inside anymore. Those walls now looked like they were made to keep me out. I felt like I had more in common with the freedom of the plains than with the structure of the city.

I didn't need the protection those walls were built to provide. Nei-

ther would anyone else if the Sixth Kenning became common. With
Beast Callers among us, Nentians could farm in the open. Start new
cities outside the king's protection. Though I suppose he would just
hire more men to run those new towns—more men like the viceroys.

Murr and Eep agreed to stay outside the city and not harass each
other. "Avoid other humans," I said. "Don't let them see you. They
might try to harm you."

It was near sundown after a day of travel, and the guards at the gate
wanted to know why I was all alone.

"My family died in a khern stampede," I explained, my voice dull.
"I'm the only survivor."

"Which family?"

"Khose." The guard looked at his checklist and found my name.
They kept track of all who left and entered the Hunter Gate as a way
of tracking who was alive or dead.

"Says here there were eight of you. Big wagon."

I nodded, said nothing, and stared straight ahead at the gate until
they opened it.

My empty house was not truly empty but haunted with reminders.
My father's fine knives. My mother's leatherwork—she made our
clothes from our own kills rather than paying to have them made;
we'd always take our own cuts from the tanner. My sister's carvings of
blurwings and flowers. Tears streamed down my cheeks as I took fresh
field bags and began filling them.

Clothes. Leather scraps and cord and needles and fabric strips. Cotton batting. Two slim notched and buckled belts of my sister's. The
cache of coins my father thought he'd hidden. Lots of beans and root
vegetables. Nothing in the way of personal items. None of it mattered
now, somehow. Word would trickle through the city that the Khose
family was no more, and the house would be looted soon. I left the
door open: I'd had to break in myself, and there was no use making
anyone else work that hard for what I was giving away.

I kept to the soft shadows of the night streets on the way to the house of my father's friend, the chaktu butcher. He would want to know. And I wanted to see his son once more before I left the city.

The butcher's son answered the door, a quizzical look on his face. His skin, a smooth orange-brown just a shade deeper than mine, glowed warmly by the light of the candelabra he held in his left hand, and cold blue highlights shone in the sleek black hair falling to his collarbone. I liked the broad curve of his jaw and cheeks, the tighter curl of his mouth, the simple light blue tunic he wore. My breath hitched for a moment to have his attention focused solely on me, but then I coughed and spoke: "Hello. I'm not sure we've ever formally met, but our fathers are friends. I'm Abhinava Khose."

Recognition lit his eyes, and he smiled pleasantly. "Ah, yes, I've seen you before. I'm Tamhan Khatri. Good to meet you finally. Did you need to see my father? He's out at the moment."

"Oh. Well, I suppose I could leave a message, then. It's just . . . well." I swallowed, and my throat grew tight. "His old friend is gone," I said. "A boil of kherns in the south."

Tamhan's mouth dropped open. "You lost your father?"

"My whole family, actually."

"What?" Shock blanketed his features. "Come in. Come in, please. You have burdens there; put them down and rest for a while. I will fix us some tea."

Grateful for the invitation, I stepped into his home, which smelled of anise and cardamom. I left my field bags by the door and followed him into the kitchen. He pumped some water into a pot—they had their own well!—stoked the hearth, and set the water to boil.

"Do you wish to talk or simply be warm and welcome? I will give what comfort I can."

"Where is your family?" I asked, noticing that the house was silent except for us.

"Dinner with Viceroy Bhamet Senesh."

I felt my eyebrows climb. "Fancy."

"Deathly boring," he corrected me. "And more than a little undignified. The pressing of lips against the viceroy's buttocks and the loud smacking noises are enough to ruin one's appetite. And pride."

"What? This is something that actually happens?"

"No." He grinned at me and waved away his sarcasm. "A figure of speech. But if one wants to supply the army with all things chaktu, as my father does, then one must smile and nod and gain the favor of the viceroy. His posterior must be blistered raw by now from all the kissing it receives."

Handsome and considerate on the one hand but a wicked wit on the other. I had impeccable taste in crushes. And since he was so willing to listen, I talked over a clay mug of tea about what happened to my family but left out my experiences in the nughobe grove. That gave him the impression that I survived three days out on the plains by sheer luck.

"So what will you do now?" Tamhan asked when I finished. "You can do anything you want."

"So can you."

He snorted. "I wish. My father expects me to be a chaktu butcher like him. Or at least a chaktu herder who will supply him cheaply."

"Don't you want to be?"

"I would rather do almost anything else," he said, and his voice dropped to a whisper to voice his secret thoughts. "I am sick of chaktu. The smell of it, the taste of it, everything disgusts me. And it's boring. I'd like to go to university, but my father says there's no money that way, no future in what you can read out of a book. He thinks my only chance at prosperity is to deal with the same few families he does, engage in the same kinds of corrupt practices, to be just like him, and that's not what I want." I knew exactly how he felt.

"Maybe seek a kenning?"

"Where? Rael? I'd never make it there."

"Not Rael. Three days' walk south of here."

"What?"

"It's difficult to explain. But pretend for a moment that there is a kenning within reach. Would you want it?"

"Three days' walk on the plains isn't within reach. That's suicide."

"I just did it."

"Right. Sorry. Still hard to believe that. But seeking a kenning is also suicide."

"Maybe. But you didn't answer. If it was within reach, would you do it?"

Tamhan sighed. "I don't know. Probably not. When you put it like that, I don't think I'm desperate enough to face death, or desire power that much. But I know a lot of people are."

"Who?"

My new friend scowled. "What do you mean, *who*? I was speaking in general. Lots of people are barely getting by and figure either death or a boat's the only way out of here. When they get tired of it, they just walk alone into the plains until something's jaws tear their meat from their spirits."

"What if people didn't have to fear the animals on the plains? Do you think that would change things?"

He laughed at me. "You're asking the strangest questions. We'll always have to fear them."

"Not if someone found the Sixth Kenning."

Tamhan sobered. "All right, you're starting to worry me."

"I'm being serious. But just supposing: If the Sixth Kenning was found and we could control animals, wouldn't that change things? We could go anywhere, right? What would happen?"

"So this is like a mental exercise, or . . . ?"

"Sure. Think it through with me."

"Well, I think people would be getting out of these sky-damned walls and starting their own farms and maybe other villages all over the place, like you see in Rael."

That was a worrisome point. What was good for the people wasn't necessarily good for the animals. People would spread out and take over the plains. Not all at once but gradually.

"Go on," I said.

"Well, it means more prosperity for everyone. Except maybe the riverboat captains, who won't be able to charge such prices for transport when people can travel by land."

"Oh, good point. The river traders wouldn't like that. Who else would be against it?"

"Anybody who profits from the way things are now and who couldn't profit from changing things up," Tamhan said, shrugging.

"The church," I said, and when Tamhan asked why, I explained that a kenning related to animals might cast doubt on the worthiness of worshipping Kalaad in the sky.

"Bones and dust, you're right. Well, that means you'd have the government against it."

"Why? Wouldn't they continue to be the government regardless of kenning or whether people lived inside city walls or not? Or regardless of what god they worship?"

"Yes, but I've been listening to my father enough to know this: the country is built on the river trade and the church. Those are the pincers of control. When those pincers have a hard time squeezing regular people, they're going to start squeezing the government instead—"

"And then the government will be squeezing the specific people who are upsetting the pincers. Got it."

"Hah! Got what? This is all dream stuff, Abhi."

"No," I said, smiling at him. "Not really."

He didn't smile back. "Tell me what you mean."

"The Sixth Kenning is real. But you can't simply be told, right? You need to be shown."

"Pfft. Of course. I can't simply take anyone's word for it."

"That's fair. Understandable. I'll show you in the morning if you want. And anyone else who wants to escape the city."

His parents returned home then, flushed with drink and apparent success; they believed a fat contract with the army was practically in hand. But that meant I had to tell my story again—the part about my family, I mean. They wouldn't hear of me sleeping alone in my house and I had no intention of doing that anyway, so I slept in their guest room and wondered, as I drifted off in comfort, if Murr and Eep were still safe.

Tamhan didn't forget our conversation and wanted to know what I was talking about, so after a solemn breakfast with his parents and after I sold my family's knives and my father's collection of finer ones, I used the coin to buy a small cart, a horse, a brush, and some feed and apples. I piled everything into the cart along with my few belongings in the field bags and bought more food and also a canvas tent, a bed-roll, and blankets. Tamhan accompanied me, asked what I was doing, and looked progressively more worried when I kept putting him off but promising a full explanation soon.

We lied to the guards at the Hunter Gate and said we were a party of two looking for bluetips and gharel hens. Once out of their earshot and safe in the grass, I undid the horse's bit but left her tied to the cart.

"Hello, my name's Abhi," I told her. She turned her head to look at me, somewhat startled to be addressed. "I won't make you wear a bri-dle anymore or whip you or anything. I'll just ask you to walk or stop and feed you apples whenever I can. I'll also make sure nothing hurts you. You have to believe me when I say that, okay, because there's going to be a bloodcat coming along soon, but he will definitely *not* hurt you."

"Look, Abhi, I understand that the loss of your family has been hard on you, but you're starting to sound less than sane here," Tamhan said.

"Walk on, please," I told the horse, and she did. I mentally searched for bloodcats in the area and saw that Murr was nearby, less than a hundred lengths away. Eep was somewhat more distant but would be able to make it in a couple of minutes. I called them both and told them not to worry or bother the man and the horse with me.

"All right, Abhi, seriously, you need to stop," he said. "Let's go back before something has us for lunch."

"Nothing will harm us, Tamhan. I found the Sixth Kenning. Didn't you see me ask the horse to walk on?"

"Yes, but horses are trained to do that all the time."

"Have you ever seen a bloodcat or a stalk hawk come when called?"

"No, of course not, but—"

"If a bloodcat and a stalk hawk appear here and walk along with us through the grass, will you believe that I have found the Sixth Kenning?"

Tamhan rolled his eyes. "Okay, sure, but that's—holy Kalaad, that's a bloodcat!" He pulled out his belt knife, and Murr, who had just appeared to Tamhan's left, laid his ears back and hissed at him.

"No, no, it's fine, put that away!" I told Tamhan, grabbing his shoulder to hold him. "Murr, stay back until I can get this guy to calm down." The horse did well; she shied and looked nervous but didn't bolt. She simply kept walking. "Tamhan, he's not going to hurt you; I already told you. Murr, you're not going to attack, right? Shake your head and say no."

Murr did so, and Tamhan's eyes changed from panic to wonder. "You really control animals?"

"I don't know if *control* is the right word, but they don't eat me and so far they don't eat other animals that hang out with me if I ask them not to."

"But you can talk to them. You called him a name."

"Yes. Now put away the knife; you're being rude."

"You're sure it's safe?"

"Very."

He sheathed his blade, and Murr's ears popped back up.

"Amazing," Tamhan said. "And there's a stalk hawk, too?"

I turned to the east, where I'd felt Eep's presence, and spied her in the air. "Yes. She's right there." I pointed. "Land on the cart if you don't mind, Eep," I called. We had to catch up a bit because the horse had never stopped walking, and Murr kept pace to the left. Once Eep backwinged and landed on the front edge of the cart and gave us a greeting chirp, Tamhan began to laugh.

"You really did it? You found the Sixth Kenning, and it's three days south of here?"

"Yes. In a nughobe grove. A pack of bloodcats will either give you the blessing or tear you up."

The bloodcat spoke up, as if to comment on that. "Murr." And for the first time that communicated something to me—not language so much as a fact that appeared in my head, like something I had always known and merely forgotten until that moment.

"For another week," I added. "After that, it . . . moves."

"What do you mean? The pack moves?"

"No, the kenning does. Different animals act as the source of the kenning, and it jumps around."

"How do you know?"

"Not sure how, but I know it."

"Huh. That would explain why nobody found it until now. You'd have to be attacked by the right animals at the right time. You were extremely fortunate."

"I don't know if I'd say that," I said, shaking my head and thinking of why I'd been in that grove.

"Oh. Kalaad, I keep saying the wrong thing. I'm sorry."

"Never mind. I understood what you meant."

"Where's it going to be next?"

I shook my head. "Don't think you want to know."

"Try me."

"Farther south, down the Khek River. You've heard about that famous pool where the pink sunfish spawn? It's supposed to be magnificent."

"Yeah."

"There's a colony of huge fish spiders down there, bigger than your head, and they dangle down from the tree branches hanging over the river to catch them, and so you would have to—"

"Ugh, never mind. You were right; I don't want to know."

"But what we spoke of last night, Tamhan, it could happen. Everyone could be free of the cities if we had enough Beast Callers."

"That's what you call it?"

"I don't know. Best I could come up with. You have anything better?"

"No, no. I like how it sounds—very intimidating. Like you would only call large animals, never songbirds or squishy caterpillars."

"But I can call anything. We could change the country. Maybe the world. Nentians don't have to be the poorest people in the world with a huge untamed land they can't use."

"Starting to think you're right. It's hard not to get excited about the thought of it. I might not want to risk a kenning myself, but I would love to live out here." He looked up at the blue and slowly turned in a circle. "The sky is so much bigger when you don't have walls around you. I could get used to this." With an effort he tore his gaze from the vastness and locked his eyes with mine. "We should go shout it in the square."

"I think it would end badly. I've been thinking about it quite a lot. This kenning is different from the other ones. We can't point to a spot on the map and say if you want the kenning, here it is, because the location changes. That means if the viceroy or the church or the river traders want to get rid of this threat to their power, all they have to do is get rid of the blessed."

"Oh. Because no one else will know where the next kenning source will be."

"Exactly. So we need to somehow get lots of people blessed without the people in authority knowing about it."

"That's going to be impossible."

"Why?"

"Because people talk. But you can probably get a few blessed without them knowing. If you give me some time to get some people together, we can start out tonight. This afternoon even."

"You know some people willing to seek a kenning?"

"It'll be easy," he assured me, and looked down at my khernhide boots. "Judging by your feet, you're even more well off than I am. Hunters always have the pick of leathers, I guess. You don't know how good you have it. But I've delivered chaktu all over the city, I've seen poverty up close, and I know that there are plenty of desperate people who would jump at the chance to improve their lives. Can you just wait a few hours? You'll be safe, right?"

I couldn't say no to him. If he came back with people, fine. If not, that was fine, too. I had much more to learn about my blessing, and my vague idea was to follow the river downstream all the way to Batana Mar Din before trying to recruit anyone.

"Tell them they need to bring six days' food and water."

Tamhan laughed and shook his head. "You really don't know. A lot of people in this city aren't sure where they're going to find their supper. But I'll bring along plenty of chaktu jerky. I know a guy." He winked at me. "And besides, if this kenning works like the others, they won't all need six days' worth, will they?"

Looking down at Murr and remembering what it had felt like to be attacked by his nest, I said, "No, they won't."

While I waited for Tamhan's return, I worked on a personal project. I wrapped two fingerlengths of sticks in cotton batting and covered both sides in leather and sewed them together, forming a small padded pillow with wooden ribs inside. The leather on the top was boiled hard, and the scrap on the bottom was soft and pliable. I rested this on my left shoulder and began to experiment with different ways to affix one of my sister's belts to the bottom of the pad and strap it on my body. I cut two slits in the bottom of the pad, and that allowed me to string the belt through it. By looping it underneath my left armpit, I was able to buckle the belt on the front side of my shoulder.

"Hey, Eep," I said. "Look what I just made. You can perch on my shoulder without scratching me now. Want to try it?"

She cocked her head at it in several different angles, checking it out before flapping over from the lip of the cart to give it a try. Her talons definitely exerted a pressure on my shoulder but didn't pierce my skin.

"Not bad, is it? You like the view?"

"Eep." She nodded to make sure I knew I had done well.

"Excellent. So what do you say, Murr? Ready for that belly rub?"

The bloodcat, who'd been watching all this with bemusement, shook his head.

Tamhan's natural charm worked well. He returned with thirty-two Seekers after only a couple of hours. They were mostly our age give or take a year, poor and clearly used to missing meals, the third or fourth children of large families if I had to guess or perhaps without parents at all. Theirs were the mouths that didn't get fed all that often. Their hair was tangled and dull, and patches of skin bore visible signs of dirt. What they considered clothing was that which provided them modesty and little else. Some were barefoot.

With Murr and Eep's help I convinced them that the Sixth Kenning was real and recounted my discovery of it and the decision to give up hunting beforehand.

"I'm not sure whether it's required to forswear killing animals before you seek the kenning, but it might help," I said. I also emphasized that I wasn't sure of the full range of my powers yet. But I knew that I could live in harmony with the animals of the plains and that that spelled a different life not only for me but for all Nentians if enough people became blessed.

"What's the success rate, sir?" a boy asked; he was perhaps only fifteen years old. His name was Madhep.

"A hundred percent so far, since I'm the first one," I said. "I honestly don't know. It could be near fifty-fifty like the Fornish, or much better odds like in Rael, or lower like in Hathrir, Brynlön, and Kauria. You're risking your life for sure—let's be clear about that. It's no small risk, but I can't tell you exactly how big or small of a risk it is."

"Doesn't really matter how small the chances are," a girl said. "At least it's a chance. I have no chance of living to see twenty if I keep going the way I'm going. Better to go out with some hope, I'm thinking."

Grunts of assent met this declaration, and all thirty-two of them followed me south. We weren't speedy, but we traveled faster than my family's wagon. The Seekers had almost nothing in the way of burdens, and my horse with its small cart was nearly brisk compared with the wart yaks. And for a night and a day it was a hopeful journey for us all. Tamhan was liked and admired by everyone, and I envied his easy way with people.

But unlike the Seekers—unlike myself—Tamhan had a family. One that had just enjoyed dinner with Viceroy Bhamet Senesh and had his ear. One that could check the records at the Hunter Gate, see that their son had left the city walls in the company of what they would consider river vermin, and force the viceroy to act.

So just after sunset on the second day I wasn't surprised to hear the rolling drumbeat of approaching hooves. With my new senses I could tell that they were horses and not some other herd of animals. Our campfires were lit—we had six—and I had looked into the blaze of ours, and so my vision had to adjust to the darkness before I could see them. I asked Murr and Eep to stay out of sight, and they melted into the darkness. My eyes shifted more quickly than they usually would, owing no doubt to my kenning, and I spied the small company of city cavalry approaching. I knew before they reined in and spoke to us why they had come: they were there for Tamhan, and it made me sad. Not sad that he was cared for—it was perfect and wonderful and right that he should be—but that the rest of us were somehow less than he, unworthy of being saved because our parents were either dead or poor. The viceroy would feed and supply and risk these cavalrymen for Tamhan, the son of his crony, but not do anything to make sure the rest of us had food.

The cavalrymen sorted themselves into an arrowhead formation. A wedge, I guess, but with nothing filling the center. They had crossbows and looked like they were searching for an excuse to use them.

The leader, in the front of the wedge, barked out a query, staring directly at our fire: "Which one of you is Tamhan Khatri?" And I wanted to shout back at him, "You already know he's the one with nice clothes!" but it wouldn't have made my life any better, so I bit back my reply.

Tamhan volunteered that he was himself, and the mounted soldier said, "We're here to escort you back to the city."

Tamhan shrugged. "That's kind of you, but I don't wish to go back to the city."

The soldier's voice dripped with condescension as he explained, "It's dangerous out here, son."

"I assure you that I'm in no danger at all and I am here of my own free will. Everyone is, in fact." He spread his hands to the seekers. "If any of you are here against your will and wish for the soldiers to take you back to Khul Bashab, please speak up now."

There was absolute silence apart from the crackle of fires and the snorting of winded horses.

"The rest of these can get eaten if they want," the soldier said, a captain if I was reading his shoulder markings correctly, "but I've been ordered by the viceroy to bring you back safely."

"Fine. I'll be heading back in a few days, and you can ride along if you want."

"Your parents—and the viceroy—want you back now."

"I don't particularly care what they want. The plains are open for everyone to walk in."

"That's true except when it's my job to bring you back. Discuss it with them."

"Let them discuss it in a few days," I said, breaking in. "Protect him if you must, and we'll return with you when we're finished. Everyone's happy that way."

"Who are you?"

"I'm Abhinava Khose."

"Oh, so you're the one who started all this. Viceroy Senesh orders you back to the city for questioning."

Snorting, I said, "About what? I've done nothing wrong."

"You've persuaded a lot of children to abandon their families, and that is worth questioning at least and sinister at worst."

"Can you name any of their families besides Tamhan's? No? I thought not. Many of them don't have a family anymore. Madhep here has been on his own for three years, and it's a rough life when you don't have a father who can send out soldiers to look after you. They want to seek a kenning of their own free will, and I'm taking them there. You can come, too, if you want."

"I'm not a gullible child. Your claims of a kenning are ridiculous, and you need to come with us now."

"Sorry, I'm not going to do that. I've broken no laws, and you have no authority to take me anywhere."

"Our authority comes from the viceroy." He raised his crossbow and pointed it at my chest, a ridiculous escalation in response to my pointing out the truth.

"But mostly from that weapon, since the viceroy isn't here."

"Come with us now."

"You speak patiently with Tamhan Khatri because his parents are privileged to know the viceroy personally, but I am immediately threatened with violence? We are supposed to be equal citizens and we are equally walking in the plains, harming no one. What are you thinking?"

"I'm following my orders, and I *will* bring you both back. How you go is up to you."

Tamhan spoke up. "We have already stated that we will gladly return with you after the Seeking. The Sixth Kenning is real."

"Let me give you a completely harmless demonstration of my abilities," I said before the captain could reply. "I will ask your horse to take two steps backward."

"Don't do that," the captain said.

"It will put your doubts to rest, and we can be more productive if we are working from the same facts." I dropped my eyes to his horse and asked it to please take two slow steps backward. It's not something a horse would think to do on its own without prodding or a fright, and the soldiers all knew that much even if the rest of the Seekers didn't. The horse obeyed, and the captain lowered his crossbow to grab its reins in a futile attempt to stop it from moving after it already had moved. The other soldiers' eyes widened, and a few of them muttered mild oaths of surprise. Unfortunately, the captain did not view this with the sense of wonder and excitement I had hoped for. He pointed his crossbow at me again.

"That's enough. Start walking back to the city now."

"Think about it, please, Captain. I might look unarmed, but you're in the Nentian plains, surrounded by animals. And as you just saw, those animals tend to do what I say."

"Don't threaten me."

I spread my arms wide, palms up. "Who is pointing a weapon right now? You are threatening me when I have done nothing wrong. You should be ashamed."

"Last chance. You can agree to walk or I'll drop you."

There was no getting through to this man. His stubbornness reminded me of my father, as did that ultimatum. And I knew what he would do when I said, "No," and I said it anyway, ready for what would come next.

The captain tensed and pulled the trigger in a syrupy slowness that was actually my quickened speed and senses. I was already moving out of the way of the shot. But as I was moving out of the way, Madhep and Tamhan were moving in, waving their hands and shouting for him to wait, and my panicked "No!" was much louder than my calm refusal to the captain. I had not been ready at all for their interference. The bolt launched and sank deep into Madhep's chest with a sickening, juicy crunch and knocked him back into Tamhan and then me. We tumbled backward together, and he coughed blood and groaned. Tamhan and I knelt over him, and I cradled his neck in my arms, searching for life in his eyes. He was still there. He looked at the bolt shaft sticking out of his chest and then up at me.

"I just wanted . . ." he said, blood bubbling on his lips, a wet cough splattering us, ". . . wanted to talk to animals," and then his eyes lost focus.

"No no no no no, not again," I murmured. Why did I never see this coming? The captain was reloading. His soldiers were bringing their crossbows to bear, pointing them in the general direction of the Seekers as an unspoken warning, and I could see the others cowering already at the display of force. And I had never wanted anyone dead so much as those uniformed men at that moment. The captain had killed

Madhep, who had done nothing to deserve a quarrel in his chest, and would have killed me for refusing to submit to his authority.

"Stand ready," the captain was saying to his men. "If anyone resists, shoot them. You, Khose. You know I'm serious now. Come along for questioning or you'll be meat."

"No, I rather think you'll be the meat here," I said, laying Madhep's head down gently and rising to my feet, fists clenched and trembling at my sides. I felt the rage building in my head so intensely that my ears buzzed with it, the air chopped with pressure, and I felt somewhat dizzy.

The captain smirked at me, utterly confident that he could casually kill us all and get away with it. "How? I don't think so."

A burrow wasp flying at top speed smacked audibly into his right check and stung him. He winced and cursed, slapping at it. Another followed, and a few more annoyed the other soldiers, and the buzzing sound in the night grew louder. The horrifying source of it flowed out of the black, a dark seething mass of wasps and other insects, glinting in places from firelight on wings or reflective carapaces, and they engulfed the soldiers like gloves made of tar. Screams ripped out of their mouths, and then they were choked off—perhaps with a flood of insects flying and crawling down their throats and up their noses. They dropped their crossbows in an effort to bat away the bugs, and the horses bucked and ran even though they were not specifically targeted. Every one of the riders fell off his horse, and the cloud of insects followed them to the ground, and seconds later the men stopped their thrashing and lay still. The horses were never bitten, only scared, and the same held true for everyone else. The Seekers scattered into the darkness with the horses, afraid that the swarms would come after them next. But I took a couple of deep breaths to calm myself and said, "Enough, be at peace," and the insects lifted away from the bodies of the soldiers and dispersed into the night. I called the soldiers' horses to come back and gather near my horse and cart and then stepped forward to examine the body of the captain, a bit tired and unsteady on my feet.

The captain's face was a swollen mass of stings, a misshapen lump of inflamed tissue. His mouth was open and filled with dead bugs, and spindly sawtoothed legs stuck out of his nostrils. "I guess that's how I'll kill you," I said, surprised more than anything else. I hadn't consciously summoned the swarms to do my bidding; in the aftermath of Madhep's murder I just wanted the viceroy's men dead, and it happened. But I supposed that made me a murderer, too. And Madhep was still gone.

Somebody made retching noises in the darkness, and I looked around. A few of the Seekers were coming back into the firelight now that the swarms had departed and discovering the ruin the insects had left behind. Their eyes swept over the bodies of the soldiers and then flicked to my face, wide and fearful, clearly wondering if they would suffer a similar fate.

"It's safe," I announced. "Nothing will hurt you."

"Abhi? You look a bit taller," Tamhan said. "And older."

I looked down at my hands as if they would reflect my accurate age. They looked no different. "I do?"

"He's right," a girl said. "You've aged a little. You're bigger."

That explained my dizziness and weariness. And it settled the question of what the Sixth Kenning could do. My earlier reflections on the potential strength of the insect world came back to me.

"You've all seen the power of the Sixth Kenning now," I said. "I am the world's first plaguebringer."

The assembled refugees on Survivor Field stood and roared their approval, giving the Raelech bard his second standing ovation. I noted that both times this had followed some adventure of Abhinava's. I hoped that this obvious delight in a Nentian hero would quell the unrest among the expatriates living in Pelemyn.

Day 9

REVELATIONS

Fintan's tale of Abhi coming into his full powers along with the portrayal of one of their viceroys as a ruthless murderer certainly entertained the refugees and the citizens of Pelemyn, but it sent the local Nentians into a fit, dashing my hopes that our obvious high regard for Abhi would soothe their wounded egos. A longshoreman sent by the pelenaut's Lung picked me up at home and recounted the night's tumult as he escorted me to meet Fintan.

"We had to move him twice in the night, and him complaining the entire time about ruining what little sleep he can get. The Nentians are paying for information on his whereabouts and sending in hired fish heads to gut him. I see you have your sword. Good."

"What? We're going to be in danger?"

"Almost certainly. You'll be delighted to hear we have a plan, though."

"Oh, indeed! My delight is boundless. So vast that I cannot think how best to express it. Do I get to hear the plan?"

"We're taking you back to the chowder house you visited a couple of days ago. It's quite busy now thanks to the bard telling everyone about it."

"It will be a terrible place to work, then."

"But a great place to be seen and attacked."

"What? I guess I should have asked if your plan was a good one. This does not sound good."

The longshoreman grinned at me. "It's going to be fine as long as you don't get killed."

"Look, that could just as easily be said of pudding or sex or life itself. It's not the hallmark of a good plan."

"It's the pelenaut's plan, all right? He wants you to live, believe me. Just have some lunch and write your story. But keep an eye on your surroundings. You wouldn't want a dagger slipped between your ribs when you're not looking."

"This is not comforting."

"Don't worry; you'll have some company keeping a closer eye on you than normal. You'll be totally safe. Probably."

"You're kind of a rotten whale dong, you know that?"

The longshoreman threw his head back and laughed. "Yes, I know." He pointed out a pair of extra mariners loitering inside the doors of the High Tide Chowder House and two more sitting at a table closer to the kitchen. There were few seats available and a line that threatened to extend outside very soon. Fintan already was seated in the far corner across from a young woman and smiled as he waved me over. It was a larger table with benches for seats, graced with two orange candles instead of one. I approved of the location and took my seat next to him with our backs to the wall; no one would be able to sneak up behind us.

"I've already ordered you a bowl and a beer," he said, and then nodded toward the woman, who had her hair cropped short around her skull and appeared to be amused. I wondered what Fintan had told her about me before I joined them. "Master Dervan du Alöbar, I present to you Gerstad Nara du Fesset. She's part of the story, actually. You'll be hearing of her adventures later." She snorted in response to this, then smiled at me, dimples on either side of a wide mouth, pearls in her ears gleaming by candlelight.

"He's exaggerating. Eating this chowder is going to be the most ad-venture I've had in months."

"Nice to meet you. A gerstad, eh? We rate an officer now?"

"For today, anyway," she said.

"Why aren't you in uniform?"

Her eyes shifted around, and then she put a hand to the side of her mouth as if someone might be lip-reading. "We're being clever," she said in a loud, dramatic whisper. "They'll never know what hit them."

"Who are *they*, exactly?"

"If they show up, we expect most of them will be dockside fish heads desperate for coin. But one of them should be a Nentian bruiser the Lung has identified as the tip of the harpoon on these attacks. He's a semiretired caravan guard from Ar Balesh, and it's his former em-ployers who are financing this."

"Old, rich expatriates of Ghurana Nent who live here for the clean water and access to hygienists?" Fintan asked.

"Precisely. He's been either spotted or reported to be involved in the attempts to assassinate you, but we haven't been able to isolate him yet."

"Why not go after the money?" I asked.

She paused while a server deposited bowls of chowder in front of us and returned with beers and a board of bread and butter. "The pele-naut likes taxes," she said, "especially right now, and the Nentian expa-triates pay plenty of them. So the objective is to go after the errand boy. If the elderly have no one to do their dirty work, then it won't get done."

"But why not put pressure on these Nentians to stop seeking my death?" Fintan asked.

"They're so obvious and loud about what they're doing that it's pointing us to criminals that the constabulary has been seeking out for a long while. They're leading us to some truly dangerous fish heads, so we don't want them to stop. But don't worry: the Lung is positioning someone to take over operations once we eliminate their current man. The Nentians will pay him to hunt you down, and he will pass on the money and information to us and do nothing. The pelenaut looks at it as a tax on their stupidity." We shared a laugh at that, and she asked to be excused for a moment. "I'd like to wash up before eating. Would that be okay?"

Fintan shrugged. "Sure."

"We Brynts can get obsessive about hygiene. Sorry. I'll be right back."

The gerstad left us, and Fintan and I clinked glasses and sampled the beer while we waited for her return. The noise drew eyes in our direction from the line, and someone near us recognized Fintan. "Hey! It's the bard!" a boy said, pointing with one hand and tugging on his mother's sleeve with the other, and I realized that the gerstad had been blocking Fintan from view until she rose from the table. At that point in Pelemyn, Fintan was *the* bard—the kid couldn't be talking about anyone else—so there were assorted gasps and tiny exclamations at spotting a famous person doing something normal, such as eating and drinking.

Fintan grinned at the boy and then the room. "The chowder's so good here, I came back for more!" he announced. He held aloft his drink and wished them good health, and many glasses were raised in return. It was very warm and congenial for a few seconds there. Then my eyes drifted to the entrance, at the back of the line, where a group of men looked less than pleased. They looked instead like predators that had just spotted their prey, brows hooding their eyes and muscles tensing along their shoulders. And when they stepped out of line and began to push past people, drawing blades of varying lengths out of their belts, I chucked Fintan on the shoulder.

"Incoming fish heads!"

I rose and drew my steel, all merriment gone, and that alerted everyone that something serious was happening, including the mariners who were supposed to protect us sitting at the neighboring table. They sprang up to intercept the fish heads, and the other two mariners stationed at the door fell in from behind. Four on four—trained soldiers against undisciplined meat. Inwardly I was relieved. They'd probably never reach us, and if they did, their numbers would at least be reduced. As the hired men and the mariners fell to it—a quick flurry of blows and grunts and howls of pain accompanied by a chorus of alarm from the lunchtime crowd that scrambled to both get away and get a better view—I noted that none of the attackers was Nentian. They were unwashed types who took on dirty jobs for quick profit, and there was an abundance of them to be found these days. And because I was riveted to the brawl at the front of the house, I completely missed seeing the man with the axe until the blade sank into the table where Fintan had been leaning forward. The axe already had been employed judging by the blood on the blade, and if I had to guess, I'd say someone in the kitchen was dead since this stout, grizzled man hadn't come through the mariners. He was definitely the Nentian bruiser we'd been warned about, his coppery skin and straight dark hair giving away his homeland. He had sent the fish heads in the front door to absorb the brunt of resistance, leaving him a clear shot at Fintan.

The bard, fortunately more aware than I, had jerked back to avoid the axe and drew a dagger from his belt. He threw it inexpertly at the Nentian, and the handle bounced off the man's chest. I swung at him, and he ducked underneath it, drawing his sword. I had nowhere to run. I was effectively trapped where I was in a terrible stance, and my swing had made it clear to the Nentian that he had to go through me if he wanted another shot at Fintan—and he did.

I batted aside his first strike but fell for a feint on his next pass as he twisted his wrist and thrust at my belly. When did other people get so bloody fast? I tried to dodge out of the way, but we were in close quarters and I felt the cold steel shiver through my left side, followed by white-hot pain. I cried out, and he yanked the blade, slicing me open further, and I toppled sideways onto the bench as my knee buckled. Fintan was wide open and defenseless now, and the Nentian raised his sword. I weakly threw mine at him; that made him flinch and pause but did nothing else. The mariners were still occupied with the fish heads. It was two against one now instead of four on four, but regardless, we'd have no help from them.

"Under the table," I said to Fintan, but I might not have enunciated well; it might have come out as more of a constipated grunt. I clutched my wound with my left hand and tried to push myself up with my right, thinking that a hot bowl of chowder in the genitals might slow the Nentian down if I could throw it in time. But I couldn't.

As the assassin's muscles bunched for a killing blow, his right ear fairly exploded with a gout of blood and then bits of brain, and he collapsed, dead before he hit the floor.

"Oh! Gah! Wait! What just happened?" Fintan said.

"I happened," the gerstad said, stepping into view, her mouth set in a tight line. Her clothes were spattered with the Nentian's blood.

"You did that? How?" Fintan asked.

"I'm a rapid," she explained. "I pulled all the water in his head to me through his ear. Tends to destroy the brain on its way out."

"Brain chowder," I mumbled, treading water in shock and edging toward delirium.

"Sorry I wasn't here to catch him before you got hurt, Dervan," she said, and her eyes trailed to the carnage near the front. "Or before I lost those men. If you can walk, we should get you to a hygienist to clean that up."

Only one of the mariners survived the encounter, though he was wounded as well. The sword hadn't punctured my stomach or guts, so it was just a painful muscle tear I'd have to live through. And stitches. And Fintan's guilt.

"I didn't mean for those men to die," he said as we limped to the hygienist's hall. "Or for you to get hurt."

"There's not a bit of blame for you here," I replied. "Or anywhere."

"I can't help feeling responsible, though."

"Nonsense. We're all Seekers of one kind or another," I said. "If it's not a kenning, then it's something else we seek. And there are thousands of people who seek to hear your story for these few who seek to silence you. I think you should grant the wishes of the thousands."

"Oh, I'm going to keep doing my job. I'm just thinking about how our causes have trouble seeing their effects until it's too late to do anything but mourn them."

Gerstad du Fesset, helping the wounded mariner to the hygienist alongside us, looked haunted by that already, lips still pressed together in regret.

"You're not the cause of this. Reactionaries from Ghurana Nent are the cause, and we are faultless." That was aimed more at the gerstad than the bard, but I'm not sure if it helped. She probably was locked in a cycle of guilt about how much better everything would have turned out if she hadn't felt the need to wash her hands, imagining scenarios in which none of the mariners was killed, ignoring the great possibility that it could have gone much worse if they had had a chance to get closer before attacking.

The hygienist we visited, an elderly lady with gray hair and bright eyes, examined my wound and ensured through her kenning that it wouldn't get infected before sewing me up. I would be in pain for a while but not bedridden. Gerstad du Fesset accompanied the bard and me to a quieter locale and guarded us on high alert while he dictated yesterday's tale to me and I wrote as quickly as possible. We had to hurry to the wall after that, and the bard began by getting them all to stomp their feet and clap on alternate beats. He was determined to lighten everyone's mood with the day's song.

> You can collect a troubled bag of burdens and brood upon them long
> You can dwell upon the woes that curdle in your sour mind
> But instead of wasting precious time on things I cannot change
> I'd rather gather up my joys and leave my sorrows far behind
>
> (Chorus)
> I'd rather gather up my blessings and my love and all my wealth
> And share them with my family and friends and wish them health
> I'd rather gather all the people I respect and I admire
> I'd rather gather you in my arms and hold you close beside the fire

You can store up your resentment cold or feed a yearlong grudge
You can cower in your room a prisoner to childish fears
You can sulk and fret away your life and I'm not going to judge
I'd rather gather with my mates down at the pub and have some
*   beers*

(Chorus)

"We haven't heard from our Kaurian scholar in a while, but that doesn't mean he wasn't busy. Today I'd like to share with you the many discoveries he made about the enemy in that uncomfortable, windless dungeon."

Fintan took the seeming of Gondel Vedd, who appeared this time with a clean set of clothes.

For want of a better name, we have taken to calling Saviič and his people Bone Giants. They are certainly not Hathrim or even related to them. They have no kenning of fire, though they have heard of it. They have heard of all the kennings, including one we have not found and another that remains a mystery.

I have made excellent progress in working out Saviič's language, but it is not fast enough to satisfy anyone, least of all myself. We moved rapidly through children's language cards that taught me the words for basic nouns and verbs. Most abstract concepts are still difficult to grasp, however, and I am often thrown off by the syntax of his language. He loads up the front ends of his sentences with nouns and objects and modifiers, and they seem to hang there, suspended and inanimate, until the verb and its modifiers are tacked on to the end. I find myself waiting for the verb so much that I lose much of what went before and have to ask him to repeat: Who died again? Where and how?

Today I thought I had learned enough to speak of where Saviič had come from. Instead of bringing *Zanata Sedam* with me into the dungeon, I brought a map of Teldwen. An incomplete map, apparently, that I was very anxious to fill in. Not least because I have been asked every day by Teela Parr where his home might be. I wonder what will consume the court's curiosity after Saviič points off the edge of the map and says, "I live over there somewhere."

For that is essentially what he did. I showed him the map and pointed to Linlauen so that he could see where he was, and after reviewing the words for directions and distances, he estimated that his country was roughly due east of Keft and off the edge of the map, far past the point where creatures of the deep would pull ships down into the dark and snack on the sailors before they had a chance to drown.

It is called Ecula, and his people are Eculans. (That being said, I doubt the "Bone Giant" nickname will go away anytime soon since the court has spoken of little else for days. It is difficult to look at him and think of anything but his stature and starved appearance. After his first gluttonous meal, his food intake has shrunk to birdlike levels.)

Saviič pointed to the archipelago between Forn and Kauria and indicated that Ecula was much like that: a series of islands with no overwhelmingly large landmass. He drew a tight cluster of five islands, named each, and claimed that there were floating bridges spanning the straits and nets at either end to keep man-eaters out of their "civil waters."

"What are the man-eaters?" I asked. He sketched pictures of bladefins and longarms and two different monstrosities that could only be classified as krakens, and I nodded, grinning.

A whole new country! Islands connected with floating bridges and protected waterways! What a sight that must be! Obviously they had a rich religious life, so think of what else they must have to offer. What did Eculan art look like? What did their music sound like? And how would we ever enjoy these things if we couldn't cross the ocean?

That inspired a new host of questions for Saviič. How did he survive the crossing? Why did he dare it, and why dare it alone?

His answer to the first question was rather flip: he survived because nothing ate him. But his answer to why stretched the limits of credibility. He claimed to be a merchant interested in trade. That would bring joy to the monied interests in the court, no doubt, but Saviič did not dress or behave like any merchant I have ever seen. For one thing, he still preferred near nudity. The merchants I know like to be dressed head to toe in the finest clothing they can afford, which is a public projection of their success as much as it is a taste for luxury. And most merchants tend not to be starved and sunburned skeletons but rather fleshy, sedentary things with jowls and wattles and jiggling bellies. They also have actual goods to sell or are willing to spin tales of what they can bring you in exchange for a bag of coin. Saviič, however, feigned weariness when I asked for details of his trade and asked to be left alone until the morrow.

I'd been expecting him to say he was the lone survivor of a larger ship pulled down by a longarm or something like that—some kind of plausible lost-at-sea story—but instead he claimed to be seeking new business all by himself across the ocean. I was beginning to think Saviič imagined me to be infinitely gullible.

Since I had the name and approximate location of his country, which was all the court really cared about, I was willing to let the matter drop. I wanted to consult with Teela Parr in any case on how I should proceed in the face of Saviič's bald lies. If he wasn't a merchant or a refugee, we had to wonder at his true purpose. I didn't wish to leap to conclusions, but here is what I had noted to that point: he was a desperate man with a deep and abiding love for his religious text. Hunger and zealotry are dangerous on their own, but combine them? Reinei bring us peace!

On a completely different note, I discovered during a lunch break that Saviič doesn't care for mustard. We may not get along very well much longer.

There is so much to learn, and it is difficult to suppress my academic urges in favor of a cold political goal. I wish to map out the morphological drift between the ancient language and modern Eculan, but I can only do bits and pieces while doggedly trying to eke out some answers from Saviič.

Teela Parr took my map and a summary of my discoveries to the mistral and I assume a coterie of assorted courtiers, all brightly dyed and coiffed and brimful of sage advice. And I must chastise myself for mocking them, for what came back was not an immediate call to send out boats or even a tempest to find the island nation of Ecula but a reasoned request for more information and some pointed and relevant questions to put to Saviič as soon as possible. Teela Parr invited me back to the posh Silverbark Room to discuss it.

"There's no reason we should discuss such things in a windless dungeon," she said, and I couldn't agree more. Someone from the palace kitchens came in with tea—our native leaf from the Teabush Range; no exotic Fornish blends served here. I actually preferred it. There were also some cakes glazed with sugar frosting drizzled with an orange clove sauce that nearly made me swoon.

"Oh," I said around a mouthful. "Mm. If this is my reward for my work, I consider myself well paid."

Teela smiled. "I'll be sure to pass on your compliments to the chef. I'm sure we can convince her to make them again."

"Please do. Her work makes me glad to be alive."

"And your work is very important, too. Mistral Kira asked me to relay her personal thanks for your efforts."

"I'm grateful she trusted me with such a project. What news from the court?"

"Anyone who's seen the Bone Gi—I mean Eculan—knows he must be lying about being a merchant. That's agreed. But the reactions to the lie are mixed. The merchant families now have serious doubts that Ecula has anything to offer. If Saviič thought we would believe he's a merchant—if being naked and destitute is a representative sample of their merchant class—then there's not much opportunity there."

I snorted. "The opportunities are endless! Why, we could start out by selling them pants. Are you telling me no one wants to become the Pants Baron of Ecula?"

She indulged me with a polite smile at my joke but pressed on. "I think the greedy lights in their eyes snuffed out once the military minds spoke up. They wondered aloud what he's really hiding. It's most likely not something we would welcome. You don't lie that badly when you want to be friends."

"No, Saviič is certainly not a trained diplomat."

"Precisely. The question is what he *is* trained for."

"So I need to get him to admit he lied and tell the truth? I'm not sure we could trust anything he says."

"Agreed. Direct confrontation on that point probably won't work. The mistral suggests that you delve into his religion since he seems so fervent about it. His zealotry may make him reveal quite a bit, and he may be less likely to lie about it. And of course we would all like to know more about the Sixth and Seventh Kennings."

Those were my orders, but Teela reassured me that they weren't going to rely on me alone thanks to the mistral's military adviser, Zephyr Bernaud Goss. "The zephyr believes—and the mistral concurs—that Saviič is part of an overall strategy to find a path over the ocean that is not plagued by krakens. He feels that dozens of small craft, perhaps a hundred or more, were sent out in hopes that a few would make it across to somewhere. It's an old idea, but no one has ever done it because if you are seeking a quick death, you might as well seek a kenning, and few people wish to volunteer to be kraken chow. So we'll be making queries up the coast, asking if anyone else has seen someone like Saviič. We might have some answers in a few weeks."

And so, fortified with tea and cake, I descended into the dungeon to resume my language lessons. Saviič's sunburned skin was peeling and blistering in places. A healer had paid him a visit and given him some ointments or creams or whatever: greasy smelly unguents that might provide him some relief. He preferred one over the others and had been given more, but that dead skin had to flake off at some point and dry, papery ridges of it crested all over him. I asked him how his skin was feeling, and after inspecting his arms, he grunted.

"Hot. Burns," he said, then pushed down the air with the flat of his hands. "Lower. Better." He pointed at me. "You burn sometimes?"

"No," and then I broke eye contact to compose my sentence for him. He was used to such pauses by now. I had to not only come up with the proper words but order them in Eculan syntax so that a simple sentence such as "I stay inside" was phrased as "I inside stay."

His next question surprised me. The words were, "Skin you black why?" and it took me a moment to realize he was asking why my skin was dark. It was a telling query; it indicated that not only had he never seen people with darker skin, he had never even heard of them before. His entire experience of the world was pale—or pink, I supposed, if they burned so easily.

But that made me wonder how he could have a religious text purporting to know about seven kennings and somehow not know that the majority of people blessed with them had dark skin of one shade or another.

I frowned at him and said, "Most people have dark skin."

He scrunched up his face. "Here only, most?"

"Not here only. In world."

He shook his head vigorously. "No. Most skin like mine."

That made no sense unless he knew much more of the world than we did. "Ecula only?" I asked.

"No. World."

That conflicted so badly with facts that I wondered if we had different conceptions of what "the world" meant.

"World is Teldwen, yes?" He nodded, so I continued. "Places in world are Ecula and—" I stopped myself and held up a hand, opening my ink pot and scrawling out a rough map of the world I knew, an in-

ferior copy of the professional map we'd used to establish the location
of Ecula earlier. I sketched our explored lands to the left and a series of
five small blobs for Ecula, leaving room on the right side of the paper
in case. I'd been so focused on finding out where his country was that
I never asked about other countries he might know—lands beyond his
own.

"This is world," I asserted, thinking he would either accept it or correct me, and he corrected me, shaking his head.

"I do not know this part," he said, pointing to the west. "But world
is more."

I handed him the paper through the bars in a wordless command to
demonstrate what he meant. He still had his own ink and quill from
our earlier language lessons.

His attempts at cartography were even worse than mine. He merely
drew three circles on the right side, each bigger than Ecula but nothing
like the size of our main landmass, and assigned names to them: Joabei
to the north, Omesh near the middle, and Bačiiš to the south. The last
one drew my attention for its linguistic relation to the old language,
but not wishing to forget our original thread of conversation, I pointed
to each circle and said, "People here. All skin like yours?"

"Yes. Most." He pushed down with the flat of his hand once more.
"Some small changes. Small differences. But not dark."

I gestured with my fingers to get the map back and then pointed to
the three new circles to the east of Ecula. "These places," I said, then
moved my finger to point to our continent. "Bigger than here?"

He shrugged, though I could not tell if it was because he didn't
know or didn't care or some combination of both.

"You go to Joabei, Omesh, or Bačiiš?"

"No."

"Those people come to Ecula?"

"No," he said, his face twisting with impatience at my stupidity and
sighing over the fact that I even had to ask. "Man-eaters in the ocean."

Yes, but so what? He had passed over those same man-eaters to get
here. Baffling. "How do you know they are like you?"

"Zanata Sedam." Ah, *The Seven Kennings.* How kind of him to bring it up. I had it with me in a leather case containing my notes, and I brought it out so that he could see it. As before, the sight of it brought him rushing to the bars, and he stuck his hand out, demanding that I give it to him.

"Those places—those people—are in here?" I asked.

"Yes. Me give."

"They have kennings?"

"Yes." His hand remained out, and for a moment Reinei's wind ceased to blow in my lungs. If they had kennings, then there must be somewhere else than the six nations where one could become a tempest or a cyclone or a fury or a tidal mariner. When I took breath again, I pointed at his holy writ.

"But this place, my people, are not in here?"

"No." His fingers curled into a fist and spread out again. "Please give."

"I cannot give. But I can read. Any part. Any page. I would like that. Would you like that?" I thought I could manage to at least pronounce the words correctly, if not recognize their meanings.

Disappointed, he withdrew his arm and scowled at me, resentful as I suppose any prisoner would be.

"Any page," he finally said. "You read." He slouched to the back of his cell, sitting on his cot and drawing his long legs up to his chest, wrapping his arms around them, and closing his eyes.

I flipped at random to a spot a little past halfway and began to read in my halting Eculan. I thought I was doing well until a low growl began in the cell and rose to a roar. "You wrong are!"

"Sorry. Please. Make me right."

It went more slowly after that, with frequent stops for subtle coaching on my pronunciation.

"Must correct say," Saviič insisted. So I concentrated on forcing my mouth to produce the sounds the way Saviič did and missed a lot of meaning; that wasn't terribly tragic since it was dry, boring stuff about being righteous. I had no complaints; I was learning and enjoying the linguistics if not the content. I kept at it for an hour before I was feeling ready for a break, but then a sentence's meaning broke through my basic decoding and translation to sink in and make me reread it. Even then it took me some time to untangle the syntax.

I muttered a quick translation in Kaurian: "In the dark of the moon the Seven-Year Ship comes to take the faithful to the . . . land? Island? . . . Of the Seventh Kenning, and there they shall know the fullness of Teldwen's . . . gifts?"

I looked up with questions in my eyes, and Saviič flashed his crooked brown teeth at me. He didn't know Kaurian, but he knew that the words were having effect.

"Best part is," he said.

"Good is," I agreed, then questioned him on the unfamiliar words to make sure my translation was accurate. *Island* was correct, but the word I thought was *gifts* was more accurately translated as *blessings*. That took quite some time to figure out, but once I was satisfied, I probed for an explanation.

"Seven-Year Ship comes?"

"Yes. My life, two times comes," Saviič said, holding up his thumb and index finger. His middle finger flicked up, and he continued, "But this time—third time—no come."

"Which time?"

He told me the Seven-Year Ship was supposed to have come last year but didn't.

"Where does the Seven-Year Ship come from?"

The Bone Giant shrugged. "Here."

"Here? No."

"Somewhere here. I not know."

Using the map, I asked if he meant the Seven-Year Ship came from Kauria; that was an improbability if he had seen the ship twice in his life yet had never seen a Kaurian. That wasn't what he meant: "Here" meant somewhere on our continent's western shores. And I gasped.

"Oh! For Seven-Year Ship you looking?"

He nodded, and I forgot myself and spoke to him using Kaurian syntax but Eculan words. He still followed me, though.

"Who is on the Seven-Year Ship? People with skin like yours?"

"Yes."

"And how many faithful go on the ship to the island of seven kennings?"

"Seventy-seven and seven. If ship come, I go. Faithful I am. But no ship. Go anyway."

Eighty-four, then. "Did all the faithful go anyway to find the Island of the Seventh Kenning?"

"Yes."

Eighty-four religious zealots climbed into tiny boats and sailed west in search of another boat. Might as well ask him again. "What is the Seventh Kenning?"

"I not know. To island faithful go, there discover."

The text could be interpreted to mean that the Seventh Kenning wasn't a separate talent at all but rather knowledge of the other six— the fullness of the kennings. Or perhaps it was something else entirely.

The only islands to the west of Ecula were the archipelago between Kauria and Forn, the island next to the Tempest of Reinei, and the Mistmaiden Isles in the north. But the only pale people on this side of the continent were the Fornish, so the evidence pointed to this mythical island being very close to Kauria. The mistral needed to know right away. I had learned so much, and it was only midafternoon. I excused myself hastily, promising Saviič that I would return soon. Rushing out of the dungeon with the scribbled map and *Zanata Sedam*, my finger jammed in the pages to mark the passage, I had a cyclone take me to Teela Parr, and on the way I wondered if the Eculans might not be some mutation of the Fornish as the Hathrim were supposed to be, caused by the Rift ages ago. It would at least account for their root language if they had at one point come from Forn's eastern shores.

Speaking perhaps a bit too quickly, I told her that there were three nations beyond Ecula, the site of the Seventh Kenning might be lo-

cated somewhere in the archipelago, and if Saviič wasn't lying, someone from Forn was crossing the ocean and going back every seven
years.

"Someone Fornish? How does he know that?"

"It's my deduction. He said the people on this ship had pale skin.
And he asked me why my skin is dark."

Teela snorted. "Guess he doesn't get out much."

"A fair assessment. But the mistral's suggestion was excellent. This
conversation blew fair because I asked him about his religion and
began to read his scripture. But you know the oddest thing?"

"It all sounds odd to me."

"Agreed, but now that I'm thinking about it, I can't remember him
ever mentioning the actual deity he follows, nor did any deity get mentioned in the portion I read."

Teela's eyes dropped to the book. "It has to be in there somewhere."

"I hope so. I have a lot of reading to do."

She asked me to walk with her and bring the map because the mistral would want to hear everything straight from me.

"We're going to see the mistral?"

"Of course. Didn't you want her to know all this?"

"Well, yes, but—" I looked down to see if I had any mustard stains
on my tunic this time. I was blessedly stain-free but still a decrepit old
scholar unfit for court.

"Don't worry about your clothes. She is well aware that you have
other priorities, unlike her courtiers."

We entered the Calm from behind the throne while the mistral was
receiving the Fornish ambassador. Apparently, a volcano had erupted
in Hathrir and the entire surviving population of Harthrad had sailed
north to land in Ghurana Nent. A serious situation, no doubt, that
could trigger the Sovereignty Accords for the first time. But as those
giants were on the other side of the continent, I could not muster very
much worry about them. The giant we had in the dungeon was far
more interesting. The mistral asked the ambassador to acquire more
information about the Hathrim before committing to anything; a pre-

cipitous action against Gorin Mogen in a time of obvious crisis could damage relationships with the other Hathrim hearthfires.

Teela Parr executed some sort of hand signal to the mistral after the ambassador bowed, and Kauria's elected ruler requested that the Calm be cleared for a private briefing. I caught many curious and perhaps calculating glances thrown my way as a result. I thought I recognized some of the faces from my first visit, though of course they were all clothed differently now and I looked like I was only a generous step away from a pauper. One man in particular was reluctant to leave. He was a broad-nosed handsome fellow in the younger half of his fourth decade who adorned the world with the muscles in his arms and spoke in one of those deep sonorous voices that sounded heavy with gravitas. "Begging your pardon, Mistral, but if this regards the Bone Giant, might I remain to hear it?" he said.

"Should it bear any relation to your concerns, Zephyr, I will consult you right away," she replied.

So that was Zephyr Bernaud Goss. He removed himself slowly not because he was incapable of speed but because there was no dignity in moving quickly. He wanted *all* the dignity. Or maybe his heavy voice slowed him down. Once all the doors closed, however, Teela moved with alacrity. She snatched the map out of my hand and stepped quickly toward the mistral.

"First is this," she said, pointing to the circles on the right before handing it over. "Three more countries we've never heard of before, all populated by people with pale skin. Second, eighty-four Bone Giants, Saviič included, sailed for our shores because they were looking for a sacred ship that supposedly sails from an island in the west every seven years—their west being our east. It didn't show up on schedule, so they got worried. They call it the Island of the Seventh Kenning. And that ship is crewed by pale people."

Mistral Kira said, "You mean the Fornish?"

Teela shrugged. "I don't know who else it could be unless we have a secret population of Hathrim living in the archipelago without our knowledge. Shall I call the Fornish ambassador back to ask about it?"

The mistral considered it, then shook her head. "No. If they have been keeping this a secret from us for all this time, we'd best not reveal that we know something about it until we know a whole lot *more* about it. Did Saviič tell you all this?" she asked me.

"Most but not all. I read some of his scripture, and the discussion that ensued was quite revelatory."

The mistral pointed at *Zanata Sedam*. "Scholar Vedd, I would like you to make a complete, detailed copy of that book, including any scribblings in the margins. Then you can give it back to him and work together on translating it."

"Certainly. Your instincts were correct: he made no effort to pretend he was a merchant once we discussed religious matters."

"My thanks for your work, Scholar." Mistral Kira shifted her eyes to Teela. "When was the last time anyone did a really good survey of the archipelago?"

"I would have to check. Certainly not in our lifetime."

"It might be worthwhile to see what's happening in there. A task to occupy the zephyr's mind." She smiled at me and raised a hand to the side of her mouth to whisper even though no one else was in the room but us. "I think being the military leader of a peaceful nation wears on him."

We all chuckled at the poor zephyr's expense, and I did feel somewhat sorry for him. All our culture and diplomacy was determined to make sure he had nothing to do. "Well, he certainly has the ships needed to carry out the task," Teela said.

"Set up a private meeting with him later tonight, and I'll get him to work on it. But not a word of this to anyone else. I don't want everyone sailing through there looking for this and alerting the Fornish." Her eyes flicked back to me to make sure I knew I was included in the silence order. "And say nothing about the three new countries, either, or any of it. We still don't know which way the wind will blow. I'll await your next report eagerly, Scholar."

"My pleasure to serve, Mistral."

"Do you have everything you need?"

"Well . . ."

"Yes?"

"Perhaps some cheese to go with that mustard you gave me?"

U početku je bilo sedam, a na kraju neče biti jed.

It is the very first line of *Zanata Sedam,* and I tremble at the translation.

If I am correct, it means: "In the beginning there were seven, and in the end there shall be one."

If this refers to the kennings—and I believe it does—then it implies a very militant philosophy on the part of the Eculans, especially when taken in context with what else I've read. They may interpret that line to mean that they should conquer all the nations of Teldwen, taking their kennings for their own. Yet there could be other meanings: Perhaps the various sources of the kennings will cease at some point to bless those who seek magical powers. Perhaps the gods themselves will expire and the kennings along with them—an apocalyptic vision, to be sure, but also consistent with their seeming lack of a deity in their holy text, for why worship gods you believe will fall? I am still not convinced they worship no god—that would contradict Saviič's holy fervor and his devotion to this religious text—but I have yet to see a god mentioned.

The simplest answer would be to ask Saviič in plain terms to name his god, but I keep thinking the next sentence I translate will give me the answer, and since the mistral ordered me to complete a copy, that is what I will do. I am translating as I go, however, rather than simply copying the text. I can't help it. I'm leaving blanks for the words and passages I'm having trouble with. My thinking is that I will be able to prioritize which sections deserve to be translated first. The temptation to return to the dungeon is almost overwhelming, and that would have been an unthinkable sentence for me to write a few weeks ago. The problem is that my progress will slow if I begin talking to Saviič. Better to continue working in my private corner of the university library.

Yet the first line disturbs me so, I hardly know how to proceed. Should I recommend to the mistral that all nations look to their borders in the near future, perhaps spurring taxes on east coast peoples in advance of an attack that will never come? Or should I keep it to myself, a private fear unworthy of larger circulation? It is too large a thing for me to decide. It's best that I pass it on to the chamberlain, like everything else, and let the people in power choose the path forward. I am merely a scholar with a taste for mustards and cheeses of a far finer quality than I can afford.

Teela Parr was quick to see me when I relayed a request for a meeting to discuss it. But her face, initially welcoming and pleasant, crushed itself into a frown after a few steps as she took in my appearance and the dirty dishes stacked on the end of the table from past meals.

"Sweet Reinei, Gondel, do you ever actually eat any mustard or do you just smear it on yourself on purpose?"

"What?" I looked down at my tunic, realizing that I was more than usually stained.

"When was the last time you went home?"

I blinked, considering. "What day is this?"

"It's Feiller."

"Then it's been days." Suddenly I missed Maron. He must have thought I'd fallen into the ocean. Or that I didn't love him anymore. Or that the government owned me now. He's always had trouble understanding that sometimes I get lost in my work. That kind of thing never happened to him, and since it was so far outside his own experience, he never believed me when I said it was a frequent hazard. He thought instead that he was not interesting enough to hold my attention, ignoring all the times I lost myself in him and neglected my work for his sake.

"I want you to go home after this meeting," Teela said. "Take a day off. Maybe two."

"But the mistral wants this translation—"

"And she'll still want it when you get back. She also wants you healthy, believe me. And don't worry about Saviič. He will be fine. Now: What have you found?"

"The translation of *Zanata Sedam* is disturbing. Portions of it also conflate with my professional interest in the origins of the Rift; apparently the Eculans know of it as well but think of it quite differently than we do. But let's begin with the very beginning. Look at this first page." I rifled through the stacks of paper and placed my translation in front of her.

"In the beginning there were seven, and in the end there shall be one. Only when there is one shall the Rift be healed and *unknown* return to the world. Then those who were *unknown* and *unknown* will thrive, and the selfish and *unknown* will perish."

Teela shifted her eyes sideways. "There are some rather important words missing here."

I don't know those yet. I was going to return to Saviič after I finished making a copy of the text."

"What's going to return to the world when the Rift is healed?"

"That's the first question I'll ask him."

"Well, why do the Eculans think the Rift is something that can be healed? I mean, we're talking about the ocean between us and Hathrir, right? It's not a wound to be stitched."

"I believe they are using the term to refer to the event rather than the ocean. The event that created the ocean, in other words, and the Hathrim if you give any credence to their version."

"You're talking about old legends."

"Yes. It's a favorite subject of mine."

The chamberlain made no comment on that but returned to the text. "I don't like this part where some will thrive and others will die. Even with the missing words it demonstrates a confrontational mindset. Label someone selfish or whatever this missing word is and you have justification for going to war. It's the sort of language the Hathrim use to justify their history of violence."

I nodded in agreement, and she continued, finally paying attention to the first sentence. "And in the end there will be one? One *what*? One nation?"

"Perhaps. I cannot say for certain, but I think it refers to the kennings."

"That's ominous."

"Indeed."

"Is there more along this line?"

"Yes, much more. Thus far it is not a scripture concerned with enlightenment and spiritual improvement. Maybe the tone will lighten soon."

"Well. I will mention it to the mistral. It's important work that you're doing, Gondel, but not so important that you need to forgo sleep or live outside of the wind. This library is little better than the dungeon."

"I find it a vast improvement."

"Go home and open the windows. With such negative words entering your mind you need to breathe peace, and there is no terrible hurry."

"That we know of."

Teela crossed her arms. "All we know at this point is coming from you. Do you see a reason to push yourself past exhaustion over this?"

I sighed in defeat. "Nothing I can specifically point to. Just a feeling."

"You're feeling tired, Gondel. Go home."

Once she said it out loud, I felt my eyelids droop, ready to sleep. "Very well."

It would be good to see Maron again even if he was cross with me. A change in the wind would be welcome.

But Maron turned out to be in no mood to breathe peace when I arrived home. A glass flew at my head and shattered against the door-jamb when I entered.

"Bastard!" he shouted. "Where have you been?"

"At Windsong and the library. Was that one of our wedding glasses?"

"What wedding? What marriage? You call this a marriage? You disappear in the middle of the night and then no word from you for weeks! I thought you were dead!"

"I'm not. I'm sorry, Maron, but the mistral summoned me, and it's been most extraordinary—"

"Oh, the mistral! So that excuses it all? Doesn't the mistral have some boys waiting around to do any little thing she wishes? You could have thought to send a message!"

"You're right. I should have. I'm so sorry."

Maron folded his arms across his chest. Still so handsome; he had aged far more gracefully than I. "I'm not sure you *are* sorry, Gondel. That's just a word you're saying because you perceive it's the time to say it, not something you truly feel. You know what you are? Distant. Inaccessible. Just like your brother."

I'd been resigned to enduring his lecture because I'd earned one, but that piqued my anger and I raised a finger. "Now that's not fair, Maron."

"Not fair because it's inaccurate? Or not fair because it hurts your feelings?"

"It's inaccurate. And you know it hurts my feelings."

"It's entirely accurate, and it hurts your feelings because you don't want it to be. But you are driven, Gondel, just like him, to the point where you don't recognize you're hurting the people around you."

Some words, aimed and thrown at the right time, are sharper than steel. Maron's pierced me, and I had to sit down, tossing my bag onto the desk and sinking into my chair. The very last thing I wanted to be was my brother. But it was true I had become so involved, so single-minded in solving the mystery that Saviič presented, that I hadn't spared my own husband a thought in all that time.

"You are right," I murmured, lowering my face into my hand because I couldn't look at him. "I've been inconsiderate and selfish and rude. And, and, I guess, if you were going to leave—well, you should leave. I deserve it. And you deserve better."

"Oh, I don't know. Maybe I do. But I want you, Gondel. I want you here. I like that you're driven. I'm glad you love your work. But when you get lost in it, I'm forgotten. I need some attention, too."

I looked up. "You have all of it now. I truly am sorry, Maron."

And I was. Because he was so very right. I am far too much like my brother. Even as he kissed me, soft and perfect and evocative of all our years together—largely blissful and joyous, a reminder of how much I loved him—I couldn't stop thinking about the apocalyptic language of *Zanata Sedam* and what poison awaited in its pages, fresh new horrors biding their time until I could translate them.

"Of course, we Raelechs and Brynts know only too well that Gondel was right to have misgivings about that text. For even as he was near collapse from exhaustion in the south, the Eculan fleets were arriving on our shores in the north, and the winds filling their sails weren't peaceful ones."

Fintan took a deep breath. "Normally I'd continue, but I've given you plenty to talk about today, and like Gondel, I have much sleep to catch up on. I'll rest up and return tomorrow to tell you what happened next in the west!"

Day 10

FIRE AND BLOOD

Though I hurried home from the wall to indulge in a well-deserved collapse on my cot, Gerstad Nara du Fesset knocked on my door right after I had shed my clothes to groan in privacy over my abdominal wound. I groaned more loudly, outraged that my rest should be disturbed so soon. Having told my body that *now* it could relax and start healing, I did not want to reverse myself and say, "But right after I answer the door and play host." But the gerstad knocked again, and I heaved myself out of the bed to answer, calling out to her to be patient while I threw on my tunic. The sun had set, and I had to light a candle in the dark before I could shuffle to the entrance.

"Oh," I said upon opening the door, blinking in surprise. "Hello, Gerstad. I thought you'd be, uh . . ." I didn't know what I thought and trailed off when I saw that she wasn't alone. The street lamps had been lit, but most of her companion's features were occluded by the darkness. I could tell little more than that he was a Kaurian dressed in loose-fitting orange and yellow robes. When our eyes met, I received a friendly flash of white teeth and a tight nod but he said nothing. "Would you like to come in?"

"Yes, please." I stood aside to let them enter and enjoyed their reactions when they saw that my home was nearly empty. To Nara's credit, she made no comment but waited until I shut the door before introducing her companion.

"Master Dervan, this is Kindin Ladd from the Kaurian embassy. He's here to protect you."

"Nice to meet—whoa, what? Protect me?"

"We've been sent by the Lung. Hopefully it's just for one night. Our mariners are stretched thin with other duties, and Kindin was kind enough to volunteer to be your bodyguard on a short-term basis."

"But—I mean, thank you, I hope I don't sound ungrateful—I'm merely confused. Why is this necessary, and why would a Kaurian diplomat double as a bodyguard?"

"I am not technically a diplomat," Kindin said, his voice mellow and measured, but his eyes darted to the gerstad to apologize for interrupting. She nodded at him to continue. "I am a Priest of the Gale. I do serve some low-level functions at the embassy, but I primarily breathe the peace of Reinei and guard the diplomats when they visit."

"Oh, you're—" I cut myself short before I said something potentially offensive. I had heard of Priests of the Gale before but never actually met one. They were commonly referred to as Talkers, but never to their faces. And Kindin Ladd, now that I could see him a bit better, had a kind face, possessed of a simple serenity that bespoke of spiritual fulfillment. Broad cheeks and a broad nose, stout and thick-necked, he'd shaven his head and regarded me from heavy-lidded eyes. "Yeah, I've heard of you guys before. Welcome. In peace. For sure. But uh, why . . . ?"

Gerstad du Fesset took over, every inch of her taut and strained. "Both Pelenaut Röllend and the Lung were appalled to hear of what happened at the chowder house today. I'm to relay their apologies to you." After a brief pause, she added, with a hint of moisture in her eyes, "And you have mine as well."

"Nara, there's no need—"

She shook her head, cutting me off and plowing ahead. She was internalizing the blame and did not want to hear that she bore no responsibility for the attack. "Toying with the Nentians was a mistake they're not going to repeat. The Lung did get his man into place as planned, and he has already been contracted by two different Nentian expatriates willing to pay for the Raelech bard's death. They will be arrested very soon—perhaps even as we speak—and their assets seized."

"Incredible. They're still angry with him even though Abhi's story represents something positive for their country?"

"Yes. Our spies have updated us, and it's primarily the portrayal of Melishev that has them incensed. One of them is from Hashan Khek and knows Melishev personally. He thinks Melishev has a real shot at becoming their king someday."

"So to spread goodwill and convince us that Nentians are nothing like Melishev Lohmet, they arrange for someone to be assassinated."

"Counterproductive in public relations, yes. But Föstyr—I mean the Lung—has concerns that various agents may be engaged already. This friend of Melishev basically got to the docks and put a bounty on Fintan's head, winner take all. So in an abundance of caution we are taking extreme care of the bard this evening and extending protection to you as well. Once it's made public tomorrow that the Nentians have been arrested and no one will be getting paid, we should have no more of this sewage."

"I see." There was a pause since none of us knew the precise thing to say next. "Uh . . . would you like some tea?" I offered.

"Thank you, no, I must be going," the gerstad said, and Kindin Ladd held up a hand and shook his head. "But before I do, how is your wound?"

"Painful but nothing that won't heal eventually."

"You should get some rest," she said.

"Yes, I fear we disturbed you. Not our intention," Kindin assured me.

The gerstad bid farewell and departed, leaving me there with the Priest of the Gale.

"Please, Master Dervan, return to your rest. If you will just leave me that candle, I will be perfectly content."

"Oh. You're sure?" I asked, handing it to him, relieved that I wouldn't have to play host.

"I've already eaten, and I imagine I can get water if I become thirsty."

"Absolutely. Do make yourself at home."

"Rest well."

For a few blissful hours I did just that. Far too exhausted to make any pretense at polite conversation with a stranger, I returned to my cot feeling that it was kind of the Lung to think of me even though it wasn't necessary.

But something woke me an indeterminate time later; it was utterly dark in the house, no soft glow of a candle coming from the other room. A few quick thumps and grunts could be heard, followed by a heavy impact on the floor, eliciting a cry of pain.

"Shhh, keep your voice down, please," the low voice of Kindin Ladd said. "Master Dervan is trying to sleep. Now, let's talk about this in peace."

"Get off me!" some man replied none too softly.

"I promise I will after we've chatted peaceably," Kindin said, his voice almost a coo. "Let's lower our voices, please."

"Drown that nonsense!" the man said, raising his voice instead of lowering it. I moaned and rose from my cot, blindly reaching out for the candles on my wardrobe while the Talker earned his nickname.

"You will not be drowning anything soon. You won't be moving, in fact, until I wish it. The quicker you calm down and quietly discuss your presence here with me, the quicker I can let you go in peace." This is what Priests of the Gale did: redirect violence aimed at them, immobilize their opponents, and then talk of peace until they were begged for mercy.

"I'm here to visit Master Dervan," the man grated out. Fury in every word, but his volume was much lower.

"A friend of his, are you?"

"Yes."

"Strange, then, that you picked the lock and snuck in rather than simply knock on the door. Is that how you commonly visit your friends?"

Silence. I got a candle lit and shuffled into the main room. The Priest of the Gale had his knee pressed down between the shoulder blades of a man much larger than he and his arms pinned to either side. The intruder had long hair coiled in snakelike ropes and queued in back with a blue band.

"Hello," I said. "What's all this?"

"Master Dervan," Kindin said, eyes flicking briefly to me. "I'm sorry to wake you. Do you know this man? He claims to be your friend."

"I've never seen him before."

"I thought that might be the case. He broke in and had a knife."

"He had?"

"It's on the floor near the kitchen now," the priest said. I took a few steps that way, candle held out far in front of me, and found it lying there, a nasty serrated piece. It appeared I needed a bodyguard after all.

Kindin questioned the man as to why he was really there, but he stubbornly refused to answer. In fact, he tried kicking himself free, and the priest found that amusing. He rolled off, let the man get to his feet, and stood in front of the door. I snatched up the knife to warn him against coming at me, but he didn't care about me anymore. He just wanted to get out, and the priest was in the way. The intruder had at least a foot of height and probably thirty pounds on the Kaurian, and it didn't look like a fair fight to me.

"No ambush this time," he snarled. "Let's see how you do when you're not attacking me from behind!"

"Yes, let's," Kindin said, perfectly bright and pleasant, as if the intruder had suggested that they go pick wild raspberries or something else delightful instead of engaging in hand-to-hand combat. The fish head lunged at him, throwing a punch, which Kindin ducked while snatching his arm and pulling him forward to slam face-first into the door. He hammered the man's ribs and midsection with his fists while he was stunned, and once he managed to turn around to attempt a counterattack, Kindin planted a leg and straight kicked him once in the stomach with the other, which caused a reflexive doubling over, and then recocked his leg and lashed out again, this time to the man's jaw. Blood and teeth sprayed from his mouth, and he dropped. Kindin settled himself down on top of the man as he had before, knee in the back and arms pinned.

"A nice stretch of the legs can be invigorating," he said in soothing tones as the man groaned. "I thought you might be laboring under the illusion you could defeat me if given a fair chance, and I hope we've settled that question now. But so many questions remain. And you will remain on this floor until you've answered them, sir."

I fetched another couple of candles to provide some more light while the priest told the intruder he regretted the violence and pain deeply and hoped we could fetch him a hygienist soon. "And in truth, sir, you've done absolutely no harm to anyone tonight apart from depriving Master Dervan of some sleep. But I imagine he'll forgive you. Won't you, Master Dervan?"

"Already forgiven." I pulled up a chair and eased myself onto it.

"There, you see? There's no reason why we can't simply let you go. But let's talk in peace first. Are you ready to answer a few questions truthfully now?"

"Uhh," the fish head moaned. The priest interpreted that as a yes.

"Excellent. Let's begin with why you really came here tonight."

"Man. Nentian man. Said he'd pay for the bard."

"And you thought the bard was here?"

"No. This guy knows. Was going to ask him."

I spoke up. "I don't know where he is. Why do you think I'd know something like that?"

"Heard you work with him." That wasn't exactly a secret at the Wellspring, but this fellow didn't look like he had acquaintances there.

"Who told you that?"

"Friend of mine. Elynea."

I frowned. "Elynea is a friend of yours? What's your name?"

He was slow to answer and Kindin did something to make him cry out. "Apologies, good sir! It pains me to trouble you when all I wish for is peace. I do wish I could apologize to you by name, however. What is your name?"

The man answered quickly now. "Garst du Wöllyr."

My eyebrows shot up in recognition. "So you're her employer? A furniture maker?"

"Not anymore."

"No longer her employer or no longer making furniture?"

"She's gone. Left a couple of days ago."

"What?" I rose from my chair and demanded, "Where is she?"

"I don't know, man; she didn't leave a note."

"Well, why did she leave?"

"Don't know that either. Maybe if she'd left a note I'd have a clue, but like I said, she just took off."

"She took her kids?"

"Yeah."

Something in the way he said that raised my suspicions. "There must have been *some* reason you can think of. You were paying her and letting her live with you, right? So why would she leave without good reason?"

Garst du Wöllyr fell silent, and before I could goad him, Kindin spoke. "We were doing so well, Garst. Let's not stop now. I'd like to refrain from hurting you anymore and escort you to a hygienist so we can all breathe peace again. Please answer Master Dervan."

He sighed, coughed, and spat blood. "I didn't mean to do it. I said I was sorry. But I hit her kid. Tamöd."

"You disgusting pink skink—"

"Master Dervan!" The priest's eyes flashed at me, and I pulled up short. "Put down the knife. We will have peace here."

I looked down, surprised to find the knife in my hand. I couldn't recall picking it up even though I must have just done so. I let it clatter on the table and took a deep breath. "You're right. Thank you." I returned to my seat and said, "Garst, thank you for telling the truth. I will tell you the truth also. I do work with the bard but have no idea where he is. He sleeps in a different place every night, and I'm not told where. Basic security measure. I can't reveal what I don't know. Now, do you have any ideas about where we might find Elynea?"

"None. I'm sorry."

"Then I would like you to lead me to your house—it's only fair since you know where I live—and I'll begin my search for her there."

"And what then?"

"And then we let you go. As the priest said, no harm was done here."

"I don't know, man; I'm feeling pretty harmed."

"I'm not sympathetic. You might wish to consider how your pain and powerlessness is exactly what Tamöd felt when you hit him. I'd say that's justice."

He agreed to lead us to his home, and while I got prepared to go out, Kindin spoke softly about how he should behave and the impossibility of outrunning a Priest of the Gale.

I blew out the candles, Kindin allowed him to rise, and Garst du Wöllyr exited ahead of us. I kept his knife. We wound through the dimly lit streets to the northeastern slums, passing the Randy Goat Inn at one point. Garst's dwelling was even more structurally decrepit, though the space above his workshop was more expansive than mine. It was dirty, though. Elynea wasn't there or her kids or any sign of their belongings. We searched the workshop, too, and found nothing of interest—not even my stolen furniture. There wasn't a lot of lumber or other pieces lying around either; if Garst was as successful as Elynea claimed at first, I would have expected to see more.

"All right," I told him. "I'll leave your knife with the baker across the street." I'd seen lights through his windows; he was baking the morning's loaves.

"Live in peace," Kindin told him, though one could tell he sort of doubted it was possible, and we left him there to find a hygienist on his own. We went to the baker's first and asked if perhaps he'd seen Elynea or the kids before leaving Garst's knife with him. No luck. We bought a pastry from his first batch and some tea while we waited for the sun to rise and the people of Pelemyn with it. Then we continued to ask after Elynea everywhere up and down the street and for blocks and blocks around. Some people had seen her but not for the last couple of days. It made me worry that perhaps something truly awful had happened to her. If we didn't find her soon, I'd be revisiting Garst du Wöllyr with the constable. But eventually we had to leave off because I had to go meet Fintan.

Kindin Ladd gave me a tired smile and hugged me. "May you find your friend and breathe peace from this day on," he said.

"Thank you. For everything. Especially the part where you stopped him from putting a knife to my throat while I slept. I owe you a legendary gift basket. I'll send it to the embassy."

He smiled. "I'll look forward to it." He was familiar enough with Brynts to know that when they said you were going to get a gift basket, you were pretty much doomed to receive one and there was no use protesting that it wasn't necessary. It was a cultural compulsion. My imagination was already composing and arranging items to give him. Maybe a nice handkerchief to offer his opponents when he had them immobilized, to wipe away their blood in style.

There were two mariners waiting at my home to escort me to Fintan. The Nentians, they assured me, had been arrested, along with some fish heads eager to do their bidding. The bard was safe. I ducked inside to get my writing materials, and we met him at a Kaurian restaurant owned by strict pacifists who served no meat of any kind, eschewing violence against animals as well as against people. We ordered marinated grilled mushroom sandwiches.

"Have an exciting night?" I asked him.

"Quite relaxing, actually," he said, his tone upbeat. "I stayed at the home of a tidal mariner."

"You mean Tallynd du Böll, or the pelenaut?"

"The former. She's delightful. Great kids. And I learned how she got that limp, which I'll share with everyone in a few days. How about you? Restful night?"

I lied and told him yes. I'd let the Lung brief him on security matters. It wasn't my place. We worked and picked at our cruelty-free food until it was time for his performance.

Fintan's voice floated over Survivor Field. "I learned a new Drowning Song last night—new to me, anyway. It's one of your old ones to which my tutor knew only a couple of verses and the refrain. If you know more verses and manage to see me, I would enjoy learning more of them. If you know this one, please join in on the refrain." He got them clapping or stomping in a slow beat, and then he began:

> When the storm blew the ship out to sea
> The mariners knew they were dead,
> Oh, yes, they knew they were dead
> And the ocean would be their bed.
>
> (Refrain)
> When the krakens rise from the deep
> Then you will be sinking down,
> You will be sinking down, down,
> And you will never be found.
>
> The currents and winds can be unkind
> And you could lose sight of the shore,
> You could lose sight of the shore, friends,
> And then you will be done for.
>
> (Refrain)

"My first tale tonight," the bard said, "will be told by a slightly younger version of myself, since I had a unique perspective on the Nentian march on Gorin Mogen. The slightly younger me had never witnessed actual battle before, and so he had a fresher face than the slightly older and wiser me."

When he took on a seeming, his clothing had changed to a nakedly martial appearance—the full hardened leather kit of Raelech armor—and his features had altered subtly to present a more youthful face—fine wrinkles gone, markers of stress as much as age.

intan

It was a slow march to the south of Hashan Khek compared to the blistering pace we'd adopted in Numa's company. The Nentian forces were sluggish at best because half of them were not professional soldiers at all but ragged people who wanted free meals and some pay in return for marching around. I am not sure they realized that they might actually have to fight. And I am not sure if the Nentian tactician, Ghuyedai, realized that if he asked them to fight, he would not get much value for his orders. They would break at the first charge or counterattack of the Hathrim.

His regular forces were much tougher; one could see the capacity for murder and cruelty etched into their features, hear it in their cynical laughter and in the targets of their jokes, which were always the weak or unfortunate. It made me reflect on the role religions play in shaping cultural attitudes to war. Those pledged to the Huntress Raena killed out of necessity only. When the words of the poet goddess failed, Raena was there to protect and rescue until words could be heard again. Hence the makeup of our party and our orders from the Triune Council: words first from the courier, and if that failed, Tarrech the juggernaut would speak in the warrior's tongue.

But to Kalaad in the sky, everything was plants or meat, and he thought of them the same way. To Kalaad and thus to the Nentians, there was little difference between cutting down a tree or a human, except in spirit. Spirits returned to Kalaad, and he distributed them again or kept them in his company. Although I'm sure that the immortality of the spirit was a comforting thought, it was a worldview that to my own admittedly biased eyes placed little value on life.

The Godsteeth grew larger and larger as we marched along the coast, defending ourselves against occasional attacks from creatures of the plains. Despite our numbers and weapons, we lost a few people to grass pumas and a small flock of cheek raptors that typically preyed on herds of ruminants and thought an army looked a lot like a herd. They dive directly at one's face, their talons designed to puncture and tear, scoop out gobbets of tender cheek meat, and fly away, leaving you to die and feed the scavengers of the plains. They killed three conscripted soldiers that way—ones who weren't wearing helmets—and then more died because a panicked volley of arrows to bring down the raptors wound up falling on the army. Others died of flesh eels burrowing into their bodies in the night.

"I fully understand why the Nentians like to stay inside their walls now," I commented, which earned me an appreciative grunt from Tarrech.

But eventually we saw walls rise from the horizon at the foothills of the mountains, and there were docks for the Hathrim fleet and glass boats deployed to intercept anyone approaching.

When Numa spied a patrol of houndsmen that obviously had spotted us, she snatched a flag of parley and ran to catch them. She had no fear of them; she could run faster than the hounds with her kenning. We saw her greet them and speak briefly.

"I told them," she said upon her return, "that Rael's delegation is traveling with but separate from the Nentian army and we wish to speak first. I requested a parley outside the walls and guaranteed their safety."

Tactician Ghuyedai was not pleased with her initiative when he demanded to know what she'd done.

"You should have consulted me first," he growled. "This is a Nentian matter on Nentian soil."

"I remind the general that we are accompanying him in friendship but are not subject to his orders," Numa said, refusing to apologize.

"You should not have made any guarantees in my name."

"I made the guarantee in *my* name. And we *will* guarantee the safety of any who come to parley with us, Tactician."

He ground his teeth and turned his back on her, calling for his junior officers. Presumably one of them would be going to parley for him.

The parley occurred an hour later, the three of us and one of Ghuyedai's junior tacticians on one side and two Hathrim women on the other. The tactician sat astride an armored horse, and we stood on foot at parade rest. Numa was in the middle, I on her left and Tarrech on her right.

One of the Hathrim women was visibly shorter than the other but had shaved her head bald and set it on fire. She was introduced as La Mastik, High Priestess of Thurik's Flame. The taller one radiated confidence and wore a smirk of condescension the entire time.

"I am Hearth Sefir of Baghra Khek, betrothed of Hearthfire Gorin Mogen. I speak for him."

Ghuyedai's tactician introduced himself as Nasreghur and said without art and with more than a little aggressiveness, "You have invaded Nentian lands, and we demand your immediate relocation to Hathrir."

The hearth blinked, but her smirk remained. If anything, it widened. "I would not call it an invasion. We have no wish to conquer, and since you have marched all this way, you're aware that we are quite some distance from any Nentian city. We are refugees who had no place else to go after the eruption of Mount Thayil and still have no place else to go. The ash cloud from Mount Thayil pollutes and sickens all of Hathrir right now. We sent spokesmen to Hashan Khek to explain and to ask for desperately needed food weeks ago, but we haven't heard back."

"We received that request and sent food immediately but have not heard back from our viceroy's representative. Are you keeping Dhingra and his men prisoner?"

"I have no idea of whom you speak. We have received no word from Hashan Khek until this moment, much less food."

It was most likely a lie but a smooth one. The tactician would need a moment to think of an adequate response, so I cleared my throat and introduced myself. Numa and Tarrech followed my lead. I noticed that Sefir's eyes flicked to our Jereh bands, visually confirming what we said aloud by checking our stones.

Numa spoke for us after that. "I notice that you have erected walls quickly with the help of Raelech stonecutters. Our information indicates that they are still in your camp. Is this true?"

"It is. Their work is a credit to your nation and their kenning."

"Kind of you to say," Numa replied. "Rael formally requests the return of those stonecutters to our care this instant regardless of work in progress."

"Of course," Sefir agreed immediately, and I almost blurted out, "Really?" but turned it into a cough instead. The hearth continued, "We will deliver them to your care as soon as our parley is finished."

That changed our objectives considerably. Our primary reason for sending the juggernaut, after all, was to rescue the stonecutters if the Hathrim refused. Now Tarrech had no reason to employ his kenning against the Hathrim, and I wondered if that was not her design all along. If she was well versed enough in our culture to read our Jereh bands, she might know much more and realistically conclude that if she gave us no reason to attack, we would refrain. Like the Kaurians, we use force only after a triggering event. It is no secret that in a way this allows us to be controlled: do nothing to trigger our military response and you will be safe. It dawned on me that her superior smirk might be deserved. At this time, anyway, she appeared to have all the answers.

Until Junior Tactician Nasreghur spoke again. "We have received reports from Forn that your houndsmen attacked their peaceful scouts without provocation."

"Then the Fornish are lying to you," Sefir said, and her expression finally hardened for a few moments. "The Fornish attacked us because we harvested a few trees to cook our food, even though this side of the Godsteeth is not part of their precious Canopy or their country. In fact, they are invaders much more than we are. We lost six houndsmen to them. We are clearly the party with a grievance here, and even though we are refugees, we reserve the right to defend ourselves."

Nasreghur was having none of that and continued with his aggressive language. "You have no rights to harvest Nentian timber or occupy Nentian land without our prior approval. Refugee status does not confer to you the right to do whatever you wish within our borders. You are in violation of the Sovereignty Accords, and your navy is also illegally blockading our national waters. We insist that you end your blockade immediately and relocate to some other place in Hathrir."

"The citizens of Baghra Khek, together with their lavaborn and military and naval forces, retain the right to defend their lives wheresoever they are regardless of official status or international treaties. And it is the height of callousness to demand that we relocate to a poisoned land on the instant. We offer you no harm and will gladly compensate you for timber harvested without permission in our hour of dire need. I formally request permission to continue timber harvesting with the understanding that we will pay in steel and glass for such resources; indeed, we would like to trade with Hashan Khek and other Nentian cities as we did in Harthrad."

I noticed the entirely unsubtle use of "lavaborn," just in case we had not yet noticed that there was a lavaborn giant standing there with her head on fire. I did not know at that time, however, if Sefir was lavaborn herself. Nasreghur shook his head and ceded nothing. "This is not a trade negotiation, though we would of course be delighted to trade once you are back in Hathrir."

"Are we not to be allowed basic needs? You would have us die because we temporarily occupy a space you are not using?"

"The fact that we do not use a space within our borders does not create a right for you to occupy it any more than unused land in Hathrir is available for Nentian use. You continue to cast yourself as the victim when it is you who are victimizing Ghurana Nent. You are occupying land you have no permission or right to occupy regardless of whether a volcano erupts in your land or not. So answer me plainly:

Will you agree to remove yourselves from this land at the formal request of Viceroy Lohmet?"

"Yes." The Hathrim hearth's smirk returned. Either she was lying or she was relying on a nebulous definition of *when* she would agree. Nasreghur was ready for that, however, and quickly moved to pin her down.

"When?"

"I'll agree when a formal request is made."

"I formally request that you leave Nentian soil immediately."

"You misunderstand. I meant I would agree to leave when Viceroy Lohmet formally requests it. You are not he, nor is your puffed-up superior over there. When Viceroy Lohmet appears here in the flesh and formally requests that we leave, we will agree to leave. The Raelech delegation bears witness."

"We do," Numa said, and I saw how we had been outmaneuvered. Hearth Sefir could speak with Hearthfire Gorin Mogen's authority, but we could not speak for the Triune nor could Nasreghur speak for the viceroy. She therefore had the advantage and could play on that.

Nasreghur ignored the exchange and tried to bluster his way through. "We are the viceory's duly appointed representatives and speak for him."

"I do not recognize this. I require his personal request."

It was a transparent delaying tactic, and we all knew it. Nasreghur continued, always probing. He might be bereft of all subtlety, but I had to admire his determination to score whatever points he could.

"Recognize my request that you dissolve your naval blockade immediately and allow ships to pass freely up and down our own coast."

"Or what?"

"Or we will be forced to make you comply."

The Hathrim hearth snorted. "You must of course do as your conscience dictates, Junior Tactician. But know that the citizens of Baghra Khek will defend themselves if you attack."

"You are the former citizens of Harthrad and have no right to be here whatsoever."

"Do send your viceroy down to tell us that in person."

"You can be sure I will."

"Is there anything else?" She turned to us with a raised eyebrow, and Numa shook her head. "Very well. I will send the Raelech stonecutters out to you as soon as I return." Her gaze swiveled back to Nasreghur, and she beamed at him. "Good day to you, friends. But I should warn you all that we have established a perimeter around our walls marked by a trench. Please do not cross that trench or we will be forced to consider it an attack on our people and defend ourselves accordingly."

"That trench is on Nentian soil and means nothing," Nasreghur asserted. "If we cross it and you attack us, then you will be at fault for beginning hostilities. This is our land, and by definition *we* are the defenders here, not you."

The hearth shrugged. "A disagreement, then."

Sefir and La Mastik bowed in concert and turned their backs on us, leaving us bemused and the junior tactician frustrated.

We reported the details to Tactician Ghuyedai, and he cursed once and spat before nodding to another one of his officers to proceed with some prearranged orders. Shouts and shuffling ensued, and it looked like they were forming ranks to march forward.

"Before you proceed, Tactician," Numa said, "may we ask you to wait until our stonecutters are returned? They are supposed to be coming directly."

"Perhaps," Ghuyedai said. "Will you march with us against the invaders?"

"We cannot directly attack without permission of the Triune Council," Numa replied, "but we can aid you in other small ways."

"How?"

"They mentioned a trench. You'll need passage over it. Tarrech can smooth the way for your troops, fill it in."

"But you won't fight with us?"

"As the junior tactician stated during the parley, it's your land to defend. You have to defend it before the provisions of the Sovereignty Accords can be triggered."

Ghuyedai was not pleased by the answer, but he couldn't argue the point. And our offer wasn't insignificant: bridging the trench quickly with Tarrech's kenning would be far more convenient than breaking out spades.

"However," I added, "if they do not return our stonecutters as they promised, that will be a different matter."

Numa and Tarrech both nodded, and Ghuyedai grunted. "Very well," he said. "Let me know when you have them back. I have preparations to make in the meantime."

We three Raelechs strode ahead to find the trench the Hathrim had spoken of. It was only a hundred lengths away from where the parley had taken place. The Hathrim had merely stepped over it with their long legs, but it was a bit too wide for us to do the same thing. Its smooth sides and the shallow stone trough in the bottom marked it as the work of our stonecutters. The trough was filled with oil. Try to cross it and the lavaborn would spark it, turning the trench into a ring of fire. And once they had fire to work with, they would spread it quickly. Whoever crossed here first would almost certainly burn to death: that was always the promise of the lavaborn.

We waited at parade rest, and the sun had sunk only a smidgen toward its home in the western ocean before we saw a single houndsman emerge from the walls with three small figures walking before him. It was our stonecutters.

"They're keeping us out of it for now," Tarrech said, a note of regret in his voice.

"Yes. They've made a huge mistake coming here, but they're playing it about as well as they can," Numa said. "We're going to get intelligence on their layout and defenses from our people, but it might not matter. It looks like they've made decent plans. Tarrech, can you tell from this distance whether they've salted everything?"

"A moment," he said, closing his eyes and visibly sinking into the earth. He was rooted up to his calves in it. While he probed at the earthen defenses of the Hathrim through his kenning, Numa and I kept our eyes on the approaching houndsman. Both rider and hound were fully armored. Tarrech raised himself back up to the surface and opened his eyes while they were still out of earshot.

"They've been blasted through," he said. "Even this trench is salted. Filling it in will require moving a lot of earth from outside the ruined area, and I'll need the stonecutters' help to do it to avoid strain. But here's a surprise: they have crops on the far side."

"Inside the trench circumference or out of it?" Numa asked.

"Inside."

"So that's obviously not salted earth. Can you do something to it from here?"

"Yes."

"Good. Wait until tonight," Numa said, "when they won't see any sign of it in progress. Then ruin those crops from underneath."

"You mean try to leave the rows intact?"

"Yes, so they'll never even know it was done. I'd prefer them to be counting on that harvest coming in so they won't make other plans for a few weeks."

When our stonecutters reached the trench and we could see their faces, they were uniformly tragic. By this time they knew how badly they'd been fooled and that they had taken money to help the Hathrim establish a city in the borders of Ghurana Nent. And there was no way for them to refund the payment and undo their work; the salting of the city ensured that any blessed Raelech would have to tear down those walls in person, and for that to happen we'd have to expose ourselves to attack.

One of them saw my Jereh band and cried out, "Oh, triple damn, they've sent a bard here! Now everyone will know about this!"

"They'll know about the incident," I admitted, "but I swear to Kaelin I'll never reveal your names."

The houndsman, a younger giant who nevertheless sported an impressive black beard, dismounted and removed several interlocking sections of wooden planks that had been slung from either side of his hound in something akin to saddlebags. When he had affixed them all together and then bound them on the sides at intervals with metal

spring clamps, he hauled the whole thing over and stretched it across
the trench. It was a portable bridge, eight feet long and three feet wide,
easy for a giant to assemble. He waved to it and stepped back, and I
wondered if they had made that here out of Nentian timber or if it
was something they had brought with them.

"Go in peace," he said, though he nearly choked on the words. They
floated down to us like dead leaves. "The people of Baghra Khek are
grateful for your aid." That was the third time I'd heard them use a
Nentian name for their walled encampment. Perhaps the Hathrim
thought if they repeated it enough, we'd think of it as legitimate. The
stonecutters made no answer but wasted no time crossing the trench,
and afterward the giant promptly lifted the bridge away and disassem-
bled it. We said nothing until he had mounted his hound and ridden
out of earshot.

"I will need to debrief the three of you and then report to the Triune Council," Numa said, breaking the silence. "And after that you will
be sent back to finish the work you were originally contracted for in
Hashan Khek. You must do everything the viceroy asks to make up for
this colossal blunder. If he asks you to complete work outside the
scope of the original contract, you are hereby directly ordered by the
Triune Council to complete it without charge."

They fairly trembled and began to apologize. Numa cut them off.

"Everyone understands that you were duped into thinking you were
building in Hathrir. Apologies won't fix the problem. Only action will.
When we rejoin the Nentians, you will *not* apologize; is that clear?
That would put us further in the Nentians' debt. The Hathrim are to
blame for being duplicitous. You will say only that you will do your
best to mend the situation."

They all nodded and assured her it would be done.

"Any idea who that houndsman was?" Numa asked.

One of the stonecutters nodded his head. "That was Jerin Mogen."

"That was Jerin Mogen? Is he lavaborn?"

"He is."

"And Hearth Sefir, too?"

"Yes."

"How many lavaborn do you think they have?"

The stonecutters looked at each other and shrugged. "Twenty?" one guessed. "Thirty or forty?"

"This is not going to end well," I said. "They'll have no problem setting us on fire."

"We should let the tactician know," Numa said. "Maybe we can convince him to hold off on the attack and think about it."

"He needs siege weapons at the very least," Tarrech agreed. "If he sends men in there now, they'll be mown down."

But there was no dissuading Ghuyedai. He wanted all nations to get involved in lancing the boil of Gorin Mogen, and to do that, Nentian blood had to be spilled defending against an invasion of Nentian soil. He was eager to be about the spilling, but the men he was going to send over that trench would not realize their role was to die; they were going to march, trusting that their general had a plan to win the day, and the horror of it grew in my mind. They would die because of a failure in diplomacy. The wording of the Sovereignty Accords required the blood of a defending army against an invading army to trigger the other countries' participation, the thinking at the time being that no one wanted to be drawn into a war over minor skirmishes or the work of pirate raiding parties, but now I was beginning to see the practical application of it here, and my stomach churned with sourness. Ghuyedai would cast away these men's lives like stones into the ocean because that would get him what the viceroy wanted.

"Give us that passage across the trench now, if you please," he said after the stonecutters had briefed him on the defenses they'd built for the Hathrim. "We're crossing before sunset."

The way we saw it, we had little choice but to accommodate him. The Triune Council wanted to aid the Nentians without risking our people, and the tactician's request qualified. The stonecutters worked in concert with Tarrech, each blessed by the earth goddess Dinae, and their combined efforts ensured that none of them had to strain. Outside of the salted zone bordering the trench, they shifted enough earth to fall into it and fill it for about twenty feet across, smothering the oil and thereby allowing an army to pass over it in narrow columns. It would have taken men with shovels an hour or more to accomplish this, but the stonecutters and juggernaut completed it in a couple of minutes, though it left dust hanging in the air for much longer. The result was a scalloped section of earth on our side of the trench that troops would dip into before rising up to cross the new land bridge. Ghuyedai gave two orders: the conscripts were to march on the city under the leadership of one of his officers, and Nasreghur was to take a company of men back to Hashan Khek with the stonecutters in tow and his preliminary report.

The setting sun warmed the right sides of our faces as we faced south and watched the Nentian conscripts cross the trench. They were armed with shields and spears. My personal belief—a nonmilitary opinion, admittedly—was that they should be armed with full pikes if they wanted a chance against the houndsmen, but perhaps they felt safer with shields.

Tactician Ghuyedai did have a company of pikemen, I noted, but he kept them in reserve along with his regulars. The ranks of spearmen marched across the trench and I kept waiting for it to ignite, all my muscles tense, but it remained cold and quiet. And so remained the city of Baghra Khek in the distance. No houndsmen formed up outside the walls unless they were mustering on the far side of the city where we could not see. No Hathrim infantry emerged to challenge the oncoming army, and we heard no alarms or saw any sign of activity from the walls. It was as if the Nentians marched on an abandoned fort.

That changed once they got into bowshot range. A flight of flaming arrows arced high over the walls, and the spearmen raised their shields above their heads to form an impromptu roof. Not a single soldier died from the arrows. They died instead from the flames.

Once the fire shafts landed among the men, thudding into shields or falling into the earth nearby, the true power of the Hathrim lavaborn was made manifest. From a distance, perhaps peeking over the tops of their walls, they spread those tiny fires to the nearest scraps of clothing. And once that ignited and they had more fire to play with, they spread it even farther, and in seconds there were ranks of men slapping at themselves or rolling on the ground, and they were so preoccupied with their pain and screaming that they never saw the second volley of regular arrows coming, never raised their shields, and those who were managing their personal fires got perforated instead.

Twice more the unseen Hathrim archers behind the walls repeated the pattern—a volley of fire arrows, spreading the flames to clothing, followed by a volley of regular arrows—and that was all it took for the army to break. The rearmost ranks wanted none of what was happening up front and pelted back to the trench, which never did ignite as we assumed it would. And as they ran from the screaming deaths of their cohorts, they did no little amount of screaming themselves. Meanwhile the lavaborn kept at their work on the front ranks, encouraging the flames to leap from soldier to soldier, alive or already dead, until all had fallen and the field was one large cook fire with greasy black smoke roiling and turning the sunset red as the fat of all those sacrificed men snapped and popped through dusk and into the night.

I hoped Ghuyedai heard it and it haunted him as it haunts me still. I hope he smelled the stench of those deaths and had it fill his lungs. I hoped he saw the terrified eyes of his men as they ran back over that trench, crying and with snot dribbling down over their lips, praying to Kalaad to spare them from being burned alive. I hoped he'd be declared unfit for duty. But I think those were all hollow hopes.

A better hope was that the Triune Council would have a good answer for what we witnessed that day, for they would need to respond to this slaughter for sure, and someone far better schooled in tactics than Ghuyedai would need to craft a plan of attack. We had seen no evidence that they had a true fury among them, but the city of Baghra Khek clearly had enough lesser lavaborn to burn whatever they wanted. With flights of arrows and fire they had slain close to two thousand men without ever exposing themselves to danger. A chill in my guts told me many more would have to die before the Hathrim were defeated.

"Meanwhile," the bard said, returning to his current self and pulling out another seeming sphere, "the world's first plaguebringer still had a Seeking to conduct in the aftermath of Madhep's death."

The figure of Abhinava Khose materialized in the smoke, and he, too, looked subtly different. Taller and older as a result of the aging penalty exacted by his kenning and with a look in his eyes that already hinted that the price of his power was grinding away his soul.

Abbi

I gave Madhep to Kalaad in the sky, but when it came to the soldiers, I looked to Tamhan with pleading eyes. He did it, giving them more respect than they had given us, and then we moved our camp. The tired kids got on the horses, and we hiked a couple of miles in the darkness before stopping once more for the night. One of them noticed aloud that she hadn't been bitten or even harassed by a single insect since she'd been in my company, and once she said that, the others realized that it was true for them as well. This small relief from a lifelong source of annoyance impressed them, I think, even more than summoning the swarms. Causing bugs to bite was not that big a deal to them. Preventing bugs from biting, though? That was miraculous.

It was wearying to pretend I was comfortable in a congregation of strangers. They all had been recruited by Tamhan, and to be honest with myself, even he was familiar only by the grace of a single day. I had known *of* him for a long time, but we hadn't really spoken until the day before, and though we got along well, he also got along well with everyone, and I couldn't assume that he felt closer to me than any of the Seekers. Because Tamhan looked to me, and I suppose because I was the one with the kenning, they all looked to me to lead them when what I wished for the most was to walk off alone and give my frustration and regret its proper voice and time. I saw in their eyes that they carried a set of expectations in their field bags that I couldn't fulfill. I couldn't make their lives better. All I could do was lead them to the nughobe grove and hope that at least one of them would be blessed.

The fear growing in my chest was that they might all die. In the eyes of the authorities of Khul Bashab, I would be responsible for killing all these kids. And I'd be responsible for the soldiers' deaths and Madhep's as well: authorities never take responsibility for their misconduct.

I already felt responsible for those men, and it was a heavy burden in my mind on top of all the others, one I would have to carry for a long time. I might have doomed all chance of being accepted or even allowed to exist by the government with a single uncontrolled flare of my temper. That one unguarded reaction might prevent me from doing so much good.

There are healers I know, for example, who believe that insects can spread disease. If that is a truth and I can stop insects from biting, then think how many lives I could *save* if only I was allowed. Would that not in time make up for the lives I took?

But already I see no path by which I can be forgiven for what happened. Madhep's family wouldn't forgive me, if any of them could be found, and Tamhan's father would make sure the viceroy didn't either. Not that the viceroy would need an incentive to turn against me after I killed a bunch of his men and took their horses.

We started small fires and tried to sleep, hoping perhaps that we would wake and find it had been a nightmare, easily banished. I took care to make sure everyone was within a sphere of my protection before picking my place to lie down, close to Tamhan but not close enough.

In the morning Madhep was still gone, my family was still gone, and I wept silently before anyone was up to see. But once it was daylight and I had to be the leader again, I spoke to the Seekers with Tamhan behind me, Murr by my side, and Eep perched on my shoulder.

"I wish to emphasize that you don't need to seek this kenning and that you may change your mind at any time," I said. "There is absolutely no obligation here. And there is also no shame. None of us is a judge, and none can decide for someone else what they should do with their life. After those who seek the kenning are finished, I will escort everyone else back to Khul Bashab so you will be safe."

They stared at me in silence and a few of them nodded, but there were no questions. No challenges, either. They merely followed me, and some of them talked with one another through prior acquaintance, but none spoke with me and none made an effort to make new friends. No one knew if they'd still be alive to continue a friendship in a few days.

None of them volunteered their names after Madhep died, and I didn't ask. Without Murr and Eep and Tamhan around to keep me company, it would have been a very lonely time. Tamhan spoke to me about what he had learned about business from his father: colluding with the viceroy and essentially bribing him through politely labeled methods ensured a tidy profit. The viceroy's cronies became wealthy that way, the other merchants just got by, and all the rest subsisted if they were lucky. The unlucky ones—well, they met a bad end in the river or outside the walls, or they were walking with us to an uncertain future. He shared so much more, and I think some of it might have been important, economics and politics and so on, but I admit that much of it barely registered. I just liked to hear him talk and encouraged him to keep going.

That ended when we arrived at the nughobe grove in the afternoon of the third day. Murr went ahead to rejoin his nest. I told him that all the people with me had come to seek the Sixth Kenning and I would send them into the grove one at a time. Using my new abilities, I sensed that there were thirty bloodcats in the nest, and it was only a quarter-mile walk from where we stood on the northern edge of the grove.

He padded into the shade while Eep remained behind with me. I got out my journal and ink pot. The sun made me squint at them as I spoke.

"And now you must decide. You may go to seek a kenning, one at a time, or remain here with me. A nest of bloodcats will determine whether you are blessed, and they are waiting a quarter mile ahead, south of here. Give me your name before you go so that if you are not blessed, I can give your name properly to Kalaad in the sky. And if you are blessed, why, then, come back and tell us!"

There was a pause while they looked at one another, waiting for someone to go first. There were no well-kept statistics on the likelihood of success in the early days of a kenning's discovery. But a man stepped forward after about ten beats and gave me his name. He gulped and looked uncertain despite being the first one to summon the will to go through with it. I smiled reassuringly at him and wished him well.

After five minutes I sent the next person willing to go after him, a girl who might have been my age but looked older. She had been worn down by life already, and her gaze was distant, seeing something from her past that spurred her forward into this desperate future in which she was willing to lay down her life for a chance at power. She half mumbled, half slurred her name and I asked her to repeat it, but she ignored me and stalked off into the grove. She had not been gone a minute before we heard distant cries of terror from the first man. Eyes flicked back and forth as the Seekers wondered if everyone else heard it.

"Making some noise is almost unavoidable," I said. "One way or another, blessed or not, you're going to get bitten. So we cannot assume an outcome from what we hear."

I kept sending them in until only Tamhan remained—no one else refused, the desperation that thick in their minds—or rather, the despair. I remembered well the hopelessness I had felt and the welcome I had given to death. I hoped now the screams we heard were one last encoun-

ter with pain before a better life began rather than a moment of fear before death. The two of us waited until we heard the last cries from the
final Seeker before walking together into the nughobe grove that had
changed my life. Eep flew from my shoulder, unwilling to let the sky go,
and screeched as she arrowed into the grass. He'd be fine until my return.

We came to the same clearing I had stumbled into the day my family died, and there we saw bloodcats at supper, tearing flesh from
splayed forms in the undergrowth. Tamhan gasped behind me and
began muttering prayers to Kalaad. I winced at the sight but had prepared myself for the reality of it. Every kenning took a steep toll, and
I had seen plenty of dead in my time as a hunter. A few of the bloodcats looked up at us, but most of them didn't bother.

"Murr?" I called. "Are you there?" I couldn't pick him out from the
rest.

"Murr," a voice replied, and then I spotted him lazing on one of the
tree branches ringing the clearing, his tail dangling below it. His muzzle
was clean. Perhaps he hadn't participated. Or perhaps he had gone first.

"Did any of the Seekers get blessed?" I didn't know what answer I
expected, but it wasn't the hand suddenly raised out of the clearing or
the two others that followed it.

Heedless of the danger—I supposed there was no danger for me—
I rushed to help. The blessed had been bitten numerous times as I had,
but unlike the others, it wasn't fatal.

"Congratulations," I told the first one I came to, speaking so that
the others would hear. "You'll heal quickly. You'll feel better in the
morning and be amazed at how well you feel the day after that."

The man at my feet shifted his eyes to the left and right. He was
about my age as they all had been, and I remembered his eyes and his
unusual hair if not his name. He had shaved the sides of his head and
left a broad stripe down the middle, which he had dyed with yellow
poppy powder and fixed with beeswax. "Is it safe to move?" he asked.

"Yes, it is." I extended a hand to help him up, and he groaned as he
grasped and pulled. "Remind me of your name again?"

"Sudhi Khorala," he said.

"All right, Sudhi," I said after escorting him to the edge of the clearing, "stay here and I'll get the others."

The other two were women, though I supposed one was more of a girl. She had been the youngest of the Seekers and reminded me of my sister. She had blood on her face and streaks through it where tears had fallen.

"I'm still alive," she whispered.

"You're blessed," I said. "Don't worry. They won't hurt you now," and I helped her up.

She sniffed and wiped at her cheek, looking around at all the dead. "I thought I'd end up like the rest of them, nothing to care about anymore."

"There's still plenty for you to care about," I said. "What's your name?"

"Adithi Ghumaal."

"Can you walk?"

"I think so." She took a couple of experimental steps. She had to limp, favoring her left leg, but she joined Sudhi and Tamhan while I visited the third person. She was already sitting up, staring at the blood-cats in outrage. It was the girl with the distant stare whose name I'd never heard correctly. She appeared quite lucid now.

"Damn it," she said. "I was supposed to die!" She picked one blood-cat nearby and pointed at her. "Hey. Why didn't you want to eat me? Do I smell bad or something? Gah, that stings!" She sucked at her teeth and looked down at her chest, which was covered in blood. Belatedly I realized she was missing a piece from her tunic. And she realized she was missing something else, and her angry voice rose to fill the grove. "One of you shits bit off my nipple! What am I supposed to do with only one tit?" She swung around to me. "Is this going to grow back? Did you fully heal?"

"Well, yes, I healed fully, but I didn't lose anything either, besides blood."

She surveyed the damage to the rest of her body, wincing. "You know, this is a messed-up way to get a kenning."

"Well, next week it's spiders, so I think this is pretty good, all things considered."

"Spiders? How do you know that?"

"I just feel it. And can kind of see it in my head. You might be able to as well now. Think about it. These bloodcats won't be the source of the kenning for much longer, will they?"

Her eyes drifted up to the sky as she thought about it. "Oh. Oh! Euuhh! Nasty!" She shut her eyes tightly as if that would rid her mind of the mental image. "I've never seen spiders that big before. You're right; this is better." She cocked her head at me. "What did you say your name was? I didn't pay attention."

"Abhinava Khose."

"I'm Hanima Bhandury. You know what's amazing—besides being alive? I'm talking and you can understand me. I didn't expect that at all! I mean, damn, everything hurts, but my mouth is working again, and that feels good."

"It wasn't working before?"

"No. Got hit on the head a couple of years back, and it did some damage. Kept me from speaking properly. I'd know exactly what I wanted to say and how to say it, but it never came out right. Everyone thought I was stupid and it wore me down till I was ready to make my exit, you know? No one would help and no one seemed to care, so I thought I might as well join my family. They all got crushed by the same building that messed up my head. But now listen to me go. I'm never going to shut up!" She grinned at the same bloodcat she had scolded earlier. "You can have my nipple. It's not like I was using it. I've got my voice back, and that's all I ever wanted. This is the best!"

Strange words to say amid all this death. But she wasn't thinking about what was going on around her. I extended a hand to her to help her up. She grasped it, groaned, and then threw her bloody arm across my shoulder. "Help me out of here, will you? My ankle's messed up, too."

Leaning heavily on me, she hopped over to the others at the edge of the clearing. They all introduced one another and shared smiles; Tamhan congratulated the blessed, and then they all looked at me expectantly. I got out my journal and turned to the page where I'd written down the Seekers' names.

"Four blessed out of thirty-three seekers, including myself," I said. "That's a pretty low success rate if that holds true." Their smiles disappeared. "Let's give them all to Kalaad in the sky."

We turned to the fallen, and I read their names one by one. Our bodies are no more than meat that falls on the plains one day and feeds some other meat, but I wished their spirits peace because I think they were all seeking that more than anything else when they followed me to the grove. Certainly Hanima had, and maybe Adithi, too. I suppose all Seekers are after peace of some kind, and make the calculation that one way or another—in death or blessing—they'll get it.

But I wondered if peace was possible for us. Even though we called ourselves blessed, I didn't see a future of bliss and contentment waiting ahead.

Plenty of chatter ensued once Fintan dispelled his seeming. Increased strength, speed, and healing as well as a connection to animals? The Sixth Kenning was truly a blessing even if it had a high mortality rate in those seeking it—the people nearest me were murmuring excitedly about Hanima's recovery. If her brain injury could be healed with a blessing, then what other infirmities might be cured?

It certainly made me wonder if my old knee injury could be fixed after all this time. I imagined so. What trouble could mere tissue be compared to the complexity of the brain? I mean, except the very large drawback that you most likely would die trying to get yourself healed. No thanks. I was fine. I had lived with my bad knee for longer than I had enjoyed a stable one, and coping with it was neither good nor bad, just a fact of my existence.

I also found it interesting that seeking the Sixth Kenning, like the Fifth, involved potentially being consumed with the trade-off of some kind of symbiosis and new physical abilities. For perhaps two seconds I marveled that this was the first time we were hearing about this, and then I realized the Nentian government would have tried to keep it quiet if they didn't control the source of the kenning. If there were still only four of the blessed and they were roaming the plains rather than spreading the word in the cities, then it was no wonder that we hadn't heard more of them. And we'd had our own problems to occupy our attention.

The bard let people talk for a while then held up his hands, a seeming stone in one hand. "Let's check in with Viceroy Melishev before we finish for the day." He cast it down at his feet, and the sour leader of Hashan Khek materialized, this time in a muted, somber tunic of black and dark blue.

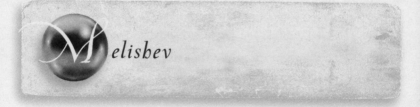

Melishev

I miss Dhingra. This new man, Khaghesh, who bubbled up from the cesspool of the bureaucracy, seems competent, but I do not enjoy the same rapport. He smells like onions and sweat. And he has an unsightly boil or mole or something growing on his face below his right eye. Perhaps it is a reservoir for his evil thoughts. Or it's a spider egg sac and one night soon the creatures will burst out and eat him in his sleep. One can only hope: I'm fairly certain he is a spy for Talala Fouz, so everything I do and say could all be reported later in writing to an unsympathetic pair of eyes. I don't know when I will find someone to confide in again. I never should have sent Dhingra away.

That Raelech courier returned today with news of what was happening to the south: two thousand burned conscripts, Ghuyedai laying a toothless siege, and the juggernaut doing nothing about it.

"Tell me, Master Courier, has Gorin Mogen, in your view, violated the Sovereignty Accords?"

"It matters little what my views are, but I think he has."

"Then by the terms of those accords, Rael is required to help us repel his invasion, is it not?"

"I am certain the Triune Council will act once I make my report. However, we were not sent here with the freedom to attack and may not act beyond the scope of our orders."

Preposterous. "Why send a juggernaut if he's not to attack?"

"A show of force is sometimes as effective as force itself and is often less bloody. And he was dispatched to safely retrieve the Raelech stonecutters who had been duped by Gorin Mogen."

"Were they retrieved? Because they still owe me work." And we'd need to have them do even more now that we had serious cause to believe we might have to defend against Hathrim.

"They were. They are en route under an honor guard of your forces handpicked by your junior tactician, Nasreghur. In the meantime, the juggernaut remains on site awaiting further orders from the Triune. And he did ruin the crops they'd sown."

"They'd sown *crops?*"

"Yes, but they'll have no harvest now."

That isn't the point at all. The fact that Mogen would be so brazen as to farm the land like it was his sends a much clearer message of his intentions than putting up walls. He intends to make his "refugee camp" a permanent settlement.

Nothing I can do except cry for help at this point, which does little for one's sense of personal self-worth. Yet it is my only option. I send the courier on her way to beg the Triune Council to intervene, and I ask the Fornish to do the same and even send word to the Brynts and Kaurians that the Sovereignty Accords have been triggered. We will see who responds first. I think the Fornish will do something before my own king does. Certainly the lily-white tree lovers will act before the Senesh cousins will. Bhamet Senesh, who likes to sit in his tower and squat on a chair like he shat the whole city of Khul Bashab out of the dank bog of his ass, sent a man asking *me* for military aid because he had some un-ruly half-naked teenagers he couldn't seem to tame. Incompetent tit.

Determined to get some satisfaction out of a frustrating day, I sum-mon my worthless healer for another attempt at treating my condi-tion. A greasy man with a fondness for mediocre boots, Malhama Poresh comes to me with his bag of stinking plant potions and reme-dies he claims are the latest medicines out of the healer community at Tel Ghanaz. He has given me unguents and oils and salves and numer-ous herbal teas to drink, smiling all the while and saying, "Try this!" but nothing cools the burning fire whenever I piss. And it has been getting worse. I have been getting fevers, chills, and sweats.

"Feeling better, I hope?" he says, flashing his teeth at me even though it should be obvious I'm not better.

"No."

"Ah! Unfortunate. Well, I have something here that might do the job," he says, already clawing in his bag.

"You have no idea what you're doing, do you? Have you ever healed anyone with these concoctions of yours?"

"Oh, yes, many people, Viceroy! Your particular affliction is just proving stubborn."

"It's more than that, I'd say. I'd say it's eating me alive. I was with a sexitrist last night and she refused to touch me, and I can't blame her. It looks like it feels—painfully inflamed."

"Apologies, Viceroy. I'm sure we can do something about it."

While he rummages about, I call over some soldiers and order him bound and gagged. We go down to the stables and get two horses. I throw him over the saddle of one and lead him out, alone, to Kalaad's Posts. It's a bit of work to tie him to one myself, but once I'm finished, I fetch a whip from my pack and give him a lick across the chest just to get the scent of his blood in the air. Then I remove his gag and let him scream a bit until he asks, "Why?"

"If you can't do your job, Malhama, then you're tonight's meal for something hungry out here."

"No! You can't just leave me to be eaten alive—"

"I most certainly can. I have been in pain for months, and it's your fault. So I think you should feel all of that pain today."

The healer's face twisted in fury. "How is it my fault? Maybe if you didn't fuck so many gut goats your cock would work just fine!"

"What?"

"You heard me, you deviant! Everyone knows where you stick that thing. Goats are just the beginning. You like gharel hens because of the way they squawk and wriggle. And then there's the legendary sessions with wart yaks."

He continues to list invented liaisons with various creatures while I scramble to my horse, draw my sword, and then hack at his neck to shut him up. His head tumbles into the grass, blood pumps from the stump a couple of times, and the horses whinny at the approach of predators. Cursing that he had been able to get to me and deny me what little pleasure I could take from his begging, I leap onto the horse and gallop back into the city.

My repeated requests for a Brynt hygienist to be sent to me from Talala Fouz have gone unheeded. The king wants me dead, I know it. Or so weak that I fail to dislodge the Hathrim and then he can remove me for that. The Fornish ambassador says there's a Brynt hygienist in Pont whom they would be happy to send except that Gorin Mogen's navy is making the passage too risky.

I have few options left. I can't leave the city to seek aid while there's an invading force on my doorstep, and there's no chance of me receiving help for days at this point. If it is Kalaad's judgment for me to die in the most humiliating way possible, I suppose I have earned it. But I will defy such an end as long as I can.

"Tomorrow our story will catch up with where we began, the night of the Bone Giants' invasion. Until then!"

Day 11

BROTHERLY LOVE

Toast, interrupted. Should anyone ever ask for a quick summary of my existence, I think that will do. The violent knock on my door as I was bringing breakfast to my mouth so startled me that I dropped my toast facedown. I could almost hear a mournful foghorn bellow through my shock as I stared at it, and I considered wailing an impromptu dirge, but the knocking continued, so I went to answer. The person responsible for destroying my breakfast was none other than Gerstad Nara du Fesset, looking grim.

"Oh, no. What's the trouble now?" I asked her.

"No imminent danger," she said. "But there's someone who needs to see you."

"Uh . . . the pelenaut?"

"Someone who works for the pelenaut. Are you ready to go?"

"More ready than I am to clean up my toast."

"I'm sorry?"

"Never mind. Let's go." I followed the gerstad down to the warehouse district surrounding the docks. She wouldn't tell me anything more about who we were going to see but instead spoke of what had happened at the chowder house.

"How's your wound? I'm still terribly sorry about that."

"It'll be fine. The hygienist says I'm free of infection. And it's not your fault. There's no reason for you to feel guilty about it."

"I see plenty of reasons. But I'm glad to hear you'll heal. And at least I have something to do now that might make up for it."

"What do you mean?"

"I'll be gone for a few days, working on something. If there are any more security worries, you'll have someone else visiting you."

"Oh. Well, I hope you'll be safe."

We turned down a narrow alley between buildings with only a sliver of sun illuminating it from above. It smelled of mold and other things that thrive in low-light, musty environments. The gerstad stopped at an unusual solid metal door with no handle on it and a slot at eye level. She knocked on it twice. The slot opened, and a pair of dark eyes peered out.

"I'm here with the professor as ordered," she said. The slot slammed shut, and then a series of clacks and clicks signaled locks tumbling open. The door scraped open, and she ushered me through first. Two gigantic mariners waited inside, blocking our path down a hallway so narrow that they almost had to stand sideways. They searched me for weapons but not the gerstad.

"Clear," one of them said.

"This is where I leave you, Dervan. Go with these men and be well."

"What? I don't understand."

"They'll take you to the man who's speaking for the pelenaut in these matters."

That didn't give me any useful information and it annoyed me, but I understood that I must be meeting someone my wife might have known. Vague sentences and security paranoia could only mean I'd stepped into state-sponsored skulduggery. I nodded a farewell, and one guard closed and locked the door behind her.

The other beefy mariner grunted and indicated that I should follow him down the hall, which was singularly strange. The floors, walls, and ceiling were all metal. There were slots and sometimes holes all along

the walls, and I glimpsed eyes watching us on the other side of them.
They could, no doubt, thrust spears or shoot bolts at us through those
apertures. Holes arranged in lines in the floors waited to receive the
metal bars of portcullises that were currently drawn up into the ceiling, allowing us to pass. Anyone trying to get down this hall without
permission would have tremendous difficulty pulling it off—even one
of the blessed. Nothing to set on fire and too narrow for a Hathrim to
navigate anyway. No earth for a juggernaut to manipulate. No plant
life for a greensleeve to twist. And the entire foundation of the building would be salted, no doubt, to prevent any trickery from below. I
wondered what defense they would have against a tempest trying to
infiltrate as the wind and soon had my answer: a series of three rooms
that functioned as air locks.

"This side of the building and the other are completely sealed off
except through these doors," the mariner explained when I asked. "No
way for a tempest to open them. They'd have to become solid eventually, and then they'd be vulnerable."

"Incredible. Even the pelenaut doesn't have this kind of security."

The mariner shrugged. "Pelenauts are easy to come by." Implying
that whoever I was meeting was more important than our rightfully
elected ruler. Interesting.

"I'll leave you here. Someone else will take you the rest of the way
on the other side. Just wave at the people on the other side of the windows. They know you're coming."

"Okay. Thanks. Have a great . . . well, do you ever have a great day
doing this?"

"Every day he doesn't die is pretty great. I think he has to be pretty
old by now."

"You mean whoever it is I'm meeting?"

He grunted and waved me through the first door. It slammed behind me, there was a hiss of pressure, and through a window of thick
glass on one side I saw a pair of mariners. I waved, they nodded, and
then they turned a wheel set in the wall that unlocked the next door in
front of me. Once I stepped through, the procedure was repeated

twice more. Once I was past the third air lock, the hallway looked considerably more friendly. A young woman waited for me in a well-lit and much wider hallway decorated with art instead of murder holes. Her clothing was a riot of bold colors, a statement of defiance against the atmosphere of doom surrounding her. She smiled a practiced smile, and her voice matched its brightness.

"Good morning, Master du Alöbar! Welcome! If you will follow me, please."

"Okay, hello. What's your name?"

She spun on her heel and spoke over her shoulder as she walked briskly down the hall. "We don't have names here. I think you're the only one in the building who does at the moment, so congratulations. You're about to meet someone known as the Wraith, if he's known by any name at all. You may simply address him as 'sir.'"

"The Wraith?" I snorted. "That's a mite pretentious, isn't it?"

"I wouldn't suggest you share your judgments with him. Please do not attempt to look at his face. If you do see him, even by accident, we will have to kill you. Is that clear?"

Her voice was so joyful that it took a moment for the import of her words to sink in. "What? You're being serious?"

"Very serious. If you see his face, you will die. Is that clear?"

"It's terrifying." She turned to look at me, the smile gone. "It's also clear," I added, and the smile came back. Approval for good behavior. "Does the pelenaut know about all this?"

"Yes. Your orders are coming from him. But the Wraith will be able to explain and discuss some things that the pelenaut cannot in court or anywhere else. This environment is much more secure."

"I'll say. It's a shrine to paranoia."

We arrived at a door that had a normal knob on it, and she paused with her hand on it, the smile erased from her face again. "Sit in the chair on the other side of this door. Do not try to explore the room. Remember, if you see him, you die. Just listen and answer and stare at the wall. When you're finished, I'll escort you out."

Wondering if I could trigger an approval response, I said, "Thank you. I will do exactly as you say." Victory! She grinned at me and opened the door.

The room was largely shrouded in darkness ahead except for an upholstered chair near the door and a small table next to it with a single candle and a glass of water. The chair faced a wall to the right of the door where two sconces with enchanted Hathrim fireglobes in them pointed to a canvas on the wall depicting a verdant, forested shoreline with a single ghostly figure standing there. A wraith among the trees. Death waiting among all the life. The message lacked subtlety, though I supposed he was at least hewing to a consistent theme.

I sat in the chair as promised, crossed one leg over the other, and stared at the painting, hands folded in my lap. I could see nothing else in the room even if I tried, but there was plenty of darkness to my left once the weak glow of the candle failed. I did hear some shallow, labored breathing and eventually a moist cough and a noisy clearing of the throat. A man's phlegmy rumble spoke from the darkness.

"Master Dervan du Alöbar. Thank you for coming."

He said it as if I'd been given a kind invitation rather than picked up by a military officer and escorted there. I'd much rather have been searching for Elynea and her children than dealing with this nonsense, so I took what petty revenge I could, perhaps driven mad by lack of breakfast. "My pleasure, Master Butternuts."

The moist cough again. "You may call me sir, or, if you must, Master Wraith."

"Oh, no, I'm not falling for that. They told me very clearly that I would die if I saw your face and I would die if I called you anything but Master Butternuts. I don't want to die, so Master Butternuts it is. I'm kind of shocked you would try to trick me like that. I don't know why I deserve any of this."

The room was silent for a while except for the wet breathing. "Someone thinks they are being funny, like divers who take their dates to see the penis corals. They point and laugh for three or four seconds and thereby waken the longarms who live among them. When that first tentacle shoots out and wraps around their wrists, they stop laughing."

He could feed his intimidation to the bladefins. "You're right, Master Butternuts. This isn't funny. Why am I here?"

He coughed, and something splattered in the darkness. Gross. "The pelenaut and the Lung grow more worried about these approaching allied armies. They may not be allies after all. The pelenaut may have mentioned this."

"Yes, he has."

"We're like a litter of kittens in a burlap sack right now. We're not sure what's going to happen next, but we're pretty sure the situation isn't good. We don't know how big the force is, nor do we know precisely where they are at the moment. We have not had time for any of our scouts to get out there and return, and we've had no additional Raelech couriers. But the bard's story is pointing to some uncomfortable possibilities. Do you know why he was there, in the west, with a juggernaut?"

"The Triune Council sent him."

"An afterthought. But sending a juggernaut was a misstep, and that was urged by a council member named Clodagh. You mentioned to the pelenaut that she was one the bard said nothing about."

"That's correct, Master Butternuts."

"Bennelin would have fallen to the Bone Giants regardless, but sending a juggernaut away just prior to an attack has damaged her influence. She's even more dangerous as a result."

"How so?"

"She'll be wanting to repair it now. She needs a big victory to overshadow that mistake. She has to gamble. She may be looking for a legacy beyond merely defending her country."

"Maybe. But I don't think the Raelech faith allows them to consider conquest."

"I agree. So they won't call it that. They'll take over and call it 'aid to an ally in need.' We'll be a 'protectorate' or a 'benign dominion' or some other euphemism that means we exist to please them, like one of their ceramic sex toys."

"Wait, back up. How would they take over?"

"They arrange an accident for the pelenaut and let things fall apart like they absolutely would without his leadership. Then they offer to help. Their forces intermingle with ours. The population becomes used to following Raelech orders. And slowly, for our own good, we do things their way instead of ours."

"That's an imaginative scenario. Uncomfortable to contemplate."

"As a fresh cob of corn shoved briskly up your anus." His throat rumbled as he tried to clear it, but nothing came of it this time and he cursed before continuing. "I'm paid to imagine such things and prevent them from happening." I suppressed a chill at his words. I'd heard Sarena speak them before, word for word. It didn't matter if she'd heard them from him or the other way around: this man had most likely been her mysterious overseer who had supervised her operations and whom she had never named.

"So you admit that you have no factual basis for this Raelech conspiracy."

"It is a fact that Clodagh has a militant mindset and is willing to send juggernauts abroad at the least provocation. It is a fact that we are still not sure how we're crossing the ocean safely to strike back at the Bone Giants, so what use is sending an army here now? And it is a fact that Fintan knows things about the Nentian viceroy he shouldn't know."

"What does that have to do with it?"

"He's a damned skilled spy. And he's here looking for weaknesses." He got excited at the end of that and raised his voice on "weaknesses," and this inspired a juicy coughing fit. I waited until he'd recovered to answer him.

"Unless he's here to tell the story like he claims."

"Of course he's here for that. But that's not the only reason he's here. He wants to take a peek at whatever he can in the palace."

"But he can't get in there. When he's not with me, he's under surveillance, is he not? You seem to have it covered."

"Maybe. What we'd all like to know is how he knows the inner monologue of Melishev Lohmet. I can't believe that Lohmet would volunteer such sentiments as we've heard so far. Contempt for his merchants, his army, and his citizens, suspicions that his king is spying on him, openly coveting the throne, and his outright murders—he'd never want that to be public. On the one hand it's as entertaining to us as a frenetic marmot orgy in the springtime. On the other it's frightening because it means the bard gained access he shouldn't have. Which means we need to guard against the same thing happening here. Imagine him talking to some other crowd of people that way about Pelenaut Röllend."

"Rölly isn't a degenerate like Melishev."

"No, he's not. But you don't get to spend more than a day being pelenaut without making a decision that will cast you in a bad light if presented at the wrong place and time. On election day it's all cake and tits and you think it's good to be pelenaut. After that it's tough."

"You've seen a few elections, then?"

"More than you. I'm an old man with a sharp mind and a soft, shitty body. I like cake too damn much. The point is that we don't want people hearing about us someday the way we're hearing about the Nentians. I want you to ask the bard straight how he found out all that shit about Melishev because this is something you can be openly curious about. Everyone's curious."

"You think he'll answer honestly?"

"No. But I think he'll give you a more thoughtful answer. Others have asked him, of course, and he laughs off the question or gives a flippant reply. I want to know what he says to you."

"All right. Is that all?"

"No. We need to keep your manuscript secure. You've written some things about our open suspicion of Rael that will be harmless later, but we don't want it to get out right now. We'll send some people over to make some modifications to your home."

"Wait . . . you've read it?"

"Of course I have. I'd be a bloody incompetent master of spies if I hadn't."

I gritted my teeth, trying to think how they could have read my manuscript without me knowing. It had to be while I slept or while I was out. I was out often enough to make it feasible. "Fine. What else?"

"Stay away from the palace from now on. If the pelenaut wants to see you, he will meet you elsewhere. That way if you show up at the palace, we'll know it's not you."

"I beg your pardon?"

"We think it likely the bard will try to impersonate you to gain access to the palace. It's all about security. Expect to be poked and prodded from now on to make sure you're not the bard."

"Understood, Master Butternuts."

Silence for a few beats, then: "I'm starting to think you may be an asshole."

"This from a man who threatens people with death if they look at you."

A snort. "Very well. You may have your petty digs against my vanity. It is the least I can do after all your wife did for me and this country. In deepest sincerity, Master Dervan, she was our finest. An excellent spy and an excellent person. I wish she were still with us. I'm very sorry about what happened."

I squeezed my eyes shut to prevent emotions from leaking out of them and spoke through clenched teeth. "And do you know what happened, Master *Wraith*? Sitting here in the dark, did you ever find out who was responsible for her murder? Or who came up with a poison our hygienists couldn't counteract?"

"No. But I haven't given up on seeking answers. I continue to devote resources to it despite our other priorities. Because the source of that poison does need to be found, and we need to muster an appropriate response."

"You will inform me of any developments?"

"You have my word on it."

I took a few deep breaths, thought of the ebb and flow of tides and the smooth sand that is left behind. I would be the beach after the tide has receded. I just needed to get out of that room and let the waves wash over me.

"You have my thanks. Am I dismissed?"

"In a moment. You'll be relieved to hear you shouldn't have to come here again. Communications will flow through the military or the Lung's staff. You may pass along any information you have through the mariners on your detail, who in fact work for me. That is all."

"Right." I pushed myself up from the chair and exited through the door, where the woman with the approval smile was waiting. She flashed it at me and led me through a bewildering maze of halls, stairways, and doors to an exit that was different from the one I had used to enter. It wasn't even the same building; we had traveled underground and come up somewhere much closer to the docks.

"I trust you can find your way home from here," she said.

I gave her an approval smile and walked away. Home wasn't where I wanted to go. Butternuts in there had opened wounds that weren't fully healed, and I wanted to fight someone. I headed for the armory because maybe Mynstad du Möcher would spar with me.

The Mynstad smiled briefly at my arrival, but then her face became wary when she saw my expression.

"Are you available to spar, Mynstad?"

"Yes, Master Dervan. Are you well?"

I clenched and unclenched my fists. "No. I need a fight. I need to have my ass kicked. It'll make me feel better."

"That doesn't make sense."

"It makes perfect sense. But if you could do it without causing any permanent damage, I'd be grateful."

"Maybe some meditation would be better, or a good stiff drink."

"I'm not some Kaurian who can just sit outside and breathe peace, and it's too early to drink. I'm a Brynt and I need to let the violence flow out of me."

She stared at me a moment, then nodded. "Very well. It so happens I wouldn't mind kicking some ass this morning. Kind of convenient that you came along, really. Training swords?" She reached for a rack of dull wooden blades mounted on the wall.

"No. Fists."

There was a moment of evident surprise, but she shrugged it off. "Okay. I hope you won't mind if I tape my knuckles."

"By all means." I taped mine as well, and when we were ready, we stepped out to the courtyard.

She took in my stance and sniffed. "You sure about this, Dervan? I could just buy you a beer and we could talk about whatever's troubling you."

"No. I need to punch something."

"Okay, then. Go ahead. Take a swing, at least."

I shuffled forward as if I was going to fight right-handed, but of course my right knee was too weak to allow that. As soon as I tried to dance back or to the side, I'd fall over. I switched my feet and fists at the last moment before jabbing left and following up with a right cross, planting my weight on my good knee. She took the jab but wasn't fooled by the switch; she stepped inside the cross and blocked it with her forearm, then hammered me in the gut and smashed her forehead into my nose. I never landed another blow. The Mynstad had speed and agility far beyond mine, as well as youth and strength, and she employed it all, robbing me of breath with body blows and then knocking me down with a couple of fists to the face that rearranged my features but thankfully left all my teeth in my mouth. My head spun, my ears rang, and I wheezed in the dust, coughing up blood.

"How's that?" she asked, standing over me, her taped knuckles bloody while mine were pristine. "Your ass been satisfactorily kicked?"

"Perfect," I said, blood and drool spraying from my lips with each syllable. "You're a good friend."

She shook her head in disgust and muttered, "Men don't make a damn bit of sense."

I started to laugh but then stopped because it hurt. "No, thank you. I feel so much better now."

"Whatever. I'll fetch a hygienist." Her boots crunched away in the dust, and I didn't even try to move. Other boots moved closer, but the Mynstad barked at whoever it was and told them to keep away from me. And so I was given some time before the hygienist arrived to lie still in the sun and feel it all, and the tears flowed out of me along with the blood and the spit as I missed my wife and mourned her yet again.

The mourning of a loved one never ends at the funeral. It comes back every so often like a stage performer eager for a curtain call and expects you to be loud about it. I gave it all the lung capacity I had.

I truly did feel better after I'd gotten that out of my system and the military hygienist patched me up. "What did you do?" he whispered to me after first making sure the Mynstad wasn't in earshot. "Did you ask her out to dinner?"

"What? No. She was doing me a favor."

He blinked. "That's a new one."

"I've heard some new ones today myself. It's that kind of morning."

I thanked him and returned home briefly to get my writing materials and then met Fintan at a Fornish greenery. Every bit of food there was imported from the Canopy, from salad leaves to root vegetables to beers. It even boasted a Fornish staff, short smiling pale people in woven clothes, all claiming to be from the Golden Tiger Clan.

"Oh, no. The Nentians got you last night?" Fintan asked upon seeing my face.

"No, I've been soundly beaten for unrelated reasons. I'll be fine." I waved a hand, dismissing it. "Looks like you were kept safe."

He nodded. "Slept well, in fact."

"Good. Wanted to ask you something that's been bothering me in going over the story so far."

"What's that?"

"How'd you get all that sewage on Melishev Lohmet? I mean, I know you met him and you were in or around the Tower of Kalaad in Hashan Khek, but I can't believe he'd share all of that voluntarily."

"You're right; he didn't volunteer it." He grinned at me. "Someone in the palace is getting nervous, aren't they?"

"The palace?"

"Yeah. Where your buddy Rölly lives."

"Unless the pelenaut has personally invited you to call him that, I'll thank you not to use his nickname."

"I beg your pardon, then. But seriously, Dervan. You're asking because the pelenaut's worried I'm a spy."

"No, I'm asking because I'm curious. I can't be the only one who's asked you."

"That's true. But let me assure you—and whoever you may wish to share this with—that I didn't infiltrate the viceroy's sanctum in Hashan Khek and sift through his sensitive documents. My opportunity came later, and in a week or so it will be part of the story and therefore part of the record. Can you wait for your answer until then?"

I shrugged. "Sure." There was no use pressing him. My personal curiosity should be satisfied with that. To pursue it would mean it wasn't my curiosity after all but Master Butternuts'.

Despite not losing any teeth, my jaw still hurt from the Mynstad's fists, so I ordered soup and pudding for lunch as we got to work.

The bard's hair blew in a breeze coming from the ocean, and he smiled as he strummed his harp. "Today is a good day, I think, for a windchime from Kauria!" he announced. "If you're unfamiliar with them, they are three verses of three with the end words of each line rotated. This is an easy one to remember. Do alter the gender to suit yourself."

> My emotions are tossed like the ocean wind
> For my love is foremost in my thoughts
> And she is a rare and dangerous treasure
>
> But it is her very danger that I treasure
> And hearing her laugh on the ocean wind
> Inspires the most distracting thoughts
>
> And now there's naught but passion in my thoughts
> For her favor is what I most treasure
> And peace never blows from the ocean wind

"Today our tales will remain here in the east, all regarding the aftermath of the Bone Giant invasion. Here's an account from the trader's daughter, Kallindra du Paskre."

Kallindra

When our wagon crested the hill above Möllerud, we expected to see the familiar domed roofs nestled against each other and softly gleaming, bronzed like baked goods frosted with sugar. We expected to see people on the road and cattle lowing in the fields outside the city. We anticipated health and prosperity and a vibrant market in which to sell our goods. What we saw instead was the aftermath of slaughter.

Some of the domes were crushed, and dark holes yawned at the sky. Rag doll bodies tossed about on stained turf fed the blackwings. Some of them were children, and I wept when I saw them, small innocents having their eyes plucked out by sharp beaks.

But the true horror for me, though I didn't realize it until later, was that nothing burned. Not a single trail of smoke curled into the sky. Somehow this made the people seem more dead.

Perhaps it is the bias of my background speaking, where the night's fire is a ritual and a comfort, but somewhere in the chaos of the city's death, a cooking hearth should have blazed out of control. At the least, someone must have grabbed a brand, or a torch, or even a poker to defend themselves and thus set fire to their surroundings in a mad bid for survival. Death should not be so cold and black and silent. A fire is both appropriate and necessary. It is the ashes that announce that the past is dead and the future is in the soil, bounty to be brought forth by the water of Bryn.

There is no hope in a blight of blackwings croaking over their bellies full of the dead.

"You're going to meet the leader of the importer clave in Fornyd, Culland du Raffert, next," Fintan said when he had returned to himself. "Like many of you here today, he lost everything at the massacre of Festwyf. But that loss was not the end of his story."

The strange smoke of his new seeming revealed a man in middle age, his skin loosened around the jaw and neck, a bit of a spread around his middle, and the beginning of a bald spot on the crown of his head. His clothing was neither rich nor poor; it was the garb of a respectable merchant, sober and prim.

Culland

My knees were fine this morning, but now they threaten to buckle with every step. My lip quivers, and my eyelids twitch. All my muscles are uncertain, reflecting the fear and trembling in my mind. I don't know whether to weep or to charge down the Merchant Trail with a sword to meet the invading army all by myself. Quartermaster du Cannym told all the clave leaders that Festwyf was lost and the evacuation of Fornyd would begin immediately to prevent us from being lost, too. We are supposed to flee before this deadly flood of giants. We have that choice.

But my son and daughter and their spouses in Festwyf were not given a choice. And neither was my wife, who had sailed downriver last week to visit them. If Festwyf was lost, then they were lost, too. And with them gone, my business was gone as well; the invaders may well be peppering their camp stew pots with my spices. Not that the business was worth a damn when my family wasn't around to make a living from it.

The furniture in my house is kindling and cloth now, nothing more, if only I remain to use it. The flowers in my wife's garden will no longer hear her humming as she weeds and prunes. The water filtration system my son made for a school project continues to drip, but it's all poison to me now. The quilt my daughter gifted to us for our twentieth anniversary: Who could possibly be comforted by it? Certainly not me. When I think that I was asleep while my family was being slaughtered, I nearly sprain my jaw from grinding my teeth together.

I will hold on to a cupful of hope until I see their bodies. And I might never see them, so that cup will always be there along with a bucket full of denial. But as time passes with no word and no spice shipments, I will have to confront that cup and bucket as the lies they are. And then what will I do, alone and shortly to be penniless?

Cry. Drink myself into oblivion. These are already attractive to me. Since I have to pack a bag and walk to Tömerhil, having no horse, I might as well fill it with liquor and money to buy more, all the money I have on hand. Strange how easily all other considerations slough away when it's just yourself to care for and you don't care much for the duty. So it's the road south for me, and if I don't receive some hopeful sign that my family may be alive after all, I'm off to Pelemyn. Long ago, when I was a young lad, before my business flourished and I met my wife, I was tempted to dive into Bryn's Lung. My commercial success and marriage banished that inclination, but I see no reason why I can't keep the date now. I have every reason to do so. And I think it's calling to me, that sound like crashing surf in my ears that no one else seems to hear.

Except perhaps some do hear a song similar to mine. When I reach the road south, I join a stream, a river of people flowing that way, their faces stunned like mine, feet going one way and their minds going in myriad others. We are wrecked survivors adrift in the flotsam of memories, incapable of rescuing or being rescued, waiting for the inevitable return to the water.

"Culland's journey has a spectacular end, and we'll return to him later in the week, when he gets to where he's going. Down in Kauria, Gondel Vedd has his own journey to undertake."

Gondel

My translation of *Zanata Sedam* is finished, or anyway, I've finished what I can. It's still full of holes, and it's time to return to the dungeon for Saviič's aid. The couple of days off with Maron had done me much good, and I returned to my work and temporary lodgings at the palace feeling refreshed and excited. It will be satisfying to finally get a firm grasp of the text. I have found several words that look as if they might be names for the Eculan deity but cannot be sure from context if they refer to gods or mortal heroes, and I'm quite curious about their version of the Rift legends. What I can be sure of is that this Eculan religion seems preoccupied with suffering as a purifying force. Pain, discomfort, starvation; these are all visible signs of devotion to their faith. It explained why Saviič looked as he did and refused comfortable clothing. He was a pious man and as such could not look or feel anything but starved and miserable. And the promised reward for such piety—if I am correct—will be a remaking of the world in the Eculans' favor. The triggering event for that upheaval had something to do with the Seven-Year Ship that Saviič was looking for. And just as I was thinking I needed to inform the mistral that these people prepared all their lives for war when we devoted all our lives to peace, I was summoned in the midst of my early-morning bladder evacuation and made a horrid mess because I was so startled by the pounding on the door. It was no ordinary lackey sent to fetch me; it was Teela Parr herself, exhaustion painting her skin a dark purple underneath her eyes.

"We need you right away," she said, then frowned. "But take a moment to make yourself presentable." I privately thought she asked for the impossible, but I tied my hair in a queue and found a stain-free tunic while she stood out of sight behind the doorway and briefed me, her voice carrying around the corner.

"We're getting reports that Rael and Brynlön have been attacked and have lost several cities already. The description of the invaders sounds like our prisoner in the dungeon."

Reinei bring us peace. "When was this?"

"Three days ago. The mistral was just informed through the Fornish ambassador." My hurried dress accomplished, she walked me through the halls and laid it out: Bennelin, Möllerud, Gönerled, and Festwyf all lost, and more to follow because the armies had moved on to the interior. They had used a coordinated strike from across the Peles Ocean using massive fleets.

"How did they cross without losing ships?"

"We'd like you to ask Saviič that very question, among others. I have a list."

She produced a sheet of paper with a numbered list of questions for Saviič, and we walked together down to the dungeon. Teela accompanied me to his cell this time, her nose wrinkling at the smell. The Bone Giant seemed pleased to see me but returned in short order to his customary entreaty.

"Give me my book, please," he said in Eculan.

"I will soon," I replied, and continued with my uncertain grasp of his language. "I am nearly finished with my copy and need your help. When I have finished a copy, I will return yours. But first, will you answer a few questions about Ecula for me?"

He flicked his eyes to Teela, registering that these questions were most likely going to be hers, but then chucked his chin at me. "Ask."

I consulted the list. "When your soldiers go to fight, do they wear . . ." I didn't know the word for "armor," so I settled for "defense." "Defense clothes?"

Saviič grimaced. "Defense clothes? You mean *oklop*?"

"*Oklop*?" I flashed my hands up and down my torso. "You wear to keep body safe?"

"Yes, yes," Saviič said. "*Oklop* made of bone. Front and back."

"And *oklop* on your head?"

"No. Paint faces like bone."

I translated this to Kaurian for Teela, and she kept her face impassive and her voice controlled, giving nothing away in her expression that Saviič could read. "That confirms it, then. It was his people who attacked."

I moved to the next question. "Does Ecula want to fight us? Attack us?"

Saviič shook his head. "No. I come to find ship. No fight. I have no *oklop*, no sword."

He hadn't answered the question. "Not you. Not Saviič. Ecula. Your home, your people. Do they want to fight us?"

The Bone giant shrugged. "I don't know. Maybe if you have Seven-Year Ship."

"We don't," I assured him, and then translated for Teela.

"Huh. Go on," she said.

"Ecula has boats," I said to him. "Bigger than yours. Boats that can cross ocean without krakens taking them?"

"Yes."

"How do you make these boats?"

"With wood." He snorted as if I'd asked the stupidest question ever.

"But krakens take our boats made of wood. Why not yours?"

He didn't answer for a while, his eyes traveling between me and Teela. "I don't know," he finally said, but once again he was a terrible liar. There was something about their boats he didn't wish to share. After turning to Teela and translating for her, I asked her a question.

"Do we still have his boat?"

"No; it was wrecked on the coral of the islands when we found him.

But I'm sure that there are boats off the coast of Brynlön now that we could investigate. Last question."

I asked Saviič, "What are Eculan leaders called?" and berated myself for not asking him earlier. So many other words had seemed more important when his leaders clearly were not accessible.

"Our leader is the *kraljic*." That was very close to the Uzstašanas word for "king." Interesting.

"What is his name?" I asked, since the suffix of the word was a masculine ending.

"Kraljic Boškov." A king, then.

"And the leader of your soldiers? What word is that?"

"The *vojskovodja*."

That completed the short list of questions. "Thank you, Saviič. I hope to see you again soon. I will bring your book next time."

We exited the dungeon and made directly for the Calm. We found Mistral Kira dressed in dark mourning grays, the gold pin of her house on her shoulder providing the only color. She welcomed me and asked what I had learned, but not until she had dismissed all other ears from the Calm. After I related my worries about the Eculan religion and added the answers to Teela's questions, she stopped me regarding Saviič's denial of Ecula's intention to attack.

"He said *maybe* they would attack if we had the Seven-Year Ship?"

"Yes."

"Well, we know we don't, and we didn't get attacked. What if they thought the Brynts or the Raelechs had it for some reason?"

"Worth investigating," Teela said.

"I have an alternative theory that we can test," I said.

"What is it?"

"According to Saviič, eighty-four of the faithful sailed west. How many returned? We know for sure that Saviič did not. What if the only survivors who returned to Ecula landed somewhere in the north? It's plausible since any who landed on the Fornish coast most likely fell prey to their forest, and our coastal waters are less than hospitable. They might assume, therefore, that the northern countries were easier to conquer. The fact that no one returned from the south was proof that it was too dangerous."

"An interesting theory but impossible to prove. Unless you talk to them," the mistral said.

"Unless I—what? Me?"

"You're practically the only one who can. I have some other old language scholars on the way here to continue speaking with Saviič. But he is obviously not aware of the Eculans' current plans, nor is he one of their leaders. I want you to travel north, find these Eculans, and talk to them."

"Oh. But if they are simply killing everyone they see, I may not be able to engage them in meaningful conversation."

"No one has tried to speak to them yet. You have some knowledge of their modern tongue now, and you have a copy of that book, *The Seven Kennings*. They will listen. And I'm sending a couple of tempests with you to keep you safe."

"Tempests?" I heard a door open behind me but kept my eyes on the mistral. It would not do to give the impression that there might be something in the room more interesting than she.

"Welcome, gentlemen," she said. "This is Gondel Vedd, a scholar I'm placing in your care."

The soft clop of boot heels on stone came to a halt to my left, and I could no longer ignore them. I turned as the tempests bowed to the mistral and saw an old man standing next to me and a younger man beyond.

The old man was my brother—an extremely aged version of him, anyway. He was ten years my junior and should have looked much better than I, but he appeared to be ancient, perhaps in his eighties or nineties, with a bent back and leaning heavily on a walking stick. He was no longer the proud tempest I had last seen many years ago. He now looked as if he would have trouble chewing his food. His voice was scratchy and tired like worn-out carpet.

"Gondel," he said with a short nod. "It's been a long time."

"Hello, Jubal," I replied, my mouth suddenly gone so dry that I had to cough. "It has indeed."

The younger tempest looked to be in his twenties, dressed in brilliant orange tied scarves, though his true age might be much younger. He could conceivably still be a teenager. "I am Ponder Tann," he said. "Peace to you."

"Now that you're all here," Mistral Kira said, "I have a mission for the three of you. Fly to the Brynt coast, beginning at Möllerud. Find out what you can about what happened. Eventually I will need you to locate one of their armies and speak to their leader. I need to know why they've invaded and if they're coming here next. If this is a matter of simple conquest, why were the Brynts and Raelechs targeted if we and Forn are closer to Ecula? And record everything, Gondel. The world is changing, and I want Kaurian eyes to be witness. Ponder will protect you on your travels. However," she said to the young tempest directly, "if you or Gondel discovers evidence that Kauria is next, I want you to fly back here and inform me immediately, understood?"

All I could manage was a nod. She hadn't mentioned what role my brother would play, but I already knew. He would fly us there, and after that his life most likely would be over.

The mistral continued, "Otherwise you may send regular reports the slow way through our ambassadors where you find them. I'm giving you a letter of introduction, Gondel, that will instruct our embassies to render you whatever aid they can. Help the Brynts and Raelechs understand what they're up against but keep Kauria's safety foremost in your mind."

She had more to say, but I missed it, my mind preoccupied with the imminent death of my brother so that it ground to a halt like gears obstructed by a pebble. I didn't hear how or when I was supposed to return, didn't hear if I would have time to say farewell to my love before we departed, didn't hear how we were supposed to survive while there. I didn't even notice that the mistral had stopped speaking until Teela Parr nudged my arm with her elbow. Startled back into the present to find the mistral looking at me expectantly, I bowed my head and said, "As you wish, Mistral Kira," and hoped that would serve. She gave a tight nod, and then I was shepherded through the palace labyrinth by Teela Parr, leaving Ponder and my brother behind with the mistral. I tried and failed to regain my focus. This wasn't the calm day of scholarly pursuit I had been looking forward to.

Teela was talking and stuffing an official-looking bag made of sturdy leather with a light lunch and a change of clothes. I caught that there was a resealable oilskin pouch inside to protect against water damage, and she put official letters in there along with additional writing supplies and my copy of *Zanata Sedam. When did she acquire that?* I wondered, but said nothing. I wanted time to sit and think, to pause and pay attention to what was happening, but Teela kept me moving, grasping me by the elbow and guiding me to the royal falconry heath, a flowered meadow on palace grounds that graced what would otherwise be the stark slash of an oceanside cliff. Jubal and Ponder were there waiting for me.

"May the wind blow gently at your back," Teela said, pushing me toward them, and I spun on her before she could leave me there, suddenly remembering.

"My husband, Maron! Tell him where I've gone and that I love him."

"I will."

She turned her back, and I had no choice but to face my future. The young tempest had a bag like mine, ready for days on the road, but Jubal had only his walking stick. We nodded greetings to each other, and then my brother said, "Give us a few moments to talk, Ponder, if you please."

"Of course," he said.

My brother and I removed ourselves twenty paces from him and stood on the precipice of the cliff, looking out at the shining ocean with the wind blowing gently on our faces, salt on our lips, and the smell of kelp in our noses. As it was our first private moment in sixteen years—our first moment of any kind, really—we spent a minute in silence, letting the wind speak first.

"Never thought you'd be working directly for the mistral, brother," Jubal began after observing the appropriate time.

"Me neither. Choosing to be a scholar instead of seeking a kenning has proved to be useful after all. I have no regrets."

"Nor I."

His note of defiance sounded a mite desperate. Perhaps he was trying to convince himself. "Jubal," I said, "you're about to die of extreme old age at fifty-two. How can you have no regrets?"

"You can't look at me and see all the good times I had getting here. But I do welcome the end."

"Why?"

"You're sixty-two now, right? I'm sure you're feeling the first pains of advanced years."

"Oh, yes. Well beyond the first pains."

"Huh. Take it from me, it gets much worse." As if to illustrate, a noise erupted from his backside, and he winced. "Sorry. Nothing pretty or peaceful about it, is there? No golden sunset, no dignified final chapter where you're sitting on a porch swing sipping lemonade with your one true love. You know what it is? Damned diapers and that look in everyone's eyes that says you've become irrelevant and a burden. This mission isn't a punishment, brother. It's a blessing—a boon!—for I'm finally going to have my peace. I asked for this assignment. Truly."

"That's good, Jubal, I suppose. But what I meant was that I don't know why you sought a kenning to begin with. I mean, after we lost Rugel—"

"It wasn't about him! Wasn't about you, either, or anyone else! It was *my* decision, Gondel, *my* life!" He was going to say more, but his face purpled and he broke into a fit of racking coughs. When he had worked it out, he moaned and spat a glob of phlegm to the ground. Then he raised his eyes to glower at me and speak in more reserved tones, but with no less passion.

"I never had your wits, nor Rugel's either. Knew that early on. Never had any passion for the sea except for the winds swirling above it. There wasn't a damn thing I wanted to do in life except fly. So it was a kenning for me or nothing. No—shut up, now. Not a word. I know I could have done something else, Gondel. I could have found something steady and boring and peaceful and lived to be just as old as I look now. I just didn't *want* to. If I had died in the Tempest of Reinei like Rugel did, I would have been fine with that. Instead I became the tempest, and they call me a hero. You don't even know why, do you?"

"Not specifically. All I heard was that you defended the nation."

"Yes, that's what they say to the population. The mistral at the time didn't want the true story getting back across the Rift; he preferred that they wonder what happened, and Mistral Kira never countermanded the order when she was elected. Not that it was ever brought to her attention. But I suppose it doesn't have to be a secret now. Sixteen years ago one of the idiot Hearthfires put together a raiding party and sailed along the Fornish coast, thinking to swing down through the islands and sack Perkau. It might have worked, too, but they were spotted by a fisherman in the archipelago, and he reported their presence to Linlauen. The mistral sent me to find them. They made it to Perkau but had only set a few buildings and people on fire before I got there. I made sure they never got home. Never showed myself in the flesh, just remained the wind. Aged a lot that day."

I remembered. It was the last time I'd seen him, after he'd aged and looked older than I did. He'd swollen with pride over some act of heroism he couldn't name and made a point of ridiculing me for wasting my life. "You're saying you killed all the Hathrim? That's what you were so proud of, resorting to violence?"

"Of course I'm proud. I'm the reason Perkau still breathes peace this morning, Gondel. I was Reinei that day. I tossed them all up into the air and then left them there. They were alive and unharmed. Technically I didn't kill them. It was gravity that did that. I let the wind die underneath their bodies, and they splattered on the beach. It was raining giants, and their heads split open like pale melons."

"That's disgusting."

"I know it is. I was sick over it and had nightmares for years and pretended it was nothing. But I hear you've been spending time in a windless dungeon. That's pretty disgusting, too, isn't it?"

"It's not the same—"

"It's exactly the same. You're doing something you loathe because you want to help."

"That much is true, but sitting in a dungeon is not violent. It's not murder."

"I'm sure you'll see plenty of violence on this mission before you're through. Somebody always has to pay the price for Kauria's peace. Sixteen years ago it was me. Right now it's those people up north. And you don't ever want it to be our people down here, so you'll do what you have to do."

"I won't kill anyone, Jubal. Ever."

"Perhaps not. But when you see someone else's violent death, it'll change you. When I saw those sparkers setting people on fire and laughing as they screamed, my nonviolent principles said they'd look the other way for a while. All I knew was that those giants had to be stopped and it was within my power to do it."

"I grant that was truly an ethical conundrum for you. But not one I'll have to face since I have no such power."

"I think you'll be surprised at your powers when you're facing death."

I made no reply. Arguing with him was wearying, yet we could seem to do little else.

He sighed, even more exhausted than I was by it. "Look, brother. It's my last chance to say this. When we get to Brynlön, I'll be beyond speech. So I want you to know now that I've always been proud of you."

"What?"

"You heard me."

"I appreciate the sentiment, Jubal, but you've always said the opposite. You said to my face that I'm a coward for not seeking a kenning. 'A worthless academic who can say nothing useful in every language'—

that's one of my favorites and apparently one of yours. It's been repeated to me by many of your acquaintances."

"I know. I know. Gondel, I apologize for every foul wind I've ever breathed about you. It was unworthy of me and undeserved."

"Then why . . . ?"

"Because, Gondel, as you have no doubt surmised by now, I am in fact a walking, talking anus. It's something I had to accept about myself after I noticed no one wanted to marry me—even after Perkau. Perhaps the violence tainted me forever and people could see it in my face. I had to accept that I am generally unacceptable. I got away with it because tempests are allowed some eccentricities and I bought a lot of drinks. Can't get away with anything now, though. All I can hope for is your forgiveness. You're my only family left and the only person who matters."

"But we never talk—"

"Anus, as I said. Trying to be a human now, to remember what it was like. It's not easy. Peace isn't as easy as everyone wants you to think it is."

That wrung a snort from me that turned into a spluttering, blubbering sniffle. "You're forgiven, Jubal. Of course you are. For everything."

My brother's lips pressed tightly together, and then he sucked them in so that they disappeared, trying to hold back a sob. He successfully kept it down, but he did tear up and gulp. "Thank you, Gondel. You've granted me a peace I probably don't deserve. And I know that you'll do your best to bring peace to the north. The mistral trusts you for good reason."

We embraced and pounded each other on the back, and I was surprised at how frail he felt when he used to be so strong. And I wanted to return to the city, find a comfortable fire in a public house, and simply sit in front of it with cider and talk and laugh with him, for we had never had that kind of moment together as adults. All we had between us was years of pointless distance. I wanted to have a brother again, but he had volunteered to die—again. And the mistral wouldn't have ordered a sacrifice like this if she didn't think speed was necessary for

Kauria's safety. We couldn't delay. Jubal said as much before I could think of a plausible reason to linger.

"We'd best be about Reinei's business," he said. "You have everything you need?"

"Yes, but—"

"Show me. What am I carrying on the wind?" He waved at Ponder. "Let's go, young man."

I held up my pack of papers and writing materials, which also included a change of clothes, a small cache of food, and Saviič's copy of *Zanata Sedam*. Jubal hefted it in his hand, feeling its weight. "That's not bad. Fastened securely. Good. Anything breakable in there?"

"An ink pot, but it's hardened Hathrim glass. And a jar of mustard."

"That'll probably smash when we land. You might want to leave it." I took it out and left it on the precipice as an offering. Jubal nodded in satisfaction. "Now just hold the bag; don't strap it to you. Can't say precisely where it'll drop, but I'll try to get it as close as possible." He turned his head. "Ready, Ponder?" The younger tempest nodded, and my brother tossed aside his walking stick. "Excellent." He grinned at the younger man and then at me, genuine glee on his face as he clapped his hands and rubbed them together. "No more pain for me. Farewell, Ponder. Goodbye, brother."

I didn't want to say goodbye but couldn't deny him his wish. "Goodbye, Jubal. May you find peace in the wind."

"I will. I'm counting on it. Peace to you forever, Gondel."

He drew a deep breath into his lungs and raised his hands dramatically, summoning or drawing the wind or whatever he called it, and a powerful gust blew us off the precipice and over the sea. I cried out in terror, expecting to fall, but we didn't. We twisted and rose and continued to float over the ocean for a few more seconds, and then I slowly lost sensation in my extremities while simultaneously feeling as if I were being stretched like a string of honey being pulled out of a jar by a spoon. And soon I carried no weight, felt no gravity, felt no wind on my face, for I was becoming one with it through the provenance of Jubal's kenning. The harsh whistle of the air became a soothing susur-

rus, and colors bled to gray and then nothing, and I lost all sense of
time and thought only of our destination, the rolling hills north of
Möllerud.

Apart from the initial terror, becoming the wind was much more
pleasant than becoming a heavy sack of fluids again uncountable
lengths to the north. It *hurt* to be flesh and bone, and in the process I
collapsed to the spongy turf of Brynlön, my knees buckling at the very
idea of having to bear my body's weight again. I heard a thud and a
gasp nearby, and my vision came back to reveal Ponder shuddering on
the turf. He was nude, as was I, and our clothes floated down behind
us. Just as I managed to raise my head, my bag hit me square in the
face, so I was spared having to look for it. I brushed it aside, looking for
Jubal. Where was he?

A whoosh behind me caused me to turn, and not five lengths away
I saw a dull gray collection of dust take the shape of a man inside a
whirlwind, one hand stretched toward me, but it never took on any
more solidity than that, no bones or skin or collection of flesh. Jubal's
tunic and pants slammed into the middle of it, scattering the dust and
dissipating the whirlwind. My brother the tempest was gone, leaving
nothing behind to bury, forever adrift in Reinei's wind.

It is strange to mourn someone you know is at peace, to cry when
they are clearly better off than you are. But I did it anyway.

The bard's last words hit most of us hard. We all thought immediately
of who we had lost and last cried for, and many of us, myself included,
welled up again. Sarena's face still haunts my dreams, and I would so
dearly love to hear her laugh again.

Gondel Vedd was only half right: it is somewhat strange to cry for
those who are now at peace except for the stark fact that we, while living, are not.

Day 12

THE UNSEEN WORLD

Apparently I am destined never to enjoy a morning again. A dour collection of longshoremen woke me by banging on my door with a hammer. Upon opening it, I beheld them waiting in the dawn with a small wagon of construction materials and furniture.

I palmed the crusty sleep from my eyes and asked how I could be of service. The one in the front thrust a sealed note at me in reply. The sun had risen just enough above the horizon to allow reading.

> Please meet the pelenaut at the home of Second Könstad
> Tallynd du Böll upon receipt. These longshoremen will be
> remodeling your home in your absence today as per our
> conversation regarding the security of your manuscript.
> *Yours in darkness,*
> Butternuts

Grunting in amusement at the signature, I asked the longshoremen if any of them knew where the Second Könstad lived. They all did, and one offered to lead me there.

"Excellent. I will get dressed and we'll go. Come on in, gentlemen."

There were six of them, all wearing woodworkers' aprons with hammers and chisels and other such tools. One of them ducked his head into my bedroom for a quick look around and then regarded me with knit brows and a frown. "You're not going to want to keep any of this, are you?"

"My clothes, I hope."

"I mean your furniture. We have enough for your entire house and were told to replace it all."

"Oh." The pelenaut had given me only bare essentials and a better lock on the door, which had still been picked by Garst du Wöllyr. "That's very generous, but why?"

"More places to hide things."

That made sense, but I didn't like the idea of being indebted in any way to the pelenaut's master of spies. I didn't see what choice I had in the matter, though.

"Do whatever you need; just leave me my personal effects."

He nodded, and I departed with an escort after changing out of bedclothes into something more appropriate for meeting the country's leader. I brought the manuscript with me since I'd be adding to it later.

The Second Könstad greeted me at the door to her home and invited me in for tea, making no comment on my battered face. She was getting her children ready for school and apologized for the fact that she wouldn't have much time to chat. The pelenaut had yet to arrive. "Please help yourself to anything from that gift basket he gave me," she said, pointing to it on the kitchen table. "I couldn't possibly take care of it all before it spoils."

"Thank you, but wait—the schools are open again?"

"A few of them are reopening today. The rest are coming. The university will reopen for the next semester, I hear."

"Extraordinary. I hadn't heard this at all."

"I imagine the faculty will be notified very soon," she replied, and smiled.

The gift basket contained foods I hadn't seen in months. I grabbed a wheel of cheese and a cured venison sausage and sliced them up on a board while she bustled about. There was a loaf of bread in the basket, and I sawed off a few slices of that as well. The pelenaut arrived as she was leaving to take her children to school.

"Ah, Dervan, it's good to see you alive after picking a fight with the Mynstad!" he said, grinning at me and then wincing once he got a better look. "Damn. She popped you good."

"She did indeed. And yes, it hurts. But I feel better anyway."

"Hmm." Tallynd and her kids shut the door and cut off their accumulated noise, leaving us alone in the house. Rölly followed me into the kitchen and pulled out a chair. I placed the board of meat, cheese, and bread in front of him and poured him a cup of tea. "So tell me what brought that on, if you would."

"Sarena. Frustrated that we still don't know who killed her."

"But you figured out why she was killed."

"No, not specifically. Just something that the Wraith had her do, no doubt."

"Any number of somethings, yes."

"Why do we even need someone like him? Haven't we been at peace with our neighbors for our entire lives?"

"Yes. But peace is something you enjoy in its season, knowing that someday it will shrivel and die. And now war is here. It will pass, too. History is full of one season or another; you know this. But how long war will last is often determined by people like the Wraith. I'm glad we had him and his network around, lurking in the dark. I inherited him, you know. From the last four elected pelenauts. He's been festering all this time."

"Ugh. You mean he's literally festering?"

"Let us say he has significant physical handicaps. The mind is keen, though. He didn't realize the bard's story would be so provocative at first, but now he's fully engaged in that and thinking ahead."

"I've noticed. Are you worried about Fintan's report of you when he returns home?"

Pelenaut Röllend shook his head. "More worried about us surviving the next few months. Fintan can tell all the nasty stories about me he wants so long as we're still here."

"You always did have your priorities straight. Well, I haven't much to report. Fintan said he didn't steal the Nentian viceroy's private thoughts from the Tower of Kalaad or anyplace in Hashan Khek, though somebody else did steal them, and he assures us that the full story of how he came by them will be revealed in the days ahead."

The pelenaut took a deep breath. "Delays upon delays. No solid information. Perhaps it is innocuous and innocent. And perhaps it is dust the Earth Shapers throw in our eyes to keep us from seeing the kick they deliver to our guts. I'm tired of trusting and hoping for the best, Dervan. Soon we will know for ourselves."

"Know what?"

"How big the Raelech army is, for one thing. And hopefully much more than that. Something about the temblor leading them would be nice. I have opened the taps, and we'll see what washes out."

We ate in silence for a moment, and I began to feel guilty. Sausage and cheese like this were exceedingly rare at this point. Tallynd deserved it, no doubt, but so did everyone else struggling to survive right now.

"How are we doing, Rölly?"

He sipped his tea before answering. "Not so bad at the moment, considering. But we're projecting serious shortages in the coming weeks. You don't shrug off losing the harvests and trade routes from so many cities even if your population is greatly reduced. And the closing of the Granite Tunnel slowed down our trade with Rael, of course. But we're reopening the schools to let the parents work a bit more during the day, giving everyone some structure and a sense of normality. I'm going to suggest tomorrow that Fornyd and the other river cities might be ready for repopulation."

"How are they ready? They're still mass graves."

"Not as bad as you'd think. I've had the river traders working on it, floating barges of bodies downriver to the ocean, and of course all the hygienists I recalled have been working on the wells and sanitation systems."

"What hygienists?"

"All of them from around the world. We needed them here, so I recalled them a few months ago to serve their country and sent most of them north, but also a few down to Göfyrd and Gönerled. We need to clean those cities up sometime, and that time is now. And we shouldn't have everyone here in case the Raelechs have other goals in mind than their stated ones. We need to spread out again. And there might be enough to salvage from the surrounding areas to help a few hardy souls get through this next winter. They might be far better off, in fact, than staying on here."

"I'm glad you're up to thinking about all this."

"It's not so different from when we were young, planning how we'd survive the winter on the streets. Identify resources, figure out how to harness them, run the figures, study the flow. It's just a difference of scale. There are a lot of people out there in worse shape than we used to be, and if I can figure out how to keep them fed and warm this winter, then we'll avoid most internal security issues."

"Meaning we'll only have to worry about the Raelechs and Bone Giants and everyone else."

"I'm letting the Wraith and the Lung do most of my worrying about that. The Könstad's doing his fair share, too. He probably wants to worry aloud, in fact, so I'd better get back to the Wellspring. Thanks for trying to get something out of the bard—keep trying."

"I will."

Fintan wanted to talk about the opening of the schools when I met him. "This is fabulous news. I'm astounded that you're ready to do this," he said.

Shrugging, I said, "I have no idea how ready we are. I just heard about it this morning. I'm largely uninformed regarding formative schools since I don't have any children and I used to teach at the university. The university hasn't contacted me yet with any updates about reopening."

"But where are all the kids on Survivor Field going? Are they coming into the city each day?"

"I don't know. I didn't ask for details. I imagine we can find out easily enough if that's a vital concern . . ."

"No, no . . . we can get to our work." I wondered why the opening of schools would be significant to him. Did it represent some kind of benchmark of organization to the Raelechs, an indication of recovery? I was used to thinking of education as a bedrock of society, but did that also indicate something to a military mind bent on conquest? Were the schools to be targets, perhaps? I'd mention his interest to the people who spent their time worrying about such things in darkness. It was too deep for me.

We were in a sandwich shop that I think perhaps Rölly had chosen for us specifically to highlight the shortages already here and those which were coming. Most of the menu had been crossed out. We could have any of the fish dishes or some tough, dried meat one would assume was of an advanced age. No fresh pork, beef, or lamb, of course; that was hardly surprising. But they didn't even have any wetland marmot meat, which was normally plentiful near the end of summer, and I mourned that shortage especially. Marinated marmot meat was one of my favorites.

"So, it looks like fish or dried shit," I said. "What'll it be?"

"Hmm. I think I'll go for the fish this time," the bard said.

Later, upon the wall, Fintan's greeting smile was distinctly mischievous as he strummed a basic chord on his harp. "One of our stories today has much to do with maps, so I thought I'd sing the old song about the Nentian heroine who discovered that the Northern Yawn was, in theory, passable by ships. We still haven't managed to sail the Northern Yawn, though we've learned more about it since the time of Khalima Chanoor. Her accomplishment remains one of the most singular in the history of the world. Sing along if you know the words!"

Indomitable, unstoppable Khalima Chanoor,
Determined to map the wooded northern shore
And survive what no one had survived before,
Struck out from Talala Fouz and left a note on her door.

"I am off," she said, "to fully explore
And map the cold and wooded northern shore,
Taking fifty people with me and more
To ensure completion of this vital chore."

Indomitable, unstoppable Khalima Chanoor
Finally mapped the wooded northern shore
And survived what no one had survived before,
Arriving in Festwyf just as she swore:

But most of her company was no more
Because she cooked and ate them by the score.
We have our map of the wooded northern shore
Thanks to hungry, hungry Khalima Chanoor.

"We'll begin today where we left off yesterday—with Gondel Vedd!"

Once Ponder Tann and I collected our clothing and dressed, we both checked our belongings to make sure they had survived the journey well. My hardened ink pot hadn't shattered while wrapped up carefully in my tunic, so that was a relief. *Zanata Sedam* was intact. They had been in good care.

But I didn't feel as well as I had before. My muscles trembled at rest and my bones felt traumatized, and for good reason. Ponder must have seen the pain on my face.

"The shock will wear off after a few minutes," he said. "Give it some time."

"Did we just age, too, or was the burden borne entirely by Jubal?"

"We aged a little, yes," Ponder said. "Riding the wind is always expensive. But Jubal paid for most of it."

"I think I'll sit, then, and wait to feel better before moving on." I half fell down and took my first good look at Möllerud below. The Peles Ocean was to our left, the green swells of Brynlön were to our right, and a gray, empty city watched over by blackwings squatted like a memorial instead of a home to many thousands. Even the bright blues and whites the Brynts favored had faded in the absence of life, and the hammered bronze domes on some of the buildings were dull and lusterless.

Dark smears fouled the grass outside the walls. Parliaments of blackwings feeding on corpses or else the rags and leftover blood of those already eaten.

"Look at that, Ponder."

"It's horrific."

"I can't imagine why anyone would do that to other people."

"That's what we've been sent to find out, isn't it?"

"I suppose it is. How much were you told about this mission?"

"Very little. We're supposed to locate the invaders, report what we see, discover if they intend to attack us, and find out why they attacked the Brynts and Raelechs."

"Correct. And you're to stay with me unless we find an imminent threat to Kauria; is that right?"

"Yes. Messages sent by ship otherwise."

The closest port was Setyrön, and the road to it, well worn by traders' wagons and horses, beckoned to us along the coast. But we had no messages to send yet beyond what the mistral already knew: Möllerud was no more.

A fleet of anchored ships with their sails furled bobbed in the ocean outside the city. That looked like a good place to start looking for clues about the Eculans' intentions. Perhaps there would be written orders that I could read.

Catching Ponder's eye, I pointed to the port, determined to get the mistral's work done and make my brother's end mean something. And maybe being driven like him was not so bad. Maybe my obsession with language would help me save lives as he had with his kenning, except through peaceful means. "Shall we begin there?"

We walked slowly, still recovering from the journey, and the smell from the city only grew in our noses as we approached. I saw bodies rent by violence and gnawed on by animals and connected it to Saviič's lunges at my person from his cell. I had felt sympathy for his imprisonment before, but seeing what his countrymen did to these innocent people without provocation, or anyway without any efforts at diplomacy, left me satisfied that he was where he should be.

A narrow, bumpy trail forked to the left to travel directly to the port, skipping the city gates. We took it and shortly discovered that the city was not empty after all. A party of six Eculans sprinted toward us from the gates, their bone armor clapping against their bodies as they moved. Their faces were painted, and they held large bent swords. We had no weapons because we never used them.

"Ponder?" I said.

"I see them."

"They do not look peaceful."

"They will be whether they wish to or not," he replied. "Stand firm here. Call out to them in their language. I will leave one with breath to speak."

"What do you mean? You won't kill them?"

"No. But neither will they kill us. Be patient and trust me."

I fumbled at the clasps on my bag and then plowed my hand into the oilskin pouch to find *Zanata Sedam*. Seizing it and holding it aloft, I cried out, "I am a follower of the Seven Kennings!"

They slowed, shot glances at one of them who must be their leader, and he barked at them, "It's a trick! Kill them!" and they resumed their charge at full speed.

"He said they should kill us," I mentioned to Ponder, feeling that might be relevant to our interests.

"Very well. Let's calm them down."

The tempest stretched out his hands to the Bone Giants, fingers splayed, and then he turned them palms up and crunched them. I don't think the gesture was necessary, but such movements helped the blessed sometimes visualize what they wished to accomplish. In this case, he pulled all the air out of the Bone Giants' lungs. They gasped to refill them and found it did them no good because Ponder was making sure the air did not cooperate. They stopped running first, then dropped their swords to clutch at their throats as if that were the source of the problem. Their throats functioned perfectly, however. Their faces turned red, then purple, and they all collapsed to their knees and then their sides as their bodies were starved of air. Ponder allowed one of them—not the leader—to resume breathing, and he took in great heaving lungfuls while his companions slipped into unconsciousness.

"There," Ponder said to me. "I've released them all. The unconscious ones will wake with headaches later and an aversion to men in orange clothing. You can talk to the conscious one now. I'll make sure he comes no closer."

"Let us speak in peace," I called. "But please remain where you are. Your friends will be fine."

He called me several names that I did not recognize—epithets that Saviič had never bothered to teach me—and suggested that my parents had been siblings and that he would resume killing me shortly.

"That's not very helpful," I said. "We wish to be friends with Ecula."

"Friends?" he spat, his chest still rising and falling visibly with the effort to regain his breath. "You steal our breath and say you wish to be friends? I don't think we can be friends now."

"You had already said you were going to kill us. We had to do something to defend ourselves. May I ask why you wish to kill us?"

He squinted at me, taking a good look. "You are different from the people who lived here."

"Yes. We are from a different land. But we know of Ecula. We know of *Zanata Sedam*. We wish to have peace."

"Ha!" he barked. "If you know *Zanata Sedam*, then you know we cannot have peace." He quoted the first line of the text after that: " 'In the beginning there were seven, and in the end there will be only one.' And that one will be Ecula."

He was framing the phrase in terms of countries rather than kennings, which I thought strange. Their plan was to destroy the six nations? The math didn't add up if they counted the additional nations beyond Ecula that Saviič drew on the map. Perhaps they didn't know we *had* six nations. "So that is why you are here? Why you killed the people who lived here?"

"Yes. It has begun just as it was set down."

I did not recall any passage detailing an invasion, but I had no doubt that they were interpreting some vague passage as explicit instructions to attack everyone who wasn't Eculan. I wanted to ask him where it was set down but feared getting mired in his religious delusions.

"But they did nothing to you, correct? These people gave you no insult."

"They have the Seven-Year Ship."

"Where?"

The Eculan shrugged. "We have not found it yet, but we are sure they have it."

"Who told you they had it?" I asked.

"Our *vojskovodja*."

"Where is your *vojskovodja*?" I asked. "I need to speak to him or her."

"He is with the army."

"Which one? There are several armies, yes?"

"This army. The one that freed this town."

"Freed?" If killing everyone was freeing them, then that word must not mean what I thought it meant.

"Yes. This is an Eculan city now."

I gestured to the cold stones, the cold bodies. "Nobody is living in the city."

The Bone Giant waved the fact away. "They will someday."

So it was to be conquest. Kill everyone but keep the infrastructure. Simply replace the Brynt population with theirs. And all for some mythical lost ship that I was fairly certain the Brynts knew nothing about. I would have liked to find it myself at this point, but not for the same reasons as the Eculans. If the owners of that ship could make the Eculans stop fighting, it was worth searching for.

"When will your armies arrive in the south?"

The Bone Giant's face pinched in confusion. "This is the southern region. There is one other army south of us. That is all."

The only other cities to the south of us that the mistral had listed as lost were the Raelech port of Bennelin and the Brynt port of Hillegöm. If this Eculan believed them to be the southernmost reaches of the continent, then they were operating with incomplete information. They must have acquired a map of Brynlön and Rael and nothing else; I had seen such regional maps before. Or else I was leaping to a conclusion. Or this man was lying to me. I could lie as well.

"I must make sure I understand," I said. "I am still learning your language."

The Eculan sneered, showing a mouthful of teeth in as poor condition as Saviič's. Did they not adhere to basic rules of hygiene? "I can tell," he said. "How did you learn?"

"One of the faithful. He was sick, and we found him. He taught me. He told me of *Zanata Sedam*."

"Who?" the Eculan asked, intensely interested. I doubted I could lie about the name. As fanatical as they were, they probably had all the names of the faithful memorized. And this might be the opening I needed.

"Saviič," I replied.

"Saviič lives?" He was thoroughly amazed and obviously recognized the name.

"Yes, yes, he does. He was injured on his journey. He is to the south and healing. Perhaps your army has already found him."

"Where is Saviič?"

I held up a hand to urge him to be patient. "Have you seen a map of this country?"

"Yes. All have seen it."

"May I see?"

"I do not have a map with me."

"Stay there. I will show you." Since we would not kill this man, we had to ensure that he reported nothing useful to his superiors later. He would not learn of Kauria from me if he did not already know of it. Searching the ground, I found a stick on the side of the road and stepped forward a few paces, sketching a rough facsimile of the Brynt and Raelech coast in the turf. I poked at places to indicate the locations of cities. I circled the one that represented Möllerud and then stepped back, motioning to Ponder that he should follow with me to keep a healthy distance between us.

"Look," I said, pointing to the ground. "Without your weapon, please. I show you where Saviič is."

The Bone Giant rose to his feet and left his sword on the ground. He seemed to be composed primarily of sinew yet rattled as he walked. Still, his easy movement and height made him intimidating. He peered down at my improvised map and said, "What is this?"

"The coast. The city in a circle is this one," I said, pointing at the ground beneath our feet. "You see three cities to the south: Hillegöm, Bennelin, and Fandlin. Saviič is in Hillegöm." By the time he discovered I was lying, I would be far away.

"My army is there now! I must tell my *vojskovodja*!"

Pasting on my best fake smile, the one I always wore to administration meetings at the college, I said, "I am happy I could help. I hope all the other faithful returned to Ecula."

It was a statement that begged to be corrected, a favorite stratagem of mine to keep people talking. Say something a person knows to be wrong and very few will be able to contain the inner pedant who simply *must* teach you how very wrong you are. The Bone Giant was no different. "No," he said, shaking his head. "Most did not. Seventy-seven and seven sailed west, but only seven returned to Ecula." He raised his fist to the sky, suddenly overcome with zealotry. "It was a sign!"

He did not say what the sign might signify or who was responsible for the sign. But instead of asking him to explain, I simply nodded, the safest reply one could make to nonsense. It was not difficult to deduce that one or more of the faithful who returned must have supplied them with the regional map of Brynlön and Rael they used for their invasion.

"Perhaps more of the faithful remain here like Saviič," I said. "Your other army to the south may discover them. Your armies to the north may discover more!"

"Why would the faithful remain here all this time?"

An excellent question. Why would these fanatics remain here? "The Seven-Year Ship," I blurted.

"Yes?"

"They may have searched up rivers for them. They go deep into the interior, very wide. Ships can sail on them."

"I had not thought of that. It is possible." Well, it was plausible, anyway, to someone like him who didn't know these lands. There was no mysterious ship crewed by white-skinned men hiding somewhere up the rivers of Brynlön.

"Can you tell me what the Seven-Year Ship looks like?" I asked him. "I have never seen it."

He pointed to the bay, where the Eculan fleet was anchored. "Different from our boats. Hull curved to slice waves, very tall. Kraken on the main sail."

"How does the Seven-Year Ship cross the ocean without being taken by krakens?"

The Bone Giant's eyes widened. "Yes, I would like to know this, too!"

"But you crossed the ocean."

"I don't know how, though. The leaders never told us. Very big secret."

I waved it away as if it were unimportant. "And when you find the Seven-Year Ship—well, then what?"

The Eculan shrugged. "Depends on what we find. But hopefully it will lead us to the Seventh Kenning. Or even be anchored next to it."

"Since I am new to *Zanata Sedam*, could you explain the Seventh Kenning to me? Saviič could not."

"It's powerful. More powerful than the other kennings."

"Yes, it must be, of course. But what is it?"

"Power."

"Fine, but how does it work? What can one blessed by the Seventh Kenning *do*?"

"Do you think I don't know?"

"I'm starting to wonder, since you do not answer." The translated (yet incomplete) text of *Zanata Sedam* had not provided me any clarity on the subject, so it was little wonder this soldier had no answers. It only said the Seventh Kenning was greater than the others, or beyond them, or a blessing past the power of speech. But on such a vague promise they had crossed the ocean.

"I do not think I should tell you. You say you follow *Zanata Sedam*, but you are not one of us." He pointedly summoned some phlegm from his lungs and spat in our direction.

"Fine. And what if you don't find the Seven-Year Ship?"

He shrugged. "Then next year we look in the other countries."

I cocked my head, alarm swelling in my head like a balloon. "What other countries?"

The Bone Giant waved dismissively in the direction of Kauria. "Farther south. The ones on the other map." He must have meant the southeastern regional map. So Kauria *was* next, along with the east coast of Forn. "But I am not worried," the Bone Giant continued. "We will find the Seven-Year Ship here somewhere. It has to be in the north."

"Why must it be?"

"The *vojskovodja* is sure, and so is the *kraljic*, so we are all sure."

Their king! "Has the *kraljic* joined you here?"

A derisive snort. "No, of course not!"

"Of course not," I said, grinning at him. "Thank you for your time. I'm glad that you and I could speak peaceably."

He jerked his head around as if suddenly remembering that his companions were still unconscious. I found it reassuring. He was not the quickest gust in the storm, and that meant he was less likely to try fooling me with misdirection. Ponder had done well to keep him conscious instead of the leader, but it was time to make an exit before his suspicions triggered a renewal of violence.

"I wish you and your companions well," I said. "They will awaken soon, so there is no need to worry. Please tell them I am sorry I had to put them to sleep. I wish we all could have spoken in friendship as you and I did."

"Where are you going?"

"Up the road to the next city. We have news to spread, after all, that some of the faithful still survive! Is there any message you wish to send along?"

"No," the Eculan said, his tone making it clear that he was unsure if that was the correct answer. "Why are you going that way? I thought you said you needed to speak to my *vojskovodja*."

Oh. I supposed I *had* said that. Shrugging, I said, "Any will do. There's another one leading the army to the north, isn't there?"

"Yes, but—"

"I will tell him of Saviič also." I waved at him and began to backpedal. "Farewell." Ponder waved and walked backward, too, and we took perhaps ten steps that way before turning our backs. A stolen glance over my shoulder showed the Eculan bending to his leader, trying to wake him up.

"We will have to take turns sleeping and hide somewhere off the road tonight," Ponder said.

"That is well. We are all still alive and breathe Reinei's peace."

"Should we not be walking to Hillegöm, where the army is? I thought we were supposed to speak to some military officer of theirs."

"There's no need. I have found out what we needed to know. Kauria is a possible target, but not until next year. We can find our ambassador in Setyrön and send word via ship to Mistral Kira. And if we can find this Seven-Year Ship they want so badly or, better yet, the source of the Seventh Kenning, Kauria will never be invaded at all. That must be our new goal."

"That was quick work, Scholar."

"Only made possible by your keeping the peace. Thank you for that. We still have much to discover and time is our enemy as much as the Eculans are, but perhaps we may find a way to baffle them yet."

"Soon after that," Fintan said as he imprinted a new stone, "Kallindra du Paskre met someone fascinating."

Kallindra

We have come into a strange morbid time of prosperity, and I am unsure that I like it. My parents are uncomfortable with it, too. There is no joy in this success. But we have sold everything that we could possibly sell at Setyrön after the Bone Giants destroyed cities to the north and south. Our inventory is empty. People were practically frenzied when we came to town—it was like we were the last family of traveling merchants that might ever appear in their lives, and I suppose I can see how that might be true for them, how that fear could wrap itself around their minds like longarms and then squeeze. But they are not cut off; there is still the sea.

And as Father pointed out, there was salvage to be had in Möllerud; that was our only available option right now.

"I don't want to go back there," Mother said. "All those dead people. It's not like they moved on. They're still rotting there in the open like they were Nentians given to the sky. And I don't loot corpses."

"I never suggested that we would be looting corpses."

"Looting their homes is the same thing!" I'd never heard such anger in Mother's voice before. "Call it salvage if you want, Lönsyr, but it's grave robbing, and we're not going to do that!"

"I think you've misunderstood what I wish to salvage. We're not looting or robbing or profiting off a single Brynt. I'd like to go down there and salvage one of those giant ships."

"What?"

"Our land trade routes are essentially gone now. How will we make our living once we've spent the money we just made? We need to become sea traders, and you saw that fleet of abandoned boats off the coast of Möllerud."

"Not to dunk your plan's head in the river, Father, but we don't know anything about sailing," I said.

"It's time we learned! Free boats don't come along all that often."

"I'm no expert, but they didn't look like any cargo boat I've ever seen."

"That's why we're going to go down there with shipwrights and sailors."

"I . . . what?" Mother said.

"We have the money to hire them right now. The plan is that we go down there and snag a boat or three. Break down one or two, modify the other into a cargo boat with cabins for us. We fly merchant colors. Sail back to Setyrön with the help of our hired crew and learn how to be merchant mariners. Sail from there to Pelemyn with our first load of cargo."

Mother shook her head. "It's too risky."

"Continuing our land route is every bit as risky, if not more. The army that took out Möllerud is still wandering around down there to the south. What if they come back?"

"Well, yes, Lön, that's an excellent question. What *if* they come back while we're down there?"

"We're not going down alone and certainly not beyond the city. There're a lot of people going. There will be scouts, and we'll have plenty of warning if they come back."

"No, I'm not buying what you're selling. What does 'a lot of people' and 'scouts' mean? Is the quartermaster sending an army of mariners along with us or what?"

"Mariners are definitely going, yes, and they'll be scouting for the enemy and cleaning up the city. Lots of families who had relatives in Möllerud will be going, too. I am sure that there will also be some who are, in fact, intent on looting."

"If any of them are part of the merchant clave, I won't speak to them again."

"As you will. But there are some who think as I do that the giants' fleet should either be put to use or scuttled. The quartermaster's one of them."

"So you have official permission?"

"I and others. We are to take what we want from the invading fleet and destroy the rest."

It took hours of Father submitting to further questioning and Mother probing to discover holes in his plans, and she did find a few, but Father knew how to handle them: "How should we address that problem, do you think?" he would ask. And in that way Mother became the architect of the future as much as he. They were an excellent team.

Though I was fairly excited by the prospect of learning new skills, the idea held little relish for Jorry. His face was long and mournful as he listened to our parents making plans.

"What's wrong?" I asked him.

"Little chance of ever seeing Mella du Bandre again if we're switching claves."

"So? There's a greater chance of seeing plenty of other girls whenever we're in port. Huge cities every time, Jorry, instead of villages and homesteads in the country. Math. Odds." I snapped my fingers in his face. "Think about them."

He squinted at me and sneered, ready to scoff by reflex, and then froze as math happened in his head. "Oh."

I rolled my eyes. His attachment to Mella du Bandre had all the depth of a lily pad. "Your happiness is chained to your groin, little brother. Set it free."

"My happiness or my groin?"

"Never mind. Shut up and stay miserable."

I viewed the return to Möllerud as a proper thing. It would not be a helpless, hopeless grind across the tracks, tears coursing down our cheeks as blackwings fatted themselves on a silent city. There would be mourning, true, but there would also be a cleansing and a slow, patient redirection to order in the wake of chaos. A steady building after quick destruction.

Mother told me that this is the pattern of life, and I have seen nothing to contradict it yet: it slowly gets better but suddenly gets worse. And so we must always work, always build, shoring up our walls against the storms that will inevitably descend.

I have been thinking about that night when Motah stole a map of the continent from us. Was that the first gust of this later storm? We haven't seen these "Bone Giants" in person, but that's what hearsay is calling them. People we spoke with in Setyrön said they got to the tops of the walls and even got into the city before they were all killed. The tidal mariner dumped most of them into the ocean before they could land, and the same thing happened in Pelemyn. But they were tall and pale and thin like that woman, and their violence was abrupt like hers. And like the man who killed most of the du Hallards. At least Tarrön was safe with an aunt and uncle in the city.

When I tried to talk about it with Father, he shushed me. "Speak no more of that with anyone."

I know his fear was that we'd be blamed somehow. The air was thick with it: Why hadn't the mariners seen this coming, or the quartermasters, or the pelenaut? But there had been nothing for us to see except for a single, starving, nearly naked lost woman. And then, of course, there had been the stories of Tarrön and Mella, which the constable had improbably dismissed as some kind of mutant Fornish pirates. She may have never even told anyone about it.

On the way down to Setyrön in an impressive if motley caravan of soldiers, merchants, and other citizens, we came across an older Kaurian man and one of Reinei's most blessed, a real tempest. I confess to staring impolitely: I do believe I was, for the first time, smitten.

The tempest—introduced as Ponder Tann—had shorn his hair practically down to his skull, and his face was likewise clean-shaven and so very pleasant to look at. He looked like a man who truly believed in the peace of Reinei. Over light brown pants and boots he wore a multitude of thin, gauzy swaths of bright orange and yellow fabric looped and tied around him. They were squares or rectangles knotted at the corners, nothing like a tunic or a shirt about him, just layers of sheer fabric. He must get cold, I thought, and then remembered that he would never be too cold or too hot unless he wished it. He had nothing to fear from the air.

His companion looked slovenly by comparison; if you didn't see the Kaurian mistral's osprey on his shoulder, you would assume that he was some kind of servant to the noble-looking tempest. The truth was the opposite: the tempest was there to protect and serve this old man.

He was largely bald but had let the gray curly hair around the temples and the back of his head grow out. He'd pulled it back into a queue behind him. His eyebrows had gone gray, too, and he had the beginnings of a curly, woolly beard sprouting on the dark crag of his jaw. His clothing was much more common and was confined to muted colors. I saw no house embroidered on his tunic apart from the osprey. He worked his way up the road, asking everyone he passed if they might have seen a Bone Giant before the invasion.

"No," Father said, and I said, "Yes, we did," at the same time. That earned me a dour glance from Father, and he asserted once more that we hadn't.

The old man's eyes shifted between me and Father. "May I introduce myself? I'm Gondel Vedd, a language scholar from the university at Linlauen." That explained why he spoke Brynt so well. He had a bit of a charming accent but had no difficulty with the words. "The reason I ask is that one of these Bone Giants landed near Linlauen and we still have him there now. I'm able to speak some of their language, so I've been sent up here to see if I can piece together what happened and perhaps help our countries avoid further violence."

Father said, "I'm sorry, but we haven't—" and then Mother chucked him on the shoulder and scowled. Father sighed and jerked his head back at me. "Talk to my daughter."

I sketched out for him what had happened that night with the giant woman who was possibly named Motah, and he asked me particulars about the map.

"Which map did you give her? A regional map of Brynlön and Rael?"

"No, it was of all six nations. A very good map—Kaurian made, in fact."

"You're positive?"

"Yes. It's the only map of the world we had, and there was a drawing of Mistral Kira and her osprey on it, I remember that."

"She probably didn't make it back, then. Or else the leaders weren't sharing the big picture with the soldiers."

"I'm sorry, what do you mean?"

"I spoke with one of them recently. There are a few in Möllerud, and I've already warned the mariners at the front of the column to beware. He has seen regional maps but not a map of all six nations."

"Oh! So our map couldn't have made it back to wherever they came from?"

"They call it Ecula. And it appears unlikely. Unless the Bone Giants are lying to their own people." He plunged his hand into a flat leather bag slung across his body and produced a strangely bound book with the foreign words *Zanata Sedam* on the cover. "Did she by any chance have a copy of this book with her?"

"No, she had a dagger with her, and that's it. I mean, she might have had a book in her boat, but we never got a close look at that." Then I remembered that I had recorded the whole thing in my diary and asked him to follow me to the back of the wagon. I crawled in, fetched my diary, then invited him to sit on the tailgate with me. I turned to the entry and showed it to him.

"Fascinating," he said as he read it, and then turned to me. "Would you mind terribly if I made a copy of this account? It's quite helpful and precisely what I was hoping to hear about."

"Sure, go ahead," I said. "And I know of at least three other families who have seen one," I added.

"Are they nearby? Might I speak with them?"

"Tarrön du Hallard is in Setyrön. But he might not want to talk about it anymore. The Bone Giant killed his family."

Gondel pursed his lips together. "I see. They can turn violent of a sudden, I've noticed," he said.

"Is the one you have in Kauria like that, too?"

Gondel nodded. "He's calm until he sees his religious text. Then he tries to get to it no matter what. A fanatic."

"Well, I did write down what the du Bandres said. It's in my entry about the clave." I leafed through the pages until I found it and showed him.

"Ah! My thanks. You are so kind to share this with me."

He produced his own paper and ink and scribbled down my entries in Kaurian, translating as he went. I let him work in silence and tried my very best not to stare at the tempest as he walked behind and to one side of the cart, keeping Gondel Vedd in sight. In my imagination he was doing the same thing I was and trying not to look at me, stealing glances out of the corners of his eyes. It was fortunate that Jorry was walking up front with the horses and saw none of this; he would tease me mercilessly about it just as I had teased him about Mella du Bandre.

When the scholar finished, he closed my diary and returned it to me with both hands like it was something sacred. "I hope you realize what you have here, Kallindra," he said.

"Just a diary," I said, taking it from his knobby, ink-stained fingers.

"It's much more than that. It's a record of a way of life that no longer exists. The end of an era. It's history. Whatever Brynlön may be in the future, it will never again be the country you wrote about there."

"Oh. I hadn't thought of it like that." The diary seemed heavier all of a sudden, and I frowned. "I suppose you're right."

There would be no clave in a cornfield for us again. No happy visits to farms and villages or the special treat of that honey-apple bacon. All our usual customers were gone. Their lives were over, and ours were forever changed.

Gondel Vedd had understood that before I did. How? What had happened to him? He looked at me with such empathy in his eyes that mine welled up and I gulped, trying to swallow a sob.

"Does your family follow Bryn or some other god?" he asked.

"Mostly Bryn, but we revere them all like many traveling people do. I'm sure you follow Reinei."

"Yes. I subscribe to peace. But it's difficult to see Reinei's work in Brynlön right now. I hope the wind will blow gently and bring you peace again soon. I will pray for you and your family if you don't mind."

"That would be very kind. Thank you."

He bowed his head to me. "It was my very great pleasure to meet you, and I hope we will meet again in this life. Please be well and happy until then, and be wary. There were a few Bone Giants still in the city when we left it."

The old scholar slid carefully off the tailgate and winced at some pain—knees would be my guess. But then he raised his hand in farewell, and so did the tempest. I waved back, carried along by the wagon, and watched them diminish as they turned to continue on their way to Setyrön. I hoped I'd see them again, but every revolution of the wagon's wheels told me that the future was too uncertain to harbor such

A PLAGUE OF GIANTS

thoughts. My only certainties at this point are that my parents love me and my brother is unspeakably horny.

The bard waved to the crowd after returning to his own form. "That's all for today! Tomorrow we hear more from your very own tidal mariner, Tallynd du Böll, as well as others!"

Day 13

DEATH AT DAWN

Immediately after the bard's performance on the wall, one of the Wraith's men approached me and handed me a set of keys. "Those will get you into your house. We've installed several security measures, and someone will tell you about them tomorrow. For now, enjoy your new home."

"My new home? What do you mean?"

The longshoreman didn't reply; he simply trickled away into the crowd like spring runoff. I made my way home as quickly as possible, curious beyond measure, as the sun edged toward one horizon and the moon peeked over the other. People in the streets were smiling, amused by Kallindra du Paskre and her assessment of her brother.

My house didn't look any different from the outside except for the front door. There were three different locks on it now instead of one, though still just the single knob. I considered the ring of keys in my hand, wondering which one belonged to each lock. I was going to look silly while I tried them out.

"Dervan?" a woman's voice called behind my back, uncertain and tremulous. I turned and beheld a familiar figure in orange.

"Elynea!" I threw my hand up in surprise and dropped the keys. "You're alive!"

She began to smile and then frowned. "You thought I was dead?"

"No, I simply didn't know; I've been looking for you."

"You have?"

"Well, yes. Excuse me." I bent down to pick up my keys. "Garst came looking for you a couple of nights ago, and that made me worry."

She put a hand to her mouth. "Oh, I was afraid of that. That's why I didn't come back."

"Are you all right? How is Tamöd?"

"He has a black eye, but we're okay otherwise. I mean—" She bit her lip, and her eyes welled a bit. "I'm feeling angry and stupid and don't know how I'll ever forgive myself for putting Tamöd in that situation, but physically, nothing permanent. We're fine."

"I'm so relieved. But please don't blame yourself. All the blame rests with Garst. And if it makes you feel any better, he received his comeuppance from a Priest of the Gale."

Elynea palmed the tears away from her eyes and said, "A Priest of the Gale? One of those Kaurian warrior monks?"

I grinned at her. "You should have seen it. He was so peaceful there at the end, so polite and cooperative with his face mashed into the floor."

"Ah!" She clapped her hands twice and returned my smile. "So justice still exists. That does make me feel better."

"Good. Are you safe now? Is there anything I can do for you?"

She looked over her shoulder. "Well, when we left you said that we'd always be welcome back . . ."

"That was true. And it's still true."

"I was hoping we could stay with you again while I look for another job."

"Oh, of course! Of course! Please do! Where are the kids now?"

She hooked a thumb behind her. "We've been hiding at Dame du Marröd's for the past few days. Do you still need furniture and . . . things?"

"Well, perhaps not. Some men were working on the house today, and I'm not sure what to expect when I open the door."

"I saw them. They were moving a lot of stuff in there."

"Oh. Shall we take a look, then?"

I asked her to hold my manuscript while I fumbled with the keys. "These are all new," I explained. "I need to figure them out." I began with the top lock and didn't get it to turn until the last key. The main lock with the knob underneath it likewise didn't turn until the second try, maximizing my embarrassment. At least I knew by process of elimination which key would turn the bottom lock. "Great. I'll take that back," I said, reaching for the manuscript. "Go on in."

She turned the knob and pushed open the door, stepping inside. Her gasp of surprise was only a beat ahead of mine.

"They did a lot more in here than I thought," I said.

The living area was fully furnished with a new sofa, chairs, and conversation table, as well as bookcases full of books that I did not own. I needed only a brief glance to confirm that it was all far above a university professor's pay. That meant I was in deep debt to the Wraith or the pelenaut or somebody before I even got into the bedrooms.

"Oh, gods, I am in so much trouble," I muttered. When the men with tool belts had bidden me farewell that morning, I had expected a few spare extras but nothing like this. I wasn't looking at simple security and convenience; I was looking at luxury. And one way or another, the Wraith would make me pay for it.

"What are you talking about?" Elynea said. "This is fantastic! Look at this fabric!" She was petting the sofa like it was a precious baby rabbit, and I had to resist the temptation to join her. It did look fantastic, but I knew that I hadn't earned it yet, and I feared what it would cost me.

I couldn't worry about it in front of her, though, so I nodded and pasted a smile onto my face. "It's very nice," I managed.

The kitchen hid new dishes and silver in the cabinets. The bedrooms had entirely new beds and frames in them, along with hardwood wardrobes that looked like they might be imported from Forn. The one in my room almost certainly was, hand-carved with intricate flourishes and probably worth more than my annual salary at the university. The second room—which would belong to Elynea and her kids—had two spacious beds in it. It had to be an upgrade from Garst's quarters or cramped shared space in Dame du Marröd's house.

"This is wonderful!" she said, and turned to me; her expression lit up. "Your new job working at the palace must be treating you very well!"

"Yes, very well," I said, ashamed that I couldn't explain that I hadn't paid for any of this. The perplexing thing was that I couldn't see any of the security supposedly installed beyond the locks. That, I supposed, meant it must be excellent security.

"May I go get the kids?"

"Absolutely! They live here with you now."

Elynea's face twisted for a moment, and then she lunged at me, clutching me tightly in a hug made awkward by the fact that I was still cradling the manuscript at my side. She had her head turned sideways against my chest, and I couldn't see her expression.

"Uh," I said, so dull that I wondered how anyone could believe I was a professor. "I'm glad you're back."

She didn't respond for a few moments, and I searched for something else to say. She saved me by murmuring, "I never should have left. You've been so kind."

"Nonsense. You've been excellent guests. It's easy to be kind."

She squeezed a bit tighter and then let me go. "Thank you. I'll be back soon."

"I'll be here."

She dashed out, and I returned to my bedroom and opened the wardrobe. My tunics were already hanging inside, and some of the shelves were occupied with folded clothes. I planted my manuscript on top of some pants and closed the doors, shaking my head. Something about the windows drew my attention: they were thicker around the edges. Drawing closer, I saw that they were new. The glass was quite thick indeed, and the frames locked on all four sides. To break in, someone would have to wield a tremendous amount of force to shatter the glass and undo the locks. Between the windows and the bolts on the front door I didn't think anyone would be stealing my furniture again.

Unless Elynea left the door open while I was gone. Or even conspired with thieves to have me robbed while I was away. I still didn't know what happened that first time.

But how odd, I thought, that the second bedroom contained two beds instead of one, just in time for her return. Almost as if the Wraith planned on me having more than a single guest. Was I, a nominal spy in the Wraith's organization and therefore the pelenaut's, being spied on in turn?

I recognized the onset of pervasive paranoia. Sarena used to have it bad, questioning whether every single person in her life might be an adversary. It hadn't served her well, so I focused on what mattered to me: Tamöd and Pyrella would be safe here, and Elynea, too. They had lost so much, and their future was so uncertain. Let them at least have a secure place to sleep at night, since that was in my power to grant them.

Stung by the thought that I had almost nothing to fix for the evening meal, I repaired to the kitchen to take stock of my stores. The pantry, I discovered, was now stuffed full. In the icebox I found a thin package of wetland marmot meat, among other things. The hearth was already lit, and a new cord of wood waited to be burned.

"How much did all this cost?" I wondered. The empty house gave me no answer. But then the front door burst open, and Tamöd rushed through the door, his arms spread wide and a joyous smile on his bruised face.

"Dervaaaaaan!" he cried. Pyrella followed close behind him, and the hugs they gave me were not awkward at all.

There may be no greater indicator of societal stress than a dearth of proper cheese. When I met the bard the next day at a south side cheese shop, the proprietor nearly wept as he recognized Fintan and apologized for having only two rather stinky varieties for us to choose from and few prospects of restocking anytime soon. Dairy was disappearing fast, and he figured he would disappear with it, since few people would pay for expensive imports.

"I might need to go into the supply side myself if I want to make it," he said. "Become the dairy farmer I need to make cheese."

His situation, as with Elynea's and so many others, made me wonder what our country would look like in the months and years ahead.

We were both at pains to assure the proprietor that we were there as much for the bread and tea as the cheese. Fintan in particular swilled the tea as he fought off a couple of yawns.

"Didn't sleep well?"

He shook his head. "I rarely do. 1 mean, I do have restful nights, but they're almost always interrupted. Nightmares, you know. I keep waking up with the stench of burning men in my nostrils. But I've been telling myself that Kaelin just needs it all fresh in my mind to do my duty and tell the tale, and once I do, those memories will stop haunting me at night. That's what I've been hoping and praying for. I'll go up on that wall today and purge it all, and then Gorin Mogen can let me sleep."

"I hope it happens as you say, for your sake," I said, but didn't feel optimistic about his chances. Once horrors take hold in the mind, they tend to clutch and linger, and it takes waves and waves of laughter to wash them away. The problem was that we still had so little to laugh about.

The view from the wall looked different when we got there. The bleachers below were still full, but something was off. It took me a moment to figure out what it was. "Oh! There're no kids."

They were back in school. Or rather they were getting out of school now but hadn't arrived in time to fill in some of the bleacher seats in advance of the bard's appearance. Looking out beyond the bleachers,

I saw some smaller figures mixed in along Survivor Field. Elynea and the kids were most likely at Dame du Marröd's now, and I wondered how the kids' first day back at school had gone.

Fintan pulled out his harp, greeted everyone, and announced he'd be performing a traditional Hathrim song still quite popular today.

"I will, in typical Raelech fashion, only perform three verses, but there are many more variations. When it was taught to me by my master during my apprenticeship, he pointed out that this particular song is important as the source of the Hathrim tendency to look upon destruction as a new beginning rather than an end. They often shrug off disaster and say that 'something better will rise from the ashes,' as we've seen with Gorin Mogen and the population of Harthrad. It makes the giants of the west a resilient people, which is admirable. But it also makes them a people willing to burn anything at a moment's notice."

> *Fire burns! And it cleanses,*
> *And something better*
> *Rises from the ashes,*
> *Like sunspot blooms*
> *On the Hearthfire Ranges.*

> *Fire burns! And it cleanses,*
> *And something better*
> *Rises from the ashes,*
> *Like hardwood saplings*
> *That will fuel our forges.*

> *Fire burns! And it cleanses,*
> *And something better*
> *Rises from the ashes,*
> *Like hot colored glass*
> *In storytelling sculptures.*

"Today's first tale is a bloody one. Let's head west to Ghurana Nent, where I was given a very rude awakening." The bard took on a seeming of himself, the slightly younger and less worn version, dressed in the Raelech red leather armor.

intan

I woke up alone at dawn to the sounds of men dying. Trust me when I say few things bring you to full alertness like the final anguished cry of a life ending in violence. Snakes in the pants or a bucket of ice water will work as well but not linger in the mind. That chorus of terror, though, still echoes in my head.

Numa was long gone, and another courier had come at sunset the day before to fetch Tarrech back to Rael, so I was the only Raelech left in the stone bunker that Tarrech had made to protect us against flesh eels and other plains creatures. The roof served as a good vantage point, so when the screams began, I peeked out the breathing vents and then emerged from the bunker to climb to the roof, where I could feel properly horrified and helpless.

To the south, the Hathrim oil trench was all lit up with flames and foul clouds of black smoke billowed into the air. Behind it, in the distance, a formation of giant infantry was shouting and pounding their chests, lifting axes and spears high.

And to the west, directly across from me, men were sprouting into flame as if their heads were the wicks of candles, and many whose heads weren't on fire had them struck off by the axes of Hathrim houndsmen, a large formation of them charging through the Nentian camp four deep, trampling, hacking, biting, and setting tents on fire.

The Nentians were caught badly off guard, many of them asleep as I had been. The houndsmen traversed the length of the camp from north to south, came to the edge where a line of sharpened stakes was ironically pointed to keep them out or slow them down, and turned around to form up for another pass, ready to mow the camp again like a field of hay. Tactician Ghuyedai had bothered to protect only the southern side of his camp, a halfhearted effort and a strategically stupid decision. Perhaps he thought that he was safe with the juggernaut nearby, but of course he no longer was. Mogen knew how to take advantage: his houndsmen had simply ridden around to the north in the darkness.

Someone rallied a group of pikemen together to stand in front of the next charge, but it was a line only two deep and not wide enough to matter. The houndsmen in the front rank were lavaborn, and they pulled up short and attacked with their kenning while the other ranks of hounds split out to the flanks, got behind the pikemen, and tore them to bloody shreds, grasping their whole bodies in their mouths and biting down, shaking their heads a few times, and then tossing their carcasses aside to land among their comrades. They were utterly destroyed, but they did get the houndsmen to stay still and broke the charge. That allowed the Nentians to charge in on their own from the flanks with pikes, not in any organized fashion but with mad abandon and desperation. And some of them were successful: they sank their pikes into the vulnerable sides of the hounds or even into their hindquarters; there were yipes and whirling hounds to attest to it.

Realizing that they were in an exposed position, one of the giants sounded a retreat to the north; they had to get out of the middle of the mob. Though one hound went down, the rest broke free to the north of the encampment where the charge had begun.

The rider of the hound that went down leapt free before it fell. It was a giantess, judging by the lack of beard, and I soon recognized her as Sefir, their hearth. She kept her hound's body to her back and then swung her axe in long, wide swaths, keeping the Nentians at bay until she could set them on fire one by one.

Once clear of the camp, the houndsmen with wounded animals dismounted and left them there while those with untouched mounts formed up anew and charged back in. The giants on foot followed in their wake, laying about with their axes, with the lavaborn continuing to spread flames. Nobody fights well while on fire except for the lavaborn themselves.

The infantry from the city approached, taking long strides across the field toward the trench, stepping over their own siege breaker walls, and soon they joined in the massacre. The whole of the Nentian army, surprised out of bed, was slaughtered before the sun was entirely above the horizon, and all I could do was watch. Another two thousand or more added to the toll of two thousand from a few days ago.

Bards are not renowned warriors, and I had no weapons apart from a belt knife and a fighting stave. In my youth I had done my martial arts training like every other kid in the Colaiste, but none of it was designed to take on mounted Hathrim houndsmen. That's what juggernauts and temblors were for. And if the Nentians, who were armed with weapons designed to take out houndsmen, could not do it without surrounding them and taking huge losses, then there was nothing I could do. I was waiting for one of the lavaborn to see me and casually set my head afire. There would be no hiding in the bunker because there was no way to secure the door. Tarrech had made it invulnerable to fire from a distance but hadn't counted on Hathrim arriving in person to say hello.

For that was what they did. The screams from the camp lessened and then were cut off altogether as the last of the Nentians died, including Ghuyedai. After that there was only the sound of cooking meat and giants laughing and blackwings calling out to one another as they circled above, eyeing the feast below. I didn't try to hide, and I fully expected to die. It was the least I could do to help things along; though I would miss Numa and regretted that I would never get to tell this story, I thought my death would at least spur the Triune Council to order something more forceful against Gorin Mogen than the rescue of the stonecutters he'd duped. I said my prayers to the Triple Goddess and consigned myself to death when one of the Hathrim pointed to me through the smoke and shouted to Hearth Sefir. He strode through the carnage in my direction, and Sefir joined him. I expected to be set aflame any moment, but instead they stopped in front of me and squatted down, removing their helmets. Thanks to this and my position on the slightly elevated roof of the bunker, we were eye to eye. Sefir nodded once to me, and smirked, her armor splattered in the blood of Nentians.

"We meet again, Fintan, Bard of the Poet Goddess Kaelin," she said. I nodded in return as the other giant removed his helmet. "I present to you my husband, Hearthfire Gorin Mogen."

The Hearthfire was likewise covered in gore, but mostly lower down. His beard was trimmed on the sides but fell from his chin in a black wave to midway down his chest plate. His eyes were ice blue under a heavy brow.

"First," he said, his voice a deep rumble, "be assured we mean you no harm, Raelech. Thank you, in fact, for staying out of the way during this messy business."

"That's what you call it? Messy business? You slaughtered those men in a sneak attack!"

"Do you believe for one instant that they would not have done the same to us if they could?"

"Any attack on Nentians here is a violation of the Sovereignty Accords. You are in the wrong no matter how you try to twist it to claim self-defense."

The giant shrugged a shoulder. "Fine. We have played long enough. We're staying here, and I want you to let the viceroy in Hashan Khek know. This city is named Baghra Khek. All peoples—especially Nentians—are welcome to trade in Baghra Khek and to live among us, as many do in Hathrim cities to the south. But make no mistake: this will either be a Hathrim city-state under my rule, the modest boundaries circumscribed by the trench, or a Nentian city of which I am the viceroy. We want logging rights to the northern side of the Godsteeth, for which we will gladly pay, and we will plant a new tree for every one we cut down. If the viceroy or the king wishes to discuss reparations for the men they lost here, I am open to discussing that. I am ready, in fact, to discuss any way forward that will allow my people to remain here permanently and peacefully. We will not entertain any demands that we leave, and any military force sent to drive us out will be destroyed without mercy just as you witnessed here this morning."

"I'm to be your messenger?"

"Yes. We're fresh out of Nentians at the moment, heh heh."

His casual disregard for their lives—making a joke out of all that death—left me slack-jawed. His hearth elbowed him and he flicked his eyes to her, and when she gave a tiny shake of her head by way of scolding him, he turned back to me and cleared his throat. "Apologies. I am often ill suited to diplomacy."

"Noted. You must know the Nentians will never agree to this."

"Not at first, no. But that's where we'll end up after they've sent some more men to die. We can hope it won't come to that, but we know that it will."

"It won't simply be the Nentians. You'll never have it this easy again."

"Oh, yes, I'm well aware we will never again have such favorable odds. Too bad your juggernaut ran off on you like that or we might have had a real fight. What was so important that he had to leave?"

"The Triune Council required his presence for something, but I don't know what."

"I hope they will have the good sense not to test my resolve. We have dealt with you fairly and harmed no Raelechs and hope that Rael will be a prosperous trading partner with Baghra Khek in the near future."

"I'll pass the sentiment along, should I get the opportunity," I said. "Though I'm not sure how I'll return to Rael at this point."

The hearth replied, "We will escort you to Hashan Khek by boat to deliver our message. We'll even pay for your services, which will hopefully allow you to arrange transport home."

I had very little choice. There was no reason to stay and every reason to leave, and they offered the only transport that wouldn't get me eaten by something on the way. But it turned out that when Sefir said "we," she had no intention of escorting me herself. She and Gorin did escort me to the city, but not inside of it, rather to their docks. They boarded me onto one of their glass boats and set a guard so that I had to stay there and not snoop around. I waited for my actual escort for more than an hour.

It turned out to be Jerin Mogen, whom I'd met before when he returned the stonecutters to us, and another giantess whom I had yet to meet. Both were armored, axes in one hand and helmets carried in the other. I noted differences in the armor: Jerin's had the same stylized bronze and copper sigil of Thurik's Flame on his breastplate that his parents wore, whereas the giantess had what looked like the head of an open-mouthed lava dragon on hers, worked in silver and gold rather than copper and bronze. The plating and shape of her armor also were different from the Mogens', the steel itself of a different color, perhaps of a different quality, though I am not qualified to judge such things. And both of them were different from what the infantry and houndsmen typically wore; that suggested to me that this giantess, whoever she was, must be high status somehow, on the level of the Mogens.

She had long red wavy hair touched with sun-bleached strands of yellow and brown eyes under elegantly arched brows. Her mouth appeared to be wide in a narrow face, and she probably had a winning smile when she had cause to give one. Meeting me, however, was not such an occasion. Her gaze took in my Jereh band and armor with interest; I was probably the first Raelech bard she'd ever seen.

Jerin, who was only slightly taller than she, introduced us. "Hello, bard. I'm Jerin Mogen," he said, "and this is Olet Kanek."

"Related to Hearthfire Winthir Kanek?"

She nodded but didn't bother to clarify the nature of her relationship. I was going to ask, but they just stepped onto the boat, put their axes down, and untied us from the dock, asking me to sit near the aft to work the tiller. They used huge oars resting in the bottom of the boat to pole us into deeper water, and then they sat and rowed us out a bit farther, pointing us north before unfurling the sails. That task done, they returned to their rowing benches, facing me in the stern but not each other, and resumed rowing as if they could not get away from Baghra Khek fast enough. They did all this in complete silence, and I witnessed it with a growing sense of awkwardness.

"Would either of you like a song or perhaps a story to fill the time?" I ventured, and Olet finally opened her mouth to speak.

"No," she said.

Jerin chuckled briefly at my disappointment, and then the void was filled only by the slosh of waves lapping against the hull and the repeated dip and splash of the oars. I noticed that they both studiously kept their eyes square with their shoulders, as if a glance near the middle of the boat would unforgivably invade the other's privacy or perhaps nightmarishly invite conversation. It was a bizarre mix of avoidance and respect.

"I'm not well versed in matters of Hathrim etiquette," I said after this stretched for a few minutes, "so please correct me if I'm wrong, but it appears that the two of you might be in the silent phase of an extended quarrel."

"Not at all," Jerin said, his tone affable, even amused. "We have yet to quarrel."

"Because you barely speak?"

"Ah, you've a keen mind. Well done."

"Why are you here, Olet?" I asked, thinking perhaps that she would be willing to speak to me as Jerin had. She cast a resentful glare at me for drawing her into conversation, then looked away, considering.

"The short answer is because I was ordered to be," she finally replied, "but the truth is I am here because Jerin and I have fathers who are driven by the kind of fire that would devour the world." She slid her eyes across to Jerin to see how he took it, and he met her gaze.

"You will hear no argument from me on that. I agree completely."

Olet stopped rowing, heaving the oar out of the ocean and setting it in its cradle before turning to face him. Jerin did the same.

"Is it your ambition to be Hearthfire of that city someday?"

"No. I'm not particularly disposed to be a Hearthfire at all."

Olet's arched eyebrows leapt up. "Have you shared that disposition with your father?"

"No. He doesn't make a habit of asking me what I want."

"All right. So what do you want?"

"Will you answer the same question?"

"Sure. You first."

Jerin hesitated, then sighed. "The truth is I like the idea of starting a new city outside of Hathrir. But I'd like to be doing it legally, not the way my father's doing it, and I'd like to do it with people from all six nations participating. And I don't want to be in charge. I just want to help build it, hammer steel, shape glass. Create something new, but not at the expense of others. The problem, of course, is finding a place to make that happen."

Olet's mouth opened and then froze that way, stunned. Jerin saw and misinterpreted. "I know it sounds stupid . . ."

"Did La Mastik—? No." Olet looked at me, her eyes narrowing. "Did the bard tell you to say that?"

"No," Jerin and I said in concert. Olet dismissed me and turned back to Jerin.

"Doesn't it burn you to be manipulated like this? Your father put us on this boat so we'd talk, and now here we are, doing what he wants."

"Yes, it burns to be manipulated, but I don't care what he wants. I got to honestly speak my mind just now, and it was refreshing. He might have wanted us to talk, but I'm sure he didn't want me to say I disagree with his goals."

"You say you disagree, yet you participated in that slaughter today."

"Yes, I did. I did indeed. And when was the last time you openly defied your father?"

Olet flinched and looked down, her voice barely audible. "You think because I'm here on this boat with you I've never defied him?"

"No. I'm sure you have. And you probably found out, as I did, that however horrible the thing was that he wanted you to do, defying him was worse."

Olet looked up. "Yes."

"What happened?"

Her eyes fell away from him, and her voice went flat. "You heard about what my father did four years ago? It was what forced the Hearthfire of Narvik to face him in single combat, made him ruler of two cities."

"Yes, I remember."

The giantess sniffed and passed a hand across her pale cheek. "That was because I defied him. I'd been a firelord for three years and serving on some ships as protection, observing that tensions between us and Narvik had been steadily increasing. One day, he told me to sail south with my crew and burn the cargo of just one ship from Narvik, and I refused, thinking of those sailors and merchants and their families at home and how desperate they'd be without that income. It would be heartless, I told him, which I thought would make him explode. I was a fifteen-year-old brat, and that was my rebellion. But his face softened, and he looked so kind, and he said, 'Oh, no, my sweet daughter, I'm trying to save lives by doing it this way. Can I show you why this is better?' and I said okay, thinking he would show me something I hadn't thought of, something outside my experience. And I guess in a way he did. He sailed south with me and was very serious, working out with me precisely what the impact would be if we burned the cargo of one ship, what the impact would be on that ship's crew and their families, and what the impact would be on Narvik as a whole. 'I'm glad you've taken the time to think this through,' he said. 'Proud, in fact. You should always weigh the consequences of your actions ahead of time.' And then we came upon ten ships—the Narvik Bloodmoon fleet, bringing up all the chipped volcanic glass knives and crystal, plus enchanted firebowls and lamps—the dragon's share of their economy. He ordered his fury, Pinter Stuken, to set them all on fire, sailors and cargo, and that sick son of a sand badger smiled. His arms just turned to gouts of flame that spanned the distance between ships, and in moments everything aboard was kindled. Two of the ships had lavaborn on them, and they snuffed out the flames on their ships as best they could, but they couldn't save everyone. So it was eight ships he destroyed and a good portion of the others. Hundreds of sailors and many of Narvik's most important merchants, gone. Eight times the economic damage I had calculated and just . . . *incalculable* damage to the lives of their loved ones."

Olet sniffed again and shook her head, and this time when tears spilled from her eyes, she let them fall. "And of course I screamed at him to stop; he didn't have to kill our own people. It was too horrible. That's when all the kindness and pride left his face and there was nothing left but this ugly, molten rage. He said, 'Their deaths are absolutely necessary, Olet. In the future, you need to also weigh the consequences of defying me. It will always be a price you never want to pay and certainly a price no one else will want to pay either. I trust you'll never be so heartless again.' So—" She splayed her hands wide. "—here we are."

"I'm so sorry. Yes. Here we are, two kids, adrift on the ocean, who don't want to grow up to be like their murderous parents."

"And who can't escape them."

"No, we can't. Well, wait. Why can't we?" Jerin flicked a finger in my direction. "We'll drop off the Raelech in Hashan Khek and then just keep sailing north into a life of adventure."

Olet smiled for the first time, and it transformed her whole person. "You mean two itinerant firelords walking among the tiny people of the world, caramelizing their onions and custard for them?"

"And fetching things off the top shelf. We'd be very helpful like that."

"I like it. Very heroic." She beamed at him for another few moments, enjoying the fantasy, before her smile crumpled and the joy leached away. "They'd never let us go. They'd send people after us, and someone would get hurt. Someone innocent."

"Yes," Jerin admitted. "I would have struck out already on my own if I thought I could. But I would just be trailing chaos behind me if I did."

Something shifted in the air between them; I could see it, even feel it. Olet cocked her head to one side, and Jerin leaned back, nostrils flared, as it hit them both at the same time: they were each sitting across from someone who didn't want them to be a Hearthfire. The same someone who could, perhaps uniquely, understand their problems.

"Are you . . . ?" Olet began, and then she frowned, shaking her head minutely. "Oh, no, no. You're like him, aren't you, being all charming, and then later you'll be a badger hole."

"What? No. Look, Olet: I'm not your father, and I'm not mine either. It's okay if you don't like me, but please make sure it's really me you don't like and not someone else."

They had themselves a staring contest, Jerin projecting earnest sincerity and Olet trying to peel back a mask with her eyes, certain that he was wearing one.

"I have trouble trusting people," she finally said, "and probably always will have."

"After what your father did, I can certainly understand why. And I'm not asking you to trust me. Just . . . reserve judgment, perhaps."

She nodded once, her eyes boring into his. "Were you aware that your father threatened to bury his axe in La Mastik's head if she said another word about returning to Hathrir?"

Jerin blinked. "No. But it doesn't surprise me. He can be ruthless and even callous, as we saw today. But he does have his admirable qualities."

"Such as? You don't mean battle, I hope."

"No. I mean he truly loves my mother. And me, too, I guess, though I didn't appreciate that until recently. When we first arrived after Mount Thayil erupted, he told me something that I think you might appreciate. He said that if you and I didn't hit it off, he'd let me out of this arrangement so that I could marry for love."

Olet's mouth gaped, and Jerin grinned at her, pointing. "That was my reaction, too! Very surprising. But maybe that will give you some comfort. If you want out, you can rest assured that there won't be any backdraft from the Mogens."

She blew out a long breath. "Only an explosion from Winthir Kanek. Thank you, though."

"Sure. But what do you want, Olet? You promised you'd answer."

"Oh. Well, it's an impossible dream. I want to be free of my father, and I don't want anyone to get hurt because of it."

"That's a fine vision for the future. I'd like the same, honestly."

"And I've thought about trying to start a new city elsewhere, too, far away from Hathrir, which is why when you said that, I couldn't believe it."

"We have plenty of time to waste talking about it. We can scheme, or we can let the bard do his thing."

They looked at me for all of one second and chose to scheme. And, unexpectedly, to smoke. Olet had a bag of personal effects and withdrew two glass pipes from it. "Do you partake?" she asked Jerin. I noted that she didn't ask me.

"Not usually."

"Neither do I. Only on special occasions. Can't stand the taste of it. Kind of lingers in the mouth."

"Indeed it does. But is this a special occasion?"

"Yes. Come on. Spark up with me and I'll explain. I don't like to smoke alone."

"All right."

Olet pinched some dried, shredded leaves out of a pouch and tamped them into the pipes. Being firelords, they sparked them with a thought, drew in the smoke, and exhaled. They both coughed a bit afterward and grinned at each other.

"Okay. Why are we doing this to ourselves?" Jerin asked.

"It's not for the fire or the taste or the smell. It's for the smoke itself."

"The smoke?"

She took a deep drag and exhaled slowly, withdrawing the pipe and pointing at the cloud birthed from her mouth. "Yes. Look at it curl into the sky, Jerin, each puff of it different and beautiful for a brief ephemeral time, like us, and then it dissipates, out of sight, gone forever and forgotten. Unless we pay attention and remember. That's what we're doing. Observing and celebrating this moment before it's gone. And using fire not to consume but to preserve." She tapped the side of her head with a free finger. "Preserving this fleeting, smoky moment in our memories."

"What are we preserving?"

"The revelation that we don't have to be what our parents want us to be. That someone else agrees with us. A small sliver of perfect accord between the Mogen and Kanek families."

Jerin stared at her for a moment, then nodded. "Okay," he said, but must have thought that wasn't strong enough, because then he added, "Yes. That's a good reason to smoke. Even if your mouth tastes horrible for days, you know why. You remember."

"That's right."

The two of them were so absorbed in each other that they never saw my jaw drop. Following a morning of screaming death with a quiet smoke on a boat was the last thing I expected that day. Not that I had expected the screaming death either.

I never got to sing or tell them a single story. Instead I had to listen to them daydream about freedom and flirt the whole distance to Hashan Khek.

I offered a prayer of thanks to the Triple Goddess when we finally sailed into port under a flag of parley. The giants delivered me into the hands of a group of soldiers at the docks and pushed off immediately. I was ushered into the viceroy's presence, where I delivered the bad news and Gorin Mogen's ultimatum and said nothing about what I had heard at sea. Thinking of what Jerin and Olet might be plotting now that they didn't have a bard along to listen in, I gave Viceroy Melishev Lohmet at least one advantage over the Hearthfire: he knew he had a problem and where it was coming from.

"The reason that the juggernaut was called back to Rael, of course, was the invasion of the Bone Giants and the loss of the Raelech city

Bennelin," Fintan said upon dismissing the seeming of his armored self. "The Triune Council saw the Bone Giants as a much greater threat than Gorin Mogen and required Tarrech's presence, for there were still plenty of Bone Giants left in the south of Brynlön, able to strike at us if they wished by skirting the southern edge of the Poet's Range."

He pulled out a sphere to imprint and grinned. "As you might expect, the viceroy of Hashan Khek was displeased to receive my report. But let's save his reaction for later. Shall we catch up with Abhinava Khose and the newly blessed Beast Callers?" Fintan asked.

All during Fintan's tale the crowd below the wall had continued to grow; the children had been dismissed from school as soon as he began and ran to join their parents and listen to the bard. They roared approval at the suggestion of more Abhi: I saw some little kids in particular jump up and down, clapping their hands.

Abbi

Hanima was true to her word and took few opportunities to be quiet. Her enthusiasm was infectious, though. She told me what it was like living under the docks by the river. "Nobody wanted me around. I was the stupid dirty girl because my mouth wouldn't work, so I had nowhere else to go." For a brief moment, her expression clouded with rage at the memory. She would not forget the treatment she'd suffered, and perhaps there would be occasion to right a wrong done to many people. The cloud cleared away, however, as she thought of her change in fortune. "But now I can talk, and I bet I'll clean up really nice. Plus there will be a respect bonus now. You know, for being blessed."

"A respect bonus," Sudhi said, a grin spreading across his face. "I like the sound of that. I'd like to just get some baseline respect, never mind the bonus."

"You're going to get it," Hanima replied, and stabbed a finger in his direction. "You watch and see. And we deserve it for getting chewed on. We're, uh . . . I don't know. Abhi, what are we again?"

"Beast Callers."

"That's right. Beast Callers. Except I don't know what I'm supposed to call or how to call them yet. Are we going to get our own bloodcats and stalk hawks now?"

I shrugged. "It's going to be a discovery for me as much as it is for you. I don't know what to expect."

We emerged from the nughobe grove where the horses waited undisturbed. They turned their heads as one to look at Adithi, who had been silent as she limped.

"Whoa," she said. "Why are they staring at me?"

"Ask them."

"Are you . . . no. Seriously?"

"Absolutely. I spoke to Murr and Eep, and they followed me." The horses nickered and approached Adithi. A bemused half smile on her face, she reached out and petted their heads. "They seem to be much more interested in you, though, than my animals were in me."

"I think I know what they're feeling or wanting," Adithi said. "Can you guys feel it?"

"No," I said, and the others chimed in with the same.

"What do they want?" Sudhi asked.

"Apples. They're bored with this grass."

"Don't horses always want apples?" Hanima said.

"This one says I can ride him!" Adithi said, her hands on the head of a spotted stallion.

"That's definitely different from me," I said. "I don't get any mental communication from Murr or Eep. They understand me but not the other way around."

"Looks like you figured out the nature of your blessing already," Sudhi said. "Congratulations."

"This is the best," Hanima asserted. "You need a tough title now, like plaguebringer but horsey."

"Well, what if she can hear more than horses?" Sudhi asked.

Adithi's smile was wide now, and she had tears leaking down her cheeks. "I'd be happy if this is all I can do."

"You could be a horsemaster!" Hanima said.

Adithi scoffed. "You mean a horsemistress?"

"Yeah, that's what I meant."

We fed the horses apples from my cart, made a camp, and spent the day there, trying to figure out the boundaries of our kenning. Adithi could make herself understood by horses just as I could, but they could "talk" back to her in a sort of fuzzy emotional language of desires. Her broader communication with horses did not extend to other animals, however. When Murr rejoined us from the grove and Eep returned from hunting in the plains, they couldn't understand her at all like they could me. They didn't understand Sudhi or Hanima either, and night fell before we could discover what new talents those two might have.

The writhing mass of snakes and eels collected around Sudhi in the morning, however, gave us a fairly decent clue about his affinity.

"Gah! Flesh eels!" Adithi cried. Not the gentlest of good mornings, but that's how I woke up. And we all scrambled to our feet, including Sudhi, who was staring at a whole lot of reptiles. Instincts and a lifetime of horror stories about flesh eels will get any Nentian off the ground in a hurry when confronted with one.

Except that none of us had to worry about flesh eels anymore, and we realized that after a few seconds of cursing. Our kenning protected us, and I had specifically protected Tamhan as well. Had I not taken care to do so, the eels would have injected their paralyzing poison, gnawed through the skin, and burrowed to the lungs while he still lived until they tore open the lungs to lay their eggs inside. In a couple of days tiny eels would slither up the windpipe and out his mouth and enjoy his face for breakfast. That is, if the lungs weren't eaten first by blackwings or other scavengers. The eels' quick gestation period and the ravenous hunger of the plains scavengers always made it a race.

"Go away!" Sudhi said to the mass of reptiles. He flipped his hands at the wrist to banish them, as if such a human gesture would be recognizable to snakes, but they began to disperse and slither off into the grass. The flesh eels obeyed as well. The significance sank in, and Sudhi turned to me, his jaw slack. "Snakes do what I say now?"

I shrugged. "Looks like maybe they do. Call one back to wrap around your arm; see what happens."

"But I don't even like snakes."

"Maybe they'll grow on you."

"Or slither on you," Hanima said. "Slither slither slither—"

"Shut up."

"Nope, I'm never shutting up again. They'll flick those little forked tongues in your ear, all tickly—"

"Ugh. If they do what I say, they won't be doing that."

"What's your title going to be, Sudhi? Serpentlord? Snakemaster?" Hanima snapped her fingers. "Ooh! How about an 'eel wizard'?"

He shook his head. "Not cool enough. I don't even know if this is it or not. But if it is? I think I'd prefer to be called a charmer."

"Oh, that's good, Sudhi," Adithi said. "I like it."

"You should talk to them, see what you can do," I suggested.

Sudhi called a wheaten constrictor to him and had it coil up on his right. There was a bulge in its abdomen where it was still digesting something. On his left coiled a kholeshar, the most poisonous serpent in the world.

"Somehow I don't think anyone will tease me about my hairstyle anymore," he said, and we grinned at him.

"This is the best," Hanima said. "Wish I knew what I was, though. Kind of weird that I've felt nothing so far. Maybe I have some kind of talent with fish and there aren't any around here. Or maybe some animals that aren't technically Nentian. Like some of those freaky creatures that live in the Gravewood. Oh! What if I could talk to gravemaws? Wouldn't that be cool?"

"I hadn't thought of that," I said. "We could explore the Gravewood without fear. Who knows what's in there? I'll bet there are animals humans have never seen before or at least creatures no one has lived to tell about."

"You're right," Sudhi said. "There is so much we can do now."

"It's true freedom, isn't it?" Adithi said. "I can get on my horse and go anywhere and not have to worry."

And during our breakfast of oats and apples, which we shared with the horses, a bee landed on Hanima's arm and did a frenetic little dance.

"Huh," she said, casually regarding it as she bit into her apple. "There's a hive back there in the nughobes about a hundred lengths from the bloodcat nest." She looked up to find us staring at her, wide-eyed, and then her eyes popped open as well. "Hey! How'd I know that? That's my thing, isn't it? Bees! I know what they're saying! Where they are! I'm a, uh . . . I'm a hivemaster! Yeah!"

"Hivemistress," Adithi corrected her.

"Whatever! That! Yes, that! You know what this is?"

"Is it . . . the best?" Sudhi ventured.

"Yes! Exactly! This is the best! You know why?"

"Why?"

"Because if someone wants to mess with me, I'll be able to say, 'Step back, man, or I am going to throw *bees* in your *face*!'"

"What? Why would you throw them?"

"Well, I will urge them to fly faceward, okay? Don't pick at my words, Sudhi; I'm all excited! I have a thing now. Bees are my thing. But not just bees!"

"What?"

"I can sense other hives," she said, her hands freezing in the air and her eyes closing. "Ants. Termites. Burrow wasps. All near here."

I stretched out with the senses of my kenning, seeking those specific creatures, and found the ants and burrow wasps at the limits of my range. "Where are the termites?" I asked.

"Three leagues to the south. The other side of the nughobes." That was a much greater distance than I could sense, as was the beehive. Hanima's affinity granted her far more sensitivity.

"What about other insects?" I asked. Can you sense them? Or spiders?"

Hanima paused and shut her eyes tight, trying to find them. "No," she finally said. "Just the kind with queens."

"Think of what we could do," Adithi said, her face glowing. "Charmers could have serpents keep fields free of shrews and voles. A hivemistress like Hanima could make crops more fruitful."

Tamhan, who'd been quiet to this point, snorted softly and said, "That won't be the first thing the viceroy will think of."

Adithi frowned. "What will he think of?"

"First, he will think of how you threaten his power. He will look at his lost cavalry and say you're too dangerous to live. He'll think of how Sudhi could send that kholeshar or a flesh eel into his bedchamber at night and end his life. And so he'll seek to control you if he can, and if he can't, he'll try to kill you and then get others blessed by the Sixth Kenning that he can control."

"Stop being a storm cloud, Tamhan," Hanima said.

"I know it's unpleasant, but we need to think about this. Do you even want to return to Khul Bashab? You don't have to. You can go anywhere."

They all wanted to return, which disappointed but did not surprise me.

"I can't go back myself," I said, "because I killed those cavalrymen and I don't want to be under the viceroy's control. But you owe it to yourselves to think about what he will want from you once you submit to him."

Sudhi's lip curled. "I don't want to submit. That's a terrible idea."

"It will be that or die, Sudhi," Tamhan said. "He won't have it any other way. So once you submit, what will he want you to do? Follow his orders. And you might not like them."

"What kind of orders do you mean?" he said.

"Well, he'll ask you to tame wild horses and put bridles on them, Adithi, so he'll have more cavalry. You'll be attached to the cavalry and have a military role. I can guarantee it."

She scowled, and Tamhan continued. "Hanima, you'll be his leverage against farmers."

"What? How?"

"If farmers don't pay enough tax or plant what he wants, you'll
keep bees from visiting their crops."

"No, I won't! That's evil."

"He would say it's good government. He'll think of some way to
exploit you that will increase his power at the expense of others. And
Sudhi, you'll be an assassin."

"No way. I'm not killing anyone."

"Not you. Your snakes."

"That's disgusting, and I would never do it. If I did that even once,
then charmers would be viewed as spies and assassins forever."

"He's not going to worry about that. In his eyes you are resources to
be used. And not just his eyes—this is how we'll be seen by any government official. We either serve them or must be eliminated."

"Where are you getting these ideas? They're horrifying," Adithi
said.

"They're not ideas. They're educated guesses. Leaders will do almost anything to hold on to their position. It's what makes them smile
in the morning, the idea that they're the boss of everything they can
see under the sky. If you can help them, they will use you; if you
threaten them, they will throw you to the wheat dogs. Since you are a
threat but also of potential use, they'll try to control you. That's how
it is in all the other countries."

Sudhi pointed out, "The blessed are sometimes in charge. The pelenaut of Brynlön is a tidal mariner. The mistral of Kauria is a cyclone."

"But they are elected and still serve the government. They are still
controlled by the responsibilities of office. They're not retiring to a
quiet life of gardening and grumbling about the weather."

"Well, I could have one glorious garden now," Hanima said, "but I
don't want to keep this to myself. I want to change things."

"There has to be a third option," Adithi insisted. "A way that we can
help people as we wish without the government controlling our lives."

"I agree that there should be," Tamhan said, nodding. "But look at every other country with a kenning. Almost without exception, the blessed serve the government's interests in some way. Especially those with the greatest powers. They are immediately conscripted into military service. The Raelech juggernauts, the Fornish greensleeves, the Hathrim furies—"

"But there are exceptions?" Hanima asked.

"There are those who serve in helpful roles but are still technically under the government's control. The hygienists in Brynlön who clean water and wounds and cure disease. The stonecutters in Rael who build walls and so on."

Adithi brightened. "My father is in a clave; he's a tanner. Clave members get paid better for their work, and the government likes it because they pay taxes regularly. And of course the government uses them when it needs something, too, but I don't think the government can force the clave to do something against its own interests. Why don't we form a Beast Callers clave? Anyone can employ our services, and we retain the right to refuse work we don't want to do."

Sudhi and Hanima liked that idea and Tamhan had no objections, so I encouraged them to try. "Apply to the viceroy and see what happens."

"Or simply announce it to as many people as possible so that the government has to acknowledge us," Adithi offered.

"Count me in," I said, "though only as a member, not an officer."

Tamhan said, "I'd make sure you have a charter that clearly defines what the government can and cannot order you to do. And it will have to be signed by the king eventually. I would get legal advice. Move cautiously when you get to town. Hide, in fact. And if they ask—actually, even if they don't ask—tell the truth about what happened. The viceroy's cavalry killed Madhep, not you, and then they were going to cover it up by killing us all. Abhi acted purely in self-defense."

"I don't think I'll ever come out again if I enter that city now," I said. "Not until I get some guarantees of safety."

They fell silent, and after a few moments Tamhan nodded. "You're probably right; you shouldn't go back now. What will you do?"

"I was thinking of following the Banighel River down to the ocean, but isn't the viceroy at Batana Mar Din a cousin or something of Bhamet Senesh?" They confirmed this. "I won't find a sympathetic ear there, then. Maybe the viceroy at Hashan Khek will be more open to working with me. And if not, I'll simply live outside the cities as a free man. Maybe explore the Gravewood like Sudhi said."

"How will you live, though?" Hanima asked.

"I've been thinking of it. I would modify my hunting skills. When grass pumas or wheat dogs take down something with a pelt—or when Murr does—I will step in after the kill and take the hide to sell, then let them eat. No waste and no death on my head, and I will have income to buy grain and apples in the cities. And what if we could establish a solid trade route between Hashan Khek and Khul Bashab? It's not a new idea. There's an old road going south from Khul Bashab to the Khek River, but no one really uses it because it's too dangerous. Beast Callers would change that. We'd protect caravans from animals; the merchants pay me less than they would for river transport, and there's no risk of bandits on the plains for them. I think I'd do very well."

"Okay," Hanima said. "I think it's good that we all have a plan. Start the clave and grow it. Improve lives in Ghurana Nent. And in the process we will allow our country to enjoy the same freedoms as the other nations."

"One more thing," I said. "Protect animals as well."

"Murr," my bloodcat said, and nodded his head in agreement. He hadn't understood the rest of the conversation, but he'd understood that.

Planning continued as we traveled north. Tamhan was quite animated as he thought aloud about how the country could, should, and would change with the Sixth Kenning. And more than the country— the whole world would be different. His excitement was contagious and we were all smiling, listening to him build us up as future legends. By the time we saw the walls of Khul Bashab, we had a rough outline of a clave in mind and a list of projects we wanted to work on. Recruitment would be put on hold until the source of the kenning moved somewhere away from the spiders, though. We didn't think anyone would want to try that, and we didn't want to watch regardless.

Sudhi adopted the kholeshar viper, which draped itself around his shoulders and neck and slept most of the time, but its bright green and yellow skin gave off a clear warning of danger against Sudhi's warm brown complexion, and it also matched the yellow stripe of his hair. Hanima, meanwhile, acquired a small swarm of bees that trailed after her and buzzed over her head in a cloud, including a young queen. "I'll get them a hive as soon as I get into town," she said. "Something I can take with me if necessary."

We parted ways well outside the vision of the guards on the wall. Adithi gave me an extra horse in addition to the one I had pulling my cart, and she would take the rest with her and return them to the viceroy's stables, though she hoped that she would be able to keep the spotted stallion for herself.

"When I get to Hashan Khek," I said, "I'll send word where you can find me. To Tamhan, I mean."

They each thanked me, and Tamhan hung back to say farewell. He opened his arms and embraced me, and I felt like I belonged there. A scant count to three, but it was perfection. When he pulled back, he kept his hands on top of my shoulders and spoke to my eyes. "Thank you for coming to me. For letting me be a part of this."

"Thank you for the many kindnesses."

"Nonsense. You will be safe and I will see you again, yes?"

"I hope so. Yes."

"I feel we should have been friends long before this," he said, and my throat closed up and all I could do was nod. "We will make up for lost time later. May Kalaad smile down upon you, Abhi."

"And you, Tamhan," I said, giving him a tight grin and a nod, letting my hands fall from him as he did the same. I'd been dwelling on the fact that when that captain had shot at me, it wasn't just Madhep who had stepped in front of the bolt. Tamhan had stepped in, too. Perhaps he felt as I did for him, or perhaps he merely had the heart of a hero. But it wasn't the time to ask.

Our eyes lingered on each other for an uncountable span, and then they fell away. He turned to join the others, they all waved, and I turned away in case my face showed how much I didn't want to be alone then.

I mounted the extra horse, and Murr and Eep followed along as I searched for the old trade road heading south. I found it after a few minutes, and through the dull ache of loneliness I felt the smallest kernel of hope for the future. Perhaps with our concerted efforts we'd be able to make life better for all Nentians. But for all the wonder of the kenning, I'd give it all up in an instant if I could have my family back.

"More from Abhi in a few days!" the bard promised. "Here's someone you ought to recognize."

He threw down a seeming sphere, and the form of Second Könstad Tallynd du Böll emerged. I watched the faces of the crowd and saw their expressions light up with glee upon her appearance. They hadn't heard from her directly since his first day on the wall. Applause erupted before Fintan said another word. He let it wash over him for a while, knowing it was for the Second Könstad as much as for him, then held up his hands to quiet them and let Tallynd speak.

Tallynd

When I surfaced near the docks at Gönerled, the smell of rot made me gag and I had to dive back underwater, take a clean filtered breath, then rise again, holding my nose. There was nothing alive except blackwings feeding on the dead. My sister lay among them somewhere, along with her family. I longed to find her if I could and return her to the sea, giving her a gentle farewell after the violence she suffered. But she would have to wait with all the others. My mission was to scout the enemy, destroy small targets where I could, and note what needed to be done in the fallen cities should we be victorious.

The note taking was quite literal: I had a waterproof satchel with writing materials, food, and fresh water inside. Pulling myself up onto the docks and wicking away the moisture from my clothing, I performed the quickest survey possible: No watchers on the walls, gates wide open, bodies everywhere, even in the wells. Structures all intact. Like Festwyf, Gönerled could be scoured and lived in again if people could bear the feeling of being haunted.

On to Göfyrd, moving at the top speed I could manage without strain, where there were most definitely sentries on the walls. The Bone Giants had decided to stay there, no doubt because of the rich food stores, and strategically it posed a problem for us. They could strike at Pelemyn, Tömerhil, or Setyrön from there. If we struck at them, we would leave our cities open to counterattack, and we didn't have ten thousand soldiers to throw at the walls anyway.

I spent the night in Setyrön, exhausted from the travel and the emotional wear, confirming for their quartermaster that Göfyrd was occupied and delivering some messages from the pelenaut and the Lung.

He told me that Möllerud was abandoned like Gönerled and he had approved an expedition of mariners, merchants, and citizens to head down there, scuttle the Bone Giant fleet, and begin cleaning up the city. I wearily noted after the next morning's journey that the city was indeed abandoned and ready for cleanup. There was only the Bone Giant ships anchored in the harbor and blackwings circling above. From there I sleeved myself to Hillegöm, where I assumed I'd find the army that had landed at Möllerud. And by midafternoon, I did find them, but they were not inside the walls.

They were walking—not marching, not in formation, but simply strolling—along the coastal road from Hillegöm to Möllerud. I had come upon them as they were leaving the city. No one was watching on the walls. They had left the gates open, and they had scuttled all the

Brynt ships in the harbor, their masts only peeking above the surface of the water.

There were . . . I don't know how many. More than I could count. All tall, pale, and dressed in clacking bones. Some with swords, some with spears—the tools they had used to slay the people of Möllerud and Hillegöm. Looking at them from the shallows, below their actual feet, all I could see was the first rank or so. There could be untold ranks behind them. Brynt cargo carts heaped high with plundered grain and other goods rolled in the middle of the column. But near the back, there was one pale giant who was unarmed and adorned in a different fashion. The skin of his torso bore swirled patterns of dark ink, and he wore no bones except for thin hollow ones strung in three levels around his neck. Unlike all the others, he had a beard, the sort one might see only on the most eccentric Hathrim. He had twirled, waxed, or somehow shaped tufts of it into pointed spikes that radiated from his face, as if his jaw were the bottom half of a child's drawing of the sun. Instead of basic strips of cloth around his groin and flimsy sandals on his feet, he had cloth pants and boots. And most important, he was reading something. Not a book or a single piece of paper but a sheaf of them, and there were more sticking out of a cloth bag he had slung over his shoulder. Plans? Messages? Whatever it was, it was unlikely to be poetry. It was much more likely to be information we could use. And even if we couldn't read their language, denying them their information was a sound strategy, and this particular giant was most likely one of their leaders. Everything about his appearance spoke of status even if the markers were strange to my eyes.

I had a glass knife. They had swords and spears and arms that were half again as long as mine, plus bodies that weren't slowing and breaking down. Combat wasn't an option, even at one-to-one odds, much less one-to-hundreds or thousands. But the Lord of the Deep had given me a kenning and now an opportunity not only to avenge my people but perhaps learn something that would help rid us of this scourge.

I sleeved myself quietly through the water, keeping only my eyes above the surface. They weren't even looking my way, their eyes on the path or on the giants in front of them. They thought themselves safe from attack. Any other day they'd be justified in thinking that.

To secure the papers I'd have to go ashore. I'd be vulnerable there, so to avoid being surrounded, I began my work at the back while I was still largely submerged. I targeted ten giants, all I could easily keep in view, and used my kenning to pull the water in their heads toward me by the width of a thumb. No screaming, no pain, just a fatal hemorrhage in the brain. Not fair, not sporting, just war, like they waged against us, using every advantage they had in size, reach, and numbers. And definitely not murder: no, just my duty.

The bones they wore rattled as they collapsed, causing the giants in front of them to turn around and see their bodies just before I scrambled their brains as well. And when they fell, that drew the attention of the leader. He was in the next group of ten, but I paused before continuing. I wanted him, at least, to see who was responsible, to see that a Brynt woman would be the end of him. So I dropped my feet, found the sand of the bay, and stood up, calling out to him. He didn't hear me at first over the tide, but someone else did and got his attention, pointing to me as I emerged from the ocean. And as soon as his eyes lighted on me, I shot out my hand toward him, an unnecessary gesture except to communicate that I was doing something, and then I pulled the water from his head much more forcefully so that his eyeballs exploded and blood and brains gouted out of the sockets.

His surrounding soldiers gasped once, and then they fell, too, ten at a time, as I rushed the shore and cleared a space for me to secure those documents. I opened my waterproof satchel as I left the surf and saw that the army was a truly huge one. There were not hundreds but thousands. My mouth dried up as I absorbed the odds of survival and instinct screamed at me to turn back now, take the death of a field commander, and call it victory. The only thing I had in my favor was surprise and perhaps, bizarrely, my comparatively small stature. None of the giants more than a rank or two back could see me over the heads and shoulders of their brothers. And in the time that it took them to turn, see that the people behind them had fallen, and look around for danger, it was already upon them, and they fell, too.

But cries of alarm spread up the column faster than I could work, and as I reached the leader and knelt down beside him, long, bony fingers were pointing in my direction and conclusions were being reached: The short woman who came from the sea must somehow be responsible for sixty—no, seventy!—dead giants! Kill her! At least that's what my imagination supplied to match their foreign words.

A rank of them took two steps, raising weapons, before I exploded their brains. A stab of pain shot between my eyes after that; I was pushing myself too hard now, aging with each new effort.

The fallen bearded officer or whatever he was smelled horrible already; it was too soon to be decay, so he must have polluted the air as part of his daily existence. Did these savages never bathe?

I had to push him over onto his back since he had fallen on top of the papers. Grunting with the effort, I looked up as I worked and put down two more groups of ten giants charging in my direction. That gave the rest of them pause, and there was some discussion on how to proceed. I took advantage and scooped up all the papers I could, cramming them into my satchel. I even reached into his tattered cloth bag and pulled out more, shoving them into my satchel and sealing it as the Bone Giants decided that spears might work and hurled a bunch in my direction.

Scrambling away from the body in a panicked crab walk on all fours, I avoided most of them. One sheared through the skin on the inside of my right calf, and another sank through the top of my left foot, pinning me to the beach. The rest thudded into the body of their leader or around it. I screamed and yanked out the spear, closing my eyes as I did so, and when I opened them, I saw a group of giants behind the foremost preparing to send another volley my way, since the first had enjoyed some success. Gritting my teeth, I pushed the water in their heads hard, disrupting their throws as they fell backward, already dead. My skull throbbed every bit as much as my foot after that, but I pushed myself up onto my right leg, testing the calf, and though it stung, it still functioned well enough. I purposely did not look at my left foot, fearing I'd faint if I saw the wound. I hopped on my right foot experimentally, holding my left foot off the ground with a bent knee, and when I didn't crash to the ground, I lunged toward the sea.

The mob of giants rippled and flowed in my direction, a roar building among them as it sank in that a single woman had killed more than a hundred of them, had stolen their leader's writings, and was both wounded and trying to escape.

In furtive glances over my shoulder, I looked for the ones with spears and pushed the water in their skulls away and let the ones with swords come on. They had some ground to cover and they would cover it pretty quickly, but not as quickly as a thrown spear. Once they closed the distance, I figured the spears wouldn't keep coming for fear of hitting their own men—and their stature would hide me from the view of others, perhaps.

Whooshing sounds, gritty impacts, and blurs in my vision told me that I didn't get all the spear throwers, but the distance and my convulsive movements made me a difficult target. The distance to the ocean would not seem so long had I two working legs, but it yawned like the abyss when I could only hop and the giants could take huge, ground-eating strides at full speed.

When I looked over my shoulder again, having made the beach, I could not see any more giants with spears; presumably they could not see me either, because my entire vision was filled with a phalanx of the skeletal figures with their swords raised, ready to cut me down. The shoulder of the nearest one bunched, his skull face snarled, and I dropped to the ground on my right side as he swung, realizing that I was already within his inhuman reach, and a line of searing pain scorched my left side as the blade sliced down my ribs. But I rolled and shoved the water of their bodies away from me, and they collapsed. Rather than try to get up, I just kept rolling into the surf, as it allowed me to get a view of my pursuers and take a few out with each revolution.

Once I hit the water and the salt stung my wounds, I sleeved myself out to sea with all speed, hearing spears plunk into the surf behind me.

As soon as I felt safe enough to do so, I surfaced and checked the seal on my satchel. It was sound, and the papers within were protected. Now all I had to do was survive my trip back. Leaking blood into the water would draw predators before long. And if I passed out from blood loss, well, it wouldn't matter that I couldn't drown. Something would eat me before I woke up.

I sleeved myself to the west, past the cold dead walls of Hillegöm and heading toward the Raelech city of Bennelin, which also had been lost to the Bone Giants. I figured it would be a safe place to see to my wounds, since the Bone Giants were heading in the opposite direction. I simply needed to give myself some space.

Crawling out onto the beach but not far from the tide, I faced the east in case any Bone Giants came running along in search of me. Then I took several deep breaths and forced myself to look at my foot, which was beginning to hurt unbearably now that the shock had worn off somewhat. There was definitely a hole there; I could see the sand through the top of my foot. I wouldn't be able to walk without a cane or crutch for a while and might never walk normally again. Blood was pumping out of it still, and I was beginning to feel light-headed. Concentrating, I used my kenning to stop the flow and trusted that my system would catch up soon enough and close the blood vessels without magical aid. I did the same for the vessels along my side and my calf. That would prevent death by blood loss, at least, but infection was still a real possibility. I'd need a hygienist to do that, and the nearest reliable one was in Setyrön.

Unready to begin the journey and desperate to find a distraction from the pain, I pulled out the papers from my satchel and took a look at what I had stolen.

It was all gibberish. Completely unreadable. It looked like the Bone Giants used letters in their writing system that we never used. I doubted anyone could read it at all; I might have risked everything and permanently injured myself for nothing.

Well, not for nothing. At least that army lacked a leader now. And more than a hundred of them would never strike at a Brynt again.

Sealing the papers away, I rolled back into the sea and began the journey back to Setyrön, keeping to the shallows to avoid large predators but remaining underwater as I passed the Bone Giant army. I didn't reach Setyrön until well after dark, and the hygienist gave me some Fornish tea as she set to work purging my blood of impurities and doing what she could to set the bones back in place.

I sent a report to the quartermaster saying that the enemy was returning to Möllerud and he shouldn't let that expedition depart, but he showed up in person at the barracks to question me about it.

"Are you positive they're heading for Möllerud?" he said, frowning at me.

"Absolutely certain. The hole in my foot bears witness."

"Bryn preserve us."

"What's the problem? Just keep that expedition you approved . . . here." I blinked, feeling incredibly tired.

"No, you misunderstood what I said," the quartermaster growled. "That expedition already left. Two days ago."

"What? You have to get them back here!"

"I'll send out riders, of course. But they'll be two days behind."

"Well then, shend out shome rapids!" I said, wondering why my speech sounded so strange. "Or I'll go myshelf!"

"You're not going anywhere," the hygienist said. "That Fornish tea I gave you was a sedative, and you'll be sleeping for a while."

"Don't worry," the quartermaster said. "We'll take care of it. Rest."

And so, having no other choice, I rested.

Fintan bade everyone a good evening after that and reminded them that the Second Könstad was fine except for a limp now. "And no gift baskets!" he chided them. "The pelenaut already took care of that!"

Day 14

THE GRANITE TUNNEL

May Bryn drown the next person who interrupts my morning toast.

I should make a habit of checking the door *before* I try to eat, because once again a loud knock at my door sent my breakfast facedown to the tile. Beyond annoyed, I shouted, "Who is it now?"

An accented and aggrieved voice replied, "Jasindur Torghala, Nentian ambassador to Brynlön. I must speak with you."

After our recent troubles there was no way I'd open my door to a Nentian. "I think you must be mistaken. I have no business with Ghurana Nent."

"I assure you that you do, so long as you be Scholar Dervan du Alöbar. Are you not he?"

"I am, but this isn't a good time. I'll contact you later at my convenience."

"My business is urgent, sir. I need to speak to you right away."

"Apologies, Ambassador, but I am not obligated to share your sense of urgency. Good day."

Someone—either the ambassador or someone with him—abandoned

the brisk knock the ambassador had employed earlier and switched to an angry pounding of my door, a clear signal that they had not come on pleasant business. "We must speak with you immediately!"

If they could break through that door with all the locks on it, then I'd speak to them, all right. I went to fetch my rapier and put on my mail shirt while they continued to hammer at my home and demand that I speak with them. Armed and protected, I returned to the living area and wondered how long it would take them to tire of knocking.

It stopped abruptly when a new voice called to them, faintly heard but plainly angry. I drew closer to the door and cocked my ear to hear the exchange better. The surly voice of the ambassador was saying, "We must speak with him regarding the representation of Ghurana Nent in his records."

"What records?" came the reply. It was the voice of Föstyr du Bertrum, the pelenaut's Lung. "You can't go around bothering private citizens like this."

"He is hardly a private citizen! He is in your government's employ, and as such we may speak with him. He kept records for the pelenaut and is now keeping a record of the bard's tales."

"So what if he is?"

"So it is bad enough that the bard is allowed to spread these lies every day about our country to your people, but it is an insult of the highest order to allow them to be written down as if they were history! As if they were *factual!*"

I supposed my involvement in the project was no secret. The pelenaut had, after all, proclaimed it to the court on the day the bard arrived. I thought it strange that it took the Nentians so long to figure it out, though, or anyway that they would get incensed enough about it now to accost me at home rather than complain through the proper channels. Obviously Föstyr had expected something of the kind and had been keeping a close eye on them if he happened to be near enough to intervene.

"An insult of the highest order?" the Lung said. "The bard's performance and its recording are by the order of Pelenaut Röllend. So your position is that the pelenaut has ordered an official insult to Ghurana Nent?"

"It is! This has gone too far!"

"Hmm. We will see precisely how far it has gone. Would you like to repeat these sentiments to the pelenaut himself?"

There was the briefest of pauses, but the ambassador must have decided that backing down would be poor form and label him as a blustery gasbag. "I would, yes."

"Very well. He shall be fetched to this very spot. Please wait here."

"Here? In the street?"

"You saw fit to start this in the street, so it will be finished here as well."

"No, that's not necessary."

"The 'highest order,' you said. Your complaint therefore trumps all other concerns, and we must not quibble about keeping the pelenaut's appointments."

Föstyr sent someone away to the palace, and then the Nentian ambassador began to speak to him in more hushed tones that I couldn't make out. Already regretting his decision, I bet. There wasn't a leader in the world who would appreciate being summoned away from his throne to deal with the tantrum of a foreign ambassador. Besides, Rölly was legendary for winning street fights of any kind, and Föstyr had cast the situation so that the ambassador was essentially calling out the pelenaut for a brawl, albeit a verbal one. Oh, this was going to be good. I put on a kettle to boil for another pot of tea while we waited for Rölly to arrive, cleaned up my fallen toast, and made myself a new piece. Tea and toast in hand, I crept to the window and peered through it to see if I could spy them.

The Lung was there in the street but pointedly not looking at any of the Nentians standing next to him. One of them, who I assumed must be Ambassador Jasindur Torghala, was talking to him earnestly, but the ambassador might as well have been a stump for all the Lung cared. They had moved across the street to stand in front of Dame du Marröd's house, an idea I would wager was Föstyr's. I'd have to go outside if I wanted to hear anything more. Happily, they were all so focused on the Lung that I could probably sneak out without them seeing me.

Nentian fashion was a little bolder than Brynt tastes; I liked it but doubted I could pull it off. Supposedly a Nentian's boots were analogous to a Raelech's Jereh band, in that they conveyed quite a bit of information about who was wearing them. Ambassador Torghala wore boots made of soft, supple khernhide with a stripe of kholesharhide inlaid along the top of the foot. Simple but wildly expensive and pretentious. Don't mess with me, his boots said, for I am wearing the skin of the world's deadliest serpent. Or maybe they said, Behold, I'm an arrogant ass. Or both.

But he still quaked in those boots when he saw Pelenaut Röllend approaching in a phalanx of mariners. That was my cue to step outside with my tea and toast. I didn't want to miss a word.

No one saw me walk right out and cross the street. The Lung and the Nentians had their eyes locked on the pelenaut's party and vice versa. I was the only one grinning. I casually took up a position behind the Nentians and sipped at my tea.

The mariners spread out a bit to give the pelenaut some room while protecting him, though in truth he wasn't in much danger. The water of all their bodies belonged to him if he wanted to call it forth. Ranged weapons could take him down, however, so his bodyguards had large shields and scanned the area for snipers.

"Ambassador Torghala," the pelenaut said. "I'm told that I've given your country an insult of the highest order."

"Yes, sir. This recording of the bard's tale must be destroyed. He continues to lie and defame our nation almost daily, and to have such a performance preserved and written down as if it were history is offensive and irresponsible."

"I disagree. The bard has been tremendously accurate regarding everything we can easily confirm here. There is no reason to believe he's being false elsewhere in his tale, especially since that would betray his duty to the poet goddess."

"There is *every* reason to believe it! He's accurate regarding Brynt matters precisely because you *can* check his facts and you are his host! Meanwhile he fabricates scandalous behavior about Nentians and paints one of our viceroys as a murderer!"

"Interesting. Do you think that he is also fabricating the clan squabbles of Forn? Or that he is sugarcoating the behavior of Gorin Mogen, who did, in fact, invade your country?"

"I cannot speak to those. But the Nentian portions of his tale are despicable falsehoods."

"Do you offer any proof of this beyond your word?"

"My word is much better than his!"

"I disagree," the pelenaut said in a flat voice. No qualifiers, no subtlety. Rölly told the ambassador that his word was held in less regard than that of a man the ambassador had just accused of being a liar. Silence fell for a moment except I crunched into my breakfast, rapt.

"So it's personal insults now, too," Torghala said. "You've been dismissive of our concerns from the beginning. And you recalled all your hygienists some months ago, thereby condemning our people to die of diesease. I see what you think of us." I nearly choked on my toast. Torghala had just made himself toast whether he realized it yet or not. Rölly's expression roiled from mild annoyance to barely controlled rage.

"I recalled hygienists from the entire world. We have a severe health crisis here right now far beyond any that might be afflicting Ghurana Nent, and Brynts' first loyalty must be to the land that blessed them. Gerstad."

One of the mariners stiffened. "Yes, sir?"

"Take the ambassador into custody—but gently, and with utmost respect. March him down to the docks and put him and his entourage here on the first ship to Rael at my expense."

"Yes, sir."

"What?" Torghala spluttered as the mariners moved to either side of him.

"You have made yourself an unwelcome guest by suggesting that I am murdering your people when I'm trying to save my own. Ghurana Nent can send another ambassador—or not—at its leisure."

"No, I never made such a suggestion! You misunderstood me."

"I don't think so. Gerstad, take him away now."

"Yes, sir."

Jasindur Torghala, an ambassador no more, shouted that this was outrageous, he'd said nothing improper, the pelenaut was acting out of all proportion, there would be dire consequences, and so on, as he was prodded forward by the mariners. Rölly gave the Lung a tight grin and a nod. "See to the details, will you?"

"I shall," Föstyr replied with a small bow, and then he trailed after the mariners, leaving me there alone with my tea and half-eaten toast staring at my old friend. He saw me for the first time and started.

"Dervan! Have you been there all this while? I'm sorry you were disturbed."

"No, that was fabulous," I said. "Thank you."

"Not at all. We knew Torghala would overstep eventually." Rölly closed the distance between us and clapped me on the shoulder.

"Why'd he wait until now to complain about the manuscript, do you think?" I asked.

"He was taking far too long discovering the information for himself, so one of Föstyr's lads made sure he found out last night."

My chin dropped and pulled my mouth wide open. "You *wanted* him to do that?"

"We didn't know how precisely he'd respond, but we knew he'd be upset and do something stupid. Worked out pretty well. I needed to get rid of him because I've gotten reports that he might be a source of renewed attacks against the bard, and I also don't need him reporting to the king what's being said about his various viceroys. Not that they've had any contact since the invasions began. Regardless, I have a feeling the story will only get worse in their eyes, and I'm tired of it."

"Bones in the abyss," I said, shaking my head. "I don't know how you think of all this."

"Flow studies," he said. "Water always finds a way through. The path may twist and fall over rocks, but it gets there. You just have to be willing to navigate the currents."

I nodded, not knowing how to respond except with the standard politeness: "Would you like to come in for some tea?"

"No, thank you. I have to get back to the palace. But I'm glad I got to see you this morning; that was a pleasant surprise. Be well, Dervan."

"You, too, Rölly."

He strode back toward the palace unaccompanied as if he were an ordinary citizen and not the leader of the country. People were too occupied with their thoughts or errands to worry about who else was walking along the street. They paid him no mind. He wasn't wearing a crown or anything especially fancy that day, and without an escort of guards to signal that he was someone important, he blended in.

It gave me hope, seeing that. Everybody was getting to work. It was time for me to do the same. I ducked back inside and wrote a letter to the chief scholar of the university, inquiring whether there might be a position for me when the new semester began.

I still felt braced for work when I met Fintan for lunch. It was in the only restaurant of its kind, a Hathrim establishment where the chef and bartender were a married couple of sparkers living far, far away from the source of the First Kenning. They used their talents to create gourmet fare: perfectly cooked food and alcoholic beverages set on fire. The ceilings were ridiculously high and the doorways quite wide, but the actual servers were Brynts in their employ. We had bladefin steaks in a salted orange demi-glace and some flash-grilled southern vegetables that must have just arrived from Forn or Kauria.

Our server must have told the owners that the bard was in the house, for after the lunch rush had passed, they both came out and loomed over us, grinning.

"Hello," said the Hathrim woman, who was dressed in a huge kitchen apron smeared with a few sauces. "I'm Hollit, and this is my husband, Orden." She was probably eleven feet tall, and he had maybe half a foot on her. "Are you the Raelech bard, sir?"

"Yes. Thank you for your work; it was delicious."

They beamed. "I'm glad to hear it," Hollit said. "And the admiration is mutual. We are very much enjoying your work."

Fintan gave them a wry smile. "You're enjoying Gorin Mogen laying waste to armies, eh?"

"No, Gorin Mogen is a fiery boil on the ass of the world," Orden said. "We're from Haradok originally, and no one south of Olenik really likes him—except for his hearth, I guess. He's one of the most arrogant Hearthfires ever. But we do like hearing about our people. Especially La Mastik, the priestess of Thurik's Flame. She sounds like someone of our mind. I wish you had told us more of her thoughts, actually. But this is all news to us, as it is to everyone else. We're enjoying it very much, and we are hoping she will be able to teach Mogen to burn clean without so much smoke and spite."

"But please don't spoil anything!" Hollit added, her huge hands splayed out in a halting motion. "We relish the suspense. We simply wanted to thank you and refuse payment for your lunch today. It's our privilege to have you visit."

"Oh, well, eating that bladefin was a privilege. Thank you."

They nodded and smiled and left us to our work. After a couple of minutes Fintan commented in a pinched voice, "They were such a nice couple. Hard to imagine them setting you on fire with a thought, isn't it? But they could."

"Ugh. Why'd you have to mention it? I don't want to think about that."

"I never wanted to think about it either. But after you see the lavaborn do that to people, you never look at them the same way. You say to yourself instead, 'If I say the wrong thing right now, will they cook me down and sweep the ashes into the trash?'"

"Stop it."

"Look at me, Dervan," Fintan said, pointing to his temple. "I'm sweating."

He was. His skin had turned ashen, and he looked sick. His hand trembled. "Lord of the Deep, Fintan, if you knew you were going to have this reaction, why did you come here?"

"I *didn't* know," he replied in an intense whisper. "I thought maybe telling yesterday's tale would put it all behind me. But obviously that hasn't happened."

"Are you going to be able to tell the story anymore?"

"Oh, I'll be fine. I'll be fine," he said. "There won't be any more of the Hathrim for a few days anyway. And telling the story is nothing like being in their presence."

"You're shaking."

"I know. I guess echoes of war can reverberate for a long time," he said. Reaching out for his pint of ale, he downed the whole thing in greedy gulps and ordered another.

"Will you be all right today?" I asked again.

He took a deep breath and nodded. "Yeah. It'll pass." He wiped his brow and tried to dismiss the spell by shaking his head. Clearing his throat, he said, "Let's get back to work."

Once he got on the wall and faced Survivor Field, you'd never know he had suffered a nervous episode. But perhaps his choice of a song had something to do with his state of mind. "Something from Rael today," he said, strumming a chord on his harp, "about seeking your own good fortune as opposed to waiting for it to happen. A traditional nine-liner."

> *Deep in stone and mineral and lime*
> *Waiting for pressure and sufficient time*
> *Are diamonds and emeralds and sapphires;*
>
> *So in our fragile hearts and minds*
> *Waiting for affection of different kinds*
> *Are virtues the goddess admires;*

But do not passively wait to thrive,
For this very moment you may strive
To whatever your will aspires.

"Switching gears now to a very different person," Fintan said. "An introduction, in fact, to a stonecutter named Meara in the northern Raelech city of Baseld, connected by the Granite Tunnel to the Brynt city of Grynek."

The figure who took shape out of the seeming smoke had the mellow brown complexion of Raelechs, with her straight black hair gently waving down to her shoulders. She was petite and had a young person's smooth skin, unweathered yet by too many years in the sun. She had a long nose and dimples on both sides of her face. Unlike the other Raelechs I had seen to that point, her clothing was more fashionable than utilitarian. Perhaps those blessed by the earth goddess to actually move the earth around carried a certain cultural cachet in Rael, a higher status. Her Jereh band had the brown sard of Dinae on the left, the master amethyst in the middle, and a maroon moonstone on the right, all set in a single person's bronze rather than the married gold.

I am a woman who loves her mud. It's an unusual affection, I know, but where most people see filth, I see potential. And not just in mud but in all the myriad forms the earth takes beneath our feet. It already shows us the vast range of shapes and colors it can take, and our imaginations, combined with the blessing of the earth goddess Dinae, can transform a sodden mess into something sublime. Or dress up the plain in fancier clothes.

Baseld is an old city, its basic structures built long ago, so my duties are split between maintenance and what I like to call sparkle work. I have been teaming with masons to face old structures with swirled marble and granite or polished mosaics of light jade, malachite, and onyx. And inside the Granite Tunnel, where many people have chosen to live and work full time, I have been often employed to help line the walls with reflective polished tiles that magnify a candle's light. It is still mud that fascinates me, though. Nothing to recommend it as a material except the shape one can give it, so it is a pure medium to my way of thinking. I have a sculpture space in the city where I create nothing but mud figures, which wash away and melt in the rain, allowing me to make new ones when the clouds part.

It is not the glamorous life that Raelechs might associate with the title of "stonecutter," but it is a peaceful, fulfilling, prosperous one, and my betrothed, a soldier in the garrison, is aggressive enough for the two of us. We balance each other out, I suppose: my calm serenity is a foil for the boiling within him, and his energy and passion ensure that I do not get bored. Plus, Gaerit is often filthy. And he has a southern accent and knows how to cook. My kind of man.

My sparkle work for the city came to an abrupt end with the visit of a courier and a temblor to my home on a misty morning.

"Stonecutter Meara, I am sent by the Triune Council with orders for you," the courier said.

"Ha! The Triune Council?" I grinned at them. "Who put you up to this? Was it Gaerit?"

"No, I'm really from the Council. An invading army approaches the Granite Tunnel from the Brynlön side. Temblor Priyit is taking a force into the tunnel to meet them, and you are to assist to the best of your abilities to prevent this army from ever reaching Baseld."

I snorted in disbelief. "Assist how? I'm no juggernaut."

"The Council is well aware. But you are the only Earth Shaper of sufficient power to make a difference. You are Rael's only option."

Dinae and Kaelin and Raena, too, she was serious. "I don't understand what you wish me to do."

The temblor spoke. "We need you to seal the Granite Tunnel. Create a wall that they cannot pass, and once they reach it, create another one behind them. Trap them in the tunnel. They will all die in a week, and Rael will be safe."

"But there are people living in the tunnel! Homes carved into the mountain!"

"We will be evacuating, of course, but that is why we must move into the tunnel to meet this army halfway," the temblor replied. "Should we meet them earlier than we planned or be surprised by advance scouts, I am taking half our garrison along to provide you time enough to seal off the tunnel. You should be in no danger."

The courier's eyes bored into mine. "The Triune Council is counting on your full cooperation, stonecutter. As is the city of Baseld and indeed the nation."

"Of course, of course, but . . . what army?" I asked, trying to catch up. "This is the first I've heard of it."

The temblor held up a hand to encourage patience. Her Jereh band was bronze, I saw, not gold. "I'll brief you in a moment." She turned to the courier. "You can inform the Triune Council that the stonecutter is engaged."

"Yes, I am," I said.

"Blessings of the Triple Goddess on you both," she said, and departed so swiftly that our hair blew in the wind of her passing.

Temblor Priyit offered up a smirk to me. She was a Nentian immigrant who'd been blessed by the Triple Goddess when she sought a kenning—one of many who came to Rael, since the Nentians didn't have their own kenning and the Fornish didn't let outsiders be Seekers at the First Tree. "What did you have planned for today? Bringing up some nice marble for a new sculpture?"

"Miners sent over a shipment of raw gold-flecked quartz from the Lochlaen quarry. I was going to shape them into translucent tiles for the interior of a dome."

"Ha! Well, never mind that. You get to save the country instead. Come with me to the garrison."

And it was during that walk to the garrison that I learned that much of Brynlön had been overrun by a people being called the Bone Giants and that the army headed our way had depopulated almost all the Brynt river cities.

"Almost all?"

"The quartermaster of Fornyd had the good sense to evacuate her people in advance. She warned the quartermasters of Sturföd and Grynek, but they were either unconvinced by the warning or unable to convince their populace of the danger. The Bone Giants move fast."

"How fast?"

"They're already in the tunnel."

"Shit!"

"If it weren't for our couriers, we'd be taken by surprise, too. And we lost Bennelin because of their surprise attack from the sea."

"Shit! Bennelin lost? As in captured or . . . ?"

"As in wiped out. Everyone dead. The juggernaut at Fandlin took out the invaders after the fact, but no one could save Bennelin."

"Goddesses, no." Gaerit was from there originally, which meant that his family would be gone. We'd been planning on visiting them after we got married; I'd always wanted to see the Brynt Sea anyway, but now I supposed that dream had been snuffed like a lonely candle.

"How is this possible? Why haven't we heard about this yet?"

"Because the city bard hasn't been told. She's being told right now, though. That's where the courier went after she left us. The Triune has been employing the couriers for a lot of scouting missions and essential military operations, and spreading news wasn't their priority. But no doubt we'll hear the bard's voice soon enough. I understand the Brynts lost several other cities as well."

I walked along with the temblor, stunned, trying to process it all, and I simply couldn't. Instead, I noticed that although the temblor had adopted Rael's customs and fought for us now, she hadn't entirely given up on her own culture's fascination for boots. I marveled at first that I could think of anything besides the tragedy of all those lives lost, but then realized that I was desperate to think of anything else, even something as insignificant as fabulous footwear. I remember the bard at the Colaiste remarking on our tendency to do that: "Small material things can be a shelter from an emotional storm," she said, "but if you hide away in them, you'll be hiding from life. Sometimes you have to face that bad weather. It will catch you out eventually."

Here I was, caught out and still trying to hide.

As we entered the stone walls surrounding the garrison, the rich voice of the city bard entered our ears, floating above the city, declaring that she had dire news and emergency instructions from the Triune Council. The tunnel must begin to evacuate immediately because of the approach of an invading army of many thousands. All soldiers were to report to the garrison. And then the details: Bennelin, lost. All but four Brynt cities, lost. No reason for the attack and no hope of negotiation. The Bone Giants appeared to have no kenning but won through surprise attacks in large numbers. And I could see heads shaking, no one wanting to believe it was true, but bards don't spread falsehoods when they speak to cities; they can lose their kenning that way, as the Lying Bard of Bechlan did, long ago. It was that thought and the thought of seeing all these people in front of me dead that broke through the shock and let me imagine what horrors must lie outside our city, which had been safe for so long. Tears escaped my eyes and dropped to the earth, emotion honoring the poet goddess.

When the bard finished speaking to the city, the temblor had me climb the steps to the garrison tower, where we found the bard waiting. Her name was Laera, and she'd been the only bard in Baseld since I'd moved there.

"Temblor, I've been expecting you," she said.

"My thanks. Can you project my voice to just the garrison, please?"

"Certainly."

Priyit first called everyone to assemble in the training ground, and while that happened another temblor joined us, an older man I think Gaerit didn't particularly like. But it was Priyit who spoke once the soldiers had mustered. "May the Huntress bless you all today. Half of the garrison will go with me into the tunnel as soon as possible to stop the Bone Giants before they get here. The other half shall remain here under command of Temblor Maerton to defend the city should we fail, provide a rear guard as citizens evacuate, and keep order in the meantime among a frightened populace. Neither duty is enviable or glorious, but they are both necessary. May I have volunteers to go into the tunnel?"

Every single soldier in the garrison volunteered, so Priyit first picked anyone who had family in Bennelin, including Gaerit, figuring they'd like to get a measure of revenge, and then gestured to the soldiers massed on the eastern side of the training ground and said, "Plus you lot. Armor, shields, and spears. No staves. Fast as you can. We leave in a quarter hour."

Gaerit and I were able to exchange a glance but not speak in advance of mobilization; we marched toward the Granite Tunnel a half hour after the temblor's orders, and they armed me, too, in spite of the fact that I hadn't practiced with weapons since my days in the Colaiste. I found Gaerit and matched pace next to him. His jaw was set like a jagged cliff, and his eyes were dark with the promise of violence.

Trying to lighten his mood, I waggled the shield and spear and said, "I hold these in front of me, right?" He didn't think it was funny; his expression even registered disgust that I would try to joke right then, and I felt alone and unloved like barren soil. But then I reflected that perhaps this was a mood that shouldn't be lightened. If ever there was a time for him to feel violent and justified in doing so, it was now. My selfish desire to have one last soft look from him before we met an uncertain future had caused me to open my mouth when it should have stayed shut.

"I'm sorry, Gaerit," I whispered to him. "I'm just nervous. Fight well for the Huntress. Be safe. I love you."

I started to lengthen my stride to catch up with the temblor near the front, but Gaerit called me back. The bunched muscles in his jaw relaxed as I waited, looking at him with a question in my brows. His shoulders relaxed, the smooth brown skin stretched over his arms arranging itself into planes I knew well, the way they did when he wasn't tense.

"Forgive me, Meara," he said. "I didn't mean to be curt with you. I'm simply upset about the news. My family . . ."

"I know, I know. All the things I want to do I can't do while we're on the march, so I said something stupid. I'm sorry."

His mouth slid into a half grin. "We'll go down to the riverbank later, roll around in the mud, and make love like otters, and we'll both feel better." The soldiers near him heard that, eyes shifting and smirks appearing on their faces, but I didn't care.

"I hope you're not just saying that, because rolling in the mud is a serious promise."

"I will keep it. Because I love you, too. Now go march with the temblor. I know you're supposed to save us all somehow."

No need for a half grin now: reassured, I beamed at him and scurried forward to join the temblor and caught up with her as the entrance to the Granite Tunnel gaped before us.

It was fretted with the ornate bas-relief sculpture of stonecutters and masons long since past, and the weight of the mountain above it never loomed so heavy. The tunnel connecting Rael and Brynlön under the Poet's Range had been the work of three hundred stonecutters, working in concert to create not only a vital and safe trade route between our countries but a wonder of the world, a testament to the power of our kenning. The same three hundred stonecutters also had created the Basalt Tunnel to Ghurana Nent underneath the Huntress Range, allowing the breadth of the continent to be connected via the Merchant Trail. It felt unwholesome to wall that up, to tarnish such a legacy and a monument in the space of minutes, to effectively destroy its function, however temporarily. But I supposed it was less unwholesome than everyone I knew dying at the sword of something called a Bone Giant.

People streamed out of the tunnel as we marched in, bundles held under their arms and slung on their backs, some pulling carts or riding horse-drawn wagons. Worried evacuees from the tunnel warrens, wondering where they should go. And some of them—quite a few of them—were Brynts who must be refugees, running in advance of the army. It was their bleak, hopeless faces that drove home to me the urgency of our mission. How horrific it must be to be forced out of your home with nothing but the clothes on your back. If we failed—more specifically, if *I* failed—to hold this army back, then everyone in Baseld and perhaps beyond would wear the same bleak expressions.

I thought perhaps I finally had an insight to what coal must feel like being pressed into a diamond.

I was marching near the front of the column with Temblor Priyit some while later when a young courier sped up from the Brynt side of the tunnel and halted in front of her, saluting and stating that he had a scouting report.

"The enemy forces are only a quarter hour away, Temblor, moving at double time."

"Size of force?"

"They are depleted—they've been drinking from the Gravewater, and it's taken a toll. But they are still an army of six or seven thousand."

We were four hundred.

The temblor turned to me. "Stonecutter Meara. Can you tell how far into the tunnel we are right now?"

"Aye. A moment." I removed my boots, closed my eyes to block out visual distraction, and stretched out with my kenning to sense the mountain above us and the long, smooth tunnel carved out of it by stonecutters long dead. I located my position within it and opened my eyes. "A little less than a quarter of the way, Temblor." The Bone Giants moved fast, indeed. Had we delayed, we might not have been able to meet them in the tunnel at all. She gave a curt nod and addressed the courier once more. "So that should mean that they are entirely within the tunnel at this point if they are marching in anything like a formation and not stretched out."

"I believe that is correct, Temblor."

"Excellent," she said with a tight grin of satisfaction. "Stonecutter, begin constructing your wall right here. When it's finished, seal them in at the other end with another wall."

"My range may not be that great, Temblor."

The satisfaction disappeared. "It's not? How far back can you build another wall?"

"I have never tried to build a wall out of my sight, so I am unsure. A thousand lengths? Two thousand, maybe?"

A frown now. "That won't trap enough of them. They could retreat and get out."

"But it would at least keep Baseld safe until the Council can send a juggernaut to finish them," the courier said.

"True enough. Stopping them is the primary objective, and elimination is secondary. Please begin, stonecutter, building from the top down. I will array my forces in front of you to give you time to complete it should it be necessary." Noises echoing off stone from down the tunnel suggested that it might. The temblor paused, listening, then continued. "Leave some room at the bottom so that we may execute an orderly retreat underneath, and once we're safe, you complete it. We'll worry about sealing them in from behind later."

She shouted orders to the column, and they marched ahead and filled the width of the tunnel in a tight formation, shields overlapping and spears pointed outward. Gaerit was among them, and he gave me the tiniest of nods and a hint of a smile as he passed by. He was in the third row, which worried me. I had to build the wall in minutes and give them enough time to retreat behind it.

I couldn't think about that pressure, though. I had to focus on the stone and soil of the mountain above and reshape it to fulfill a new purpose. This was not a simple movement of virgin earth but rather a modification of older work. The ceiling had been strengthened and solidified by the will of three hundred stonecutters. I had to break through that by the force of my will alone and then draw down a thin slice of mountain to seal off the tunnel.

The tight seals of the past did not wish to be broken, however, and they were much more powerful than I had anticipated. My forebears had shored up the ceiling as strongly as they possibly could to prevent collapse even in an earthquake. And so the temblor interrupted me as I was trying to pierce through the layers of protection because it had been several minutes, the sound of the approaching enemy was growing louder, and nothing had happened.

"What's the delay, stonecutter?" she growled. I explained and said the wall would form quickly once I broke through the protections of the past. "Hurry it up," she said, as if I had been idle.

Spreading my efforts or my focus across the width of the tunnel wasn't working; I was peeling away strips of protection like an onion, but it felt as if I was making very little progress. I tried a different tactic, focusing my kenning on a small area in the middle and drilling up through the seals. That went faster, and once my kenning touched virgin rock above, I spread out my focus across the width of the tunnel again but only a single length's thickness and attacked the seals from above, prising them apart, until they shattered into pieces like shards of glass. Nothing that anyone else could see, of course; it was simply what it felt like to me in the trance of my kenning.

With a strip of the seals gone I could now draw down the mountain, and it was then that it occurred to me that it would have been far wiser and much quicker to deal with the seals on the floor of the tunnel— which were much thinner and did not involve the potential for a cave-in once broken—and make a wall rise up instead of descend, but it was too late to begin anew and those hadn't been my orders. In the gap between switching my focus from one task to another, the outside world penetrated. Combat had been joined, and the Bone Giants fell upon our soldiers with their strange swords. Over the tops of rows of Raelech heads I saw the heads and shoulders of pale, ghastly creatures floating above them, swinging their weapons down and sometimes crashing into shields, sometimes recoiling as spears thrust out from the formation and pierced their bodies; then, when they were yanked out, the barbs pulled forth intestines through the gaps in their bone armor. The blood, I thought, looked obscene against their white skin.

The temblor, still standing nearby, looked up and saw nothing before turning to me with a snarl on her face, all her affable demeanor gone. She shouted over the din, "The wall, stonecutter! Get me that wall now or we're all going to die!"

It rocked me back into focus, and I stretched out with my senses to the strip of virgin rock and chanted the stonecutter's hymn, providing structure to my thoughts and a shape to the kenning. Rock sheared and shifted, popped and cracked as it began to slide down from the ceiling in a slab one length wide, and all my muscles tensed with the strain of containing it. The mountain above was heavy and wanted the tunnel closed.

"That's it! Faster!" the temblor said.

"I can't go faster," I explained through gritted teeth. "I have to control the descent or I won't be able to stop it."

"The floor will stop it!"

"No—you don't understand. I mean the seals are fragile now."

"As fast as you can, stonecutter. Our warriors are strong but cannot hold forever—no, don't look! Concentrate on your job."

"Quit interrupting me and I will."

The mountain wanted to heal itself; the Granite Tunnel was an open wound, and now that it felt a break in the seals keeping it out, it wanted to reclaim all that space. Letting the rock descend was easy: all my straining was to keep the edges of the seals in the ceiling intact, to prevent them from expanding.

Despite the wall descending, the clash of steel and the juicy noises of flesh being torn and blood being spilled only grew louder. Death screams floated above it all, and they chilled my spine. I kept my eyes averted from the battle, looking at the stone above, and soon it had descended low enough that I couldn't see the fight in my peripheral vision. That was some relief, but halting the descent of the slab short of the floor was a monumental effort that left me sweating and gasping with the beginnings of a headache. The soldiers would have to drop prone and roll underneath, and the temblor was yelling that the Raelechs should begin doing precisely that.

"Retreat under the wall! Your duty is done! Retreat now! Retreat!"

Soon the soldiers began to appear, and the temblor had them stand at the ready with their spears. "If one of those giants comes through, you stab him and let me know," she said, and then to me, "As soon as the enemy appears, you drop the wall the rest of the way, understand?"

"Understood," I managed, my hands braced on my knees as I bent, trying to recover my breath. My arms trembled with exhaustion. Earth shaping of this magnitude drained one so quickly; that was why they had used three hundred stonecutters in the past to do this work.

Ten warriors rolled underneath the slab and stood, their faces grim and even frightened. Another ten, and ten more, helped to their feet and deployed in ranks as the temblor continued to shout orders. Ninety warriors in all came through, and then a Bone Giant appeared underneath the stone on the far side and was immediately speared through the neck.

"Giants!" the nearby warriors cried, and even as they did so another appeared, and another, at different points across the width of the tunnel, and the temblor turned to me. "Drop the wall now, stonecutter."

"But more of our people might be coming," I said. None had come through close to our side of the tunnel, and that was the side on which my fiancé had been deployed.

"Now, stonecutter! The rest of the garrison is dead or we wouldn't see Bone Giants coming through!"

"But . . . where's Gaerit? I don't see Gaerit!"

The temblor grabbed me by the tunic and growled. "He is either here or he isn't. If he isn't, he's not going to be coming through just because you wish it. But Rael remains in danger until you do your job, so do it already!"

A Bone Giant tried to roll out from under the wall near us, and the warrior standing sentinel there promptly speared him in the throat.

The bodies of the first few giants conveniently prevented the advance of others underneath the wall, and we could effectively hold them now, but there would be no more Raelechs returning either. The temblor was right: either my fiancé was on our side of the wall and I hadn't seen him or he was already dead on the other side with three hundred other soldiers.

"All right, all right," I said to get the temblor to back off, but my eyes searched desperately over her shoulder for some glimpse of Gaerit. I didn't see him, and it drained my spirit more than my earth shaping had. Already I felt like a failure. If I had not been so slow in breaking through the seals, those warriors would not have died. Or if the courier had warned us just a little bit sooner. If we had started the process earlier in the tunnel. If I hadn't been the only stonecutter in Baseld. If we had a juggernaut to send instead.

"Hurry up!" the temblor barked.

Her peremptory command and lack of empathy punctured what little control I had, and in a momentary flash of anger I let the stone drop down abruptly, crushing anyone underneath it and sealing off the tunnel. But I had paid no attention to the seals as I released the stone, no attention to the ripple effect such a sudden shift would have on the mountain above. A shock wave tremor curled through the seals of the old stonecutters, and they shattered at the top of the wall. And that breakage triggered more and more as the pressure of the mountain rushed to fill a void, and the seals began to unravel on either side of the wall, too fast and too strong for me to contain them. The mountain fell down on top of us from the center outward, crushing everyone but me and the temblor underneath tons of granite. Our kenning ensured that we could not die by any force of earth. The rock weighed on my head and shoulders like the hand of a gentle friend, no more, and it would be the same for the temblor. Not so for anyone else. The Bone Giants were no more, but neither were the Raelechs. I had managed in a moment of weakness to kill everyone who was not already dead and turn the Granite Tunnel into a long, silent tomb. The Poet's Range had closed itself.

The enormity of it crushed me since the mountain could not. I wept in the dark and the dirt where no one could hear me, and when my breaths became short, I exerted myself and cleared some space around me so that I could take in a proper lungful of air. I realized that the temblor would need air, too, for though she could punch through almost anything with the strength of her kenning, she'd need to breathe first. After the initial trial of their kenning, temblors did not do well underground.

I could sense the human-size absence of rock nearby and shifted the earth so that I could move toward her and bring her into my hollowed-out space with a little bit of breathing room. She coughed and sputtered as the rock and sediment shifted away, taking in huge gasps of air.

"Wondered if you were going to let me suffocate," she said.

"What? Of course not!"

She coughed a few more times, and I could hear her brush rubble off her tunic, and then a scraping sound and a few sparks in the darkness announced that she had a flint and candle in her pouch. Both flint and candle, she claimed, were Hathrim-enchanted, but it still took a while to get it sparked up. Once it finally lit, she gave me a cursory glance, then looked at her long dust-covered hair with dismay. "What happened, stonecutter?"

"The seals gave way, and I wasn't strong enough to stop them all by myself. We should have built the wall from the floor up, and there wouldn't have been any danger of a cave-in."

Temblor Priyit froze, her eyes narrowing. "So I gave you the wrong orders. Is that what you're saying?"

"Yes. Ordering me to break the seals on the ceiling and build the wall from the top down was the wrong call."

"I see. So I'm to be blamed for this?"

"It's not assigning blame; it's recognizing how we got here. At the same time, I should have thought of it earlier. And I should have paid attention to the seals when I dropped the wall the rest of the way. It was my fault, and I expect the Triune will punish me accordingly."

"Punish you?" The temblor's mouth twisted into a broad grin made lurid by the candlelight, and she raised a hand, palm up. "We won! The Bone Giants are dead! Baseld is safe!"

"It doesn't feel like a win when all our soldiers are dead."

She waved my objection away. "The Bone Giants did most of that. Fewer than a hundred of them were able to retreat."

"So you can just shrug off the unnecessary deaths of close to a hundred soldiers?"

Priyit gave me an exaggerated shrug to demonstrate that she could. "I didn't kill them. It was an accident."

My mouth gaped. I had no problem taking my share of the blame, for I had indeed been responsible. What shocked me was that Priyit didn't seem to feel responsible for any part of it or even question whether perhaps we should have begun our work as soon as we'd passed the populated areas rather than go farther into the tunnel. The enemy was crushed and she was alive, and that was all that mattered to her.

The temblor handed me the candle and pulled her long hair into a knot in the back, waiting for me to say something, and when I didn't, she gestured in the direction of Baseld. "Well? Shouldn't we be going?"

"Not yet. The dead need to be spoken for. We should sing the Dirge for the Fallen."

"Oh." The temblor folded her arms and looked down. "I don't feel comfortable with that. I grew up with Kalaad, you know, in Ghurana Nent."

"But you've been blessed by the Triple Goddess, and these soldiers were under your command."

"Yes, and I'm grateful for their blessing and honored by the faith the Triune Council has placed in me. But I don't think I'm the best person to sing the dirge. You go ahead; it'll mean more coming from you."

I had never met Temblor Priyit before that day—I'd only heard what Gaerit had told me—but right then I was positive that I didn't want to know her any better. If she thought I was simply going to leave to spare her any discomfort, she was wrong. Especially since it appeared that she might not suffer any other discomfort for her role in these deaths.

A sob built in my throat as I thought of Gaerit buried somewhere nearby, unseen, and I launched into the dirge straight away, because the first verse was to the poet goddess and once past the first two lines, every singer's voice improved and could not be shaken by emotion.

> Kaelin, let not my voice falter
> As I sing this Dirge for the Fallen:
> Let not the passage of time alter
> Or diminish the honor earned,
> The victories won, the friends well met,
> Or the lessons learned.

I hoped the temblor would react to that line, but she kept her eyes downcast. I'm not sure she thought there were any lessons to learn.

> Raena, salute these warriors of Rael
> Who spat defiance at cowardice:
> They never meant to fail
> In defense of that they cherished,
> But rather fought to the limits
> Of their skill till they perished.

> Dinae, our soldiers come to your embrace,
> To rest forever in the earth:
> We shall remember their faces
> Until someday we join them there,
> And then we too will nourish life
> And leave behind all warfare.

My voice certainly broke after that. I let my sorrow cry itself out while Priyit waited. The trade-off could and would be rationalized as the temblor saw fit, I knew: four hundred lives against six or seven thousand was more than acceptable. Except that I was the one who was supposed to make sure that it would never come to that. The trade-off for me couldn't be rationalized. I would forever be bereft of a fiancé, most likely bereft of friends, and recognized as that stonecutter who was not quite strong enough to do the job, who killed nearly a hundred soldiers, created orphans and widows and robbed families of their sons and daughters, brothers and sisters. My chest felt like it was tearing apart inside.

I remained standing in place for a long, countless time, feeling the weight and loneliness of it all, and the temblor held her silence for as long as she could, the best gesture she could make, I supposed. But eventually she made a throat-clearing noise, and I oriented myself to the direction of Baseld. I parted the earth before us as we moved, letting it fall back in behind us as we passed, determined to put one foot in front of the other until we saw daylight again.

Eventually you come to a point where you have no choice but to be about the business of forever.

When the temblor and I emerged from the collapsed tunnel into Baseld, rocks and dirt parting before me, a small group of people were waiting. They had shovels in their hands and rags tied across their mouths to reduce dust inhalation. They thought perhaps the cave-in was only local and wanted to get back to their homes somewhere near the entrance of the Granite Tunnel. They had been attacking the cave-in with boundless optimism, trying to clear it away.

They started to pepper me with questions immediately, glancing at my Jereh band to confirm that I was a stonecutter and not a juggernaut or some other Earth Shaper.

"Stonecutter, what happened?"

"How far does the cave-in go?"

And then, when they saw the temblor, the questions were fired at her:

"Is the garrison all right?"

"Did the Bone Giants cause this?"

All of that at once, and more that I didn't catch. They needed answers, and I felt nothing so much as the need to hide: to collapse in bed and stay there for days. But I was trapped.

Someone pushed between the shoulders of two men, who at first looked annoyed and about to say something, but they closed their mouths when they saw her Jereh band. It was a courier but a different one from the courier who had given me orders from the Triune Council. She was shorter and sharply featured, with a bladelike nose and well-toned shoulders.

"Stonecutter Meara," she said. "Temblor Priyit. The Triune requires a report immediately. Please come with me."

I didn't want to go, not before the Triune. But I didn't want to stay, either, and face these people. So I didn't resist when the courier took my arm and escorted me through the assembled excavators, the temblor following.

"Hey, wait!" said one of them, a stout man with a thick beard. "Tell us what happened first!"

"No," the courier replied, saving me the need to respond. "The Triune will hear it first."

As soon as we got past the press of bodies and had some space before us, the courier turned to us. "I am Tuala, courier of the Huntress Raena in service to the Triune Council."

She already knew who we were, so I merely nodded and said, "Honored."

"Have you ever run with a courier before?"

I shook my head, but the temblor nodded. Tuala focused on me.

"All right. You're going to jog behind me, and it'll continue to seem like an easy jog even when we're traveling at top speed. But keep your mouth closed. You don't want a bug to fly in there while we're traveling that fast."

"No, I—oh, that's disgusting. Are they going to splatter on me?"

Tuala pointed to several discolored spots on her armor. "Yes." I almost felt like returning to answer the questions of the locals, but the courier smiled. "It's not that bad. But wear these." She pulled goggles out of her belt pouch and handed a pair to me and another to Priyit. "A bug in your eye wouldn't feel good. Plus it protects you from the wind." She had her own pair and put them on. "Come, let's be on our way."

She began to lope downhill and checked over her shoulder to make sure we followed. I jogged after her, uncertain for some reason that I was doing it right, even though I rather enjoyed jogging as a rule. Perhaps I would be doubting everything I did from now on.

For the length of two houses nothing seemed unusual, but then I noticed that the houses began to move by much faster even though I wasn't trying to run any faster. And in a matter of seconds we were traveling so quickly that I felt the skin of my face pulling back, the loose folds of my clothing snapping in the wind. It was exhilarating to experience such speed but terrifying as well. I was thinking about some of the larger beetle species of Rael and imagining the impact if one of them slammed into me.

And then it happened. I felt a hard thump against my rib cage, as if someone had flicked me with their forefinger with all the force they could muster, and it stung. I looked down and saw a green splash of entrails on my tunic. It robbed the experience of fast travel of much of its romantic associations, and I wished I had a miner's helmet.

After a while, even at the relatively slow pace I was keeping, I began to get winded. I shortened my stride and gasped out a "Sorry" to Tuala, uncertain that she would hear me. She cast a glance back at me.

"Don't worry. You can walk if you want to now. You're completely caught up in my kenning. Just don't stop."

I slowed to a walk, chest heaving, and found that it was true. We were still flying across the land, every step gobbling up fifty feet or more as the earth took our lightest step and pushed us forward. Even at that speed, however, running due south, it took us hours to reach Killae on the northern shore of Goddess Lake. When we arrived at the Triune building, which was surrounded by sculptures erected by the nation's most celebrated stonecutters and artisans, I took a few steps to become accustomed to everything moving slowly again. Tuala checked in with the cluster of guards outside the door and informed them that she had an urgent message from Baseld. I didn't speak a word to the temblor while we waited and doubted I would ever speak to her again.

The councillors had retired for the evening and would need to be summoned, but she led us to the Council chamber to wait and take some refreshment.

I drank three glasses of water and then confessed I had a dire need to relieve myself. Tuala led me to a fancy privy designed by Brynt hygienists and trimmed in polished granite flecked with metals.

Given a small space of privacy free of distractions, I let worry seize me as I did my business. What would the Triune do to me once they heard what I had done? Throw me into a salted dungeon somewhere, cut off from the song of the earth forever? Execute me for criminal incompetence? Have me work in the mines the rest of my days to pay reparations to the families of those I'd killed?

"Whatever their sentence, Meara," I whispered to myself, "you deserve it and will greet it like an old friend." I washed my hands and face, gave up on trying to make my bug-spattered clothes presentable, and composed myself to deliver the news without emotion. I even said that to my reflection in the mirror: "You will deliver the news without emotion. You have nothing left but duty." I felt strong as I left the privy, and after a short wait to allow Temblor Priyit to finish her report, Tuala introduced me to the assembled members of the Triune Council in the chamber: Dechtira, Clodagh, and Carrig.

"Welcome, stonecutter," Dechtira said. "We have already heard from the temblor but would like to hear your version of events. Please tell us what happened."

"The entire Granite Tunnel is collapsed. The Bone Giant army is destroyed as a result. But so is half of Baseld's garrison." And my betrothed, I did not say. And my shiny dreamt-of future. And my sense of self-worth.

Questions and answers followed with a close focus on why I could not control the unraveling of the ancient seals keeping the tunnel intact. The seals themselves required some explanation since none of the councillors was a stonecutter. Carrig noted drily that I had proved why we needed physical support to shore up the magic of the stone-cutters, ugly and costly as it might be. "We'll have to shore up the Basalt Tunnel as soon as possible."

And despite the fact that essentially it all came down because I cracked under pressure or that it could have all been prevented if I had simply built up instead of down, the Council did not seem especially upset about it.

"The deaths of the garrison are regrettable," Clodagh said, and the callous dismissal of their lost lives, so close to what Priyit had done, nearly took my breath away. "But Baseld is safe, at least. You saved it from certain sacking and untold civilian casualties. We shouldn't have sent you in alone to do such a massive job, but we had no choice. You are not to blame."

I knew she meant the words kindly but could not imagine her being more wrong. If I was not to blame, then who was? If I had not buckled under the strain, those soldiers would be alive. The Granite Tunnel would still be a tunnel instead of rubble. Had I thought to question Priyit's orders in time, maybe Gaerit would still be alive and we'd still be getting married in a few months.

Silence fell in the chamber as the Council stared at me and I stared back. I waited for the other members to contradict Clodagh, but they did not. Gradually I realized that they expected me to say something.

"Um. Begging your pardons, what is to happen to me now?"

"Happen to you?" Carrig said.

"Yes. I mean—" I looked down and licked my suddenly dry lips. "—my punishment."

"Punishment?" Clodagh said, her face scrunched with incomprehension. "You saved a city. We commend your service to the Triple Goddess, and now you may go back to your duties."

"Oh. So I'm to go back and face the families. I see." I nodded. "That's fit. That's just. Thank you."

"Now wait a moment," Dechtira said. "Clodagh did not speak for the entire Council right then."

"I didn't?"

"No," Dechtira said. "There is much for us to discuss in private. Stonecutter Meara, take your rest in our guest quarters, but under guard, of course."

"What?" Clodagh exploded. Dechtira ignored her.

"Return here in the morning for your punishment."

I looked to the other two councillors for confirmation, and after a moment of exchanged glances among themselves, they nodded at me to indicate they were in agreement.

Tuala led me to a room I would have appreciated in other circumstances, but I had eyes only for the bed and its down pillow. I wanted only a few hours of sleep to put the worst day of my life behind me. Every day henceforward would be miserable but not quite as bad.

There were fresh clothes waiting for me when I awoke, free of insect remains. I changed into them after visiting the washroom and then stepped into the hall, and there a guard escorted me to the Council chamber. I had to wait for a few moments but eventually was ushered in to hear my sentence.

"Our unanimous decree," Dechtira said, "is that you cross the Poet's Range in the company of the courier Tuala and aid the Brynt city of Tömerhil however they ask. Your services are to be provided free of charge. And after you are finished there, you are to travel to whatever Brynt city you wish and help them rebuild. You will have a stipend for modest living expenses from the Raelech embassy wherever you go. But you are never to return to Rael. You are banished."

No more days spent occupied with decorative flourishes, then. A lifetime of rebuilding. Yes. That would be my path to redemption. The temblor might have been awarded a medal or something, but I didn't care. She was unaware that she had anything to atone for. But I needed some way to balance out what I'd done, and the Council had given it to me. Tears sprang to my eyes, and I thanked them.

When the bard returned to his accustomed form, I was startled to discover that my cheeks were wet. And I wasn't the only one. I'd heard,

of course, that the Raelechs had collapsed the Granite Tunnel to defeat the Bone Giants because they didn't have sufficient forces at
Baseld—we'd all heard that—but I didn't think anyone knew that it
was a mistake. Or that someone out there thought of it as a disaster
rather than a victory.

What Meara had said—being about the business of forever—gave
me much to think on. I'm still not ready to move on from Sarena and
don't know that I ever will be. Perhaps my eternity is to be forever a
widower. But I had a growing hope that I would be more than that,
and I hoped Meara would be, too.

Day 15

NEW COURSES

A few days of normality and happy kids restored Elynea to the point where she bestowed at least one tired smile per evening. Sometimes more. She hadn't found another job yet but seemed much more optimistic about it. After she departed in the morning and the children were safely off to school, I grabbed my rapier and marched down to the armory to resume my training with Mynstad du Möcher. I began with an apology.

"Sorry about the other day," I said.

"Oooh," she said, wincing as she took in my bruised face. "You must have run into someone mean."

"Not at all," I said, smiling. "She was very kind and kept all my teeth in my head."

"Back for more?"

"Just training this time, if you're available. I'd rather not get rusty."

"Good. I could use the workout."

And she threw herself into it with unusual vigor and maybe a good measure of her own frustration. I recalled that she had been ready to beat someone at the time I needed a beating, and it appeared that whatever had vexed her then hadn't quite worked itself out of her system. When we called it quits, both of us gasping for breath and sweating, I suggested a trade.

"Trade what?"

"Reasons," I said. "I'll tell you why I came looking for a fight a couple of days ago if you tell me what's bothering you now."

She narrowed her eyes at me. "Okay, but you go first."

I shrugged. "It's easy enough. I was missing my wife and was enraged because I was reminded that we still have no idea who killed her. I wanted to feel any pain but that sort of impotent fury."

"Impotent fury. Yes. That's what I'm feeling, too. But look—this is between us."

"Of course." The Mynstad peered around to see if anyone was within earshot, then drew closer and lowered her voice.

"You've met Gerstad Nara du Fesset?"

"Yes, we met a few days ago."

"She's away right now, doing something for the pelenaut."

"Right, I think she mentioned she'd be on assignment for a while."

"Well, it's not widely known, but she's my lifebond."

"Oh!" Some comments and behaviors from others made a bit more sense now. "I didn't realize you were bound with anyone. But that's great. I wish you both happiness."

"Thank you. But that is what's on my mind. I worry about her more each day. She could be dead already and I wouldn't know it."

"No, surely—she's a rapid."

"It's a dangerous mission."

"I'm sorry. I know that worry can wear on you. Should she be back yet?"

"I don't even know that much about it."

"Which makes it worse, yes."

I did secure permission from the Mynstad later to write this down so that I wasn't breaking any confidence, but I offered a sympathetic ear and thanked her again for her sympathetic fists.

"It's more difficult to make new friends as you grow older," I ventured, and then my conversational ship ran aground and I flailed about, not knowing what to say next that wouldn't sound ridiculously sentimental. She saw the panic in my eyes and had mercy, smiling at me.

"I understand completely, Dervan," she said. "I'm glad we met as well."

"Right," I managed, giving her a tight nod. "See you soon."

Fintan surprised me by wishing to return to Hollit and Orden's restaurant again. "I'm paying this time," he said, "and I'm going to face this fear that's been hiding inside me."

It was busy during the lunch rush again, so busy that they couldn't keep up with demand and some people walked out. They appeared to be short-staffed, and Orden confirmed it when he came to visit our table after the madness.

"Sorry about that," he said. "Two of our staff didn't show up for work today, and we received a note that they've decided to move to Festwyf."

"Festwyf?" Fintan and I said in unison.

"Aye, the pelenaut's reopened it for resettlement as of this morning. Surprised you hadn't heard already. Should relieve some of the pressure on Survivor Field and in the city proper, I imagine."

I immediately thought of Elynea. Would she be moving back? Or would she want to remain here?

"Does that mean you need a new server or two, Orden?" I asked. "Because I know someone looking for work if so."

He eyed me. "Well, who is it?"

"Widow of Festwyf with two kids, currently living with me. She's almost thirty, I think."

"Is she going to move back?"

"I don't know. I'll ask her."

"If she wants a job, send her here, midmorning, with a note from you. If she doesn't show, I'll have to hire someone else."

"Understood."

When Orden left, I peered at Fintan. He didn't exhibit any shakes this time, but perhaps that was because he was clutching the edge of the table. He was sweating again, though.

"If it helps," I said, "I used to have similar reactions anytime someone said the word *gravemaw*." Fintan looked up at me, a querulous scowl on his face, and I realized I hadn't shared that story with him, only with Mynstad du Möcher. I waved it away. "Traumatic experience from my mariner days. Gave me my limp, nightmares, and a bad reaction for years. But the nightmares faded with time, and it's just the limp I have to live with now."

"How much time?"

"About twenty years."

"Great. Well, I'm blessed with perfect recall. My memories won't fade with time. That's essential for telling stories and recording history, but every horror and every embarrassment of my life—everything I'd like to forget—is fresh as the day it happened. I'm used to the nightmares now, as much as one can get used to them, but this is new. I'm perfectly safe and I know it, but my body is behaving like I'm back at the Godsteeth."

I didn't know what to do or how to help, because his was a special case. There was no comfort I could give him except to say quietly, "You have my sympathies."

The multitudes on Survivor Field did look somewhat less multitudinous when we looked out from the wall that afternoon, but there were still many thousands out there, and they were still clamoring to hear more of the Raelech bard's tale.

"I've heard that Festwyf is on its way to being a city again," Fintan called out. "That's excellent news. How about a traveling song, then, for all those on the road to restoring Brynlön?"

> The open road beckons, so I may not linger
> The trees in the wind wave to me like fingers

The clouds drift low like welcome banners
And the horizon greets me with good manners

So I'm off, I'm rolling on the open road
And the freedom of it always lightens my load
Don't know what I'll find when I get there
But the journey's better so I don't care

(Second verse repeated until everyone gets tired of it)

"Let's find out how Melishev Lohmet reacted to the news I delivered to him," Fintan said after the break, and took on the seeming of the Nentian viceroy.

Melishev

This situation is worse than five kherns fucking. The Raelech juggernaut got called back to Rael to deal with some strange giants invading the other side of the continent—not Hathrim but some people they're calling Bone Giants. Which means we can't expect any more help from them, not that they gave us any to begin with. And then that scrawny ball sack of a bard arrived to tell me that Ghuyedai is dead and all my army with him, completely destroyed by Gorin Mogen. Except for Junior Tactician Nasreghur, whom I suppose I must now promote to senior, and the dregs of my garrison, I am defenseless should the Hathrim or anyone else decide to take my city. The Raelech stonecutters, at least, have been returned and are already at work finishing what they started.

The Hearthfire's demands that we simply give him that land in perpetuity are so outrageous that I cannot begin to respond. Let the king do it—that's beyond my purview anyway. I've done all I can at the moment. Maybe when or if the king's forces arrive here we can take back a measure of the blood Mogen's spilled. The Fornish say through their perfumed ambassador that they're working on providing some military aid, but I don't know when or even if they'll have a force capable of countering the Hathrim.

The bard ends his completely miserable audience by saying he'll stay at the Raelech embassy and then tosses out a wish for me to "be well," which is more alarming than the news of my army's destruction. People are beginning to notice. To question my health. My sanity! My fitness to rule. Khaghesh has been making noises to the effect that I should rest and he will take care of everything while I heal. Which I never will with the king withholding his hygienist from me. So I must show them I am well. A trip to the plains with my cheek raptor! An outing under Kalaad's blue sky! Nothing makes one feel more alive or appear more normal than playing with a face-eating pet!

My forearm is wrapped in khernhide and I have a khernhide helmet with cheek guards as well, the only natural material impervious to raptor claws and far cooler than steel. Four crossbowmen accompany me; they have the same helmets on.

It's going well. The raptor's behaving, fetching a khek hare here, a grass weasel there, when a flushed Nentian courier rides out from the city. He turns out to be military; insignia on his shoulder flares identify him as a junior tactician, but he's not one of mine. I toy with the idea of offering him a commission here since I'm so poorly supplied with officers, but he looks afraid of me. If he fears me, he'd soil himself in battle and shouldn't be leading men at all. He surprises me, though.

"Viceroy Bhamet Senesh needs your help," he begins, and it's a request so out of tune with reality that I laugh at him. And then, to my horror as much as his, I can't stop. It's too ridiculous.

"Forgive me, Viceroy, but it's no joke. He really needs your help."

That keeps me going for another minute, and he has sense enough to keep silent until I can speak.

"Well, Tactician," I finally manage. "If it's not a joke—you're sure about that?"

"Very sure."

"It's quite a coincidence, then. I could use his help, too, but somehow my messages have failed to produce any either from him or from his cousin in Batana Mar Din. Has he even received them?"

"I have no knowledge of any other messages, Viceroy. I only have this one to deliver." He waggles a sealed envelope in his hand.

"Of course you don't know anything. Fine. Deliver your message." He steps forward, stretches out his arm, and extends the envelope to me at the greatest distance possible. Definitely afraid. Though maybe he's afraid of the raptor on my arm. I have one of the crossbowmen break the seal and give me the letter folded inside, which is covered in Bhamet Senesh's hasty scribble.

> *My dear Melishev,*
>
> *An extraordinary situation here forces me to ask for your aid. Please send any troops you can spare upriver from Batana Mar Din as soon as possible, preferably with my tactician.*
>
> *I sense a rebellion in the making and fear that the Sixth Kenning may be real. Only three of the thirty or so beggars who left the city as Seekers have returned, and they claim to be blessed with the Sixth Kenning, too. They call themselves Beast Callers, and I'm told through intermediaries that they want to form a clave. I haven't been able to locate them in the city, but the rumors of their abilities are awed and even worshipful. The possibility exists that they could be telling the truth since the guards at the Hunter Gate were killed in strange attacks: one suffered a kholeshar bite, and the other's face was covered in bee stings.*

*I need more men to find these kids and get them under con-
trol. My cousin has sent a few troops upriver, but it's not
enough. I pledge to return them as soon as the situation is
secure.*

*Yours in respect and service to the Crown,
Viceroy Bhamet Senesh*

Kalaad save me, not this again. "Do you know what the viceroy
asked me, Tactician?"

"I do."

"Tell me, then, what do you know of these kids who claim to have
found the Sixth Kenning?"

"Nothing for certain . . ."

"Share with me the rumors you've heard."

The tactician nods and gulps. "They say one controls bees and
wasps, one controls snakes and flesh eels, and one controls horses."

"Controls horses? Perhaps that might help answer what happened
to your lost cavalry."

"It's a possibility, yes."

"Did you know the men guarding the Hunter Gate?"

"Yes. They were under my command, Viceroy."

"Ah, so you saw their bodies."

"I did."

"And could their deaths have been accidental? A freak chance of animal aggression from the plains?"

"No, Viceroy. The bees might have been a freak attack, but if so,
why go after only one man and why only sting his face? A natural
swarm would have stung hands as well, any exposed skin. And the
other guard who got the kholeshar bite—that was on his face, too."

"A snakebite to the face?"

"Yes. One would hardly bend down to kiss a kholeshar, so that suggests the kholeshar struck from his height. Which would make sense if

the snake was coiled on the shoulder or arms of this individual as rumors claim."

Extraordinary. Bhamet might have genuine cause to worry. A bunch
of kids with power was even more terrifying than adults with power.
And for us to finally find our national birthright would necessarily
cause tremendous upheaval. "So you believe it's true—these kids have
found the Sixth Kenning after all this time?"

"I cannot be certain, but it fits the facts that we have, Viceroy."

"And they're willing to use these powers to kill guards and possibly
the missing cavalry."

"Yes. Though there are rumors about that as well."

"Oh? Do tell."

"The story that's circulating—and that must have come from the
kids—is that the cavalry accidentally killed a boy and were going to kill
all the Seekers to cover it up, so the hunter boy, the one who found the
kenning, acted in self-defense."

"So they're actually claiming credit for the lost cavalry instead of
pretending they never ran into them, and claiming the cavalry provoked a lethal response?"

"Correct."

"Very interesting. Do you think they might be telling the truth?"

The tactician shrugged. "We will only ever have their side of the
story."

"So just to make sure I have this right: Viceroy Senesh has lost men
twice to these allegedly blessed kids, and they're asking him to recognize their clave and ignore those deaths."

"Yes, Viceroy."

"Fantastic. Gentlemen," I say to the crossbowmen, "please secure
the junior tactician to one of the posts."

There is some struggle. Some protest. A quick blow to the head
with a crossbow stock stuns him and allows my men to get him secured.

"Did you know that cheek raptors can count?" I ask him, and his
head wobbles on his neck as he tries to focus.

"What are you talking about? Why are you doing this?"

"Why do children pull the wings off butterflies? Why does my cock hurt all the time? We have no reasons for all the cruelties under Kalaad's great wide sky. But we do have an answer to the first question I asked you. It's true! Cheek raptors can count. Watch this; I'll prove it to you."

I snap my fingers in front of the raptor and say "Hup!" then hold up my index finger and say, "One! One! Hup!" The raptor leaps off my protected arm and flaps over to the junior tactician, digging its talons into his left cheek and ripping it off, flying back to my arm with a bloody hunk of the tactician's face as he screams.

"There, you see? His natural instinct would be to take both of your cheeks at the same time, but he only took one! And look, he thinks you're quite delicious, Tactician. Oh, my, gone already! These plains creatures eat fast. They have to, you know. Well, he was such a good boy, we have to reward him, don't we? Hup! One! Hup!"

We leave the largely faceless tactician there after removing his military shoulder pins and return to the city. The raptor to his aerie, me to my tower to compose a suitable reply for my colleague in Khul Bashab.

> *My dear Bhamet,*
>
> *You great wide gash, we've been invaded by Hathrim and we'll all be breakfast for blackwings if I don't get some help! Pay attention—I've already informed you of this before. If you can't handle a few rebellious teenagers, then you definitely won't be able to handle Hearthfire Gorin Mogen when he comes calling. Send all your men to me now in defense of our country. And tell your cousin to do the same.*
>
> *I do have a suggestion that may solve your problems. Let it be known in your city that you will accept the Beast Callers clave and you won't have to search for the kids because they'll gladly pay you a visit to get what they want. Once you have a signed charter—actually, make it a condition of signing it—employ*

them immediately in service to the Crown and send them to me.
I will send them against the Hathrim. Either these kids will
emerge victorious and become national heroes—in which case
you can publicly "believe" their self-defense stories and forgive
the cavalry deaths—or they will die in a fire. You win either
way.

Sincere sorrow about the sudden death of your junior tacti-
cian. He was attacked by a cheek raptor outside the protection
of our walls.

In service to the Crown,
Viceroy Melishev Lohmet

I give the letter to a courier, enclosing the tactician's shoulder pins, and tell him to make haste to Khul Bashab. And then, just in case those blessed kids could change my luck, I visit Nasreghur at the garrison in person, not trusting Khaghesh to deliver the message.

"Inform every single one of your gate staff. They're to grant anyone claiming to be a Beast Caller an immediate audience." One of them under my control would catapult me to the throne for sure.

I was glad that the Nentian expatriates had already been taken care of and the ambassador expelled as well, or else we would have more violent attempts on Fintan's life to confront. That was the viceroy at his scheming worst, and the crowd muttered among themselves, wishing far worse pain upon him than a burning sensation when he urinated.

"Returning back to this side of the continent, you may recall mention of an expedition to Möllerud that concerned Second Könstad Tallynd du Böll and that Kallindra du Paskre and her family were part of that expedition."

The bard threw down a black sphere and became the sleepy-eyed teenager with her dark hair pulled back in a queue.

Kallindra

I don't think I can ever look upon blackwings again with anything but horror. They are creatures of my nightmares now, companions with death the way rain and clouds are best friends. The land is their dinner plate, and they feast upon us when we drop onto it, lifeless and rotting. They swirl and screech over Möllerud still, though it has been weeks since we passed here last and the bodies of our countrymen were freshly slain.

But they have done their work in the meantime, and the corpses outside the walls are mostly rags and bones now. If there is any mercy here, at least the faces are gone. This is an anonymous resting place, the victims mysterious and possessed of a certain distance without the substance of their flesh. I won't recognize anyone we traded with once. I can pretend for short periods that they're merely skeletons instead of former people, relics of the landscape who never laughed or cried or loved or shouted in anger.

I still think we should set the whole place on fire. Erase this excrescence from the earth, if not our memories, and let us build again, however long that takes, so that people will laugh here again instead of weep and mourn.

But I am only a trader's daughter. No one will listen to me. I think that instead of joining this clave or that, I would primarily like to become someone people will listen to. There is no clear path to that summit, however. Unless you count becoming one of the blessed. I am often amazed that Pelenaut Röllend spent part of his youth as a fish head in the dank alleys of Pelemyn. But just jump into Bryn's Lung, somehow survive to become a tidal mariner, and *you, too,* can leave behind your impoverished history and grow up to rule one of the world's largest countries!

Though I suppose we are not so large anymore. We are much reduced: the great cauldron of our people, once a mighty reservoir, has steamed away to a mere puddle.

Our caravan has paused for a while some distance away from the walls, allowing me this time to write without danger of a spilled ink pot or a scribbled word as a result of wagon wheels over rocks. The company of mariners sent with us by the quartermaster is scouting ahead, entering the city to make sure there are no traps or Bone Giants around.

I am sure they will be doing some discreet looting in advance of the rest of us to pay themselves for the danger. I am of Mother's mind in this regard: robbing the dead holds no attraction for me no matter how shiny the gold. Robbing the absent Bone Giants of a ship or five, however, sounds perfectly justified. I am not sure if that is morally defensible, but I feel it anyway. Perhaps it is just as well that no one listens to me.

We can see the silhouetted fleet anchored in the harbor from here. Father is trying to determine which ships might be in the best shape from this impossible distance and speculating aloud. Mother is ignoring him. Jorry has found a pretty girl to flirt with a couple of wagons behind us, and her parents have put him to work under their watchful eyes. The girl is extremely conscious of being the subject of a public mating ritual and uncomfortable with it as well. She's tolerating him only to be polite, but Jorry isn't picking up on any of those signals. He is little more than an ambulatory boner.

A mariner scout has just come from the west on horseback to warn us that there are small raiding parties of Bone Giants roaming around the outlying farms. "You should all head back," he said. "It's not safe." He has blood on him—not his own, though.

The men challenge him: Is this an order? Does he even have authority to order us around? How many parties of Bone Giants did he see? How many in each party? Were they actually headed this way or farther into the country? What if we head back now without the mariners in the city and these parties find us along the way?

"I'm going to report to the gerstad now," the scout said, making a visible effort to be patient. "Do as you like. I'm merely informing you that there are giants in the area and it's not safe. We may have to head back."

The father of the pretty girl Jorry was flirting with said, "Won't the mariners in the city protect us?"

That caused the scout to shed his thin veil of professionalism. His eyes grew to the size of chicken eggs, and he bared his teeth. "No! *No, they won't.* Bryn drown us all, I was in a party of five, you understand? Five men on horseback! We came upon three of the Bone Giants, and *I am the only one who escaped.* Do you see? We can't fight them. They're too big. Their reach is inhuman. If you get one, the others take you down—that's exactly what happened. We got one of them, and they got four. Blows coming from angles you can't predict, from distances you think impossible. One of them shattered my shield—" He broke off, realizing he had lost control. "But you can stay here if you like." He trotted off to the city, men shouting after him to come back and answer their questions. And once it was clear that he wouldn't stand there and be a target for them, they began to argue amongst themselves about what to do. Except for Father. He asked Mother what she thought.

"To the deep with what these others think," he said. "What do you figure we should do?"

"I think we should get on one of those ships right now and sail back to Setyrön," she said. "We're dead if they find us here. And if there are more than a few of them, then those walls and the mariners inside them won't make much difference. They didn't make any difference to all the rest of those people." She shook her head. "We never should have come down here, Lönsyr. We need to get away as fast as we can. And taking a ship was the whole idea anyway. Let's go."

He didn't argue. He nodded once and whipped the horses. I had to call to Jorry to tell him we were leaving, and he was forced to run to catch up with us. Or jog, anyway; we weren't moving all that fast.

We weren't the only ones to move. Some families decided to head for the city gates as we headed to the harbor. Some of them turned around. Some remained where they were.

Writing as we roll now, and this road we're taking is ill maintained and rough going. But Mother was right: we both need to get away and never should have come. The Bone Giants are here. Now. Coming out of distant tree lines like the pale wraiths of the Mistmaiden Isles, running across the dead fields of once-green farms. I knew that these wouldn't be like Motah, mostly naked and trying to appear harmless, but they were even more horrifying than I expected. Clacking bones and painted faces, white butchers who feed the blackwings, strange swords in their hands to slaughter us like animals. Which makes me wonder: Are we even human in their eyes? Are they in mine?

The scout is streaking for the castle, whipping his horse in panic. He has a chance to make it, I think. But the families that were headed that way behind him have largely rethought and are trying to turn their wagons around to either head for the harbor or simply go back. The ones who remained where the scout found us are definitely turning back for Setyrön. I can see some mariners up on the walls with bows. But there are more giants than archers already. They just keep coming. That mariner scout might have found an isolated party of three, but this is no isolated raiding party foaming out of the country like wave breakers. I think it must be the army come back to claim their fleet or at least occupy the city now that they've sacked Hillegöm and the interior villages. It's the tide rolling in, except it's no gentle progression of curling waters but one huge menacing whitecap, and I hope we're not on the beach when it hits.

The outcry when the bard dismissed Kallindra's seeming was swift and loud.

"Don't worry; the story continues," he assured everyone. "But I'm going to let the Kaurian scholar Gondel Vedd take it from here."

ondel

I really shouldn't eat while angry. Reinei found a way to remind me that peace is a better garden to cultivate in the mind. Ponder and I were eating breakfast at an outdoor café in Setyrön, and the people at the next table made clear through their expressions of disgust and muttered comments that I had committed a culinary crime by slathering my smoked moonscale with mustard. While I paused to glare at them, full fork raised and suspended before my mouth, a gust of wind from the sea blew that glorious mustard-covered bite right off my fork and onto my lap, beginning my day with a fresh mustard stain. The Brynts laughed at me and I laughed with them, but not for the same reason.

"Oh, no, Gondel!" Ponder said, dipping his napkin in water and offering it to me.

"No, thank you, I'll be fine. It's a gentle lesson from Reinei about what can happen when you don't maintain your peace of mind."

I had already sent a letter to the mistral on yesterday's ship to Kauria and a longer one to my husband in hopes that he'd forgive me for my sudden disappearance and an absence that may stretch out for months. I could not in good conscience return yet; there had to be a way to get ahead of this and save Kauria from an assault like the ones Brynlön and Rael suffered, and right then Brynlön was my best hope of teasing out more information from the Eculans. Saviič could help me translate the blank spaces in *Zanata Sedam*, but could not tell me any more about their plans.

Ponder agreed that we would be better off doing most anything else than trying to approach the entire army occupying Göfyrd in hopes they would opt to talk instead of kill us on sight. So it was back to Möl-lerud for us, where there was a fleet that we could examine for clues on how they crossed the ocean and perhaps there would be some written orders left behind in the city. That large party of people we'd passed on the way to Setyrön was more than enough to handle that small group of Bone Giants we had run into, so it should be a safe place to conduct our investigations.

For a couple of days as we traveled down the coast on foot, we could forget that there was a war going on and we were in a land beset by invaders. The wind blew soft and peaceful upon our skin, carrying a pleasant tang from the ocean and a gentle rain on the second night. I noted aloud that I enjoyed being outdoors for a change instead of in a library or a musty dungeon. Ponder grunted and smiled but offered little else. I thought he must have very little on his mind since he rarely spoke, but a simple question dispelled that notion.

"What occupies your thoughts as you walk along with me on this boring duty?" I asked him.

"It's not boring at all. The air here is different, and it speaks to me. I sense things you cannot because of my blessing."

"Oh. Like pressure and moisture and precise temperature?"

"Yes, but much more than that. Ghosts and voices in the wind."

"I beg your pardon?"

He cast a worried glance at me, hoping he would not have cause to regret giving his thoughts breath. "It's not something we tempests speak of very often. Cyclones don't perceive them. And I wouldn't have said anything except that you asked and this is extraordinary. There are many unhoused spirits out here."

"I guess there would be wherever humans have lived."

"No, I don't hear this kind of noise in Kauria. Most people tend to die at peace there, and their spirits become the wordless breath of the wind. But here, where there has been so much violence, the air is restless with anger and loss and yearning. Much of it ahead of us."

"I'd expect so. Do you hear actual words?"

"Sometimes, yes. Mostly it's just faint screams and roars."

"And what do you see?"

"That's difficult to explain—begging your forgiveness, Scholar. It's like asking me to describe yellow to someone born blind. But there are spirits collected in this area. Nothing that you would be able to see and nothing that will harm us. But violence leaves its echoes."

Indeed it does. On the third day, I felt out of sorts and the sky wore a somber gray skirt with dark folds of resentment pleated throughout, refusing to rain and refusing to let the sun shine through. Ponder felt it, too—more so, I'm sure. We hardly spoke the entire day, traveling in silence and our thoughts roiling like the desultory vapors above. If this was the invisible effect of the spirits he spoke of, how could anybody breathe peace in this part of Brynlön ever again? Could anyone be truly happy in close proximity to the site of a massacre?

The sky continued to churn with dark omens on the next day when we returned to Möllerud. There was supposed to be industry there if I had my facts straight—a cleanup in progress and a refitting of the anchored Eculan fleet for Brynt purposes. What we saw did not match expectations.

There were only more bodies and more blackwings gorging themselves. The remains of the caravan of wagons we passed on the way to Setyrön were now scattered outside the walls. The air was thick and sour with death, the peace of Reinei stilled on the killing field.

"I think they found more than just a few Eculans when they got here," Ponder said.

"Oh, no. That family."

"Which one?"

"The one I spoke with for a while. With the young woman who showed me her journal. I don't see their wagon."

We scanned the carnage in silence until Ponder pointed toward the port. "Over there. I think that might be theirs."

"Ah, by the ships! Yes, that's excellent! Perhaps they escaped. I'd like to check on them if we can."

Ponder squinted at the walls before replying. "I think the Eculans are in there now. I'm pretty sure I see a sentry. But we can try and leave quickly if it becomes necessary."

"Yes, let's try, please."

Hope built within my chest as we approached. I didn't see any bodies around their wagon except for the half-seen corpses of the horses. The Eculans had slain them all in their harnesses, a tremendous waste of resources. Did they not know how useful horses were? Perhaps their stature made riding horses impractical. Still, did they wish to operate plowshares on their own or pull their own wagons? It made no sense.

There were far too many ships at anchor in the bay to determine if one was missing. We had to see if we could locate the du Paskres and, if we could not, hold on to the hope of their survival.

Shouts and a familiar dread clacking pursued us before we could get there. The Eculans had spied us and sent out a party to deal with us. Seven of them, armed with both spears and swords this time.

"Ponder?" I said.

"It will be all right if that's all they send," he said. "Keep going."

I urged my ancient legs to a quicker pace, a sort of gliding half jog that would reduce stress on my knees. Appearing to flee would give them confidence and convince any officers watching from the walls that they didn't need to send anyone else to deal with us.

The Eculans steadily closed the distance between us, as they were running at nearly full speed and had a much longer stride. Ponder turned to face them, keeping one hand on my shoulder for some reason, and jogged backward. The reason for the hand became clear when he clutched my shoulder and said, "Stop!"

I did and turned to see what he was reacting to. The Eculans had decided they were close enough to hurl their spears at us in high arcs. Ponder shot a hand into the sky and uttered a simple denial at them, whipping his hand to our left as he did so. A powerful gust of wind blew the spears off course to fall harmlessly to the turf. And then he reached out with the same hand to the attackers and clenched his fist in a familiar gesture. The Eculans discovered they had no more air to breathe and collapsed after a few steps.

"Go," Ponder said. "This is under control. I'll follow behind."

Resuming my awkward and unforgivably slow top speed, I hoped to have time to discover what had happened to the du Paskres. If there were watchers on the walls, they would definitely respond to the sight of their sortie brought to its knees.

The back door of the wagon gaped open, but I could see nothing, shadows preventing me from determining if there was anything inside at all. I altered my course once I drew closer, taking an angle to see if anyone was in the front seat. My heart dropped when I saw two bodies slumped against each other. It was the father and mother I'd spoken to only briefly, large bloody gashes on their torsos, their eye sockets plucked bare, and their heads crawling with blowflies laying eggs. They obviously had never made it to the ships. That meant . . .

"No, no, no." I hurried to the back of the wagon and placed my foot on the wooden step that would allow me to peer inside. It took a moment for my eyes to adjust to the gloom inside, but I could see right away that it wasn't empty. There was a mess of things inside. An overturned ledger, pots and baskets, scattered pieces of clothing and sachets of tea, a burst container of dry beans. And at least one body, facedown. The flies would have told me that if nothing else. The feet were near me, and I pulled up the pant leg for a clue—muscular, like a man's. I didn't know who it could be, but it wasn't Kallindra. I checked behind me, and Ponder was only ten lengths away. He made a gesture with his hands to indicate that we were still okay and I could continue. There were no visible Eculans behind him; they must be prone and unconscious.

"I'm going in," I told him. "I can't see enough."

"Fine. I'll keep watch."

Grunting with the effort, I hauled myself up into the wagon and saw a knob on the left wall. There was a matching one on the right. I pulled and shoved and twisted on one until something moved—it was a slot that allowed some light to enter the interior. I did the same on the other side and reevaluated the scene. That was definitely a man sprawled facedown in front of me, but a young one. His left arm was splayed out, and there was another one underneath it, light-skinned palm up. That didn't belong to him, and the fingers were thin. Between him and the rest of the mess in the wagon I couldn't see who that hand belonged to.

More grunting to move the young man away, roll him over on his side. I expected the body to be stiff like a board, but it wasn't. He had been dead long enough for the muscles to relax again. This had happened days ago, perhaps while we were still enjoying the comforts of Setyrön.

I tossed aside a tunic and a random sheet of paper to reveal the other person underneath, and my breath caught when I confirmed it was Kallindra. I had difficulty taking a new breath after that, as often happens when peace abandons us and we are besieged by storms. I blubbered and gasped and shut my eyes to the horror of her vacant expression and open lips past which no wind moved. When strangers die, you let that knowledge flow around and past your mind, perhaps thinking "How sad," or "What a tragedy." These sympathetic thoughts never affect your breath. But when someone you know personally dies, it is like a thunderclap in the heart. And the manner of Kallindra's death was nothing more than a result of unreasoning hatred. It's an airborne poison, hatred is, for I felt it filling my lungs and contaminating my thoughts. It is how violence thrives and peace withers. I caught myself hoping that Ponder had made a mistake and withheld breath from the Eculans a few seconds too long. Unworthy and wrong of me but nonetheless fervently wished in that moment. And I remembered the words Jubal spoke to me, that once I saw violent death, it would change me, make me capable of violence myself. I hoped he was wrong, but my thoughts suggested he might have been right.

Kallindra and the young man—perhaps her brother?—had been

killed by slashes to their throats. The blood had stained her tunic and pooled underneath her neck, where her hair had become mired in it.

"Gondel. We need to be leaving," Ponder's voice floated into my consciousness and hung there until I could attach some significance to it.

"What?"

"Look." I turned around and saw that there were more Eculans coming from the city. Many more, too many to count. "I can't handle that many without resorting to violence."

I wanted to tell him to resort to it immediately. Summon winds to lift them high in the air, as my brother had to the Hathrim, and let them fall to their deaths. These monsters had no regard for peace. But it was not my place to give such orders, and even if it was, it wouldn't be in keeping with Reinei's teachings.

"Her journal," I muttered to myself. "Where is her journal?" If she had kept up with it, I might learn what had happened after I left her. I found it lying on her belly, her left arm draped over it as if to shield it from violation. I slipped it out and squeezed her cold hand. "I am so sorry, Kallindra. I hope you and your family are not haunting the winds here. Be at peace. Your story will be told."

"Scholar, we really need to go!" Ponder said.

"Coming!"

I scrambled out as best as I could, fingers pinched tightly around the journal, and Ponder lifted us up and away from the reach of the Eculans. The wind didn't carry us back toward Setyrön, however, which surprised me. Ponder instead floated us out over the harbor and set us down on the deck of one of the anchored Eculan ships, well out of spear range but still within their sight. They could try swimming out after us if they wished or board a boat to chase us, but it didn't matter. We'd have plenty of time to react to anything they tried.

"What do you want to do now?" Ponder asked.

"Report to Setyrön that Möllerud is actively occupied and all their party is lost."

"Should we do that, though, when they might see us depart and decide to follow us to Setyrön?"

"I don't think it will make a difference," I said. "They already knew the people they slaughtered came from that direction. And they saw us coming from that direction as well. We won't be giving them any new information. But Setyrön doesn't know about this. They should be warned."

"Very well. And after that?"

"We will head north. Continuing to seek information here will lead us both into a situation where we must break the peace. Let us visit Göfyrd and then the capital. Trading facts with the pelenaut might be fruitful."

The tempest nodded but said nothing. He folded his arms and frowned at the pale bodies collecting at the shore.

"Ponder?"

"Yes?"

"Do you know of any way to give the spirits you see here some measure of peace?"

He shook his head slowly. "I wish I did, Gondel."

As if in answer the wind picked up and howled about our ears. I couldn't bear to stand anymore, and I crumpled to the floor of the boat, hugging Kallindra's journal to my chest, a record of a now-extinct way of life. Once again, I had been too late to be of any help to the Brynts. I had to find some way to leap ahead of the Eculans and anticipate their next move or I would be doing nothing but writing their histories.

The bard sighed heavily when he dissolved his seeming. "That is, of course, how I came to know of the contents of Kallindra's journal. Gondel Vedd brought it here to Pelemyn. Tomorrow we'll have more from Abhi and revisit Culland du Raffert."

Day 16

BRYN'S LUNG

Tidal pools can mirror life at times, for they are simultaneously a place of beauty and wonder, yet occupied by horrors with teeth and there is no place to escape them. After I returned home from the bard's performance, I felt trapped in one.

Elynea had found a job and was positively beaming about it, her face and indeed her entire body transformed by the personal victory. But since this came as a complete surprise to me and I had walked in expecting to say that I had a job waiting for her if she wanted it, my face wasn't suffused with unadulterated joy when she said, "Isn't that great?"

It was only a second or two's delay, if that, for me to let go of my expectations and embrace her good news. But she noticed. When I said, "Oh, yes. Of course! That's fantastic!" she frowned and folded her arms across her chest.

"Are you sure? You don't seem that thrilled."

"No, I am! Honestly, congratulations. Sorry, I was just surprised because I was about to say I've found a job for you if you wanted it."

She cocked her head. "When did I ever ask you to get a job for me, Dervan?"

"Well, never—"

"That's right. I never asked. Because I didn't want your help. I wanted to get a job on my own, and I did. Drown me if I didn't."

"And that's wonderful! Seriously. I'm very happy for you. Please forgive me my presumption. Tell me about your job."

She eyed me for a moment, uncertain of my sincerity, and I admit that it hurt. It was a pain I've felt before—wounded pride, perhaps? Far too simple a label but perhaps close enough. It was more accurately an intellectual awareness that I was wrong, a fervent desire to be right from the start and go back in time to *be* right, coupled with an awareness that I couldn't do that and that in fact wishing to do so was stupid and immature, piled on top of the stupidity I already felt for assuming Elynea would want my help, and underneath it all an irrational desire to lash out in anger at Elynea when she had done nothing wrong and in truth I was angry at myself.

Sarena had trained me to identify at least what was going on in my head. She could tell what I was thinking and feeling because she'd seen the same things in the faces of men around the world. It didn't stop me from feeling any of it, but it did stop me from acting on those things the way many men would. So I restrained myself from making it worse and did what I knew to be right: give Elynea nothing but encouragement. When she was convinced I wanted to hear about it, she unfolded her arms and clasped her hands together, beaming and bobbing up and down on her toes.

"I'm formally apprenticed to a Fornish master woodworker! Eee!" She gave up the bouncing and did some full-on jumps, and that set off her kids. Tamöd and Pyrella leapt around the house, delighted because their mother's mood was so infectious, making high-pitched noises of joy and laughing.

I congratulated her again; she thanked me and then said that some post had arrived for me and she'd put it on my desk to keep it safe from the playing kids. That was my chance to escape with a shred or two of my dignity intact, and I withdrew to investigate, closing the door behind me and sighing.

"Brilliant, Dervan," I said aloud. Maybe the letter would make me feel better.

It bore the seal of the university, and I gave a surprised grunt. That was an impressively quick response. I tore it open, nearly as excited as the children for a moment, but my face quickly fell. Greetings, and then: "I regret to inform you that while the university will open again, it will do so at greatly diminished capacity and your services will not be required." I read that three times in mounting disbelief before continuing. "I hear that you have secured other important work during the hiatus, and I hope you will continue to find that fulfilling and prosperous." Best wishes and the signature of the chief scholar of my department. My hands gripped the edges of the letter so tightly that my fingers turned white at the edges and my jaw ached from clenching my teeth.

He had *heard*? What had he heard, and from whom? Was this the hand of the Wraith at work, making sure I had nothing else to do but work for him—or the Lung or the pelenaut—from now on?

I had to sit down and rest my face in my hands, letting the letter fall. My temporary employment by the government was supposed to be just that: temporary. I'd spent the majority of my professional life as a scholar and introduced myself as such; my identity was bound up with a job that made me feel proud and useful. What was I now? Certainly not a soldier, though I seemed to be in their company more often than not these days. And I couldn't tell people I was a spy even if I wanted to, and I didn't want to. No: I was *definitely* not a spy. The last thing I wanted was to follow my wife into an abyss of plots and deception and poisons.

Rölly might intervene if I asked, but I'd be ashamed to play on that association any more than I already had. Asking him to help after the university closed was what had washed me into this tidal pool in the first place. And I had the uncomfortable feeling that this arrangement was what he preferred anyway.

There was a soft knock at my door, and Elynea called through it, "Dervan? Are you hungry? I feel like cooking if you want."

Mastering my voice into something amiable, I replied, "Ah, yes, that would be grand. I'll be out to help in a moment."

I took a couple of deep breaths. Elynea's example might be the one for me to follow. She had reinvented herself; it had not been without effort, true, or a good measure of pain, but she'd proved that it could be done. Opening the door of my room, I paused at the threshold so that I wouldn't interrupt a family moment. Elynea was chopping up a carrot on a board in the kitchen, and Pyrella had frozen, staring at her. It was her intensity of expression that had caused me to freeze as well. Tamöd caught on and stopped jumping up and down on the couch, where he'd been singing the Current Chorus. The abrupt silence made Elynea look up to see what was wrong.

"What is it, Pyrella?" she said.

"You're cooking?" her daughter asked, her voice tiny.

Elynea shrugged. "Yes. You want to eat tonight, don't you?"

"But you haven't cooked in a long time."

Elynea looked down at the chopped-up vegetables and the knife in her hand, suddenly realizing it was true. Her shoulders slumped. "You're right. I'm sorry."

"It's okay, Mom," Pyrella said. "I'm just noticing. And I'm glad. Because it's like you're back now."

The knife clattered to the counter as Elynea rushed around the counter to give Pyrella a hug. They were already sobbing as they embraced, and Tamöd's mouth dropped open; he was too young to understand. As I eased backward into my room and slowly shut the door, I heard him say, "Hey! What's going on?"

Feeling guilty about eavesdropping but telling myself it was necessary so that I didn't stomp through an important time for healing, I waited until their voices resumed their happy tones and I could hear the knife thwacking on the cutting board again. Then I cleared my throat noisily as I exited my room and joined them.

Over dinner I asked if they had heard that the pelenaut had declared Festwyf open for resettlement. Elynea nodded. "But you won't be going back?"

The kids looked to their mother, perhaps a bit worried, and she caught it. "No," she replied. "I've lived there long enough and for even longer in my mind. I'm here now. *We* are here now. Time to live in the present and be thankful for what's in front of us."

Pyrella beamed at her mother. "I'm thankful."

Tamöd asked, "Is there going to be pudding in front of us after this?"

Fintan and I revisited the Kaurian restaurant where the bard had first been recognized in public. We were not so lucky as to arrive just after a shipment of oranges this time, and the menu had most of its meat entrees crossed out, replaced by new seafood dishes. They were all prepared with dry Kaurian spices and sometimes slivers of Kaurian tree nuts either baked on or garnishing the fillets. Kindin Ladd, the Priest of the Gale, was enjoying his lunch there, and we waved to each other across the dining room and traded smiles.

The bard looked a little weary under his eyes and I inquired if he had slept well. He shook his head.

"The nightmares were bad last night."

I pursed my lips, considering. I knew that many people suffered lingering mental effects after something terrible happened to them—how could they not?—and that it took many forms. Their tempers flared quickly, or they withdrew and shut down the way Elynea had until recently, or they had nightmares or vivid flashbacks of whatever trauma they experienced, or all that and more. Regardless, it crippled them to some extent. My panic attacks and nightmares about gravemaws hounded me for years and then ebbed thanks to a Kaurian principle Rölly told me about. Deciding that neither of us had anything to lose, I brought it up.

"Have you ever heard of the Kaurian practice of presence?"

"I've heard of it, but I'm not too clear on the concept. Why?"

"It helped me reduce the number and frequency of my nightmares. Or maybe it was simply a matter of time, as I suggested yesterday, though I still get them every once in a while. The problem with such horror is that some things, once seen, can never be unseen. Since you pointed out that your memories won't fade over time and I think practicing presence helped me, perhaps it might help you, too."

"I don't know," Fintan said. "If it's associated with Reinei, I might offend the Triple Goddess."

"It's not a religious practice at all," I assured him, "though of course the Church of Reinei condones anything that leads to peace, including personal peace of mind. It is simple to adapt by those of other faiths or of no faith at all. I could try to explain, but I might not do it justice. There's a Priest of the Gale a few tables over whom I know. Would you mind if I invited him to briefly outline the practice?"

Fintan shrugged. "Sure."

I waved to catch Kindin's attention and beckoned him over. After introducing him to Fintan, I asked him to explain presence and its benefits to us as laypeople.

"Certainly. May I sit? I will stay only a small while."

We begged him to be seated, and he thanked us.

"Outside the Church of Reinei," he began, "presence is a therapeutic practice that suggests one should make a conscious effort to live in the present. The reasons for this deserve to be examined regardless of one's faith. We begin with this observation: That which tends to cause us mental distress is either memories of the past or worries about the future. In such times we are not living in the present; we are missing the peace and fulfillment in every moment because our mind is absent in some other time that lies behind us or ahead. To amend this—to ease the distress we feel—we must train ourselves to be mindful of the now." Kindin leaned back and grinned. "Open your senses to this instant, friends. Is it not fine? The clank of pans and the hiss of heat from the kitchen. The chimes dangling in the wind outside the door that we can hear, a muffled yet insouciant song of the wind. The smell and taste of your food and the bounty of the ocean that makes it possible. The craftsmanship on display in this building and this very table, a beautiful hardwood improved from my home. The company you are keeping, Fintan—a Brynt and a Kaurian, with darker skin and different cultures from yours but still men who love and mourn and exult in the sun as you do. To be present, you note these things instead of ignore them. You allow—no, let me rather say, you *encourage* the wonders of the moment to occupy your thoughts rather than your past or future."

"All right; that sounds fine in theory," Fintan replied, "but if I'm to achieve that, isn't that some form of repression? I can't prevent thoughts of the past or future from happening. They won't simply go away."

"Oh, no, I'm not suggesting that!" The priest straightened in his chair, his hands held up in a placating gesture. "I'm suggesting that what you may be doing instead is *repressing the present*, and your path to peace is to simply stop doing that." He spread his arms wide. "Open yourself to it instead. Give this particular time its due." He dropped his hands and hunched forward, his eyes boring into Fintan's. "And then, when these unpleasant thoughts of the past or the future inevitably intrude, you note them, as you do the present, but when they are placed *next* to the present and the beauty of this world, you will also note they are not nearly as important as they once were." His intensity faded, and he smiled again as his body relaxed in his chair. "I am told that practicing presence has helped many people with troubled pasts. Their feelings of anxiety and panic decrease, and they even experience fewer nightmares if that is something that afflicts them. I hope it works for you as well."

Fintan gave him a tight nod. "Thank you very much."

"Should you wish further instruction, perhaps some specific techniques, you may visit or leave word for me at the Kaurian embassy," Kindin said, taking his cue. He rose from his chair and gave a little bow. "Please breathe peace."

When he was out of earshot, the bard chuckled. "I feel better already." He nodded and said more sincerely, "Thank you, Dervan. That might actually help. And I will note what I see presently for the record: you are a kind man."

I ducked my head, not knowing how to respond. But I think both of us were in good spirits after that, and it was our most amiable work session to date.

"I've noticed a little something about my diet in recent days," Fintan said upon the wall, "and you might be experiencing something similar. Here's one of your songs, one of my personal favorites."

> I had fish heads for my breakfast
> For my lunch and dinner too
> And all my friends are fish heads
> Don't know what I'm going to do
>
> I'm mighty sick of fish heads
> I'd like some fruits and veg
> But all I have are fish heads
> And a half-squeezed lemon wedge
>
> I'd trade you all my fish heads
> For an apple and a smoke
> Or just take them, I don't care,
> If I have one more I'll choke!
>
> (Coda)
> Fish heads, fish heads, they'll rot your bloody brain,
> Fish heads, fish heads, I'll never eat them again!

"We're going to hop from coast to coast today," Fintan said. "First we'll go to the west, where Abhinava Khose is about to meet the viceroy of Hashan Khek."

The bard transformed into the plaguebringer, looking a bit dusty from his travels.

$\mathcal{A}bbi$

I have been walking for a while now along the bank of the Khek River, exploring a possible land-based trade route that would give both Hashan Khek and Khul Bashab a new trading partner. And it's a very pleasant walk as long as you don't have to worry about being eaten. Easy, too, when you have a stalk hawk traveling along with you, pointing out where one can find nuts and berries. The grasses hide clumps of bushes sometimes, and though trees rise above them, they are often difficult to identify from a distance. An airborne friend definitely makes such things easier.

But my new senses help as well. I'm learning to identify what plant life might be nearby in conjunction with certain concentrations of animals and insects. I found a small clump of khanja berry bushes, for example, because I sensed the presence of khanja caterpillars feeding on them before they slept and turned into moon moths. Hunting for plant life to sustain me in this way is much more enjoyable than hunting creatures.

The old road down from Khul Bashab to the Khek River needs plenty of work. It's mostly overgrown from disuse, though it does swing by a few watering holes and end at a dock where one can tie up cargo barges. I've been counting the days and marking places along the way that might work well for waypoints. Spots that could support a fortified inn, or a trading post, or a small village someday to keep traders safe at night. I passed the spider colony that is now the current location for the Sixth Kenning and shuddered as I gazed upon it. They are larger than my head, gray and furry and no doubt capable of delivering very painful and poisonous bites. If one was to be blessed, then no doubt the poison would be neutralized almost immediately, but that wouldn't subtract from the pain and horror of being bitten. And if one wasn't blessed, why, then, I imagine it would be one of the most terrifying ways you could die, for it would not be quick or painless and you might still be alive as they began to digest you, liquefying your muscles and slurping them up, and Kalaad in the sky, I think I might be making myself sick just thinking about it. I've heard stories that somewhere in Forn there is a clan that harvests silks from spiders, caterpillars, and worms and makes their primary living from it. I hope their spiders are more sensibly sized than these.

On the positive side, it will be only a few weeks and the kenning site will shift north to the plains below Tel Ghanaz, where one can be merrily torn apart by a troop of golden baboons or else blessed by bites and maybe some hugs. I cannot speak for all, but I would take baboons over spiders any day.

Also on the positive side, I have managed not to kill anything since I left Tamhan, Hanima, Adithi, and Sudhi or do anything stupid that contributed to the death of another creature. Let Murr and Eep and all others hunt according to their nature: my nature now is to walk gently among the animals of the plains and do no harm.

I hope my fellows are safe in Khul Bashab and well on their way to creating a Beast Callers clave. Viceroy Bhamet Senesh may be unwilling to do us any favors after the mess I've made of things, but perhaps the viceroy of Hashan Khek will be more open to the idea. I will inquire when I arrive. Situated on the coast as he is, he might be interested particularly in what I can do for him in the sea, so I conducted an experiment: I waded into the river up to my ankles—not far at all—and stretched out with my kenning to discover if I could sense the animal life in the river. And I could! Sunfish. Borchatta. Clawbugs in the mud. Checking first to make sure no fish-eating birds were nearby, I asked a sunfish to leap out of the water briefly, and it did, blinding me with sunlight on its scales before returning safely to the water.

Impossible not to grin at something like that.

When I drew close to Hashan Khek, I noticed that the number of animals decreased significantly. They were more frequently hunted, of course, but also the city simply smelled bad. Like borchatta soup and . . . something worse. No wonder the animals avoided the place: humans were befouling it.

I found a small grove of nughobes well outside the walls and asked Murr and Eep to wait in the area while I visited the city, perhaps for a few days. I unhitched my horse from the cart and took both horses with me into the city to keep them safe. Murr and Eep most likely would fend very well for themselves, but two horses would be easy prey for a pack of something hungry.

The guards at the Hunter Gate could not have been more surprised to see a single unarmed man approach them and ask to enter the city.

"Who are you?" one asked. I told him. "What's your business here?"

"I've come to see the viceroy if he'll grant me an audience. I have news regarding the discovery of the Sixth Kenning near Khul Bashab."

"What nonsense is that?" They hadn't heard of the discovery, then. But perhaps they had heard of something else.

"They call themselves Beast Callers. They're trying to start a clave in the city. I'd like to discuss those developments with him."

If that didn't work, I would bring up the missing cavalry, but the guards exchanged glances after "Beast Callers" and nodded.

"We're supposed to bring anyone who speaks of that straight to him," one said. He had a marker of rank on his shoulder. "Enter and follow."

The other guard remained at the gate, and I followed the ranked soldier to the viceroy's compound, which surrounded the Tower of Kalaad near the harbor. There were some questions from other guards about my clothes, or relative lack of them, but matters of personal appearance did not matter so much as following their orders, and I was steadily passed through a series of checkpoints, gave my horses into the care of their stables, and soon was presented to the viceroy's chamberlain. He was a short man with a large gap between his front two teeth, introduced only as Khaghesh. I did not know if that was his first name or surname, but I did know that I did not trust him.

He did not think very highly of me either. I must have looked terrible, caked in dust and grass from days of walking on the plains. I might have smelled worse than the city—certainly like a horse. He smelled like some Fornish ideal of masculinity, all cloves and vanilla, but I think he had sprayed that on himself to disguise his fondness for onions, which I detected hovering about as well. He lived a pampered existence, wearing boots made of gut goats, and his lip curled in evident disgust. I should probably bathe soon.

"You are a messenger of Viceroy Senesh in Khul Bashab?"

"No, sir. I am an envoy of the Beast Callers."

"An envoy only, or are you a Beast Caller yourself?"

"I am."

His sneer communicated his disbelief. "And what proof can you offer of this rumored talent?"

"What proof would satisfy you?"

"I hardly know. There are no beasts here for you to call."

"Oh, there are plenty, sir."

"I beg your pardon?"

"There are many insects and spiders in the compound—quite nearby, in fact—and some small rodents as well. If you will agree not to strike at them when they appear, I will ask them to show themselves and do no harm to you or this guard here."

He stared at me for a moment, then looked all around at the walls and ceilings, searching for insects and the like. They were all hidden at the moment in cracks in the salt-worn masonry.

"Very well, it is agreed," Khaghesh said. "Make them appear. I will do no harm to them so long as they do not crawl on me."

I called the insects and spiders and other crawling things forth. They obliged and emerged from various hiding places in the hallway. One was a poisonous hundred-legged wheelmouth with rotary teeth that drilled into flesh and shredded it before sucking down the resulting slurry of meat.

"Ugh!" Khaghesh grunted. "I had no idea there were so many. And you said there were rodents?"

"Near the kitchen. Enjoying the food there."

His disgust deepened, but his regard improved. Grudging respect, perhaps a small hint of fear in his eyes.

"Understood. Now make them go away again. I liked them better when I couldn't see them."

I allowed the creatures to return to their shelters with my thanks.

"Wait here," the chamberlain said. "I'll inform the viceroy."

That left me alone in the hallway with the guard. He looked at me differently now, too.

"The Sixth Kenning is real, then?" he asked. "You control animals?"

"It's real," I said. "You saw for yourself just now."

"So I could seek a kenning. Any one of us could. Just like the Rae-lechs or the Fornish or whoever."

"Yes. Just like them."

The guard shook his head. "I never thought I'd live to see the day." His teeth flashed at me, and he laughed. "This is amazing."

Khaghesh reappeared and waved us into the viceroy's receiving room or whatever he called it. It was wide but even longer, with his throne, a writing desk, and a conversation table set upon a single step that spanned the room and divided the back third from the rest of the room. I still didn't know the viceroy's name, but Khaghesh took care of that with a formal introduction and a flourish of his hand: "The viceroy Melishev Lohmet."

I noticed there were several guards with crossbows posted against the walls on either side. The viceroy himself looked like he could not decide between being fashionable or martial. He wore a silken tunic in red, white, and black but with a saber belted at his side and a pauldron strapped onto his left shoulder with a flared piece designed to protect his neck from blows on that side. The robe did seem bulky and sug-gested a body far larger than the column of his neck would point to, so I imagined he had significant armor underneath as well. He nodded at me and the guard who'd brought me from the gate, standing in front of his throne with hands clasped in front of him. His eyes narrowed somewhat as he took me in, but he made no obvious signs of disgust as his chamberlain had. Up close I could see that he was sweating, a

KEVIN HEARNE

muscle twitched underneath his left eye, and his expression suggested not calm diplomacy but rather that he was barely holding on to his sanity. I almost inquired if he was well but reconsidered. Some egos are easily bruised by the suggestion that they are anything but excellent at all times, and his might be one of those.

"Report, soldier," he said to the guard, who stiffened at being addressed and barked out a quick summary of my appearance at the gate and what I'd said. While he did that, I called what creatures I could to collect silently inside the room, including the wheelmouth. I told them to keep to the shadows but be ready to move quickly into the light.

"Very well. Thank you. You are dismissed to return to your post."

The guard saluted and departed, his posture painfully erect, sweeping right past the creatures scrambling through the door, leaving me alone with the viceroy, his chamberlain, the crossbowmen, and an ever-growing collection of many-legged, toothsome allies.

"Tell me, Abhinava, what were you before you were a Beast Caller?" I thought it interesting that he did not ask me to prove my powers. He accepted that I was what I said I was.

"A hunter, sir."

"You will address him as Viceroy—" Khaghesh snapped, but Lohmet held up a hand to silence him.

"He's been perfectly polite, Khaghesh." Turning to me, he said, "'Sir' will do, but you can call me Melishev if you wish. Let's not think of titles right now; I find that they slow down conversation. Is it true you discovered the source of the Sixth Kenning south of Khul Bashab?"

"That's true." It was now due east of him along the Khek River, but he didn't need to know that.

"How many others have been blessed with the Sixth Kenning now?"

"Three others."

"So three others and yourself know where the kenning site is."

"Correct."

"Will you tell me where it is?"

"No, sir, begging your pardon."

I expected him to frown, but instead he grinned at me and rubbed his hands together. "Ah! Now we get to it. You have reasons. Reasons that no doubt have something to do with the behavior of Viceroy Senesh and his cavalry."

I responded with a curt nod and tensed. Would he try to take me into custody?

"Well, you will find that he and I are very different. He is quick to see enemies in people who would be his friends. I'm glad you came to me. Do please tell me what you want." He withdrew a journal from a pocket of his tunic below the belt and sat down at a writing desk, flipping it open to a blank page and dipping a quill into ink before looking up at me expectantly. "Please, sit. Khaghesh, bring one of those chairs over for him." He scratched "Beast Caller" at the top of a page while the chamberlain brought over a chair for me. It was all very strange and solicitous; his polite demeanor contrasted with his sweating, twitching face, and I realized that I was being hunted. These viceroys are predators, each with his own style of hunting, and Viceroy Melishev Lohmet was every bit as dangerous as Viceroy Bhamet Senesh. Perhaps more so. Senesh wielded a heavy club that you saw coming, whereas Lohmet plunged an unseen knife in your back. I checked the position of the crossbowmen again as well as that of Khaghesh. He hovered behind me, and I stared at him until it became uncomfortable and Lohmet noticed.

"Khaghesh, come over here to my side, please. Don't loom over our guest."

"Thank you." My back would be to one wall of crossbowmen, but they couldn't shoot at me without risk of hitting the viceroy, so I sat. "I first would like to say I appreciate very much your willingness to talk, sir. This is much better than confronting cavalry from Khul Bashab pointing crossbows at me." He was too sharp to miss the subtext there. The cavalry hadn't come back. The corners of his mouth played in a half smile. The muscle under his left eye twitched even faster.

"I agree. This is much preferable. Like many young people, you are not fond of authority."

"No, sir."

He looked pleased. "So what does the angry young man want? A completely new government? Some kind of endless wrangling in committee like the Raelechs have, yearly elections?"

"Not necessarily. I don't pretend to have all the answers. And let me assure you I do not want a violent revolution. If I wanted that, I would have done it already. I could take over this city without moving from this chair, which is not a threat, sir, just a statement of fact. But I don't think such chaos would help people. I do think that our country must change now that it has a kenning of its own. So many laws and customs are built around *not* having one."

The viceroy grimaced. "Yes. It's going to be an uncertain time. I cannot tell you how the king will react to this. Because as you just pointed out, you're a threat to his power, never mind mine."

"Well, perhaps speaking with you can go a long way to ensuring that we won't have any more ugly incidents. Let's be as honest as we can for our mutual benefit. Here is what we want—I mean me and the other Beast Callers."

"Go on."

"We want to help our country but not be pressed into military service."

The viceroy frowned for the first time but did not reply until he had scrawled something in his journal. "And if your country is under a grave military threat?"

"Then please request our services, detailing exactly what needs to be done, and negotiate terms of engagement, payment, and release from service through a contract. We address the threat and then are free to enter other contracts, just like Raelech stonecutters or Brynt hygienists. Treat the Nentian blessed, in other words, the same way you would the blessed from any other country. We will happily serve as contractors but refuse to be military weapons used to oppress the population and preserve the power of current rulers."

The viceroy threw his head back and laughed. "Oh, the king would definitely not respond well to that." He spared a glance for Khaghesh,

whose face looked as if he had swallowed something particularly bitter. That amused him, for his mouth smirked anew as he bent to write
some more. When he finished, he cocked his head at me. "Do you
mean to say that other countries use their blessed to oppress their pop-
ulations?"

"No. But I believe this country uses its military to do that. So I will
not join the military here except on a limited contractual basis."

"Ah! I see." He closed his journal and shifted awkwardly in his chair
to place it back into the pocket of his tunic. Khaghesh took particular
notice of this, staring at it as if he wanted to possess nothing else so
much in the world. "Blasted armor. I'm not used to wearing it here.
Have you heard what gives me cause to go armored these days?"

"No."

"We've been invaded by the Hathrim. Hearthfire Gorin Mogen has
a whole city of them to the south, just north of the Godsteeth."

I watched him to see if he was joking. He appeared perfectly serious. "The Hathrim are truly invading? With hounds and their firelords
and everything?"

"Yes." He nodded. "They've already killed four thousand of my
men. Lost my best tactician. The king is sending a much larger army
now. They should be here in the next few days, and then we march."

"I had no idea."

"I thought as much. Viceroy Senesh has been more worried about
four Beast Callers than an entire army of giants. Between you and
me," he said, and lowered his voice to a whisper, "I don't think he's
particularly good at setting priorities."

"Will the king's army be able to defeat them?"

Lohmet winced and waggled a hand in the air. "I don't think they
can by themselves. We'd have to have some major help from the Fornish, but there's a good chance we might get that since they don't like
having the lavaborn on their border."

"I'd imagine not."

"No. But don't you find it odd that Ghurana Nent finally discovers the Sixth Kenning just when we need it most? To counter our destruction by the First Kenning, I mean?"

I shrugged. "It's a coincidence."

"A fortunate one, if so. And again, I'm glad you're here. So let's do this: I will contract with you to head south and take care of this Hathrim threat, because it is dire. And when you're finished with that, we can formally set up your clave and do such other business as you wish."

That was far too glib. Far too easy. Send me off to be killed by the Hearthfire of Harthrad, would he? Ha! "Let's set up the clave first. It's not like the Hathrim are outside the walls this very moment."

The viceroy's pasted-on pleasant expression melted into a clenched jaw. "We are under an existential threat. And you have yet to prove that you can do anything except murder the cavalry of Khul Bashab. You need to make amends."

"I most certainly will. Under a contract that is permitted under the articles of the Beast Callers clave, which we will take the time to draft and sign right now."

There was no hint of amusement or even patience in the viceroy's voice as he pointed a finger at me. "I'm not drafting anything for a boy who's done nothing yet for his people. You can work for me now—as a paid mercenary—or you can fight me. And if you fight me, you will spend yourself to old age and early death. That's how these kennings work, right?"

"More or less," I admitted while simultaneously asking the spiders and assorted other insects and small creatures to move along the walls behind the crossbowmen. They were all looking up at us, not down at their feet. And the viceroy's sudden ultimatum told me all I needed to know about his true character. He was arbitrary and stubborn like my father and like that cavalry captain. "But I'm not trying to fight you. I'm trying to help you even as you help me. I can fight these giants under a clave contract. And then you and I and the other Beast Callers can usher in a new era of peace and prosperity for Hashan Khek. We both win."

The viceroy pressed his lips together and shook his head in regret. "I like it better when I win the way I want to and don't have some hunter brat thinking airy lovey-dovey Kaurian peace will spread over the world if we just be nice to animals."

That confirmed he wouldn't be negotiating in good faith. He'd be ordering those crossbowmen to act against me soon, so I commanded the bugs to crawl up the crossbowmen and chamberlain and bite at will. I had the wheelmouth crawl up the viceroy's chair and then his armored back. Khaghesh was the first to scream and start slapping at his clothes, followed shortly by all the crossbowmen, who dropped their weapons in an attempt to crush the bugs chewing them up.

"Don't move, Viceroy," I said as he gripped the arms of his chair as a prelude to lunging out of it. "There's a wheelmouth at your neck, and he will bite at my command."

Melishev sneered at me. "I think I'd know if a wheelmouth was crawling on me."

"Not through all that armor of yours. Turn your head, very slowly, and look at your left shoulder. Don't jump or try to brush him off. It won't end well."

Melishev Lohmet swiveled his head to the left and saw the gaping serrated circle of a wheelmouth's jaws facing him. That left eye muscle jumped so much that the eye simply closed and stayed that way. For the first time, I saw fear in his face rather than barely restrained malice or amusement. And because I had caused that and witnessed it, he would forever be my enemy.

"Dismiss your soldiers and your chamberlain. I'll call off the bugs." I did exactly that, except for the wheelmouth. I asked him to stay precisely where he was, ready to strike. Melishev ordered everyone out, and I added, "Leave those crossbows on the ground." They would depart with some painful bites and a lingering sense of horror but nothing worse.

"We'll be waiting for you outside," Khaghesh promised me, and I was sure they would. Once we had privacy, I leaned forward and told Melishev to look at me, not the wheelmouth.

"I'm not advocating airy lovey-dovey Kaurian peace, Viceroy. This hunter brat can be ruthless, too. I can kill you right now without spending myself at all and deal with your replacement. Or I can wipe out every single soldier in the city and simply take over. As I said earlier—I'm not sure you were listening—if I wanted to take your power, I would have taken it already. Are you listening now, and do you understand?"

"Yes to both."

"That's good. Because I came to you in a peaceful manner, and you were the one who decided to flex on me, giving me a stupid either-or decision to make. When you push me like that, I push back hard. Just ask the very dead cavalry of Khul Bashab. So now let me give *you* an ultimatum: either you write up a legal and valid Beast Callers clave charter right now and then a contract for me to fight the Hathrim or I will have the wheelmouth bore into your twitchy left eye there. What's it going to be?"

"The charter and contract," the viceroy said.

"Excellent. Thank you. The faster you work and the faster you get me out of the city safely, the sooner that wheelmouth leaves your shoulder."

He seethed for a few minutes as he got out paper and began to write, the wheelmouth looking on all the while, but after a few lines of preamble his anger melted away and he chuckled softly.

"You know, Abhinava, you're delightful."

"Am I?"

"Very. I haven't been outmaneuvered like this in so long. My own fault, really, for underestimating you, but it's refreshing. And I'm starting to think the Hathrim won't stand a chance against you."

"We'll see. Animals burn just like anything else."

"I'm sure you'll find a way to surprise them."

I wasn't fooled. The viceroy was like a wheat dog that had lunged too far, had gotten swiped on the nose, and had pulled back to circle and wait for an opening to attack again. But he wrote a fine charter and a finer mercenary contract to engage me against the Hathrim. I was to target and eliminate all the lavaborn I could ahead of the Nentian army's arrival in the south. He also drafted a requisition and took me past the chamberlain and soldiers waiting in the hall to their logistic support officer. I was given my pick of provisions, from food to tools to clothes, along with a heavy purse of coins, and they returned my horses all brushed and groomed with shining new saddles. I had the viceroy accompany me on foot out of bowshot range, and there I had him first drop his sword to the ground and then stand still while the wheelmouth climbed down his robe and scurried on its hundred legs into the grass.

"I'll see you below the Godsteeth," I said. "And I hope that afterward we'll be able to work together to improve Ghurana Nent for all its citizens."

"I'll look forward to it," the viceroy said, but his eyes already glittered with imagined violence against me.

I pointed the horses toward the nughobe grove where I'd left Murr and Eep and left him to walk back to his squalid city.

Despite the crinkle of signed and sealed papers in my new pack, I understood that nothing was guaranteed. None of my contracts would matter if I died, and that might have been precisely what he was thinking: *I can promise the boy anything he wants because the giants will burn him alive.* And the charter was good only in Hashan Khek, not the entire country; I'd have to get it signed by the king. Even if I was successful against the Hathrim, I already expected a serious attempt to have me killed. But I thought that at last I had taken some positive steps in the right direction. I couldn't help my family anymore, but I had hope that I could help everyone else's.

"And now let's move right here to the gates of Pelemyn," Fintan called out to Survivor Field, "except months ago, when Culland du Raffert arrived from Tömerhil." The smoke from the seeming stone whooshed up and resolved into a bedraggled, weary man.

Culland

Bryn's Lung, the heart of the Second Kenning, is a strange chimney of coral and rock near the palace that empties into the bay via a cave. Or, looked at the other way, the chimney is the exhalation of the underwater cave. During high tide, pressure from rolling waves would force water into the cave and up the chimney and create a sort of salty ejaculation at the surface that was the source of many sniggering jokes. It was half seriously suggested as a metaphor for the lord Bryn's life-giving powers. But officially it was his lung rather than some other organ, and the water plumes jetting out of the top were properly thought of as exhalations rather than ejaculations.

The reef surrounding Bryn's Lung was a strange little ecosystem of tidal pools and mosses and amphibians that was closely monitored by a mixed force of church and palace officials. It rose just slightly above sea level at high tide and was fed by the periodic "breathing" of the Lung. During low tide, one could dive into the chimney and attempt to swim down and then through until one emerged from the cave into the bay. You'd either be blessed by Bryn and make it—the only way to swim such a distance—or drown.

Seekers like myself had to queue up and talk to both a secular official and a church official before diving in, and during high tide, while Bryn's Lung was heaving full force, no one was allowed near it.

I arrived from Tömerhil during high tide, weary from travel and grief, my family lost for certain, and had to wait hours before the queue even began to move. The people in front and in back of me had no interest in conversation. Why try to befriend someone who most likely would be dead soon? Like me, I suspect that most people in line had little left to live for. There was only a sullen acceptance of bore-

dom. Or perhaps I was misinterpreting the silence for piety and meditation and the thinking of profound thoughts in advance of seeking a
blessing from the Lord of the Deep. In truth I can speak for no one but
myself.

The entrance to the Lung was a narrow gated hall reminiscent of a
covered bridge, and to enter the area one first had to speak to a longshoreman who had spoken the same words so many times that his
voice had become a despairing monotone.

"Welcome, Seeker," he said without a trace of welcome. "You understand that by diving into Bryn's Lung you will most likely drown
and your body be eaten by marine animals and never recovered?"

"Uh. Yeah?"

He shoved a piece of paper at me, along with a quill already wet
with ink. "Please fill out your name in the blank, last residence, and
sign at the bottom."

There was quite a bit of fine print beneath the basic blanks at the
top and the signature at the bottom. "What is this?"

"Conditional bequeathal of all your worldly possessions to the government of the pelenaut should you not have an executable will, and
of course if you are blessed, the bequeathal is null."

"All my worldly possessions? You're looking at them." Maybe I still
had a house in Fornyd. Or a warehouse in Festwyf. What did it matter?

"Someone will enjoy those clothes," the longshoreman said.

"May they bring them warmth," I said, filling out the form and
signing it.

"Thank you, citizen. Disrobe after you talk to the priest and leave
your clothes with the attendant at the end of the hall."

I thought of several quips about disrobing priests but figured the
longshoreman had already heard them all by now and asked instead,
"Is it always this busy?"

"No; it's only since the attack. Lots of people figure they have nothing to lose anymore."

"Yeah, that's me, too." I moved on so that he could repeat himself
to the next person in line.

The priestess of the Lord Bryn was a kind older woman in the traditional long robe of chromatic blues. Unlike the disaffected longshoreman, she recognized me as an individual who might have a story. But I didn't want to tell her mine, and after a minimal effort at politeness, I moved on.

The entrance to the Lung was an impressive seven feet in circumference, allowing some much-needed room to dive in without hitting the sides of the chimney. Some people gracelessly did just that, leaping too far or not far enough and catching themselves on the rocks, dashing open their heads or otherwise killing themselves before they even hit the water. The suction of low tide in the chimney ensured that they didn't remain floating on the surface, but I had heard that sometimes their bodies would remain in the chimney for a while and people had to swim past them to reach the cave. One of the blessed periodically swam up into the chimney to make sure it was clear, a vital but grisly task I would never want to call my own.

One last bored longshoreman stood near the edge of the Lung to give final instructions. "Dive in headfirst and swim straight down for the light. When you're in the cave, you'll know it and you need to swim for the open sea, which is the black hole of the cave mouth."

"What's the light? I mean what's making it?"

"The interior of the cave is coated with organisms that produce their own light."

Mincing my way to the edge of the Lung, the coral sharp against the tender soles of my bare feet, I stared down into the roiling cauldron of black water and felt a cool spray misting up from it. The water's surface rested perhaps a body's length below, and though I could see no light glowing in its depths, I felt sure it would show up eventually.

"Jump in or walk away," the longshoreman droned. "Don't hold up the line."

"A moment."

I told my dead wife and kids one more time that I was sorry for how they died, for not being there to help, for not keeping them safe. And then I remembered to be thankful for the time I did have with them, for it truly had been a blessing.

"It's all over now, though," I said, and dived into Bryn's Lung.

The shock of the cold stole most of my breath away immediately, escaping from my mouth in startled bubbles, but I kicked and parted the water with my hands, trying to push it behind me and force my body down, and then I opened my eyes to search for the light. There was none, but I kept kicking and stroking, and after a few more seconds I saw a dull gleam in the center of my vision. I kept swimming and wondered if I would reach it, but it grew in size with each passing moment. It didn't get any brighter, however—just bigger.

My lungs burned to suck in a deep gulp of oxygen and my muscles cried out for energy, and I hadn't even made it to the cave yet. Did everyone simply drown in the chimney and then get flushed into the ocean, turning Seekers into metaphorical turds? I wanted to see the cave, at least, before I drowned, so I kept going even though my arms and legs were turning into weak noodles and I was chilled to the bone.

The glow of the light abruptly expanded in my vision, extending off to my left and continuing below me until I realized I was seeing the outline of the cave, illuminated in green and blue and occasional pinpoints of white. Immediately to my right was the back wall of the cave, its bare rock beneath my fingers and devoid of any life. Fleetingly I wondered why the back would be lifeless while the walls and ceiling were covered, but that thought was pushed out by the sight of the cave floor and the silhouettes of bodies floating just above it. Drowned Seekers, including the man who'd jumped in before me—I'd be joining them shortly as my lungs couldn't take it anymore. And on the cave floor, a carpet of bones and flesh picked over by crabs and eels and other scavengers. No bladefins, though, or larger predators; the blessed must keep them out somehow. And they must also periodically clear away some of the debris or the cave would be choked with remains before long.

I couldn't hold my breath any longer and the cave mouth and surface were so very far away, but I had seen what I wished to see, and that was enough: the mystery of Bryn's Lung was revealed to my eyes, and there was no longer any need to struggle. I would give my body to the sea and eventually be borne by currents across the world. My mouth opened reflexively to gasp for air, and I welcomed the expected rush of seawater into my lungs, except that I actually drew breath instead. That first gasp was followed by another, and another, and not a single drop of water entered my mouth or my nose. It was singularly odd to be completely submerged, to feel water on my very eyeballs, yet somehow breathe only air through my mouth and nose. I was treading water, trying to figure out where the air was coming from, when a hand latched on to my hair and pulled.

There was some spirited movement after that.

The hand belonged to another Seeker swimming down through the chimney: the one who'd been behind me in line and who couldn't breathe in the water like most humans. I saw a flash of pleading eyes in the murk—terrified, really—as she tried to grab on to me and follow me wherever I was going. Not a logical move since I wasn't going anywhere, but she was panicked and rethinking her decision to drown at the worst possible time.

Belatedly, I realized that since I could somehow breathe and the water did not seem so cold anymore, I quite possibly *could* save her, and I bunched my legs against the back wall and pushed off, grasping her arm and trying to pull her along with me. My speed was far less impressive than I had hoped.

She went slack and dead before I had managed four lengths, and reluctantly I let her go. I would never make it to the surface in time to revive her, and it reminded me once again of how I'd failed my family in much the same way: I had been far too late to help.

But my breathing continued and even calmed, and the water felt pleasant instead of freezing, and it finally penetrated that I had become one of Bryn's blessed and could not drown or suffer any ills from water.

I should have been elated—I think that's the proper response—but instead I felt cheated of my peace. I would have to grieve longer and start some new career determined by the nature of my blessing. Whatever new talents I possessed, they didn't include forgetfulness.

Forty-two years old, widowed and childless, import business a ruin, but suddenly a man with prospects in an underwater cave.

Another Seeker dropped down out of the chimney, weakly clawing through the water, but I turned my back so that I wouldn't have to watch him die. There was nothing I could do except get on with being whoever I was supposed to be now.

The cave was serene and beautiful as long as you didn't look down at the floor of corpses and the clawed or writhing things feasting on them. I bet all that beauty was fed by the deaths of Seekers somehow and the soft glow of those plants was concentrated despair, fear, and desperation.

Outside the cave the water darkened, but something darted toward me in the gloom. I thought it was a bladefin at first, but it pulled up and resolved itself into a clothed woman in military colors. She was much younger than I, and when she waved and smiled, I suddenly remembered that I was acutely naked.

I hadn't cared about diving into Bryn's Lung naked, thinking I would be dead soon, but now I felt I might die of embarrassment.

She pointed up to the surface with one hand, wordlessly suggesting that we ascend, and I nodded. She offered her other hand, and I took it. Her grip was strong, and I soon discovered the reason as she pulled me up through the water not by swimming but by using her kenning to propel us. It was strange and exhilarating, moving that fast and feeling the ocean flow around us. When we broke the surface, we both took a moment to sheet the moisture away from our eyes, and she smiled again.

"Congratulations, sir! You've been blessed by the lord Bryn! You're a Water Breather."

"Thank you," I said, because I couldn't think of what else to say.

"I'm Gerstad Nara du Fesset, a rapid in the pelenaut's service. I'm going to help you figure out your blessing, and then we'll get you ashore and settled. What's your name?"

I told her, and she said it was a pleasure to meet me.

"First, cup your hand like this and scoop out a handful of water," she said, demonstrating. When I did so, treading water with the rest of my limbs, she continued. "I want you to focus on the water in your hand, not the water all around. Really concentrate on it and ask yourself if it's clean. You should be able to tell."

"Really?"

"Try it."

It looked clean to me, just like any other handful of water, but I couldn't tell anything special about it. "I don't know. I guess it's clean?"

Nara shook her head. I had guessed wrong.

"Then it's dirty water," I said, trying to recover. "Bad, naughty water."

No smile, just a raised eyebrow. "You should know precisely what's wrong with it."

"I don't. I'm sorry."

"You're not a hygienist, then. That means you're one of the fast swimmers."

"I am? I don't think so, because down in the Lung I was terribly slow."

"You wouldn't have known yet. It takes a while to develop, and even if you did get it right away, you wouldn't know how to access it. I'm going to teach you."

"All right."

"Think about putting on clothes—"

"I've been thinking about that since we met. Do you think we can get some?"

That earned a smile. "Soon; don't worry. When you put on pants, you push your leg down as you pull the pants up. Both are happening, but the pushing is in the center moving in one direction while the pulling is on the outside moving in the other. That's how you use your kenning to travel through water—you pull the water ahead of you down to your feet and then push up through the center, and you naturally move into the space ahead of you where you displaced water. So visualize your body as the foot moving through the pants leg or your fist pushing through the sleeve of a shirt. We actually call it sleeving. And what you want to do is focus on moving your center in the direction you want to go."

"What, I just think about it and it happens?"

She pinched her fingers close together and squinted. "There's a *little* more to it than that. Control takes lots of practice. But generating thrust, pulling and pushing water around? That's mostly visualization and commitment now that water is your element."

"Visualization and commitment?"

"It takes some energy on your part, just like treading water does. You'll get tired after a while. Let's try it. We'll start with a fountain." She pointed to her left, and a tight geyser of water jetted up from the surface of the ocean and continued. "See how there's a little swirly depression around the base? That's me pulling the water down, and then it pushes up in the center. Now you. Pick a place, visualize what you want and concentrate, pull the water down, and redirect it up."

Still not believing that this was possible for me, I chose a spot off to my left and pictured the same sort of fountain that Nara had made, willing the water to form a whirlpool and then fountain up in the center. Nothing happened for a few seconds, and Nara encouraged me to keep trying, to be very clear with my visualization. And then something did happen, but on a larger scale than Nara's petite fountain. The seawater circled and sucked down in a funnel the circumference of my head.

"Good! Now force the center up instead of down!" Nara said.

She made it sound so easy, but what happened instead was that the whirlpool collapsed and resulted in a sloppy splash instead of a tightly controlled jet.

"That was excellent!"

"It looked miserable."

"I told you the control takes a lot of practice, and you'll need to work on that. But now that you know it can be done, you can probably do it better, right?"

"I suppose so."

"Great. So now you're going to go much bigger, much stronger. You're going to make yourself the focus of the energy and move through the water purely on the strength of your kenning. Visualize your center as a sphere just below your ribs but above your hips. That's what you want to move. You're going to pull the water down all around you and then push it up from underneath so that you rise up out of the water, like this."

The gerstad spread her arms out flat on the surface of the ocean, and the water abruptly sucked down in a circle with her elbows marking the circumference. I could feel the water churning nearby, and then my jaw dropped open as a column of water shot her up bodily out of the ocean. She arched her back and flipped over, gracefully diving back into the water. When she resurfaced, we were both smiling.

"That was great," I said.

"Now it's your turn."

"Oh, no . . ."

"You can do it. Your first attempt was quite strong, you know. You have a good visual mind. Keep your feet together, heels flat, and make the water propel you from there."

It did look like fun, and I felt flattered that she thought I was ready so quickly. I spread out my arms, focused on imitating Nara's feat, and tried to commit, as she put it, my energy to executing the maneuver. It happened more slowly at first, but once the water began to sink and swirl around my body, I was encouraged and committed even more strongly. I remembered to put my feet together just as the water gushed up and shot me high into the air, much higher than I wished to be: about ten lengths.

Panicked instead of graceful, I splayed my legs and waved my arms and remembered how very, very nude I was and that Nara was looking. I flailed and thrashed, but it was too late to gain some kind of form, and I hit the water far closer to the horizontal axis than the vertical. The expected sting of a belly flop didn't happen, though. While there was definitely a slap of impact on the surface, the water felt like a cushion and a welcome and there was no pain. Another bonus of being blessed by the god of the sea.

When I resurfaced, Nara was laughing unabashedly.

"That was amazing!" she gasped. "Oh, I love my job sometimes."

"You did that on purpose!"

"Yes, I did. Nothing better than the newly blessed who can't control themselves."

Wounded, I said, "Isn't that kind of mean?"

"No, it's hilarious. Look, I know you're never going to be that undisciplined again, so don't worry about that. And for you it's a valuable lesson on the need to practice, to achieve that discipline. Power without control is useless. For me—well, look. I'm one of the people who has to clean the skeletons out of Bryn's Lung every so often. I need to get my laughs where I can."

Since I hadn't been hurt and she knew I wouldn't be, I supposed it *had* been funny and I could laugh with her. She coached me for a while longer on how to direct myself through the water, and once I had demonstrated to her satisfaction that I could move in any direction and stop when she said stop, she had one more test for me.

"This is the last thing we need to do. After this we'll go get you dressed and signed up in the pelenaut's service. After all that you'll be itching to get back in the ocean, trust me." She pointed to another couple that had surfaced during my practice: some other rapid helping out the newly blessed. "We need to get out of the way for this. Follow me out a bit deeper."

We sliced through the choppy waves for perhaps a hundred lengths at a moderate clip before she called a halt and we treaded water.

"Okay, face south from here. There's nothing in your way, nothing you have to steer around. Open ocean but not so deep that you have to worry about the huge predators coming up from underneath. We are going to propel ourselves south as fast as we can. Try to keep up with me—no: try to beat me. If you do pass me and you feel yourself coming apart, stop immediately."

"Coming apart? That's a thing I have to worry about?"

"It's not a bad thing—poor phrasing. I mean if you feel your body kind of letting go and you're becoming one with the water to move faster through it, just stop. Really."

"All right."

"Dinner's on me if you beat me." She flashed a grin and then shot through the water without warning, sloshing me in her wake.

"Hey!" That wouldn't slow her down, so there was only one thing to do: go that way, really fast.

The power rose faster now at my command, practice and confidence making visualization and execution nearly simultaneous. I didn't think at first I could ever catch up because she was seriously moving through the water faster than a horse could run on land, but I kept willing myself to move faster and faster and committed my whole will to surpassing her, and the gap between us narrowed. In a minute my fists were even with her feet, and in the next five seconds I had surpassed her, my heels even with her fists. It was thrilling to slice through the water like that, vast plumes of spray arcing in our wake, moving much faster than most fish could swim, and I kept going, the ocean beckoning me forward, and I realized that I was grinning in the face of it, truly enjoying my life for the first time since hearing that Festwyf had fallen. But that thought triggered another cloud bank of rage in my brain, and I was no longer swimming for the pleasure of it or for a friendly contest but in rage against those who had taken my family, adding on speed in a desperate attempt to outrun my grief.

I knew something had gone wrong when the pressure of water against my fists abruptly ceased and I could no longer in fact see my hands in front of me. I stopped wishing to move forward, and something wrenched inside of me, a stabbing pain in my chest and a throbbing vibration behind my eyes as I slowed to a stop in the water and windmilled my arms to turn around. I felt exhausted and winded and wondered where Nara had gone. I checked that I was truly facing north, and I was: the coast lay off to my left now. Where was Gerstad du Fesset? Had she perhaps passed me without my knowledge? I turned to check the south sea again but saw nothing. Growing worried, I faced north again and was relieved to see the telltale spray of the rapid's wake approaching. I sent up a fountain of water—a large but still quite sloppy one—to give her my location.

When she slowed herself and the water calmed around her, I said, "I like lobster for dinner."

A sardonic nod. "Congratulations, Culland. You're Brynlön's newest tidal mariner."

"What?"

"Only thing faster than a rapid is a tidal mariner. That's how we test. How are you feeling?"

"Worn out."

She nodded. "Tapping into that speed will age you."

"Is that the only difference between a tidal mariner and a rapid?"

"No, there are more. That's just the easiest thing for us to test. We have a tidal mariner in the palace who will train you from here. Let's head back, but at a slower pace, and we'll get you some clothes finally."

She led me back to Pelemyn and underwater near the palace. There was a locked hatch door near the ocean floor, and she spun the handle around and hauled it open. We entered and swam up through clear water through three more doors until we emerged in a pool inside the palace. A mariner was waiting nearby, and when she saw me, she plucked a robe off a hook and smiled, offering it to me. "Welcome, sir. Let's get you dry."

"Where are we?" I asked.

"You're in the Wellspring of Brynlön," Nara said, pulling herself out of the water and dripping on the marbled tile. "The pelenaut wants to meet all new tidal mariners immediately. Standing orders."

"The pelenaut? I'm going to meet Pelenaut Röllend?"

Gerstad du Fesset reached for a towel and ran it over her closely cropped head, leaving the mariner to nod and smile at me. I hauled myself out of the water and put on the robe, feeling a chill develop in the air.

"You'll want to practice doing this," the gerstad said, and as I watched, the water soaking her uniform fairly leapt out of the fabric and dropped back into the pool, rendering the towel unnecessary.

"Definitely handy."

The gerstad beckoned me to follow, and it was only a short distance to the front of the Wellspring, where a cluster of blue and white uniforms stood out against the coral of the wall and a sheet of water cascaded into the same narrow pond from which we had emerged. I felt underdressed. I couldn't see the pelenaut, and my attention was so preoccupied with trying to see him that I didn't realize the gerstad had stopped in front of me, and I ran into her.

"Oh! Sorry." There was another woman in front of me who looked a few years my senior. Lines on her neck and face and a bit of gray at the temples. She had many shiny things on her uniform, and I had no idea what any of them meant.

"No harm done," the gerstad said. "Culland du Raffert, I'd like to introduce you to Second Könstad Tallynd du Böll, our senior tidal mariner. She'll be handling your training from here."

We bowed to each other, and the Second Könstad thanked the gerstad for the introduction and dismissed her.

"Farewell, Master du Raffert," Gerstad du Fesset said. "If you are free for that dinner later, you may find me at the garrison after 1500. Otherwise, another night." She gave me a tight nod and spun on her heel, leaving me with the impressively festooned officer. My knowledge of the military was so minuscule that I had no idea what her rank meant except that it must be higher than gerstad.

"A new tidal mariner is very welcome! But you look a bit overwhelmed," she said. "Not the kind of day you expected, is it?"

"No. Rather expected it to be my last day."

Her nod was grim and understanding. "The queue for the Lung is long these days. Lots of people figuring they should have been taken with their families, and they see it as the honorable way out."

It was so precisely what I felt that I welled up and looked away, wiping my eyes. "Yes. Excuse me."

"Apologies. Who did you lose?"

"My family. In Festwyf."

"I'm very sorry. I lost my husband—not to the Bone Giants but earlier. I know the sting of that pain. We can't bring them back, but you're in a position now to save the families of many others and perhaps exact a bit of vengeance if you wish it."

"How?" The idea of revenge hadn't occurred to me before—it seemed an impossibility—but now that she had suggested it, I found the concept attractive.

"Let's get to that after we meet the pelenaut. He will simply welcome you and thank you for serving the country, so there's nothing to worry about."

I wasn't sure that I wanted to serve the country or wear a uniform, but I also didn't have an inkling of what to do with my kenning otherwise.

Meeting the pelenaut was . . . intense. When a man whose attentions are pulled in so many directions forgets everything and focuses entirely on *you*, you feel the weight of that stare. He grabbed my hand with one of his and covered it with the other and pinned me with his eyes. "Culland! Culland. Welcome. And thank you. I know that people who dive into the Lung are often beset by many troubles, and I'm sure you're no exception. But you are wanted and needed here, and I am so grateful that you are."

My throat closed with emotion *again* at the unexpected kindness, and all I could manage was a nod. Seeing this, the pelenaut continued.

"You're in excellent hands with Second Könstad du Böll. She'll have you feeling comfortable in no time. I look forward to speaking with you again. We're going to fix things and be prosperous again with your help."

"Yes, sir," I said. He seemed pleased with the affirmation, and his attention drifted to someone to his right with a uniform even shinier than the Second Könstad's.

She gave me another smile. "Not so bad, was it?"

"No."

"Come on, let's get you settled." She led me out of the Wellspring

and to the garrison barracks, during which time I noticed that she favored her left foot, moving with a significant limp. People saluted her
along the way, and she greeted them with nods and addressed them by
rank: Mariner. Sarstad. Mynstad. Gerstad. This intensified inside the
barracks themselves, but she spoke between all the salutes. "You're
going to be a gerstad so that no one can really order you around except
me, Könstad du Lallend, or the pelenaut. At the same time, we're not
going to be having you ordering a lot of people around either. You
have a military rank, but as a tidal mariner you're not really part of the
land or naval forces like the rapids or hygienists. You are a force all by
yourself and act alone. Everyone understands that."

"I didn't know that, but I guess I do now."

She nodded, allowing that such knowledge would have been outside my experience. "These barracks are on one side of an open courtyard, and on the other is the armory." She paused at one of three open
doorways on the left side of the hall and gestured inside. "Here are
your quarters. Standard gerstad accommodations. You have an office
in front, your personal space in the back."

"I have an office? For office work?" I peered through the door to find
a bare wooden desk and chair with a couple of chairs in front of it for
guests. A door behind the desk presumably led to a bedroom. I wanted
to collapse on it already but also had some anxiety about making the
bed properly afterward. I was fairly certain that I would not be able to
do it according to regulations.

"You're an officer," she said. "But you won't have much use for it.
You won't have any paperwork to speak of. Report to the armory and
see Mynstad du Möcher for a uniform and sundries. Anyone can direct
you to the mess hall for meals. I'll let you settle in for the day but report to me at the Wellspring in the morning for duty. We'll begin your
training then."

"Okay. I mean, yes, Second Könstad. Am I supposed to salute or
something?"

"I'm not a stickler for that sort of thing, but some people are. Ask the Mynstad to walk you through the proprieties so that you don't accidentally offend anyone. I'd do it myself, but I need to return."

"Right, right, you're busy. Thank you."

"If you don't mind the question, how old are you, Gerstad du Raffert?" she asked. I told her, and she remarked on how unusual it was to have a new tidal mariner in his middle age.

"Forgive me, but are you not nearly the same age?" I asked.

"No," she said, her expression turning sad. "I am twenty-nine. War always takes your life. Sometimes it's just not all at once."

I remembered that when we met at the chowder house, Fintan had mentioned that Nara du Fesset would show up in his tale eventually. I hoped she was well wherever she was and was completing her mission safely. Mynstad du Möcher got a mention, too; I'd have to congratulate her on her few seconds of fame.

Day 17

THE CLEANSING

Elynea invited me to accompany her to work to meet her new employer, so after we dropped off the kids at school, we trekked to the southwestern industrial district to the furniture workshop of Bel Tes Wey, an older Fornish woman who had planted large trees all around her building that spread their canopy over the roof. Those trees, I realized, could be seen from the wall during the bard's performances. I had assumed they indicated a public park of some kind, but no, it was a business doubling as a home. I could see structures built among the branches. Elynea followed my eyes and answered the question I was thinking.

"Yes, she lives up there, along with a couple of her clan members. A little bit of home, she says. Can't stand the thought of sleeping on ground level."

"Which clan?"

"The Green Beetles. Her nephew ships back and forth to Forn, bringing up hardwoods for her. His wife—her niece, I guess—is just a month or two away from becoming a master herself, so Bel is ready for a new apprentice and there's plenty of work right now. I showed her yesterday that I already knew a couple of things, the only thing Garst was good for, and she said she'd take me on."

The shop smelled divine even if sawdust coated almost everything. Invigorating, the scent of wood. I saw nine Brynts in the shop, all working on something or other, and two diminutive white women under five feet tall working among them. The older of them came over when she spied Elynea. Hands gnarled and face weathered by time, back somewhat bent by the weight of age and her hair gone gray, she nonetheless possessed a quick step and a ready smile.

"Ah, my new apprentice! Welcome to your first day. Who's this, then?" she asked, chucking her chin at me.

"Oh!" Elynea said, looking at me. "This is . . . my friend, Master Dervan du Alöbar."

Yes, friend: that worked. A friend and not a husband who couldn't save his dying wife. Elynea was not Sarena and didn't need me to save her. I'd taken the time last night to work that much out, at least: since I couldn't save Sarena, I'd been trying to save Elynea instead even though her situation was not remotely similar. Strange how we unconsciously steer ourselves into new spectacular mistakes while trying to avoid repeating our past failures.

"It's a pleasure," Bel said, nodding once to me out of politeness but clearly not interested. She had work on her mind and turned to Elynea. "Ready to begin?"

We waved farewell, and I took myself to the armory for a workout with Mynstad du Möcher, whose foul mood from earlier had lifted. "Nara is back!" she told me, and her grin was huge.

"Ah, excellent! She's well?"

The grin faded. "Recuperating, but it'll be fine."

That didn't sound good. "Recuperating?"

"She broke an arm, but it was clean and should heal straight. The most important things are that she's back and she feels good about whatever she did."

"She still can't tell you?"

The Mynstad shook her head. "Nope. Terrible secret. And I don't care. She's here, and she won't be doing anything like it again—she promised me that. So that's good enough for me."

It gratified me to hear that Nara felt good about the mission, whatever it was. I'd worried that she would let guilt gnaw away at her confidence until she felt worthless.

The morning went so well that I wondered if Fintan would tell me over lunch that he had good news, too: that practicing presence had eliminated his nervous condition and nightmares. That turned out not to be the case.

"I still had nightmares," he told me when I met him, "not that I expected them to disappear immediately. Still, I went to see Kindin Ladd this morning because I think the idea has merit. He led me through some mental exercises, and I'd like to go back to the Hathrim restaurant again if you don't mind."

"Not at all."

I noticed that there were new servers there, and once Orden and Hollit came out to say hello, I apologized for not sending over Elynea, explaining that she had found another job already. They waved away my concern and thanked us for coming back.

"We really enjoy the food," Fintan said. I watched him to see how he was doing. No visible signs of distress, but perhaps it would hit him once the giants left the table, as it had before. The Hathrim thanked us again and lumbered back to the kitchen and the bar, but I kept my eyes on the bard. He laid his hands flat on the table. He visibly took some deep breaths and his eyes darted around the room, but his expression remained neutral.

"Are you all right?" I asked. He wasn't sweating or shaking, but neither did he seem completely unaffected.

"I think so," he said, a tiny tug at the corners of his mouth signaling victory. "There really is something to this, living in the present, focusing on breathing peace, and all that other stuff the Kaurians are always saying. It's not just a slogan. This is working."

"How?"

"I'm breathing consciously. I'm noting that you're worried. I'm also noting that no one else is, that they all feel safe. At the same time, I'm getting flashes of the massacre of the Nentians who Gorin Mogen set on fire and men being eaten or torn apart by hounds, split in two by giant axes, imagining Hollit and Orden participating in that, all of it. That's never going away. As you said, some things you see you can never unsee, never forget. But it's not present like the rest of everything here. It's not as important as what's in front of me now. So it cannot affect me today like it did yesterday, and this is something I can do all the time. This is an improvement."

I allowed that it was. Fintan closed his eyes and took a couple more deep breaths, and when he opened them again, his smile was more confident.

"Okay," he said. "Let's get to work."

Once upon the wall, Fintan said, "Today concerns one of your country's most historic events. But it also involves a Raelech and a Kaurian, and I was thinking about Gondel Vedd, wandering around your country with the mistral's osprey on his shoulder. But I inquired at the Kaurian embassy about his house—the Kaurians all have broad family associations named after birds—and was told that he's from the house of Terns. I was taught all the House Hymns during my apprenticeship, which are brief verses of values given to Kaurians as children, and I thought I'd share Gondel's with you today.

> Dive and glide, swoop and sail,
> In your duty never fail,
> Be sustained on isles and seas,
> Soar the winds of Reinei's peace,
> In every action may you earn
> Your honor in the house of Tern.

"We'll begin with the stonecutter Meara, who came to Brynlön after the collapse of the Granite Tunnel."

eara

Few people cross the Poet's Range to get to Brynlön because it is passable only for a few months of the year and during that time it's fraught with all sorts of natural dangers. Nothing like the legendary flesh eels of the Nentian plains that take you in your sleep but other things that you will see coming before they eat you alive and screaming. Mountain wolves, for example, sound rather boring when you're not being actively chased by a pack of them. They do become exciting very quickly in such a circumstance, and for a while Tuala and I had them on our tail. But they couldn't keep up with the speed of a courier, and we soon left them behind. Still, their barking and howling attracted the attention of a chittering scurry of flying meat squirrels that *could* keep up.

They are not technically squirrels at all, though they do bear a marked resemblance and I suppose whoever named them wanted to give people nightmares when they saw the nicer ones. Meat squirrels don't eat seeds and nuts. They are arboreal carnivores, watching from the trees, and typically they prefer to gather quietly above their prey's head and simply glide down on top of them, splaying their limbs wide and letting the skin stretched between them act to slow their descent. And then, where a normal squirrel would have a nice pair of choppers for cracking nuts, the meat squirrel has a mouth full of serrated teeth for tearing flesh. But they also have tremendously powerful back legs that let them jump between tree trunks far faster than they could glide between them, allowing them to pursue running prey on the forest floor until they can get close enough to jump on top of them. I had heard of their existence before and Tuala warned me that we might wake up a scurry of them on our way, but that didn't really prepare me for the horror of them. They were cute, making little scratching noises on the trunks of snakewood pines, until they opened their mouths. That's when I saw the teeth that would scoop out gobbets of my flesh and make quick work of me, since there were twenty or more of them. I'd probably be able to defend myself with my kenning if I had to, but against that many hungry mouths all at once? If they opened up an artery, I might bleed out anyway.

When we packed for the trip, we took nothing but food and water and wooden sparring staves that took me back to my Colaiste days. There were secure and furnished shelters, Tuala assured me, built along the way for the couriers' use by stonecutters in days gone by, and of course I could build a new one for us if need be.

"I didn't know there were shelters up there," I said.

"We don't advertise their existence because we'd rather they didn't become attractive to outlaws. Better for everyone to believe there's no safety to be found in the Poet's Range."

I believed that viscerally as the first meat squirrel leapt at me from the branches of a snakewood pine, its tiny needle claws scrabbling for purchase on my shoulder and gouging deep grooves but ultimately failing to catch and falling to the trail as we churned past.

Another squirrel leapt for Tuala ahead of me. She spotted it and slapped it away with one of her staves in a move that looked almost identical to the basic warm-ups taught to first-year students at the Colaiste. I withdrew my staves, determined to follow her example, and found them immediately useful. A meat squirrel landed on the back of my neck, and I bashed it with a stave blindly until its spine broke and it stopped trying to bite its way through to mine.

It occurred to me that since the squirrels were so dependent on speed and accurate trajectory to bring us down, anything we could do to foil either one of those would keep us safe. Tuala was using her kenning to the utmost, but I had yet to contribute. It wasn't a common problem for stonecutters in the cities of Rael, trying to outsmart meat squirrels. The problem was that I couldn't really communicate effectively with the earth moving at such speed and with shoes on. But why, I thought, did I need shoes? The earth would never harm me. It was a fashion affectation more than a necessity and one I'd never understood: Were shoes invented merely to hide toes from people who found them disgusting? I definitely didn't need them or, once I thought about it, really want them. If I was to live my life in exile, I might as well be comfortable and practical and throw fashion down the deepest mine shaft underneath Jeremech. Since Tuala's kenning allowed us to travel insanely fast while only jogging, I was able to slap my shoes off my heels and then alter my gait to kick them through the air in tumbling arcs. I called to the earth then and focused on the trail ahead and threw up surface rocks and topsoil in a thin screen the width of a fingernail. It was the same principle as erecting a wall except that I didn't try to keep any shape to it. I just threw sediment up into the air that the meat squirrels were trying to navigate to get to us. Not a serious impediment unless they met face-first with a rock but perhaps enough to disorient them or scare them away from leaping at us.

Only one tried it, and I saw the whole thing. He leapt for Tuala from behind and to her left, and as he passed through the curtain of earth I was throwing up, sediment buffeted him from underneath and threw off his trajectory just enough that he sailed behind Tuala's back and in front of me, landing somewhere on the right side of the trail. His momentum carried him farther on the ground, and by that time we had passed, never slowing, and he'd never catch up. The rest of the meat squirrels, either seeing his failure or simply afraid of my kenning, gave up and ceased to pursue us. I kept up the screen for perhaps another mile and let it drop to see if we had any stubborn ones on our trail. We did not, and I thanked the Triple Goddess aloud for that.

"There's a bunker up ahead we can rest in," Tuala called back, and I responded with enthusiasm to the idea. We veered off the well-traveled trail and into dense woods for only a few hundred lengths to find a half-buried shelter constructed by some stonecutter many generations ago. Without being shown where it was, you'd never expect it to be there; it was close to the trail but not visible from it. Highly unlikely that anyone but Raelech couriers would ever use it.

The stone bunker was well ventilated but had no openings large enough to admit wildlife. There was a fireplace and a stack of wood and kindling nearby, a primitive tank privy behind a privacy curtain, and two straw tick beds resting on top of a raised platform. Not luxurious but safe.

A pedestal held a basin for washing up, but there was no water except what we brought with us. I used some of mine to wash my wounds and drank the rest.

"Are you all right?" Tuala asked.

"I imagine I will be eventually."

"Hungry?"

"Not in the least." I shuddered at the thought of eating right then, having come too close to being eaten myself.

"Well, we're not over the range yet, and it's only a couple of hours until sunset. It's unwise to run at night, so we might as well stay here. What shall we talk about?"

"Anything. But yeah, let's talk."

The truth was I preferred running for my life from the meat squirrels to being alone with my haunted thoughts. I think perhaps Tuala sensed that, and she chatted away, kindly giving me something to focus on besides mourning and pain. But eventually darkness fell, she wound down, and even the fire she had laid quieted from a lively crackle to sullen, smoldering coals. She snored softly on her bed, and I did my best to sob quietly in mine, nearly suffocating under a blanket of guilt, unable to avoid it any longer with distractions of one kind or another. The shock of what had happened in the Granite Tunnel had sloughed away in the run, and now the enormity of it oppressed me: I'd lost my love, my job, and my country in a moment. Maybe my work in the future would balance the scales somehow, but I'd never get back what I'd lost. It was not the first time I wished that I could be as unfeeling as stone.

Sleep relieved me eventually, and in the morning I felt hungry enough to eat our basic bread and dried meats and fruits. My neck and shoulder stung but not, I hoped, with the deep pain of infection.

"We'll have a Brynt hygienist look at it regardless," Tuala assured me.

"How long until we're in Tömerhil?"

"We can make it today if we don't stop and if you're up to it. Or else we rest and get there tomorrow."

"Let's try to get there today."

There were no natural threats once we descended the Poet's Range and followed a riverbank trail to Tömerhil. It was my first time in Brynlön, and it seemed like a softer land somehow than Rael, rounded leafy canopies instead of the pointed needles I was used to in the mountains, flowering bushes that held few predators and gave shelter to hares and hedgehogs. We arrived at dusk and entered a chaotic city stuffed to the walls with refugees from the river cities. The walls were in fine condition and in no danger of attack. What they needed was a few cities' worth of food and space.

Tuala led me first to the Raelech embassy rather than the quartermaster's Wellspring. There were several Raelechs in the room we were ushered into, but the lead diplomat was identifiable by his Jereh band: the white onyx of the Triune, master's amethyst, and citrine. I'd never met a diplomat myself since they were all stationed abroad. But he was very interested to meet Tuala: everyone was, I supposed. Wherever she went, she was instantly the most important person in the room since she had information no one else did. I wondered what that must be like.

I gathered quickly that Tuala and the diplomat had met many times before. They addressed each other informally with given names and cordial nods, and through that I caught the diplomat's name, Harach. He had a taut, stringy body for an older man; so many of them despair and falter at the signs of age, but he was battling defiantly to defeat them. His eyes were quick, taking in both my relative youth and my Jereh band in a single glance.

Tuala introduced me, and he welcomed me to Tömerhil. Then she proceeded to deliver the news that I had destroyed the invading Bone Giant army in the Granite Tunnel and saved Baseld. Curiously, she left out that I had also destroyed half of Baseld's garrison, and it gave Harach the impression that I was a heroine rather than a failure.

"Stonecutter Meara, I am not only honored but grateful to meet you in person," he said, and bowed to me. "Thank you for defending Baseld. I myself am from there, and most of my relations still reside in that fair city."

His gratitude was so out of tune with what I felt that I gasped, and when he looked up to see how he had erred, I struggled to control myself and muster an appropriate response.

"The honor was mine," I said. "Forgive me. I didn't expect to be commended for doing my duty."

Tuala stepped forward and pulled a folded piece of paper sealed with wax from her pack. She extended it to him and said, "From the Triune Council."

"Ah." He took it, broke the seal, and frowned as he read. "Oh." His eyes flicked up to me, and I knew that he must have read about the total destruction of the tunnel and Baseld's soldiers, along with my banishment. He continued reading and then said, "I see." He folded the paper with crisp movements, and it disappeared behind his back with his other hand as he addressed me. "I am informed that your own funds are to be converted to Brynt currency and a stipend be paid to you for services to Brynlön henceforth in perpetuity. I'm to accompany you along with Courier Tuala to visit the quartermaster and send missives to my colleagues throughout Brynlön informing them of your situation, and then you are to report monthly to the nearest embassy for your living. Otherwise you are to live and work where you see fit. Does that comport with what you've been told?"

It didn't. I hadn't been told that much. It sounded like I could simply collect a monthly stipend in any Brynt city and not actually do anything for it, which, when I looked at it from the Triune's perspective, made the most sense. I'd saved a Raelech city but at tremendous cost. Banishing me with a living was their best move politically, which I hadn't been clearheaded enough to see before. Depending on who was listening, they could emphasize either the banishment or the eternal honor they did me, and I'd never be there to contradict them. And it had clearly been Dechtira's idea. She saw that I didn't want to go back to Baseld, saw perhaps the trouble it would cause, and contrived this "punishment" as a matter of convenience more than anything else.

Not that any of that mattered to me. I would work because I needed to.

"Close enough, Diplomat," I replied.

The quartermaster of Tömerhil, when we met him soon thereafter, spat out a mouthful of wine when he heard that the Bone Giants had been completely destroyed in the Granite Tunnel and that it was closed for the foreseeable future.

"Good news and bad news," he said.

"We will, of course, let you know when it reopens, but that may not be for some long while," Harach said. Both he and Tuala left out my role in that but introduced me as someone who would help as needed in Brynlön. At that the quartermaster frowned, but in thought rather than disapproval. Or maybe he was just confused by my bare feet.

"I don't think a stonecutter would be as useful here right now as along the river cities. I'm sure the quartermaster of Fornyd could use you now, but perhaps she doesn't need you as urgently as somewhere else. The Bone Giants are not an imminent threat to her anymore. But to the south—well, that's a different story. They've taken Göfyrd, and they're occupying it. I know you're not a juggernaut, but if there's anything you can do there . . ." He trailed off and raised his eyebrows, which created several deep grooves in his forehead.

I had no idea what I could do. My career—short as it was thus far and until the Granite Tunnel—had been entirely focused on civic beautification, not military action. My Gaerit and hundreds more died because I'd been forced into a role I didn't know how to play. But that wasn't what the quartermaster wanted to hear.

"I'll do my best, sir," I told him, and his face spread into a smile. That was what he wanted to hear.

The outlying farms surrounding Göfyrd were abandoned, populated only by lonesome goats and sheep bleating at our passage, simply wanting to be milked or fed, missing their people. The reason behind their neglect struck me anew: in Baseld there were families missing their people, too.

When the road emerged from lines of trees serving as windbreaks and property markers, we saw the city of Göfyrd nestled at the river mouth below. There were hedgerows marking farm boundaries from here on but no more trees. It gave anyone atop the walls an excellent view but afforded us the same. Clouds of blackwings circled above and around the city.

At the edge of a once-prosperous family farm, Tuala crouched down with me behind some sort of native shrubbery with waxy dark green leaves and white four-petaled flowers, and we scanned the walls from a distance. It was difficult to tell whether they were manned.

"We're too far away. I'm going to need to scout."

"Watch out for earthwork traps."

"Always." She flashed a quick grin at me and departed in such a rush of displaced air that I was blown over sideways. I laughed and got up and brushed myself off, and then a flash of movement in my peripheral vision jerked my head to the right. Six Bone Giants had emerged from the nearby farmhouse and were running directly toward me, the clatter of their armor becoming clearer and louder with every step. The farms were not quite as abandoned as I thought, and I saw the cleverness: they were using farms to set little infantry traps for scouts.

"Tuala!" I called, but she was already out of hearing. I had my staves but was a year out of practice with my combat training. Six-to-one odds didn't look good either, and they were moving fast. The Bone Giants weren't meat squirrels, but maybe a little dirt in their eyes would at least slow them down. I threw up some sediment in their path, and it did make them lose a few steps as they clawed at their faces and spat, but I hadn't stopped them. I didn't know what else to do; the juggernauts were trained to use their kenning in a military fashion, but stone-cutters weren't. Could I make rocks erupt from the ground to hit them directly in their, uh, rocks? Perhaps when I was more skilled.

Better, perhaps, to disrupt the ground they had to cross to get to me. Throw up obstacles. They were bunched up, swords raised, and looking at me rather than at their feet. I called on a patch of the earth to ripple and shake in front of them, just a handbreadth of topsoil made uncertain, and they tumbled in a heap of gangly white limbs. One of them accidentally cut deeply into another with his sword, and an awful scream split the air, illustrating why parents always tell their children not to run with sharp objects. But that didn't stop them. All except the hacked one got up again, even more determined to cut me down. They came more slowly now, careful of their footing, but they kept closing the distance. When I shook the ground beneath them once more, they wobbled but remained on their feet and would soon be able to take a swipe at me. A different tactic, then.

Focusing on the leader, I had the sod leap at him from all sides, trapping him at the waist, so that it appeared he was erupting out of an enormous anthill. That held him motionless, the weight of the earth too much for him, but that still left four, and the effort of moving and shaping that much ground so quickly left me winded. When the others stopped to check on him, he shouted and gestured that they should keep going without him.

Repeating that maneuver would be pointless. It took too much effort, and there would still be three left in range to take me out. If I was going to move that much earth, I might as well take them all out at once. Grunting with exertion—pain like a diamond blade stabbed me between the eyes—I tore lose a broad strip of sod, roots, and soil two hands deep and curled it back toward me. The egg-white eyes bulged in their painted black sockets, but they kept coming, and so I pushed that roll of earth back as hard as I could, flattening three of the four, their cries of alarm cut off as the sod covered them in a final blanket. Spots swam in my vision, and I fell backward onto my rear, legs suddenly unable to support my weight. Stonecutters were not supposed to move that much earth with such violent force. We could move tremendous weight, erect walls and more, so long as we did it at a measured pace. Whenever we moved too fast, something went wrong: the collapse of the Granite Tunnel, for example, or my current collapse. The one giant who had managed to retreat in time, avoiding the slap-down, saw me blinking furiously on the ground and charged, thinking that I was too drained to react in time.

He was right. I knew I was in danger but couldn't think of what to do about it, the pain in my head was so fierce. And perhaps I was hallucinating, for the Bone Giant's legs seemed absurdly long and thin, stepping over land like a crane mincing through the shallows of a pond, and the rattling of his bone armor clapped in my ears like applause for my imminent death.

His sword flashed above his head, and the hallucination continued, for there was a wet, percussive crunch and the Bone Giant's body caved in sideways, practically folding in half like a rug beaten by a rod as something blurred behind him, and once he fell over next to me, broken and twitching, a knife handle sprouted underneath his jaw, the blade rammed up through his mouth and into the brain. And then Tuala was standing over him, chest heaving and her right arm looking strange at the shoulder.

"Are you okay?" she asked.

"Alive," I managed. "Your arm . . ."

"Dislocated it just now when I hit him."

"Oh! That was you . . ."

"Yes. You're out of it. Hold on; I have to get the others."

"Others?"

Tuala picked up the strange sword that the Bone Giant had dropped and carried it in her left hand, jogging toward a mound with a tall white man stuck in it that I suddenly remembered creating. "Oh, yeah," I said. "I think that guy was gonna kill me." Tuala circled around to his left, got behind him, sped up, and his skull was split abruptly down the middle. She left the sword embedded in his flesh at the top of his rib cage, the two halves of his head and neck resting on his shoulders like the open petals of a blood lily. "Well, he probably won't kill me *now*," I said, "but this headache might."

I tried to locate Tuala after that and discovered she had gone to finish off the wounded one who'd been injured by one of his fellows. I blinked a couple of times, and she was right next to me.

"Meara, can you stand?"

"Hm? Stand. On my feet. Maybe? Help me up." I raised a hand, and she grasped me by the arm with her left hand, pulling me to my feet. The movement did nothing good for my headache. A sudden wave of nausea overcame me, and I vomited on the body of the Bone Giant.

"Aww. That was such a good breakfast, too."

"I'm sorry, Meara."

"Don't be. I think that's what I needed, honestly. I feel better already."

"Good. Then you can help me put my arm back in its socket."

"How'd you do that?"

"I hit that Bone Giant with a stave at top speed," she explained. "Deadly to him but not without consequence to me."

"Uh . . . I don't know how to do this."

"Both hands firmly on my biceps, then roll it back in."

"I take it you've done this before?"

A tight nod. "Happens a lot."

Tuala hissed when I grabbed her arm but nodded. "Do it. Do it!"

I tried to do it, and judging by the sounds Tuala made, I was doing it wrong. I was simultaneously trying to push and roll it in, as she said, but that wasn't accomplishing anything except more pain for her.

"No, no, just . . . hold it steady and I'll roll it in from my end, all right? Just put my arm in your strongest grip and hold it still."

We both gritted our teeth, though mine was more in sympathy as Tuala grunted, shifted her torso, and rolled that socket onto the end of her arm bone with a dull pop.

"Ahh! Much better, thank you. Now observe the city."

"Why?" I turned my head toward Göfyrd, and my question was answered. A largish group of Bone Giants were streaming out of the gate and running our way. "Oh, goddess. That looks like more than six."

"A lot more than six," Tuala agreed. "There's a whole army in there. Sentries on the walls, towers fully staffed, and they saw me make my scouting run. I'm fast but not invisible. So what do you want to do?"

"I'm not sure."

"We can run, easy. That's an option."

We hadn't run in the Granite Tunnel, and I didn't want to run here, either. We had a short time to think because the city gates were more distant than the farmhouse. I felt taxed already to my limits; that searing pain, faded now, was the signal one was aging and should back off. I had pushed the kenning too far. Thinking of that brought up a memory of my temblor in the Colaiste, Temblor Kavich, growling out military history through his beard: "The earth will nourish you until it is time to return and nourish it yourself, and your enemies will either send you back early or press you, like the earth would, into gemstones."

I thought it unlikely I'd ever be a gem. But maybe this confrontation would harden me from soft soapstone into granite. I wished Temblor Kavich were here to counsel me now.

"Stand next to me," I said to Tuala, beckoning her to follow me three lengths away from the Bone Giant's body.

"What are you going to do?"

"What I should have done in the tunnel. Build from the ground up."

The farmland near the coast was rich and aerated and relatively free of rocks, having been plowed and harvested and fertilized for many years. A modest earthwork should be manageable, especially since I had the luxury of a full minute or so rather than a few seconds in which to do it.

I scrunched my toes in the turf. It was springy soil, watered well by recent rains and ideal for shaping. I reached out with my kenning and pulled it underneath us in a generous circle, and we rose on a thick pillar of earth as the first rattle and clack of bones reached our ears. By the time we could easily count them, our feet were already above their heads, though not by much.

"You know they climb walls, right? Stand on one another's shoulders?" Tuala asked.

"I heard, yes. Bennelin and others. I have a plan."

"Glad to hear it. I think there are close to fifty of them coming."

"Right. I'd get your staves out just in case they decide to jump. How's the shoulder?"

"Well enough to smash fingers."

I braced myself for the headache to come but did what prep work I could as the Bone Giants clacked and snapped closer, macabre skull faces promising all that they had to deliver. Through my feet, through my kenning, I could feel the earth all around my tower and urged it to loosen up, especially in the direction from which the Bone Giants were coming. And once they got in range, I commanded the earth to loosen more, become like sand pulling at their feet, reducing their speed. The leaders tripped, and that tripped up some behind them, and then the challenge began. I commanded the earth to hold on to their feet, even draw them down into it up to their knees, a very different process from throwing earth up to their waists. Smarter to allow the earth to give way and then firm up, compact around their ankles and calves, a far more efficient operation that froze them in the ground. Except that I had to do it nearly fifty times while still urging the pillar to rise higher. After the tenth giant had been frozen in such a manner I felt that headache coming back. And the rest of them were at the base of the tower—sinking into the earth mostly but able to steady themselves, and one leapt onto the back of another braced against the pillar and lifted himself up to where he could take a hack at us.

Tuala was ready. She sped herself up and rotated at the hips as she swept her staves left, the left one smacking away the sword as it came for her and the right one busting open the real skull under all that paint. He tumbled away, and Tuala said as she peered down, "They're surrounding us. I won't be able to catch them all if they come from all sides. Might need to revise your plan."

That wasn't it: I just needed to commit to hurting myself to hurt them more. I pushed hard with my kenning to loosen the softened earth even more around the base of the pillar so that it wouldn't bear their weight, and they sank up to their knees as I wished. That set off a mass vocalization of alarm and surprise, along with a lance of pain through my head and torso that brought me to my knees.

"Good, that's working, but they can still get out if they try," Tuala said. "Close them up now."

"Hhk . . . can't," I said, clutching at my chest. "Feels like I'm burning from the inside."

Tuala spared me a fleeting glimpse. "Oh. Yeah, that's about right. Burning your life away when you strain your kenning." She turned away to gaze down at the enemy. "Well, with the ground all soft like that I don't think they can do their spooky ladder trick effectively. But maybe get over here and just do one at a time. We don't want them to figure this out."

Splaying flat on the top of my improvised tower, I dragged myself to the edge, grunting as I went, until I reached the edge and peered over. The Bone Giants were doing their best to win free of the soil only to find that there was no such thing as solid land nearby. They could force their way out of the affected area, perhaps, if they thought to do that, but they were still trying to get to us instead. They would try clawing their way up the tower, I guessed, since it was earth and not solid rock.

Wincing, anticipating more pain, I targeted one of the attackers and gently prodded the soil around his legs to compact and firm up. The screaming fire I felt didn't increase, but it didn't decrease either. The Bone Giant squawked when he realized there was no more give to the ground and he was truly stuck.

A ragged sigh of relief escaped me, and I continued to trap them one by one, working from the base of the pillar outward. The spots came back into my vision by the end of it and the nausea returned as well, but I had nothing left in my stomach to evacuate, and I was convulsed by dry heaves while Tuala knelt next to me with a comforting hand on my shoulder.

"Relax now. You did it," she said. "Just listen to them complain." The Bone Giants were shouting at us and one another in their incomprehensible language, and it made me smile for a moment until I remembered there were many more inside the walls of Göfyrd.

"If any more come after us, we run. I can't do that again."

"Yes, I agree." She fetched my canteen and made me drink some water. "Just relax and regain your strength."

"What should we do next?"

"Let's eat lunch in front of them while they cook in the sun."

It hurt to laugh, but I did anyway, and Tuala helped me sit up. We sat on the edge of the tower, legs dangling in the air, and chewed through some salted dry meat and biscuits as the invaders hurled insults and dire promises of murder at us. We smiled and waved, and by the end of the meal I felt better if not actually good.

Tuala waved a hand at them. "Notice anything weird about this group besides them being tall, pale, and obsessed with death?"

I took a moment to survey them with a critical eye before observing, "They're all men."

"Good, so it's not just me."

"It's really strange now that I think of it. Don't their women fight? I didn't see anything like the whole army in the Granite Tunnel, but the ones I saw there were all men, too."

The courier shrugged. "Maybe they're in the city running things."

"If so, it's a criminal war they're waging. Killing children and the elderly."

Tuala shook her head. "You ever go to Bennelin?"

"No, I never got down there."

"It was wonderful. Thriving market down by the docks. Best seafood in Rael, you know, right off the boat. There was one fishmonger in particular I liked to visit whenever I was in town. Nicest old woman you'd ever meet; she must have been seventy-odd years old, her spine all bent with age, a good number of her teeth missing, but she was down there every day, rain or shine, and just happy as could be. She braided her hair with shells, had shells around her neck, too. She also spoke fluent Brynt and knew their sea chants and Drowning Songs and taught a bunch of them to me. That helped me get along in Brynlön and make fast friends, you know. She did so much good for me, and I never learned her name. She smiled and I smiled back, and we talked and sang, and I always bought some fish to cook later, always assuming that I'd see her again. And now I never will. Because of them." Her head bobbed down at the Bone Giants. "Well, not them specifically but another army of them. They're all stone killers."

"They are," I agreed.

"We have to be the same. We can't leave them like this or they'll dig themselves out. I can go down, speed up, and knife them in the kidney."

"No, don't do that."

"We don't have a choice. They'll kill anyone they meet."

"I meant, don't do that specifically. I have a better idea. I'll finish what I started."

"How so?"

"Watch that one there," I said, pointing to a Bone Giant gesticulating at me with what I assumed were rude gestures in his culture and bellowing what I guessed were promises of a gnarly death. Placing the soles of my feet against the side of the earthen tower, I commanded the earth to convulse underneath his feet, loosening and dropping, and then compact once more around his body. It worked so well that I repeated it. The effect was that he was being gulped down into the earth, a hand span or two at a time. His aggressive tone and demeanor changed the farther down he sank. He kept his arms up and held on to his sword, I noticed. When he was buried up to his belly, he fell silent and despair gripped him as he saw his end approach. But once he sank to his armpits, he raised that sword high above his head and shouted a phrase as inspiration to the others, for they raised theirs in answer and repeated the phrase back to him in unison. Two more gulps and his head disappeared from view. I let it go one more gulp after that, leaving only his forearm and hand above the ground, still clutching that sword in defiance. It quivered, spasmed, but held on to the handle tightly even when it grew still. The remaining Bone Giants watched that in silence once he went under, but as soon as they were sure their fellow soldier was dead, they all turned to face me and shouted that phrase again.

"What is that they're saying?" Tuala wondered aloud. "It's all kind of a garble at the beginning, but then they say 'Zanata sedam.' Maybe that's the word for their king or queen or god. Or their country."

"I don't know. But the good news is that wasn't too rough on me. I think I can do that forty more times or so." I picked the invader nearest the tower to be next. He stubbornly died the same way as the first, sword in the air, and so did the next two. The fifth giant broke the pattern and appeared to beg me for mercy, but he was quickly shamed by the others into dying with what they considered to be dignity. He raised his sword like the others and died like the others. There were no more entreaties until I got to the very last one. Seeing forty-seven die ahead of him—forty-eight counting the one Tuala brained with her stave—had robbed him of his convictions. Or else he figured there was no one left to witness his plea for mercy and judge him.

I would show him the exact same mercy that his people showed Bennelin and all the Brynt cities, that is to say, none at all. And I would ignore the twinge of my conscience. "There is no such thing as moral high ground in war," Temblor Kavich told me once. "There is only high ground, and as a Raelech stonecutter, you don't take and hold it. You make and mold it."

From my high ground I sank that Bone Giant into the rich farmland of Brynlön to join the others, leaving only their wrists and swords standing in the air. The worms would be at the rest of them soon enough.

Fintan returned to himself and said, "Let's step backward in time that very same morning right here in Pelemyn, where the newly commissioned gerstad Culland du Raffert had an appointment with Second Könstad Tallynd du Böll."

This time the importer was dressed in a very smart and overly stiff uniform.

ulland

Pressed pants with a crease that audibly crackles as I walk: I hate this uniform already. But I move it and all its stiff, scratchy, crunchy noises to report on time to the Second Könstad at the Wellspring, hoping that she will give me some excuse to take it off and go swimming. People salute me as I walk now that I have shiny things on my breast indicating my rank, and I remember to respond only half the time and probably salute improperly when I do. Mynstad du Möcher confirmed via her expression yesterday that I'm definitely not military material, and she may have suffered a crisis of faith as a result: What was Lord Bryn *thinking*, making me a tidal mariner?

She's not the only one asking herself that question.

No close encounters with the pelenaut this time: Tallynd du Böll meets me at the entrance to the Wellspring and guides me back around the throne to the small pool that leads to the Lung's Locks and the bay.

"Gerstad du Fesset reports that you're competent at sleeving and swimming in general now. You will not have had much practice at dry direction, though."

"You're right. I don't even know what that is."

"It's any exertion of your kenning while on dry land. The pulling and pushing of water on your person or elsewhere."

"Okay."

"Hop into the pool, get yourself soaked, and climb back out."

"All right." I noticed that her uniform, while appearing quite sharp, didn't make all the noise that mine did. I gladly leapt into the pool just to stop the itching and make that material loosen up. I climbed out, dripping, and she smiled.

"Feels better, doesn't it?"

"So much better."

"Good. Now I want you to pull that water out of your clothing and let it fall back in the pool."

"How do I . . . ?"

"It's focused visualization and exertion of will, just like moving yourself through water. Your kenning will do most of the work."

My first attempt gets the water out of my uniform, but it doesn't all go in the pool. Instead it radiates out in all directions from my body, spraying down the Second Könstad and the mariner standing guard there and splashing against the wall behind me as well. I apologize to them both, horrified and embarrassed. Tallynd du Böll just laughs, says it's no problem, and wicks away the moisture properly from both herself and the mariner.

"This is why we call it dry direction," she explains. "It's the direction that takes work. The nature of water is to take the easiest path. Forcing it to take a path of your choosing takes a bit more effort. Not exertion, mind—just an effort of concentration. Wrapping your mind around the totality of the water you wish to affect, allowing none of it to behave as it would wish but as *you* would wish. Again, Gerstad—and again and again until you can do it flawlessly."

It takes me nine attempts to perform it to the Second Könstad's satisfaction. It was, as she suggested, much more of a mental exercise than a physical one. Water will try to leak out of any container, physical or mental.

"But at what point," I ask her, "does this kind of thing become a physical exercise? I mean, when do we get the physical consequences— the aging?"

Tallynd du Böll shrugs. "Difficult to say. At some point you pass a threshold of moving volume or creating pressure that triggers the cost. No one has ever wished to experiment with their lives to measure it precisely. The effect is that we try to get along with the minimum possible. You live longer that way."

She dives into the pool and waves at me once she surfaces. "Come on; we'll head out to the ocean now. I have some things to show you."

We cycle through the locks, and once we're out of the harbor, we pause and tread water. "Before the invasion and my promotion, the majority of my work involved current adjustment and reef farming."

I shook my head. "I don't know what you mean."

"All those people who dive into Bryn's Lung—you saw what happens to the bodies, right?"

"Yes. Crabs and scavengers on the bottom. Glowing fungus on the walls."

"Right. It's a tremendous source of both food and waste. We have to keep that moving out of there, and I used to work with the rapids and hygienists to maintain it. Lots of particles can be used elsewhere; the hygienists analyze the contents of the water and work with me on moving it out. We feed the coral reefs and shellfish beds, those in turn feed the fish, and as a result we have the world's most fecund fishing waters. And thank goodness because I think it might be all that keeps us going when we run out of everything else. Follow me down. I'm going to show you Pelenaut Röllend's personal reef."

"He has his own reef?"

"Yes. He sneaks out every morning and tends it. Takes a small net sometimes and catches his breakfast. And he allows a small daily harvest of the pelenaut's reef to be sold at the Steam Spire restaurant. Have you ever been there?"

"No, but I've heard legends about its high quality and higher price tag."

"Well-deserved legends, both. Follow." She bends at the waist and dives, propelling herself to the south, and I trail after, opening my eyes and enjoying the swim. We don't descend very far; we stay in the shallows where we still have light to see. I'll have to ask her how she handles going deeper where the sun doesn't penetrate. Do our eyes adjust due to some gift of the kenning or do we need luminous bulbs of some kind, like the fungus living on the walls of Bryn's Lung?

She slows down as we approach a reef teeming with schools of shining fish, rays cruising along the sandy shallows, colorful banded eels, and all kinds of pulsing, feeding, crawling, squirming things I had never seen or even heard of before.

When we surface, she smiles. "Is that not beautiful?" I agree that it is. "You see his attention to making sure all the creatures thrive. It's a consuming interest of the pelenaut's, the flow and equitable distribution of resources, his passion for infrastructure as the basis of prosperity. He's taught me so much. I have my own reefs being fed by currents, and they do well, too, but not so well as his. That's primarily what tidal mariners do with our kenning in the absence of war." Her face turns somber. "But there are obviously aggressive tactics. Ways to use water as a weapon. That method we use to pull the water out of our clothes, for example. What do you think would happen if you applied the same principle and forcibly pulled the water out of someone's head through their ear?"

"Gods, they'd be dead before they dropped to the ground."

"Exactly."

She swims closer to me and speaks quietly. "People are mostly water to begin with. But tidal mariners are a bit more so. You belong to Bryn of the Deep now."

"I, uh . . . I don't follow."

"You're not going to leave anything behind you when you die except water."

"Wow, this has taken a pretty dark turn all of a sudden. You mean . . . ?"

"I mean to say I know you wanted to die when you jumped into Bryn's Lung. And you can still die if you want. But not before every last Bone Giant in Göfyrd dies first."

"You mean I have to go down there and do the exploding ear trick to every last—"

"No. That would take too long, and they'd overwhelm you. You'll think of something else."

"Oh. Of course."

"They represent an imminent threat. We've seen scouts or messengers coming our way, and we've managed to pick them off so far. But eventually they're going to figure out that Pelemyn and Tömerhil remain untouched and march against us. So there's no time like the present."

"Right, right. I understand."

"You do?"

"Yes, indeed." They'd been waiting for someone like me to come along, someone willing to return to the sea and take the enemy with him. I'm not saying the Second Könstad wasn't willing to make sacrifices—she'd aged much in defense of Pelemyn, and I learned from Mynstad du Möcher that she got that limp from a spear in her foot, earned while stealing Bone Giant documents near Hillegöm—but she has kids to raise, and I don't. "Leave it to me. Currents keep you safe, Second Könstad."

"And you as well, Gerstad."

She salutes me and then propels herself back to the Lung's Locks. I tread water for a minute, taking a last look at Pelemyn's domes and spires, and then decide I'm not quite ready to go just yet. I sleeve myself along the surface but do not return to the locks. I head for the docks instead and climb out there, wicking the water out of my uniform to drop back into the harbor. Longshoremen and fish heads alike look surprised and give me tight nods and wide berths. I walk back to my quarters, enjoying the morning sun, and once there I fetch a log book, ink and a pen, and a waterproof satchel issued to me by a surly sarstad at the armory. I check the contents of my purse, which is slightly swollen from the gerstad's stipend paid to me, and realize that I have enough for one last glorious, ridiculous meal at the Steam Spire Loose Leaf Emporium. They have a table for me on the second level, where I indulge in their rarest Fornish tea and a selection of fresh raw fish from the pelenaut's reef, cooked in citrus acids. A month's pay and more blown on breakfast. But it is an excellent place to record some final thoughts in the log.

I'm not sure how I'm supposed to carry out my orders—for they are orders, even if not explicitly spoken—but then I don't think the Second Könstad knows either. There's no precedent for any of this. But what I do understand is that I'm probably going to die in the attempt regardless of how successful I am.

Few people get a single chance to choose the time of their passing, let alone a second chance. I think today will suit me just fine. For as marvelous as Bryn's blessing is, as beautiful the white-ribboned blue sky, as exquisite the tea, and as filling the breakfast, I'm still empty and alone. Life is for those graced with love and ambition. My life no longer features such graces, so I'm ready for oblivion rather than a hollow existence. For me, the deep awaits.

I put the log safely inside the satchel, slung it across my shoulder, and left my entire purse on the table. I fell backward off the docks, waving Pelemyn goodbye, and sleeved myself most of the way to Göfyrd on my back, looking up at the sky and marveling at how something so empty could contain so much.

It was past midday when the bay began to narrow, and I flipped over to see my target better. I had yet to see those creatures who had destroyed so many lives. There were some, perhaps, on the walls, but I couldn't see them well. I didn't want to get too close, either, not knowing what their capabilities were, so I avoided both the docks and the Lung's Locks, choosing to walk out of the sea on a beach well outside the city walls. I had been there only a few moments, beginning to wonder how I was supposed to eliminate a whole army by myself and also wondering why there was a strange earthen tower near the road leading north, when I saw a woman approaching me impossibly fast. Impossible, that is, until I realized she must be a Raelech courier. She had a Jereh band on her right arm, and couriers were the only Earth Shapers who could move like that.

She slowed down to normal human speeds and waved in a friendly manner before I could worry that she had come to attack. I noted that she stopped a good distance away, however, and shouted a greeting to me in accented Brynt.

"Hello! May I approach and speak with you?"

I nodded at her, and she darted forward, flashing a grin at me when she halted a length away.

"I am Tuala, courier of the Triune Council," she said.

"Gerstad Culland du Raffert, tidal mariner," I replied.

Her eyes widened. "You're a tidal mariner?" Her gaze took in my decidedly unmilitary body, and doubt clouded her expression.

"Yes. I'm here to do something about . . ." My hand writhed at the city like a beached eel. "That. Them. This."

"Ah! We thought Brynlön would be doing something soon, but we thought we'd see an army instead of just one person."

"Who's we? You mean Rael?"

"No, I mean me and the stonecutter who raised that tower."

I looked past her at the tower, then at the city, thinking the view from that tower might be far superior to the one I currently had. "Is the stonecutter still up there? I mean, can I have a look at the city from there?" I asked, pointing.

"Sure. Let's go. She doesn't speak Brynt, but I'll translate if you need me to."

She pulled me along with her by using her kenning, moving as fast over land as I could move through the water. When we reached the base, I saw the strangest crop one will ever see in farmland: pale thin wrists and bony fingers clutching swords, sprouting from the ground, bunched together near the base but trailing away toward the city like the tapered tail of a river lizard.

"Are those . . . ?"

"Bone Giants? Yes. Meara just got finished burying them. I was worried about her for a while, but she's a stone killer."

"Can't wait to meet her."

At the top of the steps spiraling around the tower, I met Meara, who looked to be in her midtwenties and weary beyond measure.

We nodded helplessly at each other, unable to speak except through our eyes. Hers had pain in them, and she didn't smile at me the way the courier had. Perhaps she had lost her family in Bennelin the way I'd lost mine in Festwyf. We wouldn't get to trade tragedies, however.

The view of the city was better but not good enough. I could see sentries on the walls much more clearly now but not into the city itself. Perhaps the stonecutter could mend that.

I turned to Tuala and asked, "Can Meara get me a look down into the city? Raise the tower, maybe, until I can see over the battlements?"

After Tuala's translation, that turned out to be something Meara could do. The tower lurched for a moment under my feet, then rose as the ground built beneath us.

I don't know precisely how high we climbed, because I never took my eyes off the city. As we rose above the walls, I could finally see them and understand what they'd done. Being told is one thing, but seeing it is another. Milky ghouls on sticklike legs, teeming in the streets, and . . . dragging bodies around. Brynt bodies, men, women, and children, all murdered by those horrible creatures like wraiths made flesh.

"Why?" I murmured, not really expecting an answer, but Tuala gave me one.

"Because they thought they could get away with it," she said.

"But what are they doing? With the people?"

The courier shrugged. "I don't think they're going to bury them in the ground or in the sea like you and I would. They appear to be dragging them all into one big pile. See there? My guess is they're going to burn them."

"Burn . . . ?" My fingers twitched first, but the tremors spread all over my body, just as they had when I'd heard the news about Festwyf. All those poor people, hauled around like so much meat, only to be melted down to ashes, denied their return to the ocean. My family was little better off, still left where they were slain in Festwyf. My thumb caught on the edge of the satchel in its restless quivering, and I unslung it from my shoulders, handing it to the courier. "That's the last of me," I told her.

She stared at me, uncomprehending. "What am I supposed to do with this?"

"Whatever you like. It's yours now. I'm going to practice my dry direction."

"I don't know what that is."

Sunlight glinted on the scalloped surface of the bay as if a school of moonscales had surfaced to feed. "The people of Göfyrd deserve to be buried properly at sea," I said, "and the Bone Giants deserve to drown in it."

I didn't talk any more after that, though Tuala tried to get me to explain. She would see for herself soon enough.

All my trembling rage and despair I channeled into calling the waters of the shining blue bay. And it resisted because what I wanted was not the path of least resistance, but I poured my emotions into it and pulled, and it pulled back until I quaked with the effort. Still the waters receded from the shore and built into a wave—no ordinary wave but one shaped by my will to do the right thing. To bring Göfyrd vengeance and peace. Justice and a final rest. A reaping, yes, but also a cleansing.

Needles of pain fired hot and bright throughout my body, the toll for such a kenning already being exacted, but I kept calling the water anyway. How strange that the process of liquefying your organs should feel so blasted hot.

The roar of that building water matched the roar in my ears and the roar tearing from my throat—or maybe it was all one, the same roar I'd heard back in Fornyd, calling to me even then, and I understood that it had always been the Lord of the Deep, calling me to this duty, calling me home to the sea.

Without a word, Fintan threw down a black sphere and changed seemings directly back to the stonecutter Meara.

M eara

This strange Brynt man who looked so uncomfortable in his military uniform was in fact a tidal mariner: the Second Kenning's equivalent of a juggernaut. I didn't speak the language—yet—so we did little more than make eye contact and nod. I wished I could have talked to him, though. He looked like he could relate to the week I'd had.

Mild mannered at first, he transformed after he saw the Bone Giants from on high, moving Brynt bodies around. His jaw clenched, he gave his satchel to Tuala, and then he looked out at the bay as if he could slay the whole ocean with a snarl. I followed his gaze and saw nothing but calm waters, so I checked him again and he was quivering, head to toe. Sweat glistened on his brow and his upper lip, and I worried that perhaps he was having some sort of physical episode, maybe even a seizure. What reason could he have, after all, to glare at the bay with such fury? I turned back to look, and it was different: the waters were receding from the tongue of the shore to form the most massive single wave I have ever seen. A wave much taller than the walls of Göfyrd, even seen from farther out in the bay, and heading straight for the city. The building roar of it reached our ears later than the sight, and both the size of the wave and the volume of the roar grew as it approached the occupied city. Furthermore, it was oddly shaped: not a wide bank of blue-green with a foam-capped leading edge spanning the width of the bay but rather a fat whirling cylinder that looked like it might fit perfectly inside the walls.

"That has to be terrifying," I whispered, looking at the distant figures on the walls pointing out frantically to the oncoming wave. They could see it coming to get them but could not possibly get out of the way in time or do anything to stop it. The base rushed forward, all that weight slamming into the seaside wall, more than any stonecutter would prepare for, and the massive cylinder of whirling water crested over the wall and fell inside, crushing rooftops and the much more fragile bodies they sheltered. Anyone not immediately killed by the weight of it would surely drown, for the water filled up the city walls like a soup ladle filling a bowl, but instead of herbs and vegetables floating in soup we saw rubble and bodies bobbing to the surface of the churn.

The tidal mariner cried out, and I turned just in time to see his face ripple like there were waves underneath his skin, and then there *was* no skin or anything really solid beyond a sodden lump like wet ashes, for he came apart and splashed inside his uniform, his head fountaining briefly, and he watered the soil of the tower as the Second Kenning destroyed the vessel through which it worked. His empty mariner clothes smacked wetly to the earth, and I sank down next to them, seized by revelation.

He had just achieved the impossible because he didn't care about the consequences. He knew he'd die instantly for straining his kenning like that, and he did it anyway. And if I had thought to do the same thing in the Granite Tunnel, I could have made those seals hold and prevented the collapse. I could have saved those soldiers if only I had been willing to sacrifice as this man had. I would have returned to the earth, someone would have sung the Dirge for the Fallen for me—not Temblor Priyit but someone, surely—and I wouldn't be an exile, this legendary example of how not to be a stonecutter.

Tuala shook me gently by the shoulders. "Meara, it's okay. He meant to do that. He knew it was going to happen."

"I know," I said, wiping at my nose and realizing that I had become a mess of tears and snot. But not, as Tuala thought, because this man had died but because I hadn't. "I should have done what he did. If I had committed everything, I could have saved them."

"No. No, Meara. If you had, you wouldn't have been here to help him. He needed this tower to be here. You helped him and thereby helped Brynlön, as you pledged to do." She snorted at a sudden thought. "I know it may not feel like it, but the Triple Goddess may be working through you. Do you not realize you have been instrumental in destroying two armies? And now you will help the Brynts even more."

"How?"

"Get up. Look at that," Tuala said, pointing to the city. Waves of Brynt bodies were returning to the sea, which was every bit as important to Brynts as burial in the ground was to us. "That's history right there. A turning point, as was the Granite Tunnel. And it needs remembering. I will tell what happened here and bards will repeat it, but you will make it last forever. Because you're going to work on this tower and make it a monument to this tidal mariner. What he did, right here, deserves your best effort."

"I never caught his name. It just didn't penetrate."

"Culland du Raffert."

"Okay. You're right. I will do my best sparkle work—"

"What?"

"Never mind. Hey," I said, pointing to something in the sky above Göfyrd. "I don't think those are blackwings over there. Those look like flying men."

"We must step back just a wee bit from that point," Fintan said, "and pick up with Gondel Vedd and Ponder Tann."

*G*ondel

There are a few rolling hills south of Göfyrd, and I crested them with Ponder Tann one morning to witness the most awe-inspiring work of the Second Kenning I'd ever seen or even heard of. We knew something strange was going on as soon as we saw a rather incongruous tower to the north of the city, rising above the walls yet not made of stone—it appeared to be raw earth.

"What purpose does that tower serve?" Ponder wondered aloud. "It's not in an ideal spot for a lighthouse."

"An archers' tower, perhaps?"

"Too high for that. And any archers you put up there would be cut off in an attack."

"Well, I think there are people on top of it."

The tempest squinted. "I think you're right. Three, perhaps. Difficult to tell at this distance."

We could see much more clearly that there were Bone Giants on the walls of Göfyrd, pale bodies clearly visible against dark stone. There was no telling how many more might be inside the city; all we could see was rooftops from our angle.

"I hate to ask, Ponder, but might you be able to get us closer? Quickly, I mean, yet without straining yourself?"

"Sure. We could fly over there without much strain if you don't mind a rough ride. Where would you like to land?"

"Perhaps within hailing distance of the people on the tower. We can at least ascertain if they are friend or foe. And if they are the latter, I suppose we must fly away quickly again."

He nodded. "All right. I'll take us over the city to get a better look inside."

"Out of bowshot range, I hope."

"Arrows won't fly straight when I'm directing the wind," he said, "so no need to worry about that. I don't think the Bone Giants have bows anyway. Better secure whatever you need to hold on to before we go."

My carisak was already strapped to me, but I rechecked to see that the clasp was securely fastened and tightened everything before nodding to the tempest. "Ready."

He closed his eyes and took a couple of deep breaths, and on the third inhalation a phenomenal gust blew up from the valley below and lifted us into the air, chilling my nethers abruptly and sending my stomach into sloshing nervous fits. We dipped and twisted and flipped, and in short order I was hurling my breakfast into the wind.

We managed to straighten out to at least a semihorizontal trajectory by the time we reached Göfyrd, some alarming swoops aside. Looking down directly into the streets and squares, I saw that the city was well populated with Eculan invaders. Some of them spotted us and pointed, but no one tried to shoot us out of the sky.

"Oh, Reinei preserve us," I breathed when I saw the bodies. On the northern edge of the city, the Eculans were dragging the slaughtered bodies of all the Brynts and piling them against the inside of the wall. The streets leading to it were smeared with their blood. I caught something of the smell as we passed over, and my guts heaved again even though my stomach was already empty.

Tears streamed out the corners of my eyes as we approached the wall. How could the Eculans believe that they were just and righteous in this behavior? For they surely did, using their religion as their excuse. What was I missing in *Zanata Sedam* that gave them permission to kill without remorse?

Now closer to the strange tower, we saw that there were indeed three figures on top: two women and a man. The women were easily identified as Raelechs thanks to their bare arms and the Jereh bands worn on the right.

The man, middle-aged and stout, wore a blue and white uniform that looked like it might be Brynt military, though I couldn't tell what rank; I am unfamiliar with such customs anyway, and he might simply have liked crisp blue and white clothing. He appeared to be in some kind of distress: his expression was strained, and his clenched fists shook. He was staring out at the bay, and the Raelechs were staring at him; none of them saw us approaching. I turned my head to follow their gaze and saw that the waters were behaving strangely. They were receding from the shore quite rapidly. I pointed it out to Ponder and shouted through the wind, "Look at the bay! That's not normal, is it?"

He stared. "No. That's unnatural. Where is it going—oh! He must be a tidal mariner!"

"Why? What do you—oh, sweet kraken tits." Ponder's eyes were better than mine, and I was a bit slow in discerning that the waters were receding only to form a wave able to crush the entire city underneath its weight, dumping a large portion of the bay right over the walls and obliterating the entire occupying force of Eculans in a matter of seconds. It crashed through the wall facing the sea, and eventually the water returned there, taking the bodies of the Eculans and the Brynts with it.

My mouth ran dry with fear despite the fact that we were looking down upon so much water.

Ponder spun us around and held us aloft in a juddering plume of air. "Think of the power that would require!" he said, ignoring that he was already doing what only a handful of people could do with their kenning.

I thought of my brother, already aged near to death, who had died transporting us to this continent. The tidal mariner had not been nearly so old, but the power he must have summoned to do that—to wipe out an entire city with a single wave, for that is what he just did—would surely bring him near to death if not kill him outright.

Tearing my gaze away from the city to peer at the tower, I saw that there were only two figures on top of it now: the Raelechs, one of them on her knees. Where was the Brynt man? Had he fallen off the tower? As I watched, the other Raelech moved to comfort the one on her knees. Had she loved the Brynt man?

"Ponder! Can you take us to the tower?" I called.

He glanced over at me briefly and then returned his gaze to the ruined city, perhaps determined to fix the sight in his mind. But he nodded, and moments later the wind shifted and carried us toward the tower.

"Do you speak Raelech?" I asked Ponder.

"No."

"All right. I will try to summarize as needed."

"If that tidal mariner is still alive, I'll be surprised," Ponder said as we began our descent. "That kenning probably finished him."

Both of the Raelech women were on their feet now, looking at Göfyrd, but as we neared, one of them spotted us and pointed. I waved to let them know we were friendly, and they braced themselves as the first gusts of Ponder's wind reached them. Then they flattened themselves to the top of the tower to reduce their profiles and avoid being blown over the side.

They rose and slapped dirt off their clothes once we landed, and I saw by their Jereh bands that one of them was a stonecutter and the other was one of the Triune's couriers. Meara and Tuala were their names. Meara looked as if she'd been crying recently. The Brynt man's uniform lay crumpled and drenched between us, but there was no sign of his body.

"I'm Gondel Vedd, and this is Ponder Tann," I said in the Raelech tongue. "We serve Mistral Kira of Kauria, here to witness and report, and we have witnessed something truly remarkable. Where is the tidal mariner?"

My question caused the stonecutter to sob openly. She covered her eyes with her hands and turned away.

"He's dead," Tuala replied, gesturing at the uniform. "He just melted. Dissolved—whatever. The kenning drank him up, liquefied even his bones. And it was so strange because it was like he wanted to die."

"Who was he?"

"His name was Culland du Raffert." She waggled a small leather journal in her hand. "He gave me this, said it was the last of him."

"May I take a look at it? For scholarly purposes."

"You can read Brynt?"

"I am fluent in all the languages, as you are."

"Why did the mistral send you up here with a tempest?" she asked, but handed the journal to me.

"Because I can also speak with the Eculans."

"Who?"

"The Bone Giants."

That interested her, and we traded information. The destruction of the northern army was news to me; everything I knew about the Eculans, including the Seventh Kenning and the Seven-Year Ship, was news to her. Tuala wanted to leave right away to inform the Brynt pelenaut at Pelemyn what his tidal mariner had done and then return to Rael to report to the Triune Council. But Meara, it seemed, would be staying. She wanted to turn the tower into a memorial for Culland. I'd not yet read his journal and knew nothing of him, but I'd seen what he'd done and agreed that such a moment should be preserved.

Before Tuala left us, I asked her to report also to the Kaurian embassy in Pelemyn and let them know I'd be coming and would deliver Culland's journal to the Wellspring after I'd made a copy.

The courier departed, and I seated myself on the tower top with Ponder, paging through the tidal mariner's journal and also keeping an eye on Meara as she frowned and set about her work, converting the earthen tower to stone by slowly calling up the rock from deep in the earth and fitting it around the circumference of the tower until it reached the top. Later, she said, she would let all the earth drain from the middle and build a spiral staircase inside so that people could visit the spot, and she would work with masons to create a mosaic floor to walk on. Culland's uniform, along with the dirt around it to a depth of three fingerlengths, was not to be touched or moved, and eventually sealed under glass. But she needed to work with a Raelech mason to do the fine decorative work she had in mind, and she would go with us to Pelemyn to find one once she had the basic structure completed.

Ponder and I thought it an excellent plan. The tempest probably listened to ghosts on the wind while I read Culland's journal and made a copy in Kaurian.

When I got to his last entry, I exclaimed and startled everyone, including myself.

"What is it?" Ponder asked.

"A possibility. A small gust of hope that I can do some actual good here." I pointed to a passage in Culland's journal. "It says here that another tidal mariner stole some Eculan documents from the *voj-skovodja* near Hillegöm and brought them back to Pelemyn. If they will let me see them, I can help translate! Perhaps there will be something there to help us anticipate the Eculans' next move."

I dearly hoped there would be. Some shred of vital information that would mean my brother had good reason to die to get me here. Something that would save lives and validate my decision to breathe in all the words of the world instead of the wind.

Meara finished the basic tower structure near sundown but wasn't ready to leave then. "We need something to explain what's here. An obelisk, I'm thinking, which I'll decorate later. But I want the words finished today. You can help with that?" she asked me.

"Of course."

There being no stairs at present, we leapt off the tower together and Ponder caught us in the wind, lowering us gently to the ground. At the base, near where she would later create an entrance to the tower, she erected a polished granite obelisk with a Raelech-language inscription chiseled into the base through her kenning. I translated it for her into Brynt, Fornish, and Kaurian, and she etched the same message on the other sides of the obelisk in those languages:

> On this spot on 17 Barebranch 3042, witnessed by two Rael-echs and two Kaurians, tidal mariner Culland du Raffert sacrificed himself to call the wrath of Bryn down upon the city of Göfyrd, held by the Eculan invaders known as Bone Giants. The wave he summoned crashed through the seaside wall of the city, drowned the occupying army, and washed them out to sea, along with their victims, who returned to Lord Bryn.

"Gerstad Culland du Raffert, friends," Fintan said, returning to his shape in a cloud of smoke. "His memorial can be found in that spot if you ever get down to Göfyrd. And you will find the stonecutter Meara there, too. She's made it her life's work to rebuild that city."

Day 18

UNHINGED WRATH

I'd been looking forward to going home and asking Elynea about her first day as an official apprentice, but my plans were drowned by a longshoreman in coral livery. After the bard's tale, he thrust some fancy paper our way and informed both of us that we were invited to join the pelenaut at the Nentian embassy in town for dinner.

"You're expected to attend. Formal dress if you can manage it," the longshoreman said.

The invitation promised a "rare dining experience" and varied company.

"How is this possible?" I asked. "The pelenaut expelled the Nentian ambassador and his staff four days ago. They're on a ship heading for Fandlin."

"This isn't hosted by the ambassador. These are some fat yaks from Ar Balesh who paid the Raelechs to take them over the Poet's Range since they couldn't go through the tunnel."

"Who are they?"

The longshoreman shrugged. "Rich fat yaks. Not diplomats. That's all I know. Except they just got here. So they wouldn't have heard anything about that murdering viceroy with the diseased tadpole hose."

I caught Fintan's eyes. "Could be fun."

"Could be heinous. Why do I have to go?"

"Pelenaut Röllend wants your perfect recall. But he may also need your language skills. We're not sure how many of them speak Brynt, and the pelenaut does not speak Nentian."

"Well, I want someone to taste everything first and see if they die."

The longshoreman grinned. "That's being taken care of. The entire preparation will be supervised. And there will be hygienists in attendance, of course."

We arrived punctually, which turned out to be early. Four Nentian merchants, dressed in their floofy and poufy best, welcomed us and were delighted that the bard could speak Nentian. They could hardly wait to put drinks in our hands, but Fintan protested that he'd best wait until the rest of the party arrived. He relayed to me their names and what their particular business was, but then much of the talk swirled around me like thin word soup and I didn't have a spoon to enjoy it.

The merchants were entertaining at least. Jovial, ebullient types, lacking the restraint of diplomats and projecting a sincere rather than a feigned warmth. None of them resembled a fat yak, but they did appear to be rich. Poudresh Marekh was the shortest of the lot and had taken the trouble to grow a mustache that spread to his sideburns, leaving his chin bare. He represented a collective of Nentian llama ranchers and sold everything from their curly wool to combs carved from their hooves. Ghurang Bokh was quite clearly into tanning and leathers of all kinds, and he was the sort to wear his products as a walking advertisement. Even his hair was plaited and run through broad tooled leather circles fastened with a wooden pin. Subodh Ramala was an older man, comfortable with his jowls and wattled neck and perhaps the most tense of the lot despite the smile pasted onto his face. He was a distributor for smoked and cured Nentian meats such as chaktu, khern, and even borchatta. The last merchant was tallest of the lot and had grown a scraggly goatee on his chin in an attempt to hide the apple in his throat. Fintan said he was "a purveyor of fine footwear—a bootmonger, if you will," and his name was Jahm Joumeloh Jeikhs.

"He gave you three names?"

"He did. Said it helped people not blessed with perfect recall remember him."

"The boots help, too, no doubt," I said, for they were undeniably rich, the uppers sparkling with mosaics of inlaid semiprecious stones. "Why are they here and so anxious to meet the pelenaut?"

"I'm afraid to ask."

And we didn't get to, at least right then, for the pelenaut arrived with his entourage, and the introductions could begin anew. He had three hygienists with him, and apparently another had been in the kitchen all day with a couple of mariners and longshoremen as the food was being prepared. The three newly arrived ones immediately set about checking the liquors for poisons, and once they declared them safe, everyone relaxed a bit. The pelenaut proposed a toast to our distant friends the Nentians, and no sooner had we drunk than a longshoreman announced that dinner was ready and we moved from the parlor into the embassy's dining room.

Platters of Nentian charcuterie and sliced rounds of chaktu cheese waited there, thanks to Subodh Ramala, but I was far more excited to see the Brynt foods spread out there: some meats and vegetables I hadn't seen in some time—or, indeed, ever. There was an entire scurry of roasted meat squirrels, for example. Hunting them must have been extraordinarily dangerous. There was also fresh broiled moonscale, fire-glazed swamp duck, and some rare wild fyndöl mushrooms sautéed in even rarer Fornish cream butter. These merchants had really spared no expense to impress us. That only made me more curious about what they wanted.

Jahm Jeikhs couldn't wait to get to that and began to speak of it in halting Brynt as soon as we sat down, clearing his throat and saying, "Pelenaut Röllend, I'd like to speak of some vital matters in Ghurana Nent—" but Rölly held up a hand to stop him.

"Time enough for that after we've eaten, Jahm. I'm famished, and that's a vital matter as well. Let's enjoy this extraordinary meal."

"Surely we can do both?" Certainly not a diplomatic reply; he'd been given an undeniable cue to wait until later but chose to ignore it. My friend just smiled at him.

"We could, but a dinner like this is a rare treat. Please eat first and then we'll talk."

"Eat first? We didn't travel all this way to eat, but all right." The bootmonger's long fingers darted forward to the swamp duck resting in a shallow pool of orange glaze, and he tore off a wing and crammed it into his mouth. "I'm eating," he said, his words muffled by the food, and everyone stared at him, aware that he was jumping into a pool of embarrassment but unable to do anything but look on. "Mmm! So good! Delicious! I want some more of that!" He grabbed the swamp duck with both hands and simply tore at either breast in a fantastically rude spectacle and moaned as he brought the hunks of greasy meat to his mouth. "Oh, mmm! So saucy!" His cheeks bulged with the flesh, and he kept cramming it in faster than he could chew. Trickles of the sticky orange glaze dribbled down his chin and soaked his goatee, turning it into a glistening rope of hair. When he couldn't fit any more in, he glanced at his countrymen, who universally wore expressions of horror at his behavior, and he laughed, necessarily spitting some of the duck out to do so. That only made him laugh harder.

"Aha ha ha ha!" he cried, duck bits spraying across the table, but when he took a breath to continue, his eyes boggled in panic and he wheezed, spitting the rest out without even trying to keep it in. He clutched at his throat and attempted to breathe but couldn't.

"Hygienist!" Röllend barked, worried that the food might have been poisoned somehow after all and perhaps a hygienist might still be able to purify his blood. One of the hygienists rushed to the Nentian's side and placed a hand on his neck, using her kenning to search for poison in his system. Jahm continued to struggle, slowly turning blue from lack of oxygen and pointing at his throat as if we weren't aware there was a problem. The hygienist shook her head.

"He's not poisoned. He's choking." She began to pound him on the back, not being gentle about it either, and Jahm's choking noises changed tenor but didn't cease. The bone he must have inhaled was lodged firmly in his airway and refused to budge. Duck bones can be broad and flat, and even if they are hollow, they are excellent at blocking air. The Nentian's complexion continued to go pale and blue until his eyes rolled up and his head crashed to the table, his long fine hair mired in swamp duck meat, causing both Poudresh and Ghurang to leap up and join in pounding the abyss out of his back to eject the bone.

They failed, and Jahm Joumeloh Jeikhs died there in front of us, ending the dinner before it truly began.

The surviving merchants and the pelenaut all floated experimental sentences to express their shock and deep regret, having never been trained in what to say when someone dies at your dinner party.

I turned to the bard on my right and said in a low voice intended only for him, "That was certainly a rare dining experience. I've never seen someone kill himself with a glazed duck before."

"You realize I can't let him die like that for nothing, don't you?" the bard whispered back to me.

"What do you mean?"

"I mean I have to write a song about this. Kids can learn a lesson from poor old Jahm. Take your time eating and chew your food."

"Fintan. No."

"How can I pass this up? 'The Saucy Fire-Glazed Swamp Duck Death of Jahm Joumeloh Jeikhs.' The tale of his demise will live longer than he did!"

The pelenaut asked a question that distracted both of us from possible morality songs. "Might any of you know what he was so anxious to talk about?"

The merchants all nodded, and Subodh spoke for the others in Nentian, which Fintan then translated. "We were hoping we could convince you to send at least a few hygienists back to Ghurana Nent. Our people are suffering and our businesses flagging without their aid."

"It saddens me to hear that, and it's regrettable," Pelenaut Röllend said, "and I do hope to allow our hygienists to resume work abroad in the future. At present, however, we need them here to recover from the devasting aftermath of the invasion."

"But you have so many here tonight," Subodh protested. "Four of them when one would have sufficed. Surely you can spare one or two for Ghurana Nent. I ask not merely for myself but on behalf of the viceroys and even the king, who helped us get here."

"I can't spare them, no. They are here tonight after working all day in Survivor Field as a favor to me. And tomorrow they will go out there again. I wish I could give you better news, but you have my assurances that we will send hygienists abroad as soon as we can afford to."

"Sir," Poudresh Marekh pleaded in Brynt, his mustache quivering, "at the risk of leaving my llamas out to play with bloodcats, it's the king. He's not well. And it threatens us all. We need a hygienist for the king."

"What's wrong with him?"

"He's unstable. Going mad, in fact, though I will thank you not to repeat that to him. And he has our families. If we don't come back with a hygienist, he has promised to strap them to the posts of Kalaad and let his cheek raptor tear their faces off."

The pelenaut snorted. "We're talking about Bhadram Ghanghuli, right? Since when does he have a cheek raptor? That sounds like Viceroy Melishev Lohmet."

The Nentians all traded looks of alarm and bemusement, and Fintan, I noticed, covered his eyes with one hand. Ghurang Bokh was the first to venture, "But it *is* Melishev Lohmet."

"Who is?"

"The king," Subodh said. "Melishev Lohmet is the king now."

The pelenaut and I and every other Brynt in the room turned to Fintan. Rölly said, "Fintan, is this true?"

"Yes," he admitted.

The pelenaut gaped, then shouted, "Why didn't you tell me?"

"I'm sorry, but I thought you knew! How could you not?"

"Well, we've been a bit busy, and the Nentians never use their king's name, do they? They just call him the king. So I rely on the ambassador to tell me when there's someone new sitting on the throne."

"You threw him out a few days ago," I pointed out.

"He didn't know anyway. He was still calling Melishev a viceroy. And with the Granite Tunnel closed it's no wonder we haven't heard anything. We've had almost zero trade from Ghurana Nent since then. When did this happen?"

The question was directed at Fintan, but Subodh answered. "Two months ago."

"Two *months*? Neither I nor the ambassador heard anything for two months? How is that possible?"

"Like you, we have been busy," Subodh said, shrugging helplessly. "In the worst possible way."

The pelenaut fumed and took a couple of deep breaths before saying, "Fintan."

"Yes?"

"I don't suppose Melishev's coup is part of your tale in the coming days?"

"It is."

"And Bhadram Ghanghuli, the former king? What happened to him?"

"Do you want all the details?"

"No; just give me the short version."

"He's dead."

The pelenaut grimaced and clenched his fists. "Do you have any idea how angry I am with you right now? I want to beat you senseless with the biggest kraken cock in the abyss."

"I'm very sorry, sir. I truly thought you would have been informed through other channels, and we just haven't gotten to that part of the story yet."

The pelenaut said, "Oh, you can be sure I'll be following up through other channels. Never mind the Nentian embassy. Why hasn't the Raelech embassy spoken to me about a change of leadership in Ghurana Nent? Or the Fornish, for that matter?"

"They may not know either, sir," Subodh said, drawing all eyes to him. "I mean, now that I think about it. The king has been, uh. What's the word?" He said something in Nentian, and Fintan translated.

"Paranoid."

"That's it, thank you," Subodh said. "Paranoid. And violent. He is not well."

"Yes, we've been hearing about that from the bard." Röllend turned sharply to Fintan and said, "You're not embellishing him, right? He truly is the shitsnake you've described?"

"He is. If anything, I've been casting him in the best possible light."

"Bryn drown me, then." He returned his gaze to Subodh and the others. "I have to tell you, kind sirs, I'm not inclined to help him. He's a casual murderer and cares nothing for the suffering of his people."

Panic grew in the Nentians' eyes, and they all spoke at once some variation of "But sir, our families—"

Pelenaut Röllend held up a hand to silence them. "I didn't say I'm not inclined to help *you*. I'm just not inclined to help Melishev Lohmet. Let me think on this, consult with some advisers, and try to come up with a solution." He looked down at the body of Jahm Joumeloh Jeikhs, whose face was still planted in his plate of decadent swamp duck sauce. "I assume Melishev has his family, too?"

The Nentians nodded, and Ghurang added, "He has three children."

"I'm sorry it ended like this. I didn't realize what was at stake. But I understand now and thank you for speaking candidly with me. I assure you that I'm engaged and will be in touch soon."

Rölly took his leave, and Fintan and I followed close on his heels, leaving behind the Nentians, their sumptuous feast, and the body of Jahm Joumeloh Jeikhs in the middle of it.

When Fintan took the stage the next day, he had two additional musicians with him, both with lutes—one bass and one rhythm. He lifted up his feet one by one and pointed at them. "I got new shoes!" he exclaimed, and I felt unobservant for not noticing earlier. They were simple brown leather but undeniably new. "I wanted to sing about them, but sadly I don't know any shoe songs. Fortunately, the Nentians have a celebratory song about boots, and I was reminded of it by a

Nentian bootmonger I met briefly yesterday. We're going to perform that for you today." The musicians launched into an up-tempo tune, and Fintan picked a blistering melody above it on his harp until he began to sing:

> My hens all died and my plow is broke
> My well is dry and my yak just croaked
> My farm's all rotted straight down to the roots
> But I don't care because now I can wearrrrr—!
>
> My worldwide, superglide, yellow-dyed, verified,
> Certified, ratified, justified and dignified,
> Qualified ironside, fortified and purified,
> Bona fide, amplified, khernhide boots!

"Let's begin today with Abhinava Khose, who has a contract to fulfill at the Hathrim city of Baghra Khek."

Abbi

There are so many bones to the north of the Hathrim city. Charred, blackened, and some with strings of gristle left on them, but mostly just helmets and mail draping skeletons. An army's open grave. I remained far out of range. If that mass of men could be burned at such a distance from the walls, I could be, too. I came upon another battlefield first where some bodies were burned but most had been halved or quartered by huge blades. There were still some scavengers in the neighborhood, but they left us alone. Murr and Eep hunted some of them for their next meal, and I led the horses around to the east, planning to circle the Hathrim city at a healthy remove until I reached the foothills.

I saw the reflected glare of glass boats down by the shore but no actual giants until I'd nearly reached the bottom of the Godsteeth. I'd never seen one in the flesh before because they had little reason to visit Khul Bashab. I saw a group from a distance that was clearing the timber closest to their walls on the forest side, the south side.

More than their stature—which was awesome, to be sure—I noticed their skin and hair. So pale you'd think they'd burn up in the sun. And their hair wasn't just dark like ours; some of them had light yellow or red hair. I did see at least one who was bald, except his—or maybe her—skull was on fire. Definitely one of the lavaborn there. I doubted the others would be so helpful in identifying themselves. I'd never heard that fire skulls were how you could tell a blessed giant from a merely huge one. I think it was a woman, and for some reason she wasn't pitching in but rather talking to the workers. Perhaps I could figure out more if I watched, but I couldn't just stand there and be spotted.

The sawgrass was high and I could hide myself completely in it if I crouched, but the horses could be seen above it. Before that crew took a good look around to the east, I dismounted and asked the horses to lie down for a few minutes so that I could think in safety.

"Murr. Can you smell the large people near here? I mean, do they have a specific smell?"

The bloodcat tipped his snout into the air, and his nostrils flared as he took in a few deep breaths. Then he looked at me and tossed his chin in a nod.

"Can you smell any of them closer to us than they are?" He checked again and nodded. "Where? I mean, in which direction? Can you point with one of your paws?"

He turned south to face the Godsteeth and lifted his right front paw in that direction. I rose somewhat from my crouch so that I could peek over the grass. A hundred or so lengths away, the plains gave way to hills that rose to mountains, and they were covered in shorter grasses, shrubs, and grand moss pine trees. Tans and browns and some leafy greens mostly, so the gray and white movement among it all caught my eyes.

Two Hathrim houndsmen on patrol, returning to the city at a leisurely walk. Unbelievable to see a predator that size—the hounds alone were the size of kherns! I couldn't tell whether the armored giants astride them were lavaborn, but either way they posed a challenge. I'd have no chance against them without my own kenning. Now that I'd seen the hounds with my own eyes, I reached out with my kenning to see if I could locate them. They weren't native to Ghurana Nent, so I wanted to make sure it would work, and it did. I sensed the hounds, felt their barely contained ferocity, and knew that I could use it to my advantage. I suggested to the hounds that the lavaborn with the fiery skull was extraordinarily delicious but only one of them could get there first, and they took off at top speed, much to the surprise of their riders. One of them held on, though just barely, and the other toppled from his saddle onto the ground, axe and all.

The houndsman who managed to stay mounted yanked hard on the reins, but his hound fought it, twisting and shaking its head from side to side and then spinning in a circle to try to reach the rider on its back. That was certainly entertaining, but I wanted to see what happened with the free hound. It had descended from the trees and charged full speed through the grass toward the working giants next to the city walls. Kalaad, what power there! But it was not a stealthy charge. The Hathrim outside turned and saw it coming and raised the alarm, and one bearded giant stepped forward to meet the charge. He was not armored, but he did have one of those huge axes, and he set it aflame, demonstrating that he was lavaborn also. Though the lavaborn were supposed to be my targets, it would not end well for the hound and I told it to stop and forget it; none of those giants were tasty after all.

In fact, he should sit down until his rider could catch up, and I told the other hound to calm down as well. I knew that those hounds most likely would be involved in the battle later, but I could muster no more anger toward them than I could toward the horse that bore the man who shot Madhep. Let the king's army worry about them: I hadn't been sent to hunt hounds, only giants blessed with the First Kenning. But what could the Sixth Kenning do against fire? I knew of no fire-proof animals.

The giant who'd fallen off his mount groaned audibly and clambered to his feet. He said some things that I assumed were curses and began to jog after his hound, his heavy footsteps crashing through the underbrush. The more competent rider was berating his hound in an angry tone while the lavaborn was standing in place, ready to defend the workers should either hound resume its charge. He was a valid target.

I searched the area with my new senses, hoping a solution might present itself. High up in a grand moss pine perhaps three or four ranks up from where they were clearing trees, a hive of moss hornets reminded me of something Hanima once said: if anybody gave her cause, she'd throw bees in their face. That might actually work. Moss hornets were supposed to be pretty nasty: it was said you felt only the first sting because their venom numbed your nerves and eventually paralyzed you. Didn't know if that would necessarily be true for a giant, but if it didn't work, that hive was probably going to be dead in a few days anyway. I let them know that their hive was in danger and that it was the guy with the fiery axe who had it in for them. It took perhaps half a minute, but a cloud of iridescent black and green descended on that particular giant's head. He roared and flared up, burning some of the hornets, but then the toxins overcame him and the flames died, shortly followed by the rest of him. I supposed with enough moss hornet venom in you everything went numb, including the heart. He keeled right over, and the hornets departed, leaving a shocked and bewildered work detail behind him, and more than a few shouts for help.

Several of the giants worked together to lift the body of the fallen lavaborn and carry him into the city through some gates on the south side; it was good to know they were there. I heard quite an uproar after that—anguished voices raised in lamentation—and then a huge blossoming cloud of flame rose into the air.

"Huh. He must have been someone important," I said to my companions.

"Murr."

"Eep."

The houndsmen went into the city, following everyone else, and for the moment we had the plains to ourselves. I told the horses they could get up.

"Let's put a bit more distance between us and the giants," I said to them all. "I doubt I'll have enough hornets to do that again. Getting rid of the rest of the lavaborn is going to require some study. Preferably out of sight."

With Murr's excellent nose we identified where the limits of the houndsmen's patrol route was in the trees and went a bit farther east to be safe. It didn't matter if the hounds caught our scent the next time they came through; they couldn't tell their riders about us, and I could tell them to go away if they got too close.

We found cover for the horses among the trees, just slightly uphill from the great plain, and I made a dry camp and the futile offer of a belly rub to Murr. Bedding down with a blanket over some piled pine needles, I stared at the rising moon and stretched out with my kenning every so often, counting the animals to get myself to sleep. It was less effective than I hoped. Worry about what to do kept me awake until the moon was directly overhead, when I became aware of some new creatures moving into my range. That gave me an idea that could either work or get me killed. Since all my other ideas would just get me killed, I called it good enough and sighed, finally able to relax and drift off to sleep.

"So who was that lavaborn?" Fintan asked his audience. "Let's find out!" He threw down a sphere and took on the seeming of Gorin Mogen.

Gorin Mogen

The five children that Sefir and I lost to the boil in Olenik died as giants should: by forces larger, stronger than ourselves. Volcanoes, lava dragons, the axe of a worthy foe, or the ever-increasing weight of time—these are noble ways for a giant's fire to be extinguished. We should not die in a cloud of blasted insects!

And yet my son is dead. Seeing him carried in on the shoulders of the work detail, I recognized his beard, but the rest of his face was swollen, blackened and purpled with poison, mountains of fluids and pus bubbling underneath the skin.

My legacy—hope for the future—oh, I will burn them! *Burn them all.* And dump their ashes in the ocean to dwell in cold darkness forever.

Jerin was an artist and a warrior, kind until the very moment he had to be ruthless, already showing that he could be a better man than me. I could not be more proud of him or have loved him more. And now he is ruined.

This city, all the plotting and killing I've done to make it rise from the grasses—what does it matter now? It's all worthless, all for naught, because my son is dead. By triple-damned insects.

Someone had to explain to me what they were because I had never heard of moss hornets before. We have large and poisonous insects in Hathrir, but none behave as these hornets did. No provocation was given, yet they attacked a single target as if they bore a personal grudge: Who has ever heard of such a thing? It wasn't natural. Someone was responsible.

Kill them all.

Immediately before this attack two houndsmen lost control of their hounds. Or more accurately, the hounds did their very best to charge the work detail clearing trees outside the south gates, one of them throwing off his rider completely, and then they both stopped as abruptly as they began. To have two such freakish occurrences happen suggests that it was planned somehow. Both occurred within or at the edge of the woods. I don't know how they did it, but I'm sure it's the Fornish. They must be in the woods, high up the mountain, and they have some kind of pollen- or plant-based devilry to drive creatures into a murderous frenzy. And they plan to attack at dawn or soon after.

Unless it was La Mastik. She might have arranged this to free Olet Kanek from her obligations. She'd be able to return to Tharsif without placing Winthir Kanek in my debt. And she was on the detail with Jerin.

I grabbed my axe and stalked over to her. "La Mastik!" She whirled around at the rage in my tone, and her eyes grew wide as she saw my axe, saw me raise it, saw my intent. "You killed him!"

"What? No, Hearthfire, it wasn't me!"

She took a step back and said something else; I don't remember what, and it doesn't matter. I was going to have that shaved head separated from her shoulders. An inchoate roar ripped loose from my throat as I leapt for her, the axe raised high, already anticipating how much better I'd feel once I heard the crunch of it take her miserable life. "Graaahh!"

Someone rammed into me from the left side, unseen, and caught me off balance; the impact knocked me sideways to the ground, my axe hand trapped under me. Whoever it was followed me down and planted their weight on top of me, guaranteeing only that they would die shortly before La Mastik did.

"Gorin! Gorin!" the person shouted, and it took me a moment to connect that voice to Sefir. It was Sefir who had knocked me down and pinned me, and her hair dangled in my face as she spoke into my ear in lower tones. "You need to stop. La Mastik did nothing."

"She did! She killed him!" I did not bother to modulate my tone.

"No, Gorin. She had nothing to do with it."

"That was no accident! Someone killed him!"

"You're right about that. But it wasn't La Mastik."

"No—" I turned my eyes toward the priestess, who was still backing away, guilt written large on her face.

Sefir's hand cupped my cheek and forced me to turn back to her. "Gorin. We will find out who did it and cut them down together." Tears spilled down her cheeks. "Together, you hear me? But now we need to set him free in flame. We have to say goodbye and let him go."

No!

The rage boiled over, and I exploded in fire. Sefir joined me, and a plume erupted from us both, billowing into the sky as we cried for our son, his lost hopes, all the glass and steel he would never shape, all the battles he would never fight. And when we exhausted ourselves, we were just a bit older, the ground was scorched black in a circle around us, and we were alone.

We did not ask La Mastik to perform the rites. We did not invite anyone to participate in his last fire. He was *our* son. Even when Halsten approached, we shook our heads at him and he understood. He kept everyone else away.

Together we took Jerin's body to our hearth and laid him out on the ground. No longer lavaborn, he would ignite now, his spirit freed from the confines of flesh, and nothing would be left but ashes and his lava dragon hides. We stood over him, and Sefir took my hand in hers.

"He made me proud," she said.

I nodded my agreement and added, "He would have been a stronger Hearthfire than either of us."

"He would have ruled well."

"His art would have been the envy of the world."

"Yes. That magnificent hound and rider he crafted showed the blaze of his gift. Glass of smoke and flame and amber, with blue steel for the rider's axe. I wish we still had it. We lost so much to Mount Thayil."

That was true, but I thought we had lost still more. To insects. *Burn them all.*

"Is it time to tell him?" I asked.

Sefir squeezed my hand. "Yes."

We addressed Jerin directly, in concert: "We love you, Jerin, and your memory will forever burn bright in our hearts. And now we set your spirit free and bid your flesh farewell."

Together we set him alight and watched in silence as he burned away in the night, a process of hours. I know not what Sefir thought during that time, but all I could think of was the vengeance I would wreak on the Fornish. For Sefir was right: La Mastik could not have done this. I had been seized by madness when I attacked her; perhaps I am still in its grip.

I have not slept this night, and it has occurred to me that perhaps I am being alarmist, that the death of my son has banished my reason. But no: the naval watch reported moments ago that the Nentians are sending a significant army against us, marching through the night, and they'll be here at dawn as well, coming from the north. I hope they will be able to see the bones of the first army they sent against me. The Nentians would not be coming unless their Fornish allies were waiting for them on the slopes of the Godsteeth. They no doubt see themselves as the hammer to the Fornish anvil.

I want to burn them all. And I will.

That may, in fact, be the smartest move. Before the Fornish can move against us, we should set the mountainside aflame and see if the light illuminates any greensleeves lurking in the brush. Let them choke to death on the smoke of their precious trees. Or let them run out of the forest and into the blade of my thirsty axe.

Volund is back from Tharsif, having successfully delivered timber to Hearthfire Kanek and secured enough food to last us for months. I will send him up the coast to harass the Nentians on the instant. Let them burn before they even get here.

It is time to armor up. Sefir and I will show them what it means to provoke a Hearthfire. If they want to end the Mogen line, we will make sure they all meet their end with us.

"If we turn back the clock just a wee bit while that was going on, we'll find out what the Fornish were up to under the leadership of Nel Kit ben Sah."

Nel

A successful garden blooms again and again, as the saying goes. Having confronted the Hathrim twice and survived, the sway decided that I'm to be Forn's first Champion in three hundred years or so. Or rather, the First Tree decided. There was some argument at first about who was to lead a party against this city the Hathrim were calling Baghra Khek, with Rig Wel ben Lok of the Yellow Bats and Nef's uncle, Vin Tai ben Dar, arguing strongly in my favor, among many others, but of course the Black Jaguars and the Blue Moths objected and were ready to die upon the hill of Anybody-But-Nel. After an hour of circular wrangling, another voice, rarely heard, spoke in the sway for the first time in living memory, though we all instantly knew to whom it belonged. Slow, rumbling, and strong, vibrating through my silverbark and in my skull, the First Tree said, "Nel Kit ben Sah. You are my Champion. Serve the Canopy well."

The naysayers had to be silent after that. If they protested, they'd be contradicting the First Tree. And if I made the high-pitched noise I wanted to make or went up to Pak Sey ben Kor and spat "Ha!" in his face, I would not be remembered as a dignified Champion.

I consulted strategists, asked the western clans to send me one picked greensleeve each and a bunch of grassgliders and thornhands, and requested siege crews from the Invisible Owl Clan.

Pen was very upset that I did not include her on the team.

"Only one greensleeve from each clan is participating," I explained, "and I'm the one from the White Gossamer Clan."

"But I *need* this, Nel! What they did to my brother—"

"I know, Pen. If you want to see action against the Hathrim, I can station you in the south, where the timber pirates make regular raids. But you're our clan's only other greensleeve. We can't risk both of us on something like this." She huffed, and I continued. "Speaking of risk . . . just in case, I have something for you." I took from my vest a small wooden box and put it in front of her.

"What's this?"

"Every new greensleeve gets one from an elder of their clan. I'm not sure when I'll see you again, and I didn't want you to miss out. Open it but don't touch what's inside."

Pen carefully pushed open the hinge and saw the bantil plant seed inside. "Is this . . . ?"

"Yes. Keep it with you always in case you need it to defend the Canopy." I planted a kiss on her forehead. "I'm proud of you, cousin. I wish I could stay, but I won't have much rest until Gorin Mogen is defeated. After that I can get you properly trained. Perhaps we can spend some time in the south together."

"I would like that," she said.

And I would like it, too, since Nef was from there and I'd have the opportunity to see him more often. We had enjoyed only a single, interrupted outing together, slurping noodles in a swing-by soup cradle, laughing together and almost kissing. We were leaning toward each other, slowly, enjoying the anticipation, when a thornhand found me and said I was needed at the Second Tree for the sway where I was to be named Champion.

"To be continued," I said. Now he was under my command again, part of my siege crew, and we would have to wait a bit longer. That was fine: everything has its season, and budding promise has as much beauty as full flower.

High up on the slopes of the Godsteeth days later, I was in charge of a small army of the blessed intended to soften up the Hathrim before the Nentians, who were marching from the north, arrived in overwhelming numbers. I had my doubts and insecurities. I heard echoes of the criticisms levied by the Black Jaguars and the Blue Moths that I was too young, too inexperienced, to be given such responsibility. I worried that I would lead our forces into disaster or that the Nentians would arrive too late or prove ineffective and the giants would be firmly rooted here forever. But being named Champion by the First Tree appeared to have given everyone else complete confidence in my abilities.

At sundown, grassglider scouts lower down the mountain reported that a huge fireball had risen from the city, generated by two giants, but they had no idea what it signified.

Patrols of houndsmen passed underneath the scouts, unaware of their presence. For all that we are unused to attacking the Hathrim outside our borders, they are just as unfamiliar with defending against us. They are so used to looking down on everything that it never occurs to them to look up into the trees for silent watchers.

Rig Wel ben Lok asked to lead the first siege crew downhill, and I gave him the go-ahead at midnight. Grassgliders positioned themselves around the Invisible Owls, who all had portable pieces of a light catapult that would launch payloads of choke gourds over the walls, and they moved together in utter silence thanks to their kenning. Pods of thornhands with a grassglider each also streamed downhill to chosen locations.

I nodded with satisfaction as each crew and pod quietly mobilized. This is what the Canopy teaches us: grow while they're not looking, silent and strong, and then, just as your competitors become aware that you may pose a problem, you grow thorns and choke them out, and they will fall by necessity.

I caught Nef smiling at me for no reason, his eyes keen to drink in the light of mine. I gave him only the tiniest grin in response, conscious of being watched, before sending him down with a few other grassgliders to spread bantil seeds in front of the southern and eastern gates. He makes me laugh, and it is easy to imagine being happy with him. Nef and Nel. Oh, that would be almost impermissibly adorable.

Bah—I have no time to dream of something that cannot bear fruit now. My mind should be employed anticipating what surprises the Hathrim will throw at us. I am certain they will do something horrific.

"Tomorrow: the Battle of the Godsteeth!" Fintan said.

Day 19

BELOW THE GODSTEETH

This time, at least I got to finish my toast. But my dream of a pleasant morning was crushed as soon as a huge mariner I recognized knocked on my door after breakfast. He was one of the hallway guards in the Wraith's spooky facility.

"He needs to see you now," the mariner said. The thought was as appetizing to me as a spoonful of squid shit.

"He told me I wouldn't have to visit him again." The mariner shrugged. "Right. I'll be out in a moment."

We entered the secret complex by a different route, a door hidden behind some stinking barrels of fish heads and entrails that nearly made me vomit up my delicious toast. Labyrinthine security procedures had to be endured once again before I was dumped into the care of Approval Smile. She had no approval for me this morning, just a crooked finger as a summons to follow her. Ushered into the same dark room with the same dark chair, I was surprised to find a different picture hanging on the wall for me to stare at. No wraith among the trees this time: it was a landscape portrait of Goddess Lake in Rael, with the city of Killae shining on the shore. On the table next to the chair, resting near the single candle, was a journal bound in red leather. A blue ribbon marked a certain page.

The hoarse, wheezing rumble of the Wraith's voice said without greeting, "I'll ask you to look at that journal in a moment. First, are you familiar with Gerstad Nara du Fessett?"

"You must know that I am."

The Wraith attempted a modest clearing of his throat, but it only inspired an epic fit of mucus-filled coughing. He groaned once and apologized when it finally subsided. "You know that she was away on assignment and that now she's returned."

"Yes. A broken arm, I've heard, but otherwise all right."

"More than all right. She's pulled off one of the most stunning espionage missions ever. One that I will tell you about because I made you a promise. But you must understand first that this information can never leave the room. You most especially must share no hint of it with the bard even though you will be sorely tempted to do so."

"The only promise you made me was to tell me if you learned anything about my wife."

"That's correct. I doubt this knowledge will do you any good. I fear it may ruin what little peace you have."

"I have no peace to ruin."

"That's nonsense. After you read the marked page in that journal, you'll look back at yesterday as a time of carefree bliss. Go ahead and read it if you truly wish to know what happened to your wife. Or you could leave it alone and be assured that I—that we—will respond."

I didn't hesitate. I picked up the journal and flipped to the marked page, which had a folded sheet of paper inserted there as well. A flowing script in the Raelech tongue slowed me down.

"Can you read Raelech?" the Wraith asked.

"A little. I'm not as fluent as I'd like to be."

"There should be a Brynt translation in there for you."

When I unfolded the paper, a neat hand in Brynt provided the date: Shalech, Bloodmoon 9, 3041. The autumn before the Bone Giant attacks. The autumn Sarena fell ill.

Master herbalist from Aelinmech believes that a new tinc-
ture, when added to drink, will finally work as a slow-acting
poison that Brynt hygienists will be unable to counteract.
The poison will collect in the liver and remain there, bond-
ing to tissue, rather than flow free in the bloodstream. Liver
failure and death will follow in a few months. I think that
troublesome spy from Brynlön would make an ideal test
subject.

Sarena had died at the end of Barebranch, her skin turning yellow
from jaundice and no help for it as her liver failed. "Whose journal is
this?" I asked, for I was already planning a trip to Rael.

"I will tell you, but there is nothing you can do about it."

"Well, you can toss that notion into the abyss. Whoever this Raelech
is, they're going to die a horrible death."

"Dervan, that is the personal journal of Clodagh of the Raelech
Triune Council."

"*Clodagh*? The militant councillor you said was dangerous now?"

"The same. Though that journal confirms that she has been dangerous all along, working in deep waters."

"Does Fintan know that she ordered my wife's poisoning?"

"I very much doubt it. But you can't ask him about it or even allude
to it, because then Rael would know that we've stolen it. And that
would be an unhappy revelation for us right now seeing as they have
an army already within our borders and marching this way."

I shut my eyes, and my whole body clenched at the effort not to
scream my frustration.

"The last time you looked like that," the Wraith said, "you went to
get your face smashed by Mynstad du Möcher. And it's not healed
yet."

"That won't happen this time. I was helpless to do anything then."

"You still are. You can't do anything right now except wait."

"There has to be more we can do!"

"Clodagh is untouchable right now, but her term ends soon. Her service ended, she'll be returning to her family in the country and be quite vulnerable. And this master herbalist she mentions in Aelinmech needs to be found, records destroyed if possible. We can hope that the formula for this poison has been kept secret."

"Surely they'd figure we were responsible."

"Accidents happen."

I tasted bile in the back of my throat and felt polluted then, as if I'd tried to cleanse a foul cistern by shitting in it. His nonchalant talk of arranging murders placed him in the same moral cesspool as Clodagh—and if I pursued it on my own, I'd be joining them. Had Sarena been one who organized such accidents for others? Whether she had or not, working for the Wraith had gotten her killed. And if I pressed him, he'd say that the good she had done for the country in secret had been worth her early death. But it would never be worth it for me.

My body remained tense for another few moments of anger, but it relaxed when I decided I wouldn't swim anywhere near these long-arms if I could help it. Where would be my profit? I could never fill the emptiness of my wife's absence with Clodagh's death, and I'd come away from the experience forever stained and might not even feel any better afterward. Taking a deep breath and sinking back into the chair, I placed the journal back on the table.

"Thank you for keeping your promise," I said, my voice flat. "Am I dismissed?"

"What? No, I need to make sure you understand how to approach the bard now. You cannot bring up the subject of Clodagh or her journal, and be very careful not to betray anything if he brings it up. I expect he will once their embassy hears about the theft, and that might be soon if they suspect us and sent a courier right away. He could try anything: claim that the journal is blue or that it was a series of papers or anything just to see if you contradict him. He may also bring up your wife's death again to see how you react to that. Just be careful not to betray any knowledge of this journal to anyone. We are in no shape to start a war with the Earth Shapers."

No, we weren't. That made me wonder why he had taken the risk of sending Nara on such a mission. What if she'd been caught? How had she done it? Obviously she had used her blessing to move quickly up the river to Goddess Lake and thence to the capital and back again, but how had she infiltrated the Council chambers? I opened my mouth to ask but thought better of it. If I didn't know, I couldn't betray anything.

"I'll be careful," I said instead, and the Wraith was silent for a while as he considered—well, silent except for his wet, ragged breathing.

"Currents keep you safe," he finally said, and I was free to return to the dubious care of Approval Smile. She led me to the exit by the docks again, and instead of going home or to the armory, I went down to the end of the quay where one could rent a remembrance craft and purchase a basket of white rose petals.

Raelechs like to erect monuments and stone edifices to mark where their people returned to the earth; Kaurians raise flags to blow in the wind; the Fornish plant something unusual when one of their own returns to the roots; the Hathrim have special candles to commemorate the dead; and the Nentians give everything to the sky. But we Brynts consign our dead to the sea, and so when we wish to remember them, we sail out a short way and spend some time alone bobbing on the waves, adding our salt tears to the salt ocean and spreading white petals on the surface, small fragile craft that bear the weight of our thoughts and memories for a while before sinking into the deep to join our loved ones.

I told Sarena that at least we knew who killed her now but I hoped she would forgive me if I left any vengeance to the Wraith.

"That's not the way my river flows," I said. "I suppose I'm not well suited to being a man of action anymore despite my occasional wishes to be. I'm too old, and my knee literally won't stand for it. I know there are those who say if you are not strong, then you are merely a victim in waiting, but I think that's the violent man's way of justifying the evil he does. And it is profoundly simplistic, the sort of thing we heard from the fish heads who used to beat me and Rölly when we were young and living on the streets. I never wanted to believe in that or be the sort of person they were, and I don't think Rölly did either. I think—and it is something I have thought about for a while—that there is a measure of heroism in providing safe harbor. Not actively saving anyone so much as providing the space for them to save themselves. It takes a lot of effort and patience and kindness and a resignation that while you may be thanked, you will never be celebrated for it. Though you did notice every so often. You used to tell me that our home centered you after your missions; it was dependable like the sunrise, the one true and solid thing in your life. For me, that was better than any medal I could have won in a war. Well, I can't be your safe harbor anymore, but I'm trying to be one for another family now. It's the only sort of heroism that suits me in my middle age. And it'll do more good than seeking revenge."

I scattered the rose petals onto the soft churning blue of the ocean, where they bobbed like curling white flags snapping in a distant sky. "I'm still here," I said, "though I'll join you soon enough, my love."

During the row back into shore I determined to record what happened that morning and see if it survived the attentions of the Wraith. He no doubt had keys to my place and perused my manuscript regularly. Perhaps he would see, after tensions were not so high, that keeping the secret was moot. Clodagh had had my wife killed, and we had the proof. Let the Raelechs make a stink like a fishmonger if they wished. Sure, we stole their stuff. But the Earth Shapers could hardly point fingers at us and claim they stood on holy ground. Not anymore.

Fintan seemed especially cheerful when I met him for lunch and work, and I asked him why. "Numa's here," he said. So it was just as the Wraith had predicted: a courier would arrive to inform the Raelech diplomats that some valuable intelligence had been stolen.

"Oh? News from home?"

He shrugged. "I assume so. She's at the embassy now and will meet with the pelenaut later, no doubt. I'll get to see her tonight after the performance."

"That's excellent," I said, and prepared myself for probing questions or statements about the contents of the journal tomorrow. I doubted Fintan was a party to Sarena's murder or even knew that Clodagh was responsible. But he was oath-bound to support the person who murdered her and not, therefore, someone I could trust.

Fintan brought a full complement of musicians with him to the wall for the day's song, which was largely instrumental and an old favorite at Brynt dances. It had only one verse, sung between long breaks of foot-stomping, furious music with a famous flute melody skirling above the rhythm, and the rule was that every time it was sung, the band had to play faster afterward and the dancers had to keep up. People would boast for years about any time they made it beyond six verses without collapsing from exhaustion, and musicians likewise bragged if they could play beyond eight. The words weren't anything special, but by long-standing tradition, whoever sang it had to begin calmly and get progressively angrier with each repetition:

> Well, the sun and the sea and stars up above
> You can always take for given,
> But you never know what will happen next
> With the mariner men and women!

The Raelech bard's band made it to nine repetitions along with two young dancing couples of extraordinary endurance, and then everybody needed a break before he began the day's tales. He started with Hearthfire Gorin Mogen, fully armored, face half obscured by a helmet, and carrying both an axe and an enormous shield that must have been six feet tall.

Gorin Mogen

The Fornish had their plans, no doubt, little scheming weeds they planted with the Nentians, which they hoped would grow and choke us out. The last thing I should do is wait for them to proceed. A warrior's duty, above all, is to shit on the enemy's plans.

Before dawn even grayed the sky, I lit an arrow and shot it over the walls to fall into the needle-covered ground of the mountainside. And then, standing on tiptoe to peer over the walls, I accelerated that fire and spread it along the ground in a line parallel to the wall, illuminating the front ranks of trees, which revealed a Fornish siege crew putting together the interlocking pieces of a catapult. I knew it! *Burn them all.*

I urged the flames up the mountain to surround the crew and then ignite them. Their screams tore into the night, and it was better than birdsong to my ears. Those who killed my son and would kill me and all my people deserved to die in pain.

There would be more of them, no doubt, unseen in the darkness, farther up the mountain. I spread the flames directly uphill from that crew and saw nothing, but they had to be out there. I needed to take them out before they could get set. It turned out that only Sefir and I were armored and ready to go, however. The city had gone to sleep while Sefir and I set Jerin's spirit free. I roared the alarm: we were under attack and needed hounds in the hills, hunting at will.

Halsten got four out the southern gate in a hurry, but they ran into the same flesh-eating plant that the Fornish used on Jerin's patrol. One made it through and up into the hills, but for the others it was a grim business. Three of them immediately showed signs of distress, their paws pierced by those barbed toothy things that grew inside them and ate their muscles and organs. One rider was thrown from his mount, and two held on; I thought perhaps they would have time to jump free, but the hounds spun and caved in on themselves, trying desperately to nip out the pain in their paws, and they flipped onto their sides. One rider's leg was crushed and trapped by his hound going down, and once he hit the ground, I saw one of those horrible toothy blossoms take a mouthful of him as well, and he was helpless to free himself. The other rider leapt clear of his hound before it went down and shouted something at me, looking at the ground beneath his boots, but I couldn't make out the words over the noise the hounds and the trapped rider were making. Soon he was high stepping as if his own feet were in pain; a barbed seed must have pierced through the sole of his lava dragon boots. He was a sparker, though, and before he crumpled to the ground, realizing that they were all dead anyway and he could help clear the way, he set the hounds and himself on fire as well as the land all around the gates. He was immune to the flames until he died, but the third rider, who had been thrown from his mount, was not. He howled as his hair and beard ignited, but strangely, he didn't move otherwise. He must have broken his spine in the fall and become paralyzed.

I ground my teeth. The eastern gate no doubt would be seeded as well. Better to burn through this first gate since the fire was already started, make sure the plants were exterminated, and plow through with armored lavaborn to take on the Fornish.

I added to the flames in front of the southern gate to hasten the end both for the plants and for the houndsmen.

"I want all the lavaborn with me!" I shouted. "Armor and shields and axes! And Halsten, get the rest of your riders ready. Once we're through, you follow behind with the houndsmen!"

I sought out Olet Kanek after that. She was with La Mastik and, seeing me coming, stepped in front of her. She was already armored and carried a sword, I saw, rather than an axe. Serviceable, even fine work, but not up to the Mogen standard.

"I'm not here to fight either of you," I said, putting them at ease.

"Now that Jerin is gone, Olet, your father will no doubt wish you to return to Tharsif. That being the case, I will not ask you to leave the walls with us. But the Fornish have catapults and may try to lob something over the walls. I hope you won't mind burning whatever they send, using your blessing to protect people."

They both stared at me, looking for deception, and I was content to bear it. Most of the lavaborn were still struggling into their armor anyway. Finally, Olet gave me the barest nod. "We will, Hearthfire."

"My thanks." I peered past her to lock eyes with La Mastik. "My apologies for earlier. My anger was . . . misdirected."

She didn't reply, only nodded acknowledgment, but that was good enough. I had a proper focus for my fire now. It was right outside the southern gate. The Fornish would be scrambling to do what damage they could before dawn even as we were scrambling to prevent them. We had traded a few casualties so far, but I looked forward to tipping the scales in our favor. The Fifth Kenning was meant to be burned by the First, and once we dealt with them, the Nentians would be routed just as before, and Baghra Khek would be secure.

Eschewing previous practice, Fintan did not dispel the seeming but put on another one, transforming directly into the greensleeve Nel Kit ben Sah.

I had to stifle a cry when I saw Rig Wel ben Lok and his siege crew combust, their screaming silhouettes outlined in fire. How had Gorin Mogen known we were creeping down the mountain? The grassgliders were making sure we moved in silence. Did this have anything to do with the huge fireball we'd seen rise into the sky near sunset after they'd stopped chopping down trees for the day? Something must have upset him, made him suspicious, eager to lash out.

I thought of recalling the attack, for the element of surprise was gone now and it simply wasn't our season, but if I did that, the Nentians would have no support when they arrived. The Hathrim would huddle behind their walls and wait for them to get close enough to set aflame, and when it was over, they would be nearly impossible to uproot.

So I had to order everyone forward. Speed was our best chance of success now.

I sent Nef Tam ben Wat downhill to the other crews to relay my orders: run directly east, keeping to the trees and the darkness, and then go down to the southeast corner of the city where the clusters of thornhands waited. Mogen might be able to spy the lowest crews at first, but once out of his immediate line of sight, they'd disappear into the darkness and make no sound as they ran thanks to the grassgliders. I withdrew from the kenning of my own crew's grassgliders so that I could be heard and called out for Vin Tai ben Dar, who was the greensleeve for the crew below mine. I doubted Mogen would hear me above the anguished cries of Rig Wel ben Lok's crew.

"Would you accelerate the growth of the bantil plants at the south gate? He's going to send out some houndsmen soon, and if we can clog that gate, it will buy us some time."

"Aye, Champion," he replied—a title I was still getting used to—and fell back with his crew so that he could send out his shoots safely and communicate with the bantil plants. I moved back into the sound bubble of my grassgliders, and together we picked up our pace until we were running at a full sprint, heading east on the mountain. The other crews below were doing the same thing, trying to keep themselves shrouded in darkness. Sometimes they tripped as a result, which I managed to do myself—a fine display of leadership. Any light we used from our glowing fungi bulbs could attract the Hearthfire's attention or that

of the spotters he no doubt would have watching soon, so we kept
them covered.

Once we cleared the fire, we had to descend rapidly at dangerous
speeds to get to the catapults in range. We wouldn't be able to cover
the entire city in spores anymore, but we could at least choke off the
eastern gate and force the Hathrim to use only the southern gate if
they wanted to get at us. And they would. The spores inside the eastern walls would prevent them from targeting us with fire while standing behind them; they'd have to come out to play, and that was the
whole point. Send out your lavaborn where the thornhands can reach
them.

Four houndsmen erupted out of the southern gates, and three of
them were caught by the bantil seeds, taking them out without endan-
gering us. But we were having our own troubles. Moving so quickly
down the steep mountainside, one siege crew went down in a tumble
of limbs and wood and suffered broken bones and in one case a broken
neck. That meant there were only eight crews left, including Vin Tai
ben Dar's, who were still high up on the mountain. He would be moving now, though, his work at the gate with the bantil plants finished.

At the southern gate, nothing more had emerged but the flames had
bloomed higher. They were scouring the area, cleansing it of bantil
plants and seeds. When they felt safe enough, the lavaborn would walk
right through that fire and attack our positions. Our crews needed to
assemble, launch, and retreat if they could, leaving the Hathrim exposed to Nentian archers. But we would never have the luxury of that
time: Mogen had chosen to deal with us first, before the Nentians
could get involved. It was up to us to eliminate the lavaborn.

The black sky dissolved to cobalt in anticipation of the dawn, giving
just enough light to allow our eyes to secure our footing and speed our
descent. I could pick out silhouettes of crews below and the clusters of
the thornhands. One crew had cleared the trees and was busy assem-
bling its catapult just east of that southeastern corner of the Hathrim
city. I dispatched Nef, who already was winded from his prior run,

with orders to have them fire at the eastern gate first. Another team arrived and stationed itself a bit farther east but more forward, constructing its catapult to fire deeper into the city. Another and another, and soon I drew close enough to speak my orders to the thornhands without relays.

"We're going to keep them from coming out at the east, so watch the south—two pods can drift that way now. Lavaborn will be coming out first, and we need them taken out. Then watch for the hounds once they snuff the fires at the gate, and remember there's already one houndsman up in the trees."

I urged my crew forward as the thornhands moved to take up positions behind the trunks of grand moss pines. The first siege crew to set up was ready to fire its first payload of spore gourds at the eastern gate as I passed it, and I noted that it was the crew of the greensleeve sent by the Black Jaguar Clan, Lan Del ben Huf, who was a vast improvement over Pak Sey ben Kor. I nodded at him in passing and watched the first volley wobble into the air, five gourds lobbed north and just slightly west. Four landed inside the eastern gate, and one fell outside of it, an excellent shot, and I heard the soft crack of the shells and the hiss of the escaping spores. The gates had actually begun to open but halted as the gourds fell, spores floating up and into the noses of the giants behind them, burning their sinuses and swelling their throats so that their airways would be choked. We were protected by the Fifth Kenning and had nothing to fear from the spores. I led my team out past all the others, way beyond the trees and fully on the eastern side of the city. We would aim for inside the northern wall, opposite the southern gate. The more giants we could push out into the open, the better for the Nentians.

Looking back as the crew began its assembly work, I saw all the remaining crews either launching or preparing to launch except for Vin Tai ben Dar's lagging group, which was only now emerging from the trees and heading in our direction. He had done us a tremendous service by slowing down the giants at the southern gate,

but as he grew closer, I could see that he had paid for it, pushing the
bantil seeds so fast from such a distance. He looked much older and
moved more slowly, crags on his face appearing like the rugged bark
of the grand moss pines. He called a halt next to my crew, and I gave
him a quick hug and murmured words of praise as he took heaving
breaths. We broke apart as the shrieking song of thornhands split
the dawn: Mogen's lavaborn had poured through the fire of the
southern gate, armor and axes aflame, and charged to the east to
take out our catapults.

That was around the corner of the wall from me, though, so I
dashed back toward the trees to see what new poison they were sprouting.

Fintan returned to himself and held out his hands, forestalling any applause.

"As this was happening, Gorin Mogen's trusted firelord, Volund, had
taken a glass boat north and spotted the dark mass of the Nentian
army advancing on the Hathrim city in the early dawn. He was the
only lavaborn among a crew mainly employed in rowing against the
prevailing current. But a single firelord can do tremendous damage
with the ability to spark, stoke, and spread flames. Squeezing a mixture
of dung and hay around the tip of an arrow, he used his kenning to
ignite it and shot it in a shallow arc to the grasses of the plains. Since
most of the Nentians were already looking at the inferno combusting
the flanks of the Godsteeth, few of them saw the single flicker off to
the west, and when it disappeared into the grasses, there was no need
to comment or raise the alarm. But Volund had only begun his work.
Dropping his bow to clatter in the bottom of the boat, he stretched out
with his kenning and pushed those flames through the grasses toward
the Nentian army, and once they reached the westernmost flank of the
forces, he spread them to the north and south to illuminate them, relieving the dim silhouettes of early morning. Shouts of alarm spread

among the ranks, and near the front, where the mounted men were bunched, the horses shied and whinnied, and Volund grinned. The flames gave him a glimpse of a Nentian armored in bright, beautiful colors, no doubt their leader, and Volund directed the flames to spread in his direction, and once they arrived under the horse carrying him, he pushed hard and fanned those flames to engulf both horse and rider. He could hear their screams carry across the plains and the water, and he smiled, taking a moment to rest. The effort had drained him, and the Nentian forces churned and reared and shouted in panic. The fire was still there, waiting to be directed or simply burn on its own, and he could afford a short span of time to marshal his strength for another push.

"Except he discovered a short six breaths later that he was profoundly mistaken. The mass of men behind the cavalry rippled, a wave of shadow passed among them, and then the sky darkened from a deep blue to black off to the east. A massive light-sucking flight of arrows blocked out the nascent sunrise, and Volund's mouth dropped open as he recognized his mistake. Whoever he had killed, it wasn't the only person capable of assessing the situation and giving quick, efficient orders. There was no evasive maneuver they could execute, no shields they could raise above their heads. He spoke a quick prayer to Thurik, and then the shower of arrows rained upon him and his crew, cutting them down and leaving their lifeless boat at the mercy of the western ocean tides.

"Volund's mistake was this: the immolated Nentian had not been the King's Tactician Diyoghu Hennedigha but rather Junior Tactician Senesh—younger brother of Viceroy Bhamet Senesh—dressed purposely in the brightest regalia possible as a decoy. It was a position of honor precisely because of its danger. And so the Nentians marched on toward the Godsteeth and Baghra Khek."

Fintan threw down a seeming sphere and changed back into Gorin Mogen, this time dressed for battle, axe and armor aflame and teeth clenched in a savage grin.

Gorin Mogen

In my youth, before I became a Hearthfire, I used to be a timber pirate until I rose to captain my own ship and then take over Harthrad from my sire. We had to deal with thornhands as a matter of course when we raided the Fornish coast, and I had forgotten how much I enjoyed thwarting them. They are freakish creatures who become instruments of death at the sacrifice of their own lives. But they are not unstoppable. No Fornish hardwood can penetrate Mogen steel.

Sefir and I led a cluster of lavaborn, six-foot-high shields carried purposely on our right sides as an impenetrable barrier, the wall of the city on our left as we jogged east to take out the catapults that were launching spores into the city. We heard the thornhands before we saw them. They chose their targets and quite literally planted themselves, the bones of their legs and feet cracking and transforming into strong taproots plunging into the earth, and from those roots they drew strength to trigger the rest of their violent metamorphosis, a shuddering, excruciating, and fatal process of converting flesh and blood to wood and sap and flame-resistant resin. As they died, the thornhands sent up a spine-shivering wail both from their throats and from the abrupt growth of their arms from muscled sinews into spined spears that shot out from a melting body to seek out a target, find soft flesh to pierce, invade, and sprout new thorns until something vital was shredded. Four from the first pod attacked our formation, lethal branches of thorns penetrating our wreath of flame, searching for weakness, but only one slipped through shields and axes and armor to pull down a giant.

Sefir and I were both targeted, but I batted away one thorned spear with my axe and we deflected the others with our shields. The formation shifted and closed up to take the place of the one fallen giant, and we advanced in lockstep, because there is a silken unconscious flow to battle at times, when there is nothing but blood to let and blood to lose and all senses are tuned to survival rather than conversation. The wit departs, and instinct takes over. And it was my instinct to kill all the Fornish I saw for killing my son.

I sparked the arm of the nearest catapult, and once it kindled, I directed fingers of flame to lance out and ignite the hair of all the crew. I made sure to spread an extra portion to the greensleeve, igniting his silverbark arms as well as his hair, and as he and his crew cried out in pain and horror, I knew that we would prevail so long as we could outlast the thornhands.

There is no preventing their transformation; one cannot preemptively kill them before they take their shot, because even while on fire, they have enough time to strike back before they die. All one can do, therefore, is survive their attacks, and flame-resistant is not the same as flameproof.

Searching for a new target, my eyes slipped past the next couple of catapults to a diminutive blond woman, a greensleeve, staring at me with her fists clenched. A dark-haired man who wasn't a greensleeve but might have some other kenning demanded her attention and pointed to something on the eastern side of the city, out of my sight around the corner of the wall. She nodded at him and jogged that way, which made me curious. What were the Fornish up to around the corner, and who was this man to give her orders? I thought that greensleeves ran things among the Fornish in the field. Perhaps she was the leader after all and he had merely delivered a message. The man remained behind, staring at me, but I let my attention refocus on the catapults; though he was no threat, they were.

I set the next crew on fire as Sefir barked a warning that another thornhand attack was incoming. We were ready and deflected them all this time, the thorns unable to penetrate our shields and then unable to quest beyond or around them as our protective flames blackened them to char.

My awareness of fire registered the conscious snuffing of the flames behind us at the southern gate. Halsten and the houndsmen were ready to ride, and I heard them yip in excitement as he gave the order. We were not the only ones who heard that: movement in the trees revealed the next pod of thornhands, who were moving to intercept and let us pass by—not a bad decision strategically. The hounds would be more vulnerable, with significant gaps in their armor and no shields or axes. But the houndsman who had escaped in the first sally and disappeared uphill returned, plowing into the pod, with the hound snapping up a thornhand in its jaws; the rider's long poleaxe cut two more in half with a single sweep of steel and sprayed blood, leaving only one who had ducked with an opportunity to exact revenge. She screamed as the change shook her, and her hands and arms first lengthened and then shot into the backs of both the hound and the rider, in the hound's case entering directly underneath the tail. They convulsed but kept going because of their momentum as the thorns grew and spread inside them, and it was only a bare second longer until they passed the limit of the thornhand's accelerated growth. Their immense combined mass pulled her roots out of the ground, but the thorns also pulled out of the hound and rider, yanking steaming entrails with them into the dawn and toppling them both; all three died together.

It was a grisly and distracting reminder of what a thornhand can do if one is not vigilant. And two full pods chose that moment to attack us simultaneously—eight suicidal tree fanatics willing to die to take just one of us down because we might need firewood someday. Except that this time more than one of us fell. There were so many thorned spears coming at once, creaking and popping the way wood does, that it was overwhelming. Sefir and I were scratched, and deeply, but nothing hooked and held on because we crouched behind our shields, took the impact of the spears, swept the edges with our axes, and flared up until the thorns lost their animation. Sefir glanced at me, dressed in flame and steel, blood sheeting down one cheek, a small grin on her face.

"Burn them all," I said.

"For Jerin," she replied, "and for us. For our people."

She will always be my love.

We rose together, our formation tightened behind us again, and we continued east along the southern wall. Sefir and I sparked the next catapult and its crew together just as it launched, which was delightful overkill. The music of their screams drowned for a moment a building thunder in the ground. We felt it before we heard it, and we heard it before we saw it. Out past the dark-haired Fornish man who'd sent the blond greensleeve out of sight, tall shapes loomed above the grasses, gray-skinned things difficult to see in the gray twilight. They were singular in that they appeared to be my height—twelve feet, easily. And they were coming straight at us.

Massive beasts, wicked horns and tapered snouts, moving at speed, and we had no cover—

"Sefir, run! We must make the corner!" I said, and lengthened my stride. The Fornish man turned around, saw them coming—saw the *kherns* coming; that's what they were called—and scrambled out of sight the same way the greensleeve had gone. "Hug the wall!" I said, and shuffled a few strides to the left, thinking that perhaps the kherns would pass by us. But they altered course to match us—this was no natural stampede! It was a calculated attack, just like the attack on Jerin. The Fornish must have found the Sixth Kenning and gained control over animals—confirmed, almost as I thought it, by Halsten's swearing behind me. I looked over my shoulder and saw that the houndsmen, who had been charging right behind us, were now fighting their hounds as they turned around and ran directly west, toward the ocean.

No matter. There was another way to control animals. "Burn them, Sefir!" I said, and we sent gouts of flame toward the vanguard, lighting up the fine hairs on their heads and setting their skin to bubbling. They bellowed and keened but kept coming, shaking the ground as they churned through the remnants of the burned catapults, smashing them to splinters, grinding the bodies of the Fornish crews into paste. I drew a line of fire in the grass ahead, and Sefir added hers to it until it rose to our height, a wall of flame to dissuade the kherns from continuing. But they plowed through it, snuffed it as they came, and we had not yet reached the corner.

Panic gripped me as I realized that I could not stop them after all, and I did not know if I could make the corner. Gorge rose in my throat at the thought of a collision. I doubted I'd survive it, and even if I did, there were more of them behind the leaders; if I went down, I'd be trampled by the boil, and even my armor might not protect me against such weight and force. A better death than moss hornets, to be sure, but I did not want it to be mine. "Come on!" I roared to Sefir, and sped up without a care for protecting myself against thornhands, having no other choice. If I played it cautious now, I would be bowled over and churned into the earth.

Thunder and fire, horns and steel, sprinting to outrun a crushing death: I had never felt so alive. I saw the small black eyes of the kherns focused on me and felt their desire to ram their horns through my guts. The ground shook, my lungs heaved, and my legs strained, the corner only a couple of lengths away, the leading fire-mad khern a couple of lengths beyond that.

He wanted the collision because he knew he would win, and I wanted desperately to deny him.

"Gorin!" Sefir cried, fear in her voice. "We won't make it!"

I couldn't look around, couldn't lose an inch of momentum. "We will! Just . . . jump!"

My muscles convulsed as I reached the corner and leapt out of the path of the oncoming khern, to my left and its right, its bellow deafening me as it realized it was going to miss. One of the horns knocked against the wall with a hollow thunk, and then there was the crash, scrape, and shudder of flesh and bone against stone and steel. When I hit the ground, I kept rolling out of the path in case any of the kherns following chose to pursue me, but they kept going straight on. By the time I stopped and rose to one knee, they were past. There were pods of thornhands emerging from their cover in the foothills and following the boil, presumably to make sure the houndsmen were contained. They ignored me, which I thought strange: Weren't the lavaborn their primary concern? There were four more catapults here, unprotected except by their greensleeves, and they were highly flammable.

"Sefir!" I called. "They're past. Where are you?"

No answer. I didn't see her either. I clambered to my feet to get a better view, since she was probably lying prone in the grass. But I didn't see her at all. "Sefir?" She had been right next to me, perhaps a step behind on my right shoulder. She should have made it. "No, no . . ."

Returning to the corner, I peered around it and beheld ruin. The leading khern we had set on fire was sprawled on the ground, gouges in the wall and in the earth, its corpse smoking, its end hastened by Sefir's axe in its skull. The rest of the boil had trampled through and was still moving to the ocean, thornhands jogging behind them. My lavaborn littered the ground in their wake, including Sefir. She was not merely unconscious—she was broken, her bones caved in, vital organs punctured by crushed ribs, the once beautiful face inside the helmet a shapeless pulp, a smashed fruit.

My love—all I had left to live for—was a bloody ruin.

"Sefir . . . I am so sorry." Had anyone attacked me then, I would not have fought. Tears welled, spilled into my beard. "I was wrong to bring us here." I set her body aflame to set her free of the flesh. "I won't be far behind." I set all the lavaborn alight, apologizing to them as well, and realized that was why the thornhands had written me off. Only I had escaped the boil of kherns, and weighed against a pack of houndsmen, how much damage could one giant do?

I would show them.

Shrouding myself in fire, shield shifted to my left arm and axe in my right hand, I roared and turned on the four remaining catapults.

Fintan threw down a black sphere, shrinking down directly once more from Gorin Mogen to Nel Kit ben Sah.

The thornhands made a mistake that might have killed us all—an understandable mistake, but no less dire. A boil of stampeding kherns thundered past, slamming into the lavaborn and presumably on to a pack of houndsmen that I heard baying, and they chose to pursue them rather than make sure all the lavaborn were dead. Perhaps they were drawn by the fact that the kherns appeared to be under the control of a single Nentian man riding on the back of the rearmost khern, black straight hair streaming behind him, a hawk of some kind cruising in the air just above him and a single bloodcat, of all things, trailing behind the boil. It made my jaw drop open at the implications: Had the Nentians finally discovered, at long last, the fabled Sixth Kenning? Did they have control over animals and not really require our help to defend their lands?

But Gorin Mogen missed all this when he got to his feet. He glanced briefly in our direction, then went to discover what had happened to the rest of the lavaborn. When he found out, he would come for us, and our siege crews had no thornhands to fight him: only four greensleeves and the lesser blessed, such as grassgliders and culturists, who had few fighting skills.

I followed branches of strategy to their ends, and none would support any weight except for the most desperate one, though why should it give me pause when thornhands had to confront the reality of it as soon as they were blessed by the First Tree?

Mogen set the bodies of the fallen lavaborn aflame, or at least I think he did, since I could see only him and not their bodies. But the flame shooting from his axe pointed down, and his body wilted like a water-starved violet, so I doubted he was attacking anyone. When he was finished, though, his giant form blossomed into orange flame and he turned our way with a roar audible even over the distance and the din. Nef Tam ben Wat was directly east of him, and Mogen's eyes found him for a single fearful moment and then slid past, dismissing the grassglider as a threat because several members of the closest siege crew had the brilliant idea of lobbing some gourds his way. Mogen destroyed them in midair with fireballs, but the effort visibly tired him; it was too much energy to expend at once, unlike sparking something small and spreading it. He did that next, setting the catapult aflame and then spreading it to the crew, as he'd done with the others. Three catapults remained, but their crews hadn't seen Mogen coming yet, so intent were they on fulfilling their mission and forcing the Hathrim out into the open. My head turned to the north, where the first sun's rays revealed a smudge of the approaching Nentian army on the horizon. We needed to flush the giants outside their walls to make them easy targets for the Nentian archers; the Hearthfire needed his people to stay in there if he wanted a chance to prevail, so he needed those catapults destroyed, and he was justified in thinking he could do it all by himself.

The Hearthfire charged with his teeth bared, hefting his axe and keeping his shield in front of him. He took huge strides, building up speed, passing by the writhing figures of the crew he'd just set aflame and forgoing his kenning altogether to attack the next crew with an axe he probably had forged himself. And running on a course that was not exactly parallel but still coming my way, shouting and waving his hands, was Nef Tam ben Wat, trying to warn the next crew that they were in mortal peril. Over the din of the field I couldn't hear him as his mouth moved silently, speaking doom like distant lightning whose thunder never reaches your ears.

The greensleeve in charge of the crew, a member of the Green Beetle Clan, finally heard Nef's shouted warning in time to witness but not avoid the blow coming from his blind side, a scything sweep that cut the greensleeve in half and smashed the light wood of the catapult to kindling. The surviving members of the crew bunched

together around the catapult attempted to scatter, but Mogen killed
four at once by leaping horizontally and landing on his six-foot shield,
flattening them underneath it with an audible crunch and then an
awful silence. Nef flinched at the horror of it as Mogen rolled and
rose like a grinning avatar of death with the gore of our countrymen
sliming his shield. But then Nef resumed his run to warn the next
crew that Mogen was coming, and he did so with utter unconcern
for his own safety, since the Hearthfire could see him and set him
aflame whenever he wished. Nef didn't care; he was putting others
first. And in that moment, completely out of its proper season, the
small sprouts of springtime affection I had nurtured for him bloomed
into summertime love. He was a truly good man. Together as Nef
and Nel we would be almost sickeningly cute. But there were only
two catapults left. And only two Fornish truly capable of stopping
Gorin Mogen.

Vin Tai ben Dar, the greensleeve from Nef's clan who had taken
him to his Seeking years ago, saw Mogen coming and ordered his
crew to scatter with a gourd each, leaving the catapult unguarded.
"Surround him and throw your spores!" he shouted, and they spread
out to encircle him. Mogen came to a halt, stood in place, and peered
down at them, apparently unconcerned, maybe even slightly amused.
Trying to take him out with the spores wasn't a terrible stratagem
except that Mogen was clearly ready for it. He waited and watched
Vin, his eyes daring the greensleeve to proceed. And Nef, seeing that
I was watching this unfold, came to a halt himself. My siege crew still
had no idea and continued to work on launching gourds over the
walls.

Vin called out for his crew to throw their gourds, and Gorin Mogen
took a deep breath, crouched, and expelled a wave of fire from him in
all directions as the gourds came his way. They melted or exploded,
and any spores that escaped were singed in the air, never reaching him.
A few members of the crew, including Vin, were caught in the fire blast
and fell away, rolling in the grass and trying to smother the flames.

After that effort, however, Mogen's face was a mask of pain and he was slow to get to his feet. The exertion of that kenning exacted a heavier toll, perhaps, than he had expected, and it did nothing to improve his mood despite saving him from a likely defeat. When he did rise from his crouch, he took his anger out on the catapult with his axe, reducing it to splinters with repeated blows and ignoring the Fornish, who presented no threat to him. I surged forward and told my crew to abort the mission and run for cover in the forest, taking any surviving member of Vin's crew with them if they could. Then I backed away from the catapult, fading as much as I could back into tall grasses. There was only one way to stop him, and none of the others had thought to do it because greensleeves are taught to think of preservation above all, including self-preservation. But while I had much to lose, Gorin Mogen no longer had anything to lose: I assumed he lost his hearth to the boil of kherns, because she was lavaborn, too. So he would kill and kill until the plains were scourged clean of his enemies or one of them found the courage to do what needed to be done.

Vin Tai ben Dar was in no shape to do it, and his actions already had demonstrated that he did not see the only branch leading to victory. If I did not do it, no one would. Mogen would destroy our catapults, retreat inside his walls, burn the Nentian army, and wait for reinforcement from Hathrir. The Canopy would be forever in danger from Hathrim predation if I did not stop him. How could I refuse such a clear duty? I sent out silverbark shoots from both my shins and my forearms to plunge into the earth. I sent out all of them.

"What are you doing?" a tiny voice broke through the noise. It was Nef, suddenly running toward me again, one hand outstretched, pleading. "Nel, don't try it!"

My mouth twisted in regret. He and I would have been such a winsome couple. The garden we would have grown together would have been lush and fragrant and nurturing, and I truly should have kissed him when I'd had the chance. I longed to kiss him now. But I could not possibly place my happiness above the safety of the Canopy. "I'm sorry,

Nef," I said softly, doubting he would hear me, but I imagined he could read my lips well enough, and that would have to be our farewell.

I tore my eyes away and heard him shout "No!" but he didn't matter anymore. All that mattered was defeating Gorin Mogen. The roots, at least, were already there, coaxed from the trees on the hills to lash the catapults in place by each crew's greensleeve. But now they must do more, take on girth and strength, for Mogen was not inanimate timber; he was a giant firelord. Making that happen, channeling that energy and forcing that rapid growth so far from the Canopy, required will and strength I might not actually possess.

My fingernails dug into my palms as I concentrated and let my consciousness meld with the trees, forcing pulp and sap to move and grow by my command. The buildup began as Mogen finished dismantling Vin's catapult. The roots bulged and stirred underneath it, the earth bubbled, and then the first thick rope whipped out toward the Hearthfire even as he lifted his gaze to seek his final target. The pine root twined around Mogen's left leg, and he immediately kindled it, setting his body and armor aglow with new fire. He raised his axe to hack at it, an awkward proposition because it was in his right hand and he could not easily target the root behind him on the left. He tried to pivot to get a better angle, but I had never stopped building and growing: more roots erupted from the earth to encircle his right leg and hold him in place. I was sweating, my entire body ached, and my nails had opened up cuts in my palms, but that was fine. Mogen wrenched his left leg free with a roar and took a step before fresh roots shot out of the ground to entangle him anew.

The eye sockets of his helmet were fireballs, nothing human in them anymore, only rage, and they scoured the area for the source of this attack—it had to be a greensleeve. He remembered seeing Vin Tai ben Dar, searched for him, and found his body smoking in the grass yet still moving. He sent a fresh blanket of fire out from his axe to alight on him, making sure he would perish, and then he sparked my catapult, the last one, which was a useless hulk without a crew to operate it anyway. The roots still held him and indeed kept thickening in spite of his efforts to burn them away, so he let his gaze roam farther afield. That was when he saw me and perhaps recognized me. Our eyes had met briefly after he'd destroyed the first catapult, then Nef had come to tell me my crew needed me to lash the catapult down with roots. Yes, he recognized me, perhaps even understood that I was the Fornish Champion. He certainly understood that the shoots leading from my silverbark into the earth meant I was the one wrapping him up in pine.

He snarled and pointed his axe in my direction, and a gout of flame blossomed and arced toward me. It was a significant distance to project, fifteen lengths, perhaps, so I saw it coming and knew what would happen. I gritted my teeth around a sob and sent my final instructions through the roots with concentrated fury: fury that he thought he could take whatever he wanted, that he had in fact taken so much already, that he would take my life as well.

The trail of fire split into three fingers as it neared me while behind Mogen thicker roots emerged from the earth and reached out for him like longarm tentacles. That was when the flame landed on me, and I shrieked my pain into the suffocating heat, my body a pillar of orange blossoms on a black bough, my skin crisping and melting, my silverbark turning into glowing coals, my final defiance and the dregs of my strength carried through the shoots before they crumbled into ash. Through the flames, I saw the roots wrap themselves over the giant's shoulders, underneath his arms, and around his neck. His bellow of outrage was cut short as the roots constricted his throat. A moment later, my last command was executed and the roots convulsed, squeezing in concert and pulling in five directions. Gorin Mogen's four limbs ripped free of his torso, and his head popped off, extinguishing his fires and showering the grasses with his blood, and though I still burned and felt only pain, cried only pain, I saw the sky, and it was so blue now, no longer gray, except it was moving and going dark at the edges, all black—

Fintan dispelled the seeming of Nel Kit ben Sah and spoke into silence:

"To Nef Tam ben Wat's ears, there was no finer sound than the final heavy clank of Gorin Mogen's armor hitting the ground. And there was nothing more horrifying than the sound of Nel screaming as she burned. She toppled backward, crying out, wreathed in orange and yellow, billowing black smoke, and Nef could think of nothing to do but kick dirt on her in an effort to smother the flames. He kept at it even after her screams passed into silence and her body crumpled and shifted as it was consumed. He kept at it so that something of Nel would remain long after Mogen's corpse had rotted and fed the scavengers of the plains.

"When he finally subsided, chest heaving and tracks of tears streaking his dusty cheeks, the fire was snuffed and what remained was only a vaguely human-looking mound of dirt. A shout caused him to look up. One of the Invisible Owls of Nel's crew was pointing to the city. There, waving above the walls, a ragged white tent canvas affixed to a narrow pine trunk signaled surrender.

" 'Good,' Nef said, nodding once. He had forgotten that there were still plenty of giants hiding behind those walls, and just as quickly as he'd been reminded, he forgot them again. He knelt next to Nel's body and waited for something to move. When it did, he leaned over and gently blew dirt away, brushing off small clumps of it with the tips of his fingers so that the leaves of the rapidly growing silverbark sapling could drink in the morning sun. Nef made a strangled sound halfway between a laugh and a sob, then smiled as fresh tears spilled down his face. 'There you are, Nel,' he said, his voice almost a whisper. 'There you are.' "

Fintan sighed and said nothing for a few moments, and some sniffles could be heard. Maybe one or two of those were mine. I thought perhaps he would end there, but instead he withdrew a new black sphere and held it aloft between his fingers. "The Mogens defeated, most of the lavaborn slain, and surrender indicated, the Battle of the Godsteeth was over. But for the aftermath, we'll hear from that young Nentian man who trampled over the lavaborn with a boil of kherns." He dropped the sphere, and a plume of black smoke rose around him.

bbi

For both the hunter and the hunted, there is always terror right before death. The hunter terrified he won't eat, the hunted terrified of being eaten. There is defiance and desperation and even bloodlust. But those kills are quick. A torn throat, a snapped spine, or a spear to the heart, and the suffering is over. There is no reveling in pain and grinning at screams the way the Hathrim do when they set people on fire.

The smell of those poor burned Fornish people is in my nose, and I may be sick. And the khern that died in the charge—I was so involved in directing it to trample the lavaborn that I felt its agony and its confusion at what was happening as it burned and then took an axe to the head. That was my fault. I was responsible. I would add it to my toll.

And the Hathrim, too, of course. Though I supposed that my efforts, together with those of the Fornish, had prevented the Nentian army from suffering much in the way of casualties. By taking twenty or so lives I had perhaps saved thousands. I still wished it hadn't been necessary.

We drove the houndsmen to the sea, where I commanded the hounds to sit down in the shallows while the kherns formed a wall, an intimidating front in case any of the Hathrim had ideas about charging on foot. Most of them, unable to stay comfortably in the saddle when their mounts were sitting and refused to stand, dismounted and stood next to them in the shallows.

Thornhands joined us, standing in front of the kherns, daring the Hathrim to try anything. If any of them were lavaborn, they didn't reveal it. They didn't surrender, but neither did they fight. We just stared at one another, promising violence if the other made any advances, and I was content to let that stand until someone thought of a way to defuse tensions. The white flag that waved over the walls of the city, signaling surrender, caused a ripple of dismay to run through the houndsmen, but they made no comment. I asked them politely to drop their weapons into the surf or the thornhands might have to take it as a given that they would attack, and after one of them with silver thread in his mustaches translated, they complied. We did nothing else, though, since none of the Fornish thornhands were in a position to accept surrender and neither was I as a contracted mercenary. We had to wait for the Nentian army to arrive.

Viceroy Melishev Lohmet rode up eventually, along with a senior tactician he called Hennedigha and a somewhat short Raelech man carrying nothing but a harp. He looked at me sitting on top of a khern, a stalk hawk sitting on my shoulder and a bloodcat waiting patiently below, and his eyes grew to the size of dragon eggs. I smiled and waved at him so he would know I was friendly.

The viceroy apparently had met one of the houndsmen before, a flame-haired brute who scowled as soon as the viceroy appeared.

"Hello again," Melishev said as he reined in behind the thornhands. "Your Hearthfire and hearth are both dead. The city has surrendered. Have you surrendered as well?"

"We have not."

He craned his neck to look up at me. "Where are their weapons?"

"I made them drop them into the tide." So the giant was all bluster.

"Perhaps you should rethink not surrendering," the viceroy said, turning back to him, "considering the odds and the fact that your hounds won't obey you." The giant flicked a murderous glare up to me but said nothing. "Tell me your name again."

"Lanner Burgan. Where is Korda?"

"He died in a terrible accident, I'm afraid. My condolences. So! Lanner. Who's in charge of your city now? Who speaks for you?"

He spat into the ocean. "I don't know. We don't even know who waved those surrender flags."

"Well. I'll give you the same deal I'm going to give them: you can get on those glass boats and sail the fuck away from Ghurana Nent, or I have all these archers who are just itching to bring down a giant. You choose."

His eyes flicked to the giant with threaded mustaches standing next to him, indicating that perhaps he wasn't the actual leader here, but then he scoffed. "Let me know who's in charge in the city and what they say. Then I'll give you my answer."

A play for time. The viceroy craned his neck to look up at me. "Are you okay with standing guard a while longer?"

"I think the thornhands will do just fine, along with the kherns. Neither they nor the hounds will move until I say so. I'll come with you." Melishev didn't look pleased by that, but he could hardly cast any doubt on my abilities thus far. I needed to stay close to him so that he couldn't give an order to have me meet with an unfortunate accident. And besides, I wanted to see the inside of this Hathrim city and talk to the Raelech, so I hopped down, realizing too late that normal people don't hop off the backs of kherns. The bard was waiting.

"I'm Fintan, Bard of the Poet Goddess Kaelin," he said. "And you are?"

"Abhinava Khose. A plaguebringer . . . of the Sixth Kenning, I guess."

"Plaguebringer! Fascinating. I do hope we get to talk more."

"I'd be delighted. This stalk hawk is Eep, and this bloodcat is Murr."

We followed the viceroy and tactician into the "city," which was nothing more than a wall surrounding a bunch of tents and fire pits and a very large well. There were, to be fair, a couple of buildings under construction: a forge, no doubt, and perhaps a public house. Still, it had potential as a city site now—a Nentian one. We could benefit from those walls and the well, too.

The mass of Hathrim had collected against the walls nearest the harbor gates, away from where the Fornish had launched those exploding gourds full of spores. Some of them were prone and coughing up blood anyway, loud racking heaves that sounded like imminent death.

"Who's in charge?" Hennedigha called to them. Two women came forward. One was twelve feet tall and had some light armor on but no helmet. She had red hair and might have been attractive if she weren't so huge. The other was a couple of feet shorter but was completely bald. She had earrings and a brightly colored chain leading from her nose to her ear and wore a shimmering dress of white and orange.

"I am Olet Kanek," the redhead said, "daughter of Winthir Kanek, Hearthfire of Tharsif, and this is La Mastik, Priestess of the Flame."

We introduced ourselves, including the Raelech, and then the viceroy asked Olet, "Are you lavaborn?" The priestess would be by default.

"Yes. I'm a firelord."

"Can you put out that fire on the mountain?"

She looked at the blaze for a few moments and shook her head. "Not by myself. But I can contain it, keep it from spreading."

"That would be appreciated," he said. "We'll let you get to that in a moment. But first, why is a daughter of Winthir Kanek here?"

"I was betrothed to Jerin Mogen."

"I see. And where is he?"

"Dead. And his parents with him, I imagine."

"Right you are. So, the terms of your surrender are simple: Stop the fire. Then get on your boats and sail back to Hathrir. Or die here."

She glowered at him for a moment, then nodded. "May I offer a third option that will be to our mutual benefit?"

He made her wait before saying, "Go ahead."

"There is nothing for me—or for many of us—back in Hathrir. My father will simply arrange another political marriage for me, and most of us can expect less welcome than that. We will choke on ash from Mount Thayil, and our keeping will be begrudged. But we can be of use to Ghurana Nent, and you can offer us a home—in the Gravewood."

Hennedigha gave a short bark of laughter. "In the *Gravewood*? Nonsense." He shook his head, but the viceroy pretended he hadn't spoken.

"What did you have in mind?"

"A city surrounded by rich resources open to people of all kennings or of no kenning. Far in the north, above Ar Balesh. We'll build the road to the northern coast as we go. All the taxes benefit Ghurana Nent, and you will have a new center of commerce in addition to this site's potential. We few Hathrim can help fuel your country's expansion."

Melishev looked perplexed. "But you'll be eaten by gravemaws or worse."

"Even gravemaws are afraid of fire."

"If it were that easy, it would have been done already."

"You have not heard me say it would be easy. You are correct that we may die. And if we do, what do you care? But if we succeed, Ghurana Nent's coffers will be filled. To us it is preferable to returning to Hathrir. Please consider it. We were not brought here of our own free will. We came with the Mogens because they had a way to escape Mount Thayil, that is all. Now they are dead, and we reject their plan to take this land by force. We have no desire to invade but a desire to coexist and fill the coffers of your government—with your permission."

"Let me think on it," the viceroy said. "How many more lavaborn do you have?"

"There are only we two," Olet said, hooking a thumb at the priestess. I wondered why she shaved her head.

"If I may," the bard broke in, "which tent was Gorin Mogen's?" Olet pointed out a large one near the southern gate. "May I look inside?"

The giantess shrugged. "Of course. Take whatever you like. They are gone. They are no relations of mine. We have no interest in their possessions or secrets."

The bard spun around immediately and ran at top speed for the tent. He emerged a short while later carrying a journal, and it reminded me that Melishev carried one as well. I stole a glance at his tunic and saw the telltale outline of it in his pocket. He only had eyes for Olet Kanek.

"Stop the fire," he said to her. "Remain here until the morning. Understand that you're surrounded by twenty thousand men and your good behavior will go a long way toward deciding what we choose. We'll give you an answer then."

She nodded, and we departed, returning to the standoff at the oceanside. Once we explained, Lanner and the other houndsmen agreed to throw in their lot with Olet Kanek, and then, much to everyone's surprise, I said I'd join them.

"You'll join . . . the Hathrim?" Melishev said.

"Well, if they'll have me, sure. I'd like to see the Gravewood if you let them do that. I can protect everyone from the animals there. And I'll be out of your way, Viceroy." I saw immediately that this idea appealed to him.

"As you wish," he said, and the sly look in his eyes told me he'd do his best to make sure we met misfortune somewhere along the way.

A horrible accident when the archers were taking target practice.

An unfortunate food poisoning—I must have eaten some spoiled meat on the plains!

An outright ambush arranged somewhere around Ar Balesh.

And it occurred to me then that if I could imagine the viceroy doing such things so easily, he should not be a leader at all. Tamhan would do so much better. Though I may simply be paranoid.

Fintan dispelled the seeming of the plaguebringer and sighed. "The aftermath of a battle will haunt you; it certainly haunts me. The bodies you see are the ends of so many stories, and most of them never get told. It was my duty to collect what stories I could—a duty drilled into me as an apprentice—but as I went about it, I felt somewhat guilty, as if I were a blackwing picking over bones. Gorin Mogen's journal was mine to take, the viceroy caring nothing for the machinations of a

dead man. I'll tell you more as my former self," he said, and transformed to his armored, slightly younger seeming.

intan

Abhinava Khose told me much of his personal journey that morning
after dismissing the kherns, and he allowed me to read what he'd written
in the journal his aunt gave him. I determined to follow him around for
a while—how could I not? It had been millennia since a new kenning had
been found. We met Nef Tam ben Wat together after inquiring about
the small saplings the Fornish were guarding. While the Nentian army
was setting up camp around the walls of Bagrha Khek and Olet Kanek
was busy containing the fire Gorin Mogen had started, Nef moved
quickly up the mountain, around and above the fire, to the cache the
Fornish had left before the battle—a standard practice of theirs. Nel Kit
ben Sah's journal was buried there, and he fetched it down for me. If I
was going to tell all these other stories, he wanted hers to be told also.

"She was our Champion, you see," he said, placing it gently in my
hands with both of his. "And it was she who brought down Gorin
Mogen for the Canopy—and our Nentian allies." He stared at the small
journal, and I didn't move it, sensing that he had something more to
say. Finally, he wrenched his gaze up to mine. "I read some of it. She
didn't know, but she was well loved."

I nodded. "Of course she was. Tell me more of her?" I asked, and
invited him to sit with me and Abhi. He told me much of what happened during the battle since most of it had happened out of our sight
and coached me on what Nel looked and sounded like. He and most of

the Fornish were going to return to Forn the next day, carrying back their dead to return to the roots, but some would stay behind to look after the silverbark saplings. "Once they're strong enough for the journey, they will be transplanted to grow in the Canopy."

Noon passed us by before we knew it, and Nef bid us farewell to rejoin his countrymen.

"You now have my journal, Gorin Mogen's, and Nel Kit ben Sah's," Abhi noted after he departed. "Everything a bard would need to tell the story of this battle but the journal of Viceroy Melishev Lohmet. Would you like to take a look at that?"

"Sure. Does he have one?"

"Yes. And I'm pretty sure I can get you a look at it. But you have to be ready to leave right now."

"Right now?"

"Right now. We get on our horses and ride north all the way to Talala Fouz. It will be perfectly safe."

"All right. I'm game."

Packing only water skins, we walked out past all the soldiers, and then the plaguebringer called a couple of horses to us from somewhere—they were his, apparently, waiting for him to hail them. Once we mounted, the young man searched the skies above and then turned his gaze toward the trees to the south still untouched by fire.

"What are you looking for?" I asked.

"A cheek raptor," he replied, then smiled. "Found one. Look over there."

He pointed, and I saw a cheek raptor take to the sky.

"Give me a few moments," he said, "and I'll see if we can get that journal."

Picturing what Melishev Lohmet looked like that day—a gold and sky-blue tunic over armor with a significant rectangular outline in the right-hand pocket draped over the thigh—Abhi sent that image to the cheek raptor so that he could spot his target. And he felt in turn what the raptor felt: flying high, searching, spying Melishev so easily among all the drab colors, then spiraling, diving, cries of alarm before the sweet tearing, the clutching, the escape, and wails of regret behind. Finding the man who wanted it, opening the feet, letting it go, circling back to the roost—

The viceroy's journal dropped near Abhi's horse, and he dismounted to fetch it. He flipped through the latter pages until he found the one Melishev had been writing on the day Abhi came to Hashan Khek. There were some scribbled notes about his demands and then, on the next page, a written reminder: "Kill the Khose boy at first opportunity."

Abhi read that aloud to me then said, "Well, that's all I need to know." He tossed the journal to me. "Here," he said. "New stories for you."

We rode north together, glad to be shut of the Godsteeth for a good long while.

The bard grinned at the audience, and many of them grinned back at him. "That's how I became the traveling companion of the world's first plaguebringer. We will hear plenty more from Abhi in days ahead, though for obvious reasons I will have no more of the viceroy's personal reflections to share. Meanwhile, as Abhi and I made our way north, Gondel Vedd and Ponder Tann arrived here in Pelemyn for a brief while. Gondel found out some rather startling news, and I assure you ahead of time that I have permission to share it."

The Wellspring of Pelemyn was so humid that one could almost feel clouds parting as one walked through the vapor. To be charitable, I supposed no one ever felt like their skin was drying out, but taking a

deep breath of air was impossible without inhaling a good measure of
sea salt in the bargain. Thank goodness it was quite cool or else it
would have been unbearable.

Soon after my arrival in the city and the return of Culland du Raffert's journal to his superior, Second Könstad Tallynd du Böll, she
brought me the documents she'd seized at Hillegöm. The Brynts had
been unable to make sense of them, but I immediately recognized the
Eculan language. As with translating *Zanata Sedam*, there were words
here and there that escaped me, but they were not enough to keep the
basic meaning out of reach, and the Eculans had not bothered to use a
code.

My discoveries warranted a meeting with Pelenaut Röllend and his
Lung, Föstyr, as well as their chief military officer, Könstad du Lallend.
The Lung started with a minimum of formality.

"Scholar, thank you for your work. Please share what you've found."

I handed over a copy of the documents translated into Brynt to him,
which he immediately passed to the pelenaut. "What the Second Könstad stole was the Eculan invasion plans, much of which you already
know because it happened. But what you did not know is that they
sent two additional fleets in search of the Seven-Year Ship. One landed
at the Mistmaiden Isles, and one went to some ill-defined place in the
Northern Yawn."

Könstad du Lallend swiveled his head to the right. "That means they
could still be out there."

"We'll check the Mistmaiden Isles," the pelenaut said. "Actually, I'd
like you to do that tomorrow, Tallynd, very carefully, if you would not
mind."

"Of course," she replied.

"But I'm sure the wraiths took care of them for us or we would have
heard from them by now. The other army worries me more. A force
that size could conceivably make its way south through the Gravewood, and we have Fornyd repopulated and some new settlers on their
way to Festwyf."

"There was nothing about which side of the Poet's Range the army may have landed on?" Föstyr asked me. "Are they north of us or north of Rael or even Ghurana Nent?"

"They were unsure of their final destination. They were looking for some landmark along the coast, the sort of thing where they would know it when they saw it."

"What sort of landmark?"

"It's never described, only named in their language as the 'Nest of Man-Eaters.' I've translated it as 'Kraken's Nest' since that is what the Eculans typically mean when they say 'man-eater,' though it could also refer to bladefins or longarms. I have no idea, unfortunately, what that might look like, nor have I ever heard of such a landmark along the northern coast."

Pelenaut Röllend turned to the Lung and said, "Dervan du Alöbar is an historian. Ask him if he remembers ever hearing of it."

"There's more. The Eculans have a contact here in Pelemyn."

Silence, widened eyes, and then the Lung said: "A traitor?"

"I assume so. A contact by the single name of Vjeko."

"This never leaves the room," the pelenaut said, making eye contact with each of us in turn. "You tell no one. I mean *no* one, Föstyr."

"Understood."

Pelenaut Röllend tapped the copy of the report I'd given him. "Gondel, do you know where I can find mention of Vjeko in here?"

"Page ten, I believe."

He began to flip through the papers. "Any other contacts listed besides him?"

"No."

"Exactly how were they to contact him?"

"That's not mentioned, unfortunately."

"Very well. Thank you, Gondel. We're very grateful for your assistance, and I'm going to take some time to absorb this. You'll remain in Pelemyn for a few days at least in case I have questions?"

"Both Ponder and I are at your disposal until duty calls us elsewhere," I said. "We'll be staying at the Kaurian embassy."

Ponder had no difficulty with the decision; the handsome lad had many admirers already. For my part, I longed to return home to Maron and call my duty done: no one would question it except for me. If I returned now, I would always wonder if I could have done something more to save lives and to prevent Kauria from ever suffering the way Brynlön has. So I determined to stay and wrote Maron a love letter instead so that he would know that yes, I was still driven, still consumed by my work, but I was thinking of him, too, and though I might seem lost, one day I would be found again in his arms.

The mood is justifiably dark and bleak here, and I can see the pelenaut straining to see a way through for his people. In addition to what I've seen with my own eyes—the slaughter at Möllerud and Göfyrd, the loss of so many families like Kallindra du Paskre's—I've since learned that it was just as bad in the north.

Amid so much ruin I prayed that Reinei would, in some near future, gasp a labored breath of peace.

Continued in volume two, *A Blight of Blackwings*

APPENDIX

JEREH TABLE

This is the latest table according to Fintan, the Raelech bard. By looking at the three colored stones on a Raelech's Jereh band, one can tell immediately a person's status and profession. The left stone always identifies the goddess or other affiliation, and the middle stone indicates rank; the right-hand stone will signal one's profession or status when combined with the left affiliation stone. A Jereh band that reads brown, purple, and white, therefore, would indicate that the wearer is affiliated with the Goddess Dinae as a master healer. A journeyman tanner would wear yellow, blue, and brown; an apprentice hunter would wear red, brown, and evergreen, and so on. Visitors must also wear cheaper, temporary bands, the first stone usually green (foreign) or white (unskilled, at least in Raelech eyes). Relationship status is indicated with the metal of the band: bronze means single, gold means married.

AFFILIATION (LEFT STONE):

(Ruby) Red:	Hall of the Warrior Goddess Raena (usually called the Huntress)
(Sard) Brown:	Hall of the Earth Goddess Dinae
(Citrine) Yellow:	Hall of the Poet Goddess Kaelin
(Malachite) Evergreen:	Foreign National
(Obsidian) Black:	Criminal
(Onyx) White:	Triune Council/Ward of the Triune

RANK (MIDDLE STONE):

(Sard) Brown:	Apprentice
(Sapphire) Blue:	Journeyman/Laborer
(Amethyst) Purple:	Master
(Jade) Apple Green:	Protected by the Goddess (Raelechs from ages nine to twelve)
(Obsidian) Black:	To be determined/Probationary Status/ Stripped of Rank/Foreign skill
(Onyx) White:	Unskilled/Tradeless/Raelech children up to age nine

PROFESSIONS (RIGHT STONE) ACCORDING TO AFFILIATION, ALWAYS SUBJECT TO CHANGE/EXPANSION:

COLOR/STONE	RAENA	DINAE
Red/Ruby	Soldier	Farmer
Brown/Sard	Constable	Miner
Yellow/Citrine	Temblor	Shepherd/Cowherd/etc.
Blue/Sapphire	Archer	Fisherfolk
Purple/Amethyst	Navigator	Laborer
Orange/Fire Opal	Army Officer	Miller
Green/Malachite	Hunter	Forester
White/Onyx	Enforcer	Healer
Black/Obsidian		
Dark Blue/Sodalite	Naval Officer	Herbalist
Violet/Charoite	Architect	Dyemaker
Apple/Jade	Scout	
Green/Emerald	Mercenary	Gardener
Sepia/Smoky Quartz	Juggernaut	Stonecutter
Light Blue/Chalcedony	Sailor	
Mother of Pearl	Courier	Brewer/Distiller
Pink/Rose Quartz	Jurist (Lawyer)	Sexitrist
Gold/Tourmaline	Engineer	Beekeeper
Grey/Howlite	Siege Crew	
Silver/Quartz	Jailer	
Turquoise	Bailiff	
Mauve/Rhodolite Garnet	Clergy	Clergy

Please note that some terms are catchalls: Hospitality, for example, includes a multitude of professions, from bartenders and innkeeps to household employees of all kinds. Almost all professions involved in food production are given a ruby in Kaelin's Hall, but curiously (at least to me) is the inclusion of Brewers and Distillers in Dinae's Hall. Fintan's explanation for this is a Raelech legend in which Dinae supposedly outdrank her sisters one fine Felech evening three thousand years ago, and thus became the patron goddess of hopheads everywhere. —*Dervan*

KAELIN	FOREIGN	CRIMINAL	TRIUNE
Chefs, Butchers, Bakers	Mercenary		Colaiste Master
Tanner	Lawyer		Magistrate
Bard	Diplomat		Diplomat
Potter	Herald	Jereh Fraud, Other Fraud	Herald
Hospitality	Laborer		Laborer
Merchant	Merchant	Thief	Coiner/Banker
Woodcraft		Despoiler	
Papermaker	Student		Student
		Murderer	
Chandler	Official of State	Smuggler	Adviser
Glasswork		Fence	Teamster
Armorer	Head of State		Tax Official
Weaver			Hygienist
Mason			Clave Poobah
Blacksmith	Tradesman		Stevedore
Dancer/Acrobat/Artisan			Council Member
Thespian		Organized Crime	
Jereh/Gemcraft	Scholar		Scholar
Tailor	Tourist	Poison/Drug Offenses	Harbor Master
Cobbler		Violent Crimes	Postal Service
Clerk/Printer	Clerk	Conspiracist	Clerk
Clergy	Clergy		

KAURIAN CALENDAR

Though Ghurana Nent insists on a different timekeeping system for their internal use, the Six Nations otherwise use the Kaurian Calendar. It begins on the day of the Spring Equinox and ends on the last day of winter. It uses eight-day weeks: ten months have four weeks, but months six and twelve have three, for a total of 368 days. A few days are usually subtracted from the last week of the year to ensure that the Spring Equinox falls on Bloom 1, which means in practical terms that Thaw is often only twenty-one to twenty-two days long. Bloodmoon 1 is usually the day after Autumn Equinox.

The Giant Wars began in the winter of 3041 with the eruption of Mount Thayil and the destruction of Harthrad, followed closely by the du Paskre Encounter and the capture of Saviič in the east.

SPRING SEASON

Bloom (32)   Rainfall (32)   Foaling (32)   (96 days)

APPENDIX

SUMMER SEASON

Sunlight (32)   Bounty   (32)   Harvest (24)   (88 days)

AUTUMN SEASON

Bloodmoon (32)   Amber   (32)   Barebranch (32)   (96 days)

WINTER SEASON

Frost (32)   Snowfall (32)   Thaw (21)   (85 days)

DAYS OF THE WEEK

Kaurian Language

Deller, Soller, Tamiller, Keiller, Shaller, Feiller, Beiller, Reiller

Raelech Language

Delech, Solech, Tamech, Kelech, Shalech, Felech, Belech, Ranech

Acknowledgments

I've had the Raelech bard in my head a long time—longer than the Iron Druid, in fact. The idea of nightly, serial storytelling has fascinated me ever since I learned that this was something Homer might have done in ancient Greece, and it took me about ten years to figure out how to simulate that experience in a novel. It could not have been done without the following:

1. My wife's constant belief that I could pull this off. Thank you, Kimberly.
2. My editor's keen insights and tremendous patience while I figured things out. Thank you, Tricia.
3. My good friend Alan O'Bryan, who read extremely early versions of the story, provided feedback, and helped think through the Raelech Jereh system. Thank you, Alan.

Many thanks to you for reading, and I hope you'll return for the rest of the bard's tales.

ABOUT THE TYPE

This book was set in Dante, a typeface designed by Giovanni Mardersteig (1892–1977). Conceived as a private type for the Officina Bodoni in Verona, Italy, Dante was originally cut only for hand composition by Charles Malin, the famous Parisian punch cutter, between 1946 and 1952. Its first use was in an edition of Boccaccio's *Trattatello in laude di Dante* that appeared in 1954. The Monotype Corporation's version of Dante followed in 1957. Though modeled on the Aldine type used for Pietro Cardinal Bembo's treatise *De Aetna* in 1495, Dante is a thoroughly modern interpretation of that venerable face.

extras

www.orbitbooks.net

about the author

Kevin Hearne lives with his wife, son, and doggies in Colorado. He hugs trees, rocks out to heavy metal, and will happily geek out over comics with you. He also thinks tacos are a pretty nifty idea.

kevinhearne.com
Facebook.com/authorkevin
Twitter: @KevinHearne

Find out more about Kevin Hearne and other Orbit authors by registering for the free monthly newslettter at www.orbitbooks.net

interview

When did you first come up with the idea for *A Plague of Giants*?

About ten years ago! I had a first draft written before I wrote my urban fantasy series, in fact. It was both huge and hugely awful. Thankfully I learned quite a bit while writing the Iron Druid Chronicles. When I came back to *Plague*, I scrapped almost the entirety of the first draft, keeping only twelve lines and the world itself. That was 250K words I kissed goodbye, but I really like the twelve lines I kept.

Did you need to approach the writing of this book in a very different way to writing the Iron Druid Chronicles?

Absolutely. Epic fantasy is significantly different from urban fantasy to begin with, and since I have eleven first-person points of view that also jump back and forth a bit in time, trying to organize that in Word would have driven me insane. I used Scrivener to compose this, since it allows one to create folders for each chapter and then those folders can be easily rearranged with a click and drag, whereas moving things around in Word requires a lot of scrolling, highlighting, copying, and pasting.

What was your inspiration behind using a bard as the framing device for a much larger tale?

That came from my desire to render in prose the experience of an audience listening to a bard like Homer performing the *Iliad* or *Odyssey* a chapter at a time. Those old epics were the popular culture of the ancient world, and the closest thing we have now is binge-watching a series on Netflix, which is somehow a comedown. We've lost something magical since we let bards pass into obsolescence, and I wanted to recapture a smidgen of that if I could.

The magic system you've come up with is very original. What were the challenges of creating this system?

The challenge to creating any magic system is maintaining internal consistency. The challenge of presenting that system is how much to reveal and when, and in this case, we have narrators who possess only one kenning or none at all, so there is never an opportunity for someone to explain everything—not that you would ever want that. And kennings are at once simple but mysterious: tremendous power available to all at tremendous risk and cost, but no one is sure *why* such power is available, or how it came to be there apart from vague assertions that the gods must be responsible. Discovering that, along with the precise nature of the Seventh Kenning, will occupy part of the narrative of the next two books.

If you were to seek a kenning, which one would you go for?

Oh, egad! I think I'd be too afraid to be a Seeker; I rather like my chances of staying alive without risking that. But if I did seek one, I suppose I'd go for the Second Kenning and dive into Bryn's Lung. There's a whole lot of fun to be had in the water.

Is there a character you most identify with in this book? Who was your favourite to write?

I probably identify most with Olet Kanek, daughter of the giant Hearthfire Winthir Kanek. She is a minor character in the first book but a major point-of-view character in the second. She'd like to see her generation follow a different path than their parents have and I feel that quite strongly myself. I think you see that in current US culture and around the world as well—we frequently see articles about how Millennials are not conforming to the values of the Baby Boomer generation or even Generation X, and every time I see such an article I think, "Good on them." But the greatest joy for me to write was the voice of Nel Kit ben Sah, the greensleeve who loves her forest so much. There's a lightness and poetry infused in her language that made her headspace a treat to inhabit.

What can we expect from the next Seven Kennings novel?

A Blight of Blackwings will pick up where *A Plague of Giants* leaves off, for while some crises have been dealt with there are bigger ones coming. You will see new narrators (such as Olet, mentioned above), the world's reaction to the new power risen in the west, and a rather frightening demonstration of the Seventh Kenning.

if you enjoyed
A PLAGUE OF GIANTS
look out for

THE FIFTH WARD: FIRST WATCH

by

Dale Lucas

In the cramped quarters of the city of Yenara, humans, orcs, mages, elves and dwarves all jostle for success and survival, while under-staffed watch wardens struggle to keep the citizens in line.

Enter Rem. New to the city, he wakes bruised and hungover in the dungeons of the fifth ward. With no money for bail – and seeing no other way out of his cell – Rem jumps at the chance to join the Watch.

Torval, his new partner – a dwarf who's handy with a maul and known for hitting first and asking questions later – is highly unim-pressed with the untrained and weaponless Rem. But when Torval's former partner goes missing, the two must learn to work together to uncover the truth and catch a murderer loose in their fair city.

CHAPTER ONE

Rem awoke in a dungeon with a thunderous headache. He knew it was a dungeon because he lay on a thin bed of straw, and because there were iron bars between where he lay and a larger chamber outside. The light was spotty, some of it from torches in sconces outside his cell, some from a few tiny windows high on the stone walls admitting small streams of wan sunlight. Moving nearer the bars, he noted that his cell was one of several, each roomy enough to hold multiple prisoners.

A large pile of straw on the far side of his cell coughed, shifted, then started to snore. Clearly, Rem was not alone.

And just how did I end up here? he wondered. *I seem to recall a winning streak at Roll-the-Bones.*

He could not remember clearly. But if the lumpy soreness of his face and body were any indication, his dice game had gone awry. If only he could clear his pounding head, or slake his thirst. His tongue and throat felt like sharkskin.

Desperate for a drink, Rem crawled to a nearby bucket, hoping for a little brackish water. To his dismay, he found that it was the piss jar, not a water bucket, and not well rinsed at that. The sight and smell made Rem recoil with a gag. He went sprawling back onto the hay. A few feet away, his cellmate muttered something in the tongue of the Kosterfolk, then resumed snoring.

Somewhere across the chamber, a multitumbler lock clanked

and clacked. Rusty hinges squealed as a great door lumbered open. From the other cells Rem heard prisoners roused from their sleep, shuffling forward hurriedly to thrust their arms out through the cage bars. If Rem didn't misjudge, there were only about four or five other prisoners in all the dungeon cells. A select company, to be sure. Perhaps it was a slow day for the Yenaran city watch?

Four men marched into the dungeon. Well, three marched; the fourth seemed a little more reticent, being dragged by two others behind their leader, a thickset man with black hair, sullen eyes, and a drooping mustache.

"Prefect, sir," Rem heard from an adjacent cell, "there's been a terrible mistake..."

From across the chamber: "Prefect, sir, someone must have spiked my ale, because the last thing I remember, I was enjoying an evening out with some mates..."

From off to his left: "Prefect, sir, I've a chest of treasure waiting back at my rooms at the Sauntering Mink. A golden cup full of rubies and emeralds is yours, if you'll just let me out of here..."

Prefect, sir... Prefect, sir... over and over again.

Rem decided that thrusting his own arms out and begging for the prefect's attention was useless. What would he do? Claim his innocence? Promise riches if they'd let him out? That was quite a tall order when Rem himself couldn't remember what he'd done to get in here. If he could just clear his thunder-addled, achingly thirsty brain...

The sullen-eyed prefect led the two who dragged the prisoner down a short flight of steps into a shallow sort of operating theater in the center of the dungeon: the interrogation pit, like some shallow bath that someone had let all the water out of. On one side of the pit was a brick oven in which fire and coals glowed. Opposite the oven was a burbling fountain. Rem thought these additions rather ingenious. Whatever elemental need one had—fire to burn with, water to drown with—both were readily provided. The floor of the pit, Rem guessed, probably sported a couple of grates that led right down into the sewers, as well as the tools of the trade: a table full of torturer's implements, a couple of hot braziers, some chairs and manacles. Rem hadn't seen the inside of any city dungeons, but he'd seen their private equivalents. Had it been the dungeon of some march lord up north—from his own country—that's what would have been waiting in the little amphitheater.

"Come on, Ondego, you know me," the prisoner pleaded. "This isn't necessary."

"'Fraid so," sullen-eyed Ondego said, his low voice easy and without malice. "The chair, lads."

The two guardsmen flanking the prisoner were a study in contrasts—one a tall, rugged sort, face stony and flecked with stubble, shoulders broad, while the other was lithe and graceful, sporting braided black locks, skin the color of dark-stained wood, and a telltale pair of tapered, pointing ears. Staring, Rem realized that second guardsman was no man at all, but an elf, and female, at that. Here was a puzzle, indeed. Rem had seen elves at a distance before, usually in or around frontier settlements farther north, or simply haunting the bleak crossroads of a woodland highway like pikers who never demanded a toll. But he had never seen one of them up close like this—and certainly not in the middle of one of the largest cities in the Western world, deep underground, in a dingy, shit- and blood-stained dungeon. Nonetheless, the dark-skinned elfmaid seemed quite at home in her surroundings, and perfectly comfortable beside the bigger man on the other side of the prisoner.

Together, those two guards thrust the third man's squirming, wobbly body down into a chair. Heavy manacles were produced and the protester was chained to his seat. He struggled a little, to test his bonds, but seemed to know instinctively that it was no use. Ondego stood at a brazier nearby, stoking its coals, the pile of dark cinders glowing ominously in the oily darkness.

"Oi, that's right!" one of the other prisoners shouted. "Give that bastard what for, Prefect!"

"You shut your filthy mouth, Foss!" the chained man spat back.

"Eat me, Kevel!" the prisoner countered. "How do *you* like the chair, eh?"

Huh. Rem moved closer to his cell bars, trying to get a better look. So, this prisoner, Kevel, knew that fellow in the cell, Foss, and vice versa. Part of a conspiracy? Brother marauders, questioned one by one—and in sight of one another—for some vital information?

Then Rem saw it: Kevel, the prisoner in the hot seat, wore a signet pendant around his throat identical to those worn by the prefect and the two guards. It was unmistakable, even in the shoddy light.

"Well, I'll be," Rem muttered aloud.

The prisoner was one of the prefect's own watchmen.

Ex-watchman now, he supposed.

All of a sudden, Rem felt a little sorry for him...but not much. No doubt, Kevel himself had performed the prefect's present actions a number of times: chaining some poor sap into the hot seat, stoking the brazier, using fire and water and physical distress to intimidate the prisoner into revealing vital information.

The prefect, Ondego, stepped away from the brazier and moved to a table nearby. He studied a number of implements—

it was too dark and the angle too awkward for Rem to tell what, exactly—then picked something up. He hefted the object in his hands, testing its weight.

It looked like a book—thick, with a hundred leaves or more bound between soft leather covers.

"Do you know what this is?" Ondego asked Kevel.

"Haven't the foggiest," Kevel said. Rem could tell that he was bracing himself, mentally and physically.

"It's a genealogy of Yenara's richest families. Out-of-date, though. At least a generation old."

"Do tell," Kevel said, his throat sounding like it had contracted to the size of a reed.

"Look at this," Ondego said, hefting the book in his hands, studying it. "That is one enormous pile of useless information. Thick as a bloody brick—"

And that's when Ondego drew back the book and brought it smashing into Kevel's face in a broad, flat arc. The sound of the strike—leather and parchment pages connecting at high speed with Kevel's jawbone—echoed in the dungeon like the crack of a calving iceberg. A few of the other prisoners even wailed as though they were the ones struck.

Rem's cellmate stirred beneath his pile of straw, but did not rise.

Kevel almost fell with the force of the blow. The big guard caught him and set him upright again. The lithe elf backed off, staring intently at the prisoner, as though searching his face and his manner for a sign of something. Without warning, Ondego hit Kevel again, this time on the other side of his face. Once more Kevel toppled. Once more the guard in his path caught him and set him upright.

Kevel spat out blood. Ondego tossed the book back onto the table behind him and went looking for another implement.

"That all you got, old man?" Kevel asked.

"Bravado doesn't suit you," Ondego said, still studying his options from the torture table. He threw a glance at the elf on the far side of the torture pit. Rem watched intently, realizing that some strange ritual was under way: Kevel, blinking sweat from his eyes, studied Ondego; the lady elf, silent and implacable, studied Kevel; and Ondego idly studied the elf, the prefect's thick, workman's hand hovering slowly over the gathered implements of torture on the table.

Then, Kevel blinked. That small, unconscious movement seemed to signal something to the elf, who then spoke to the prefect. Her voice was soft, deep, melodious.

"The amputation knife," she said, her large, unnerving, honey-colored eyes never leaving the prisoner.

Ondego took up the instrument that his hand hovered above—a long, curving blade like a field-hand's billhook, the honed edge being on the inside, rather than the outside, of the curve. Ondego brandished the knife and looked to Kevel. The prisoner's eyes were as wide as empty goblets.

Ingenious! The elf had apparently used her latent mind-reading abilities to determine which of the implements on the table Kevel most feared being used on him. Not precisely the paragon of sylvan harmony and ancient grace that Rem would have imagined such a creature to be, but impressive nonetheless.

As Ondego spoke, he continued to brandish the knife, casually, as if it were an extension of his own arm. "Honestly, Kev," he said, "haven't I seen you feign bravery a hundred times? I know you're shitting your kecks about now."

"So you'd like to think," Kevel answered, eyes still on the knife. "You're just bitter because you didn't do it. Rich men don't get rich keeping to a set percentage, Ondego. They get rich by redrawing the percentages."

Ondego shook his head. Rem could be mistaken, but he thought he saw real regret there.

"Rule number one," Ondego said, as though reciting holy writ. "Keep the peace."

"Suck it," Kevel said bitterly.

"Rule number two," Ondego said, slowly turning to face Kevel, "Keep your partner safe, and he'll do the same for you."

"He was going to squeal," Kevel said, now looking a little more repentant. "I couldn't have that. You said yourself, Ondego—he wasn't cut out for it. Never was. Never would be."

"So that bought him a midnight swim in the bay?" Ondego asked. "Rule number three: let the punishment fit the crime, Kevel. Throttling that poor lad and throwing him in the drink...that's what the judges call cruel and unusual. We don't do cruel and unusual in my ward."

"Go spit," Kevel said.

"Rule number four," Ondego quickly countered. "And this is important, Kevel, so listen good: never take more than your share. There's enough for everyone, so long as no one's greedy. So long as no one's hoarding or getting fat. I knew you were taking a bigger cut when your jerkin started straining. There's only one way a watchman that didn't start out fat gets that way, and that's by hoarding and taking more than his fair share."

"So what's it gonna be?" Kevel asked. "The knife? The razor? The book again? The hammer and the nail-tongs?"

"Nah," Ondego said, seemingly bored by their exchange, as though he were disciplining a child that he'd spanked a hundred times before. He tossed the amputation knife back on the table. "Bare fists."

And then, as Rem and the other prisoners watched, Ondego, prefect of the watch, proceeded to beat the living shit out of Kevel, a onetime member of his own watch company. Despite the fact that Ondego said not another word while the beating commenced, Rem thought he sensed some grim and unhappy purpose in Ondego's corporal punishment. He never once smiled, nor even gritted his teeth in anger. The intensity of the beating never flared nor ebbed. He simply kept his mouth set, his eyes open, and slowly, methodically, laid fists to flesh. He made Kevel whimper and bleed. From time to time he would stop and look to the elf. The elf would study Kevel, clearly not simply looking at him but *into* him, perhaps reading just how close he was to losing consciousness, or whether he was feigning senselessness to gain some brief reprieve. The elf would then offer a cursory, "More." Ondego, on the elfmaid's advice, would continue.

Rem admired that: Ondego's businesslike approach, the fact that he could mete out punishment without enjoying it. In some ways, Ondego reminded Rem of his own father.

Before Ondego was done, a few of the other prisoners were crying out. Some begged mercy on Kevel's behalf. Ondego wasn't having it. He didn't acknowledge them. His fists carried on their bloody work. To Kevel's credit he never begged mercy. Granted, that might have been hard after the first quarter hour or so, when most of his teeth were on the floor.

Ondego only relented when the elf finally offered a single word. "Out." At that, Ondego stepped back, like a pugilist retreating to his corner between melee rounds. He shook his hands, no doubt feeling a great deal of pain in them. Beating a man like that tested the limits of one's own pain threshold as well as the victim's.

"Still breathing?" Ondego asked, all business.

The human guard bent. Listened. Felt for a pulse. "Still with us. Out cold."

"Put him in the stocks," Ondego said. "If he survives five

days on Zabayus's Square, he can walk out of the city so long as he never comes back. Post his crimes, so everyone sees."

The guards nodded and set to unchaining Kevel. Ondego swept past them and mounted the stairs up to the main cell level again, heading toward the door. That's when Rem suddenly noticed an enormous presence beside him. He had not heard the brute's approach, but he could only be the sleeping form beneath the hay. For one, he was covered in the stuff. For another, his long braided hair, thick beard, and rough-sewn, stinking leathers marked him as a Kosterman. And hadn't Rem heard Koster words muttered by the sleeper in the hay?

"Prefect!" the Kosterman called, his speech sharply accented.

Ondego turned, as if this was the first time he'd heard a single word spoken from the cells and the prisoners in them.

Rem's cellmate rattled the bars. "Let me out of here, little man," he said.

Kosterman all right. The long, yawning vowels and glass-sharp consonants were a dead giveaway. For emphasis, the Kosterman even snarled, as though the prefect were the lowest of house servants.

Ondego looked puzzled for a moment. Could it be that no one had ever spoken to him that way? Then the prefect stepped forward, snarling, looking like a maddened hound. His fist shot out in front of him and shook as he approached.

"Get back in your hay and keep your gods-damned head down, con! I'll have none of your nonsense after such a bevy of bitter business—"

Rem realized what was about to happen a moment before it did. He opened his mouth to warn the prefect off—surely the man wasn't so gullible? Maybe it was just his weariness in the wake of the beating he'd given Kevel? His regret at having to so savagely punish one of his own men?

Whatever the reason, Ondego clearly wasn't thinking straight. The moment his shaking fist was within arm's reach of the Kosterman in the cell, the barbarian reached out, snagged that fist, and yanked Ondego close. The prefect's face and torso hit the bars of the cell with a heavy clang.

Rem scurried aside as the Kosterman stretched both arms out through the bars, wrapped them around Ondego, then tossed all of his weight backward. He had the prefect in a deadly bear hug and was using his body's considerable weight to crush the man against the bars of the cell. Rem heard the other two watchmen rushing near, a flurry of curses and stomping boots. Around the dungeon, the men in the cells began to curse and cheer. Some even laughed.

"Let me out of here, now!" the Kosterman roared. "Let me out or I'll crush him, I swear!"

Rem's instincts were frustrated by his headache, his thirst, his confusion. But despite all that, he knew, deep in his gut, that he had to do something. He couldn't just let the hay-covered Kosterman in the smelly leathers crush the prefect to death against the bars of the cell.

But that Kosterman was enormous—at least a head and a half taller than Rem.

The other watchmen had reached the bars now. The stubble-faced one was trying to break the Kosterman's grip while the elfmaid snatched for the rattling keys to the cells on the human guard's belt.

Without thinking, Rem rushed up behind the angry Kosterman, drew back one boot, and kicked. The kick landed square in the Kosterman's fur-clad testicles.

The barbarian roared—an angry bear, indeed—and Rem's gambit worked. For just a moment, the Kosterman released his hold on the prefect. On the far side of the bars, the stubble-faced watchman managed to get the prefect in his grip and yank him backward, away from the cell. When Rem saw that, he made his next move.

He leapt onto the Kosterman's broad shoulders. Instead of wrapping his arms around the Kosterman's throat, he grabbed the bars of the cell. Then, locking his legs around the Kosterman's torso from behind, he yanked hard. The Kosterman was driven forward hard, his skull slamming with a resonant clang into the cell bars. Rem heard nose cartilage crunch. The Kosterman sputtered a little and tried to reach for whoever was on his back. Rem drew back and yanked again, driving the Kosterman forward into the bars once more.

Another clang. The Kosterman's body seemed to sag beneath Rem.

Then the sagging body began to topple backward.

Clinging high on the great, muscular frame, Rem realized that he was overbalanced. He lost his grip on the cell bars, and the towering Kosterman beneath him fell.

Rem tried to leap free, but he was too entangled with the barbarian to make it clear. Instead, he simply disengaged and went falling with him.

Both of them—Rem and the barbarian—hit the floor. The Kosterman was out cold. Rem had the wind knocked out of him and his vision came alight with whirling stars and dancing fireflies.

Blinking, trying to get his sight and his breath back, he heard the whine of rusty hinges, then footsteps. Strong hands seized him and dragged him out of the cell. By the time his vision had returned, he found himself on the stone pathway outside the cell that he had shared with the smelly, unconscious Kosterman. The prefect and his two watchmen stood over him.

"Explain yourself," Ondego said. He was a little disheveled, but otherwise, the Kosterman's attack seemed to have left not a mark on him, nor shaken him.

Rem coughed. Drew breath. Sighed. "Just trying to help," he said.

"I'll bet you want out now, don't you?" Ondego asked. "One good turn deserves another and all that."

Rem shrugged. "It hadn't really crossed my mind."

Ondego frowned, as though Rem were the most puzzling prisoner he had ever encountered. "Well, what do you want, then? I can be a hard bastard when I choose, but I know how to return a favor."

Rem had a thought. "I'm looking for work," he said.

Ondego raised one eyebrow.

"Seeing as you have space on your watch rosters"—Rem gestured to the spot where they had been beating Kevel in the torture pit—"perhaps I could impress upon you—"

Ondego seemed to appraise Rem honestly for a moment. For confirmation of his instincts, he looked to the elf.

Rem suddenly knew the strange sensation of another living being poking around in his mind. It was momentary and fleeting and entirely painless, but eminently strange and unnerving, like having one's privates appraised by the other patrons in a bathhouse. Then the elf's probing intellect withdrew, and Rem no longer felt naked. The elfmaid seemed to wear a small, knowing half smile. Her dark and ancient eyes settled on Rem and chilled him.

She knows everything, Rem thought. *A moment in my mind, two, and she knows everything. Everything worth knowing, anyway.*

"Harmless," the elfmaid said.

"Weak," the stubble-faced guardsmen added.

The elf's gaze never wavered. "No."

"You don't impress me," Ondego said, despite the elf's appraisal. "Not one bit."

"No doubt I don't," Rem said. "But, by Aemon, sir, I'd like to."

The watchman beside Ondego leaned close. Rem heard the words he whispered to the prefect.

"He did get that brute off you, sir."

Ondego and the big watchman continued to study him. The elf now turned her gaze on the boisterous prisoners in the other cells. A moment's eye contact was all it took. As the elfmaid turned her stone idol's glare on each of them, they fell silent and withdrew from the bars. Bearing witness to the effect the elf's silent, threatening stare had on those hard, desperate men made Rem's skin crawl.

But, to his own predicament: Rem decided to mount a better argument—he certainly couldn't end up in any more trouble, could he?

"You're down two men," Rem said, trying to look and sound as reasonable as possible. "That man you were beating and the partner he murdered. Surely you can give me the opportunity?"

"What's he in here for?" Ondego asked the watchman.

Rem prepared himself to listen. He was still trying to reason that part out himself.

"Bar brawl," the stubble-faced watchman said. "The Bonny Prince here was casting dice with some Koster longshoremen. Rolled straight nines, nine times in a row. They called him a cheat and he lit into them."

It was coming back now. Rem remembered the tavern. He'd been waiting for someone. A girl. She hadn't shown. He'd had a little too much to drink while waiting. He vaguely remembered the dice and the longshoremen—two tall fellows, not unlike the barbarian he'd just tussled with in the cell.

He couldn't recall their faces, or even starting a fight with them... but he did remember being called a cheat, and taking umbrage.

"I wasn't cheating," Rem said emphatically. "It was just a run of good luck."

"Not so good," Ondego said, "seeing as you're here in my dungeon." To the guardsmen beside him: "Where are the other two?"

"Taken to the hospital, sir," the big man said. "Beaten senseless by the Bonny Prince here."

"And a third Kosterman, out like a light on my dungeon floor. What is it with you and these northerners, boy?"

Rem shrugged. "Ill-starred, I guess."

Ondego seemed to appraise Rem anew. Three Kostermen on their backs was bold, and he couldn't deny it. "Doesn't look like much," the prefect said, as if to himself, "but he can hold his own in a fight."

Ondego was impressed with Rem—no thanks to the stone-faced watchman laying that damned "Bonny Prince" label on him. Rem guessed that Ondego's grudging respect might work in his favor.

"I don't like being called a cheat," Rem said, "first and foremost because I don't cheat. Ever."

Ondego nodded toward Kevel, limp in his chair. "Neither do we," he said.

"So I see," Rem answered.

A long silence fell between them.

"Get him on his feet," Ondego said. "We'll try him out."

Without another word, the prefect left.

Rem looked to the tall man. He felt a smile blooming on his face, then suddenly felt the pain of his brawl the night before. A swollen, split lip; a bruised nose; at least one missing tooth, far back in his mouth; the taste of old blood.

The big man offered a hand and yanked Rem to his feet. Upright, Rem swooned for a moment, his vision briefly going black again before finally clearing.

"Don't look so pleased with yourself, my bonny boy," the stubble-faced watchman said. "You've no idea what you're in for walking the ward."